THE TENTH JUSTICE

Landmark Cases in Canadian Law

Since Confederation, Canada's highest court – first the Judicial Committee of the Privy Council in England and then the Supreme Court of Canada – has issued a series of often contentious decisions that have fundamentally shaped the nation. Both cheered and jeered, these judgments have impacted every aspect of Canadian society, setting legal precedents and provoking social change. The issues in the judgments range from Aboriginal title, gender equality, and freedom of expression to Quebec secession and intellectual property. This series offers comprehensive, book-length examinations of high court cases that have had a major impact on Canadian law, politics, and society.

Other books in the series are:

Flawed Precedent: The St. Catherine's *Case and Aboriginal Title* by Kent McNeil

Privacy in Peril: Hunter v Southam *and the Drift from Reasonable Search Protections* by Richard Jochelson and David Ireland

From Wardship to Rights: The Guerin *Case and Aboriginal Law* by Jim Reynolds

For a list of other titles,
see www.ubcpress.ca/landmark-cases-in-canadian-law.

LANDMARK CASES
IN CANADIAN LAW

THE TENTH JUSTICE

Judicial Appointments, Marc Nadon, and the Supreme Court Act Reference

Carissima Mathen
and Michael Plaxton

UBCPress · Vancouver · Toronto

29 28 27 26 25 24 23 22 21 20 5 4 3 2 1

Printed in Canada on FSC-certified ancient-forest-free paper (100% post-consumer recycled) that is processed chlorine- and acid-free.

Library and Archives Canada Cataloguing in Publication

Title: The tenth justice : judicial appointments, Marc Nadon, and the Supreme Court Act Reference / Carissima Mathen and Michael Plaxton.

Names: Mathen, Carissima, author. | Plaxton, Michael, 1975- author.

Description: Includes bibliographical references and indexes.

Identifiers:
Canadiana (print) 20200174347 | Canadiana (ebook) 20200174657 | ISBN 9780774864275 (hardcover) | ISBN 9780774864282 (softcover) | ISBN 9780774864299 (PDF) | ISBN 9780774864305 (EPUB) | ISBN 9780774864312 (Kindle)

Subjects: LCSH: Nadon, Marc. | LCSH: Canada. Supreme Court. | LCSH: Judges – Selection and appointment – Canada.

Classification: LCC KE8293.A6 M38 2020 | DDC 347.71/03534 – dc23

Canadä

UBC Press gratefully acknowledges the financial support for our publishing program of the Government of Canada (through the Canada Book Fund), the Canada Council for the, and the British Columbia Arts Council.

This book has been published with the help of a grant from the Canadian Federation for the Humanities and Social Sciences, through the Awards to Scholarly Publications Program, using funds provided by the Social Sciences and Humanities Research Council of Canada.

UBC Press
The University of British Columbia
2029 West Mall
Vancouver, BC V6T 1Z2
www.ubcpress.ca

Contents

Acknowledgments

Many persons assisted us in the writing of this book. We are indebted to Adam Dodek, John Mark Keyes, Dwight Newman, Benjamin Oliphant, Bob Tarantino, and Leonid Sirota for providing comments on previous drafts; to the two anonymous reviewers for UBC Press; and to Howard Anglin, the Honourable Louise Charron, John Ivison, and the Honourable Marshall Rothstein, who spoke to us.

We also extend special thanks to Justice Marc Nadon for graciously agreeing to speak to us.

Our friends and families provided much-needed support and encouragement. Carissima would like to acknowledge Charles Feldman, the Honourable Michael Moldaver, and Jason Kee. Michael would like to thank his parents, Charles and Tom, and Katrina.

THE TENTH JUSTICE

INTRODUCTION

On 21 March 2014, the Supreme Court of Canada released its opinion in *Reference re Supreme Court Act, ss 5 and 6.*[1] Most of the public knew the case by another name: the Nadon Reference.[2] For six months, the man at the heart of the case – Marc Nadon – had quietly waited offstage while politicians, journalists, lawyers, academics and, ultimately, the Supreme Court debated whether, as a Federal Court judge, he was eligible for a seat on the bench of Canada's highest court.

Now it was over. By a six-one majority, the court concluded that section 6 of the *Supreme Court Act* precluded the appointment of Federal Court judges to one of the three seats reserved for Quebec jurists.[3] More shockingly, the majority advised that the Act could not be unilaterally amended by the federal government. There might yet have been ways for Marc Nadon to be appointed – in particular, by retiring as a Federal Court judge and reapplying to the bar of Quebec. But he didn't seem interested in pursuing that course. If anything, he sounded relieved that the episode was over. In an interview with Global News, Nadon said: "I've been living in limbo ... since October ... [A]t least this has ... ended the uncertainty."[4] It didn't, however, end the controversy.

It is not always easy to tell which cases will be regarded as landmarks. The Supreme Court may issue a sweeping statement of principle that makes headlines across the nation and then proceed to water it down over a period of years. What seems like an important precedent may be distinguished by later decisions into virtual irrelevance or overruled altogether.[5] Today's dissent may be tomorrow's majority opinion.[6]

Some decisions, though, are instant classics. In a stroke of the pen, they change the way we make sense of whole bodies of law,[7] and even entire institutions.[8] Indeed, they may affect how those institutions understand themselves and how others in the political sphere relate to them.[9]

Not surprisingly, some of the most canonical decisions involve assertions of power by the judiciary vis-à-vis other branches of government. Think of the US Supreme Court's decision in *Marbury v Madison,* in which it articulated its own authority to issue binding rulings on the meaning of the Constitution.[10] Or *Fuller's Case,* in which Lord Coke emphatically denied that the King had authority to "adjudge any case," holding that the common law was supreme.[11] *Roncarelli v Duplessis,* an indisputably canonical case in Canada, concerned the authority of the courts to review exercises of discretionary power by executive actors.[12] These cases are bigger than the disputes that gave rise to them. They provide a lens through which to see our entire constitutional order differently or with new clarity.

There is a reasonable argument that the Nadon Reference sits alongside those other landmarks in terms of its legal significance and wider cultural importance. This book makes that argument.

The Supreme Court of Canada is the highest appellate court in the country. First created in 1875, it has come to occupy an increasingly important position in Canadian society. The court's power over its first sixty years was limited because of Canada's strong ties to the United Kingdom. Those ties meant that cases could be appealed to the Judicial Committee of the Privy Council. It was only in 1949 that the Supreme Court came to occupy the apex position in the judicial system.

The court, though, did not immediately assume more importance in the eyes of Canadians. The pivotal moment came in 1982, when Canada made important changes to its Constitution. Through the *Constitution Act, 1982,* Canada guaranteed that individual and group rights would be protected, primarily in the *Charter of Rights and Freedoms.*[13] As a result, Canadian courts were called upon to scrutinize the validity of legislation and government decisions more frequently than before. The Supreme Court led the way, ushering in a distinctive approach to constitutional interpretation and issuing landmark decisions in every area, from equality rights and freedom of expression to privacy and Indigenous Title cases.

Over the last four decades, the Supreme Court has become more familiar to Canadians. Its role in holding governments and legislatures to account has been identified as one of the features of the Canadian legal and political system that gives Canadians confidence. To be sure, the court issues controversial decisions, and its increased power has spurred criticism from those who think that courts should not intervene in policy matters. Nonetheless, it is impossible to deny that the Supreme Court has assumed a function in Canadian society that would have been unimaginable, say, fifty years ago.[14]

Given the role and function of the Supreme Court, the process by which persons are appointed to it matters a great deal. Yet the appointments process has traditionally been a quiet affair. The fierce confirmation battles that characterize appointments to the US Supreme Court are not part of Canada's political or constitutional culture. Supreme Court of Canada appointments are generally in the hands of the prime minister. And though, in the years just prior to the Nadon appointment, there had been greater scrutiny of judicial appointments, the idea that they might give rise to a court challenge – or, in fact, that they could run up against any sort of legal barrier at all – was virtually unthinkable. Until 2014, when the unthinkable happened.

As a matter of constitutional law, the Nadon Reference established that the Supreme Court of Canada is an essential part of Canada's "constitutional architecture" and that its core features cannot be changed through an ordinary Act of Parliament. It is because of the Nadon Reference that there is now controversy and uncertainty about whether eligibility to the Supreme Court of Canada can be formally restricted to those who are functionally bilingual in Canada's official languages, or whether a seat can be reserved for an Indigenous jurist. That alone makes the decision noteworthy. But the idea of constitutional architecture was also important in itself; shortly after the Nadon Reference, it was deployed in the Senate Reference as a basis for finding that most kinds of Senate reform require the consent (either substantial or unanimous) of the provinces.[15]

The Nadon controversy began as a dispute over statutory interpretation, and much of the reference is an exercise in just that. But even in this notoriously technical – some might call it dull – area of the law, the reference is striking. In holding that Parliament may use over-inclusive rules to achieve a particular goal, the Nadon Reference rejected a widely held view about what it means to engage in purposive interpretation, namely, that it requires lawyers and judges to give relatively little weight to the text of a statute when it is in tension with Parliament's aim in enacting the statute in the first place. This aspect of the decision continues to generate a great deal of skepticism, and even hostility.

Apart from its significance for the law, the reference was a noteworthy moment in the history of the relationship between the judicial and the executive branches of government. When Prime Minister Stephen Harper first announced Marc Nadon as his choice, many onlookers saw it as an attempt to make the Supreme Court more deferential to the executive and legislative branches. At the time, there was a perception that the Harper government had suffered a number of high-profile losses in the high court. The Nadon Reference itself was followed by a remarkable attack on Chief Justice Beverley McLachlin. Furthermore, in the wake of the reference, there was an almost unprecedented leak of the appointments short list from which Nadon's name had been selected.

The entire episode focused the public's attention on the judicial appointments process to an extent we had not seen before, and it arguably gave rise to a new legal field: judicial appointments law. Following the Nadon controversy, there was increased discussion about challenging certain judicial appointments on constitutional grounds – for example, Justice Robert Mainville's appointment, in 2014, from the Federal Court of Appeal to the Quebec Court of Appeal (which some thought was a precursor to further elevation to the Supreme Court of Canada) and Justice Russell Brown's appointment to the Supreme Court of Canada. Most recently, the Canadian Bar Association was prepared to challenge, on constitutional grounds, any attempt to replace Justice Thomas Cromwell (who came to the Supreme Court from the Nova Scotia Court of Appeal) with someone who was not drawn from the Atlantic provinces. It may have been because of this, at least in part, that Justice Malcolm Rowe, a Newfoundlander, was ultimately appointed to replace him.

Though relatively new, the Nadon Reference is indeed a landmark. *The Tenth Justice* explains how it came to be a case, how it was argued, and why it matters. We look to media coverage, legal scholarship, and political commentary to capture the public mood and debate surrounding the case as it developed and as arguments emerged and to contextualize the decision within a broader public conversation about the Supreme Court appointments process. In Chapters 1 and 2, we consider the controversy surrounding Marc Nadon's appointment to the Supreme Court of Canada. Chapter 1 looks at some of the things that were cited about Nadon as a basis for objecting to his appointment. Most, if not all, of these bases were, at best, overstated and, at worst, unfair. The reasons for taking issue with his appointment were grounded, by and large, in political and legal forces quite outside Nadon's control – in particular, they had to do with Quebec politics, with the fact that Supreme Court appointments were made under conditions of great secrecy, and with the perception that the prime minister, Stephen Harper, had a somewhat antagonistic relationship with the courts, which is examined in Chapter 2.

Chapter 3 explores the early legal questions that swirled around Nadon's appointment – that is, those concerning the interpretation of section 6 of the *Supreme Court Act.* It is reasonably clear that the prime minister and minister of justice were broadly aware that Federal Court judges might be ineligible for appointment under that provision. From the moment Marc Nadon was introduced to the Canadian public, the minister of justice sought to foreclose attacks on the legality of his appointment by wielding a memorandum written by former Supreme Court justice Ian Binnie. We discuss that memorandum in Chapter 3 and the many criticisms levied against it.

Chapter 4 discusses the next phase in the Nadon controversy, when the federal government introduced declaratory legislation purporting to resolve the interpretive dispute over section 6. At the same time, the government referred two questions to the Supreme Court of Canada – one concerning the proper interpretation of section 6, and one concerning the constitutionality of the new declaratory provisions. We explore the issues arising out of this two-tiered approach.

Chapters 5 and 6 focus on the written and oral submissions made by the attorney general of Canada and the interveners in the reference, as well as the court's decision. We discuss the arguments that had the greatest (and least) amount of traction and the criticisms directed at the majority decision after its release. Chapters 7 and 8 examine events that took place after the reference. Chapter 7 looks at the remarkable public dispute between Prime Minister Harper and then Chief Justice Beverley McLachlin, the leak of the short list from which Nadon's name was selected, and the government's subsequent dismantling of its own judicial appointments process and the Trudeau government's new, more transparent one. Chapter 8 considers the reference's impact on how politicians, lawyers, the media, and the public at large view Supreme Court appointments – through a legal and political lens.

Finally, Chapter 9 looks at the reference's potential effect on future attempts to reform the appointments process. In holding that matters concerning the composition of the Supreme Court can be changed only with a constitutional amendment, the majority protected the court as an institution. It cannot be unilaterally abolished or stacked through an ordinary Act of Parliament. But the opinion also presents formidable hurdles to those wishing to make the court more reflective of the diversity of Canada. Henceforth, efforts to statutorily enshrine gender, race, or regional diversity on the court, or to make bilingualism an express criterion of eligibility, may well meet with the objection that they are unconstitutional. To this extent, the reference has cast the Supreme Court in amber.

1

What's So Bad about Marc Nadon?

On 2 October 2013, the Canadian public was introduced to Marc Nadon, Prime Minister Stephen Harper's nomination for the Supreme Court of Canada. Appearing before an ad hoc committee of parliamentarians in a suit and bow tie, Nadon was an unassuming figure. He spoke about his humble roots in Saint-Jérôme, Quebec – "a tiny village north of Montreal, in the Laurentian Mountains" – and about his family: his grandparents, father, mother, wife, and son.[1] He discussed his path to legal studies, his initial hopes to practise criminal law, and his ultimate diversion into transportation and maritime law. Nadon spoke about his work on the Federal Court and the Federal Court of Appeal. He reflected on the life of a judge as a "life of intellectual pursuits." And he discussed the role of the Supreme Court of Canada in Canadian society, the importance of the rule of law, and the significance of lawyers in the administration of justice. Nadon closed his introductory remarks with an anecdote about a speech given by Lord Chancellor Elwyn-Jones to a group of civil lawyers in Paris, in which they mistranslated "common lawyers" as "ordinary lawyers."

It was by all accounts a perfectly charming, if suitably dry, appearance by a man who, most assumed, was set to become Canada's next Supreme Court justice. Nadon inadvertently invited controversy by seeming to have suggested that he had been drafted by the Detroit Red Wings.[2] (He hadn't.) Otherwise, though, Marc Nadon came across as pleasant and good-natured.

Yet in the weeks and months that followed, Nadon would be at the centre of one of the great legal and political controversies in modern Canadian history. National columnist Jeffrey Simpson wrote a scathing op-ed in the *Globe and Mail* in which he concluded: "Justice Nadon is undoubtedly a nice man and perhaps a competent judge, but he is not qualified enough to sit on the Supreme Court of Canada ... [H]is is at best an ordinary appointment, and at worst sub-par."[3] In a longer piece by Sean Fine, reflecting on what Nadon's appointment "says about the Supreme Court's future," a number of distinguished legal academics were remarkably candid about their lack of regard for him as a jurist. Professor Jamie Cameron, who made a point of noting that she was breaking "a rule not to comment publicly on the attributes of appointees," observed that "the appointment shows ... the Prime Minister's lack of respect for the Supreme Court as an institution." She stated: "[T]his appointment unquestionably weakens the court."[4] Professor Robert Leckey quipped that Nadon was on no one's short *or* long list.[5]

One cannot overstate just how unusual it is for any appointment to the Supreme Court of Canada to be subjected to the sort of withering criticism that Marc Nadon received in fall 2013. Traditionally, the bar, legal academics, and the media have been strenuously careful not to call into question the merits of appointees. That was not the case with Justice Nadon.

So what happened? How could such an apparently mild-mannered judge of twenty years' standing, the coauthor of a book on maritime law, provoke such a cascade of criticism?[6]

To understand the political and legal firestorm that greeted Marc Nadon's appointment, one needs to situate the appointment in a wider context. In fact, the controversy was rarely about Nadon himself, though ungenerous insinuations were sometimes made about his character as a judge. The controversy, rather, was about the person who appointed him, the legal framework surrounding judicial appointments in Canada, and an array of other political debates about, among other things, diversity, criminal justice, francophone-anglophone relations, and the long-term direction of the Supreme Court. It may help to begin by taking a brief moment to consider the man Justice Nadon was appointed to replace: Justice Morris Fish.

SO LONG, JUSTICE FISH, AND THANKS

On 22 April 2013, almost six months before Marc Nadon nostalgically reflected on his erstwhile hockey ambitions, Justice Morris Fish announced that he would be retiring from the Supreme Court of Canada.[7] In making sense of the controversy that would swirl around Marc Nadon, it helps to appreciate the stature of the man he was supposed to replace on the Supreme Court and the important role that his predecessor played.

Justice Fish had been appointed to the Supreme Court after spending fourteen years on the Quebec Court of Appeal. An expert in criminal law, committed to civil liberties, his elevation in August 2003 was widely celebrated.[8] When Justice Fish was named to the court (replacing Charles Gonthier), Michel Robert, chief justice of the Quebec Court of Appeal, described him as a person with "a passion for defending the rights of the accused, though he's not always in favour of the accused's rights. I think he's got some equilibrium and balance."[9] Justice Fish had a strong reputation as a criminal law expert even before his appointment to the bench in the late-1980s. Prior to sitting on the Court of Appeal, he had periodically taught criminal law at the law faculties of the University of Montreal (1969–71), the University of Ottawa (1971–74), and McGill (1973–80, 1986–89). Justice Fish had been active in law reform initiatives and received a number of honours for his contributions to criminal justice.[10] In a Supreme Court news release issued upon news of his retirement, Chief Justice Beverley McLachlin stated: "Justice Fish has served on the court with wisdom, and made enormous contributions to the court and to Canada. He is a wonderful colleague and friend who will be greatly missed."[11]

Those are the sorts of comments one might expect from a chief justice whenever any member of the court departs. But well before Justice Fish officially announced his retirement, the wider legal community had quietly reflected on what his departure might mean for the court and for civil and legal rights in Canada. After all, the court's docket is dominated by criminal cases – many of which are heard as a matter of right – and so the loss of a judge with expertise in the area would be felt especially keenly. In a 2012 article for the *Globe and Mail*, Kirk Makin reported the concerns of many lawyers – particularly those working in criminal defence. They worried about the tough-on-crime agenda of Prime Minister Stephen Harper and the effect that a more "conservative" or "hawkish" appointment might have on the Supreme Court's effectiveness as a guardian of the Charter rights of criminal defendants. Justice Fish was arguably the last link to an era when the court was regarded as the stalwart defender of those rights. As Makin wrote: "Judge Fish has carried on the legacy of the Gang of Five – a faction of Supreme Court of Canada judges whose orientation toward the rights of the accused in criminal cases dominated the court in the 1990s."[12] Since Beverley McLachlin had become chief justice, it was generally acknowledged, the court had adopted a far more deferential posture, leading to a perceived softening in rights protection.[13] Justice Fish was a vocal critic of the court's direction, frequently dissenting on matters concerning the scope of Charter protections in criminal investigations.[14]

Indeed, a month after he announced his impending retirement, Justice Fish chastised future chief justice Richard Wagner for failing to appreciate that a defendant should have been permitted to leave the partial defence of provocation with the jury in a murder case – describing Justice Wagner's analysis as "incomplete and flawed."[15] Makin, reporting the jab for the *Globe and Mail*, observed: "As its ranking expert in the field [of criminal law], Justice Fish's imminent departure from the court is a major concern to the defence bar, which perceives him as the only judge on the court who consistently advocates for the rights of the accused."[16] Makin further reported public remarks by Justice Fish that were taken as a thinly veiled rebuke of the views of Justice Michael Moldaver, who had suggested that defence lawyers were using the Charter to make specious arguments and to string out the trial process. Justice Fish took issue with that claim and urged lawyers to make Charter arguments whenever doing so would advance the interests of clients.[17]

Justice Fish's departure left the court short of expertise in criminal law, and Marc Nadon's appointment did not compensate for that loss. Moreover, his own areas of expertise – maritime law and transportation law – were of less obvious use on Canada's highest court. As Jeffrey Simpson wrote: "[M]aritime law cases might make it to the Supreme Court once in a quarter-century."[18]

There were also suggestions that Nadon, by then a supernumerary judge on the Federal Court, lacked the necessary vigour for a position on the Supreme Court.[19] Sean Fine wrote at length that Nadon had been effectively pulled out of semiretirement. Whether intentional or not, he conjured an image of Nadon practically leaping at the chance to "work about half his usual hours and still receive his full pay." Fine quoted Frederick Vaughan, coauthor of a history of the Supreme Court, who stated: "It's a strange, strange appointment, frankly." He continued, "Why would you go with a supernumerary when he's indicated that he's halfway to retirement?"[20] The impression cast was of a judge who would be no more than a marginal figure in the life of the court.

Those comments were somewhat unfair. For his part, Nadon denied that his supernumerary status was akin to semiretirement. Under questioning by Françoise Boivin, Nadon argued that he had taken supernumerary status so that he could devote more time to complex cases, rather than thinly spreading his time across a wider number of simpler but less interesting cases. He stated: "The supernumerary status allows us to hear fewer cases and work fewer weeks as a result ... It can also help us dedicate much more time to our cases, should we choose to. So we are not talking about an early retirement."[21] To illustrate his point, he observed that, shortly after taking supernumerary status, he had spent two months working full-time on "a complicated Charter case" concerning equality rights.[22] Under light pressure, he continued: "I knew those weeks or days of rest would disappear when I accepted this appointment to the Supreme Court. I did not accept the Prime Minister's offer lightly. If this goes well, I am ready to do the work and devote all my time to it."[23]

Again, all these questions about energy and vigour may have been unfair. It is not so difficult to believe that a person might find the work at the Supreme Court of Canada more interesting and attractive than work at many lower courts. But there were other questions surrounding Nadon as a jurist. It was widely suggested that he had been selected principally because he would be inclined to defer to the government and legislature in Charter cases. His dissenting opinion in *Canada v Khadr,* in particular, was frequently referenced.[24]

THE KHADR CONTROVERSY

Omar Khadr is a Canadian citizen who, at the age of fifteen, was taken prisoner by US forces in Afghanistan and subsequently held at Guantanamo Bay. He was subjected to a sleep deprivation program to make him more pliable while under interrogation. Knowing this, Canadian officials nonetheless questioned Khadr and shared the information they obtained with the Americans. On that basis, the Supreme Court of Canada in 2008 held that the Canadian government had violated Khadr's rights under section 7 of the Charter. At the time, this finding was reached only by way of concluding that the government had a duty to disclose the information to Khadr and his lawyers. On the strength of the finding, however, Khadr argued that the government also had a Charter obligation to seek his repatriation to Canada. Prime Minister Harper had emphatically stated in a press conference that he had no intention to do so.[25]

And so Khadr sought an order from the Federal Court to force the prime minister's hand. At the trial level, Justice James O'Reilly found that the government had infringed Khadr's section 7 rights and ordered it to request his return to Canada. A majority of the Court of Appeal upheld the order. But Justice Nadon dissented. He found that the Canadian government had "taken all necessary means at its disposal to protect Mr. Khadr during the whole period of his detention at

Guantanamo Bay."[26] In a lengthy passage that surely would have appealed to the prime minister, Nadon noted that the Canadian government had advocated for Khadr's fair treatment on numerous occasions and that it "continued to monitor Mr. Khadr's situation and kept in contact with US officials in that regard."[27]

Justice Nadon noted that Canadian authorities had requested that Khadr be provided with medical assistance and had paid him frequent "welfare visits." He concluded: "Other than the fact that Canada ... should not have proceeded with interviews in 2003 and 2004 and should not have provided the information obtained therefrom to US authorities, I cannot see how Canada's conduct can be criticized."[28] Even if there had been a Charter violation, Nadon continued, it would be inappropriate to remedy the violation by ordering the government to request repatriation. Observing that matters pertaining to foreign affairs lie at the core of the Crown's traditional prerogative powers, Justice Nadon stated that O'Reilly's order was contrary to the separation of powers. It is worth noting that, although the Supreme Court of Canada ultimately agreed with O'Reilly's finding that there had indeed been an infringement of Khadr's Charter rights, the court somewhat endorsed Nadon's analysis of the remedy. Rather than order the government to seek repatriation, which was regarded as too intrusive a remedy, the court issued a declaration that the government had violated Khadr's rights.[29]

Nadon's dissenting opinion in *Khadr* was often trotted out as an example of the deferential stance he could be expected to adopt when appointed to the high court.[30] At the very least, it was suggested, Prime Minister Harper had selected Nadon in the expectation that he would issue decisions and cast votes "friendly" to the government. Sean Fine, discussing the inferences that might be drawn from Nadon's decision in *Khadr,* stated:

> Thirteen Canadian judges ultimately heard the case ... On interrogating a teenager without counsel present, and turning information over to his jailers, the court said: "[This behaviour] offends the most basic Canadian standards about the treatment of detained youth suspects."

> Only one judge called Canada nearly blameless: Justice Nadon. Foreign policy, he wrote in a stylish and confident defence, is one of "the forbidden areas" in which judges have no right to question government.
>
> Clearly he was no bleeding heart. He had nerve. And he was on the government's side.[31]

When assessing a judge's entire career, one shouldn't make too much of a single case. It is not clear whether Nadon himself considered his opinion in *Khadr* representative. He did submit it to the judicial selection committee as an example of his work, but some of his comments on the separation of powers before the ad hoc committee on his appointment are at least broadly consistent with his reasoning on the remedy.[32]

The other cases Nadon submitted to the committee do not reflect any particular or obvious skepticism of Charter review or an especially deferential attitude to the government. One possible exception is *Canada v Jodhon.*[33] There, the claimant, who was legally blind, alleged that websites operated by the Treasury Board, Statistics Canada, and the Public Service Commission of Canada were not accessible to persons with visual impairments, and to that extent infringed section 15 of the Charter. The trial judge agreed that there was a section 15 violation, which was not saved under section 1, and ordered a supervisory order – or structural injunction – whereby the court remained seized of the case until the violation was effectively fixed.

Justice Nadon, writing for the court, found no error in the trial judge's conclusion that there had been a violation of section 15. He did, however, conclude that under the circumstances the supervisory order had been unjustified and needlessly intrusive. The order was based on evidence that was dated, and this was the first case of its kind, meaning that there was no reason to think that the government would fail to take necessary and timely steps to make the websites accessible to the visually impaired.[34] More interesting, Nadon again appealed to separation-of-powers considerations: "[T]he judge's remedy ventures into the realm of the executive ... [A] contempt proceeding would have been available to the Attorney Generals and would have constituted a more appropriate way to deal with government disobedience or further inaction rather than a supervisory order because it would intrude less on executive jurisdiction."[35] Under the circumstances, Nadon concluded, a declaration of unconstitutionality was an appropriate remedy.

It is, of course, possible to draw broad parallels between *Jodhon* and *Khadr*, especially in Nadon's consideration of the remedy. But structural remedies are rightly rare,[36] and it is hard to see Nadon's rejection of one here as particularly noteworthy.

Martin v Canada likewise involved a section 15 claim.[37] The main thrust of the litigation was that the *Employment Insurance Act*, by limiting parental leave to thirty-five weeks per pregnancy, as opposed to per child, discriminated against the parents of, for example, twins. Nadon, writing for the court, found that the parents of multiple children did not represent a historically disadvantaged group and that the restriction was not based on stereotyping. Moreover, the restriction did not deny "access to fundamental institutions or a basic aspect of [their] full membership in Canadian society." On this basis, the Federal Court of Appeal rejected the Charter challenge. Section 15 is a tricky area of law, but it is difficult to see the opinion as especially problematic or even controversial. A similar conclusion could have been reached by judges embodying a variety of philosophical perspectives. It is hard, therefore, to know what, if anything, one should read into it.

Finally, there is Nadon's ruling in *Mugesera v Canada*. A deportation order was issued against the applicant broadly on the basis that he had incited hatred, murder, and genocide of the Tutsi ethnic group and had misrepresented his involvement in a crime against humanity to obtain status in Canada. The order was upheld by the Appeal Division of the Immigration and Refugee Board. The applicant sought judicial review of that decision in the Federal Court. Nadon was the trial judge. He found that a number of factual conclusions by the adjudicator and Appeal Division were unreasonable and sent the matter back to the Appeal Division for reconsideration. Furthermore, he certified two questions of law for consideration by the Federal Court of Appeal. The case itself is interesting – concerning, among other things, the definition of various serious criminal offences – and it ultimately found its way to the Supreme Court of Canada.[38] It is, however, difficult to see any particular judicial philosophy at work in Nadon's ruling.

One other case, which to our knowledge was not presented by Nadon to the selection panel, is also of interest. In 2011, Elizabeth May, leader of the federal Green Party, had sought judicial review of a policy by the Canadian Radio-Television and Telecommunications Commission (CRTC) that not every leader of a political party needed to be included in election debates.[39] To expedite the review process, May sought an order requiring the CRTC to amend its guidelines for election debates and an order requiring the television networks covering the debates to allow her to participate. Nadon rejected the application, for the most part on what might be regarded as technical grounds – for example, May's failure to challenge the policy in a more timely fashion and her failure to name the attorney general of Canada as respondent. But Nadon also took the view that the underlying merits of May's case were relatively weak, and he found her Charter claim – that the CRTC's policy interfered with her right to effective participation in the electoral process – particularly unpromising. This case was mentioned in the media on at least one occasion.[40] Again, though, the case hardly suggests that Marc Nadon had especially strong political convictions. At most, it suggests a concern for legal process and, in the absence of a compelling justification, a disinclination to throw the election debates into chaos only twelve days before they were scheduled to take place.

For all the fuss over Justice Nadon's opinion in *Khadr*, then, the rulings that were made available to the judicial selection committee do not reveal anything especially problematic about his judicial philosophy or his attitude to constitutional rights or civil liberties. Indeed, there were several occasions during the hearing when it seemed as if his questioners were confused about why he had included some of the cases. Moreover, academics and commentators did not produce other cases by way of demonstrating Nadon's infirmities as a judge. On the contrary, few onlookers had ever thought to ask themselves about his judicial merits prior to his appointment. He was on nobody's radar. Jeffrey Simpson remarked: "The country's law associations and professors knew so little about such an unknown judge that they fell silent."[41] That is not exactly high praise, but it underscores that Nadon was hardly a notorious figure before the national spotlight was turned upon him.

DIVERSITY AND QUEBEC REPRESENTATION

Some of the criticism heaped upon Justice Nadon during the weeks and months following the prime minister's announcement was no doubt driven by the fact that his appointment would do nothing to improve either gender or racial diversity on the court. Concerns had been expressed, well before Nadon's nomination, that the Harper government had a tendency to appoint men to the high court, leading to a decrease in gender parity. Since 2006, when Harper took office, there had been four vacancies on the court, and all but one of the replacements had been men.[42] As a result, the complement of women on the court had dropped from four to three. At the same time, commentators had noted a wider trend in judicial appointments across the country – one suggesting, at worst, deliberate disregard for the value of diversity among judges.[43] To those onlookers, Nadon's appointment could be justified only if he had an especially distinguished record on the bench. The heightened scrutiny he received can be understood in this light as well – even if this was somewhat unfair to Nadon, who had hardly appointed himself to the Supreme Court.

There was an additional, very different diversity issue in play. Quebec is entitled to have three judges representing it on the Supreme Court of Canada. Nadon was to be one of those judges. As a Federal Court judge, however, he was not a current member of the Quebec judiciary or bar. This created a legal problem. It also created a political problem. The whole point of the legal requirement of Quebec representation was arguably to ensure that there would be voices on the

Supreme Court prepared to speak on behalf of Quebec's unique culture and traditions. For Quebec's political establishment, section 6 was symbolically important. Nadon's appointment therefore embroiled him in, of all things, the political dynamic between the federal government and Quebec. He arguably became the unwitting symbol of the federal government's willingness to stampede over Québécois rights, values, and culture.

What, then, was so bad about Marc Nadon? In an important sense, the answer is clear – nothing. Certainly, there was nothing to suggest a lack of competence. Nadon had written a few opinions that were arguably on the conservative side but none that could be described as radical. He had reduced his workload on the Federal Court of Appeal by assuming supernumerary status but was still active on the bench. His name may not have been on the lips of the profession and professoriate before his appointment was announced, but there was nothing in his record to justify the abuse he endured in the popular press. After all, the merits of one judicial candidate relative to another are not always easy to assess. Nadon had served as a judge for more than twenty years; he was familiar with the demands of the job. He was sometimes caricatured as a mere "maritime lawyer." As he pointed out in a conversation with us, however, his work on the bench was hardly limited to maritime law issues – he had dealt with cases pertaining to tax, patents, and constitutional questions.[44] And, he was far from the first Federal Court judge to be so elevated.

There was, of course, a further reason to subject Marc Nadon's qualifications to special scrutiny. From the outset, it appeared, there might be a legal barrier to his appointment. To some commentators, that raised the question: Why appoint someone who raised issues of legal eligibility unless he was not just superior but obviously superior to everyone else? A competent judge, Nadon had not been a particularly prominent or distinguished voice. He had not developed an especially strong identity, authored noteworthy opinions, produced influential scholarship, or in other ways demonstrated the particular combination of skills and qualities that many people hope to see reflected on the Supreme Court. To his critics, he was ordinary and workmanlike. And that was taken to reflect a decision, by the prime minister who appointed him, that the court itself should be more ordinary and workmanlike too.

2

The Prime Minister's Prerogative

JUSTIFIED OR NOT, PEOPLE had concerns about Justice Nadon as a replacement for the retired Justice Fish. Those concerns were amplified by the fact that it did not seem that there was anything that could be done about it. Since the creation of the Supreme Court of Canada, the appointments process has been largely marked by secrecy and all-but-untrammelled discretion.

It may come as a surprise, but the *British North America Act, 1867* – the document that created the Dominion of Canada – does not say anything at all about a Supreme Court of Canada. On the contrary, at the time of Confederation, it was anticipated that the final court of appeal would remain the Judicial Committee of the Privy Council, in the United Kingdom. Section 101 of the *BNA Act* conferred upon Parliament the power to create a "general court of appeal for Canada."[1] But there was no legal requirement on Parliament to do so, and any court created pursuant to section 101 would still be subject to the oversight of the Privy Council. Parliament created the Supreme Court not by a constitutional process but by an ordinary statute: the 1875 *Supreme and Exchequer Courts Act.*[2] For much of the court's history, it was open to Parliament to radically change, or even abolish, the Supreme Court; there was nothing in the Constitution to prevent it.

Section 4(2) of the *Supreme Court Act* states that judges are to be appointed by the governor general, acting on the advice of the governor-in-council – that is, the federal Cabinet. In practice, it has generally been understood that the matter is entirely in the hands of the prime minister.[3] At least three ministers of justice, including the minister who shepherded Marc Nadon's appointment, have articulated this understanding.[4] There are few legal limits on the prime minister's exercise of this prerogative power. Section 4(1) stipulates that there must be one chief justice and eight puisne judges. And sections 5 and 6 of the *Supreme Court Act* state:

5. Any person may be appointed a judge who is or has been a judge of a superior court of a province or a barrister or advocate of at least ten years standing at the bar of a province.
6. At least three of the judges shall be appointed from among the judges of the Court of Appeal or of the Superior Court of the Province of Quebec or from among the advocates of that Province.

Thus, the Act mandates that there be nine judges on the court, three of whom must come from Quebec and all of whom must satisfy the qualifications set out in section 5. These provisions represent – or, anyway, were thought to represent – the extent of the statutory limits on the prime minister's appointment power. In addition, there were and are conventions of regional representation – though the precise parameters of those conventions have always been a matter of some dispute. For example, it is often thought that the province of Ontario must also be represented by two or three judges on the court, the Atlantic provinces must be represented by one judge, and the western provinces must be represented by at least two.[5] Furthermore, there has arguably developed over the last thirty years a convention of rough gender parity on the court, though it may be too early to say how far such a convention has solidified.[6] There is certainly no convention of racial or ethnic diversity, though there has been increasing dismay and frustration about the court's homogeneity.[7]

So there are few legal constraints on the prime minister's prerogative over judicial appointments to the Supreme Court. But even more striking has been the traditional absence of political constraints. Until relatively recently, the process was conducted in strict secrecy, with all the suspicion that engenders. Adam Dodek has observed that "[m]ore was known about the process for electing a new Pope than about the process for selecting a new Supreme Court justice."[8] Similarly, Jacob Ziegel described the process as one "shrouded in vagueness, and unsubstantiated rumour and gossip."[9]

THE POLITICS OF JUDICIAL APPOINTMENTS

Given the lack of transparency, and the limitless discretion accorded the prime minister, there has always been a risk that appointments to the court would be awarded on a patronage basis.[10] Indeed, for the first seventy-five years of the Supreme Court's history, more than a few appointments were nakedly political.[11] Consider the appointment of Louis-Philippe Brodeur in 1911. Ian Bushnell, discussing Brodeur's appointment, remarked: "[Brodeur] had been speaker of the House of Commons from 1901–04, following which he had been a member of the government until his appointment to the court. The appointment was an obvious and dramatic return to one in which the political background dominated."[12]

Robert Taschereau's appointment in 1940 also smacked of patronage. Taschereau was a prominent member of the Liberal Party. His father was Louis-Alexandre Taschereau, the former premier of Quebec. According to Bushnell, Robert Taschereau "had a high political and social profile, and had been heir-apparent to his father's political power until Duplessis' victory of 1936."[13] He had no judicial experience before his appointment. An even more controversial appointment, Douglas Abbott, was a federal Cabinet minister when he was appointed to the Supreme Court in 1954.[14]

Perhaps the most blatant example was in 1963, when Chief Justice Patrick Kerwin died just as the Diefenbaker Conservatives were in the middle of a collapse. The prime minister himself was offered the vacant position on the court in exchange for stepping down as leader of the Conservatives. He refused, and ultimately Justice Wishart Spence was appointed – after Parliament was reconstituted with a new government.[15]

Beyond such notorious episodes, politics has long played a role in the appointment of Supreme Court judges. How extensive a role it plays is unclear, largely because of the lack of transparency.[16] Empirical research published in 1967 showed that, among federal judicial appointments generally, the vast majority were politically affiliated with the governing party.[17] From 1984 to 1988, when Mulroney was prime minister, 47.4 percent of federal judicial appointments "had a known association with the Conservative Party."[18] A further study of federal appointments from 1989 to 2003 indicated that 30.6 percent had "probably" donated money to the party of the prime minister who appointed them.[19] As David Schneiderman notes in *Red, White, and Kind of Blue?*, "The numbers across both Conservative and Liberal federal administrations were nearly constant."[20]

At the Supreme Court level, outright lobbying on behalf of certain candidates has been rare. There have, however, been exceptions. Following the sudden death of Justice John Sopinka in November 1997, there was blatant jockeying in favour of two Ontario Court of Appeal justices: John Laskin and Rosalie Abella.[21] The struggle was engineered by their supporters rather than the judges themselves, but it had a political character that some onlookers regarded as unseemly. Prime Minister Jean Chrétien eventually appointed Ian Binnie, a renowned lawyer and senior partner at a national firm. Like Sopinka, Binnie had not previously been a judge before his ascension to the Supreme Court.

None of this is to suggest that brute partisan political considerations drive judicial decision making in a straightforward or predictable fashion.[22] Nor have there been indications that the public's respect for the judiciary has been significantly undermined by the secrecy surrounding the process.[23] A Focus Canada survey in 1989 found that 76 percent of respondents had at least some confidence in the Supreme

Court as an institution.[24] A Gallup poll conducted in 2001 showed that "Canadians had greater respect for and confidence in the Supreme Court than they did in almost all other Canadian institutions, including ... the federal government, the House of Commons, and provincial governments."[25] In *The Last Word: Media Coverage of the Supreme Court of Canada,* Florian Sauvageau, David Schneiderman, and David Taras reported: "When asked whether courts or legislatures should have the final say on key questions in public life, Canadians supported the courts by a margin of two to one."[26] This was the case in spite of allegations of judicial activism, often from conservative commentators.[27] A 2010 poll found that 69 percent of Canadians had confidence in the Supreme Court, compared with 42 percent who felt that way about Parliament.[28]

Yet one cannot assume that Canadians are entirely satisfied with how Supreme Court justices are appointed. Sauvageau, Schneiderman, and Taras observed: "Despite efforts to appear independent and non-partisan, the public views the Supreme Court as being deeply enmeshed in politics."[29] They cited a 2001 Ipsos-Reid poll that suggested that "seven out of ten of those surveyed believed that the court was influenced by partisan politics" as well as a 2003 poll showing that an "astonishing" two-thirds of respondents "believed that party politics either always or sometimes played a role."[30] Canadians, it appears, do have concerns about the process by which high court judges are selected, if not about the judges themselves.[31]

THE TURN TOWARDS TRANSPARENCY AND ACCOUNTABILITY

In 1949, Canada abolished appeals to the Judicial Committee of the Privy Council. The Supreme Court became the country's court of last resort. As a result, it was thought important to dispel any hint of partisanship in the court's appointments.[32] In 1969, Prime Minister Trudeau wrote: "Judges should not be regarded as representatives of several different governments which could conceivably be allowed to appoint them."[33] And in the Charter era, it became still more difficult to justify a Supreme Court appointments process that appeared in any way to rely on partisan considerations.[34] In 2004, following a request by the minister of democratic reform in Paul Martin's Liberal government, the process was scrutinized by the House of Commons Standing Committee on Justice, Human Rights, Public Safety and Emergency Preparedness.[35] It concluded that there should be an appointments advisory committee with representatives from each of the official parties, the provinces, the judiciary, the bar, and the lay public. That committee would provide a short list of candidates for the minister of justice, who would later appear before the committee to explain the process and the qualifications of the individual ultimately selected from the list.[36] There were dissenting voices from the other parties, but few disputed the need for more transparency and accountability.

The new process was unveiled in 2005, and it empowered an arms-length advisory group to produce a short list of three candidates. Except in extraordinary circumstances, the minister of justice and prime minister would choose someone from the list. Candidates, however, would not be subject to questioning, and the advisory group would sign confidentiality agreements regarding the list.[37] Finally, the minister of justice would appear before a committee to explain the process and selection.[38]

The new procedure took effect when Justice John Major retired. After the short list for his replacement was assembled, however, Stephen Harper's Conservatives were voted into government. Justice Marshall Rothstein was selected from the list and – in a departure from the prescribed process – the nominee himself was asked to answer questions before a parliamentary committee.[39] The hearing was televised. Justice Rothstein entertained questions on a wide variety of subjects, including Indigenous Rights and their relationship to the Charter, the appropriate treatment of lower courts by appellate ones, the importance of precedent, the increasing role played by nonlegal experts in complex litigation, the wisdom of relying on foreign judgments and international law, and the role of personal experience and biases in judging.[40] He emphasized the need for judicial restraint and deference to Parliament's judgment, stating:

> [T]he important thing is that judges, when applying the [Charter], have to have recognition that the statute they're dealing with was passed by a democratically elected legislature, that it's unlikely the legislature intended to violate the charter. Sometimes it happens. But they have to be aware of that, and therefore they have to approach the matter with some restraint. But the most important thing is that they apply a rigorous and thorough analysis, and if they do that, then I would say they are doing their job. If they depart from that, it might be a different matter.[41]

There is room to wonder just how much Canadians learned about Justice Rothstein as a result of this process.[42] Professor Peter Hogg chaired the proceedings and (for reasons we will see) was clearly intent on ensuring that they would not degenerate into anything like an American-style confirmation hearing. The chair cut off questioners and the respondent numerous times, no doubt in the interest of fairness but sometimes at the expense of a substantive dialogue.[43] Nonetheless, insofar as the hearing introduced Canadians to their newest Supreme Court justice and humanized him, the innovation could be regarded as a modest success.

Two years later, in 2008, a broadly similar process was undertaken when Justice Michel Bastarache announced his retirement. But the advisory committee, when presented with the minister of justice's long list, was "beset by partisan bickering."[44] Frustrated, Prime Minister Harper opted simply to nominate Justice Thomas Cromwell (then of the Nova Scotia Court of Appeal). At first, the intention was that Cromwell would not be formally appointed until he participated in a Rothstein-esque hearing before a parliamentary committee. Shortly after announcing the nomination, however, Harper asked the governor general to dissolve Parliament. Following an election campaign, which the Harper Conservatives won, the governor general prorogued Parliament.

More than three and a half months after nominating Cromwell, Harper gave up on the hearing, and officially appointed him.[45]

A process broadly similar to that used in the appointment of Rothstein was used again in 2011, when Justices Ian Binnie and Louise Charron both decided to retire. There were minor changes. For example, in addition to consulting with the Ontario attorney general and leading members of the Ontario bar, the minister of justice invited members of the public to suggest possible candidates through a government website.[46] But the nominated candidate, chosen from a short list settled upon by an advisory committee of five members of Parliament, would still be required to answer questions at a public hearing. The chosen replacements, Justices Michael Moldaver and Andromache Karakatsanis, did just that – as did Justice Wagner when he was selected to replace Justice Deschamps in 2013.

Thus, by the time Justice Fish retired, in 2013, there was a broadly settled process in place for appointing Supreme Court justices. The main innovation of the Harper government was, of course, the public hearing. Plainly, the point of this was to mimic the Senate confirmation hearings used in the United States for the appointment of federal judges. In the United States, nominations for federal courts, including the Supreme Court, must receive the "advice and consent" of the Senate. Since the 1950s, nominees have appeared before senators.[47] In principle, one can see why, in an era when the Supreme Court of Canada sometimes issues decisions that have a political hue, nominees should be required to publicly answer questions addressed to them by elected representatives from all the major political parties. The fear, however, is that those very representatives will treat the nomination as simply another zero-sum political debate – in which one party's success, by definition, requires another party's failure – and conduct the questioning in such a way that the public will come to regard judicial decision making as driven by partisan political considerations rather than legal ones. Indeed, Canadian jurists and legal commentators are often horrified by US confirmation hearings, which, at least since the failed nomination of Judge Robert Bork in 1987, have been viciously fought by both Republicans and Democrats.[48] For this reason, the Canadian Bar Association, in 2004, flatly opposed any sort of parliamentary review of Supreme Court nominations.[49] Retired Justice Claire L'Heureux-Dubé, providing evidence to the Standing Committee on Justice, Human Rights, Emergency Preparedness, and Public Safety, did the same.[50]

The appointments process devised by the Harper government was intended to provide a degree of transparency and accountability without undermining public respect for the judiciary. At bottom, though, the process in 2013 was hardly more transparent than that which had existed before Paul Martin's government initiated reform in 2004. Canadians were none the wiser as to the criteria for selecting candidates, the nature of the consultation process (i.e., who would be consulted and the extent to which the input from consulted bodies could be disregarded by the minister of justice), the role to be played by the public, the number of names on the long list assembled by the minister of justice, and whether and to what extent the prime minister's final decision would be guided by the opinions of the minister of justice.[51]

Perhaps more to the point, none of the changes made to the process really constrained the prime minister's discretion. The advisory committee could not consider anyone not included on the minister of justice's long list – which, it seemed, did not need to be terribly long.[52] Moreover, the government controlled who was on the advisory committee; since 2011, a majority of MPs on the committee were Conservatives, and the proceedings of committee hearings were entirely secret.[53] They were given only two to three days' notice to scrutinize the candidates on the long list.[54] What is more, the parliamentary hearings themselves did not exert much of a pull on the prime minister's appointment power. Prime Minister Harper announced the appointments of Justices Moldaver, Karakatsanis, and Wagner, within a day of their respective hearings, giving no indication that the opinions of the parliamentarians who attended them had made any difference.[55] Indeed, legal scholar Adam Dodek pointed out that, "[i]n one case, the Chief Justice announced the swearing-in dates for the new justice before the

Prime Minister had formally appointed the 'nominee,' thus demonstrating the *pro forma* nature of the hearings."[56] In an editorial for the *Globe and Mail*, it was suggested that the prime minister regarded the hearings as a mere formality.[57] And why wouldn't he? After all, the MPs who asked questions during the hearing were typically those who served on the advisory committee that created the short list. It is unlikely that they would take serious issue with a candidate they themselves had notionally approved.[58]

Insofar as anyone was made accountable by the process, it was the judges who were nominated, not the prime minister who appointed them. In 2006 and 2011, respectively, Justices Rothstein and Moldaver were challenged about their lack of facility in French. Justices Karakatsanis and Wagner faced questions regarding their relative lack of judicial experience.[59] To a degree, this is precisely what critics of public hearings feared: turning Supreme Court judges into political punching bags. (As we have already seen, Justice Marc Nadon hardly got off lightly during his own hearing.) There will always be some metric by which someone other than the person ultimately chosen could be regarded as "better." To a degree, weighing one prospective judge against another is a matter of subjective taste rather than objective fact.[60]

For now, we would simply note that the appointments process, whatever else it may have achieved, did not make the prime minister more accountable. If anything, it turned the nominee into a kind of proxy target for critics of the prime minister, encouraging frustrated committee members from opposing parties to direct their criticisms at the appointee, not the appointer. It may have had a similar effect on media commentators who, lacking much insight into the process by which the nominee was selected, were reduced to reporting any issues of substance that happened to float to the surface.

THE PRIME MINISTER

The appointments process in 2013 did nothing to dispel the notion that the prime minister was under no legal constraints, and few political ones, in selecting new Supreme Court of Canada judges. This only magnified concerns that Prime Minister Harper would use his power to appoint someone who would thwart judicial review of his conservative agenda. Harper had a track record for pushing up against the legal limits of his authority. In 2008, he asked the governor general to prorogue Parliament, apparently to avoid an inevitable vote of non-confidence that would bring down his (newly re-elected) minority government.[61] In the waning days of 2009, he again asked the governor general to prorogue Parliament during February's Olympic Winter Games, ostensibly to allow Canadians to focus on the event, but possibly to hinder a parliamentary investigation of Canada's treatment of detainees in Afghanistan.[62] On both occasions, the prime minister would have known that, by and large, the governor general does not refuse such requests, irrespective of the reasons for making them. Without diminishing the complexity of the issues raised in these episodes,[63] or suggesting that one or both of these prorogation requests were illegitimate,[64] they nonetheless suggested a willingness to push against the limits of the law.

These are far from the only examples. Legislation concerning criminal justice was often introduced through private members' bills, rather than government bills, in order to circumvent requirements that the Department of Justice vet them for Charter compliance.[65] Relatedly, in 2013, Edgar Schmidt, former general counsel in the Legislative Services Branch of the Department of Justice, sued the Office of the Attorney General for failing to apply a proper test for Charter compliance.[66] So long as there was a credible argument that legislation was constitutionally valid, Schmidt alleged, it would be waived through. Ultimately, in 2016, Justice Noel of the Federal Court found that the governing legislation did not require a more searching standard.[67] But the allegations fit within a broader public narrative that Harper was someone who did not feel obligated to respect the spirit of the government's legal duties, rather than its letter. Likewise, the Mike Duffy expenses scandal, which had been slowly burning since 2012, suggested that the prime minister had exploited a loophole in the residency requirement for Senate appointments.

This track record suggested that Harper would be prepared to push his prerogative authority to appoint Supreme Court judges to its limits, without regard for legal or political niceties. Moreover, there was some reason to think that Harper might at least try to make radical changes to the court. Since taking office in 2006 – and, indeed, before – Harper's Conservatives had had a contentious relationship with the judiciary. He was, after all, the man behind the now defunct Reform Party's *Blue Books* of the early 1990s. The 1991 *Blue Book* stated: "The Reform Party supports more stringent and more public ratification procedures for Supreme Court judges in light of the powers our legislators are handing to the courts. Our Draft Constitutional Amendment calls for Senate ratification of Supreme Court appointments."[68] Other figures close to Harper and the Reform movement – such as Preston Manning and Ted Morton – frequently assailed the Supreme Court as too political.[69]

As president of the National Citizens Coalition, Stephen Harper had written an op-ed in 2000 explaining his decision to challenge election advertising laws on Charter grounds. He stated: "I share many of the concerns of my colleagues and allies about biased 'judicial activism' and its extremes. I agree that serious flaws exist in the Charter of Rights and Freedoms, and that there is no meaningful review or accountability mechanisms for Supreme Court justices."[70] (Harper ultimately fought the case up to the Supreme Court of Canada – and lost.)[71]

His outlook did not seem to change once he became leader of the Opposition. In 2004, Conservative Party members of a committee considering possible reforms to the judicial appointments process insisted, in a dissent, that Supreme Court appointments should be subject to parliamentary ratification.[72] As David Schneiderman has observed, one can draw a direct line from the early Reform Party *Blue Books,* driven by a suspicion of decisions such as *Morgentaler,*[73] to the Conservative position in 2004.[74] Moreover, at around this time, Justices Rosalie Abella and Louise Charron were appointed to the court. Their appointments were seen by some, including people in the Harper government, to be part of a "Liberal conspiracy" to ensure that the court remained committed to a particular political agenda.[75]

The conspiracy claim was directly tied to the Same-Sex Marriage Reference. By March 2004, three provincial courts of appeal had found the opposite-sex definition of marriage to be unconstitutional.[76] The federal government decided not to appeal any of these decisions and directed the Supreme Court to hear a reference concerning draft legislation entrenching a new definition of marriage.[77] This decision rendered moot the work of a parliamentary committee conducting hearings on the issue. The executive, working in cahoots with the judiciary, seemed to have taken the issue out of Parliament's hands.[78] Critics speculated that the appointments of Abella and Charron were intended to ensure that the court would approve the Liberal government's draft legislation.[79] Stephen Harper adopted a particularly aggressive tone, as illustrated in the following excerpt from an interview:

> I think it's a typical hidden agenda of the Liberal party ... They had the courts do it for them [change the definition of marriage], they put the judges in they wanted, then they failed to appeal – failed to fight the case in court ... I think the federal government deliberately lost this case in court and got the change to the law done through the back door.[80]

Since taking office, Harper had undertaken significant reforms of the judicial appointments process. In 2006, the government changed the way that judicial candidates were ranked from "highly recommend," "recommend," and "unable to recommend" to simply "qualified" and "not qualified." This gave the government much more leeway in terms of selection.[81] The government also added a fourth government representative – a member of law enforcement – and gave itself a working majority by denying a vote to the committee chairperson except in the event of a tie. These changes were made over the objections of the Canadian Bar Association, the Canadian Judicial Council, and the Federation of Law Societies of Canada. Chief Justice McLachlin, writing in her capacity as chairperson of the Canadian Judicial Council, called for "an immediate process of consultation on the proposed changes with the judiciary, Canadian Bar Association, the law societies and other interested parties ... to protect the interests of all Canadians in an independent advisory process for judicial appointments."[82] Nonetheless, the reforms were made. In 2007, Harper stated: "We want to make sure we're bringing forward the laws to make sure we crack down on crime, that we make our streets and communities safer ... We want to make sure our selection of judges is in correspondence with those objectives."[83]

There were also what might be described as collateral attacks on the role of the Charter and the courts. In 2006, the Harper government largely abolished the Court Challenges Program of Canada.[84] This was a program that funded litigation that challenged the constitutionality of legislation. It is reasonable to think that this policy change was driven by suggestions made by well-known "Charter skeptics" Ted Morton, Rainer Knopff, and Ian Brodie (who would become Harper's assistant chief of staff) that the program benefitted a particular group of equality-rights advocacy groups.[85] Similarly, many have construed the Harper government's decision to abolish the Law Reform Commission – "a body whose task was to propose possible legislative changes, which was seen as duplicating the work of government in a generally unconservative way" – as a way of narrowing the ability of unelected judges to influence policy.[86]

Finally, much of the legislation enacted as part of the Harper government's tough-on-crime agenda worked to constrain the role of judges in the criminal justice system – particularly at the sentencing stage of proceedings. Mandatory sentences of imprisonment precluded judges from issuing sentences that might be perceived as too soft. Likewise, judges were obligated to impose victim surcharge fees without considering extenuating circumstances, the offender's ability to pay, or even whether there was a clear-cut victim.[87] The point, to a large extent, was to tie a judge's hands. Moreover, much of the legislation was introduced through private members' bills rather than government bills. In a recent paper, James Kelly and Kate Puddister have suggested that Harper – a leader notorious for centralizing governmental power in the Prime

Minister's Office – supported such private members' bills precisely because they were not scrutinized for Charter compliance by the Department of Justice.[88]

There were reasons for thinking, then, that Harper would want to appoint judges to the Supreme Court who would favour – or at least not interfere with – a conservative agenda. It is important to note, though, that these fears had been expressed virtually every time there was a vacancy on the court and, as far as anyone could tell, they had not been borne out.[89] In 2006, the prime minister appointed Justice Rothstein from a list of candidates assembled before Harper took office. Thomas Cromwell, appointed in 2008, did not appear to be particularly conservative. In 2011, after Justices Binnie and Charron announced that they were retiring from the court, Kirk Makin wrote in an article titled "The Coming Conservative Court":

> Legal experts now believe Mr. Harper will use his choices to usher in a decades-long course of conservative Charter of Rights rulings and low-key deference to Parliament. That prospect is sure to delight those who view activist judges as anathema and the Charter with suspicion. At the same time, it conjures up a potential nightmare for the political left and civil libertarians who look to the Supreme Court to strike down laws that offend the Charter and to safeguard the rights of the accused.[90]

Makin suggested that Justice Rosalie Abella, as the only "liberal" voice on the court, might become isolated – or simply leave out of frustration or disillusionment. Law professors Allan Hutchinson and Jamie Cameron both echoed these concerns. And yet there was an unmistakeable tension in Makin's article. The concern was not simply that Harper would mould the court into his political image but that it had already become too conservative in outlook and, indeed, had been that way since Beverley McLachlin was made chief justice (by Jean Chrétien) in 1999. Makin noted that the McLachlin court had a well-deserved reputation for deference – at least in choosing remedies for Charter violations. The problem, in other words, was not just that Harper's appointments would make the court more conservative but that they would squelch hopes of making it more liberal. Ultimately, however, Harper appointed Justices Moldaver and Karakatsanis, both justices on the Ontario Court of Appeal, to replace Justices Binnie and Charron. Neither appointment could be construed as strikingly ideological.[91]

The following year, when Justice Richard Wagner of the Quebec Court of Appeal was nominated to replace the retiring Justice Marie Deschamps, there would again be suggestions that Harper was attempting to pull the Supreme Court to the right. Wagner had been an appellate court judge for only one year, though he had been a superior court judge for roughly seven years before that, and had a strong reputation in Quebec's legal community. There was also some controversy surrounding the decision not to appoint a woman to replace Deschamps. But Wagner was hardly seen as a radical conservative. Sean Fine reported: "Based on Judge Wagner's relatively short judicial record and impressions from friends and acquaintances, he is likely to be a court centrist who is neither staunchly conservative nor a strong believer in advancing the law through creative judgments."[92]

Tom Flanagan has recently said that Harper "didn't do the job well of changing the complexion of the judiciary. The only [Harper appointee] with a reputation as a conservative was Russ Brown [appointed in 2015]."[93] At the time, Justice Nadon's nomination was not obviously the latest in a string of transformative conservative appointments. But there was a perception that Harper was attempting to shift the court in a more conservative direction, however tentatively. This aggravated concerns that he would exploit the lack of legal and political checks on his appointment power and arguably heightened suspicion of Justice Nadon himself.

3

Memos

HISTORICALLY, THE PRIME MINISTER'S power to make appointments to the Supreme Court of Canada was not subject to meaningful legal or political limits. The new process devised by Stephen Harper's government did not seriously constrain the prime minister's discretion. He could change or abandon it at will – as when he chose simply to forego the hearing for Justice Cromwell. The *Supreme Court Act* imposed some statutory limits, but they were hardly onerous. They precluded the prime minister from appointing more than nine judges – as US president Franklin D. Roosevelt had threatened to do in the 1930s in response to the US Supreme Court's invalidation of New Deal legislation. They also blocked him from appointing a junior lawyer or someone with no legal training at all. Finally, they required that he ensure that three of nine judges represented Quebec. Otherwise, his hands were untied. And in the unlikely event that the statute prevented him from getting his way, there was a simple (if not easy) answer: amend the *Supreme Court Act.*

The legal limits were so few that the potential issue with Justice Nadon's appointment was spotted early on. To avoid leaving Quebec with fewer than three judges, anyone appointed to replace Justice Fish would need to satisfy the eligibility criteria set out in section 6 of the *Supreme Court Act.* But an individual could be appointed under section 6 only if he or she was either a judge on a Quebec superior court or a member of the Quebec bar for at least ten years. The Federal Court of Appeal categorically is not a Quebec superior court.[1] Moreover, once appointed to a Federal Court, an individual ceases to be a member of the Quebec bar. That would be unproblematic if section 6 conferred eligibility upon those who had at some point been a member of the Quebec bar for ten or more years. The text of the provision, though, could be read as limiting eligibility to those who were current members of the Quebec bar. On that reading, no Federal Court judge could be eligible to fill one of the Quebec seats on the Supreme Court of Canada.

Federal Court judges had been elevated to the Supreme Court of Canada before, but always under section 5. Justice Frank Iacobucci, for example, had been chief justice of the Federal Court prior to his appointment to the high court in 1991. Marshall Rothstein was on the Federal Court before his elevation in 2006. More interestingly, Justice Gerald Le Dain, a Quebecer, was also appointed to the Supreme Court of Canada from the Federal Court. But Justice Le Dain was not appointed to fill a Quebec seat – he was appointed to fill one of the so-called Ontario seats and therefore needed only to satisfy the requirements of section 5.[2] The legal problem of appointing federal judges under section 6 had never squarely arisen.

THE PROBLEM WITH APPOINTING A FEDERAL COURT JUDGE

And there was a legal problem, at least for Prime Minister Harper. Because it is now clear that, for whatever reason, he was deeply interested in appointing a Federal Court judge to replace Justice Fish. The long list assembled by the minister of justice, and submitted to the selection panel, had only six names on it. Four were Federal Court judges. Assuming that the selection panel shortened the list to three, as it was called upon to do, there would be at least one Federal Court judge on it. Some of the Federal Court judges included on the list were perfectly credible candidates. Justice Mainville, for example, was (and is) a well-respected judge who, as a lawyer, had represented Indigenous groups and authored books on Aboriginal law.[3] (Justice Mainville would eventually be appointed to the Quebec Court of Appeal.)[4] But the list also included Michel Shore, a judge with the Federal Court's trial division, who had notoriously copied large extracts from government briefs into his judgments.[5] He may have been included just to give the selection panel someone to cut, but it is hard to escape the conclusion that Prime Minister Harper had a strong interest in appointing someone from the Federal Court.[6]

It is also clear that the prime minister and the minister of justice knew there was a potential legal issue with appointing a Federal Court judge. The selection panel, responsible for shortening the initial list of names assembled by the minister of justice, had consulted with the chief justice of the Quebec Court of Appeal as well as the chief justice of the Quebec Superior Court. Apparently, both advised the panel that there was an eligibility issue.[7] Indeed, it emerged that the chief justice of Canada, Beverley McLachlin, had contacted the minister of justice and the prime minister to advise them of the section 6 issue. This was confirmed in a statement released by the executive legal officer of the Supreme Court:

> On July 31, 2013, the Chief Justice's office called the minister of justice's office and the Prime Minister's Chief of Staff, Mr. Novak, to flag a potential issue regarding the eligibility of a judge of the federal courts to fill a Quebec seat on the Supreme Court. Later that day, the Chief Justice spoke with the minister of justice, Mr. MacKay, to flag the potential issue. The Chief Justice's office also made preliminary inquiries to set up a call or meeting with the Prime Minister, but ultimately the Chief Justice decided not to pursue a call or meeting.[8]

The chief justice herself stated: "Given the potential impact on the Court, I wished to ensure that the government was aware of the eligibility issue. At no time did I express any opinion as to the merits of the eligibility issue. It is customary for chief justices to be consulted during the appointment process and there is nothing inappropriate in raising a potential issue affecting a future appointment."[9]

Those comments were made by way of deflecting suggestions that the chief justice had acted improperly. But propriety is not our concern here – what matters is that the minister of justice and Prime Minister Harper knew that there was a legal issue surrounding the section 6 eligibility of Federal Court judges, including Marc Nadon.[10] Minister of Justice Peter MacKay signalled his awareness in an August 2013 interview: "There are provisions right now that could be [mistakenly] interpreted as excluding federal judges from Supreme Court appointments. This act literally goes back to Confederation. Suffice to say, there's a need to update some of the provisions."[11]

In an interview, Howard Anglin – who was senior adviser on legal affairs and policy at the time – told us that the government had sought advice from both the Department of Justice and the Privy Council Office. (He could not recall whether the Privy Council Office had provided a formal opinion or just memoranda.) Both, he said, had been emphatically of the view that section 6 of the *Supreme Court Act* permitted the appointment of Federal Court judges.[12] The Privy Council Office, Anglin recalled, had taken the view that McLachlin's warning was overly cautious – and it had noted that she had not actually said that Nadon was categorically ineligible. Though the office had not ruled out the possibility of a legal challenge, Anglin continued, it had clearly regarded any such challenge as frivolous and vexatious.[13]

All this was quite promising. The government, however, wanted to put to rest any controversy surrounding the legality of Nadon's appointment before it could erupt. It wanted a legal opinion that it could show to the wider public. The government could, of course, release the opinions provided by the Department of Justice and the Privy Council Office, but it was reluctant to set a "precedent" by which internal legal opinions would be expected to be made public in the future. So the government took the unusual step of seeking outside legal advice – from individuals with unimpeachable credentials. It approached two retired Supreme Court justices – Ian Binnie and Louise Charron – and the eminent constitutional lawyer Peter Hogg.[14] According to Anglin, the government was particularly interested in the opinion of Louise

Charron. Though she occupied one of the Ontario seats as a Supreme Court judge, the government took the view that her status as a francophone would give her opinion special weight under the circumstances. It was also useful to seek an opinion from someone in a position to read and interpret both the French and English versions of the provisions.

In an interview with us, Louise Charron recalled that she had been approached by Department of Justice counsel on a confidential basis.[15] Charron was asked whether sections 5 and 6 permitted the appointment of a Federal Court judge to one of the Quebec seats on the Supreme Court and, if not, whether a retired judge who rejoined the bar would thereby become eligible. The government, she observed, was in a clear hurry to get an answer: they approached her on a Monday; she delivered her opinion later that same week.

Charron gave an oral briefing to six to eight people.[16] She was of the view that the suggestion that Federal Court judges might be ineligible under sections 5 and 6 was without merit. (In our interview, she used the phrase "no-brainer.") There were discussions about formalizing her opinion into a written memorandum. Charron informed the government that because she was not a member of a provincial bar association she could not provide, strictly speaking, a legal opinion. According to Charron, the government asked her to consider rejoining the bar, suggesting that it could offer some assistance in doing so. She declined. Charron was paid as a consultant, and the request for a written opinion was withdrawn.

At this point, the government decided to approach Ian Binnie.[17] According to Anglin, Binnie was given the same questions as those posed to Charron and was not told what she had decided.[18] (Charron confirmed with us that she did not share her opinion with Binnie beforehand.) Nonetheless, Anglin told us, Binnie's opinion was more or less identical in substance and conclusion. The minister of justice shared Binnie's memorandum with Charron and Hogg, who orally agreed with his reasoning.[19] Charron was asked if her verbal opinion could be disclosed to the public; despite some reservations, she agreed.

In an article about the Nadon controversy, law professor Hugo Cyr stated: "Clearly, the government knew that the nomination was going to be controversial. We may assume that it is precisely because of the potential controversy that could ensue from such an appointment that the government took those extraordinary measures."[20] The above account, though, does not suggest that the government proceeded recklessly in appointing Marc Nadon. According to Anglin, the government had in hand opinions from the Department of Justice, the Privy Council Office, two former Supreme Court judges, and Peter Hogg – all strongly supporting the conclusion that Marc Nadon was eligible under section 6.[21] The Binnie memorandum, on his account, was far from the only opinion relied upon.

In an interview with us, Marc Nadon stated that he had been advised of the eligibility issue when the government first informed him that he was to be appointed. Though the offer of appointment came as a complete surprise, the eligibility issue did not altogether come as a shock. There had been another Quebec vacancy the previous year, following Marie Deschamps's retirement, and the idea that Federal Court judges might be ineligible for a Quebec seat under section 6 of the *Supreme Court Act* had already been a matter of some discussion among his colleagues. According to Nadon, it was suggested that he might need to return to the Quebec bar for a period of time to mute the eligibility concerns. Nadon balked at the idea of giving up his seat on the Federal Court of Appeal: "I didn't like that; I didn't sleep well." He told the government that it would need to appoint him from the Federal Court of Appeal, or not at all.[22]

On 30 September 2013, the government announced Marc Nadon's appointment.[23] That same day, it publicly released the Binnie memorandum. Indeed, two days later, the minister of justice referenced the memorandum at considerable length before introducing Marc Nadon at the latter's parliamentary hearing. It is worth setting out Peter MacKay's remarks on the Binnie memorandum in their entirety:

> The Prime Minister's news release announcing the Honourable Marc Nadon as nominee for the Supreme Court of Canada also included a backgrounder with an opinion that was prepared by the Honourable Ian Binnie, a former judge of the Supreme Court of Canada.

For those of you who've had the opportunity to review that opinion, I'm sure you will agree that it was written in very clear and unequivocal language – as some might say, in "plain-speak" – in English. It was also, of course, made available in the language of Molière, *en français.*

In short, Mr. Justice Binnie – as he then was – was asked to review certain provisions of the *Supreme Court Act* as they pertain to the appointment of judges representing the province of Quebec, and specifically to address the issue of eligibility of judges from the Federal Court of Appeal as Supreme Court of Canada justice nominees.

As many of you will know, we have several judges on the Supreme Court of Canada who were in fact appointed directly from the Federal Court of Appeal, so there is precedent. Those justice appointees would include Mr. Justice Rothstein, Mr. Justice Iacobucci, and many years before that Mr. Justice Le Dain. I also note that we've had a number of justices who were appointed directly from private practice, including Mr. Justice Sopinka and more recently Madam Justice Arbour.

Having said that, there has not been an appointment from the Federal Court directly to the Supreme Court of Canada from Quebec. The purpose of this exercise of having Mr. Justice Binnie examine this issue was to provide the government with an opinion as to whether a person who has been a member of the Quebec bar for at least 10 years and is now a judge of the Federal Court or the Federal Court of Appeal would qualify as one of these three judges from the province of Quebec.

The conclusion, as I mentioned earlier, was clear and unequivocal. Mr. Justice Binnie stated that as long as the candidate has been a member of the Quebec bar for at least 10 years, he or she would qualify for an appointment to the Supreme Court of Canada as a representative of the province of Quebec. He went on to say that this would clearly include a judge of the Federal Court or the Federal Court of Appeal – and I would again emphasize – as long as that judge has been a member in good standing of the Quebec bar for at least 10 years immediately prior to his or her appointment as a judge.

I would add that this opinion was reviewed by several eminently qualified individuals, including the Honourable Louise Charron as a former judge of the Supreme Court of Canada herself. The opinion was

> also reviewed by Professor Peter Hogg, a recognized constitutional expert and author. Both of them expressed unequivocal support for Mr. Justice Binnie's conclusions.[24]

We have set out these comments at length precisely because their length is so remarkable. Prior to the Nadon hearing, Canadian judicial confirmation hearings were by and large treated as opportunities for appointees to introduce themselves to the wider public. As we have seen, there were isolated moments when this or that judge was subjected to discomfiting questions about his or her experience (Karakatsanis, Wagner) or bilingualism (Moldaver). But none of those questions went to the nominee's legal eligibility. The idea of holding a hearing for a nominee whose eligibility was so in dispute that it called for such a lengthy discussion of a publicly released legal memorandum – complete with assurances of its accessibility for a lay readership – was extraordinary. Indeed, Françoise Boivin quipped during the hearing: "You [Nadon] are the first person to be appointed and have a legal opinion at the same time."[25]

The next day, Prime Minister Harper officially confirmed Marc Nadon's appointment. Four days later, on 7 October 2013, he was sworn in. That day, a Toronto lawyer named Rocco Galati, as well as the Toronto-based Constitutional Rights Centre (of which Galati is executive director), filed a challenge against the appointment in Federal Court.[26] The foundation of the challenge was that sections 5 and 6 of the *Supreme Court Act* ruled out the appointment of Federal Court judges. More than this, though, Galati claimed that, by purporting to appoint a Federal Court judge, the prime minister had effectively contravened constitutional principles. The federal government could not unilaterally alter the composition of the Supreme Court – that is, it could not, on its own, decide to change the conditions of eligibility. It would need first to amend the Constitution, which in this instance would require the unanimous consent of the provinces. Proceeding as the government had was contrary to the unwritten principles of federalism, constitutionalism, and the rule of law. Finally, it was argued that permitting the prime minister to unilaterally alter the composition of the court would offend the notion that judges must be independent of other branches of government. Less plausibly, Galati claimed that the appointment constituted a violation of section 7 of the Charter.

Galati's challenge set in motion a chain of events that, with the benefit of hindsight, made the reference inevitable. As soon as the challenge was launched, it arguably became untenable for Justice Nadon to participate in the life of the Supreme Court of Canada. The following day, the court announced: "Mr. Justice Marc Nadon has decided, in light of the challenge to his appointment pending before the Federal Court, not to participate for the time being in matters before the Supreme Court of Canada."[27] This, of course, meant that, until Nadon's case was resolved, the court would sit with no more than eight judges and would have only two Quebec judges.

Such a state of affairs was wholly unacceptable to the Quebec bar. Its president, Johanne Brodeur, observed that it could take more than five years for the case to wind its way through the courts.[28] The bar association urged the federal government to seek an advisory opinion from the Supreme Court. The Quebec National Assembly unanimously adopted a resolution deploring the prime minister's decision to appoint Nadon. On 17 October 2013, the Quebec government announced that it would seek an advisory opinion from the Quebec Court of Appeal, effectively joining Galati's court challenge.[29] Like Galati, the Quebec government's position was that section 6 precluded the appointment of a Federal Court judge.

Shortly after Galati's challenge was filed, several academics (including us) publicly took issue with Ian Binnie's analysis of section 6 of the *Supreme Court Act*.[30] This helped to fuel a broader debate on the legality of the appointment, increasing calls in the House of Commons for a reference to the Supreme Court of Canada to resolve the legal question once and for all.[31] Throughout this period, the minister of justice and others repeatedly defended the appointment of Justice Nadon by referencing Ian Binnie's memorandum. Under questioning by Stéphane Dion in the House of Commons, on 17 October 2013, MacKay responded:

> The eligibility and the opinion that we have received from Mr. Justice Ian Binnie, which has also been endorsed by Supreme Court Justice Louise Charron, as well as a noted constitutional expert Peter Hogg, is very clear. In fact, we believe that Justice Nadon is eminently qualified. We are certain that he will serve the court and the country with distinction and will receive the clearance he needs to join his colleagues on the Supreme Court of Canada.[32]

The next day, Robert Goguen made virtually identical remarks.[33] These comments were made expressly by way of rebuffing calls by Opposition MPs for a reference to the Supreme Court of Canada.

THE BINNIE MEMORANDUM

Much turned, then, on the memorandum produced by Ian Binnie. From the moment Marc Nadon's appointment was announced, the memorandum was used by the Harper government to ward off suggestions that the appointment was invalid. Though it was a legal memorandum, its purpose was largely to provide a political justification. So what did it say?

Binnie's core insight was that section 6 of the *Supreme Court Act* cannot be read in isolation. It must be read alongside section 5.[34] With that as his point of departure, Binnie's memorandum focused – perhaps, we will see, too much – on section 5, explaining why it does not restrict eligibility to current members of the bar.

In construing section 5, Binnie considered both the English and French versions.[35] The French version reads: "Les juges sont choisis parmi les juges, actuels ou anciens, d'une cour supérieure provincial et parmi les avocats *inscrits* pendant au moins dix ans au barreau d'une province" (emphasis added). The word "inscrits," Binnie acknowledged, "*could* be interpreted to mean current membership."[36] That is only true, however, insofar as one examines the term in isolation from its English counterpart. The English version of section 5 states: "Any person may be appointed a judge *who is or has been* a judge of a superior court of a province or a barrister or advocate of at least ten years standing at the bar of a province." The English version is "clear and unambiguous" in allowing someone to be nominated so long as he or she "*has been* ... a barrister or advocate of at least ten years standing."[37] Where one version of a statutory provision is ambiguous but the other clear, the clear version is generally taken to reflect the shared meaning of both.[38] With that in mind, Binnie concluded, past members of the bar could satisfy the eligibility criteria of section 5.

Why think that section 5 has anything to say about the ambit of section 6? Recall that the English version of section 6 states: "At least three of the judges shall be appointed from among the judges of the Court of Appeal or of the Superior Court of the Province of Quebec or from among the advocates of that Province." If one were to read this section in isolation from section 5, Binnie observed, strange results would follow – for example, a person could be appointed to one of the Quebec seats despite having only been an advocate of the province for a single day.[39] Clearly, section 6 presupposes that "advocates" must be read in light of the eligibility criteria set out in section 5. Binnie further remarked that "[i]f Parliament had intended to specify *current* membership it could easily have said so in both official languages."[40] This suggests that, in interpreting section 6, we should not read "among the advocates" as requiring nominees to be current advocates.

Binnie returned to section 5 and the use of "inscrits" in the French version – which he plainly regarded as the only plausible basis for concluding that section 6 is restricted to current members of the Quebec bar. This time, he focused on legislative history. The "inscrits issue," as he put it, only emerged in the 1952 version of section 5.[41] The 1927 French version stated: "Peut être nommé juge quiconque est ou a été juge d'une cour supérieure de l'une des provinces du Canada, ou un avocat qui *a exercé* pendant au moins dix ans au barreau de l'une des provinces" (emphasis added). It could not plausibly be said that, by replacing "a exercé" with "inscrits," Parliament intended to narrow the range of nominees to exclude former advocates. This is especially so given that the English versions of the 1927 and 1952 provisions were identical.[42] The only reasonable inference to draw, Binnie concluded, was that the changes amounted to nothing more than legislative housekeeping.

Ultimately, Binnie argued, sections 5 and 6 of the Act were not designed to arbitrarily restrict candidates for the Supreme Court. The eligibility criteria set out in those sections had a purpose – specifically, to ensure that candidates had a minimum level of experience.[43] Since one could have the requisite experience without being a current member of the bar, Binnie concluded, there was no basis for reading either section more restrictively than the English version of section 5 permitted. He wrote:

> The *Supreme Court of Canada Act* established a final appellate body for Canada. Parliament's obvious concern in ss. 5 and 6 was to exclude from consideration men and women who lack the appropriate skills and experience. Exclusion from possible appointment of the talent pool of Federal Court judges conflicts with this purpose. Take for example a lawyer who practices for 15 years in Montreal from 1970 to 1985, then sits as a Judge on the Federal Court of Appeal from 1986 to 2000. Such an individual is clearly better qualified in 2000 after 14 years on the bench than he was in 1985 prior to the initial appointment. Yet the objection to the appointment of Federal Court judges attributes to Parliament the view that Federal Court experience is a detriment not an asset. Equally, on the contrary view, an appointment to the International Court of Justice at the Hague would present an insurmountable barrier to appointment, despite decades of earlier practice at a provincial bar. Any interpretation of ss. 5 and 6 of the Supreme Court of Canada Act that leads to such an absurd result should be rejected.[44]

This reasoning was repeated by others, including Professor Benoit Pelletier when he appeared before the Senate Standing Committee on Legal and Constitutional Affairs in November 2013.[45] When asked point blank whether he accepted Binnie's analysis, Pelletier replied, "Yes, entirely."[46]

Former Supreme Court justice Michel Bastarache, who also appeared before the Senate Committee, likewise shared Binnie's view. He claimed that "section 6 ... cannot disqualify a person who is already qualified under section 5. Its purpose is simply to ensure that three of the persons contemplated in section 5 shall represent Quebec."[47] He thought it absurd to interpret section 6 so as to preclude the appointment of Federal Court judges:

> It would be utterly illogical for a member qualified under section 5 to be disqualified on the day he or she is appointed to the Federal Court, just as it would be illogical for a 20-year-old admitted to the Barreau du Québec for one day suddenly to be eligible for appointment to the Supreme Court of Canada. The rules of interpretation strictly provide that an absurd interpretation must always be avoided.[48]

For those keeping track, this meant that no fewer than three retired Supreme Court of Canada judges had weighed in and accepted that Federal Court judges could be appointed under section 6 of the Act.[49] Needless to say, this provided at first glance a compelling basis for thinking that Marc Nadon's appointment was valid.

CRITICISMS OF THE MEMORANDUM

But not everyone agreed.[50] Few took issue with Binnie's interpretation of section 5.[51] Nor did they take issue with the proposition that section 6 must be read in light of section 5 and certainly not with the idea that we should resist "absurd" interpretations of statutes. But serious concerns remained. Those concerns tended to dwell on four issues.

First, though sections 5 and 6 must be read together, it doesn't follow that every person who is eligible under section 5 must, for that reason alone, be eligible under section 6. Indeed, it clearly doesn't mean that. Section 6 plainly limits eligibility to individuals who are advocates of Quebec, or judges on Quebec's Superior Court or Court of Appeal – it refers to a *subclass* of the broader class of persons who are eligible under section 5. Importantly, neither Binnie's memorandum nor the submissions of Bastarache or Pelletier take issue with that. How could they? Doing so would mean that section 6 serves no purpose at all, since the Quebec seats could be filled with anyone eligible under section 5, including a lawyer practising in Newfoundland or Winnipeg.

So section 6 clearly refers to a narrower class of individuals than that recognized in section 5. The critical question is: How much narrower? Does that narrower subclass contain past members of the Quebec bar, or does it only contain current members of the bar? (For ease of reference, let's call the first interpretation the "inclusive reading" and the second the "exclusive reading.") If the latter, then federal and provincial court judges are ineligible under section 6, even if they are eligible under section 5 – they may fill one of the six non-Quebec seats on the court but not one of the three Quebec seats. If the former, then federal and provincial court judges may be eligible under both sections.

The text of section 6 would seem to provide some mild support for the exclusive reading. After all, the provision contains the clause "from *among* the advocates" – a person who is no longer an advocate hardly seems to be *among* advocates. Moreover, as Professor Paul Daly observed in his Senate submissions, the language in section 6 is far less permissive than that contained in section 5; whereas section 5 uses the word "may," section 6 uses the word "shall."[52] This suggests that the prime minister has less discretion with respect to section 6 appointments than he or she does with respect to section 5 appointments.[53] Again, though, this does not in itself tell us much about how much less discretion the prime minister has – that is, whether the exclusive reading is the correct one. Realistically, one must look beyond section 6 to the wider statutory context to determine – or even make an educated guess – whether the inclusive or exclusive reading is preferred.

This brings us to the second complaint concerning Binnie's memorandum. Though Binnie insisted that section 6 must be read in light of section 5, he ignored the potential significance of another provision in the *Supreme Court Act:* section 30. This section sets out the circumstances under which someone may be appointed temporarily as an ad hoc judge where, for whatever reason, the Supreme Court would otherwise lack quorum in a given case. Under section 30(1)(a), ad hoc judges can be drawn from the federal courts. But section 30(2), which governs the appointment of ad hoc judges where an appeal is from a judgment rendered in Quebec, is quite different. It states: "Unless two of the judges available fulfill the requirements of section 6, the ad hoc judge for the hearing ... shall be a judge of the Court of Appeal or a judge of the Superior Court of [Quebec]."[54]

Strikingly, there is no mention of the federal courts. If Parliament wanted to include these courts under section 30(2), it could easily have done so. The fact that it chose not to do so suggests that it regarded Federal Court judges as inappropriate representatives of Quebec on the Supreme Court. Indeed, there is historical precedent arguably suggesting that Federal Court judges (or their equivalents) were intentionally excluded under section 30(2). Paul Daly, arguing for the significance of section 30(2), relayed the story in his submission:

> [T]here was a significant controversy which erupted shortly after the adoption of this provision for the first time in 1918. At the time, a civiliste, Louis Arthur Audette, was one of two judges on the Exchequer Court (the predecessor to the modern federal courts). There was a political backlash from the common-law provinces against the possibility that civil-law judges would dominate the bench on appeals touching matters of common law. Accordingly, Audette was never appointed as an ad hoc judge. The ad hoc appointments were made solely from the Québec superior courts. That appointments were made only from the Québec courts even though a highly qualified civiliste was available at the Exchequer Court is clearly significant. It suggests that the understanding was that federal court judges could not be appointed to the Québec seats on the Supreme Court of Canada.[55]

Daly suggested that, insofar as a civil lawyer on the Exchequer Court was not regarded as eligible to serve as an ad hoc judge in Quebec cases where there was not a quorum of Quebec judges on the Supreme Court, one should construe section 30(2) as categorically excluding judges on the Exchequer Court's modern-day equivalent – federal courts.

This is certainly a plausible argument. But it is not the only way to understand the Audette episode, or section 30(2). Months later, in his submissions as an intervener before the Supreme Court of Canada, Professor Sebastien Grammond – representing three retired Federal Court judges – offered an alternative interpretation.[56] According to the 1912 legislation, there were only two judges on the Exchequer Court: a "judge" and an "assistant judge." When the original version of section 30 was passed into law, it provided that the judge of the Exchequer Court should be asked, when necessary, to sit as an ad hoc judge on the Supreme Court. If he was unavailable, then a judge of a superior court would be sought to provide quorum. The assistant judge was ineligible. As there is today, however, there was a special rule in place for cases from Quebec in which the (then) two judges on the Supreme Court were unavailable. In such cases, the ad hoc judge would be drawn from a Quebec superior court – and not from the Exchequer Court.

At the time, Audette was the assistant judge on the Exchequer Court. His ineligibility upset Quebec politicians, especially since the common law judge on the Exchequer Court would be eligible – and, indeed, the first to be invited – to sit on Quebec cases, even when quorum had been lost as a result of a lack of Quebec judges on the court. There was an understandable concern that, in such cases, there would be a lack of civil law competence on the Supreme Court.[57] And so two distinct procedures were devised – one applying to Quebec cases in which quorum was lost for want of a Quebec judge on the Supreme Court (in which Exchequer Court jurists were simply excluded as ad hoc judges) and one for all other cases where there was a lack of quorum (in which any member of the Exchequer Court could so serve). Section 30(2) was born.[58]

It is difficult to know what to infer from all this. On one hand, section 30(2) appears to be a pragmatic compromise, designed to ensure that civil lawyers could not serve as ad hoc judges in common law appeals – and vice versa. This in itself hardly suggests an intention to restrict eligibility under section 6 to current members of the bar or to categorically exclude Federal Court judges under section 6. On the other hand, the fact remains that Parliament chose to make this compromise by excluding Exchequer Court – and, by implication, Federal Court – judges from serving as ad hoc judges in Quebec appeals where Quebec representation would otherwise be lacking. At the very least, this is a point that deserved attention by Binnie in his memorandum, for the very fact that such a choice was made suggests that the language used in section 6 was not an accident but a deliberate decision by Parliament to exclude Federal Court judges.

One further point warrants mention. The Supreme Court was created through the *Supreme and Exchequer Courts Act.* The Exchequer Court was, therefore, front and centre in Parliament's mind. If Parliament had meant to include judges from the Exchequer Court in what would become section 6, it could (again) have easily done so. Legislative history suggests that it had good reasons – or, at least, what it would have regarded as good reasons – for wanting only Quebec superior court judges (in the section 96 sense) and current members of the Quebec bar to be "appointable" to the Supreme Court.[59]

The third objection to Binnie's argument was that serious attention had not been paid to the legislative history of section 6. Here, we should acknowledge that this is, so far as anyone can tell, not necessarily a problem with the memorandum that Binnie gave the government but a problem with the memorandum made public by the government. In the memorandum, Binnie referred to two appendices in which he set out the legislative history of sections 5 and 6.[60] Those appendices were not included when the government released the memorandum to the wider public.

The decision not to release the memorandum in its entirety was unfortunate, because a great deal turned on precisely why Parliament had decided to enact section 6 in the first place. To those favouring the inclusive reading of section 6, such as Binnie, Bastarache, and Pelletier, the point of section 6 was clear: to ensure that at least three judges on the Supreme Court of Canada had expertise in civil law. On that understanding of the purpose of section 6, there is no sound reason to exclude individuals merely because they are no longer current members of the Quebec bar. A person does not lose expertise in civil law simply by ceasing to be an advocate – and certainly does not lose it by virtue of having been appointed to a federal or provincial court. That understanding of the purpose of section 6 explains the focus, by Binnie and others, on section 5. There is little doubt that section 5 is grounded in a concern with ensuring that Supreme Court judges have legal competence generally. Once one concludes that section 6 is also concerned with ensuring competence, albeit of civil law specifically, it is natural to suppose that if section 5 treats past members of the bar as no less competent than current members, section 6 must do so as well.

To critics of the Binnie memorandum, though, section 6 was not merely concerned with ensuring competence in civil law. It served an additional purpose – one that the Parliament of 1875 thought it could achieve only by restricting section 6 eligibility to current members of the Quebec bar. To get insight into that additional purpose, it is necessary to dig into the legislative history.

The original progenitor of section 6 of the *Supreme Court Act* was section 4 of the *Supreme and Exchequer Courts Act*.[61] The relevant part of that provision is: "[T]wo of [the judges] at least shall be taken from among the Judges of the Superior Court or Court of Queen's Bench, or the Barristers or Advocates of the Province of Quebec." This language found its way into the Act after Toussaint Laflamme, member of Parliament for Jacques Cartier, Quebec, introduced it during the third reading of the bill in the House of Commons. Hansard reports his comments as follows:

> [H]e believed under the peculiar circumstances in which the Province of Quebec was situated, and its special system of laws, of which the Judges from the other Provinces who might be selected for the composition of this court would be entirely ignorant – it was essential in order to arrive at a good and sound interpretation of the laws of that Province, that two of these Judges, at least, should be selected from the bar of Lower Canada. He believed there was no Province in the Dominion which stood in this peculiar position. If their laws had been

> the same as those of the other Provinces, certainly no one in Quebec would have pretended to demand this representation.[62]

Laflamme's reasoning was explicitly endorsed by several members of Parliament, including Sir John A. Macdonald.[63]

Others members of Parliament resisted.[64] Luc-Hyacinthe Masson observed that, carried to its logical conclusion, Laflamme's argument meant that only judges drawn from the Quebec bar should hear Quebec appeals.[65] Acalus Palmer "was quite willing to admit that two of the Judges of the Supreme Court should be taken from Quebec, but he would be sorry to see that made a part of the Act."[66] McKay Wright "admitted the peculiarities in the laws of the Province of Quebec" but nonetheless took the view that the bill should not have any "sectionalism."[67]

Ultimately, though, Laflamme's amendment was adopted. Tellingly, no one is recorded as suggesting that Laflamme's reasoning was flawed, although some MPs disagreed that the Act should be changed. Moreover, a subsequent proposal to amend the Act by requiring at least one judge from British Columbia was rejected.[68] The scholar Frank Mackinnon observed that the latter amendment "was lost because of the feeling on both sides of the House that the representative principle was not of the same importance to the other provinces as it was to Quebec."[69]

Even before the amendment was introduced, the House of Commons debates concerning the creation of the Supreme Court indicate that Parliament was preoccupied with the question of whether the court would be able to effectively deal with appeals turning on points of Quebec civil law. Political scientist Peter Russell has observed: "[H]ostility to the Supreme Court's review of provincial court decisions, especially the decisions of the Quebec courts dealing with Quebec's Civil Code, ran throughout the debate and was the central theme of most French Canadian criticism of the Act."[70] Louis François Georges Baby, five days before Laflamme introduced his amendment, noted that the right of Quebec to have legal issues pertaining to property, civil rights, and civil procedure dealt with in its own courts would now be subject to appeal at the Supreme Court. That meant that "the decisions of Judges fully acquainted with the French law" could be set aside by a panel composed of a majority of judges not so acquainted.[71]

Before proposing what would become section 6, Laflamme suggested an amendment that would have "forb[ade] appeals in all private law cases from Quebec (excluding commercial law cases) in which two Quebec courts had been unanimous."[72] Other amendments, likewise intended to make it impossible for four common law judges to overturn decisions on Quebec civil law reached by jurists more familiar with it, were proposed but rejected.[73] Russell states:

> [T]his kind of concern about the Supreme Court's appellate jurisdiction was almost entirely confined to French Canadian representatives of Quebec ... The French Canadians showed no inclination to couch their criticism of the Supreme Court in federalist terms. On the whole, the rationale of their case turned much more on an interest in preserving their own culture than on the logic of federalism.[74]

While the legislative history does not conclusively reveal the intent behind section 6, it suggests that Parliament's purpose was to ensure that at least some members of the Supreme Court had familiarity with Quebec's civil law.[75] That does not mean that section 6 requires judges with an up-to-date grasp of civil law. But in the context of a new confederation, in which the people of Quebec were suspicious of a high court with jurisdiction over civil law appeals, it is entirely plausible that Parliament would have wanted Supreme Court appointments from Quebec to have a current understanding of Quebec civil law and that they would have wanted this understanding demonstrated with ongoing membership in the Quebec bar or status as a judge in one of its domestic superior courts. Given Russell's point that the objection of French Canadians was grounded in cultural rather than federalist concerns, the symbolic importance of drawing Quebec appointments only from its currently practising bar or from its superior courts should not be dismissed out of hand.

In 1949, when the Supreme Court of Canada was made the "court of last resort," it was expanded from seven judges to its current complement of nine. Section 6 was likewise modified to require three judges from Quebec rather than two. The debates in both the House of Commons and the Senate suggest, again, that Parliament's intention was to guarantee a measure of expertise in Quebec civil law. The minister of justice, replying to objections that Quebec was receiving special treatment that would be "resented" by the other provinces, stated:

> So far as the reference in the clause to there being three appointees from Quebec is concerned, the necessity for that arises, as my honourable friend knows, from the fact that in that province they have a system of civil law which is altogether different in character from the common law that we inherited from England, and which prevails in the other provinces. While the clause says that the third judge shall be appointed from Quebec, the real purpose is to get upon the supreme court, when it becomes the court of last resort for Canadian lawsuits, three lawyers trained in the civil code rather than in the common law.[76]

The character of Quebec's legal order was also raised in another context. In 1949, the Canadian Bar Association passed a resolution "that the rule of *stare decisis* ought to continue to be applied with respect to past decisions of the Court, as well as with respect to past decisions of the Judicial Committee."[77] Some parliamentarians argued that such a rule, if incorporated into the *Supreme Court Act,* would be incompatible with respect for Quebec's civil law tradition.[78] The impact of the court on Quebec was in the forefront of legislators' minds.

To some critics of the Binnie memorandum, the legislative history brought out a difference between section 5 and section 6 as regards bar membership. When a criterion for appointment was based primarily on the need to ensure a minimum level of legal expertise, as was clearly the case with section 5, it did not necessarily matter whether one had acquired that expertise recently or in the past. Thus, it is not surprising that section 5's reference to ten years' bar membership was not restricted to current members.

But section 6 arguably reflected more than a concern for technical expertise in civil law. It may also have reflected the need to assure Quebecers that members of the Supreme Court have that expertise. With that in mind, it may indeed have been thought important to draw candidates not only from civil law experts but also from the community of lawyers and judges practising in Quebec. On Binnie's reading of the *Supreme Court Act,* it would be possible to appoint a person who had practised law in Quebec for fifteen years but who had, for the past ten years, lived and practised in Vancouver, ensconced in the common law system.

To the extent that section 6 is designed only to ensure civil law expertise, that result is entirely unobjectionable. But if the point is to assure Quebecers that the Supreme Court can draw on judges who are familiar with and sensitive to French Canadian legal traditions, that result looks more problematic. The present-tense language of section 6, read in conjunction with the language of section 30(2) and viewed against the legislative history all cast significant doubt on the idea that "among the advocates" includes past advocates.

Fourth and finally, the arguments that had most traction in legal and political circles were those that emphasized the apparent absurdity of the exclusive reading of section 6. These arguments ran in two directions. First, Binnie pointed out the absurdity of excluding Federal Court judges from eligibility under section 6, given that their time on the bench should, if anything, enhance their qualifications and, thus, their desirability as judges. Given the Supreme Court's role as "a final appellate body for Canada," Binnie claimed, Parliament's "obvious concern" was "to exclude from consideration men and women who lack the appropriate skills and experience."[79] Exclusion of Federal Court judges "conflicts with this purpose." As we have seen, he illustrated the absurdity of the exclusive interpretation with a hypothetical example of a person who, despite having practised in Montreal for fifteen years, is declared ineligible because she had served on the Federal Court for ten years, even though the additional experience ought to have made her a better candidate.

The absurdity argument ran in the other direction as well. Supposing that section 6 excluded those who were past members of the bar, there was a simple way for Federal Court judges to circumvent the restriction – step down as a judge and rejoin the Quebec bar. One might think that the availability of such a simple step would resolve any real concerns that the exclusive reading would unduly narrow the talent pool from which section 6 appointments could be drawn. In fact, though, the step was regarded as too simple. If Parliament intended to exclude Federal Court judges from eligibility under section 6, argued Binnie, why make it so easy for them to become eligible? If section 6 was intended to provide meaningful constraints on Federal Court judges being elevated to the Supreme Court, then it was obviously inadequate. Why suppose that Parliament had intended to impose a trivial procedural hurdle that did nothing to ensure civil law expertise? According to Binnie, such a "two-step expedient" made "no practical sense" and was "not compatible with the dignity of the office being filled."[80]

This last observation by Binnie introduces a further dimension to the absurdity argument. Simultaneously barring Federal Court judges from being appointed under section 6 and making it easy for them to circumvent the restriction made the appointments process, Parliament, and the Supreme Court look absurd. It put those who would be appointed to the highest court in the land in a position where they would need to, in effect, exploit a "loophole" in order to circumvent a statutory restriction. It is in this sense that the two-step expedient is not compatible with the dignity of the office being filled.

The difficulty with these arguments from absurdity is that they prove both too much and not enough. They prove too much because, on the reasoning employed by Binnie, there is no reason to limit eligibility under section 6 to members of the Quebec bar or judges on the bench of the Quebec Superior Court or Court of Appeal. Indeed, there is no reason to exclude those who have never set foot in Quebec or taken any legal training there. If the point of section 6 was merely to guarantee expertise in civil law, then why focus on members of the bar and bench in Quebec and not use broader language permitting the appointment of civilly trained lawyers or legal academics from, for example, Louisiana, Scotland, or Paris?

Perhaps more to the point, it is far from clear that the inclusive reading of section 6 isn't itself absurd, if we take seriously the fact that Parliament intended to restrict eligibility to those with a real and ongoing connection to the province. Professor Benoit Pelletier quite fairly alluded to this problem in his submissions to the Senate Standing Committee on Legal and Constitutional Affairs:

> [U]nder the interpretation that I propose and that Justice Binnie proposes, people who have not been domiciled in Quebec for several years may be appointed.
>
> In the context in which Quebec takes it for granted that it is entitled to three of the nine seats, I wonder whether we can still consider that a judge who has not resided in Quebec for several years, no longer practises in Quebec and no longer lives in Quebec still comes from Quebec. That is another problem because the act itself does not refer to residence or domicile. I am perfectly aware of that. I am talking here about historical gains that Quebec believed it had made within the Canadian federation and that are very much undermined by the current situation, by the way matters have developed, by the creation of the Federal Court, the Federal Court of Appeal, the Court of Quebec and so on.[81]

As Pelletier noted, once we read section 6 in the inclusive sense, there is nothing to prevent the government from appointing people to fill Quebec seats whose present connection to the province is tenuous. This rightly troubled Pelletier because, intuitively, it fails to pay due regard to the notion that section 6 provides for Quebec seats. The difficulty is that, if we read section 6 as intended to guarantee only civil law competence, we appear to be logically committed to the idea that ongoing residence or connectedness to the province of Quebec is really beside the point.

Binnie's argument from absurdity also proves too little. Let us suppose that it really would be absurd to read section 6 in such a way that a Federal Court judge could become eligible by simply retiring and then rejoining the Quebec bar for a day. One response would be to read section 6 in such a way that it precludes this sort of gamesmanship. The "rejoin for a day" example assumes that section 6 is intended to provide maximum discretion for the prime minister. But as Daly observed, the section uses language that seeks to restrict discretion, at least to some extent.[82] So we might well wonder if Binnie's conclusion on this point is too quick. Alternatively, we might ask whether the sheer act of rejoining the Quebec bar for a day does serve one of the purposes intended by Parliament. Plainly, it does nothing to make a prospective candidate more competent in civil law. If, however, the intention is also to ensure that only individuals with a particular connection to the province and its traditions are appointed to one of the Quebec seats, then the act of rejoining the Quebec bar arguably serves a worthwhile symbolic function.

In any case, the most important point to take from this discussion is not that this or that result would or wouldn't be absurd but that talk of absurd results presupposes that we already know Parliament's intention in enacting section 6 in the first place. After all, the question is not whether we would find a result absurd, but whether Parliament would find the result absurd given the intentions that animated its enactment of the statutory scheme. If a result is broadly consistent with those intentions, then it cannot be characterized as absurd – at least for the purposes of statutory interpretation – no matter how objectionable we might find them.

Arguably, an even more fundamental point underpins all of these responses. Binnie's argument, at times, seems to suggest that, insofar as section 6 excludes competent people from being eligible, it is necessarily absurd. But even if we think that the sole purpose of section 6 was to ensure that three judges on the Supreme Court have expertise in civil law, it does not automatically follow that it must – on pain of absurdity – recognize the eligibility of any and all competent, even highly competent, *civilistes.* Why? Because, as both we and Paul Daly have argued, section 6 amounts to an exercise in line drawing.[83] And lines can be drawn in different places and in different ways, without being irrational or arbitrary. Parliament could have enacted section 6 so that it read: "At least three judges on the Supreme Court must have expertise in Quebec's civil law." It didn't do that. Perhaps the legislators feared that to do so would place debatable questions such as "What counts as expertise in civil law?" and "How much expertise is enough?" in the hands of the prime minister, effectively giving him or her the power to appoint judges who would not be recognized by Quebec jurists as appropriately representative. Rather than take that approach, Parliament set out a bright-line rule for distinguishing eligible candidates from ineligible ones, a rule that seeks to guarantee civil law expertise without requiring the prime minister to decide for him- or herself whether a given candidate has that expertise.

There is nothing unusual in such an approach. Consider, for example, legislation that restricts the franchise to those eighteen years of age or older.[84] We might say that this kind of provision is designed to ensure that only people who have achieved a certain level of maturity will be able to vote in federal elections. But the age rule doesn't ask officials to decide, on an individualized basis, who has sufficient intellectual maturity and who does not – that is, to decide whether some sixteen-year-olds meet the standard or whether some twenty-five-year-olds do not. And though reasonable people may disagree on this point, there may be good reasons not to codify that sort of open-ended standard. A legislature might reasonably worry that such a provision would enmesh officials in deeply contentious arguments about precisely which individuals are "worthy" to vote, ultimately casting a pall over the legitimacy of elections and our democratic institutions. Rather than set out the desired state of affairs in the statute, the legislature could reasonably conclude that it is better for the statute to impose an age-based restriction. This rule would be, in a sense, arbitrary – Why eighteen and not seventeen? Why not eighteen years less a day? – and so would permit the inclusion of some immature over-eighteens and the exclusion of some mature under-eighteens.[85] But the advantage to the political process, in crafting a bright-line rule rather than a more open-ended standard, makes the legislative decision to use such a rule entirely rational.[86]

Our point is not to defend the use of bright-line rules over standards in the context of section 6 or elsewhere. We only want to emphasize that there is nothing intrinsically irrational or absurd in the idea that Parliament would use such rules to structure the discretion of officials. That being the case, one cannot assume that the precise text used in section 6 is disposable – that it was intended to confer more discretion upon the prime minister than its language suggests. In crafting the text of section 6, Parliament decided to use a particular means of distinguishing the eligible from the ineligible, and it is far from clear that this can or should be disregarded when interpreting the provision. The Supreme Court of Canada, from the moment of its birth, was a controversial institution,[87] particularly among French Canadians.[88] It is far from obvious that Parliament would have wanted a statutory provision requiring overt scrutiny of French Canadian candidates for their grasp of civil law. With that in mind, arguments claiming that the exclusive reading are absurd might be thought to gloss over aspects of the text and its legislative history that shed significant light on Parliament's intentions.

Ian Binnie's memorandum, in many respects, drove the debate surrounding Marc Nadon's eligibility. But as we have seen, the memorandum – at least in the form in which it was released to the public – was far from perfect. Its reasoning was open to attack on a number of grounds, putting the government in an awkward position. For the first few weeks after Nadon's appointment, the minister of justice and other Conservative MPs tried to deflect suggestions that he was ineligible simply by pointing to Binnie's arguments. That would change – the government ultimately decided to settle the interpretive dispute once and for all by referring it to the Supreme Court, thereby raising the stakes considerably. But the Binnie memorandum always loomed large in the controversy over Nadon's appointment.

Seventy-five years earlier, a similar interpretive debate had occurred in the Department of Justice.

In January 1940, Mackenzie King's government was seeking to replace Justice Arthur Cannon, who had died the previous month.[89] The vacancy was for one of the (at the time) two Quebec seats on the Supreme Court. Ultimately, the position went to Robert Taschereau, a highly "political" appointment, given to the son of the former premier of Quebec.[90] Mackenzie King's diaries suggest that the decision was between Taschereau and Lucien Cannon – Arthur's brother.[91] In the end, King appears to have reasoned that Taschereau was "the abler lawyer," "would be more welcome to the Bar," and "[w]ould make a better Judge of the Supreme Court."[92]

But a Department of Justice file in Library and Archives Canada shows that there was likely another candidate under consideration.[93] The file contains two memoranda, followed by a brief response to the second. The first, written by Deputy Minister of Justice W. Stewart Edwards and submitted to Minister of Justice Ernest Lapointe, expressly states that the question being deliberated "is whether the Chief Magistrate of the Province of Quebec is qualified for appointment to the Supreme Court of Canada."[94] The chief magistrate at the time was Ferdinand Roy, who also served as the dean of Laval's law school.[95]

The question of his eligibility arose because of section 6 of the *Supreme Court Act.* At the time, that section read: "Two at least of the judges shall be appointed from among the judges of the Court of King's Bench, or of the Superior Court, or the barristers or advocates of the province of Quebec." The Magistrate's Court was the precursor of the Provincial Court and, later, the Court of Quebec. It was not, therefore, a superior court within the meaning of the section. Could Roy be appointed as a barrister or advocate?

Edwards took the view that he could not, arguing that, since the section explicitly singles out judges of the Court of King's Bench and the Superior Court, "judges of other courts or persons holding other judicial positions are disqualified whether or not they would come technically within the description 'barristers or advocates.'" He noted that, according to the rules of the bar of Quebec (as with other provinces), "when a person accepts judicial office he ceases to be a barrister or advocate in the ordinary sense." Edwards concluded: "A search has been made as far back as 1903 and no precedent has been found for appointing anyone other than a judge of the Court of King's Bench or Superior Court, or a barrister or advocate of the Province of Quebec."[96]

The next day, Charles Stein submitted a memorandum of his own.[97] To some extent, he sought simply to offer further support of Edwards's view. Stein observed that section 267 of the *Quebec Courts of Justice Act* provided that those appointed as district magistrates "shall, upon their appointment, cease practising."[98] This reinforced Edwards's conclusion that district magistrates could not be regarded as barristers or advocates within the meaning of section 6 of the *Supreme Court Act.* But Stein also cast some doubt on Edwards's reasoning, drawing on section 5 of the Act, which read: "Any person may be appointed a judge who is or has been a judge of a superior court of any of the provinces of Canada, or a barrister or advocate of at least ten years' standing at the bar of any of the said provinces." Stein observed that section 5 permitted anyone who "has been" a barrister or advocate for ten years to be appointed to the Supreme Court.[99]

In reply, Edwards stated: "But [Stein's] argument does not get over the difficulty presented by the language of section 6. Section 5 deals with the judges generally, but section 6 provides a special rule to be followed with regard to appointments made from the Province of Quebec." He continued with the observation that section 4 of the *Judges Act* (as it was then) already provided that a person could not be appointed a judge of a "superior court or of a circuit, county or district court ... unless ... he has been admitted to the Bar of one of the provinces for at least ten years." On Stein's reading of section 5 of the *Supreme Court Act, any* judge of a circuit, county, or district court must be eligible for the Supreme Court. Yet section 6 pointedly restricts eligibility to judges of the Court of King's Bench or the superior court. That suggests that not everyone who would otherwise be eligible under section 5 remains eligible under section 6. Edwards stated: "It seems to me there is an irresistible inference that judges of other courts are not qualified, even though they have necessarily had ten years standing at the bar."[100]

Over time, of course, the statutes referenced by Edwards and Stein changed in various respects. But the core of their dispute is, in some respects, remarkably similar to that which took place more than seventy years later. At bottom, Stein argued (if only as devil's advocate) that section 6 of the *Supreme Court Act* should be read in light of section 5 and that, since the latter allowed the appointment of former members of the bar, so should section 6. Edwards, by contrast, took the view that section 6 provided a "special rule" for the Quebec seats and that the reference to "barristers and advocates" must be construed in light of the fact that only judges of certain courts were mentioned. In effect, their argument concerns the significance of the fact that section 5's language ("has been") is more expansive than that contained in section 6. Does that mean that section 6 should be read in a more expansive fashion than its text, standing alone, would otherwise suggest? Or does it mean that section 6 is simply narrower than section 5?

There are real differences between the behind-the-scenes debate in 1940 and the all-too-public debate of 2013–14. Edwards and Stein were preoccupied with the text of sections 5 and 6 and not with the purposes that had animated their enactment. Neither, moreover, was concerned that his interpretation would lead to absurd results – though one might wonder if the entire debate was spurred by the intuition that there was something distinctly odd in allowing the appointment of a practising lawyer with ten years' standing, but not the chief magistrate of Quebec. There is no discussion of the Hansard debates or other legislative history surrounding section 6. But those additional pieces of information hardly resolved the fundamental question. The 1940 file is, to some extent, the 2013 debate distilled to its essence.

The very existence of the file raises intriguing questions. Perhaps the Department of Justice was unaware of it. But we located it after discovering a reference on the Library and Archives website, and making a simple request. Concerns about solicitor-client privilege were clearly not thought to be engaged. Yet, throughout the Nadon controversy, the Edwards-Stein memoranda were never mentioned. To be clear, the file is hardly fatal to the case for Nadon's eligibility – enough had changed, not just in the relevant statutes but in the way that courts interpret them, that the Edwards position had arguably become obsolete. But the file raises questions that would have been pertinent to the Nadon controversy. The fact that it languished in obscurity while the Binnie memorandum was paraded before the media and the public is, if nothing else, unfortunate.

4

Asking and Telling

On 22 October 2013, the government introduced two new clauses to a pending budget bill:

471. The *Supreme Court Act* is amended by adding the following after section 5:

    5.1 For greater certainty, for the purpose of section 5, a person may be appointed a judge if, at any time, they were a barrister or advocate of at least 10 years standing at the bar of a province.

472. The Act is amended by adding the following after section 6:

    6.1 For greater certainty, for the purpose of section 6, a judge is from among the advocates of the Province of Quebec if, at any time, they were an advocate of at least 10 years standing at the bar of that Province.[1]

These were eyebrow-raising provisions for a number of reasons.

First, the very fact that they were part of a much larger (i.e., 323-page) budget bill made them noteworthy – and somewhat problematic.[2] After all, as part of a supply bill, it would be extremely difficult for members of Parliament to sensibly challenge them – to do so would risk bringing down the government. Moreover, Supreme Court appointments were among a wide variety of matters that Bill C-4 addressed, making it difficult for MPs to focus on them.[3] Omnibus bills had long been a matter of criticism, even if there was no rule (strictly speaking) forbidding them.[4] Nonetheless, over the course of the previous few years, the Harper government had introduced, to considerable controversy and over the objections of Opposition members of Parliament, an increasing number of omnibus bills.[5] In 2010, for example, it had produced a budget bill of more than 900 pages, covering a vast range of topics.[6] In 2011, an omnibus bill was more than 650 pages.[7] In 2012, there were two omnibus bills that each ran to more than 400 pages.[8] By the time Bill C-4 was introduced, "omnibudget bills"[9] had become "routine."[10]

The legislation was problematic for a second reason. Sections 471 and 472 did not purport to amend sections 5 and 6. The legislation did not, for example, rewrite section 6 so that instead of saying "from among the advocates" it read "from among those who are or have been advocates." Insofar as the prime minister sought to fix any legal problems with Marc Nadon's appointment, that approach would not have achieved his end: if section 6 indeed excluded Federal Court judges at the time Nadon was appointed, then his appointment was invalid at the time it was made, and it would remain so even if an amendment of section 6 ensured that future appointments of Federal Court judges would be perfectly lawful. What Prime Minister Harper needed was legislation that could reach back and retrospectively make Marc Nadon's appointment valid (assuming for the sake of argument that it wasn't already).

THE DECLARATORY LEGISLATION

Of course, the government could have amended sections 5 and 6 in the manner above or by expressly making Federal Court judges eligible and devising an additional provision saying that the change would be retroactive. But this approach would have been politically problematic. The prime minister and minister of justice had, from the outset, insisted that Federal Court judges were already eligible under section 6 and defended Marc Nadon's appointment on that basis. Given that the government had already been embroiled in controversy with respect to Senate appointments, it was no doubt eager to avoid further embarrassment.

And so Bill C-4 took a third path – that of declaratory legislation. Sections 471 and 472 would seek to clarify the law as it always existed – giving guidance to the courts on how they should interpret sections 5 and 6 of the *Supreme Court Act* but not purporting to amend them.[11] That way, the legislation would achieve two seemingly incompatible goals: it would send a clear legal signal to the courts that they ought to construe sections 5 and 6 in an inclusive fashion, and it would do so without sending a political signal that the government had already made an appointment contrary to the law.

Declaratory legislation can raise separation-of-powers concerns. Generally, it falls to the courts – not the legislature – to interpret the law. In telling the courts how to interpret sections 5 and 6 of the *Supreme Court Act,* Parliament stepped out of its traditional role. In *Canada Bread,* decided only six weeks before the introduction of Bill C-4, a majority of the Supreme Court emphasized the sense in which declaratory provisions represent an exercise of judicial power by the legislature:

> In enacting declaratory legislation, the legislature assumes the role of a court and dictates the interpretation of its own law ... As a result, declaratory provisions operate less as legislation and more as jurisprudence. They are akin to binding precedents, such as the decision of a court ... Such legislation may overrule a court decision in the same way that a decision of this Court would take precedence over a previous line of lower court judgments on a given question of law.[12]

Such an exercise of power may be problematic in some instances, particularly when a declaratory provision is intended to correct a decision that has already been reached by the courts. In such a case, declaratory legislation does not simply tread on the courts' interpretive function, it threatens to interfere with their adjudicative role – their responsibility to settle disputes that have arisen between specific parties. Declaratory provisions that seek to overturn final judicial rulings in particular cases are, for that reason, impermissible.[13]

What about pending cases? This was an important question. Remember, Rocco Galati had already begun proceedings in Federal Court seeking a ruling on Marc Nadon's eligibility for the Supreme Court of Canada. Would it be wrong in principle for sections 471 and 472 to clarify the meaning of sections 5 and 6 while that case was in litigation?

The short answer is no. The Supreme Court in *Canada Bread* made it clear that declaratory provisions "have an immediate effect on pending cases" and that that is an acceptable use of legislative power.[14] Though declaratory provisions may disrupt the expectations of the parties to particular litigation, insofar as they alter the legal landscape, the legislature is presumed to have weighed the costs of disruption against the benefits of settling a legal question in the manner in which it sees fit.[15] The courts, when they hear affected disputes, must accordingly defer to the legislature's judgment on the matter. As Paul Daly noted in his submissions to the Senate Standing Committee on Legal and Constitutional Affairs, this attitude distinguishes Canada – with its "traditional conception of parliamentary sovereignty" – from countries such as Ireland, which regard legislative interference with pending litigation as unacceptable.[16]

The declaratory legislation would seem to have resolved the interpretive issue: section 472 would indeed make clear that former advocates of Quebec – including Federal Court judges such as Marc Nadon – are eligible for appointment under section 6 of the *Supreme Court Act*. And, as we have seen, declaratory legislation is retrospective in nature and applicable to pending cases. But that didn't end the problems faced by the prime minister. It some ways, it made them bigger. Arguably,[17] the practical effect of sections 471 and 472 was to change the eligibility criteria. It was not at all obvious that, as a constitutional matter, Parliament could do such a thing.

COULD PARLIAMENT CHANGE THE ELIGIBILITY CRITERIA FOR APPOINTMENTS?

The *Supreme Court Act* was (at least to all appearances) an ordinary piece of legislation. The Supreme Court of Canada was a creature of statute; there is nothing in the *Constitution Act, 1867* requiring the creation of the court as an institution. Section 101 of the Act, moreover, states that Parliament has the authority to provide "for the Constitution, Maintenance, and Organization of a General Court of Appeal for Canada" – suggesting that it may unilaterally change the rules for appointing Supreme Court judges. One might think, on these bases, that there could be nothing to stop Parliament from amending the *Supreme Court Act* or otherwise changing its import.

That, however, would be too hasty, because it neglects Part V of the *Constitution Act, 1982.* In that part, section 41(d) provides that any changes to the "composition of the Supreme Court of Canada" require a constitutional amendment for which there is unanimous provincial consent. Under section 42(1)(d), any other change to the court requires the agreement of seven provinces representing 50 percent of the population.

There was some question as to whether and to what extent these provisions posed any sort of obstacle to changing the *Supreme Court Act.* The prominent constitutional lawyer Peter Hogg had long argued that, by itself, Part V had nothing to say on the matter.[18] Since the rest of the Constitution says nothing at all about the Supreme Court of Canada, he took the sections mentioning the court to be more or less dormant – suggesting that they would only become active if and when there was a decision to expressly entrench the court in the written text of the Constitution. This has been described as the "empty vessel" theory.[19] Benoit Pelletier made a similar argument.[20]

Hogg's view has troubled some scholars, because the very idea that a section of the Constitution has no operational effect whatsoever runs contrary to standard intuitions about the interpretation of legal instruments. Intuitively, the whole point to sections 41(d) and 42(1)(d) must have been to restrain Parliament's power to change some aspects of the Supreme Court of Canada without provincial consent. They were, after all, meant to answer the concerns of the "gang of eight" – the provinces that had opposed Trudeau's constitutional reforms. As Patrick Monahan and Byron Shaw remark in *Constitutional Law:*

> The underlying purpose of the amending procedure [in Part V] ... is to protect the provinces from having their rights or privileges negatively affected without their consent. This includes provincial interests in the design and operation of key national institutions such as the Senate and the House of Commons. Yet, by treating section 41(d) as ineffective, the provinces are granted absolutely no protection when it comes to the Supreme Court, a key institution of the federation.[21]

As we will see, Monahan would later argue for this position before the Supreme Court. Monahan and Shaw did not suggest that all aspects of the *Supreme Court Act* were effectively entrenched by Part V – only "those key characteristics of the Court that implicate fundamental provincial interests." They gave, as one example, "the requirement that three members of the Court be appointed from the bar of Quebec."[22] In support of such a contention, one could cite (among other things) the explanatory notes accompanying Part V of the *Constitution Act, 1982,* which "suggest that modifications to the selection criteria for Quebec judges were intended to be subject to the unanimity procedure of s. 41."[23] In the end, the aim was straightforward: to identify the broad ends or "telos" that Part V was intended to achieve and read it in accordance with that understanding, rather than get hung up on the fact that little about the Supreme Court of Canada had been expressly constitutionalized.[24]

Monahan's view was one of several approaches that Professor Paul Daly described as intermediate – in the sense that it struck a balance between a purely purposive approach that gave little free-standing significance to the text itself, and the formalist "empty vessel" theory that treated Part V as all but meaningless. Peter Oliver adopted a view broadly similar to that of Monahan, arguing that Part V could be used to protect Quebec's interest in being represented on the Supreme Court of Canada.[25]

For his part, Warren Newman observed that, on several occasions, "attempts to entrench substantively the composition and essential characteristics of the Supreme Court in the Constitution of Canada were proposed and failed to be ratified."[26] This was a point later emphasized by the attorney general of Canada in written submissions to the Supreme Court. Part IV of the 1971 *Victoria Charter* "included 21 provisions which would have established the Court and its composition, prescribed the professional qualifications required for appointment, and provided for a nomination and selection process that included a consultative role for provinces."[27] But the *Victoria Charter* fell apart after failing to get sufficient provincial consent. Several years later, Bill C-60 contained provisions that would have also constitutionalized the Supreme Court in various respects. After a reference to the Supreme Court of Canada, however, Bill C-60 was not enacted into law.[28] As we have seen, the *Constitution Act, 1982* did not expressly entrench the Supreme Court of Canada or any particular "essential" features – there is only the bare reference in Part V to the court's "composition." The Meech Lake Accord "would have entrenched the qualifications for appointment to the Supreme Court in the Constitution," but it was not ratified. As the attorney general of Canada noted in written submissions to the court, even if the accord had been ratified, it "would have reserved to Parliament the power to make laws under section 101 'except to the extent that such laws are inconsistent' with what was proposed to be entrenched."[29] That suggests an understanding that Parliament's power to alter the Supreme Court of Canada had not been affected by Part V of the *Constitution Act, 1982*. Likewise, in 1992, there were proposals to entrench eligibility criteria in the Charlottetown Accord, but these also went unratified.

For the attorney general of Canada, one could not read Part V of the *Constitution Act, 1982* as though all of these attempts at entrenching aspects of the Supreme Court of Canada had somehow succeeded. To do so would fail to respect the provinces' role in the process of constitutional amendment. Similarly, constitutional lawyer and scholar Warren Newman argued that it would be strange if we could effectively read limits into Parliament's authority to change the court's composition or eligibility criteria "directly into the text of the Constitution" – that is, by adopting an aggressively broad interpretation of Part V, ostensibly in the name of "purposivism" or "teleology" – as if forty years of failed attempts at amending the Constitution had never happened.[30] Unlike the attorney general of Canada, though, Newman did not straightforwardly endorse Hogg's view either. Instead, he looked to the structural role of a court of last resort in Canada's constitutional system.

As Newman pointed out, it was unnecessary at the time of Confederation to set out the features of a general court of appeal, or to require Parliament to create one, because Canada already had one: the Judicial Committee of the Privy Council. The *Constitution Act, 1867* thus presupposes that there will be a "court of last resort." Given the legal problems bound to arise in a federal state, it is impossible to read the Constitution as permitting the abrogation of the Supreme Court. Once appeals to the Privy Council were abolished in 1949, "the appellate jurisdiction of the Supreme Court of Canada became essential."[31] In effect, Newman claims, the mention of the Supreme Court in Part V "crystallized" its constitutional status and made it impossible for Parliament to change those attributes that were "essential" to it as of 1982.

Many jurists and commentators found it difficult to countenance the idea that the Supreme Court of Canada received no constitutional protection at all. Daly noted:

> [I]f certain essential elements of the *Supreme Court Act* are not protected from unilateral amendment, Parliament could accomplish sweeping changes to the nature of the institution. It could pack the Supreme Court of Canada with sympathetic jurists by amending s. 4 to increase the number of judges. It could do away with the requirement that appointees to the court be lawyers by amending s. 5 of the *Supreme*

> *Court Act.* It could remove the three Quebec seats altogether by repealing s. 6. By unilateral federal action the court could thus variously be stacked with pro-government judges; be re-fashioned as a constitutional court in the French tradition, a body on which politicians sit, for which legal experience is not a necessary prerequisite; or be shorn entirely of its Quebec judges. Or, indeed, it could be abolished altogether.[32]

None of this was likely to happen. But that was beside the point – the very idea that it was constitutionally open to Parliament to embark on those courses of action was itself unthinkable. The questions remained: How could one explain and defend the intuition that court stacking and wholesale abolition of the court are constitutional nonstarters? Assuming they are, what else would be off limits?

A number of scholars appearing before the Senate Standing Committee on Legal and Constitutional Affairs claimed that Part V implicitly distinguished between matters pertaining to the composition of the court and those pertaining to the qualifications of its members. On this reading, Parliament was precluded from unilaterally abolishing the Supreme Court, stacking it with government-friendly judges, or (crucially) stripping away Quebec's entitlement to three judges, but it was free to change the eligibility criteria for the appointment of judges – for example, by introducing a requirement that judges be bilingual. Thus, former Supreme Court Justice Michel Bastarache remarked:

> If the government wanted to reduce the number of Quebec representatives to two ... that would affect the composition of the court. If qualifications are the issue, that does not change the representation. One year ago, the Government of Quebec requested a change to qualifications to ensure that all judges appointed to the Supreme Court would be bilingual. If that did not require a constitutional amendment, why would this require one?[33]

Likewise, co-author Carissima Mathen testified that although "the specific mention of composition in a part that requires unanimity at the very least confirms the current practice of the special reserve of seats for Quebec[,] I do not believe that composition in this case includes qualifications."[34]

The line separating composition from qualifications was not easy to track. It was not clear, for example, whether requiring a certain number of judges to be women or members of certain racial or ethnic groups would amount to a change in one or the other. Nor would it allay concerns that Parliament could unilaterally decide to make non-lawyers eligible for appointment to the Supreme Court of Canada.

More importantly, it was unclear whether the line between composition and qualifications could be sustained in principle. Section 6 illustrated that point. In a sense, one could say that the requirement of three Quebec judges went to composition, whereas the requirement of expertise in civil law went to qualifications. But what was the point of having a requirement of three Quebec judges if Parliament could unilaterally declare that those three judges did not need to have any grasp of civil law or Quebec legal traditions? In what sense would those judges be *representative* if they lacked any significant connection to the legal traditions they were meant to represent? The distinction that some asserted between composition and qualifications would arguably confine the scope of Part V – ensuring that the court could be protected and also, at some future point, reformed (if necessary) by ordinary statute. It also, however, raised fears that Parliament could strip the substance out of Quebec's "right" to be represented on the court by appointing persons who might not be accepted as having a sufficient connection with the province. As we will see, the idea of that connection would be important when the Supreme Court heard the reference in 2014.

THE REFERENCE QUESTIONS

It was hardly obvious that sections 471 and 472 were a constitutionally valid means of removing any eligibility hurdles created by section 6. And so, on the very day that it introduced clauses 471 and 472, the government finally yielded to public demands that it seek an advisory opinion from the Supreme Court of Canada. But it didn't only ask whether sections 5 and 6 made Federal Court judges eligible for appointment. The government asked a second question as well:

1. Can a person who was, at any time, an advocate of at least 10 years standing at the Barreau du Québec be appointed to the Supreme Court of Canada as a member of the Supreme Court from Quebec pursuant to sections 5 and 6 of the *Supreme Court Act?*
2. Can Parliament enact legislation that requires that a person be or has previously been a barrister or advocate of at least 10 years standing at the bar of a province as a condition of appointment as a judge of the Supreme Court of Canada or enact the annexed declaratory provisions as set out in clauses 471 and 472 of the Bill entitled *Economic Action Plan 2013 Act, No. 2?*[35]

The decision to ask the second question – a question about the constitutional validity of the proposed amendments – was rather curious. It was made necessary by the addition of sections 471 and 472 to the budget bill. But if there was some doubt as to the constitutional validity of those provisions, why enact them before obtaining the Supreme Court's advice on the matter? The whole point to receiving advice on such issues, after all, is surely to avoid making unconstitutional legislation in the first place.

The matter was raised with the minister of justice in the House Standing Committee on Justice and Human Rights:

> *Mr. Sean Casey:* My question for you is whether you would be amenable to delaying the impact of [clauses 471 and 472] to allow the Supreme Court to speak unimpeded.
>
> *Hon. Peter MacKay:* Not at all. Absolutely not. Our intention is to clarify what we believe is the case and what we believe the Supreme Court will affirm.
>
> *Mr. Sean Casey:* So as I understand what you just said to me, you are not in favour of delaying the implementation until the Supreme Court has spoken. You want to have Parliament amend the legislation to say

that this is the state of the law, and then ask the Supreme Court what the state of the law is. Do I have that right?

Hon. Peter MacKay: Well, Mr. Casey, you've been here a little while now, and you recognize that there is something called the supremacy of Parliament when it comes to the passing of laws. So yes, that's exactly what I'm saying. We are telling the Supreme Court this is what the legislation means. We're putting in place a declaratory provision to bring about a greater understanding of the eligibility rules, and at the same time we have sought an opinion from the Supreme Court. That's how it works, sir.

Mr. Sean Casey: So we're going to ask them and tell them at the same time.

Hon. Peter MacKay: You got it.[36]

Why proceed in this way? The answer, it seems, is that the government wanted to ensure that the Supreme Court would have the declaratory provisions before it when deciding the first question – that is, in order to guarantee that the court construed sections 5 and 6 in an inclusive fashion. Since the court would presumably rely on the declaratory provisions for guidance only if it was satisfied of their constitutionality, the government decided to simply put that higher-level question on the agenda as well.

With the benefit of hindsight, that was probably unwise. Certainly, the government could have taken a more cautious route. It could, for example, have chosen not to add the declaratory provisions and – armed with a legal opinion that had received the imprimatur of three retired Supreme Court of Canada judges – sought a definitive ruling on the meaning of sections 5 and 6. There was a possibility that the court would invalidate Nadon's appointment, but the government would then have further options. It could appoint someone else. Or it could enact the declaratory provisions and try again to appoint Marc Nadon. The government didn't need to bring the constitutional question to the court just yet.

Politically, though, the Harper administration may have thought it important to draw a line under the Nadon controversy. As Professor Hugo Cyr has noted, the government had already been embroiled in controversies surrounding Senate appointments.[37] A ruling that it had failed to make a legally valid appointment to the Supreme Court would have been politically embarrassing (to say the least). To avoid that result, the government sought to stack the deck in its favour – by adding the declaratory provisions. Yes, this raised the stakes by presenting the court with a constitutional question. As we have seen, though, there were reasonable arguments that the federal Parliament could unilaterally amend sections 5 and 6 of the *Supreme Court Act* – either because Part V of the *Constitution Act, 1982* presented no barrier at all or because it limited Parliament's ability to change the composition of the court and not the eligibility criteria for its members. To the government, this might well have seemed a good bet to make.

Still, the decision to enact the declaratory provisions at the same time as the government sought an advisory opinion on their validity was seen, by some at least, as provocative. In their testimony before House and Senate standing committees, a number of expert witnesses weighed in on the appropriateness of seeking a reference on the meaning of sections 5 and 6 of the *Supreme Court Act* at the same time as the government purported to authoritatively "declare" an answer to that question in legislation. Some took the position that this "belt and suspenders" approach was simply superfluous; it was, they argued, so obvious that the court would interpret section 6 in an inclusive fashion that the declaratory provisions were wholly unnecessary in any event.[38]

But several were also of the opinion that the approach was, at the very least, unsavory. Appearing before the House Standing Committee on Justice and Human Rights, Professor Adam Dodek testified that the dual-track strategy was untenable. He expressed concern over the fact that the attorney general, by permitting clauses 471 and 472 to be inserted into the budget bill, had implicitly vouched for its validity at the same time as asking the Supreme Court for an opinion on that validity. Carissima Mathen and Michel Bastarache expressed broadly similar concerns.[39] In a society committed to the rule of law, it was unacceptable for Parliament to purport to enact a law that it knew or reasonably believed to be unconstitutional.

Commentators observed on several occasions that Parliament had only once before referred a question on the constitutionality of legislation at the same as it purported to enact that same legislation: the *Anti-Inflation Act*. That was a very different piece of legislation, enacted under quite different conditions more than thirty years earlier – not a declaratory provision intended to prevent mere political embarrassment, but legislation intended to address an imminent economic emergency.[40] One could not draw ready parallels between that case and this one. In considering the strange situation before the court, Mathen suggested that the court might exercise its discretion simply to refuse to answer the second question about the declaratory legislation. Admittedly, this prospect was unlikely. Nonetheless, the Supreme Court had refused to answer reference questions in the past. If the court decided that the current versions of sections 5 and 6 did not pose an obstacle to Nadon's appointment, it might conclude that the declaratory legislation was basically redundant, which would obviate the need to provide an answer to Question 2.

In the end, objections to the dual-track strategy did not shift the government from its course. Bill C-4 was passed, and the reference questions were put to the Supreme Court of Canada. In the weeks that followed, others sought and received leave to intervene in the matter. Almost immediately, the Quebec government expressed its interest in intervening. It emerged that the attorney general of Ontario would also make submissions on the legal issues before the court, as would the Canadian Association of Provincial Court Judges, three Federal Court judges, Rocco Galati, and the Constitutional Rights Centre. The hearing was scheduled for 15 January 2014.

As for Marc Nadon, the Supreme Court issued a statement that, until the matter was resolved, it would have no further contact with him. In a letter issued on 1 November 2013, the deputy registrar of the court stated:

As questions concerning the legality of Justice Nadon's appointment are pending before the Court, it has adopted the following measures to ensure that justice is both done and is seen to be done in an independent and impartial manner:

1. Justice Nadon will not have contact with the members of the Court.
2. Justice Nadon will continue not to participate in the work of the Court.
3. Justice Nadon will not occupy his office or attend at the Court.

The court confirms that none of its members has discussed the merits of the challenge or the reference with Justice Nadon.[41]

5

The Legal Showdown

THE REFERENCE WAS HEARD on 15 January 2014. Strictly speaking, there were no parties as such. References differ from live cases or appeals precisely in that they lack moving and responding parties. References are initiated by the executive branch to obtain judicial answers to questions of its choosing.[1] They are merely advisory.

That said, many references do present clearly opposing interests and points of view. In this case, it is fair to see the principal opponents as the attorney general of Canada (Canada) and the attorney general of Quebec (Quebec). Aside from them, there were few interveners. Those that did appear are best described as an eclectic bunch with very different priorities and concerns. They include the attorney general of Ontario (Ontario); three former Federal Court judges intervening in their own names;[2] the Association of Provincial Court Judges; Rocco Galati, the Toronto lawyer who first challenged the appointment; and the nonprofit Constitutional Rights Centre (CRC), with which Galati was closely associated. Before getting into their arguments, and how and why each became involved in the case, it is necessary to note an issue concerning one member of the Supreme Court panel.

THE RECUSAL OF MARSHALL ROTHSTEIN

Perhaps not surprisingly, given that the case concerned the composition of the Supreme Court of Canada, allegations of bias were made. One of the sitting judges, Marshall Rothstein, had himself been appointed to the court from the Federal Court of Appeal (in his case, under section 5). Rocco Galati asked that Justice Rothstein not be assigned to the case. As it happened, Rothstein had already recused himself from the entire proceeding. At the time, he provided no reasons for his decision to do so. In a telephone interview, however, Rothstein explained that the primary motivation behind his decision to recuse himself was his close friendship with Marc Nadon – a former colleague on the Federal Court.[3] He recalled that his wife had asked him whether he planned to sit on the panel, pointedly observing, "Well, he's your friend." He was, Rothstein remembered, somewhat conflicted at the time. "When things involve a judge personally," he reflected, "it takes time to get one's head around the issue." In the end, though, Rothstein concluded that the "perception [of bias] would be difficult" if he didn't recuse himself.[4] As for Galati's motion, he recalled in our interview that it was "inconsequential" and "not a factor for me."

There was an additional reason for Rothstein to recuse himself. Had there been a panel of eight judges, of course, it would have been possible for the court to reach a four-four split.[5] This would not have been so problematic in an ordinary appeal – in such a case, the lower court decision would stand. But in a federally initiated reference, there is no lower-court decision.[6] Cabinet simply exercises its authority to put an issue before the court *de novo.* In the case of a tie, Canadians would simply have been left with no answer as to the meaning of section 6, or the validity of Justice Marc Nadon's appointment. This plainly would have been an unacceptable result. It was critical to know whether he was a member of the Supreme Court of Canada. Moreover, Chief Justice McLachlin would not want to have to exercise her administrative authority as chief justice to remove one member of the court from the panel: in such a politically charged case, it would not do to create even the perception – however unreasonable – that the outcome turned on the composition of the panel. Rothstein's recusal solved this problem. By stepping aside, he dispelled the possibility of an evenly split court and did so without creating the impression that the chief justice was in any way involved.

In our interview with Rothstein, he acknowledged that the desire to avoid an even number of judges on the panel had played a role in his decision. He was not under pressure by the chief justice to step aside; there was, he recalled, no protocol requiring an odd number of judges. According to Rothstein, Chief Justice McLachlin took the view that any member of the court who wanted to sit on a case could do so, even if that meant an even-numbered panel. But, he continued, it was obviously desirable to avoid even the possibility of a four-four split. With that in mind, and in light of his relationship with Marc Nadon, Rothstein recused.

One further possible argument for recusal deserves mention, if only to explain why it may be set aside. Given the reference questions and the declaratory legislation, the court was required to interpret not just section 6 but section 5 as well. It was theoretically possible for the court to conclude that neither section permitted the appointment of a Federal Court judge, as Justice Rothstein had been at the time of his elevation.[7] As we have seen, the Binnie memorandum and other arguments urging a broad construction of section 6 focused on the language contained in section 5. Few jurists or legal scholars took seriously the idea that section 5 precluded the appointment of federal or provincial court judges. But the arguments made by Rocco Galati were such that the court would need to decide the point. That being the case, Rothstein would effectively have been called upon to pass judgment on his own eligibility.

This explanation, however, can be discounted. In conversation with us, Rothstein noted that that he did not take seriously the argument that section 5 precluded the appointment of Federal Court judges to the Supreme Court of Canada. In his view, the truly interesting legal questions surrounded the proper interpretation of section 6 and its implications for the Quebec seats. The section 5 arguments were not irrelevant to Justice Rothstein's decision to recuse, but they were no more than background considerations.

CANADA VERSUS QUEBEC

As expected, the federal government pressed hard on both Questions 1 and 2. It argued that Nadon had always been eligible because, in its view, current bar membership was not a requirement for either section 5 or section 6: "[W]hen read in context, and in light of the purpose of the provisions and of the Act as a whole, sections 5 and 6 provide that a person who is or has been, at any time, an advocate of the Barreau du Québec of at least 10 years standing is eligible to be appointed as one of the three members of the Court from Quebec." Canada emphasized the point made by Binnie and others: that section 6 could not be read in isolation from section 5 and did not impose a special currency requirement. In doing so, Canada offered additional interpretive evidence. Specifically, it noted that the predecessor of both sections 5 and 6 was a single provision – which in 1875 was numbered as section 4.[8] That evidence alone suggested that one should not read the current versions of sections 5 and 6 in isolation from each other. Notwithstanding that the rules for all judges and the rules for Quebec judges were separated into two clauses in 1886, Canada argued, they had a continuing relationship. In Canada's view, section 5 set out the qualifications for Supreme Court judges. Section 6 merely ensured that a certain number of appointees would hail from Quebec. Nothing of significance turned on Parliament's use of the phrase "from among" or "parmi."[9]

Setting aside the predecessor provision, Canada continued, the current text of section 5 – in both English and French – suggested that both current and former barristers or advocates of ten years' standing were eligible.[10] This point was argued at length, though it was far from clear how it answered the central criticism levelled at Binnie's memorandum – namely, that a focus solely on section 5 does not really tell us much about its relationship with section 6. Indeed, it is not until page 15 of the attorney general's factum that section 6 is mentioned as a provision of free-standing significance – and that was, at best, glancing:

39. As for section 6, the English and French versions have changed little since 1886. As noted above, it was in 1886 that the various components contained within section 4 of the 1875 enactment were separated. The portions relating to professional qualifications became subsection 4(2) whereas the portions relating to the number of Quebec judges on the court became subsection 4(3).
40. The history of the revisions demonstrates that the discrepancies between the two versions of section 5 were the result of ordinary revision exercises rather than a deliberate attempt to change the law. These discrepancies cannot be taken to have altered Parliament's intention in 1886 to make clear that current membership in the bar of a province was not required.

Although not quite as stark as Binnie's memorandum, it is impossible to read Canada's factum without concluding that, so far as the government was concerned, section 6 had very little to do with the underlying issue. All of the "meat" was in section 5.

With respect to section 30's treatment of ad hoc judges, Canada argued that that was simply a historical anomaly. As we have noted, there was an argument that this section was intended to ensure that in a common law appeal where quorum was lost because of the absence of a common law judge, the panel would not have a majority of civil law judges. This was the position essentially adopted by the attorney general of Canada.[11] Any amendments to that section in subsequent years, Canada argued, were minor, not concerned with the status of Federal Court judges and, thus, not indicative of any underlying legislative intent about them.

In oral argument, counsel for Canada met with resistance early on. Echoing earlier concerns about the government's dual-track strategy (enacting declaratory legislation at the same time as initiating a reference), Justice Louis LeBel queried why the court's input was needed at all. Wasn't the declaratory legislation sufficient?[12] Canada responded that the new provisions did represent a directive to the court but that it would be helpful to know the court's answer to Question 1, as that would determine whether it needed to answer Question 2. LeBel appeared skeptical. The attorney general conceded that the situation was unusual, noting that "[t]here is a context here, and everyone knows what it is."

Next, Chief Justice McLachlin and Justice Cromwell raised the issue of the Act's different treatment of the Federal Court, particularly with respect to ad hoc judges under section 30. Canada repeated the long history of that section. But its answer to the query of why the Federal Court is mentioned in section 30(1) but not section 30(2) did not seem to satisfy at least some of the judges. The most Canada could offer was that, given its inability to locate "truly relevant debates" about the specific amendments, the matter may not have been fully considered. But, Justice Wagner pointed out, the most recent amendment to section 30 had occurred in 2002 and was undertaken to reflect changes in the structure of the Federal Court.

Canada also relied on wording found in other statutes governing judicial appointments, namely, the *Federal Courts Act* and the *Judges Act*. Both pieces of legislation, it said, conditioned eligibility for the bench on bar membership completed at any time prior to appointment, using language similar to that in the *Supreme Court Act*. In addition, it argued, language proposed by actors at various points contemplating the Supreme Court's entrenchment in the Constitution had not suggested currency as a requirement.[13]

Finally, Canada recited the arguments of absurdity that had been so well-rehearsed in Binnie's memorandum. In oral argument, Canada raised the absurdity argument relatively early in response to a question from Justice Abella. She wondered why, if Canada's approach was correct, the sections were in separate provisions and used somewhat different wording. Reiterating its written argument, Canada noted that interpreting the provisions in isolation of each other would lead to the absurdity of a candidate being eligible for a seat on the day of their admittance to the Quebec bar. Justice Wagner immediately shot back with the question: But isn't there at least an equivalent absurdity if someone can be appointed under section 6 who, after his call to the Bar, repairs to New York for twenty years? Justice LeBel jumped in, too, asking whether someone who had been disbarred from Quebec (but still had ten years) would also be eligible. Canada responded that the rule simply meant that thousands of lawyers living and working in Quebec were statutorily eligible to serve on the court. Whether they were actually suitable to do so was a decision for the executive branch, which would actually make the decision to appoint or not.

Justice Wagner then pressed Canada on the ultimate intent of section 6; specifically, whether it was intended to reassure Quebecers as much as it was intended to guarantee the civil law expertise of at least three judges. Canada responded with the observation that several former Quebec members of the Supreme Court – Chief Justice Lamer, Justice Fauteux – were not *civilistes* at all. What made them suitable? Justice Wagner quickly countered that those jurists, regardless of their subject-matter expertise, had been ensconced in the Quebec legal community. Counsel for Canada was frank: he could not understand how a Quebec judge, appointed to the Federal Court, as a Quebec judge, did not also have that experience.

Turning to Question 2, Canada's position was that section 101 of the *Constitution Act, 1867* disposed of the issue. Recall that section 101 states that the "Parliament of Canada may, notwithstanding anything in this Act, from Time to Time provide for the Constitution, Maintenance, and Organization of a General Court of Appeal for Canada, and for the Establishment of any additional Courts for the better Administration of the Laws of Canada." Section 101, Canada said, grants Parliament plenary power that has never been modified. It exists notwithstanding anything else in the Constitution. In 1949, Canada said, the section had been used to eliminate further appeals from the Supreme Court to the Judicial Committee of the Privy Council. Faced with a provincial challenge to the move, Lord Jewitt had proclaimed the power under section 101 to be "unqualified and absolute."[14] The power exists so long as it is not abrogated through formal amendment. None had occurred, it argued. Nothing in the *Constitution Act, 1982* had the slightest effect on section 101. Indeed, Parliament "has continued to amend the *Supreme Court Act* as necessary since 1982."[15] With respect to Part V of the *Constitution Act,* Canada adopted the Hogg approach.[16] That is, the reference to the Supreme Court in the amending formula was intended to apply in the event that the court was entrenched; it did not itself entrench the court. Section 101, Canada stated, offered a complete answer to Question 2.

Canada urged the court not to view the Nadon controversy, or the legal status of the declaratory legislation, as an opportunity to engage in broader constitutional soul-searching. Those who were trying to turn the reference into a grand examination of the court's status, it argued, were misguided:

> This reference is not about the constitutional status of the Court or its fundamental features, including the number of judges of the Court who, by tradition or statute must be drawn from Quebec. Acceptance of the propositions advanced here will not require the Court to address or provide its opinion on those broader questions ... *The constitutional issue in this reference is narrow and discrete.*[17]

These sentiments were repeated in oral arguments. Consistent with its factum, Canada tried to downplay the significance of the case. It was not at all necessary, it said, for the court to consider grand constitutional theory. Question 2 asked merely whether Parliament could confirm a reading of sections 5 and 6 that was already in place. In the alternative, should the legislation represent a true change, it was a minor one, clearly falling under section 101.

At that point, numerous questions were posed by the chief justice, as well as Justices Abella, Cromwell, Karakatsanis, LeBel, and Wagner. The most dramatic moment may have been the LeBel and Wagner queries as to whether, under section 101, Parliament could abolish the court altogether. Canada replied: "That's the million-dollar question, and we won't answer it today."[18]

The federal government resolutely refused to entertain any arguments about the broader status of the court because, it insisted, the proposed changes to sections 5 and 6 were entirely mundane. Even if aspects of the court are now constitutionally protected, it argued, that would not be because of Part V of the *Constitution Act, 1982.* It refused to engage with a suggestion that there might be a constitutional convention at work. And it pushed back, hard, on the suggestion that section 6 was enacted to ensure a "contemporaneous connection" between the candidate and the bar. That phrase would continually emerge at the hearing, though it did not, ultimately, make its way into the opinion.

As the initiator of the reference, the attorney general's position largely defined the issues in play. At least so far as the constitutional question was concerned, its strategy was one of minimization.[19] It tried to distract from broader questions of constitutionality, federalism, and underlying political agreements. There is nothing intrinsically illegitimate in such a strategy – many lawyers would regard it as the wisest path. But Canada had put the broader constitutional issues on the table in the first place, by introducing the declaratory provisions. It was difficult to argue now that the court should ignore the broader implications of those provisions.

THE ATTORNEY GENERAL OF QUEBEC

Unsurprisingly, Quebec's approach to both the interpretative and constitutional questions was diametrically opposed to that of Canada. It stressed the legislative history and the importance of ensuring a current connection between Quebec nominees and the province. It also took pains to stress the unique competence of Quebec jurists, not only to adjudicate issues dealing directly with civil law but also to properly use its tenets to influence the development of the common law. Quebec's attorney general quoted Robert Décary (one of the former Federal Court judges intervening in the reference), who observed:

> [L]a culture québécoise ne se confine pas, en matière juridique, au droit civil pur, et qu'au contraire elle s'étend à tout ce qui émane du législateur québécois et imprègne même ces lois que le législateur emprunte à d'autres systèmes juridiques. Ainsi, par exemple, la Loi de la protection du consommateur est aussi "civiliste" que le Code civil, et la responsabilité des municipalités et des corporations, quoiqu'établie par des lois inspires de la *common law,* doit s'apprécier en termes "civilistes."[20]

At the hearing, Quebec stressed the need to obey not just the letter of section 6 but its spirit. On that basis, it took an especially unyielding approach to the need for what it called a "contemporaneous connection." Most significantly, it stressed that bar membership must not only be current at the time of appointment but also continuous. In this way, it manoeuvred around the one-day argument applied to the reinstatement of a previous member. In response to a question by Justice Moldaver (gamely posed in French), Quebec replied that Nadon "had left the Quebec legal milieu" some twenty years previous and could not be considered as a candidate. Justice LeBel pointed out that bar membership could be interrupted by events quite beyond a candidate's control, such as wartime service. (Presumably, advocates' status would be paused during such activity.) Quebec remained unmoved. Its argument was uncompromising and gave the court a clear picture of the options before it.

With respect to the constitutional status of sections 5 and 6 of the *Supreme Court Act,* Quebec adopted a bluntly incorporationist argument,[21] claiming that those provisions were effectively entrenched in the Constitution by section 41(d) of the *Constitution Act, 1982.*[22] Citing the interpretative principle that constitutional text is not inserted in vain, Quebec stressed that sections 41 and 42 could not have a null effect on the current status of the Supreme Court. Rather, they entrenched those aspects of the court considered essential to its function, including its composition.

THE ATTORNEY GENERAL OF ONTARIO

It is difficult to consider Ontario's involvement in the reference without also noting who was serving as its deputy attorney general at the time: Patrick Monahan.[23] Monahan was a former law professor and dean who, as we have seen, had written extensively about the significance of Part V of the *Constitution Act, 1982.*[24] It is easy to imagine him being eager to argue, before the Supreme Court, a position he had advocated for many years as an academic.

Looking back, Ontario may have had the greatest effect on the reference as a whole. It pushed for a particular understanding of the

Supreme Court of Canada, one rooted in a broader argument about constitutionalism and the rule of law. Its focus was on Question 2. It did not stake out a position on the interpretation of section 6, a provision that applied only to Quebec in any case. Ontario did, however, take the view that section 5 permitted the appointment of candidates based on ten years' bar membership acquired at any time. This was not because federal courts counted as "superior courts" for the purposes of section 5, but by virtue of the past bar membership. It would be inconsistent with the purpose of section 5, it continued, for an otherwise qualified lawyer to lose eligibility solely by virtue of his or her appointment to the federal courts, which "have been established by Parliament as superior courts of record with broad and complex jurisdiction." Indeed, Ontario argued, some of the country's "most eminent jurists" have been on the Federal Court. It would be "quite extraordinary" to conclude that they are or would have been ineligible.[25]

The main purpose of Ontario's intervention, though, was to address Question 2 – the question of Parliament's constitutional authority to pass the declaratory legislation. Monahan presented the argument personally. He did not disagree with Quebec's analysis of section 41 and its effect on the power of Parliament to unilaterally amend certain provisions of the *Supreme Court Act.* But, he said, there was a "far more profound" argument for the court to consider: under section 101, Parliament has a continuing duty to maintain the Supreme Court as a general court of appeal for Canada. This duty "includes the maintenance of those characteristics that nourish and are essential to the fulfillment of its unique role." These "include, at a minimum, the qualifications necessary for appointment, including the fact that at least 3 judges of the Court must have training in civil law." Since the duty was rooted in section 101, that section would need to be amended in order for Parliament to change certain aspects of the *Supreme Court Act.*[26]

Ontario's argument was grounded in the way in which the Canadian constitution had evolved since the court's creation:

> As this Court has held, Canada's "constitutional history demonstrates that our governing institutions have adapted and changed to reflect

> changing social and political values." As Canada evolved from a colony to an independent state, the Supreme Court assumed a growing role as the impartial, ultimate arbiter of federal-provincial differences, as an institution for ensuring uniform interpretation of the Constitution and federal laws, and as a vehicle for promoting cross-fertilization between Canada's two legal traditions (the common law and the civil law). In 1982, the Court took on an additional role as the ultimate arbiter of the fundamental rights promised to Canadians through the enactment of the Canadian Charter of Rights and Freedoms and the protection of the Aboriginal and treaty rights of the Aboriginal peoples of Canada. Accordingly, the Court's role has grown and matured to the extent that it now serves as a fundamental constitutional linchpin that is essential to the proper functioning of our entire scheme of government.[27]

Monahan made specific and detailed reference to the Constitution's architecture, language that would assume great significance in the court's opinion and, later, in the *Senate Reform Reference.* In his view, the Supreme Court had become a central part of that architecture. And, essential to the court's ability to fulfill its role is its actual complement of nine judges, three of whom must come from Quebec. Quebec representation was fundamental to the court's establishment in 1875, and it remained fundamental to the exercise of its plenary jurisdiction as a court of general appeal. Here, Monahan seized upon Canada's unwillingness to say whether Parliament could, under section 101, simply abolish the court. He suggested, forcefully, that it could not.[28]

The chief justice wondered how Monahan's argument could be reconciled with the history of the Supreme Court of Canada. After all, the court was not considered central to the constitutional order in 1875. Monahan agreed, but pointed out that what *was* created in 1875 was a unitary court system under the oversight of a body – at the time, the Judicial Committee of the Privy Council – that could not be abrogated by Parliament. As the Supreme Court's role evolved and changed – beginning at least in 1949 with the elimination of further appeals, continuing through 1975, when its appellate jurisdiction was changed to a largely "by leave" process, and finally confirmed in 1982 – it gradually assumed a more central constitutional status.[29]

For her part, Justice Abella asked about the place of the *Supreme Court Act* in Ontario's analysis. Monahan responded that the Act itself was incidental to his argument but fully supported by it. He adopted a point articulated by Justice Cromwell: section 6 reflects a constitutional imperative but does not embody it. Abella asked whether there was anything in the *Supreme Court Act* that might be inconsistent with the court's "essential features or functioning" and, if so, how the analysis would deal with it. Could the architecture argument be used to strike down aspects of the *Supreme Court Act* itself?[30] Though Abella did not raise this example, one might ask whether the mandatory nature of the court's advisory (reference) function, set out in section 53, interferes with the court's ability to act as a neutral arbiter of, say, federalism.[31] One might make a similar argument about Parliament's ability to designate certain matters as appeals "as of right." (We consider some of these questions in Chapter 9.)

The chief justice asked whether there was a guiding principle that could determine which features are deemed essential and which are not. Monahan turned to the unwritten constitutional principles – particularly federalism, which requires an independent arbiter of disputes between orders of government, and constitutionalism, which implies a fundamental precondition of legitimacy. But throughout his submissions he carefully avoided taking a position as to whether rules ostensibly requiring Quebec appointees to be current members of the bar for ten years were essential in light of those principles.[32]

Some members of the panel seemed nervous at the idea of using unwritten principles to constitutionalize the court. Abella, notably, asked Monahan if it would not be wiser for the court to follow Quebec's lead and ground its analysis in Part V, which was entrenched in the Constitution of Canada through known democratic procedures. Monahan explained that he was not using unwritten constitutional principles as the basis for entrenching the court's essential features. Rather, the unwritten constitutional principles helped make sense of

Parliament's duty, in section 101, to maintain those particular features of the Supreme Court.[33]

Monahan's reluctance to weigh in on the meaning of section 6 gave a hesitancy to some of his arguments. He emphasized, however, that if Parliament wished to alter the qualifications of Quebec jurists, it needed to amend the Constitution. The question of who gets to sit on the court, Ontario argued, is fundamental to its operation. Justice Cromwell asked whether Parliament could declare that its intent was to prevent a disbarred lawyer or removed judge from being nominated to the court. Monahan replied that the response would depend on whether such a declaration amounted to amending the Act; if it did, formal amendment was the only possible route. Justice Moldaver asked why the definition of "who comes from Quebec" counts as an amendment under section 41 (requiring unanimity) rather than section 42 (which does not). Monahan declined to get into the specifics, but suggested that, at a minimum, no change to the provisions governing the appointment of Quebec judges could proceed without that province's consent.[34]

Without question, Monahan made an impression. At one point, Justice Abella asked him to clarify what his theoretical arguments had to do with the actual questions posed to the court. Over laughter, Monahan apologized for adopting a "professorial" tone. Abella responded, "It was a great seminar." LeBel added, "At least, it was interesting."[35]

ROCCO GALATI AND THE GRAMMAR OF SECTION 5

Rocco Galati, of course, brought the lawsuit that precipitated the entire affair. A Toronto litigator, he had quickly responded to Nadon's appointment with a motion in Federal Court challenging its legality. Galati had a history of challenging a variety of executive decisions.[36] He had also been vocal on issues pertaining to judges and judicial ethics. He was joined by the Constitutional Rights Centre, represented by Paul Slansky, with whom Galati had worked on a number of previous occasions. Galati, though, was the principal actor.

In public, Galati maintained that his challenge of Marc Nadon's appointment was "nothing personal." He remarked: "In fact, I like Justice Nadon. I was tormented by bringing the challenge. I thought he was a good judge. I got along with him. That's not the point. If it was my father, I would have brought the challenge."[37] He was galled at the fact that so few lawyers were prepared to challenge the legality of an appointment he regarded as plainly unconstitutional: "[T]here are about 300,000 lawyers in Canada. I think 299,995 think they're all going to the Supreme Court and they don't want to blow their chances. They're worried about their reputation."[38]

But Galati was undeterred. A highly complimentary profile in the *Globe and Mail* suggested that he had a secret advantage in that "he knew the *Supreme Court Act* inside and out."[39] In *Felipa v Canada,* Galati had successfully challenged a practice whereby former superior court judges, over the retirement age of seventy-five, could be asked to act as deputy judges on the Federal Court. A majority of the Federal Court of Appeal concluded that the practice "is so inconsistent with the legislative scheme that the statutory interpretation upon which it is based cannot stand."[40] His experience in that case, the *Globe and Mail* interview suggests, gave him special insight into the *Supreme Court Act* and emboldened him to challenge Marc Nadon's appointment. In the end, though, he regarded its unconstitutionality as in itself a reason to litigate the point.

Indeed, Galati had taken part in a number of high-profile cases alleging that judicial practices were unconstitutional in some way, shape, or form. There was the above-noted *Felipa* case in 2011. Galati was also involved in several cases involving the Canadian Judicial Council (CJC), of which he was a vocal critic. In 2012, Paul Slansky brought a complaint to the council, alleging that a judge was "biased, rude, abusive, and bullying." The CJC denied the complaint. Slansky took the extraordinary step of bringing an application for judicial review of the CJC's decision, arguing that its investigation was flawed and anemic. He also claimed that the entire process by which judicial ethics complaints are made is unconstitutional because it involves judges investigating judges. Galati represented him.[41] In an interview with *Canadian Lawyer,* Galati stated:

> It's easier to get a constitutional amendment than to remove a judge ... Judges are human beings. They don't descend from the sky or heaven, and some need to be removed. If the public knew the kinds of things some judges do, I think there would be more action taken. They make life hell not only for lawyers, but the people that have to come in front of them.[42]

Galati later made broadly similar remarks during the controversy surrounding the disgraced judge Robin Camp.[43] And in 2012, Galati was involved in another judicial review proceeding against the Canadian Judicial Council, this time representing the independent counsel responsible for presenting evidence in the Lori Douglas case.[44]

Following the reference, moreover, Galati would continue to litigate judicial appointments, both in and out of court. He would challenge the appointment of Justice Robert Mainville to the Quebec Court of Appeal, relying heavily on the reasoning employed by the majority in the reference. In 2015, Galati publicly criticized the appointment of Grant Huscroft, an internationally respected legal academic, to the Ontario Court of Appeal.[45] According to Galati, Huscroft did not qualify as a barrister or advocate within the meaning of the federal *Judges Act,* since he had not practised law or performed legal services for a number of years. In his view, the terms "barrister" and "advocate" should be construed narrowly. This was, as Adam Dodek pointed out, an idiosyncratic interpretation of the *Judges Act* – if accepted, the argument would effectively preclude many talented jurists from being appointed to superior courts across the country.[46] But, as we will see, it was a position that fit well with the argument he ran in the reference.

As all of this suggests, Galati was not at all intimidated by judges. He and Slansky would later argue that the government should be ordered to pay all of the costs he had incurred in the course of litigating the Nadon matter. They provocatively told the judge that, if they were not awarded full costs, it would signal that the court was in bed with the government.[47] The Federal Court of Appeal would later describe that suggestion as "gonzo."[48] It does, however, give some insight into the take-no-prisoners approach to litigation adopted by Galati and Slansky. Galati's submissions in the reference were blunt and, in some respects, just as provocative.

Galati's argument was simple: both section 5 and section 6 restrict eligibility to current members of the bar or current superior court judges. And that is so in spite of Parliament's use of the phrase "has been" in section 5. In his words, "has been" "is the 'continuous present' tense in the English language in which an action or state of being commenced at some point in the past, and continues into the present."[49] Galati pointed out a number of examples in which "has been" may be (and often is) used in this sense:

> (a) it has been raining all day or since yesterday;
> (b) s/he has been (sitting as) a Federal Court Judge since 1993;
> (c) it has been impossible to amend s. 101 of the Constitution Act 1867, and
> (d) s/he has been an Advocate (practicing) for 10 years.[50]

Properly speaking, Galati argued, Marc Nadon and other federal and provincial court judges "had *previously* been" members of the bar.[51] In support of his grammatical reading of section 5, Galati invoked the linguistic work of Noam Chomsky and his notion of substructure. Without repeating that analysis, it is enough to say that, if the court was not already prepared to accept Galati's understanding of "has been" in section 5 as being in the continuous present tense, the references to Chomsky or substructure were unlikely to persuade it. In oral arguments, the panel did not take him up on his invitation to discuss the point at greater length.

In support of his reading of section 5, Galati noted that the attorney general of Canada's argument led to absurd results. It would, for example, permit the appointment of individuals who had been disbarred or judges who had been removed from office. It would also permit the appointment of persons with only a paper connection to a particular bar. Some of Galati's written submissions were remarkably acerbic. He was dismissive of Canada's position, describing it as "challenged." At one point, he observed that appointments made under sections 5 and 6 relate to "a Judge or lawyer, disjunctively *and not by means of travelling through time and space.*"[52]

With respect to the second question, Galati's position was, again, straightforward: the declaratory provisions, he argued, did more than merely "clarify" sections 5 and 6. To the extent that they permitted the appointment of individuals who were neither current members of the bar nor current superior court judges, the declaratory provisions changed the composition of the Supreme Court. This was, argued Galati, contrary to Part V of the *Constitution Act, 1982.* Referencing the views of several legal scholars, Galati acknowledged that there was a reasonable difference of opinion as to the constitutional status of the Supreme Court. In the end, though, he appeared to conclude that it would be inconceivable to leave the court exposed to "the *manipulation and stacking* of the Court by the Federal Executive, whereby the Court, in its composition, is gutted of its Federalism safeguards and protections, and certainly in perception, and possibly in fact, *the court becomes a puppet on a string* of the Federal Executive."[53] In oral arguments, Galati stated his agreement with the provincial attorneys general that the 1982 constitutional package had, in some way, changed the status of the Supreme Court. This, however, was not the principal focus of his written or oral submissions, which were broadly preoccupied with the interpretation of sections 5 and 6.

During oral arguments, Justice Moldaver asked what would happen if someone "has been" a member of the bar for ten years but then "foolishly" accepts a position at the Federal Court. To join the Supreme Court, would he have to complete a further ten years first? Galati said, yes. Justice Moldaver, clearly incredulous, noted that such a person could be appointed so long as he was first catapulted onto a section 96 court – was *that* a problem? Galati responded that in such a circumstance the law did not appear to impede such an appointment. He reminded the panel that it was important not to personalize the legal question before them – that is, not to dwell on whether it was fair "that certain categories of judges might be statutorily and constitutionally barred from appointment to the Supreme Court of Canada." It was not a constitutional imperative, Galati said, to ensure that "every single lawyer in the country gets a fair crack at the Supreme Court."[54] The case turned on the constitutional relationship between the Supreme Court of Canada and the other branches of government, and the court should approach it in that spirit.

THE JUDGES

Only two other interveners appeared. The first was an ad hoc group composed of three former judges of the Federal Court of Appeal: Robert Décary, Alice Desjardins, and Gilles Létourneau. The second was the Canadian Association of Provincial Court Judges. Each filed its own factum, but both were represented by the same counsel: Sebastien Grammond, an experienced advocate and former law dean. (Grammond would himself be appointed to the Federal Court in 2017.)

Though the two sets of interveners represented the interests of judges on two different courts, they shared one key feature in common: neither provincial nor federal courts are superior courts within the meaning of sections 5 and 6 of the *Supreme Court Act*.[55] Moreover, it is well established that federal and provincial court judges cease to be barristers or advocates as soon as they are appointed to the bench. If, and to the extent that, sections 5 and 6 restrict eligibility to current members of the bar, neither provincial nor federal court judges can be appointed.

Judges rarely participate in litigation as interested parties. The risk of bringing the administration of justice into disrepute is enough to keep them well away from the adversarial process.[56] The reference did not raise issues related to judicial, administrative, or institutional independence. It was, therefore, unlike previous proceedings where judges have felt compelled to respond. It is somewhat understandable, though, that some would do so here, given the clear effect of the reference on their future choices and opportunities.

The two groups were obviously coming from somewhat different perspectives, yet they shared some interests. Both sets of interveners urged that their members should be eligible for appointment to the Supreme Court. They pointed to the expertise of provincial and federal court judges, as well as the unintended, and undesirable, consequences of excluding them from the court. Neither of the groups took a position on Question 2.

The former Federal Court judges, following Binnie, stressed that sections 5 and 6 must be read together to avoid absurd results. Most of these arguments from absurdity are, by now, familiar and will not be repeated here.[57] The provincial court judges, for their part, emphasized the need to maintain as large a talent pool as possible without needlessly constraining the discretion of the prime minister:

> Hence, the criteria found in section 5 of the *Supreme Court Act* must be considered as threshold eligibility requirements. They are not meant to identify the person best suited to hold office on the country's highest court. They are merely an initial filter that screens out persons who do not have basic qualifications. As such, they should not be interpreted too rigorously or technically, as that would risk excluding candidates who might in fact be qualified. In a system in which legislation sets out only threshold eligibility requirements, the task of selecting the best candidate falls primarily with the executive.[58]

There is an important difference between the two positions. By virtue of the *Judges Act,* all federally appointed judges (whether acceding to courts included in section 96, 98, or 101) must have a minimum of ten years' legal experience. Thus, so long as that experience need not be current, members of the Federal Court are per se eligible under section 5 or section 6. Provincial court judges, though, are not uniformly subject to the same requirements. There may be current provincial court judges whose bar membership is shorter than ten years. For that reason, the association urged against a reading of the provision that would be too rigorous or technical. Rather, the limits should be read as establishing threshold requirements, without determining ultimate appointability.[59]

Grammond used much of his time to explore the historical idiosyncrasies that produced distinctions between categories of judges – distinctions that, in his view, should not carry present-day weight, certainly not if they led to the exclusion of entire categories of jurists. He took care to explain the odd history of section 30, which authorizes the appointment of ad hoc judges. He also explained why superior court judges had been treated separately in the first place: in 1875, those courts had not required ten years' bar membership, but the framers accepted that good candidates for the Supreme Court could proceed from that bench. Thus, the Act was structured to ensure that such judges would not be *per se* excluded.[60]

Like other advocates on that day, Grammond pressed the absurd results that could flow from too narrow a reading of sections 5 and 6. He urged the court to consider that subsequent constitutional negotiations suggested that the relevant constitutional actors had not regarded Federal Court judges as uniquely unsuitable to represent Quebec on the Supreme Court. The Meech Lake Accord, which was accepted by Quebec, would have included Federal Court judges (although Justice Wagner pointed out that the accord would also have granted Quebec more control over section 6 appointments). How is it, Grammond asked, that someone like Marc Nadon could be so unacceptable to the province of Quebec when it previously had been prepared to accept those who occupied a similar position?[61]

A thoughtful and skilled advocate, Grammond was given a respectful hearing. He later said that he had expected the court to confirm Nadon's appointment and was surprised by its ultimate decision.[62]

On reviewing the majority opinion, it is striking that it scarcely mentions the arguments that featured most prominently at the hearing. If one were to do a word cloud of the oral submissions and questioning, the words "one day rule" and "continuous and contemporaneous connection" would likely appear in the largest font. Both were discussed extensively by parties on both sides of the argument and seemed to spark significant interest from the bench.

Yet the majority barely mentioned the "one day rule" argument, only commenting briefly in the final paragraph discussing Question 1:

> We note in passing that the reference questions do not ask whether a judge of the Federal Court or Federal Court of Appeal who was a former advocate of at least 10 years standing at the Quebec bar could rejoin the Quebec bar for a day in order to be eligible for appointment to this Court under s. 6. We therefore do not decide this issue.[63]

The majority's disinclination to discuss the issue did not go unnoticed. In his dissent, Justice Moldaver called it out explicitly and stated that the clear implication of the majority's interpretation of section 6 was that the one-day strategy was, indeed, an option.[64]

The question of whether one's bar membership under section 6 need be continuous was not addressed by the majority at all – not even to acknowledge that it had been argued. Justice Moldaver again pointed that out.[65] As for the question of the quality of the connection between a particular lawyer and Quebec legal culture, including whether it should be contemporaneous to the time of the appointment, none of the judges saw fit to refer to it directly.

When we watched the hearing live, it appeared a somewhat sleepy affair. In hindsight, the event provided hints of the controversy swirling just under the surface. Justices Wagner and LeBel were, throughout, the most exercised. As the two Quebec jurists on the court, they were clearly convinced that section 6 was not a mere gloss on section 5 or a simple guarantee of civil law expertise. Justice Abella was concerned with legitimacy, with text, and with interpretative norms. Justices Karakatsanis and Cromwell and the chief justice asked fewer questions, but tended to challenge those defending the validity of Nadon's appointment. Justice Moldaver, by contrast, telegraphed his eventual dissent.

6

The Opinion and Its Critics

On 21 March 2014, the Supreme Court of Canada delivered its advisory opinion in *Reference re Supreme Court Act, ss 5 and 6.* By a majority of six to one, the court concluded that section 6 of the *Supreme Court Act* did, indeed, require a Quebec appointee to be a "current" member of the Quebec bar, meaning that Justice Marc Nadon was statutorily excluded.[1] Insofar as section 6.1 of the *Supreme Court Act* purported to make a declaration to the contrary, it was constitutionally invalid. Any change to the eligibility criteria set out in the *Supreme Court Act,* the court continued, would need to be made according to the procedure set out in section 41(d) of the *Constitution Act, 1982* – that is, it would require the unanimous consent of Parliament and the provincial legislatures.

Justice Moldaver issued a stinging dissent. He concluded that the majority's interpretation of section 6 failed to reflect the text and legislative history of the *Supreme Court Act* and that it led to absurd results. That being the case, Moldaver found, it was unnecessary to express any opinion on the circumstances under which the composition of the Supreme Court could be altered. But this ever-so-brief summary of the judgment hardly tells us much. As we have seen, a range of arguments were provided on each of the questions posed to the court. Which resonated with the majority?

THE COURT'S REASONING

To begin, the court *unanimously* rejected Rocco Galati's interpretation of section 5. The majority had no trouble accepting that section 5 of the *Supreme Court Act* contemplates the appointment of both current and former barristers or advocates of at least ten years' standing at the bar of a province. Under previous legislation, only current barristers or advocates were eligible for appointment. The change in wording was clearly intended to expand the category of eligible individuals beyond current members of the bar. In light of the plain meaning of the English version, there was nothing in the French version of the provision that cast serious doubt on the ambit of section 5. Given that the aim of section 5 "is to ensure that appointees to the Court have adequate legal experience," there was no reason to give the section a narrow reading.[2] Practically speaking, this meant that Federal Court judges could be appointed to the Supreme Court of Canada, insofar as they would occupy one of the non-Quebec seats.

Section 6 was another matter. The majority agreed that section 6 needed to be interpreted in light of section 5. But it did not follow that the two sections were mirror images of each other. On the contrary, the text and legislative history of section 6 suggested that it must be given a narrower interpretation – one that confined the scope of eligible Quebec appointments to those who were current members of the Quebec bar. Whereas section 5 of the Act uses the phrase "is or has been," section 6 states that Quebec judges must be chosen "from among the judges" of the Quebec superior courts or "from among the advocates" of the Quebec bar. These phrases suggest that the pool of eligible appointees cannot be drawn from former judges or former advocates. Moreover, whereas the language of section 5 had been changed so that it could encompass former members of the bar, no such alteration had been made to section 6.[3]

Just as importantly, the majority found that the narrow reading of section 6 made sense in light of its purpose. If the aim of section 6 was merely to ensure that Quebec appointees were competent in civil law, there would be no reason to restrict eligibility to current members of the bar. But the majority concluded that the provision had a somewhat larger objective, namely, "to ensure that Quebec's distinct legal traditions and social values are represented on the Court, thereby enhancing the confidence of the people of Quebec in the Supreme Court as the final arbiter of their rights."[4] Section 6 purported to protect "both the functioning and the legitimacy of the Supreme Court as a general court of appeal for Canada."[5]

The majority endorsed this analysis by Peter Russell:

> [T]he antipathy to having the Civil Code of Lower Canada interpreted by judges from an alien legal tradition was not based merely on a concern for legal purity or accuracy. It stemmed more often from the more fundamental premise that Quebec's civil-law system was an essential ingredient of its distinctive culture and therefore it required, as a matter of *right,* judicial custodians imbued with the methods of jurisprudence and social values integral to that culture.[6]

The majority expounded at length on the historical reluctance of Quebecers to accept a new Supreme Court of Canada. This concern, it found, was grounded in large part on their skepticism of the court's ability to competently settle cases turning on questions of civil law. In light of that nagging concern, it was not enough merely to provide technical guarantees of competence that would be appreciated by informed members of the legal community but not by the wider public; rather, it was necessary to provide the sort of strong assurances to that effect that would be apparent to the relatively casual onlooker.

The majority cited these remarks by Joseph-Aldéric Ouimet, a member of Parliament for Laval: "In Quebec an advocate must have ten years' practice before he can be a Judge. The Judges from the other Provinces *might have the finest intelligence and the best talent possible and yet not give such satisfaction to the people of Quebec as their own judiciary.*"[7] The majority concluded:

> Viewed in this light, the purpose of s. 6 is clearly different from the purpose of s. 5. Section 5 establishes a broad pool of eligible candidates; s. 6 is more restrictive. Its exclusion of candidates otherwise eligible under s. 5 was intended by Parliament as a means of attaining the twofold purpose of (i) ensuring civil law expertise and the representation of Quebec's legal traditions and social values on the Court, and (ii) enhancing the confidence of Quebec in the Court. Requiring the appointment of current members of civil law institutions was intended to ensure not only that those judges were qualified to represent Quebec on the Court, but that they were perceived by Quebecers as being so qualified.[8]

Writing in dissent, Moldaver claimed that this characterization of the purposes of section 6 was inconsistent with its text. Why restrict the pool of potential appointees to those who are current members if the aim is simply to guarantee that they would "in fact bring Quebec's legal traditions and social values to the Court"? Former members of the bar would (or, anyway, could) be just as conspicuously well qualified. An esteemed member of the bar, well known for his or her grasp of the subtleties of civil law and deeply immersed in Quebec's legal traditions and culture, does not suddenly lose that aura of accomplishment upon retirement. With that in mind, the majority's narrow reading of section 6 might well appear needlessly "under-inclusive when measured against the provision's objectives."[9] Without explicitly saying so, Moldaver adopted the entirety of Binnie's argument from absurdity.

But the majority was unpersuaded. It observed that Parliament could choose from a range of different means of achieving the competence and assurance objectives it pursued. It might, for example, have required merely that three appointees to the Supreme Court complete a written test or oral examination in civil law. It might have required appointees to be drawn from those who had been members of the Quebec bar for fifteen years rather than ten. The fact that Parliament chose one means of assuring the public that Supreme Court judges would have civil law competence rather than another in no way undercut the conclusion that it intended to achieve that result. The majority stated:

> Parliament could have adopted different criteria to achieve the twofold objectives of s. 6 – for instance by requiring a qualitative assessment of a candidate's expertise in Quebec's civil law and legal traditions – but instead it chose to advance the provision's objectives by specifying objective criteria for appointment to one of the Quebec seats on the Court. In the final analysis, lawmakers must draw lines. The criteria chosen by Parliament might not achieve perfection, but they do serve to advance the provision's purpose.[10]

The majority was careful not to suggest that Federal Court or Federal Court of Appeal judges necessarily lacked expertise in civil law. The opinion simply emphasized that, irrespective of any expertise they may have in fact, they failed to satisfy the technical eligibility criteria set out in section 6 of the Act.[11]

Finally, the majority took the view that the "broader scheme of the *Supreme Court Act* reinforces the conclusion reached through a textual and purposive analysis."[12] It noted that, under section 30 of the Act, Federal Court judges are ineligible to sit as ad hoc Supreme Court judges in Quebec appeals when the quorum (of at least five) does not include at least two judges appointed under section 6. This suggests that section 6 imposes eligibility criteria more restrictive than those set down by section 5 and that Parliament did not intend to make Federal Court and Federal Court of Appeal judges eligible for appointment under section 6.[13] The majority rejected claims that section 30 could be disregarded because it had gone unused for almost one hundred years. Parliament had never abrogated the section – even in the face of other revisions to the Act that referenced the Federal Court. As the majority said: "[T]he exclusion of judges of the Federal Courts as ad hoc judges for Quebec cases was not a mere oversight."[14]

Here, too, Moldaver disagreed with the majority's conclusion. He expressly endorsed Sebastien Grammond's argument that section 30 was a "historical anomaly" that had not been revisited or updated by

Parliament since its enactment. In Moldaver's view, one could draw from it few if any inferences about the meaning of section 6.[15] But he was alone in reaching that conclusion.

In short, so far as the interpretation of section 6 was concerned, the majority rejected the arguments presented in Binnie's memorandum, as well as the submissions of the attorney general of Canada and the Federal Court judges who intervened. And to the extent that Galati rested his interpretation of section 6 on his grammatical reading of section 5, his argument, too, was rejected. By contrast, the majority accepted the position adopted by the attorney general of Quebec. Ultimately, the majority held that section 6 restricts eligibility of Quebec appointees to those who are current members of the Quebec bar, making Federal Court judges ineligible under that section.

But what about section 6.1? Here, the majority's analysis was not just eyebrow-raising but downright jaw-dropping. The majority concluded that section 6.1 was constitutionally invalid, inasmuch as Parliament purported to unilaterally affect the composition of the Supreme Court of Canada through ordinary legislation. The majority stated:

> Parliament cannot unilaterally change the composition of the Supreme Court of Canada. Essential features of the Court are constitutionally protected under Part V of the *Constitution Act, 1982.* Changes to the composition of the Court can only be made under the procedure provided for in s. 41(1) of the *Constitution Act, 1982* and therefore require the unanimous consent of Parliament and the provincial legislatures. Changes to the other essential features of the Court can only be made under the procedure provided for in s. 42(2) of the *Constitution Act, 1982,* which requires the consent of at least seven provinces representing, in the aggregate, at least half of the population of all the provinces.[16]

In reaching this conclusion, the majority expressly adopted Patrick Monahan's suggestion that the court had become part of Canada's constitutional architecture.[17] In a country where powers are divided between the federal Parliament and the provincial legislatures, there must be some judicial body capable of authoritatively resolving jurisdictional disputes.[18] In the absence of such a body, the majority suggested, Canada's constitutional system of arrangements would be unworkable and possibly incoherent. As it stated:

> With the abolition of appeals to the Judicial Committee of the Privy Council, the continued existence and functioning of the Supreme Court of Canada became a key matter of interest to both Parliament and the provinces. The court assumed a vital role as an institution forming part of the federal system. It became the final arbiter of division of powers disputes, and became the final word on matters of public law and provincial civil law. Drawing on the expertise of its judges from Canada's two legal traditions, the Court ensured that the common law and the civil law would evolve side by side, while each maintained its distinctive character. The court thus became central to the functioning of legal systems within each province and, more broadly, to the development of a unified and coherent Canadian legal system.[19]

Thus, the majority suggested that, even by 1949, the Supreme Court of Canada's constitutional status had been elevated.

But that did not end the matter. In 1975, Parliament amended the *Supreme Court Act* so that there were no longer appeals as of right in civil cases. This ostensibly signalled an intention to reorient the court away from mere error correction and towards broader consideration and development of general legal questions.[20] Its constitutional importance grew. Repatriation solidified the Supreme Court's constitutional status. Section 52 of the *Constitution Act, 1982* states that "any law that is inconsistent with the provisions of the Constitution is, to the extent of the inconsistency, of no force or effect." Insofar as this provision presupposes a judicial body that can settle questions of constitutional validity, it reinforces the essential role of the Supreme Court of Canada. As the majority put it: "The existence of an impartial and authoritative judicial arbiter is a necessary corollary of the enactment of the supremacy clause. The judiciary became the 'guardian of the constitution' ... As such, the Supreme Court of Canada is a foundational premise of the Constitution."[21]

Moreover, section 41(d) of the *Constitution Act, 1982* "expressly makes changes to the Supreme Court and to its composition subject to constitutional amending procedures."[22] The majority concluded that this effectively constitutionalized sections 4(1), 5, and 6 of the *Supreme Court Act,* since these provisions "codify the composition of and eligibility requirements for appointment to the Supreme Court of Canada as they existed in 1982." The majority observed that Part V of the *Constitution Act, 1982* was based on the "April Accord" of 1981. The explanatory notes to the accord indicated that the intention behind what would become section 41 was to ensure that changes to the composition of the Supreme Court could not take place without the unanimous consent of the provinces. "Pointedly," the majority continued, the explanatory notes suggested an intention to "ensure that Quebec's representation was given special constitutional protection."[23] To the majority, this was not surprising: "The objective of ensuring representations from Quebec's distinct juridical tradition remains no less compelling today, and implicates the competence, legitimacy, and integrity of the Court."[24]

The majority found the attorney general of Canada's argument, that these provisions were effectively dormant, unsustainable. Under that argument, Part V excluded the court from "constitutional protection."[25] Why would a provision intended to constitutionally "freeze the status quo"[26] expose the court to the risk of unilateral change? The majority regarded the suggestion as absurd:

> Accepting this argument would have two practical consequences that the provinces could not have intended. First, it would mean that Parliament could unilaterally and fundamentally change the Court, including Quebec's historically guaranteed representation, through ordinary legislation. Quebec, a signatory to the April Accord, would not have agreed to this, nor would have the other provinces. Second, it would mean that the Court would have less protection than at any other point in its history since the abolition of appeals to the Privy Council.

> This outcome illustrates the absurdity of denying Part V its plain meaning. The framers cannot have intended to diminish the constitutional protection accorded to the Court, while at the same time enhancing its constitutional role under the *Constitution Act, 1982.*[27]

As we have seen, the attorney general of Canada had also argued that although the Meech Lake and Charlottetown Accords would have constitutionally entrenched eligibility requirements for the Supreme Court of Canada, these proposed amendments were not adopted. Therefore, existing eligibility requirements were clearly not entrenched. The majority likewise had little time for this argument. The accords had proposed a reformed process for appointing judges to the Supreme Court. The mere fact that those proposals had not been adopted, the majority reasoned, tells us little about the constitutional status of the eligibility requirements then in place.[28]

For all these reasons, the majority found that Parliament could not unilaterally change the eligibility requirements set out in sections 5 and 6 of the *Supreme Court Act.* Section 6.1 was, therefore, of no force and effect. Former members of the Quebec bar – including judges of the federal courts – could not be appointed. In the part of the opinion that received the least attention but, in many ways, had the most practical significance, the majority declared Justice Nadon's appointment null and void.

SUPREMELY FLAKY?

Supreme Court rulings are often controversial. Nevertheless, the reaction to the Nadon Reference was unusually vociferous. To many people, the reference was an easy case with an obvious answer. To them, there was no good reason to exclude Federal Court judges from serving on any of the Supreme Court's seats. The proceedings had been initiated *after* Marc Nadon had been sworn in. And the court was reviewing the exercise of a highly discretionary executive power that had never before been challenged. That the court would actually reject Nadon was, clearly, unthinkable to a great many people.

Professor Grant Huscroft, who was later appointed to the Ontario Court of Appeal, stated in an op-ed: "The Supreme Court of Canada's decision in the Nadon Reference is as bad a decision as the Court has made in recent memory." Huscroft argued that Moldaver's dissenting opinion was, by far, the more convincing. To him, the "single day" argument from absurdity was particularly significant: "This, we are told [by the majority], was a major constitutional moment in the Supreme Court of Canada, but all that was at stake was a single day. The majority of the court explicitly refused to address this point, no doubt out of embarrassment."[29]

Huscroft was unpersuaded by the majority's appeal to the purposes underlying section 6. Judges, he pointed out, are generally expected to be impartial and leave their personal values at the proverbial door when they decide cases – why would we hold Quebec judges to a different standard? The majority had not done enough to establish that this was the purpose of the provision. Even if it was, there was no reason to think that Marc Nadon lacked the "social values" of other Quebecers, assuming they have a shared, distinctive, and uniform set of values in the first place. In the end, Huscroft argued, the majority's decision threw "the Federal Courts and their Quebec judges under the bus ... Following the Court's decision in the Nadon Reference, Quebec lawyers with aspirations to sit on the Supreme Court of Canada are far less likely to be willing to serve on the Federal Courts."[30]

Andrew Coyne likewise did not mince his words. "[T]his is," he stated, "just the sort of flaky decision the Court is capable of."[31] In Coyne's view, Parliament would have been much more explicit if it had intended to reserve the Quebec seats for current barristers or advocates. Section 5 refers to "any person" – not "any person outside Quebec." Coyne endorsed Moldaver's "single day" argument from absurdity. He also seconded Moldaver's observation that, by holding that section 5's ten-year membership requirement applied to Quebec appointees, while simultaneously imposing a currency requirement that is not recognized in section 5, the majority was engaged in cherry picking. Coyne was also underwhelmed by the evidence relied upon by the majority to support its findings about section 6's underlying purpose:

> Unsupported either by statute or logic, the majority's interpretation cannot even appeal to the legislative record. While the principle of reserving a number of the judges to Quebec was part of the original legislative bargain that created the Court, and while the majority correctly quotes a raft of sources on how critical this was, not only to its proper functioning but to its perceived legitimacy in the province, it provides no similar citations in support of the claim that appointments to the Court from Quebec are and always have been restricted to current members of the bar or bench, or were ever intended to be. It doesn't because it can't: as Judge Moldaver notes, "there is nothing in the historical debates that suggests any such thing."[32]

Coyne's most scathing criticisms were reserved for Prime Minister Harper. As Coyne observed, Harper knew there was a legal issue in appointing a Federal Court judge, yet he proceeded anyway. That might make sense, Coyne went on, if Nadon had been "some world-beating legal superstar." But Nadon was only a "semi-retired maritime law specialist." The willingness of the prime minister to risk such a debacle for such an undistinguished choice, Coyne continued, was another mark against his judgment. That his government refused to rule out reappointing Judge Nadon – perhaps after sitting for a day on the Quebec Superior Court – was sheer lunacy. In the end, he concluded, the problem was with the appointments process itself, which "trusts so much to one person's discretion."[33]

Professor Leonid Sirota similarly took issue with the majority's interpretation of section 6, broadly sharing the concerns expressed by Huscroft and Coyne. He criticized the suggestion that the *Supreme Court Act* had become constitutionalized in the absence of any express entrenchment of it, and he questioned why eligibility criteria go to composition. Sirota also observed that the majority's decision would limit the pool of jurists who could fill the Quebec seats and might undermine efforts to impose bilingualism requirements. Like Coyne, though, Sirota laid much of the blame at the door of Prime Minister Harper – while also giving some to the province of Quebec:

> Of course, it is the federal government and the Prime Minister who are ultimately responsible for the shambles that Justice Nadon's nomination has become. They wanted to pick a fight with the legal community – they got it, and the country will be worse off as a result. But the same can be said of Québec's friends and defenders, who will have ended up undermining the province's representation on the federal courts and perhaps the Supreme Court too, not to mention making impossible the enactment of legislation requiring judicial bilingualism which many of them deemed desirable or even necessary. Be careful what you wish for.[34]

In the months that followed, others would criticize the ruling. Notably, former Supreme Court Justice John Major stated in an interview that he did not agree with the majority's reasoning.[35] This raised the total of present and former Supreme Court judges who expressed a view different from that of the majority to five – six if one counts Marc Nadon himself. In conversation with us, Louise Charron made it clear that she still believes that the question of statutory interpretation was a no-brainer and would have signed onto Moldaver's dissent. But, she added (echoing Justice Robert Jackson of the US Supreme Court), the majority doesn't need to be right; what matters is that they are final.[36]

Not everyone was critical of the decision. Paul Daly stated: "This is a ringing declaration from the Supreme Court of Canada on the importance of Quebec's distinct character and how important it is to protect it."[37] Adam Dodek was similarly enthusiastic.[38] And even those who were less enthused about the decision did not, as we have seen, shy away from criticizing the government for putting the court in such an awkward position in the first place. Political scientist Emmett Macfarlane, who penned a cautious and even-handed op-ed shortly after the decision was released, stated:

> In many ways, today's decision was a mess of the prime minister's own making. The appointment of Nadon was not only unusual because he was a Quebec appointee from a Federal Court, but also because he held a supernumerary (semi-retired) position. The fact that the Supreme

> Court was able to block the appointment in this case should not give Canadians any comfort about the integrity of a broken, opaque selection process. If anything, today's decision makes all the more clear that it is time for meaningful reform.[39]

In the weeks and months that followed, the prime minister and minister of justice would become the main targets of criticism for their role in the debacle. Within days of the decision's release, amid speculation that Harper might try to find an alternative route to appointing Marc Nadon to the Supreme Court, Nadon publicly stated that he was not interested in pursuing such a course.[40]

IN (QUALIFIED) PRAISE OF RULES

Critics of the majority's interpretation of section 6 tend to focus on its apparent absurdity. Insofar as sections 5 and 6 of the *Supreme Court Act* are intended to ensure that three judges on the court have expertise in civil law, many commentators found it absurd that the provisions would exclude Federal Court judges – whose time on that bench, after all, hardly diminishes their expertise. In effect, critics claim that the majority's reading of section 6 requires the prime minister to ignore a salient fact about the learnedness and experience of Federal Court judges.

In Chapter 3, we explained why that conclusion is, at the very least, too quick. Legal rules are not irrational or absurd merely because they require decision makers to ignore certain facts in favour of other ones. There are often compelling reasons for constraining decision makers in this way. Indeed, this is so even if, in a particular case, ignoring certain facts does not advance the policy objectives that animated the creation of the rule in the first place.

Consider offences targeting speeding. Such offences are (surely) animated by a legislative concern about unsafe driving. Yet exceeding the speed limit is enough to establish the offence regardless of whether it is unsafe to speed at the time in question (e.g., because there are no other cars on that stretch of road or because every other car on the road is also speeding). A police officer or judge administering the offence would be expected to ignore those facts, even though the law is intended to address unsafe driving and even though there was nothing unsafe about the motorist's conduct under the circumstances. The legislature, after all, may not want to leave it to the individual motorist to determine whether and when it is safe to drive at certain speeds; the driver might overestimate his own judgment or skill or might neglect relevant considerations, putting himself and other motorists at risk. Indeed, the legislature may have decided to target speeding as opposed to dangerous driving precisely to forestall such dangers.

There are additional concerns. Since reasonable people might disagree about the dangers of driving faster than the speed limit under particular conditions, leaving that decision in the hands of police officers, prosecutors, and judges effectively expands the amount of discretion they have. There is a heightened risk that official power will be exercised inconsistently, unpredictably, and arbitrarily. By contrast, a bright-line rule stating categorically that it is an offence to drive faster than, say, one hundred kilometres per hour makes the law more predictable, easier, and cheaper to apply – since there is no need to engage in a detailed assessment of the background circumstances – and less susceptible to abuse.

As this example illustrates, bright-line rules have several advantages over more open-ended standards. First, they may lead to better decision making, especially in contexts where human reasoning is liable to go astray.[41] Open-ended standards, by their very nature, invite decision makers to consider a wide array of factors, some of which may be misinterpreted or given too much weight. A bright-line rule limits the range of factors that can be considered, blinkering the decision maker, and thereby minimizing the risk that she will be distracted by irrelevant matters. A rule that prevents decision makers from considering a person's race or gender may ensure that biases and stereotypes do not warp their judgment.[42] A rule that prevents decision makers from considering anecdotal evidence of isolated disasters may keep them from exaggerating the risks associated with a policy or course of action.[43] Even where the decision maker is an expert in her field, her all-things-considered judgment will often be inferior to a relatively myopic algorithm or formula.[44] In criminal trials, juries are often prevented from hearing certain kinds of evidence precisely because they would give it too much weight or significance.[45]

Second, bright-line rules facilitate certainty.[46] It may be difficult to predict what conclusion a decision maker will reach in a particular case if she is empowered to consider any and all relevant facts and to determine the weight to give to each. Bright-line rules, insofar as they require the decision maker to consider only a single factor or (if the rule is somewhat dimmer) a narrow band of factors, may produce greater certainty and predictability.

Finally, and relatedly, rules constrain official discretion.[47] When a lawmaker uses standards-based directives to guide decision makers, they confer a kind of jurisdiction upon the latter – to consider and weigh a wider range of factors by way of promoting the lawmaker's objectives. Bright-line rules, precisely because they narrow the scope of what can be considered, circumscribe that jurisdiction.[48] Importantly, even if we think that a decision maker would be well placed and well equipped to make all-things-considered judgments about what would advance the lawmaker's objectives under the circumstances, it may be better that she not have that power.[49] A law authorizing police officers to arrest individuals for conduct that is simply described as wrongful without further elaboration, for example, would be problematic whether or not the officers had the training, perspective, and sensitivity to apply such a directive in a sensible and restrained fashion.[50] Likewise, a law entitling doctors to substitute their own judgment for the decision of adult patients to withhold consent to medical treatment would strike most people as unconscionable.[51] Bright-line rules, inasmuch as they narrow the discretionary authority of decision makers, both reflect and reinforce the idea that certain decisions do not rightfully belong to them.[52] In this sense, rules are "tools for the allocation of power."[53]

The second and third justifications arguably find expression in the majority's reasoning in the reference. The majority suggested that section 6 of the Act was intended to assure members of the Quebec public and bar that three seats on the Supreme Court would be occupied by jurists familiar with and sympathetic to Quebec's civil law and traditions – that is, to ease the concerns of a francophone public that the Supreme Court of Canada would simply become an instrument of Anglo-federalist domination. On that understanding, Quebecers would not necessarily have been happy leaving the decision entirely in the hands of the prime minister, who might fail to correctly identify experts in civil law; select experts whose understanding of Quebec civil law was regarded, by members of the Quebec bench and bar, as highly idiosyncratic; or select experts broadly unsympathetic to Quebec values. Quebecers would want a degree of certainty that the prime minister could neither make a mistake nor use his discretion to fill the three seats with ringers. They might reasonably want that discretion narrowed, even if it would mean excluding qualified candidates in the future.

Of course, the above discussion has no answer for the critic who simply does not accept that section 6 was animated by such concerns. But we take this to be something on which reasonable people can disagree. Our point here is simply that the mere fact that a rule is over- or underinclusive is no reason, in itself, to doubt its rationality.

Critics of the majority opinion might also observe that there are real drawbacks to the use of rules. By precluding consideration of salient factors, rules may lead decision makers to act in ways that strike observers and affected parties as unfair.[54] The reference itself provides an illustration. The practical effect of the majority's interpretation of section 6 is that federal and provincial court judges are treated differently from section 96 judges irrespective of their experience and expertise.[55] That, understandably, gave rise to a palpable sense of indignation among some federal and provincial court judges, both before and after the decision.[56] We agree: it is important not to pretend that bright-line rules entail no trade-offs – both moral and political. But it is a long way from that commonsense proposition to the position that it would be absurd for Parliament to devise a rule intending to make such trade-offs. Indeed, legislators make these kinds of hard choices all the time.[57]

There is a further possible line of attack. Many critics, as we have seen, seized upon Justice Moldaver's one-day argument as a basis for dismissing the majority's interpretation as absurd. To some extent, the point of such criticisms is that Parliament didn't enact a bright-line rule: it created a rule so easily circumvented by a crafty prime minister that it provides neither certainty nor constraints on power. We are (literally) of two minds as to whether such a manoeuvre would be legally available. But let us assume for the sake of argument that it is. The mere fact that a rule can be "gamed" does not make it absurd to enact it. It is often the case that cynical actors can push up against the limits of rules, or exploit loopholes, precisely because it is relatively easy to see when they apply and when they do not.[58] In the specific context of section 6, a reasonable legislator could suppose that the political optics of having one's preferred candidate readmitted to the Quebec bar for a day, just so he could be appointed to the Supreme Court, would be so sufficiently poor that only the most desperate prime minister would attempt it.

Finally, it is one thing to say that Parliament could reasonably devise a bright-line rule in an ordinary statute and quite another to say that the same rule should be effectively constitutionalized. Here, criticisms of the majority's interpretation of section 6 blur into criticisms of its interpretation of Part V of the *Constitution Act, 1982.* Many would say that the point of a constitution is to precommit a society to a particular set of institutional arrangements and limitations, thereby ensuring that they will be honoured even when doing so is contrary to short-term concerns or interests.[59] To that extent, we might say that a constitution is a natural habitat for bright-line rules. But insofar as constitutions impose bright-line rules at all,[60] they do so on the basis that the values they protect are, in an important sense, timeless. By contrast, a legislature might reasonably enact a bright-line rule today in the belief that doing so will allow an institution or set of values time to take root while anticipating that it may be abrogated at some later date. The majority's decision in the reference, critics may well contend, takes a rule that is rational when viewed as part of a piece of ordinary legislation and, by constitutionalizing it, turns it into something that is irrational.

We will return to this (very real) difficulty with the majority opinion in Chapter 9. For now, it is enough to note that this, too, is a matter about which reasonable people can disagree. Who is to say when it is finally safe to expand the prime minister's discretion to appoint jurists to represent Quebec on the Supreme Court? Who is to say whether and when Quebec no longer needs to be assured of the court's legal and cultural competence vis-à-vis civil law issues? Canada is a federal state, and the provinces' confidence in the Supreme Court is critical to its institutional legitimacy. And whatever else L'affaire Nadon shows, it is that Quebecers and the Quebec Legislative Assembly are not indifferent to how its seats on the court are filled.

7

The Aftermath

Leading up to the hearing, there had been an uncomfortable question hanging over the proceedings. Marc Nadon had sworn an oath of office before Chief Justice Beverley McLachlin. To some observers, that suggested that at least one (highly influential) member of the court had either already prejudged the matter or had sworn into office someone she believed to be ineligible. Ian Greene, a political scientist, was quoted in the *Globe and Mail* as saying: "It looks like a conflict of interest," though he continued with the observation that, under the circumstances, "there is no other practical resolution of this problem."[1]

Indeed, when Rocco Galati first filed his challenge to the appointment of Marc Nadon in Federal Court, he named Chief Justice Beverley McLachlin as one of the parties to the action – on the basis that, as the individual who had administered the oath to Marc Nadon, she was partly responsible for the appointment. Even after the Nadon Reference, Galati maintained that she bore some of the blame for the Nadon controversy: "I don't think the chief justice should be left off the hook in this sense – she should never have administered the oath."[2] Emmett Macfarlane, discussing the awkwardness of the case for the Supreme Court itself, observed that "a reasonable question might be posed as to why the Court swore him in when his eligibility was in doubt."[3]

Professors Dennis Baker and Rainer Knopff, after the ruling, were aghast at the suggestion that the narrow reading of section 6 was obvious. If that were true, they asked, why on earth would the chief justice have administered the oath? After all, if the government proposed a non-lawyer for a seat, presumably the sitting judges would refuse to swear the candidate in and would "presumably warn the government of this consequence. If Nadon's nomination was a similarly unambiguous error, the chief justice should have issued such a warning."[4]

These remarks were prophetic. It would emerge that the chief justice had indeed attempted to give just such a warning. But the circumstances under which this would come to light were remarkable indeed.

THE HARPER GOVERNMENT VERSUS McLACHLIN

For many Conservative members of Parliament, the majority's decision in the reference fit all too well into a broader narrative in which the Supreme Court of Canada was promoting a liberal agenda and thwarting the policy choices of the democratically elected government. Some tied the Nadon ruling to the court's unanimous decision in *Bedford* – in which three prostitution-related offences were struck down on Charter grounds – a decision released only three months earlier.[5] John Ivison reported that although there was reluctance to directly engage the court in a firefight, government MPs were bitter, reportedly saying: "It's clear that Canadians don't make laws through their governments any more. Instead, they watch while unelected courts override important community standards."[6]

The old complaint – that the Liberals had stacked the judiciary with left-leaning judges – was repeated.[7] One Cabinet minister suggested that the majority's decision in the Senate Reference, in which it held that it would be unconstitutional for the federal government to unilaterally impose term limits on senators, had been animated by a concern that similar limits could be imposed on Supreme Court judges. Nonetheless, Ivison reported that these senior Conservatives were "wary of being seen as vindictive and no action is planned ... [T]here seems little that the government can do. There is little upside for Mr. Harper in making the Supreme Court rejection of his policies a political issue."[8] As a biographer of Stephen Harper wrote:

> Harper was furious with the [Nadon] ruling. The court had set itself up as the unofficial opposition to his prime ministership ... As far as Harper was concerned, the court under McLachlin had resolved to dismantle as much of his government's agenda as it could get away with, and was immune to criticism for doing so. Not only that, he was convinced McLachlin had opposed Nadon's appointment to the court and had meddled in the selection process in order to frustrate his appointment. Staff talked the prime minister down from launching a full, public assault on the impartiality of the court, but he still went pretty far.[9]

For all the wariness of Conservative ministers to launch a full-frontal attack on the Supreme Court of Canada, John Ivison claimed, they were not-so-quietly wafting accusations against the chief justice. According to Ivison's piece, published on 1 May 2014, journalists were being told that the chief justice had "lobbied against the appointment of Marc Nadon" and that she was claiming that "the Harper government ha[d] caused more damage to the court as an institution than any government in Canadian history."[10] Effectively, Ivison reported, senior Conservative figures were encouraging journalists to present the Supreme Court as an overtly political institution. Ivison, in conversation with us, suggested that the openness with which these figures spoke created the distinct impression that their comments reflected discussions taking place at the highest levels of government, if not Cabinet.[11]

That alone was remarkable. In the course of researching his article, though, Ivison brought the rumours wafted by Conservative ministers to the Supreme Court.[12] In conversation with us, Ivison confessed that he did not expect the court to respond, particularly given that these were unattributed accusations. Surprisingly, though, the chief justice did issue a response through the court's executive legal officer, to the effect that she had merely been consulted by the parliamentary committee and had engaged in no lobbying.[13] Chief Justice McLachlin's statement asserted that "the question concern[ing] the eligibility of a Federal Court judge for appointment to the Supreme Court under the *Supreme Court Act* was well-known in legal circles." For that reason, and "[b]ecause of the institutional impact on the Court," the chief justice said that she had advised Peter MacKay and the prime minister's chief of staff of the issue.[14] She maintained that she had expressed no opinion on the merits of the issue. She steadfastly denied having disparaged Harper's impact on the court. All this was reported in the Ivison piece.

According to Howard Anglin, former deputy chief of staff to the prime minister, who spoke to us about the matter, the government was taken entirely by surprise by the chief justice's remarks.[15] As Ivison noted, it was not obviously necessary for the chief justice to respond to unattributed accusations. He speculated that the rumours had already reached the ears of the court, observing that "Ottawa's a small place."[16] Early that evening, the Prime Minister's Office responded with the following statement: "The Chief Justice initiated the call to the minister of justice. After the Minister received her call he advised the prime minister that given the subject she wished to raise, taking a phone call from the chief justice would be *inadvisable and inappropriate.* The prime minister agreed and did not take her call." The statement went further: "Neither the prime minister nor the Minister of Justice would ever call a sitting judge on a matter that is or may be before their court."[17]

Anglin insisted that the remarks were meant innocently. On his account, Stephen Harper, one of the few people to hold the office of prime minister who did not have a law degree, was unusually cautious about engaging directly with the Supreme Court. Harper thought it was likely that the legal validity of an appointment from the federal courts would be litigated, notwithstanding the fact that – according to the advice he had received – such a challenge would be frivolous. That being the case, Harper ostensibly decided, the ethical course of action was not to speak to the chief justice. But, Anglin emphasized, the point of Harper's public statement in May 2014 was not to accuse the chief justice of unethical behaviour in *making* the call but to stress that it would have been unethical for him to *take* the call. Moreover, since the legal issue was already known to the prime minister, there was nothing to be gained by discussing the matter further (a point that would also be made by Bob Dechert in an interview with Evan Solomon).[18]

Whatever the intention, the statement was taken as an insinuation that Chief Justice McLachlin had inappropriately approached the prime minister about pending litigation.[19] If true, this would be a shocking breach of judicial ethics. The problem was exacerbated when, at a news conference the following day, Harper stated:

> I think the suggestion ... that if people thought that the prime minister, other ministers of the government were consulting judges on cases before them, or even worse consulting judges on cases that might come before them, before the judges themselves had the opportunity to hear the appropriate evidence, I think the entire opposition, entire media and entire legal community would be outraged.[20]

In the ordinary course of events, judges avoid getting into public spats with politicians.[21] The chief justice, though, responded directly. According to an interview she gave after retiring from the court: "I was worried that any such allegation could tarnish the administration of justice, could tarnish the office of chief justice, could tarnish the court."[22] The court issued an official news release, which made it clear that the chief justice had never communicated with the Prime Minister's Office about a pending case. McLachlin's overtures to the prime minister had occurred on 31 July 2013, well before Nadon's appointment.[23] She concluded:

> Given the potential impact on the Court, I wished to ensure that the government was aware of the eligibility issue. At no time did I express any opinion as to the merits of the eligibility issue. It is customary for chief justices to be consulted during the appointment process and there is nothing inappropriate in raising a potential issue affecting a future appointment.[24]

We would observe that nothing in this account is incompatible with Anglin's or Dechert's. But the controversy was only beginning. It was now clear that the chief justice had not contacted Harper or MacKay about pending litigation. Yet the allegations were not withdrawn. Indeed, on 5 May, the minister of justice repeated them: "My office was contacted by the office of the Chief Justice. After I spoke with her on that call I was of the considered opinion that the prime minister did not need to take her call. Neither the Prime Minister nor I would ever consider calling a judge where that matter is or could be before the court of competent jurisdiction."[25] Shortly thereafter, the prime minister and several members of the Conservative caucus claimed that the statement issued by the Prime Minister's Office had been made necessary by the chief justice's initial comments in the Ivison article.[26] Peter MacKay would defend the statement issued by the Prime Minister's Office by hinting that it was simply parrying an attack by the chief justice: "I also note for the record that this entire subject began when a Supreme Court spokesperson released a statement to the press, to which we felt it was incumbent to respond and clarify."[27] This is notwithstanding the fact that McLachlin's initial comments did not obviously accuse Harper and MacKay of anything and (more contentiously) might well have been needed to dispel the anonymous allegations reported by Ivison.[28]

The prime minister's conduct towards the chief justice was widely regarded as unprecedented and deeply problematic on separation-of-powers grounds.[29] As Lorne Sossin, then dean of Osgoode Hall Law School, observed in *The Walrus:* "The opposition and the legal community, meanwhile, were more or less apoplectic."[30] Eleven former presidents of the Canadian Bar Association, as well as the Canadian Council of Law Deans, publicly urged Harper to withdraw his accusation against the chief justice. An open letter was subsequently released by 650 lawyers and law professors from across Canada.[31] The Advocates' Society also released a letter stating: "The comments at issue here can only serve to undermine the respect and confidence of ordinary Canadians in the proper administration of justice, and we therefore urge you to make a public statement advising Canadians that the chief justice did not conduct herself inappropriately in any way."[32] Former prime ministers Joe Clark and Paul Martin as well as Jean Chrétien's former chief of staff all rushed to McLachlin's defence, noting that her conduct had been entirely appropriate – indeed, that she had a duty to alert Harper to any potential legal issues surrounding the appointment of a Federal Court judge.[33] But the prime minister did not withdraw his remarks.

Later, the matter was brought to the attention of the secretary general of the International Commission of Jurists (ICJ),[34] which subsequently found that the chief justice had not acted inappropriately.[35] The secretary general also criticized Prime Minister Harper for his remarks:

> The ICJ considers that the criticism [by the prime minister and the minister of justice] was not well-founded and amounted to an encroachment upon the independence of the judiciary and integrity of the Chief Justice ... Such public criticism could only have a negative impact on public confidence in the judicial system and in the moral authority and integrity of the judiciary, and thereby on the independence of the judiciary in Canada.

The ICJ also expressed the view that the judicial appointments process needed overhauling, that it should be an "open process with prescribed criteria based on merit and integrity and without discrimination."[36]

The minister of justice acknowledged the ICJ's conclusions but otherwise made it clear that it was drawing a line under the whole affair.[37] Within a few months, the chief justice herself said that she had moved on.[38]

It is difficult to know what to make of all this. If Anglin's account is accurate, Stephen Harper – far from trying to undermine the prestige of the court and the chief justice – was in fact trying to emphasize the importance of the separation of powers. From his point of view, it may well have seemed as though he was being criticized for acting ethically. Perhaps ironically, then, the Harper-McLachlin contretemps will be remembered as an unprecedented attack upon the judiciary by the government. John Ibbitson, in his political biography of Stephen Harper, stated: "[T]he prime minister had set a dangerous precedent, undermining the separation of executive and judiciary powers on which the whole democratic system of government is based."[39] He concluded that Harper's criticism of the chief justice was one of his "most discreditable acts as prime minister."[40] The chief justice, ultimately, was largely praised for her handling of the affair.[41] At an event celebrating McLachlin, who had retired, her former colleague Louis LeBel obliquely suggested that the episode represented a critical moment for judicial independence.[42]

NO MORE DOG AND PONY SHOW

After the appointment of Marc Nadon was declared a legal nullity, it might well have been expected that the prime minister would simply appoint someone else – either going through the selection process anew or drawing upon one of the runners-up. But an extraordinary thing happened. The long list submitted to the selection panel, as well as the short list presented to Prime Minister Harper, was leaked to the media.[43] This was stunning on a number of levels. First, members of the selection panel had signed a confidentiality agreement. This point was emphatically made by the government in response to written questions by Irwin Cotler:

> The consultations were not made public and in fact all individuals consulted were asked to sign a Confidentiality Agreement. A legal opinion of the consequence(s) of breaking the undertaking of confidentiality has not been sought. The confidentiality agreement signed by members of the Selection Committee included an undertaking not to disclose any information to anyone except to members and staff of the Selection Panel, the Commissioner or Deputy Commissioner for Federal Judicial Affairs, the Judicial Affairs Advisor to the Minister of Justice or the Minister of Justice.[44]

As we have seen, the judicial appointments process in place in 2013 had not been designed for meaningful transparency.[45] There was clearly no intention, on the part of Prime Minister Harper, to tie his own hands by allowing the public at large to scrutinize the candidates placed before the panel. The fact that the panel members were required to sign a confidentiality agreement underscores that point.

Separate and apart from this breach of confidentiality, though, the leak was remarkable on its own terms. Rarely had Canadians been given such an opportunity to peer inside the appointments process. Before 2014, they might hear rumblings or gossip about the names being considered by the prime minister, especially if they were well-connected members of the legal profession in the region from which the appointment would be drawn. But to have a list of names confirmed by someone who was responsible for actually reviewing and refining it for the prime minister? That was almost unprecedented.[46] In many respects, of course, this was a welcome development, casting daylight into a traditionally murky (and many would say suspicious) process. It was, however, also an intrinsic challenge to the idea that Supreme Court appointments were a prerogative of the prime minister – that he was free to choose who he wanted and that the very existence of the selection panel represented nothing more than a gracious (if decidedly limited) concession to Parliament and the Opposition.

And then there was the political embarrassment. As we have already seen, the leaked names on the long list included no fewer than four Federal Court judges out of six. Once the list was published, it became difficult to convincingly argue that Marc Nadon's selection had everything to do with his individual merits and nothing whatsoever to do with his being a Federal Court judge. On the contrary, Prime Minister Harper plainly had a preference for candidates drawn from the federal courts rather than Quebec's Superior Court or Court of Appeal. Politically, this was embarrassing because there was no shortage of legal talent on the Quebec benches; focusing so myopically on Federal Court judges suggested, at best, an inexplicable fetish and, at worst, an intention to appoint someone who would defer to the government on rights issues. (Whether warranted or not, Federal Court judges had a reputation in some legal circles for being too deferential to government.)[47]

Perhaps most importantly, the leak placed Harper in a difficult position. Everyone now knew that there had been three options placed in front of him: Marc Nadon, Johanne Trudel, and Marie-France Bich. Justice Trudel, like Nadon, was a judge on the Federal Court of Appeal. The reasoning in the reference, therefore, made it impossible to appoint her. That left Justice Bich of the Quebec Court of Appeal. Justice Bich was (and is) a highly respected judge with a great deal of experience as a law professor and on the bench. By all accounts, she was regarded by members of the Quebec bar as a top contender for the vacant position on the Supreme Court of Canada.[48] Sean Fine described her in these terms: "She is known for writing powerful judgments with an academic bent ... She is difficult to pigeonhole as a liberal or conservative. She is the consensus pick of the Quebec legal community."[49]

When the short list was leaked, there were many (and vocal) calls for Harper to simply appoint Bich rather than start the appointments process from scratch. Leaving aside the fact that, for whatever reason, Harper may not have wanted to appoint Bich, it may well have been galling for him to find his discretion subjected to political pressure – particularly given the possibility or even likelihood that an Opposition member of Parliament had leaked the short list in the first place.

In the end, Harper did not succumb to the pressure. On 3 June 2014, he appointed Clement Gascon of the Quebec Court of Appeal. Justice Gascon had been on the Court of Appeal for less than two years, having spent about a decade on the Superior Court. At the age of fifty-four, he was relatively young, but there was little sense that his appointment was at all controversial in and of itself. What was interesting was how he was appointed. The process that Harper had used since 2006 was abandoned. No selection panel. No US-style confirmation hearing before an ad hoc committee of parliamentarians.[50] Harper simply made the announcement, apparently while "*en route* to Poland," as if to emphasize that this was his choice to make and that no one else had anything to say about it. Harper's announcement included a note that he had consulted with "Quebec's head judges of the senior trial and appellate courts, as well as the Canadian, Quebec and Montreal bar associations."[51] As Tonda MacCharles observed, there was one name conspicuously absent from the list of consultees: Chief Justice Beverley McLachlin.[52] A statement released on behalf of the minister of justice was clear that the reversion to the pre-2006 process had been prompted by the leaks of the long and short lists: "These appointments have always been a matter for the executive and will continue to be so. As we are concerned about recent leaks from what was intended to be a confidential process, we are reviewing the process for future appointments."[53]

Later, in November 2014, Harper made another appointment to the Supreme Court of Canada, this time to replace the retiring Justice LeBel – another Quebec judge. Once again, the appointments process used for most of the preceding ten years was scrapped: Harper simply announced that Suzanne Côté, a high-profile commercial litigator with a national profile, would fill the spot.[54] And the following July, Harper made a further appointment, this time for one of the "Western seats" vacated by the retiring Justice Rothstein. He tapped Justice Russell Brown, of the Alberta Court of Appeal, on the shoulder and once again did so without any selection panel or public hearing.[55] The clear signal was that, at least so far as Harper was concerned, reform of the judicial appointments process was no longer a priority. Within months of Justice Brown's appointment, though, Harper's Conservatives were voted out of office.

JUDICIAL APPOINTMENTS UNDER JUSTIN TRUDEAU

In October 2015, when the Liberal Party came to power in a surprise upset win over Stephen Harper, the new prime minister, Justin Trudeau, assumed responsibility for federal judicial appointments. The jewel in that particular crown was, of course, the Supreme Court of Canada, and the prime minister, as we have seen, had an unusual degree of latitude to shape the judicial branch.[56] In 2015, however, the court was not anticipating turnover for some time. The next judge to reach retirement age would be Beverley McLachlin, the chief justice. But that wouldn't be until September 2018. Replacing the chief justice would be a formidable challenge. At least, it seemed, Trudeau would have a few years to think about it.

But he was thrown a curveball. On 22 March 2016, a full ten years before his mandated retirement, Justice Thomas Cromwell indicated that he would leave the court in September. Cromwell gave the prime minister many months to figure out a way forward. Nonetheless, the government now faced an unanticipated situation involving a very high-priority task.

Over the spring of 2016, the Prime Minister's Office conducted informal consultations with a number of scholars and other persons.[57] Staff appeared keen to turn the page on the Harper era and seemed open to a variety of ideas. The scope of parliamentary involvement, the constitutional constraints on the prime minister, and how the government could design a process consistent with its stated commitment to openness and transparency were all points of interest.

In July 2016, the Prime Minister's Office decided to craft a new process that featured (a) a list of qualifications and assessment criteria that a successful candidate should meet and (b) a questionnaire for applicants that could, eventually, be released to the public. Candidates would be assessed on the basis of their knowledge of the law; analytical skills; ability to resolve complex legal problems; awareness of and ability to synthesize information about the social context in which legal disputes arise; clarity of thought, particularly as demonstrated through written expression; ability to work under significant time pressures and diligently review voluminous materials in any area of law; and commitment to public service. As for personal qualities, the following were specifically noted: irreproachable personal and professional integrity; respect and consideration for others; the ability to appreciate a diversity of views, perspectives, and life experiences, including those relating to historically disadvantaged groups in Canadian society; moral courage; discretion; and open-mindedness.

Finally, the documents stated that the new process would strongly consider certain institutional needs: ensuring a reasonable balance between public and private law, bearing in mind the historic patterns of Supreme Court appeals; expertise in any specific subject matter that regularly features in appeals and is currently underrepresented on the court; and ensuring that members of the Supreme Court are reasonably reflective of the diversity of Canadian society.[58]

On 2 August, in an op-ed published in the *Globe and Mail,* the prime minister announced the new process. He explained that selecting Supreme Court jurists was "one of the most important decisions a prime minister makes." The court's decisions, he said, "affect us all – they influence our economy, our cultural mores and our definition of our individual and collective rights and responsibilities." Therefore, the nine people who sit on the Supreme Court must be extraordinary: "jurists of the highest calibre," "functionally bilingual," and representative of "the diversity of our great country." To achieve those goals, Trudeau said, it was time for a new process that "is open, transparent and will set a higher standard for accountability."[59]

The process had several components.[60] First was the creation of an independent, nonpartisan judicial advisory committee to vet applications from candidates and recommend three to five to the prime minister. Gone were the days of a secretive backroom process. Instead, the committee, chaired by former prime minister Kim Campbell, would be composed of seven members, four of whom would be chosen by nongovernment entities: the Canadian Judicial Council, the Canadian Bar Association, the Federation of Law Societies, and the Council of Canadian Law Deans. The remaining three would be chosen by the minister of justice and would include two nonlawyers.

The application process itself would change. Interested candidates would be invited to apply via a questionnaire. Their application would be assessed in accordance with the qualifications and assessment criteria outlined above. In submitting the questionnaire, the candidates would have to agree to have selected portions released to the public, should they ultimately be selected by the prime minister.

There would also be broader consultation. After receiving the short list, the minister of justice would meet with a number of stakeholders, including the chief justice of Canada and relevant attorneys general. The minister would appear before the House Committee on Justice and Human Rights,[61] and she and the chair would also appear before a special joint House-Senate committee to explain the process and the choice. And, the nominee would appear before a committee of parliamentarians to answer questions.[62]

Furthermore, within the month following the appointment, the advisory board would provide a report to the prime minster "outlining information about the process, including statistics related to applications received, the manner in which the board executed its mandate, and the costs associated with the process."[63] This report would be made public.

The appointments process outlined by the prime minister represented an important break with past practice. First, it delegated the short list to a separate nongovernmental, nonlegislative body. In the past, the prime minister and justice minister either picked the nominee themselves or provided a list (of varying length) to a committee composed of MPs (a preponderance of whom were from the governing party). Instituting the advisory committee, particularly a relatively large one with nominees from disparate groups, made it difficult for the government to entertain any expectations that it could infiltrate, influence, or coerce its work. Appointing as chair a respected, fiercely independent and famously free-speaking former prime minister was an even greater sign that the government was prepared to be quite hands off.

Second, and perhaps more strikingly, the new process depended on qualified individuals to apply for appointment. The days of the discreet tap on the shoulder or late-night phone call were gone. Instead, anyone moved to serve on the Supreme Court would need to come forward, and indicate that clearly, filling out a questionnaire with numerous challenging queries – for example, "What would you regard as your most significant contribution to the law and the pursuit of justice in Canada?" Both Justice Sheilah Martin and Justice Malcolm Rowe's questionnaires were tens of pages – thousands of words – long.[64] These questionnaires would provide a far richer basis for the committee's deliberations than, say, a mere review of the candidate's jurisprudence.

As simple as that step is, it was nonetheless a radical change to a system that had always relied on a strictly arms-length approach, declining all direct interaction with candidates until the prime minister phoned to offer the job.[65] In 2016, the advisory committee chair noted, there had been thirty-one applications. Forty-two percent were from women, and a significant proportion self-identified as a member of a minority.[66] In 2017, the committee received fourteen applications. Unquestionably, one of the most important innovations of the new system was that the candidates were formally interviewed. In 2017, for example, the committee interviewed eight persons to replace Beverley McLachlin.[67]

The process has not escaped criticism. In a symposium at the Supreme Court of Canada in October 2017, Bob Rae said that it risked alienating excellent candidates:

> I think there are a lot of people who wouldn't necessarily apply because they think they might not be considered, and I think there are other people who wouldn't apply because they understand it's a competitive process ... I've had one judge say to me, "If they think I'm the right person they should ask me if I want to do it or not, and if they don't think I'm the right person then I'm not going into a lengthy competition to do it."[68]

This criticism is fair enough, at least to a point. There is no guarantee that suitable candidates will apply or that the candidates who do apply will represent a diverse pool. The very thing that ostensibly makes the process a radical shift from past practice – its relative passivity – also raises concerns. Rae's co-panelist at the symposium was none other than Kim Campbell – the chair of the advisory committee. In response to his criticism, she suggested that certain individuals might be contacted and urged to apply – blurring the line between the tap-on-the-shoulder approach and the sit-back-and-wait approach.

The final distinguishing features of the new process were the various mechanisms for dialogue with Parliament. The prime minister and justice minister appeared to view this as a form of accountability. It can be misleading to use the term "accountability" when describing the relationship between the executive and legislature in regard to judicial appointments. Nonetheless, the executive branch made itself far more available to parliamentarians than it had at any previous time, with the exception of the Abella and Charron appointments in 2004, when Justice Minister Irwin Cotler appeared before the committee. Not only that, it ensured that the advisory committee chair would appear. Indeed, when the government sought to replace Justice Cromwell, the questioning from MPs – specifically, as to whether the government intended to depart from the "Atlantic seat" regional convention – was so intense that it might actually have influenced the outcome.

The process is still new, and it is too early to say whether it will lead to better appointments.[69] But this move towards greater transparency in judicial appointments is significant and can to some extent be traced to controversies surrounding the Harper-era process – particularly the process used in the failed appointment of Marc Nadon.

8

Judicial Appointments Law

THOUGH LONG A MATTER of public interest, judicial appointments have not traditionally invited serious discussion as to their legality or constitutionality. As we have seen, such matters have generally been regarded – quite reasonably – as entirely within the prerogative powers of the prime minister and therefore immune to serious challenge on legal grounds. That deferential (or fatalistic) attitude changed following the Nadon Reference. In the months and years that followed, questions of legality and constitutionality came to dominate the public discourse surrounding judicial appointments, particularly Supreme Court appointments. These questions were rarely litigated, but they often exerted an enormous pull on the course of the process.

THE MAINVILLE REFERENCE

Shortly after the Nadon ruling was released, the Harper government appointed Justice Robert Mainville to the Quebec Court of Appeal.[1] At the time of his appointment, Mainville was on the Federal Court of Appeal. Section 98 of the *Constitution Act, 1867* states: "The Judges of the Courts of Quebec shall be selected from the bar of that province."[2] Mainville's appointment to the Quebec Court of Appeal was challenged, once again by Rocco Galati, on grounds similar to those used to challenge Nadon's appointment to the Supreme Court of Canada: as a Federal Court judge, Mainville could not be regarded as a current member of the Quebec bar and was, therefore, ineligible. This was somewhat ironic, given that during the public debates surrounding Justice Marc Nadon, Mainville was sometimes mentioned as the very sort of Federal Court judge who belonged on the Supreme Court. He was regarded by many as a talented jurist, and some commentators thought it problematic that a narrow reading would effectively exclude someone of his calibre from elevation to the high court.

The Quebec government sought the opinion of the Quebec Court of Appeal, referring two questions: first, whether the reference to "Courts of Quebec" in section 98 of the *Constitution Act, 1867* includes the Court of Appeal and, second, whether a Federal Court judge can be a member of the Quebec bar for the purposes of section 98. Put simply: Did section 98 restrict those who could be appointed to the Quebec Court of Appeal to current members of the bar?

At first glance, it might seem that the Nadon Reference had settled these questions. It was very easy to (mis)read that judgment as standing for the proposition that Federal Court judges lack a sufficient connection to Quebec's values and traditions and are, for that reason alone, disqualified from acting as "Quebec judges." That being the case, why not conclude that they are just as ineligible for appointment to the Quebec superior courts? Furthermore, since judges of Quebec's superior courts are eligible for appointment to the Supreme Court of Canada, the view that Federal Court judges can be appointed to Quebec's superior courts would seem to be in tension with the reference. On this basis, several jurists and commentators – including Robert Décary, one of the Federal Court judges who intervened in the reference and maintained afterwards that it had been wrongly decided – argued that the ruling led inexorably to the conclusion that Justice Mainville was ineligible for appointment to the Quebec Court of Appeal.[3]

The notion that Federal Court judges lack a sufficient connection to Quebec's legal values and traditions was brought out in oral arguments before the Court of Appeal. It was claimed that "a lawyer could only remain steeped in Québec's 'social values' and be an effective representative of Québec's legal tradition if he or she remained a member of the Québec bar or its bench."[4] Leonid Sirota, observing the proceedings, reported that:

> Québec's lawyer, Francis Demers, emphasized the importance of the judges' representative functions, warning of judges who have, in the past, been tempted to introduce common law concepts into Québec's civil law. Questioned during his reply, he would not even grant that one of the Supreme Court's Québec judges could be appointed to the Québec Court of Appeal if he or she so chose. Rocco Galati compared the potential appointment of a federal court judge to a Québec court to "a drop of cyanide" that would poison Québec's legal tradition, and warned that if one such judge could be appointed, more could follow, since "there is no shortage of them." Paul Slansky, for the Centre for Constitutional Rights, insisted that Québeckers cannot have confidence in a judge who served on one of the federal courts, in the same way as, in the first half of the 19th century, they could not have confidence in British judges appointed to serve in the courts of a province about which they knew nothing. Even though the judges of the federal courts also apply Québec's law, he said, they do so in the name of Canada, not Québec, and people, "separatists" especially, could take it badly should one of them be appointed to the Court of Appeal.[5]

As Sirota suggested, all of this was deeply unfortunate. The Nadon Reference does not, at bottom, stand for the proposition that there is anything intrinsically objectionable about Federal Court judges being appointed as Quebec judges – whether on the Supreme Court or on Quebec's superior courts. The case, most fundamentally, is about statutory interpretation. The majority's reading of section 6 of the *Supreme Court Act,* as we have seen, rested in large part on the fact that the provision uses particular language ("from among"), uses language distinct from that employed in section 5, took colour from the wider statutory scheme (specifically, section 30), and was informed by purposes going beyond merely ensuring competence in civil law.

The Mainville Reference concerned an altogether different provision – section 98 of the *Constitution Act, 1867.* As the Quebec Court of Appeal noted:

> As interesting as [the Nadon Reference] may be, the opinion in that case is not directly relevant, and therefore not conclusive as to the answers to be given in this case. It certainly cannot be deduced, by an analogy amounting to extrapolation, that the opinion determined the meaning of s. 98 of the *Constitution Act, 1867* and that it dictates a negative answer to the question whether "that section allow(s) the appointment of persons who are members of federal courts."[6]

The Court of Appeal observed that whereas the Supreme Court of Canada in 1875 represented a novel institution towards which Quebecers were broadly suspicious, the same could not be said of superior courts in 1867. By then, it had long been established that judges of superior courts would have expertise in civil law; therefore, the sorts of public concerns animating section 6 of the *Supreme Court Act* simply did not come into play with respect to section 98 of the *Constitution Act, 1867.*[7] It followed that, in construing section 98, one did not need to proceed on the basis that it was aimed at assuring or instilling confidence in Quebecers. One could give the section a broader interpretation – one more in alignment with the Supreme Court's reading of section 5 of the *Supreme Court Act.*

In the end, the Quebec Court of Appeal concluded that section 98 did not impose a "contemporaneity" condition on eligibility for appointment and that Federal Court judges could therefore be appointed to the courts of Quebec – including the Quebec Court of Appeal. Mainville's appointment was valid. On further appeal, the Supreme Court of Canada issued a perfunctory judgment, in which it accepted the Court of Appeal's reasoning. Importantly, the court stated: "The arguments based on [the Nadon Reference], do not stand up to analysis.

As the Court of Appeal mentioned ... this appeal concerns different constitutional and statutory provisions, and the reasoning and conclusions from that reference do not apply to it."[8]

The Mainville Reference demonstrates that the Nadon Reference was, in many respects, a quite narrow ruling, settling a discrete question of statutory interpretation. In fact, it was so narrow that it did not, in the end, even affect Justice Mainville – one of the Federal Court of Appeal judges who, it was once thought, would be ineligible for appointment to the Supreme Court of Canada. For all the concerns expressed about the Supreme Court of Canada's narrow construction of section 6 – that is, its tendency to prevent talented legal minds on the federal courts from being appointed to the highest court in the land – it is not clear that the decision made much of a difference to him. After all, as a judge on the Quebec Court of Appeal, he is now eligible for appointment to the Supreme Court of Canada, should a Quebec vacancy arise.

Indeed, many commentators initially thought that the appointment had been motivated by a desire on the part of Stephen Harper to circumvent the barriers thrown up by the Nadon Reference.[9] Justice Mainville, recall, had been one of the names included on the list from which Justice Nadon was ultimately selected.[10] Moreover, his was one of the more highly regarded names on that list.[11] It was tempting to see the appointment of Mainville to the Quebec Court of Appeal as a way for Harper to finally get his way.

As we have seen, that didn't happen. When Justice LeBel retired, Harper appointed Suzanne Côté, a commercial litigator with no judicial experience but who was nonetheless quite well thought of in the Quebec bar.[12] Even if it had been Harper's intention to elevate Justice Mainville to the Supreme Court of Canada, the very fact that his eligibility for the Quebec Court of Appeal was in doubt for roughly ten months would have dissuaded him from following through on it. Arguably, if it had ever been Harper's intention to elevate Justice Mainville to the Supreme Court, that plan was scuttled the moment Rocco Galati filed his challenge.

To critics of the majority opinion in the Nadon Reference, the very fact that such a manoeuvre could have succeeded merely underscores its absurdity: why construe section 6 in such a way that it excludes Federal Court judges, if one can easily circumvent the exclusion simply by appointing them first to a superior court – perhaps only for a day or even an hour?[13] How would Quebecers' confidence in the Supreme Court be enhanced by requiring potential appointees to jump through these technical hoops or by allowing the government to circumvent them so easily?

These questions, intended to be rhetorical, were raised by way of casting doubt on the suggestion that a narrow construction of section 6 was correct as a matter of statutory interpretation. But one could turn this objection on its head: yes, it is technically possible for the government to circumvent the eligibility hurdles posed by section 6, but it does not follow that such a course of action is ethical or in the spirit of the statute.[14] Even accepting the point emphasized by the joint majority opinion that section 6 represents an exercise in line drawing, one may well ask whether it is appropriate for the government to exploit, and bring attention to, the merely technical nature of the eligibility criteria. Doing so could well highlight the political nature of the appointments and threaten the public's perception of the Supreme Court of Canada as above petty partisan politics, as, in a sense, Olympian.

REGIONAL REPRESENTATION

Like the Nadon case, the Mainville episode was unusual in part because it found its way into the courts at all. Otherwise, constitutional and legal debates about judicial appointments have largely occurred in the media and the public sphere. They never made their way into the courts because the constitutional issues did not, by and large, concern the eligibility criteria set out in the *Supreme Court Act*. Rather, they concerned constitutional conventions governing (or thought to govern) the appointment of Supreme Court judges.

Constitutional conventions are "binding rules of constitutional behaviour which are considered to be binding by and upon those who operate the Constitution, but which are not enforced by the law courts (although the courts may recognise their existence), nor by the presiding officers in the Houses of Parliament."[15] As this definition suggests, conventions are distinct from the ordinary law of the Constitution inasmuch as they are not judicially enforceable. In the words of A.V. Dicey, conventions "consist ... of customs, practices, maxims, or precepts." For that reason, he took the view that they "make up a body not of laws, but of constitutional or political ethics."[16] He also suggested, for much the same reason, that constitutional lawyers had little need to pay attention to conventions.[17] But that is a mistake. It is simply not possible to grasp our constitutional system of arrangements by looking to the written, enforceable parts of the constitution in isolation.[18] Eugene Forsey has observed:

> The law of our Constitution confers enormous power on the Queen and her representatives, the Governor-General and the Lieutenant-Governors. A foreigner, reading only the [written] law, would conclude that we live under a despotism. In fact, these powers are exercised by Ministers responsible to the House of Commons, which in turn is responsible to the people. But the law of the Constitution barely mentions the most powerful Minister, the prime minister; it says nothing about how he is appointed or removed; it confers on him only two powers, both very minor. The other Ministers are not mentioned at all; nor is the Cabinet; and of the Cabinet's responsibility to the House of Commons there is not one syllable.[19]

It is not only that conventions sit alongside written constitutional rules. As Andrew Heard points out, conventions can "negate some existing legal power or duty."[20] Moreover, the fact that conventions are not judicially enforceable does not make them meaningfully different from other constitutional rules.[21] They are still obligations binding the political actors to whom they apply. Indeed, many of the written laws presuppose conventional understandings.[22]

As we have seen, a number of conventions govern – or at least have been long thought to govern – Supreme Court appointments. In particular, there are a number of unwritten conventions pertaining to regional representation. The *Supreme Court Act* says only that Quebec must have three representatives on the court. In practice, though, it is generally accepted that Ontario, too, must have three judges. In addition, there must be at least one judge from the Maritime provinces. Until recently, it was sometimes said that Manitoba, Alberta, and Saskatchewan should be represented by one judge between them – with each province alternating in turn – and that British Columbia should have the post that remained.[23] Since the Nadon Reference, these conventions have been the subject of much public attention and have given rise to considerable controversy, particularly as they have come into tension with contemporary views about the value of gender and racial diversity.

Obviously, the regional conventions had little to say about the appointments of Justices Gascon and Côté, since Quebec representation was statutorily required. But with respect to appointments made since 2014, regional considerations have loomed large. In 2015, when the Harper government was seeking a replacement for Justice Rothstein, many suggested that the province of Saskatchewan was due – by convention, they claimed, it was Saskatchewan's turn.[24] After all, the province had not been represented on the Supreme Court of Canada since the retirement of Justice Emmett Hall in 1973.[25] There were also skeptics who argued that, for precisely that reason, no such convention existed. As one commentator observed: "If there is a convention that the next appointment should come from Saskatchewan, it is hardly rock-solid – and arguably shouldn't be. The very fact that the last four Western Canadian appointments have come from Manitoba and Alberta could be taken as evidence that no such convention exists. (Such is the nature of conventions: they guide until they don't.)"[26] At the very least, it was noted further, "[A] government that is prepared to push against the boundaries of convention, or game them somewhat, [could] credibly say that it is not bound to make its next selection from a Saskatchewan pool."[27] Ultimately, Harper appointed Justice Russell Brown of the Alberta Court of Appeal.

The issue of regional representation took on far greater public significance in 2016, when Justice Cromwell announced his retirement. This time, the concern was that Atlantic Canada might lose its representative on the court, in that Prime Minister Trudeau might appoint an Indigenous person from outside the region. The worry was fuelled, first, by the prime minister's suggestion that the new application process would be open to "any Canadian lawyer or judge who fits the criteria."[28] The Prime Minister's Office later confirmed that the appointment might not go to someone from Atlantic Canada.[29] Shortly thereafter, in a CBC interview, the minister of justice, Jody Wilson-Raybould, remarked: "We are opening up the appointment process to people who aren't just specifically from Atlantic Canada."[30]

There was also Trudeau's mandate letter to the Independent Advisory Board for Supreme Court Appointments, which stated:

> I ask that the Advisory Board develop and submit to me, by no later than September 23, 2016, a list of three to five qualified and functionally bilingual candidates that *includes* candidates from Atlantic Canada, for my consideration for this position. In making your selection, I would ask that you *consider* the custom of regional representation on the Court as being *one of the factors* to be taken into consideration.[31]

The highlighted portions of the passage, directed at the advisory board itself, strongly indicated that Trudeau was prepared to appoint someone from outside Atlantic Canada. Finally, Wilson-Raybould acknowledged, before the Standing Committee of Justice and Human Rights, that there was a convention of regional representation for Atlantic Canada but conceded that the "next appointment to the Supreme Court of Canada will not necessarily be a person from Atlantic Canada."[32]

There were expressions of discontent from both the Premier of Nova Scotia and the justice minister for Newfoundland and Labrador.[33] Conservative member of Parliament Lisa Raitt suggested that the prime minister's announcement reflected a view in government that Atlantic Canada was a backwater.[34] Professor Wayne MacKay stated in an interview: "I think it's a really big mistake to go against the long-standing convention of regional representation on the court, it's one of our most important policy-making institutions now, and to have no Atlantic voice in that institution would be contrary to the basic principles of Confederation."[35] The Canadian Bar Association issued a public letter, stating:

> Our highest court must continue to represent all regions of Canada, including Atlantic Canada. Consequently, we urge you to amend the mandate of the Advisory Board outlined in your August 4, 2016 letter, to ensure that the Atlantic Canada vacancy is filled by a meritorious candidate from that region. We also urge you to honour regional representation in filling future vacancies on Canada's highest court.[36]

In an interesting twist, Chief Justice McLachlin – who was making remarks before the annual conference of the Canadian Bar Association – refused to comment on the possible departure from the convention of regional representation.[37] She did, however, state that such a move could be challenged in court: "[F]rom what I see, it could be something that might someday come before [the Supreme Court of Canada], but this is a question I think I have to leave aside." She continued: "I'm the last to know what will come before the court."[38] To the Trudeau government, these were no doubt ominous words.

And to a point the chief justice's prediction came to pass. On 19 September 2016, the Atlantic Provinces Trial Lawyers Association announced that it had filed an application with the Nova Scotia Supreme Court.[39] In obvious reliance on the Nadon Reference, the association sought a declaration that "the Prime Minister's proposed departure from the constitutional convention of regional representation on the Supreme Court of Canada amounts to an amendment to the Constitution that requires unanimous consent of the provinces."[40] That was almost certainly a bridge too far: though the court might well agree that there was a convention of regional representation, it is difficult to imagine it holding that the convention was part of the "law" governing Supreme Court appointments and as such could not be changed without constitutional amendment. After all, the court has been careful to distinguish between conventions and law precisely on the basis that the latter is enforceable whereas the former is not.[41] In any event, the case was rendered moot by the appointment of Justice Rowe, who hailed from Newfoundland. But it is interesting to wonder what might have been.

The real turning point occurred not in a courtroom, but in the House of Commons. The Honourable Rob Nicholson, former minister of justice, made a motion that "the House call on the government to respect the custom of regional representation when making appointments to the Supreme Court of Canada and, in particular, when replacing the retiring Justice Thomas Cromwell, who is Atlantic Canada's representative on the Supreme Court."[42] Nicholson remarked:

> I am speaking on behalf of Atlantic Canada, but indeed I believe everyone across this country has a stake in the constitutional convention that makes up the Supreme Court of Canada. If one is from western Canada, I am sure it would be as completely unacceptable if the Prime Minister started questioning whether we should have a seat on the Supreme Court of Canada. I believe that would be the case.[43]

He continued:

> This has been a constitutional convention for over 140 years and is something that has worked well and is only appropriate. This is a vital part of this country. It has always been since this country's creation. There are 2.3 million Atlantic Canadians, and to say that they will now not have that constitutional convention of having a representative on the Supreme Court of Canada is not acceptable.[44]

Perhaps surprisingly, Minister of Justice Wilson-Raybould replied by saying that she supported the motion. It quickly became clear, however, that this was because she had a quite flexible understanding of the convention of regional representation. The convention, she suggested, required only that the government place weight on regional factors when considering who should be appointed. Much of her speech emphasized the importance of flexibility, and she produced several examples of appointments that may have violated the convention, strictly understood, but were nonetheless generally regarded as positive.[45] Ontario judge Wishart Spence, for example, had been replaced by BC jurist Willian McIntyre – meaning that, for a time, western Canada had three judges on the court instead of two. Furthermore, Ronald Martland, originally from Alberta, was replaced by Ontarian Bertha Wilson. Wilson-Raybould noted that "[w]ithout flexibility, Canada's three territories will forever be without representation on our country's highest court." And surely the convention did not preclude the government from appointing two justices from Atlantic Canada? Finally, Wilson-Raybould observed that many lawyers and judges have practised in more than one region in Canada or work in a part of Canada where they did not grow up or take their legal training. Quite simply, a rigid application of the convention was not appropriate in light of the mobility of the modern legal profession.[46]

At the conclusion of the debate, the Liberal MPs joined with the Opposition in supporting the motion.[47] But it is difficult to know how to read this. Given the position taken by the minister of justice, that respect for the convention does not require the government to actually appoint someone from the traditionally represented regions of Canada, it is difficult to say that anyone definitively won or lost. At the time, it was thought significant that Judge Mary Ellen Turpel-Lafond – an Indigenous jurist living in British Columbia, who was widely discussed as a potential appointee – proclaimed that, in light of the feelings of those in Atlantic Canada, she would stand aside. (In her words: "I never go where I'm not invited.")[48] In reality, Turpel-Lafond was almost certainly not eligible.[49] Nonetheless, her public declaration that she would honour the convention likely placed additional pressure on the prime minister to select a candidate from Atlantic Canada.[50] Shortly thereafter, Justice Malcolm Rowe was appointed.[51]

The issue of regional representation was reopened with the retirement of Chief Justice Beverley McLachlin. At the outset, Trudeau announced that the government would comply with the convention of regional representation – or, at least, one reading of it. The press release stated:

"Candidates may demonstrate that they satisfy the geographical requirement by reference to their bar membership, judicial appointment, or other relationship with Western Canada (British Columbia, Alberta, Saskatchewan and Manitoba) and Northern Canada (Yukon, Northwest Territories and Nunavut)."[52]

Immediately, the president of the Canadian Bar Association expressed gratification at this development.[53] Moreover, there were expressions of approval at the decision to include the territories in "western Canada."[54] But some were unhappy at the idea that British Columbia, which for more than twenty-five years had held a seat on the court, might find itself with no distinctive representative of its own.[55] Some commentators insisted that the court should have a member who was familiar with British Columbia's unique culture and traditions. (Ironically, such suggestions vaguely echo those of Arthur Bunster who, in 1875, argued that British Columbia, like Quebec, should have a statutory guarantee of representation on the Supreme Court.)[56]

The need for regional representation tied into calls for more (i.e., some) Indigenous representation on the court. Tasneem Karbani remarked:

> With McLachlin's departure, British Columbia no longer has representation or a voice on the Supreme Court. This lack of representation also ties in with the concerns about Indigenous representation. The issues that involve Indigenous groups in British Columbia are often unique from those in the rest of Canada. The Supreme Court stands to lose out on both a British Columbia perspective and Indigenous perspective by having a judicial appointment that neither represents the region or Indigenous peoples.[57]

These suggestions were sometimes echoed after Justice Sheilah Martin was appointed to replace Chief Justice McLachlin. Murray Rankin, the justice critic for the NDP, took serious issue with British Columbia being shut out of the court. As reported by Laura Lynch: "Rankin said B.C.'s unique issues involving First Nations and conflict over resource use make the province different from the Prairies even though it is considered part of the West."[58] Others, such as BC attorney general David Eby, were less troubled.[59]

What about Saskatchewan? Justice Georgina Jackson of the Saskatchewan Court of Appeal was often mentioned as a front-runner but was ultimately not selected.[60] As matters stand, the two western Canadian seats on the court are both occupied by former judges on the Alberta Court of Appeal. As Tasneem Karbani observed, western Canada may not have another vacancy on the court until 2040, when Justice Brown reaches the age of seventy-five.[61] Assuming that no other convention of regional representation is broken in the interim, Saskatchewan will not have had a representative on the court for almost seventy years.

DOGS THAT DIDN'T BARK

In the immediate post-reference period, there was heightened awareness among politicians, the media, and the public of the legal and constitutional rules governing judicial appointments, and Supreme Court appointments in particular. It is, however, worth acknowledging the limits of this claim. Some serious legal and constitutional questions were either missed or ignored. On at least two occasions, for example, Judge Mary Ellen Turpel-Lafond was repeatedly referenced as a possible appointment – as a potential replacement, first, for Justice Cromwell and then for Chief Justice McLachlin.[62] This was the case even though Turpel-Lafond, a provincial court judge with less than ten years' standing at the bar, was clearly ineligible according to section 5 of the *Supreme Court Act.*

Perhaps more troubling was the lack of attention paid to the appointment of Russell Brown, which was announced six days before Prime Minister Harper advised the governor general to dissolve Parliament.[63] The appointment took effect in the middle of a long and bitterly contested election that the Harper Conservatives would lose.

A Supreme Court appointment had not been made while Parliament was dissolved since 1958, likely because making an appointment in these circumstances represents a violation of the caretaker convention. It is central to the idea of responsible government that ministers of the

Crown must act with the confidence of Parliament. Once Parliament is dissolved, there is still a need for government. But ministers cannot be presumed to have the confidence of the House of Commons. For this reason, there is an understanding that, once the election writ is drawn up, the government assumes a more modest caretaker role. It can (and must) govern, but it must do so with restraint, generally restricting itself to activities that are routine, noncontroversial, reversible, or urgent.[64] There is good reason to think that the convention precluded making an appointment – a far-from-routine, irreversible, and non-urgent matter.[65]

This might be a mere technicality but for the fact that Trudeau's Liberals ultimately won the election, meaning that the appointment would have been his to make. Yet the matter went largely undiscussed in the media and was not made an issue in the campaign. To some extent, this is a good thing – no one wants to see Supreme Court judges turned into partisan election issues. But given that this was a period in which the legality and constitutionality of Supreme Court appointments was a matter of general interest, and given the level of attention paid to other aspects of Justice Brown's appointment,[66] the lack of scrutiny on this issue is strange.[67]

To be clear, the issue is not whether Turpel-Lafond or Brown had the requisite legal expertise and other qualities needed to be an effective Supreme Court judge. We only observe that, under the circumstances, and in light of other legal controversies surrounding Supreme Court appointments following the reference, the lack of attention to these legal questions is noteworthy.

Since at least 2004, increasing public attention has been paid to the Supreme Court appointments process. Before the reference, it was implicitly understood that the appointment of a Supreme Court justice was to be assessed in political terms and not legal terms. One could, in principle, debate the merits of an appointment – though even this was a matter to be approached with delicacy, lest one risk undermining respect for the judicial branch. Questions of validity or constitutionality were hardly mentioned. The reference changed that. After Marc Nadon's appointment was declared null and void, lawyers, politicians, and the media began to pay closer attention to statutory and conventional limits on appointments. There is, however, a flip side to this increasing preoccupation with legality – the reference may well foreclose a number of reforms to the Supreme Court of Canada.

9

A Court Frozen in Amber

IN ANY LEGAL SYSTEM, an opinion like the one offered by the Supreme Court in the Nadon Reference – that one of its members had been appointed contrary to the law – would be an extraordinary event. Remarkably, that is not the most stunning aspect of the reference. Instead, pride of place goes to the court's conclusions about itself and its relationship to the Constitution of Canada. The court effectively inserted itself into the Constitution with nary an amendment in sight. Moreover, it is striking that the court did not expressly rely on previously recognized unwritten principles – most notably, judicial independence – to justify the conclusion that there are limits on Parliament's authority to change its composition and essential features.[1]

Concerns about court stacking, for example, surely reflect worries that the executive branch would be in a position to dominate the court and drive its agenda. Furthermore, we suspect that the value of and pull towards judicial independence helps to explain the boldness of the majority opinion. It may be, ironically enough, that the court avoided mentioning judicial independence because it did not want a repeat of the sort of controversy that followed the Provincial Judges Reference, in which the court used the principle to hold that judicial compensation had to be determined through a process operating at arm's length from the government.[2] Whatever its reasons for taking this approach, the court's overwhelming reliance on constitutional architecture was remarkable and has produced many unanswered questions.

THE COURT'S ROLE

An Architectural Digest

In reflecting upon the reasoning of the majority, and particularly its reliance on the idea that the Supreme Court is built into Canada's constitutional architecture, it is important to observe that there is nothing novel in the idea of architecture itself.[3] The court in the past has suggested that our Constitution has a basic structure that lends coherence to its written provisions. Back in 1938, in *Reference re Alberta Statutes,* Chief Justice Lyman Duff observed that the written provisions of the *Constitution Act, 1867* "manifestly contemplate a House of Commons which is to be, as the name itself implies, a representative body."[4] He continued:

> The statute contemplates a parliament working under the influence of public opinion and public discussion. There can be no controversy that such institutions derive their efficacy from the free public discussion of affairs, from criticism and answer and counter-criticism, from attack upon policy and administration and defence and counter-attack; from the freest and fullest analysis and examination from every point of view of political proposals.[5]

Plainly, Duff was not resting his analysis on anything expressly articulated in the Constitution. Rather, he proceeded on the basis that the written provisions would not make structural sense unless some broad right of free political expression was implied. On this basis, Duff concluded: "Any attempt to abrogate this right of public debate or to suppress the traditional forms of the exercise of the right (in public meeting and through the press) would, in our opinion, be incompetent to the legislatures of the provinces, or to the legislature of any one of the provinces."[6]

Almost twenty years later, these remarks were endorsed by Justice Ivan Rand in *Switzman v Elbling,* who likewise opined that it would not be open to the provincial legislatures – and, he hinted, even Parliament – to abrogate citizens' right "to free discussion and debate."[7] These remarks, in turn, were accepted in principle by the Supreme Court in *Ontario v OPSEU,* a case concerning whether, and to what extent, the legislative branches of government were entitled to impose limits on political speech:

> There is no doubt in my mind that the basic structure of our Constitution, as established by the *Constitution Act, 1867,* contemplates the existence of certain political institutions, including freely elected legislative bodies at the federal and provincial levels ... [N]either Parliament nor the provincial legislatures may enact legislation the effect of which would be to substantially interfere with the operation of this basic constitutional structure.[8]

There are other examples. In *Roncarelli v Duplessis,* Justice Rand referenced the "rule of law as a fundamental postulate of our constitutional structure."[9] On this basis, he held that it would be repugnant to our constitutional system of arrangements to permit judicially unreviewable exercises of arbitrary power. Rand's point was picked up by the Supreme Court in *Reference re Manitoba Language Rights:*

> Additional to the inclusion of the rule of law in the preambles of the *Constitution Acts* of 1867 and 1982, the principle is clearly implicit in the very nature of a Constitution. The Constitution, as the Supreme Law, must be understood as a purposive ordering of social relations providing a basis upon which an actual order of positive laws can be brought into existence. The founders of this nation must have intended, as one of the basic principles of nation building, that Canada be a society of legal order and normative structure: one governed by rule of law. While this is not set out in a specific provision, the principle of the rule of law is clearly a principle of our Constitution.[10]

Indeed, the Nadon Reference was not even the first time that the Supreme Court had recognized the judiciary as a fundamental part of the basic structure of the Canadian constitution. In the Provincial Judges Reference, the court stated:

> [P]olitical institutions are only one part of the basic structure of the Canadian Constitution. As this Court has said before, there are three branches of government – the legislature, the executive, and the judiciary ... Courts ... are equally "definitional to the Canadian understanding of constitutionalism" ... as are political institutions. It follows that the same constitutional imperative – the preservation of the basic structure – which led Beetz J [in *OPSEU*] to limit the power of legislatures to affect the operation of political institutions, also extends protection to the judicial institutions of our constitutional system. By implication, the jurisdiction of the provinces over "courts," as that term is used in s. 92(14) of the *Constitution Act, 1867,* contains within it an implied limitation that the independence of those courts cannot be undermined.[11]

Most famously, the Supreme Court of Canada recognized four structural features of the Canadian constitution in the Quebec Secession Reference: "federalism, democracy, constitutionalism and the rule of law, and respect for minority rights." These defining principles, the court held, "function in symbiosis." They are "the vital unstated assumptions upon which the text [of the written Constitution] is based."[12] Reinforcing this point, the court observed: "Our Constitution has an internal architecture, or ... a 'basic constitutional structure.' The individual elements of the Constitution are linked to the others, and must be interpreted by reference to the structure of the Constitution as a whole."[13] Six years later, in *Demers,* the court recognized a fifth defining principle: respect for human rights and freedom.[14] This became part of Canada's basic constitutional structure as a result of the incorporation of the Charter of Rights and Freedoms.

Glass Houses

The court's reliance on the idea of constitutional architecture or basic structure, then, was hardly a bolt out of the blue. By 2014, the architecture metaphor had a long pedigree. Even leaving aside the cases we have mentioned already, the notion of structural argumentation is implicit in federalism decisions reaching back to the early days of the *Constitution Act, 1867*. It was employed by the Judicial Committee of the Privy Council before the Supreme Court ascendancy, and it has been used in other Anglo-American democracies with written constitutions.[15] Why, then, might it seem controversial when deployed in the reference?

First, structural arguments have tended not to be used to strike down legislation. In cases such as *Switzman* and *Roncarelli,* structural arguments were used to quash administrative decisions.[16] There are, as we have seen, comments suggesting that it is possible to do so, notably in *Reference re Alberta Statutes.* But these remarks are generally made either in *obiter* or only after the court has already found that the statute conflicts with a written constitutional provision.[17] By contrast, the majority in the Nadon Reference appeared to rely, to an extraordinary degree, on the structural features of the Constitution as a basis for concluding that the declaratory provisions were *ultra vires* Parliament because they conflicted with Part V.

Second, it is not obvious that one *can* look to structural features of the Constitution to strike down duly enacted legislation when two key structural principles are democracy and parliamentary sovereignty.[18] In *Babcock,* the Supreme Court held that "unwritten principles must be balanced against the principle of Parliamentary sovereignty."[19] Likewise, in *British Columbia v Imperial Tobacco,* the court observed that the principles of "democracy and constitutionalism ... very strongly favour upholding the validity of legislation that conforms to the express terms of the Constitution."[20] This reasoning has been employed by a number of appellate courts by way of refusing to strike down legislation on such a basis.[21] The reference represented a manifest departure from that.[22]

To be fair, the reference posed some genuinely stark questions. Whether intentionally or not, the attorney general of Canada's arguments begged the question: What if Parliament actually *did* pass legislation purporting to either abolish the Supreme Court of Canada or change its jurisdiction from that of a general court of appeal? If the court held that it could not strike down legislation purporting to impose such radical constitutional changes, leaving it to political actors to fix (or not), that would open the door to dangerous constitutional crises in the future. That possibility was remote, but the judges on the court may have wondered if they could take that chance.

Once one leaves the realm of stark all-or-nothing choices, though, it is less obvious that the courts should foreclose tinkering by the elected branches of government. It is exceptionally difficult to amend the Canadian constitution.[23] It is important not to treat the Constitution as an exhaustive list of rules that exist independent of deeper values and norms that hold those rules together and lend them coherence as a system of governance. At the same time, however, not every norm and established practice is or should be constitutionally protected in such a way as to prevent political actors from making what they think will be modest improvements to the way in which Canadian government functions. This need for flexibility is why it has traditionally been thought important that constitutional conventions and usages are not enforceable in the fashion of constitutional laws (strictly understood).[24]

That leads to a third reason for being skeptical of the majority's reliance on structural principles in the reference: the court distinguishes essential from nonessential features but adopts a seemingly quite expansive understanding of the former. One may agree that the Constitution forbids the prime minister from engaging in court stacking but hesitate to agree that it bars Parliament from changing any aspects of its composition – including all eligibility criteria whatsoever. As we will see, constitutionalizing those aspects of the *Supreme Court Act* that set out eligibility criteria may have the effect of making perfectly legitimate reforms impossible in the absence of constitutional amendment.[25]

To some extent, this problem is exacerbated by the majority's narrow interpretation of section 6. Earlier, we make the point that it is often reasonable for Parliament to adopt bright-line rules – not just in spite of the fact that they are, by nature, overinclusive, but *because* they are overinclusive. But it is one thing to say that legislatures can reasonably employ overinclusive rules to achieve important objectives, and quite another to say that those rules have become constitutionalized. The majority was clear that its reading of section 6 was based on the need to reassure the Quebec public and bar that the Supreme Court of Canada would be alert to the province's civil law traditions and values. On its reasoning, that had been an urgent concern in 1875. It strikes many onlookers, however, as (dare we say it) absurd to suggest that Quebecers, in 2014, continued to have such a profound lack of confidence in the Supreme Court of Canada and would do so for the foreseeable future. The bright-line rule may make a good deal of sense when understood as a response to a concrete concern at a specific moment in Canadian history, but appear preposterous when understood as a structural feature of the Constitution.

It is troubling, too, that the reference may thwart the sorts of reforms that would make the court more representative, legitimate, and effective and that it may undermine efforts to make the appointments process more transparent. The effects of the reference depend on the type of change being discussed, and in the discussion that follows we do not wish to be taken as endorsing any change or changes in particular. Nonetheless, it is difficult to deny that, in at least some cases, the reference has greatly complicated the prospect of future reform in a way that, ironically, could harm the very federation that the court was so keen to protect.

Essential Features

The reference has offered some clarity. It seems clear, for example, that changes to the number of judges, whether in total or just those from Quebec, would fall under the term "composition" and thus be unachievable absent unanimous provincial consent. Changes to the court's overall jurisdiction, such as whether it might cease to function as a final court of appeal in some matters, would without a doubt count as a change to its "essential features" and be protected by the general amending formula requiring, in addition to Parliament, the consent of seven provinces representing 50 percent of the population of the provinces (the "7–50 rule"). That leaves a host of matters, large and small, for which the constitutional implications remain murky.

As a preliminary observation, it is worth noting that not all of the Supreme Court of Canada's features are contained in the *Supreme Court Act.* The *Criminal Code,* for example, sets out circumstances under which there is an automatic right of appeal: "691(1). A person who is convicted of an indictable offence and whose conviction is affirmed by the court of appeal may appeal to the Supreme Court of Canada ... (a) on any question of law on which a judge of the court of appeal dissents."[26] When the conditions in this section are satisfied, the defendant is entitled to appeal his or her case to the Supreme Court of Canada, regardless of whether the court would have otherwise chosen to hear it. Between 2007 and 2017, appeals as of right accounted for about one-quarter of the court's overall caseload.[27] After the reference, one may well ask whether it is open to Parliament to unilaterally alter the scope of as-of-right criminal appeals or to set the parameters of appeals by changes to other federal legislation. Doing so would not affect the court's jurisdiction, but it could radically change the court's power to shape its own docket.

There are other examples. The *Judges Act,*[28] which applies to all federally appointed judges, contains important provisions governing the court – such as judges' salaries and the grace period during which they may continue to participate in judgments after they retire.[29] Could Parliament unilaterally abolish the grace period? And what now is the status of funding agreements reached by the court and the government of Canada? Can they be changed? On what terms?

Finally, myriad rules in both the *Supreme Court Act* and the associated Rules of Court govern Supreme Court of Canada litigation and practice. These rules concern important matters such as granting leave to appeal, motions to intervene, the admission of fresh evidence, and the ability to make oral argument. But they include plenty of other things too. As S.A. Scott put it, if the Act is part of the Constitution of Canada, so too is everything in it, up to and including the rules about the colour of factum covers.[30] Does the Constitution really preclude Parliament from requiring litigants to use purple factum covers instead of green ones? Surely, one might object, the Constitution has better things to do.

For that matter, what about the court's advisory function? Since 1875, the court has enjoyed a special jurisdiction to entertain questions put to it by the executive in the absence of a live case.[31] The Nadon Reference itself was one such proceeding. References have been extremely important to the development of Canadian jurisprudence. Yet their function is not without controversy or need of reform. For example, they create an unusual relationship between the court and the executive. Only the executive can refer questions, leaving the legislature out of the picture.[32] Suppose that there was a demand to give authority to Parliament to refer questions. Would that count as a change requiring constitutional amendment? Again, the answer depends on the degree to which one regards the current arrangements concerning the reference function as part of the court's essential features. There seems little doubt that the reference jurisdiction itself has become sufficiently central to the court's role that any attempt to abolish the function altogether would require application of the general amending formula.[33]

But other changes are far less clear. The answer may depend on (a) the degree to which a change would affect the court's independence and (b) the degree to which a change could be said to implicate provincial interests. For example, the current arrangement whereby provincial reference opinions may be appealed to the Supreme Court is extremely important to the provinces. They currently enjoy those appeals as of right. If Parliament decided to amend the *Supreme Court Act* so that the provinces would thereafter need to seek leave, the impact on their interests would be such that, surely, a constitutional amendment reflecting some measure of provincial consent would be needed.

A CHILLING EFFECT

Bilingualism

For many years, people have sought to make bilingualism an eligibility criterion for Supreme Court judges.[34] Justice Moldaver was subject to criticism, both during and after his confirmation hearing, for having failed to become proficient in French.[35] In 2010, the Canadian Bar Association resolved that litigants appearing before the Supreme Court of Canada should be entitled to speak in either official language – hinting that the court itself must be broadly bilingual.[36] The bar of Quebec has long taken this view.[37] Francophone advocates have expressed concern, at both a functional and symbolic level, about the effect on the court of unilingual (which, generally, means English-speaking) jurists. In a widely discussed article, Sebastien Grammond and Mark Power argued that "Francophone litigants before the Supreme Court face a challenge that is not shared by their anglophone counterparts: to attempt to persuade judges who do not understand the language in which arguments are presented."[38] The two have spoken eloquently about the demoralizing effect of appearing before the court and feeling like their arguments have not been fully understood.

There is, in addition, the straightforward point that Supreme Court judges may be unable to do their work properly unless they have a degree of fluency in both languages. In the context of statutory interpretation, it is well established that the meaning of a provision should be construed in light of both the French and English versions – that their meaning is shared.[39] Judges on the court may be called upon to read untranslated decisions by the Quebec Court of Appeal. Leaving aside the feelings of francophone lawyers and litigants, there are hard-headed reasons to think that the basic work of appellate judging in Canada requires reasonable facility with both official languages.

The Liberal government has been officially committed, since 2016, to appointing bilingual jurists to the Supreme Court of Canada. Following Justice Cromwell's announcement that he intended to retire from the court, the government released a list of qualifications in which bilingualism was prominent:

> The Government has committed to only appoint judges who are functionally bilingual. The Supreme Court hears appeals in both English and French. Written materials may be submitted in either official language and counsel may present oral argument in the official language

> of their choice. Judges may ask questions in English or French. It is expected that a Supreme Court judge can read materials and understand oral argument without the need for translation or interpretation in French and English. Ideally, the judge can converse with counsel during oral argument and with other judges of the Court in French or English.[40]

Trudeau's mandate letter to the Independent Advisory Board for Supreme Court Appointments asked the board to identify "a list of three to five qualified and functionally bilingual candidates."[41]

In December 2015, François Choquette, an NDP member of Parliament for Drummond, introduced a private member's bill purporting to amend the *Supreme Court Act* to make bilingualism one of the essential criteria for eligibility.[42] Given the Liberal government's commitment to bilingualism in the Supreme Court of Canada, one might expect the legislation to have passed. Yet the bill failed at second reading on 25 October 2017. Marco Mendicino, parliamentary secretary for the minister of justice, set out why the government opposed the bill even though Liberal policy was to require Supreme Court appointments to be functionally bilingual. The answer had everything to do with the Nadon Reference:

> [T]he composition of the Supreme Court, including the eligibility requirements for appointment, may very well be constitutionally entrenched and thus beyond the reach of legislative measures enacted by Parliament acting alone.
>
> [Translation] Under the circumstances, to proceed with Bill C-203 at this time, in light of the evident constitutional concerns its enactment would raise, would be, in the government's respectful view, unwise and ill-advised. If enacted, Bill C-203 would provoke needless controversy and very probably, protracted litigation.[43]

There are good reasons to think that the reference does indeed preclude this sort of change without a constitutional amendment. Currently, no formal rule requires the judges to be bilingual. Enacting legislation to do so would therefore change who the prime minister can appoint to the court. In our opinion, it would certainly go to the candidates' eligibility no less than the requirement that they be lawyers. It is unclear whether such a change properly relates to the court's essential features or its composition. But there clearly is a strong basis for arguing that such a change would trigger the application of Part V of the *Constitution Act, 1982.*

There are, however, arguments to the contrary. One has been offered by Sebastien Grammond.[44] In his view, it is a mistake to read the reference as a case purporting to set out a broad presumption that matters going to eligibility are off limits. We should instead try to "understand the reasoning in [the] case and ... see which parts of it can be applied to the issue of bilingualism."[45]

Grammond's argument runs as follows. The majority treated Part V as, among other things, a provision designed to protect Quebec's representation on the court as well as the court's continued role as guardian of the Constitution. To the extent that sections 4 to 6 of the *Supreme Court Act* preclude Parliament from stripping away Quebec's representation on the Supreme Court, or block outright abolition or court stacking, they go to the protected core of Part V, and Parliament may not unilaterally amend them. But *only* to that extent. The court, Grammond observes, never declared that the *Supreme Court Act,* or even sections 4 through 6, was constitutionally entrenched. Insofar as Parliament seeks to amend those sections in a way that does not implicate the protected core of Part V, then, it may do so without having to seek a constitutional amendment. Since a bilingualism requirement would neither compromise Quebec's representation on the court – quite the contrary! – nor undermine the court's independence or legitimacy, it is open for Parliament to proceed.

The argument is ingenious but not entirely convincing. Grammond gives short shrift to the actual text of Part V, which refers only to composition while focusing on the imputed intentions of the court and the framers of the *Constitution Act, 1982.*[46] That approach might be necessary to avoid the conclusion that many post-1982 amendments to the *Supreme Court Act* are constitutionally invalid. But so what? If the amendments are unconstitutional, then so be it. The fact that it is inconvenient or embarrassing to acknowledge their invalidity is not obviously a reason to change our understanding of the Constitution. (As Leonid Sirota put it, such a line of reasoning would amount to "legislative competence ... by adverse possession.")[47] Moreover, the court was alerted to those changes by the attorney general of Canada, and this did not deter the court from reading Part V in an expansive fashion.

Even accepting Grammond's broad approach to reading the reference and Part V, it is far from clear that a bilingualism requirement would fall outside the protected core. Consider an argument by Kate Glover-Berger.[48] She agrees with Grammond that Part V protects the "essence of what enables the Supreme Court to perform its current role"[49] and that those matters that are "crucial to [the court's] ability to function effectively and with sufficient institutional legitimacy as the final court of appeal for Canada."[50] On this basis, she concludes: "[S]ection 41(d) covers matters relating to composition that are *constitutionally significant* and the eligibility criteria tied to them. That is, it covers only those aspects of composition and eligibility that are necessary to ensure the Court's competence, legitimacy, integrity, and proper role and functioning."[51]

Constitutionally significant changes do not include routine matters or "all aspects of the Court's institutional design." The trouble is that there is nothing routine about a bilingualism requirement. A requirement of that sort, she claims, would be significant because it would be "directed at enhancing the Court's legitimacy within a federal constitutional culture that is officially bilingual" and in relation to "its constitutional role as the final court of appeal for all legal issues and for all Canadians." It "would suggest that appointing judges with a legal background is no longer sufficient to ensure the Court can fulfill its role and preserve its integrity; rather, proficiency in both languages is needed."[52]

There is a good deal of force to Glover-Berger's argument. Formally requiring judges to be functionally bilingual changes their set of competencies in a manner that is more than trivial. Grammond's position seems to be that, so long as a change to the court would enhance its legitimacy among the francophone community, Parliament should have more leeway to make it. But why think that? After all, it is not clear precisely what a bilingualism requirement would demand. Grammond (and others) would no doubt be pleased if the court was composed of jurists who are, at least, functionally bilingual. They would (presumably) be less pleased if a lower threshold – say, passively bilingual – was legislated. They would (again, presumably) be still less pleased if bilingualism was recognized as an asset for candidates – to, say, break a tie between two otherwise equally matched persons – but not made a strict condition for appointment.

The questions surrounding a bilingualism requirement raise legitimate concerns for other provinces and interest groups. One should not assume that the only perspective to consider is that of Quebec or parties or advocates of francophone heritage. The very nature of the federal compact makes that inadequate. Instituting a requirement for mandatory bilingualism will, inevitably, diminish the pool of eligible appointees in regions outside Quebec.[53] It may also conflict with other initiatives to improve the court's diversity, such as the appointment of Indigenous candidates.[54]

To be sure, and many persons have said this, *all* criteria will exclude someone. Furthermore, it is no secret that bilingualism is generally required for employment in the federal public service. Those replies, however, miss the point – which has nothing to do with fairness to potential candidates for Supreme Court appointment and everything to do with the fact that provincial actors may be owed an opportunity to give or withhold consent to a proposed change to eligibility criteria. A requirement of official bilingualism may impede other important diversity-based goals for the court, such as the appointment of racial minorities or an Indigenous jurist.[55] Can such a decision be made by Parliament alone? The reference suggests that the answer may be no.

Other Forms of Representation

The Supreme Court is one of the most visible symbols of the justice system. Its members shape the law and, in interpreting and applying it, have enormous impact on the lives of Canadians. It is, therefore, only to be expected that who occupies the court's nine seats has become a matter of public comment and concern. Increasingly, such concerns are not limited to questions of technical expertise and legal knowledge but deeper (and more controversial) issues of identity.

There have been increasing demands for Indigenous representation on the Supreme Court of Canada, and there is clearly a principled case for it. The relationship between Indigenous Peoples and Canada is one of the primary narratives of this country, and it continues to be a site of both historical mistreatment and national remorse. Indigenous persons are incarcerated at a rate that is disproportionate given their numbers in the wider community.[56] Indigenous Peoples also have distinct constitutional rights, such as to land title and the duty to consult, that require special knowledge and expertise. Moreover, many think it pivotal for the court to have a real grasp of Indigenous legal traditions if a proper "reconciliation" is to occur. To that extent at least, the argument for Indigenous representation broadly resembles the case for Quebec representation made in 1875. More and more, the country appears to be awakening to the reality that civil and common law were not the first, or even primary, legal orders in this land. Having an Indigenous jurist on the court could do much to assure Indigenous communities that the law will take into account their perspectives, experiences, and voices.

The desire for an Indigenous jurist has been expressed numerous times over the last three decades.[57] Meeting this goal has been complicated by the remarkable lack of diversity in the lower courts, both in the provinces and federally. In 2016, it was estimated that the number of Indigenous jurists was between 1 and 3 percent.[58] In 2016, during the search for Thomas Cromwell's replacement, it was widely thought that the Trudeau government was keen to appoint an Indigenous jurist – so much so that it deliberately left the call for applications open so that someone from outside Atlantic Canada could be considered. This was perceived as significant because the judiciary in the Atlantic region was not particularly diverse and did not include anyone of Indigenous background.[59]

It was not to be. Trudeau went for another kind of "history making," appointing the court's first-ever judge from Newfoundland and Labrador (Malcolm Rowe). The prime minister got another opportunity a year later, when the chief justice herself announced her retirement nine months before her seventy-fifth birthday.[60] Numerous media stories suggested that "now may be the time." There was again wide speculation about who, in the Indigenous legal community, might be selected – with particular attention being focused on Professor John Borrows and former Saskatchewan provincial court judge Mary Ellen Turpel-Lafond.[61] In a television interview, Lorne Sossin stated that the possibility of an Indigenous appointment was "very likely."[62]

Again, it did not happen. The prime minister announced instead that the ninth seat would be occupied by Sheilah Martin, a white, female judge on the Alberta Court of Appeal.[63] Martin was a highly respected and accomplished figure, and no one doubted that she would make an excellent Supreme Court justice. But that did not diminish the disappointment and frustration felt by many that another opportunity to appoint an Indigenous jurist had fallen by the wayside.[64] This disappointment was exacerbated by media reports stating that no Indigenous individuals had been on the short list.[65] Speaking on behalf of the Indigenous Bar Association, Brooks Arcand-Paul stated that Trudeau's "decision neglects the importance and urgency of including Indigenous lawyers and judges and academics within the judiciary."[66]

Although it is not rooted in the same constitutional expectations as Indigenous jurists, the call for more parity on the court with respect to gender and race also has become more urgent. The two types of representation are not equivalent.[67] Most obviously, while there have been significant moves to appoint more women, the court remains racially homogeneous. Arguably, that difference itself has created very different expectations.

When a female jurist retires, there may well be an expectation among a significant number of Canadians that the prime minister will appoint a woman to replace her or, at least, have a convincing reason to not do so. When Prime Minister Harper replaced Marie Deschamps with

Richard Wagner, it altered the court's gender split from five–four (male-female) to six–three. The balance did not change until the appointment of Suzanne Côté, in 2014, as a replacement for Louis LeBel. Apart from that period, there have been four women on the court since the dual appointments of Rosalie Abella and Louise Charron in 2004. The court, however, has never had *more* than 50 percent women. One cannot help but wonder what the reaction will be when a prime minister eventually is moved to appoint a fifth, or even sixth, woman.[68]

The Supreme Court has yet to have a justice who is a member of a racial minority. That, increasingly, is a source of consternation. The degree to which such a move is expected tends to be twinned to the region that is in play during a particular appointment. It seems that Ontario and British Columbia have the most diverse practising bars and, as a corollary, benches to choose from. But the number of racialized judges in Canada remains vanishingly small.

The rationale for appointing jurists of diverse backgrounds is to ensure that the court is reasonably representative of the country and the legal profession. The case for gender parity is in part a recognition of the traditional silencing of women, their exclusion from positions of public power and, in particular, their chronic erasure from the legal and justice system. There are, more controversially, arguments that lived experience as a woman can give rise to different approaches to judging itself.[69] As for racial diversity, the court's legitimacy depends, to some extent, on it reflecting the broad diversity of the country. To the extent that the court's decision making appears to be rooted in an exclusively white experience of the world, that is a concern – no matter the skill, expertise, and other important experiences brought by the various judges.

With all this in mind, the question of whether the reference permits or restricts Parliament's ability to respond to these increasingly urgent political demands is important. As with proposed bilingualism requirements, it is hard to believe that such matters do not go to eligibility or, perhaps, even composition. After all, if Quebec representation is a matter of composition why not other kinds of representation?[70] Taking seriously Grammond's argument, it may be that this sort of change would be perceived to have a more routine character, so much so that none of the provinces would regard themselves as potentially disadvantaged by it. But that is not obvious. The reference appears to set forth a template: the court, as an arbiter of federalism, cannot be subjected to the whims of only one order of government if a contemplated change would affect its ability to perform that role with the confidence of all relevant actors. What has yet to be decided is whether the court also embodies other important constitutional roles, such as arbiter of human rights or the treatment of minorities (some of whom are also recognized by unwritten constitutional principles). In such matters, perhaps, it may be considered appropriate to acknowledge the seat of federal law-making (Parliament) as having its own distinct legitimacy to make such changes without the overarching need to secure additional provincial consent. At present, there is no clear answer.

The Regional Conventions

As we have seen, there have been a number of controversies in recent years concerning the regional representation conventions. What is the constitutional status of these conventions in light of the reference?

To begin, keep in mind that, by definition, constitutional conventions are not enforceable by the courts. A court may clarify what conventions exist in our constitutional system of arrangements, as in the Patriation Reference, but it cannot require political actors to act in accordance with them. This raises an interesting problem right at the outset. Can a constitutional convention count as a feature of the Supreme Court within the meaning of the reference?

If the answer is yes, then the regional representation conventions would surely qualify as essential. After all, the provinces themselves would hardly regard changes to their own representation on the Supreme Court with indifference. They certainly would not treat such changes as routine. Reading Part V in light of the federal principle, there is good reason to think that a constitutional amendment would be needed to alter the regional representation conventions. Moreover, there is a reasonable argument that the conventions go to the court's essential features and, possibly, composition. This, however, leads to the striking conclusion that the regional representation conventions have ceased to be conventions and are now rules of constitutional law.

Indeed, if the regional representation conventions are features of the court, then it would be problematic even to make rules purporting to codify existing practice. Because constitutional conventions are unwritten, reasonable people may disagree about their precise content. British Columbia, for example, might well argue that, as a matter of existing practice, it is entitled to a seat of its own. In October 1962, there was a debate within Cabinet on this very question.[71] Saskatchewan might well argue that the convention requires reasonable rotation among the Prairie provinces.[72] And so on. The very fact that the provinces would fight over such questions strongly suggests, again, that the proposed codification could not be regarded as routine. But that would suggest that the Constitution precludes Parliament from enacting a law that is consistent with the Constitution.

The most elegant solution may be to say that the regional representation conventions do not count as features of the court – because they are conventions. Certainly, there is nothing in the reference suggesting that the court intended to transform conventions into enforceable constitutional law. That, however, carries a strangeness of its own. Are we really prepared to say that Quebec's seats are protected forever, whereas Ontario's seats can be given away by the prime minister, or that Newfoundland could be given all six of the non-Quebec seats? The reference does not provide the resources to answer these questions with much confidence.

The Appointments Process

As discussed, the Supreme Court appointments process has undergone significant changes since 2004 and even more significant ones since 2016. It is now largely in the hands of an independent, nonpartisan body, which forwards a short list to the prime minister. The prime minister is not bound to select one of the short-listed candidates, but the process creates significant expectations that he or she will. In addition, candidates now must apply and are assessed against a standard list of qualifications.

In ceding a measure of control to an independent advisory committee, Prime Minister Trudeau arguably diminished his own constitutional authority such that a formal amendment was required under Part V. The comparison some might draw is to the Senate and to remarks made by the Supreme Court in the Senate Reform Reference. There, the federal government argued that instituting consultative elections in the provinces would not constitute a change to the Constitution so long as the prime minister held the final word as to who to appoint. In rejecting that argument, the Supreme Court said: "[I]ntroducing a process of consultative elections for the nomination of Senators would change our Constitution's architecture, by endowing Senators with a popular mandate which is inconsistent with the Senate's role as a complementary legislative chamber of sober second thought."[73]

Would the same caution apply to the new process for appointing Supreme Court judges? The concern was raised during the justice minister's appearance before the House Standing Committee on Justice and Human Rights by the leader of the New Democratic Party, Thomas Mulcair. After criticizing the government for the way that it had announced the process, he said:

> We are trying, unsuccessfully, to figure out whether this involves a substantive change, as the Supreme Court indicated in Nadon. In its decision, the court deemed such a substantive change ultra vires of Parliament itself. The ultra vires finding is even more applicable when you have the executive branch making substantive changes of this nature ...
>
> Mr. Chair, in our parliamentary system of government, openness and transparency start with a discussion with duly elected representatives of the public. The minister contends herself, as she just said, that she is talking to us now, but she is talking to us after they've already announced the result. There's no consultation with Parliament. Let's be clear on that. This was decided *in vacuo* by members of cabinet, and a letter was simply sent to two chosen newspapers.[74]

In assessing the above complaint, it should be recognized that the remarks were made in a parliamentary committee hearing. In other words, one would be forgiven for treating them more as political rhetoric than true and cogent questioning. Nonetheless, we think they are worth taking seriously, not least because they were posed by a former leader of the Official Opposition who is legally trained.

And yet we think that the specific constitutional complaint outlined above is tenuous. To the extent that the objection rests on the premise that the prime minister is taking something away from Parliament, it skirts the fact that Parliament does not enjoy formal input into the selection of Supreme Court judges. Indeed, successive justice ministers have argued that under section 96 of the *Constitution Act, 1867* the executive power of appointment *cannot* be shared with the legislature. Irwin Cotler, for example, made this argument in 2004. At that time, one could challenge the assertion because the appointment power was contained in the *Supreme Court Act* (then understood to be mere ordinary law). It seemed a bit too convenient for the government to argue that its hands were tied in terms of giving Parliament greater say when, presumably, it could simply introduce legislation that would amend the Act.

But now, of course, the situation has changed. The appointment power granted to the prime minister under section 4.2 of the Act must be counted as one of the court's essential features and may well relate to its composition. Therefore, to the extent that Mulcair was referring to the previous practice (post 2004) of permitting parliamentarians to produce a short list, the idea that the practice had been constitutionalized is not persuasive.

Mulcair, though, also queried whether the new appointments process constituted a change in any sense contemplated by the reference. That is a fair question. After all, the prime minister himself trumpeted the groundbreaking nature of the change. Did his new process, especially in relation to the independent advisory committee, change things in the constitutional sense as well?

That's unlikely. The most important reason is that the final choice remains with the prime minister as, under the Constitution, it clearly must. Now, one could argue that delegating an appointment power affects it to such a degree that the power itself is altered in a (constitutionally) significant way. That was the flaw that the court identified with the prospect of consultative elections for senators. In the Senate Reform Reference, the federal government argued that there was, in effect, no change to the appointments process because the prime minister still held the last word. But the court believed that injecting electoral considerations into the process, however secondarily, would fundamentally change the nature of the Senate itself, because the Senate was expressly designed to not reflect ordinary democratic wishes and aspirations in the way that the House of Commons does. It was designed as a "chamber of sober second thought" precisely to *complement* the function of the other chamber. Therefore, even consultative elections to appoint Senators would require a formal amendment to the Constitution.

Now, there is no question that submitting the appointments process for the Supreme Court to a similar electoral process would immediately be ruled out of bounds – albeit for different constitutional reasons. Such a move would threaten the court's independence, which is itself an unwritten constitutional principle.[75] But we do not think that outsourcing the consideration of applicants to an expert committee, who are themselves guided by qualifications and assessment criteria designed and approved by the executive branch of government, represents a similarly profound change. It does not, we think, change the nature of Supreme Court appointments, although it clearly is designed to make them better. The new process reflects a considered choice by Prime Minister Trudeau as to how he wishes to exercise his appointment authority, privileging an expertise-based approach to one that is strictly political. Either would be consistent with current constitutional arrangements.[76]

In pursuing the dual-track strategy of enacting its declaratory legislation while seeking the court's *post facto* opinion about that legislation's validity, the Conservative government set in motion a sequence of events that has greatly affected the court and the Constitution. In recognizing its constitutionally protected status, the court drew on the underlying norm of federalism which, increasingly, it has used to ensure that provincial concerns and input are not subsumed by federal goals. A commitment to the basic coherence of the Constitution may well be incompatible with allowing the court to be subject to unilateral abolition by Parliament, judge stacking, or the removal of Quebec's seat entitlement. But by reconciling those entirely plausible assertions with the particular wording of Part V, the court has arguably rendered all but the most mundane changes to it beyond ordinary law. That may be wise for intergovernmental relations, but it may prove to be a millstone that obstructs all manner of reform. Regardless of whether one agrees with the substance of the reforms above, though, it would be regrettable if the perceived impossibility of achieving them meant that they were not considered worthy of serious discussion.

Conclusion

It has been six years since the Supreme Court of Canada released its opinion in *Reference re Supreme Court Act, ss 5 and 6.* That is not a long time in which to assess the impact of a court ruling. But much has happened during that period. The reference changed the national conversation surrounding judicial appointments. It showed that such appointments could be matters of high drama, that these are not dry, bureaucratic affairs. They are political decisions involving the exercise of power. And, like other exercises of power, they can run aground on the rocks of legality and constitutionality.

To anyone keeping track of the changing role of the Supreme Court of Canada over the last forty years, it will seem quaint or dangerously naive to think that politics or power was ever separate from the judicial appointments process. But Canada never had the high-profile appointment battles of the United States. For much of the modern history of the Supreme Court, appointments have been presented as purely merit-driven endeavours – a matter of finding the lawyer with the best curriculum vitae. Even when the process was reformed early in the new millennium, the idea that one would critique an appointment from a political vantage point was regarded as largely off limits. Though conservatives have long argued that, in the Charter era, the court itself has assumed a political role, they have tended not to politicize individual appointments or scrutinize the political values and beliefs of individual judges.

The Nadon appointment changed that. From the moment his name was announced, Marc Nadon was subjected to intense (and arguably unfair) political scrutiny. As the public heard more and more about how he came to be selected in the first place, the political nature of the process became more exposed. Canadians learned that, at least in some circles, Federal Court judges were regarded as too deferential and pro-government, whereas Quebec Superior Court judges were regarded as too progressive and interventionist. There was talk of moving Justice Mainville to the Quebec Court of Appeal to circumvent the legal barriers presented by section 6. In the years that followed the reference, calls for more diversity on the bench – Indigenous, racial, gender, regional, ideological – have grown louder. The prospect of appointing a justice from outside Atlantic Canada to replace Justice Cromwell was a matter of debate in the House of Commons. If it could ever have been said that Supreme Court appointments were above politics, it cannot be said now.

Exposing the place of politics and power at the heart of judicial appointments means confronting the unnerving fragility of our constitutional order, one in which the guardians of the Constitution are selected by the very people whose decisions will come under review. Law is frequently envisaged as a check on raw power, but the two have never been neatly severable. Behind every judicial decision, presented as a neutral exercise in legal reasoning and interpretation, is a decision made by a politician that *this* person should hold *that* authority – that he or she has the values and skills "suitable" for someone holding judicial office and that others, with perhaps equally impressive credentials, do not. One need not be a dyed-in-the-wool legal realist to think that these decisions have implications for the kinds of judgments reached by courts, though the extent to which that is true remains a matter of intense disagreement.

But the reference raised questions that were even more unsettling. Though Prime Minister Harper never expressly claimed that Parliament had the power to abolish the Supreme Court of Canada or alter its composition in fundamental ways, that seemed an obvious implication of his position that the *Supreme Court Act* could be rewritten to widen eligibility. However much the attorney general of Canada sought to downplay the significance of the reference, it was hard not to see troubling possibilities lurking offstage – for example, Roosevelt-like attempts at court stacking or the removal of bar membership requirements – designed to shift the ideological direction of the court or otherwise undermine it as an institution.

Such possibilities could not be dismissed because, for all the attention paid to Canada's written constitutional instruments, much of its Constitution is unwritten. Just as the prime minister and Cabinet go unmentioned in the Constitution Acts, so the Supreme Court finds almost no formal recognition. To all appearances, the court was a pure creature of statute. Any legislative attempt to abolish the court, or diminish its role in our legal order, would clearly pose an urgent constitutional problem – but not obviously a legal one. After all, Parliament is sovereign. And so the court looked dangerously vulnerable just as it had reached the peak of its authority and prestige. In retrospect, the contretemps between Prime Minister Harper and Chief Justice McLachlin fuelled the sense, among many, that the court had been right to worry.

For better or for worse, the reference set things straight. The court articulated, clearly and emphatically, that it is no mere appendage to Canada's constitutional order, subject to amputation whenever the political mood shifts. In the process, it removed some of the fragility in the Constitution.

It also removed some of its flexibility. Given that it is notoriously difficult to amend the Constitution, the architecture metaphor has seemed to forestall – by rendering moot – all talk of fundamental reform to the Supreme Court. Even relatively modest, and widely sought, changes to the court have been dismissed as impracticable. In using the language of architecture, the court may have wished to evoke the image of a house; in practice, it may turn out to be a prison.

This brings us full circle. We began with the observation that the reference, and the events preceding and following it, exposed the role of politics in judicial appointments. But "politics" is not a dirty word. In ensuring that Parliament could not undermine the court, the reference had the perhaps unintended side effect of choking off reforms that arguably would have heightened the court's legitimacy and effectiveness. To those who feel, with some justification, that the court lacks diversity and that its judgments reflect a blinkered vision of life in Canada, the architecture metaphor might evoke another less-than-positive expression: "The master's tools cannot dismantle the master's house."

⁂

There is a photograph in Library and Archives Canada. Taken in 1994, it shows Marc Nadon being sworn in as a Federal Court judge. Surrounded by other judges of the court, including future Supreme Court justice Marshall Rothstein, Nadon has a slight smile on his face. He appears rightly pleased. He could have had no way of knowing that, years later, this would be the precise moment when he ceased to be eligible for the Supreme Court of Canada.

After his retirement in 2016, Justice Thomas Cromwell gave an interview in which he reflected on the reference. He expressed kind words for Marc Nadon, who he said was no more than the very unfortunate victim of a technicality: "Justice Nadon is an experienced and highly respected judge. The case was about some very technical requirements in the *Supreme Court Act* and the Constitution, for the composition of this court. It had absolutely nothing to do with his suitability. And I think it's regrettable that that seemed to get lost often in the discussion." He continued: "I would feel bad for that happening to anybody, of course. It's an unfortunate, very unfortunate, thing. And I thought that, No. 1, the court exhibited its independence and impartiality, both the majority and the dissent, I think we showed we were doing our job. But I feel very sorry that that happened to any judicial colleague."[1]

As we saw earlier, similar sentiments were expressed by others involved in the decision. Rocco Galati, the man who started the legal proceedings in Federal Court, insisted that his decision to challenge the appointment was "nothing personal."[2] To many commentators, Marc Nadon – who was neither a party nor an intervener in the case that would decide his fate – has been done a great disservice, if not by the court than by the government that appointed him.[3] Throughout the entire episode, though, Nadon himself cut a figure of quiet dignity. He continues to serve on the Federal Court of Appeal.

In an interview with us, Justice Nadon looked back on the whole affair with good humour.[4] He recalled having been completely surprised when told that the government planned to appoint him. He had never lobbied for the job; he never asked for it. At the time, Nadon said, he and his wife were spending several months each year in Arizona, and he was enjoying his life as a supernumerary judge on the Federal Court of Appeal. In the end, he accepted the appointment out of a commitment to public service. The ensuing controversy, he remarked, wasn't easy. But he withstood it, in part with the support of his wife and in part because he had not sought the appointment in the first place. Nadon admitted to occasionally wondering if the spot on the Supreme Court was "worth all the hassle." There were, however, worse things in life, he told us with a laugh.

So far as Nadon is concerned, the reference was wrongly decided as a matter of law. He agreed with the argument outlined in Ian Binnie's memorandum. Had he been on the panel hearing the reference, Nadon told us, he would have signed on to Moldaver's dissent. In his view, the interpretation of section 6 adopted by the majority led to absurd outcomes. There was little or no evidence, he suggested, that the people of Quebec wanted their judges on the Supreme Court subject to a unique standard of eligibility. He felt bad for his francophone colleagues on the Federal Court who, he thought, were treated by the majority as somehow "less Québécois" than their colleagues on the Quebec Superior Court or Court of Appeal.

He remains surprised that the majority declared his appointment void *ab initio.* Advisory opinions are, by definition, nonbinding and involve no parties formally seeking redress. For that reason, there were never any written or oral arguments concerning the legal status of Marc Nadon's appointment to the Supreme Court. "No arguments were made, and I was not represented," he said. He likes to joke with students that "I may still be a Supreme Court judge in law" – a tenth justice. The order-in-council appointing him was never revoked. "If I had a hundred thousand dollars to burn," Nadon mischievously remarked, "it would be fun to challenge" that aspect of the opinion. Ultimately, he suggested, it would have been better if the continued validity of his appointment had been properly litigated in the Federal Court – if Rocco Galati had been allowed to proceed with his initial claim.

Nadon said it felt strange to return to the Federal Court of Appeal: "I thought I was in the Twilight Zone." But Nadon's colleagues, he recalled, were very nice to him, and he was told to take a pace with which he was comfortable as he settled into his old job. He was even given three maritime law cases. Since returning to the Federal Court of Appeal, Nadon told us, he has not spoken publicly about his appointment or the reference. His willingness to speak to us, he said, may have much to do with his approaching retirement. He is currently working on his memoirs.

APPENDIX

130 Adelaide St W
Suite 2600
Toronto, ON
Canada M5H 3P5

T 416-865-9500
F 416-865-9010
www.litigate.com

September 9, 2013

Hon. Ian Binnie, C.C., Q.C.
Direct line: 416-865-3737
Direct fax: 416-865-9010
Email: ibinnie@litigate.com

VIA EMAIL AND COURIER

Department of Justice
Rm. 4159
284 Wellington St.
Ottawa, ON K1A 0H8

RE: Eligibility of Federal Court Judges for Appointment to the Supreme Court of Canada

You have asked for my opinion on the following:

1. Is a sitting judge of the Federal Court qualified for appointment to the Supreme Court as a Québec member, pursuant to *Supreme Court Act* ss. 5 and 6, assuming that the judge had been a member of the Québec Bar for ten years prior to appointment to the Federal Courts?

   Answer: Yes

2. Based on the same explicit assumption as question one, if a Federal Court judge resigns and is forthwith readmitted to the Québec Bar, would he or she be eligible for appointment to the Supreme Court as a Québec member, pursuant to the *Supreme Court Act* ss. 5 and 6?

   Answer: Yes

The questions have their origin in an alleged dissonance in the meaning of the French and English text of section 5 and 6 of the *Supreme Court of Canada Act*, RSC 1985 c. 5-26, which currently provide as follows:

5. Les juges sont choisis parmi les juges, actuels ou anciens, d'une cour supérieure provinciale et parmi les avocats inscrits pendant au moins dix ans au barreau d'une province.	**5.** Any person may be appointed a judge who is or has been a judge of a superior court of a province or a barrister or advocate of at least ten years standing at the bar of a province.

BARRISTERS

LENCZNER SLAGHT ROYCE SMITH GRIFFIN LLP

September 9, 2013
Page 2

6. Au moins trois des juges sont choisis parmi les juges de la Cour d'appel ou de la Cour supérieure de la province de Québec ou parmi les avocats de celle-ci.	**6.** At least three of the judges shall be appointed from among the judges of the Court of Appeal or of the Superior Court of the Province of Quebec or from among the advocates of that Province.

Clearly the Federal Court is not one of the Courts named in sections 5 and 6 and the issue therefore is whether it can be said that a Federal Court Judge who spent at least 10 years at the Québec bar qualifies for appointment to the Supreme Court as an advocate of at least ten years standing even though not a *current* member in good standing of the Québec bar.

There does not appear to be any jurisprudence at any level of court addressing the precise questions you have posed, although Justices Gerald LeDain, Frank Iacobucci, and Marshall Rothstein were appointed directly to the Supreme Court from the Federal Court of Appeal without any s. 5 controversy.

In addition, Louise Arbour was appointed to the Supreme Court of Canada directly from the post of Chief Prosecutor of the International Criminal Tribunal for Rwanda in Arusha and the International Criminal Tribunal for the former Yugoslavia in The Hague prior to which she had been a member of the Ontario Court of Appeal and prior to that a law professor. She was therefore neither a judge of a court specified in s. 5 nor a practicing member of a provincial bar at the time of her appointment.

Notwithstanding past practice it is necessary to approach the problem of statutory interpretation from first principles.

Applicable Principles of Statutory Interpretation

The "golden rule" is that the text of particular sections is not to be read in isolation.

The Supreme Court of Canada has repeatedly endorsed as correct the *Driedger* approach formulated as follows:

September 9, 2013
Page 3

> the words of an Act are to be read in their entire context and in their grammatical and ordinary sense harmoniously with the scheme of the Act, the object of the Act, and the intention of Parliament (E.A. Driedger, *Construction of Statutes* (2nd ed. 1983), at p. 87)

See, for example, *Stubart Investments Ltd. v. The Queen*, [1984] 1 S.C.R. 536, at p. 578, per Estey J.; *Québec (Communauté urbaine) v. Corp. Notre-Dame de Bon-Secours*, [1994] 3 S.C.R. 3, at p. 17; *Rizzo & Rizzo Shoes Ltd. (Re)*, [1998] 1 S.C.R. 27, at para 21; *R. v. Gladue*, [1999] 1 S.C.R. 688, at para 25; *R. v. Araujo*, [2000] 2 S.C.R. 992, 2000 SCC 65, at para 26; *R. v. Sharpe*, [2001] 1 S.C.R. 45, 2001 SCC 2, at para. 33; and *Bell ExpressVu Limited v. Rex* [2002] 25 SCR 559 at para 29.

Any interpretation that leads to an absurd result is to be avoided.

When dealing with issues of bilingualism:

1. The English and French version of a statute are equally authentic and authoritative.
2. If the French and English texts are in apparent dissonance, the court searches for a "shared meaning".
3. If one version is ambiguous and the other clear, the clear version provides the shared meaning, and is to be adopted.

See *Canadian Charter of Rights and Freedoms* s. 18; *The Official Languages Act*, RSC R.S.C., 1985, c. 31; *R. v. Mac*, [2002] SCJ 26, [2002] 1 SCR 856 at para 5, 6; *R. v. Daoust*, [2004] S.C.J. No. 7, 2004 SCC 6, [2004] 1 S.C.R. 217 at para 27 to 29 (S.C.C.); Bastarache, Metallic, Morris, Essert *The Law of Bilingual Interpretation* (LexisNexis 2008) at pp 21, 24, 38, 47, 56, and 70.

Application of the Principles

The *Driedger* approach is often canvassed in terms of text and context of the statutory provisions under consideration and the "scheme and object" of the Act itself.

(i) Text

Eligibility for appointment to the Supreme Court of Canada is governed, as stated, by sections 5 and 6 of the *Supreme Court of Canada Act*. Section 5 presently reads as follows (with emphasis added):

5. Les juges sont choisis **parmi les juges, actuels ou anciens,** d'une cour supérieure provinciale **et parmi** les avocats **inscrits pendant au moins dix ans** au barreau d'une province.	**5.** Any person may be appointed a judge who **is or has been** a judge of a superior court of a province or a barrister or advocate **of at least ten years standing** at the bar of a province.

The argument against appointments from the Federal Court is that s. 5 requires a potential nominee to the Supreme Court to be either a judge of one of the named courts, or an advocate *currently* practicing at the bar, and that a Federal Court Judge meets neither criterion.

In the English version the words "is or has been" refer grammatically to both judges and advocates. If an individual has "at least ten years standing at the bar of a province" he or she "is or has been" such a member, and despite a lapse of time while serving on the Federal Court, the s. 5 requirement is met.

In the French text, an advocate who was "inscrits pendant au moins dix ans" does not lose that experience or status or qualification when appointed to the Federal Court. The word "inscrits" does not point unequivocally to past or present membership. Grammatically the text embraces both possibilities.

The rationale for excluding Federal Court judges therefore has to be that use of the words "barrister or advocate" (ou "avocat") itself connotes *current* membership in good standing in a provincial law society at the time of appointment.

While it is true that the French text taken in isolation, *could* be interpreted to mean current membership, any ambiguity in the French text is to be resolved by seeking a "shared meaning" with the English text. The English text, in my opinion, is clear and unambiguous. The shared meaning, according to the rules governing bilingual statutory interpretation, is satisfied by an individual "who is *or has been*… a barrister or advocate of at least ten years standing at the bar of a province."

If Parliament had intended to specify *current* membership in the bar it could easily have said so in both official languages.

Accordingly, in my view the *text* of s. 5 does not require *current* bar membership.

(ii) Context

The danger of reading sections in isolation is illustrated by reference to s. 6 of the *Supreme Court of Canada Act,* which, as stated earlier, provides

6. Au moins trois des juges sont choisis **parmi les juges** de la Cour d'appel ou de la Cour supérieure de la province de Québec ou **parmi les avocats** de celle-ci.	**6.** At least three of the judges shall be **appointed from among the judges** of the Court of Appeal or of the Superior Court of the Province of Quebec **or from among the advocates** of that Province.

Read in isolation, a Québec advocate of zero years standing would be eligible to be appointed to the Supreme Court of Canada the day after his or her call to the bar. This would clearly be a nonsensical result. Sections 5 and 6 have to be read together.

An important contextual consideration is legislative history. Attached as Appendices hereto are the relevant legislative histories of sections 5 and 6. The historical evolution of the sections indicates, in my opinion, that Parliament's concern has never been with current membership but with a minimum length of experience at the bar.

The "inscrit" issue was introduced into s. 5 by the 1952 Consolidation of the Statutes of Canada. In the prior 1927 text neither the French or English versions of s. 5 contemplated current membership. The 1927 version of s. 5 read as follows:

5. Peut être nommé juge	5. Any person may be appointed a

September 9, 2013
Page 6

quiconque **est ou a été** juge d'une cour supérieure de l'une des provinces du Canada, ou un avocat **qui a exercé pendant au moins dix ans** au barreau de l'une des provinces. S.R. 1906, c.139, art. 5.	judge who **is or has been** a judge of a superior court of any of the provinces of Canada, or a barrister or advocate **of at least ten years' standing** at the bar of any of the said provinces.

It cannot reasonably be contended that the formulation "a exercé" points unequivocally to current bar membership.

The 1952 Consolidation introduced into the French text the word "inscrit" which, together with the comma after the words "provinces du Canada," is said to give rise to the requirement of "current standing." However, if such a substantive change were intended a corresponding change would have been made in the English text, but there was no change at all in the 1952 English text:

1927 Text	**1952 Text**
5. Any person may be appointed a judge who **is or has been** a judge of a superior court of any of the provinces of Canada, or a barrister or advocate **of at least ten years' standing** at the bar of any of the said provinces.	5. Any person may be appointed a judge who **is or has been** a judge of a superior court of any of the provinces of Canada, or a barrister or advocate **of at least ten years' standing** at the bar of any of the said provinces.

This observation is not surprising. The argument against appointment of Federal Court judges places too much emphasis on "statutory consolidations" which generally deal with legislative housekeeping not changes in meaning. Section 4 of the *Revised Statutes of Canada, 1985 Act* so provides:

> The Revised Statutes shall not be held to operate as new law, but shall be construed and have effect as a consolidation of the law as contained in the Acts and portions of Acts repealed by section 3 and for which the Revised Statutes are substituted.

The Supreme Court of Canada has held that in cases where (as here) the revision only modifies one of the two linguistic versions of a provision of a statute, the presumption of

September 9, 2013
Page 7

continuity of meaning is even stronger: *R. v. Popovic,* [1976] 2 S.C.R. 308; see also *Flota Cubana de Pesca (Cuban Fishing Fleet) v. Canada (Minister of Citizenship and Immigration),* [1998] 2 F.C. 303 (C.A.) and Côté, Pierre André, *The Interpretation of Legislation in Canada,* 4th ed. (Toronto: Carswell, 2011) at 61.

At the time of the 1952 consolidation neither the Federal Court nor the Federal Court of Appeal existed. It is not surprising these courts were not referred to in the 1952 Consolidation. Membership in the predecessor court, the Exchequer Court of Canada was never considered a bar to appointment to the Supreme Court of Canada.

The "context" therefore reinforms the textual reading of ss. 5 and 6 that current membership of the Québec bar is not a requirement of eligibility for appointment to the Supreme Court.

(iii) Scheme and Object of the Act

The *Supreme Court of Canada Act* established a final appellate body for Canada. Parliament's obvious concern in ss. 5 and 6 was to exclude from consideration men and women who lack the appropriate skills and experience. Exclusion from possible appointment of the talent pool of Federal Court judges conflicts with this purpose. Take for example a lawyer who practices for 15 years in Montreal from 1970 to 1985, then sits as a Judge of the Federal Court of Appeal from 1986 to 2000. Such an individual is clearly better qualified in 2000 after 14 years on the bench than he or she was in 1985 prior to the initial appointment. Yet the objection to the appointment of Federal Court judges attributes to Parliament the view that Federal Court experience is a detriment not an asset. Equally, on the contrary view, an appointment to the International Court of Justice at the Hague would present an insurmountable barrier to appointment, despite decades of earlier practice at a provincial bar. Any interpretation of ss. 5 and 6 of the *Supreme Court of Canada Act* that leads to such an absurd result should be rejected.

Question 2: Resignation, Rejoining the Bar, Making the Appointment

Clearly a judge of the Federal Court who resigned and rejoined the Québec bar is eligible to be appointed subsequently to the Supreme Court. However, any hypothesis that requires of a person who starts the week as a Federal Court judge to rejoin the Québec bar mid-week for a day or two in order to "qualify" for appointment to the Supreme Court by the end of the week, makes no practical sense. Parliament's manifest intent in the *Supreme Court of Canada Act* was to identify minimum qualifications for an important job. Accordingly, the answer to Question 2 is yes but with the *caveat* that such a two-step expedient is nether required nor compatible with the dignity of the office being filled, in my opinion.

Conclusion

In my view there is nothing in the *Supreme Court of Canada Act* that would prevent the direct appointment to the Supreme Court of Canada of a judge of the Federal Court of Canada or the Federal Court of Appeal.

I would be glad to discuss any aspect of this matter with you at your convenience.

Yours truly,

Ian Binnie

Hon. Ian Binnie, C.C., Q.C.

IB/sa
Encl.

Notes

INTRODUCTION

1 *Reference re Supreme Court Act, ss 5 and 6,* 2014 SCC 21.

2 Throughout this book, we refer to the ruling as "the Nadon Reference" or as simply "the reference."

3 *Supreme Court Act,* RSC 1985, c S-26, s 6.

4 Laura Stone, "Justice Marc Nadon Speaks 'At Least This Has Certainly Ended the Uncertainty'" *Global News* (25 March 2014).

5 See *Bedford v Canada,* 2013 SCC 72; *Carter v Canada,* 2015 SCC 5. For a review of important changes to the constitutional landscape, see *Schmidt v Canada,* 2018 FCA 55 at paras 90–97.

6 Compare *R v O'Connor,* [1995] 4 SCR 411 and *R v Mills,* [1999] 3 SCR 668.

7 See, for example, *Brown v Board of Education,* 347 US 483 (1954).

8 See, arguably, *Crevier v AG (Québec) et al,* [1981] 2 SCR 220.

9 *McCulloch v Maryland,* 17 US 316 (1819).

10 *Marbury v Madison,* 5 US 137 (1803).

11 *Fuller's Case,* 12 Co Rep 63, 65, 77 Eng Rep 1342, 1343 (1607).

12 *Roncarelli v Duplessis,* [1959] SCR 121.

13 *Constitution Act, 1982,* being Schedule B to the *Canada Act 1983* (UK), 1982, c 11; *Canadian Charter of Rights and Freedoms,* Part I of the *Constitution Act* (*ibid*).

14 For examinations of the court's history, see Ian Bushnell, *The Captive Court: A Study of the Supreme Court of Canada* (Montreal and Kingston: McGill-Queen's University Press, 1992); James G. Snell and Frederick Vaughan, *The Supreme Court of Canada: History of the Institution* (Toronto: Osgoode Society for Canadian Legal History, 1985).

15 *Reference re Senate Reform,* 2014 SCC 32, [2014] 1 SCR 704.

CHAPTER 1: WHAT'S SO BAD ABOUT MARC NADON?

1 Department of Justice, Judicial Appointments, "Ad Hoc Committee on the Appointment of Supreme Court of Canada Justices," online: <http://www.justice.gc.ca/eng/news-nouv/ja-nj/2013/doc_32972.html>.

2 *Ibid*, "During my youth, my ambition in life was to become a hockey player. Looking at me, that may seem surprising, but those days were different. In fact, I was drafted by the Detroit Red Wings when I was 14, and I'm now going to make an admission, which may be fatal to me here in Ottawa, that I'm neither an Ottawa Senators fan nor a Montreal Canadiens fan. However, when I was around the age of 16, my father read me the riot act and said that I had to decide whether I wanted to study or play hockey. I opted for studying. It now seems that I made the right decision." For a sample of the news coverage, see Chris Carter, "Justice Marc Nadon Drafted by Harper – and Red Wings?" *CBC News* (3 October 2013), online: <http://www.cbc.ca/news/politics/justice-marc-nadon-drafted-by-harper-and-red-wings-1.1894191>.

3 Jeffrey Simpson, "The Supreme Court Deserves Better" *Globe and Mail* (26 October 2013), online: <https://www.theglobeandmail.com/globe-debate/the-supreme-court-deserves-better/article15027360/>.

4 Sean Fine, "What Justice Nadon's Appointment Says about the Supreme Court's Future" *Globe and Mail* (3 January 2014), online: <https://www.theglobeandmail.com/news/national/what-justice-nadons-appointment-says-about-the-supreme-courts-future/article16192045/>.

5 Tristin Hopper, "Marc Nadon Caught Stephen Harper's Attention with Dissent Khadr Ruling in 2009" *National Post* (21 March 2014), online: <http://nationalpost.com/news/politics/marc-nadon-caught-stephen-harpers-attention-with-dissent-khadr-ruling-in-2009>.

6 William Tetley and Marc Nadon, *Marine Cargo Claims* (Toronto: Butterworths, 1978).

7 Supreme Court of Canada, News Release (22 April 2013), online: <https://scc-csc.lexum.com/scc-csc/news/en/item/4282/index.do>.

8 Harold Levy, "A Judge Who Has Always Made a Difference; Top Court Appointee Noted for Fairness Morris Fish Made Mark in Several Influential Cases" *Toronto Star* (10 August 2003) A04; "Former Tough Quebec Lawyer Boosted to Nation's Top Court," *The Guardian* (Charlottetown) (1 August 2003) A09; L. Ian MacDonald, "Morris Fish Is a Supremely Wise and Popular Choice" *Montreal Gazette* (4 Aug 2003) A19.

9 Gail J. Cohen, "Fish Announces Retirement from Supreme Court," *Canadian Lawyer Magazine* (22 April 2013), online: <http://www.canadianlawyermag.com/legalfeeds/author/gail-j-cohen/fish-announces-retirement-from-supreme-court-5091/>.

10 Supreme Court of Canada, biography of Morris J. Fish, online: <https://www.scc-csc.ca/judges-juges/bio-eng.aspx?id=morris-j-fish>.

11 Supreme Court of Canada, News Release (22 April 2013), online: <https://scc-csc.lexum.com/scc-csc/news/en/item/4282/index.do>.

12 Kirk Makin, "End of an Era Looms on the Supreme Court" *Globe and Mail* (18 April 2012), online: <https://www.theglobeandmail.com/news/politics/end-of-an-era-looms-on-supreme-court/article4210348/>.

13 See, for example, her majority decision in *Alberta v Hutterian Brethren of Wilson Colony*, 2009 SCC 37 (adopting a more deferential approach to the minimal impairment test for s 1); *R v Mills*, [1999] 3 SCR 668 (on the "dialogue" between courts and legislatures in the interpretation of Charter rights); and *Canada (Prime Minister) v Khadr*, 2010 SCC 3 [*Khadr*], *R v Conway*, 2004 SCC 20, and *Vancouver v Ward*, 2010 SCC 27 (construing remedial powers under s 24(1) in light of statutory scheme or executive decisions).

14 See, e.g., *R v Singh*, 2007 SCC 48 (arguing for a Charter right to silence that is more expansive than the common law confessions rule) and *R v Gomboc*, 2010 SCC 55 (arguing that warrantless requests to a power company for authority to install a digital ammeter to measure electricity usage engage s 8 of the Charter).

15 See *R v Buzizi*, 2013 SCC 27 at para 17.

16 Kirk Makin, "Retiring Supreme Court Justice Scolds Junior Colleague" *Globe and Mail* (20 May 2013), online: <https://www.theglobeandmail.com/report-on-business/industry-news/the-law-page/retiring-supreme-court-justice-scolds-junior-colleague/article12032641/>. Note that the suggestion is not that Justice Fish advocated for specific defendants appearing before the court on appeal but that he advocated for a particular interpretation of Charter and common law protections.

17 *Ibid.*

18 Simpson, *supra* note 3.

19 *Ibid.*

20 Fine, *supra* note 4.

21 Department of Justice, *supra* note 1.

22 *Ibid.* Nadon submitted some of these cases to the committee.

23 *Ibid.*

24 *Khadr*, *supra* note 13.

25 "Harper's Comments on Omar Khadr 'Deplorable': Lawyer" *CTV News* (10 July 2008), online: <https://www.ctvnews.ca/harper-s-comments-on-omar-khadr-deplorable-lawyer-1.307875>.

26 *Khadr*, *supra* note 13.

27 In July 2004, Canada informed the United States that it expected that Mr. Khadr would be entitled to judicial review of his detention before a court of law, in accordance with due process and international law. In January 2005, upon receipt of

reports that physical and psychological coercion were being used against detainees at Guantanamo Bay, Canada advised the United States that it expected detainees to be treated humanely and that perpetrators of mistreatment would be brought to justice. *Ibid* at para 99.

28 *Ibid* at para 101.

29 *Ibid* at paras 46–47.

30 It bears noting that Rocco Galati, the Toronto lawyer who first challenged Nadon's appointment in Federal Court, had represented Omar Khadr's brother Abdurahman Khadr: "Marc Nadon's Appointment to Supreme Court of Canada Faces Legal Challenge by Toronto Lawyer" *National Post* (8 October 2013), online: <http://nationalpost.com/news/politics/marc-nadons-appointment-to-supreme-court-of-canada-faces-legal-challenge-by-toronto-lawyer> ["Marc Nadon's Appointment"].

31 Fine, *supra* note 4.

32 Department of Justice, *supra* note 1.

33 *Canada (Attorney General) v Jodhon,* 2012 FCA 161.

34 *Ibid* at paras 178, 180–83.

35 *Ibid* at para 179.

36 For a critique of such remedies, see the dissent by Justices LeBel and Deschamps in *Doucet-Boudreau v Nova Scotia (Minister of Education)*, [2003] 3 SCR 3, 2003 SCC 62.

37 *Martin v Canada (Attorney General)*, 2013 FCA 15.

38 *Mugesera v Canada (Minister of Citizenship and Immigration)*, [2005] 2 SCR 91, 2005 SCC 39.

39 *May v CBC/Radio Canada,* 2011 FCA 130 (CanLII).

40 "Marc Nadon's Appointment," *supra* note 30.

41 Simpson, *supra* note 3. See also Sean Fine, "Committee Grilling New Supreme Court Judge Faces Severe Time Crunch" *Globe and Mail* (1 October 2013), online: <https://www.theglobeandmail.com/news/national/committee-grilling-new-supreme-court-judge-faces-severe-time-crunch/article14648112/>. Fine quotes law professor Kathleen Mahoney: "I don't know who this fellow is ... I'm just Googling him right now."

42 The appointments were Thomas Cromwell, Michael Moldaver, Andromache Karakatsanis, and Richard Wagner.

43 See Rosemary Cairns Way, "Deliberate Disregard: Judicial Appointments under the Harper Government" (2014) 67 SCLR (2nd) 43.

44 Marc Nadon, telephone interview, 4 June 2018.

CHAPTER 2: THE PRIME MINISTER'S PREROGATIVE

1 *British North America Act,* 1867, SS 1867, c 3, s 101.

2 *Supreme and Exchequer Courts Act,* RSC 1886, c 135.

3 *Supreme Court Act,* RSC 1985, c S-26. Jacob Ziegel, "Merit Selection and Democratization of Appointments to the Supreme Court of Canada" in Paul Howe and Peter H. Russell, eds, *Judicial Power and Canadian Democracy* (Montreal and Kingston: McGill-Queen's University Press, 2001) 131 at 139.

4 See Anne McLellan, "Foreword" (2000) 38 Alta L Rev 603 at 604; Irwin Cotler, "The Supreme Court Appointment Process: Chronology, Context and Reform" (2007) 58 UNBLJ 133; Tonda MacCharles, "Supreme Court Pick Defends Qualifications: Justice Marc Nadon Concedes He Doesn't Meet Any Diversity Expectations for Upper Chamber" *Toronto Star* (3 October 2013) A28.

5 Compare J.R. Mallory, *The Structure of Canadian Government* (Toronto: Macmillan, 1971) at 293 to Richard Devlin and Adam Dodek, "The Achilles Heel of the Canadian Judiciary: The Ethics of Judicial Appointments in Canada" (2017) 20 Leg Ethics 43 at 49.

6 See, generally, Rosemary Cairns Way, "Deliberate Disregard: Judicial Appointments under the Harper Government" (2014) 67 SCLR (2nd) 43. See also Kirk Makin, "Supreme Court Needs More Women, Departing Judge Says" *Globe and Mail* (2 February 2013), online: <https://www.theglobeandmail.com/news/national/supreme-court-needs-more-women-departing-judge-says/article8149711/>, quoting remarks by retiring Justice Marie Deschamps.

7 Rosemary Cairns Way, "Deliberate Disregard: Judicial Appointments under the Harper Government" (2014) 67 SCLR (2nd) 43; CBA Resolution 05-01-A, "Recognition of Legal Pluralism in Judicial Appointments"; James C. Hopkins and Albert C. Peeling, "Aboriginal Judicial Appointments to the Supreme Court of Canada" (Indigenous Bar Association Research Paper, April 2004), online: <http://caid.ca/AboJudAptSCC2004.pdf>.

8 Adam Dodek, "Reforming the Supreme Court Appointment Process, 2004–2014: A 10-Year Democratic Audit" (2014) 67 SCLR (2nd) 111 at 118–19.

9 *Ibid*, citing Jacob Ziegel, "Merit Selection and Democratization of Appointments to the Supreme Court of Canada" (1999) 5:2 Choices 3 at 6.

10 David Schneiderman, *Red, White, and Kind of Blue? The Conservatives and the Americanization of Canadian Constitutional Culture* (Toronto: University of Toronto Press, 2015) at 242.

11 Ian Bushnell, *The Captive Court: A Study of the Supreme Court of Canada* (Montreal and Kingston: McGill-Queen's University Press, 1992) at 209.

12 *Ibid* at 189.

13 *Ibid* at 263.

14 Michael Plaxton and Carissima Mathen, "Purposive Interpretation, Quebec, and the *Supreme Court Act*" (2013) 22 Const Forum Const 15, n 8; Supreme Court of Canada, Judges, "The Honourable Douglas Charles Abbott," online: <https://www.scc-csc.ca/judges-juges/bio-eng.aspx?id=douglas-charles-abbott>.

15 Bushnell, *supra* note 11 at 343; John G. Diefenbaker, *One Canada: The Tumultuous Years, 1962–1967* (Toronto: Macmillan, 1977) at 157–58. Donald Fleming is also said to have coveted the post: Patrick Nicholson, *Vision and Indecision* (Don Mills, ON: Longmans, 1968) at 254.

16 See William H. Angus, "Judicial Selection in Canada: The Historical Perspective" (1966) 3 Can Legal Stud 220; Martin Friedland, *A Place Apart: Judicial Independence and Accountability in Canada* (Ottawa: Canadian Judicial Council, 1995) at 236; Martin Friedland, "Appointment, Discipline and the Removal of Judges in Canada" in H.P. Lee, ed, *Judiciaries in Comparative Perspective* (Cambridge: Cambridge University Press, 2011) 46 at 52; Canadian Bar Association, *Report of the Canadian Bar Association on the Appointment of Judges in Canada* (Ottawa: Canadian Bar Foundation, 1985) at 57.

17 See John Willis, "Methods of Appointing Judges: An Introduction" (1967) 4 Can Legal Stud 217.

18 Peter H. Russell and Jacob Ziegel, "Federal Judicial Appointments: An Appraisal of the First Mulroney Government's Appointments and the New Judicial Advisory Committees" (1991) 41 UTLJ 4 at 19, as discussed in Schneiderman, *supra* note 10 at 243.

19 Troy Riddell, Lori Hausegger, and Matthew Hennigar, "Federal Judicial Appointments: A Look at Patronage in Federal Appointments since 1988" (2008) 58 UTLJ 39 at 57, as discussed in Schneiderman, *supra* note 10 at 243.

20 Schneiderman, *supra* note 10 at 243.

21 Alec Scott, "The Supremes" *Saturday Night* 120:3 (April 2005) 44.

22 See Benjamin Alarie and Andrew Green, "Policy Preference Change and Appointments to the Supreme Court of Canada" (2009) 47 Osgoode Hall LJ 1 at 28; C.L. Ostberg and Matthew J. Wetstein, *Attitudinal Decision Making in the Supreme Court of Canada* (Vancouver: UBC Press, 2007). But see Donald Songer, *Transformation of the Supreme Court of Canada* (Toronto: University of Toronto Press, 2008) at 109–11.

23 See Donald J. Savoie, *What Is Government Good At? A Canadian Answer* (Montreal and Kingston: McGill-Queen's University Press, 2015) at 85.

24 Shirley Ouellet, *Public Attitudes towards the Legitimacy of Our Institutions and the Administration of Justice* (Ottawa: Department of Justice, 1991).

25 Florian Sauvageau, David Schneiderman, and David Taras, *The Last Word: Media Coverage of the Supreme Court of Canada* (Vancouver: UBC Press, 2006) at 26–27, citing Josephine Mazzuca, "Armed Forces, Supreme Court and Public Schools Top Institutional List for Respect and Confidence" (28 May 2001) 61 Gallup Poll 30.

26 Sauvageau, Schneiderman, and Taras, *supra* note 25 at 27, citing Joseph Fletcher and Paul Howe, "Public Opinion and Canada's Courts" in Howe and

Russell, *Judicial Power and Canadian Democracy,* 255 at 260–64 [Fletcher and Howe, "Public Opinion"].

27 Dodek, *supra* note 8 at 144, citing Fletcher and Howe, "Public Opinion," *supra* note 26 at 260–64.

28 Environics, *Focus Canada 2010: Public Opinion Research on the Record – Serving the Public Interest,* at 19, online: <https://www.environicsinstitute.org/docs/default-source/project-documents/focus-canada-2010/final-report.pdf?sfvrsn=6ec8c1d3_2>.

29 Sauvageau, Schneiderman, and Taras, *supra* note 25 at 27.

30 *Ibid,* citing Kirk Makin, "Canadians Believe Supreme Court Rulings Are Influenced by Politics: Poll" *Globe and Mail* (3 July 2001) A1 and Janice Tibbetts, "High Court Too Partisan: Survey" *Canada.com* (12 May 2003).

31 Sauvageau, Schneiderman, and Taras, *supra* note 25 at 27–88; Dodek, *supra* note 8 at 146.

32 See James G. Snell and Frederick Vaughan, *The Supreme Court of Canada: History of the Institution* (Toronto: Osgoode Society for Canadian Legal History, 1985) at 194, 204; Peter H. Russell, *The Supreme Court of Canada as a Bilingual and Bicultural Institution* (Ottawa: Queen's Printer, 1969) at 44–45.

33 Pierre Elliott Trudeau, "The Constitution and the People of Canada: An Approach to the Objectives of Confederation, the Rights of People and the Institutions of Government (1968)," reproduced in Anne F. Bayefsky, ed, *Canada's Constitutional Act 1982 and Amendments: A Documentary History* (Toronto: McGraw-Hill Ryerson, 1989) 78.

34 Schneiderman, *supra* note 10 at 238–39.

35 Dodek, *supra* note 8 at 122, citing Letter to Mr. Derek Lee, Chair, House of Commons Standing Committee on Justice, Human Rights, Public Safety and Emergency Preparedness (16 March 2004), online: <https://www.publicsafety.gc.ca/lbrr/archives/ua%2010.5%20r47%202004-eng.pdf>.

36 See House of Commons, House of Commons Standing Committee on Justice, Human Rights, Public Safety and Emergency Preparedness, *Improving the Supreme Court of Canada Appointments Process* (May 2004) (Chair: Mr. Derek Lee); Dodek, *supra* note 8 at 122.

37 The Honourable Irwin Cotler, "Proposal for the Reform of the Supreme Court of Canada Appointments Process" (Address, 7 April 2005), online: <http://www.justice.gc.ca/en/news/sp/2005/ doc_31432.html>.

38 Dodek, *supra* note 8 at 123–24.

39 See House of Commons, Ad Hoc Committee to Review a Nominee for the Supreme Court of Canada, News Release (27 February 2006), online: <http://www.canada-justice.ca/en/news/sp/2006/doc_31772_3.html> [Ad Hoc Committee]; Peter W. Hogg, "Appointment of Justice Marshall Rothstein to the Supreme

Court of Canada" (2006) 44 Osgoode Hall LJ 527. Prime Minister's Office, News Release, "Prime Minister Announces Appointment of Mr. Justice Marshall Rothstein to the Supreme Court" (1 March 2006), online: <https://www.canada.ca/en/news/archive/2006/03/prime-minister-announces-appointment-justice-marshall-rothstein-supreme-court.html>.

40 Ad Hoc Committee, *supra* note 39 at 1400, 1505, 1435, 1535, 1555, and 1600.

41 *Ibid* at 1420.

42 Compare Michael Plaxton, "The Neutrality Thesis and the Rothstein Hearing" (2008) 58 UNBLJ 92.

43 *Ibid.*

44 Dodek, *supra* note 8 at 127.

45 *Ibid* at 127.

46 *Ibid* at 128.

47 Schneiderman, *supra* note 10 at 252; Lee Epstein and Jeffrey A. Segal, *Advice and Consent: The Politics of Judicial Appointments* (Oxford: Oxford University Press, 2006) at 88.

48 See Benjamin Wittes, *Confirmation Wars: Preserving Independent Courts in Angry Times* (Lanham, MD: Rowman and Littlefield, 2006); Schneiderman, *supra* note 10 at 253–56. The most recent episode was the extraordinary hearing of President Trump's nominee, Judge Brett Kavanaugh, in 2018.

49 Canadian Bar Association, "Supreme Court of Canada Appointment Process," March 2004, online: <https://www.cba.org/CMSPages/GetFile.aspx?guid=62718bd3-2ed4-4497-b7da-66dce82fa975>.

50 House of Commons, Standing Committee on Justice, Human Rights, Public Safety and Emergency Preparedness, 37th Parl, 3rd Sess, No 8, Evidence (30 March 2004) at 1650, online: <https://www.ourcommons.ca/DocumentViewer/en/37-3/JUST/meeting-7/evidence>.

51 Dodek, *supra* note 8 at 148–57.

52 *Ibid* at 158.

53 *Ibid* at 158–59.

54 *Ibid* at 160.

55 *Ibid* at 159.

56 *Ibid* at 159.

57 Editorial, "Harper v Harper" *Globe and Mail* (4 October 2012) A14.

58 Dodek, *supra* note 8 at 162–63.

59 The questions about Justice Karakatsanis's fitness for the role did not end with her appointment. See Editorial, "Weak Process for Weighty Choices" *Globe and Mail* (4 April 2013) A16. See also the responses: Patrick LeSage and Susan Lang, "Both Merit Praise" *Globe and Mail* (5 April 2013) A16; Morris Chochla, "Unwarranted" *Globe and Mail* (10 April 2013) A16.

60 Allan C. Hutchinson, "Looking for the Good Judge: Merit and Ideology" in Nadia Verrelli, ed, *The Democratic Dilemma: Reforming Canada's Supreme Court* (Kingston: Queen's University Institute of Intergovernmental Relations, 2013) 99; Carissima Mathen, "SCC Appointments" (19 October 2011), *Blogging for Equality,* online: <http://www.bloggingforequality.ca/2011/10/scc-appointments.html>. See also Carissima Mathen, "We Don't Need Hearings to Help in Appointment of a New Supreme Court Justice" *Ottawa Citizen* (18 May 2016) A09.

61 See Michael Valpy, "The 'Crisis': A Narrative" in Peter H. Russell, Lorne Sossin, and Adrienne Clarkson, eds, *Parliamentary Democracy in Crisis* (Toronto: University of Toronto Press, 2014) at ch 1, 3.

62 The episode was widely discussed. For a sample, see Mark D. Walters, "The Law behind the Conventions of the Constitution: Reassessing the Prorogation Debate" (2012) 5 JPPL 127; Kenneth Munro, "The Turmoil Surrounding the Prorogation of Canada's 40th Parliament and the Crown" (2009) 18 Const Forum Const 13; Bruce M. Hicks, "British and Canadian Experience with the Royal Prerogative" (2010) 33 Can Parliamentary Rev 18; Andrew Heard, "The Governor General's Decision to Prorogue Parliament: A Chronology and Assessment" (2009) 18 Const Forum Const 1; Eric Adams, "The Constitutionality of Prorogation" (2009) 18 Const Forum Const 17; Melissa Bonga, "The Coalition Crisis and Competing Visions of Canadian Democracy" (2010) 33 Can Parliamentary Rev 8; Edward McWhinney, "The Constitutional and Political Aspects of the Office of the Governor General" (2009) 32 Can Parliamentary Rev 2; Bradley W. Miller, "Proroguing Parliament: A Matter of Convention" (2009) 20 Pub L Rev 100; Hon. Edward Roberts, "Ensuring Constitutional Wisdom during Unconventional Times" (2009) 32 Can Parliamentary Rev 13.

63 See Hugo Cyr, "De la formation du gouvernement" (2013) 43 RGD 381; Hugo Cyr, "Implementing Electoral Reform: Specific Issues with Regard to Forming and Maintaining a Responsible and Legitimate Government in Our Parliamentary Democracy" (Brief submitted to the House of Commons Special Committee on Electoral Reform, 27 July 2016), online: <http://www.ourcommons.ca/content/Committee/421/ERRE/Brief/BR8397335/br-external/CyrHugo-e.pdf>.

64 Notably, the 2008 request was triggered by the possibility of a coalition between Stéphane Dion's Liberals and the NDP, which struck many ordinary Canadians as fishy. See Grace Skogstad, "Western Canada and the 'Illegitimacy' of the Liberal-NDP Coalition" in Russell, Sossin, and Clarkson, *Parliamentary Democracy in Crisis,* 163.

65 See James B. Kelly and Kate Puddister, "Criminal Justice Policy during the Harper Era: Private Member's Bills, Penal Populism, and the Criminal Code of Canada" (2017) 32 CJLS 391.

66 Doug Beazley, "The Whistleblower" *CBA National Magazine* (21 November 2013), online: <http://www.nationalmagazine.ca/Articles/November/The-whistleblower.aspx>.

67 See *Schmidt v Attorney General of Canada,* 2016 FC 269. The decision was affirmed on appeal: 2018 FCA 55.

68 Reform Party of Canada, *Principles and Policies: The Blue Book, 1991,* online: <http://contentdm.ucalgary.ca/digital/collection/reform/id/2193/rec/1>.

69 See, e.g., F.L. Morton, "Judicial Appointments in Post-Charter Canada: A System in Transition" in Kate Malleson and Peter H. Russell, eds, *Appointing Judges in an Age of Judicial Power: Critical Perspectives from around the World* (Toronto: University of Toronto Press, 2006) 56 at 61; F.L. Morton, "The Meaning of *Morgentaler:* A Political Analysis" in Ian Gentles, ed, *A Time to Choose Life: Women, Abortion and Human Rights* (Toronto: Stoddart, 1990); F.L. Morton and Rainer Knopff, *The Charter Revolution and the Court Party* (Toronto: University of Toronto Press, 2000); Preston Manning, "Parliament Not Judges, Must Make the Law of the Land" *Globe and Mail* (16 June 1999) A23.

70 Stephen Harper, "Why I Hate Gag Laws" *Globe and Mail* (13 June 2000), online: <https://www.theglobeandmail.com/opinion/why-i-hate-gag-laws/article768270/>.

71 *Harper v Canada,* 2004 SCC 33.

72 House of Commons, *Improving the Supreme Court of Canada Appointments Process: Report of the Standing Committee on Justice, Human Rights, Public Safety and Emergency Preparedness,* Derek Lee, MP, Chair, May 2004, Dissenting Report (Ottawa: Communication Canada, 2004), online: <https://www.ourcommons.ca/DocumentViewer/en/37-3/JUST/report-1/page-36#160>.

73 In the *Morgentaler* decision, a majority of the court struck down Canada's criminal abortion law on the basis that it violated s 7 of the Charter: [1988] 1 SCR.

74 Schneiderman, *supra* note 10 at 246–51.

75 This claim was perhaps more to be expected vis-à-vis Abella than Charron, as the former has been identified with progressive views for decades. For example, she is credited with devising the term "employment equity" as a Canadian counterpart to "affirmative action." See Rosalie Silberman Abella, *Equality in Employment: A Royal Commission Report,* Royal Commission on Equality in Employment (Ottawa: Minister of Supply and Service Canada, 1984).

76 *Halpern v Toronto (City)* (2003), 65 OR (3rd) 151 (CA) (held the definition to be invalid and ruled that same-sex marriage licences immediately be granted); *EGALE Canada v Canada (AG),* 2003 BCCA 251, 13 BCLR (4th) 1 (CA) (found the common law definition unconstitutional and issued a two-year delay before effect); *Hendricks c Québec (PG),* [2004] RJQ 851 (CA) (affirmed lower

court ruling of unconstitutionality and struck two-year delay ordered in that court).

77 *Reference re Same-Sex Marriage,* [2004] 3 SCR 698. Initially, the reference concerned only the constitutionality of the draft legislation; in other words, it asked whether the federal government could expand the definition of marriage but not whether such a definition was constitutionally required. Eventually, a fourth question was referred to the court, more or less replicating the issue that had already been argued in various provincial courts.

78 Carissima Mathen, "Developments in Constitutional Law: The 2004–2005 Term – A Court in Transition" (2005) 50 SCLR (2nd) 89 at 137.

79 *Ibid* at 90.

80 Alexander Panetta, "Harper Accuses Liberals of Setting Up Court Losses on Gay Marriage" *Canadian Press* (4 September 2003) (ProQuest). While Harper was speaking specifically about Liberal appointments to provincial superior and appellate courts, the argument certainly would extend to the Supreme Court.

81 Tasha Kheiriddin, "Law and Order in the Harper Years" in Jennifer Ditchburn and Graham Fox, eds, *The Harper Factor: Assessing a Prime Minister's Policy Legacy* (Montreal and Kingston: McGill-Queen's University Press, 2016) 196 at 209; Carissima Mathen, "Choices and Controversy: Judicial Appointments in Canada" (2007) 58 UNBLJ 52 at 61; Kirk Makin, "Appointment of Judges Too Political" *Globe and Mail* (16 May 2005) A7.

82 Canadian Judicial Council, News Release, "Canadian Judicial Council Calls on Government to Consult on Proposed Changes" (9 November 2006), online: <https://www.cjc-ccm.gc.ca/english/news_en.asp?selMenu=news_2006_1109_en.asp>.

83 Canada, *House of Commons Debates,* No 110 (14 February 2007) at 1400.

84 The Conservatives continued to fund challenges on language-rights grounds but otherwise ended the program.

85 Morton and Knopff, *supra* note 70 at 97; Ian Brodie, "Interest Group Litigation and the Embedded State" (2001) 34 Can J Political Science 357.

86 Kheiriddin, *supra* 82 at 208.

87 *Ibid.* The victim surcharge was recently struck down by the Supreme Court in *R v Boudreault,* 2018 SCC 58.

88 Kelly and Puddister, *supra* note 66.

89 See Emmett Macfarlane, "Conservative with the Constitution? Moderation, Strategy, and Institutional Distrust" in J.P. Lewis and Joanna Everitt, eds, *The Blueprint: Conservative Parties and Their Impact on Canadian Politics* (Toronto: University of Toronto Press, 2017) 221 at 234–35.

90 Kirk Makin, "The Coming Conservative Court: Harper to Reshape Judiciary" *Globe and Mail* (13 May 2011), online: <https://www.theglobeandmail.com/news/

politics/the-coming-conservative-court-harper-to-reshape-judiciary/article 595398/>.

91 One could argue that Justice Moldaver's record, and public remarks, indicated a somewhat conservative approach to criminal justice. He was, however, a highly regarded justice on the Court of Appeal; one did not need to appeal to ideological considerations to explain his elevation.

92 Sean Fine, "Harper Nominates Quebec Judge Wagner to Supreme Court" *Globe and Mail* (2 October 2012), online: <https://www.theglobeandmail.com/news/politics/harper-nominates-quebec-judge-wagner-to-supreme-court/article4582006/>.

93 Kheiriddin, *supra* 82 at 209. See also Leonid Sirota, "Both Stephen Harper and His Critics Misunderstand the Nature of the Judiciary and Judging" *Policy Options* (5 October 2015), online: <http://policyoptions.irpp.org/magazines/october-2015/stephen-harper-and-the-judiciary/there-will-be-no-harper-revolution/>.

CHAPTER 3: MEMOS

1 Federal courts are created by statute (specifically authorized under s 101 of the *Constitution Act, 1867* (UK), 30 & 31 Vict, c 3) and have no inherent jurisdiction. Superior courts, by contrast, being modelled on English courts, predate the written Constitution and enjoy inherent jurisdiction that may be added to, but not diminished by, ordinary law.

2 Similarly, Justice Louise Arbour had been legally trained in Quebec but appointed to the Supreme Court of Canada to fill an Ontario seat – after having sat as an Ontario Court of Appeal judge for a number of years.

3 See, e.g., Brian A. Crane, Robert Mainville, and Martin W. Mason, *First Nations Governance Law,* 2nd ed (Toronto: LexisNexis, 2008).

4 The appointment, and the controversy that ensued, is discussed in Chapter 8.

5 See *Bennett v Canada (AG)*, 2013 FCA 161 (CanLII); *Es-Sayyid v Canada (Public Safety and Emergency Preparedness)*, 2012 FCA 59 (CanLII). Interestingly, Justices Mainville and Trudel (another name on the long list) were both on the panel in *Bennett.*

Only two months after releasing its decision in the reference, the Supreme Court issued its ruling in *Cojocaru* – a case concerning the acceptability of judges "cribbing" from the written submissions of a party when crafting opinions. Without mentioning him by name, the court cited an opinion written by none other than Marc Nadon, in which he set out the reasons such a practice should be avoided. See *Cojocaru v British Columbia Women's Hospital and Health Centre,* 2013 SCC 30. See Alain Roussy, "Cut-and-Paste Justice: A Case Comment on *Cojocaru v British Columbia Women's Hospital and Health Centre*" (2015) 52 Alta L Rev 761.

That case, in turn, was an appeal from the decision of Justice Michel Shore, who had "reproduced verbatim, without so saying, approximately 100 paragraphs, including many of the headings, the underlining, the footnotes and the references to the evidence." See *Apotex Inc v Janssen-Ortho Inc*, 2009 FCA 212 (CanLII). Small world.

6 See Sean Fine, "The Secret Short List That Provoked the Rift between Chief Justice and PMO" *Globe and Mail* (23 May 2014), online: <https://www.theglobeandmail.com/news/politics/the-secret-short-list-that-caused-a-rift-between-chief-justice-and-pmo/article18823392/>.

7 *Ibid.*

8 Supreme Court of Canada, News Release (2 May 2014), online: <https://scc-csc.lexum.com/scc-csc/news/en/item/4602/index.do>.

9 *Ibid.*

10 One must therefore take, with a large grain of salt, suggestions that the prime minister had no idea that there might be a legal barrier to appointment until after the Supreme Court of Canada's ruling. Such claims were frequently made. See, e.g., the answer in Order/Address of House of Commons, Q-437 (1 April 2014), online: <http://www.macleans.ca/wp-content/uploads/2014/05/Q-437.pdf> [Q-437]. "The prime minister was first informed that there was a different rule for the appointment of judges from Quebec when the Supreme Court of Canada released its decision (the Nadon decision) on Friday, 21 March 2014. Whether the prime minister sought, received, or reviewed legal advice on this issue, apart from the legal opinion of the Honourable Ian Binnie, is a matter protected by solicitor-client privilege. The legal opinion of Justice Binnie and views of Justice Charron and Professor Hogg were obtained to confirm the government's view on this issue, and the legal opinion of Justice Binnie was made public."

11 Sean Kilpatrick, "Peter MacKay Insists Conservatives Are Not Moving Canada toward U.S.-Style Justice" *National Post* (17 August 2013), online: <https://nationalpost.com/news/politics/peter-mackay-insists-conservatives-are-not-moving-canada-toward-u-s-style-justice>. See the discussion in Chapter 5.

12 For greater clarity, we have not seen these legal opinions and cannot vouch for their content.

13 Howard Anglin, telephone interview with authors, 11 May 2018.

14 It is unclear whether the government sought the legal advice of any Quebec jurists on the eligibility issue. In response to questions by Irwin Cotler, the government asserted solicitor-client privilege over this information. See answers to (j) (i) to (iii), (k), (o) (i) to (iii), (p) and (dd) in Q-437, *supra* note 10. An Access to Information Act request for documents pertaining to the outside consultations, running to 460 pages, was likewise found to be protected by solicitor-client privilege. The sheer number of documents, however, is telling. Alison Crawford, "Judges' Advice on Marc Nadon Supreme Court Appointment Cost $11K" *CBC News* (25

January 2014), online: <http://www.cbc.ca/news/politics/judges-advice-on-marc-nadon-supreme-court-appointment-cost-11k-1.2511202>.

15 Obviously, that confidentiality has since been waived by the government's disclosure of her retainer, which is why she was prepared to speak to us.

16 Louise Charron, telephone interview with authors, 17 May 2018.

17 Howard Anglin, telephone interview with authors, 11 May 2018.

18 The Binnie memorandum contains questions identical to those that Charron says she was asked, corroborating Charron's recollection that she was not asked about the prospects for reforming the law.

19 In response to a question by Irwin Cotler, the government stated: "Both Justice Charron and Professor Hogg indicated that they agreed with the conclusion reached that: a) a person who has been a member the Quebec Bar for at least 10 years, but is now a judge of the Federal Court or Federal Court of Appeal (occupying one of the positions set aside for members of the Quebec Bar pursuant to s 5.4 of the Federal Courts Act) is eligible to occupy one of the 3 positions set aside for the province of Quebec pursuant to s 6 of the *Supreme Court Act* and that b) it is not necessary for that person to apply or rejoin the Quebec Bar prior to his or her appointment as one of the three judges from Quebec to the Supreme Court of Canada." See answer to (ff) in Q-437, *supra* note 10.

20 Hugo Cyr, "The Bungling of Justice Nadon's Appointment to the Supreme Court of Canada" (2014) 67 SCLR (2nd) 73 at 75.

21 According to the government's account, Hogg did not provide a separate opinion but indicated his support of Binnie's memorandum.

22 Marc Nadon, telephone interview, 4 June 2018.

23 Susana Mas, "Justice Marc Nadon Chosen for Supreme Court" *CBC News* (30 September 2013), online: <https://www.cbc.ca/news/politics/justice-marc-nadon-chosen-for-supreme-court-1.1873360>.

24 Department of Justice, Judicial Appointments, "Ad Hoc Committee on the Appointment of Supreme Court of Canada Justices," online: <http://www.justice.gc.ca/eng/news-nouv/ja-nj/2013/doc_32972.html> [Ad Hoc Committee]. Note that the reference to Louise Arbour proceeding from the private bar is an error – she was appointed from the Ontario Court of Appeal.

25 *Ibid.*

26 *Galati v Harper,* 2014 FC 1088.

27 See Supreme Court of Canada, News Release (8 October 2013), online: <http://scc-csc.lexum.com/scc-csc/news/en/item/4401/index.do>; Sean Fine, "Justice Nadon Steps Aside While Legal Challenge Heard" *Globe and Mail* (9 October 2013) A3; Tobi Cohen, "Supreme Court Appointment Challenged; Judicial Review; Activist Lawyer Argues Nadon Not Qualified" *National Post* (9 October 2013) A5.

28 "Quebec Bar Urges Quick Hearing on Justice Marc Nadon's Eligibility" *CBC News* (11 October 2013), online: <http://www.cbc.ca/news/quebec-bar-urges-quick-hearing-on-justice-marc-nadon-s-eligibility-1.1991948>.

29 Patrick Bergeron, "Cour suprême: Québec va contester la nomination de Marc Nadon" *La Presse* (17 October 2013), online: <http://www.lapresse.ca/actualites/justice-et-faits-divers/201310/17/01-4700699-cour-supreme-quebec-va-contester-la-nomination-de-marc-nadon.php>.

30 Michael Plaxton and Carissima Mathen, "Purposive Interpretation, Quebec, and the *Supreme Court Act*" (2013) 22 Const Forum Const 15.

31 See Francoise Boivin, 28 October 2013, Ad Hoc Committee, *supra* note 23.

32 Peter MacKay, 17 October 2013, Canada, *House of Commons Debates,* 41st Parl, 2nd Sess, No 2 (17 October 2013), online: <http://www.ourcommons.ca/DocumentViewer/en/41-2/house/sitting-2/hansard#Int-8098417>.

33 Robert Goguen, 18 October 2013, Canada, *House of Commons Debates,* 41st Parl, 2nd Sess, No 2 (18 October 2013), online: <http://www.ourcommons.ca/DocumentViewer/en/41-2/house/sitting-3/hansard#Int-8099258>.

34 Memorandum from the Honourable Ian Binnie (9 September 2013) at 5 [Binnie Memorandum], in the Appendix to this volume.

35 *Ibid* at 3. There is clear Supreme Court authority for the proposition that the two versions must be read together so that they share a single harmonious meaning: see *R v Daoust,* [2004] 1 SCR 217 at para 28.

36 Binnie Memorandum, *ibid* at 4 [emphasis in original].

37 *Ibid* at 4–5 [emphasis in original].

38 *R v Daoust,* [2004] 1 SCR 217 at para 28.

39 Binnie Memorandum, *supra* note 34 at 8.

40 *Ibid* at 5 [emphasis in original].

41 *Ibid* at 5–7, citing *Supreme Court Act,* RSC 1952, c 35, s 5.

42 *Ibid* citing *Supreme Court Act*, S.C. 1926–27, c. 38, s. 1.

43 Binnie Memorandum, *supra* note 34 at 5.

44 *Ibid* at 7.

45 Senate Standing Committee on Legal and Constitutional Affairs, 42nd Parl, 1st Sess (27 November 2013) at 1:23–25 [Senate Standing Committee].

46 *Ibid* at 1:27.

47 *Ibid* at 1:43.

48 *Ibid.*

49 Much later, another retired member of the Supreme Court of Canada, Justice Jack Major, also suggested that he had accepted Binnie's reasoning: Tonda MacCharles, "Former Supreme Court Judge Critical of Both Harper and Court's Ruling on Marc Nadon" *Toronto Star* (27 May 2014), online: <https://www.thestar.

com/news/canada/2014/05/27/former_supreme_court_judge_critical_of_both_harper_and_courts_ruling_on_marc_nadon.html>.

50 See, e.g., Michael Plaxton and Carissima Mathen, "Purposive Interpretation, Quebec, and the *Supreme Court Act*" (2013) 22 Const Forum Const 15.

51 See Paul Daly's submissions to the Senate Standing Committee, *supra* 45 at 1:32: "Section 5 is not at the heart of this. I think everyone who has looked at this question agrees that s 5 allows anyone who has practiced for any period of 10 years to become a member of the Supreme Court of Canada, and that includes judges of the federal courts." But note Rocco Galati's submissions to the Supreme Court of Canada.

52 On the significance of the difference, see *Interpretation Act,* RSC 1985, c I-21, s 11.

53 Paul Daly, "Submissions to Senate Standing Committee on Legal and Constitutional Affairs re Modifications to the Supreme Court Act" (19 November 2013), online: <https://papers.ssrn.com/sol3/papers.cfm?abstract_id=2357273> at 6.

54 *Supreme Court Act,* RSC 1985, c S-26, s 30.

55 *Ibid* at 7–8. See also his oral submissions, Senate Standing Committee, *supra* note 40 at 1:32.

56 Robert Décary, Alice Desjardins, and Gilles Létourneau, Supreme Court of Canada, Factums on Appeal, No 35586, *In the Matter of Section 53 of the Supreme Court Act, RSC 1985, c S-26,* online: <https://www.scc-csc.ca/case-dossier/info/af-ma-eng.aspx?cas=35586>.

57 One way for Parliament to fix this problem would have been to legislate that either the judge or assistant judge could sit as ad hoc judges on the Supreme Court of Canada, whether the case was from a common law or civil law jurisdiction. That solution, however, would lead to the reverse problem: in a non-Quebec case where quorum had been lost as a result of the absence of common law judges, there might well end up being a majority of civil law judges on the panel. This potential outcome was unacceptable to anglophone parliamentarians. Moreover, there was nothing requiring the judge to be from a common law jurisdiction or the assistant judge to be from a civil law background. Declaring in legislation that one must be eligible in some appeals, while setting out that the other must be eligible in others, would be fraught with danger.

58 Ian Bushnell, *The Federal Court of Canada: A History, 1975–1992* (Toronto: Osgoode Society for Canadian Legal History, 1997) at 95–97. See also Reynald Boult, "Ad Hoc Judges of the Supreme Court of Canada" (1979) 26 Chitty's LJ 289.

59 See Chapter 6, note 3 and accompanying text.

60 Binnie Memorandum, *supra* note 34 at 5.

61 *Supreme and Exchequer Courts Act,* SC 1875, c 11, s 4.

62 Canada, *House of Commons Debates,* 3rd Parl, 2nd Sess, No 20 (30 March 1875) at 970–71.

63 *Ibid* at 972 (Hon. Mr. Mills, Hon. Sir John MacDonald).

64 *Ibid* at 971.

65 *Ibid* at 972.

66 *Ibid* at 971.

67 *Ibid.*

68 *Ibid* at 974 (Mr. Bunster).

69 Frank Mackinnon, "The Establishment of the Supreme Court of Canada" in W.R. Lederman, ed, *The Courts and the Canadian Constitution* (Toronto: McClelland and Stewart, 1964) 106 at 112. See also James G. Snell and Frederick Vaughan, *The Supreme Court of Canada: History of the Institution* (Toronto: University of Toronto Press/Osgoode Society for Canadian Legal History, 1985) at 8.

70 Peter H. Russell, *The Supreme Court of Canada as a Bilingual and Bicultural Institution,* Documents of the Royal Commission on Bilingualism and Biculturalism, vol 1 (Ottawa: Queen's Printer, 1969) at 13.

71 Canada, *House of Commons Debates,* 3rd Parl, 2nd Sess, No 20 (25 March 1875) at 921–22.

72 Russell, *supra* note 70 at 14, citing *ibid* at 937.

73 *Ibid* at 14.

74 *Ibid.*

75 See also P.B. Waite, *Arduous Destiny: Canada, 1874–1896* (Toronto: McClelland and Stewart, 1971) at 38–39. As minister of justice, Blake immediately became interested in the new Supreme Court of Canada, established in the session of 1875 after a number of false starts. Blake asked Macdonald as early as 1868 if the Conservative government was going to establish a Supreme Court. Macdonald said, "Yes, certainly," and that he hoped a bill would be introduced in the session of 1869. A bill was introduced in 1869, but it was deferred; in 1870, Blake again asked questions. The Conservatives never did bring it in because the French Canadian wing of the party – led by Cartier, Langevin, and Chapais – opposed it, saying that only two of the proposed seven judges would be French Canadian and that the others would be unfamiliar with French Canadian civil law. Chapais, at least, was not opposed to an outrance, and rather than upsetting the government, he would have accepted the Supreme Court, but Macdonald never pressed the issue that far.

76 Canada, *House of Commons Debates,* 21st Parl, 1st Sess, No 20 (4 October 1949) at 662. He continued at 662–63: "We knew that when we created the supreme court as the court of last resort for Canada we would have to have appointed

to the membership of that court enough civilians or judges trained in the civil law so that, in the event of there coming from Quebec a case involving any matters other than criminal law, it would be decided without a stalemate, having one civilian judge on one side and one civilian judge on the other. That necessitated the appointment of three judges trained in the civil law on that court of last resort."

77 See *1949 Yearbook of the Canadian Bar Association and the Minutes of Proceedings of the Thirty-First Annual Meeting* (Ottawa: National Printers, 1949) at 54–55.

78 See, e.g., Canada, *House of Commons Debates,* 21st Parl, 1st Sess, No 20 (4 October 1949) at 509; Canada, *Debates of the Senate,* 21st Parl, 1st Sess, No 20 (19 October 1949) at 132.

79 Binnie Memorandum, *supra* note 34 at 7.

80 *Ibid* at 8.

81 Senate Standing Committee, *supra* note 45 (21 November 2013).

82 Daly, *supra* 51 at 6.

83 Michael Plaxton and Carissima Mathen, "Purposive Interpretation, Quebec, and the *Supreme Court Act*" (2013) 22 Const Forum Const 15; *supra* note 53.

84 *Canada Elections Act,* SC 2000, c 9, s 3.

85 On the over- and underinclusiveness of legal rules, see Frederick Schauer, *Playing by the Rules: A Philosophical Examination of Rule-Based Decision-Making in Law and in Life* (Oxford: Clarendon, 1991) at 31–44.

86 See *ibid* at ch 5. Sometimes, of course, the legislature will want to encourage people to reflect on the background reasons for doing or not doing something. Under those circumstances, it may be sensible to incorporate open-ended standards into the text of a statute. For discussion, see Jeremy Waldron, "Vagueness and the Guidance of Action" in Andrei Marmor and Scott Soames, eds, *Philosophical Foundations of Language in the Law* (Oxford: Oxford University Press, 2011) 58.

87 See Snell and Vaughan, *supra* note 67 at chs 1 and 2.

88 See Russell, *supra* note 68 at 14.

89 Ian Bushnell, *The Captive Court: A Study of the Supreme Court of Canada* (Montreal and Kingston: McGill-Queen's University Press, 1992) at 263.

90 *Ibid* at 263.

91 Diaries of William Lyon Mackenzie King, Library and Archives Canada (LAC), Item 21272, online: <http://www.bac-lac.gc.ca/eng/discover/politics-government/prime-ministers/william-lyon-mackenzie-king/Pages/item.aspx?IdNumber=21272&>.

92 *Ibid.* King also noted that this "would solve the question of further consideration of Taschereau himself for the Senate which, on personal grounds, and because of his long public service, [he] would like to have given him."

93 Memorandum of Deputy Minister of Justice to Minister of Justice, 29 January 1940, at 1, LAC, RG 13, Department of Justice, file number 141312 [DMJ Memorandum]. On file with the authors.

94 *Ibid.*

95 "Roy, Ferdinand," *Directory of Quebec's Cultural Heritage*, online: <http://www.patrimoine-culturel.gouv.qc.ca/rpcq/detail.do?methode=consulter&id=9612&type=pge#.XVAn_pNKjOQ>.

96 DMJ Memorandum, *supra* note 92 at 2.

97 Memorandum of Charles Stein to the Deputy Minister of Justice, 30 January 1940, LAC, RG 13, Department of Justice, file number 141312 [CS Memorandum], on file with the authors. For a short biography of Stein, see Mélanie Brunet, *Out of the Shadows: The Civil Law Tradition in the Department of Justice Canada, 1868–2000* (Ottawa: Department of Justice, 2000) at 31, online: <https://www.justice.gc.ca/eng/rp-pr/other-autre/civil/index.html>.

98 *Ibid* at 1–2.

99 *Ibid.*

100 *Ibid.*

CHAPTER 4: ASKING AND TELLING

1 *Economic Action Plan 2013 Act, No 1* SC 2013, c 33.

2 Adam Dodek, "Omnibus Bills: Constitutional Constraints and Legislative Liberations" (2017) 48 Ottawa L Rev 1; Louis Massicotte, "Omnibus Bills in Theory and Practice" (2013) Can Parliamentary Rev 13 at 16–17.

3 It should be noted that some of the pernicious effects of omnibus bills on debate were curbed by referring different aspects of Bill C-4 to different standing committees. Thus, the House Standing Committee on Justice and Human Rights heard evidence on ss 471 and 472, even though, as a budget bill, it would have ordinarily been scrutinized by the Standing Committee on Finance.

4 Dodek, *supra* note 2 at 14–18.

5 Aaron Wherry, "Twenty Years of (Expanding) Budget Bills" *Maclean's* (28 October 2014), online: <http://www.macleans.ca/politics/twenty-years-of-expanding-budget-bills/>; Aaron Wherry, "Another Omnibus Budget Bill and a Test of Parliament's Will" *Maclean's* (15 May 2015), online: <http://www.macleans.ca/politics/another-omnibus-budget-bill-and-a-test-of-parliaments-will/>; Aaron Wherry, "Speaker Splits Up Liberal Omnibus Budget Bill, Thanks to New Liberal Rule" *CBC News* (8 November 2017), online: <http://www.cbc.ca/news/politics/omnibus-liberals-speaker-analysis-wherry-1.4393690>; Aaron Wherry, "New Liberal Budget Bill Raises Old Concerns about Omnibus Legislation" *CBC News* (24 April 2016), online: <http://www.cbc.ca/news/politics/budget-omnibus-wherry-1.3550676>.

6 Bill C-9, *An Act to implement certain provisions of the budget tabled in Parliament on March 4, 2010 and other measures,* 3rd Sess, 40th Parl, 2010.

7 Bill C-13, *An Act to implement certain provisions of the 2011 budget as updated on June 6, 2011 and other measures,* 1st Sess, 45th Parl, 2011.

8 Bill C-38, *An Act to implement certain provisions of the budget tabled in Parliament on March 29, 2012 and other measures,* 1st Sess, 41st Parl, 2011–12; Bill C-45, *A second Act to implement certain provisions of the budget tabled in Parliament on March 29, 2012 and other measures,* 1st Sess, 41st Parl, 2011–12.

9 See, e.g., Kady O'Malley, "Omnibudget Watch: So Now What?" *Inside Politics Blog* (31 October 2012), online: <http://www.cbc.ca/newsblogs/politics/inside-politics-blog/2012/10/omnibudget-watch-so-now-what.html>.

10 Dodek, *supra* note 2 at 6.

11 *Régie des rentes du Québec v Canada Bread Company Ltd,* [2013] SCJ No 46, [2013] 3 SCR 125, 2013 SCC 46, at paras 28, 48 (SCC) [*Canada Bread*].

12 *Ibid* at para 27.

13 *Ibid* at para 29, citing *Western Minerals Ltd v Gaumont,* [1953] 1 SCR 345.

14 *Canada Bread, supra* note 11 at para 28.

15 *Ibid* at para 2.

16 Paul Daly, "Submissions to Senate Standing Committee on Legal and Constitutional Affairs re Modifications to the Supreme Court Act" (19 November 2013), online: <https://papers.ssrn.com/sol3/papers.cfm?abstract_id=2357273> at 17, citing *Buckley v Attorney General,* [1950] 1 IR 67.

17 See the discussion in Chapter 3.

18 Peter Hogg, *Constitutional Law of Canada,* 5th ed Supp (Toronto: Thomson Carswell, 2007) at 4–21.

19 *Ibid; Reference re Supreme Court Act, ss 5 and 6,* 2014 SCC 21, [2014] 1 SCR 433 at para 97 [*Supreme Court Act Reference*].

20 Benoit Pelletier, *La modification constitutionelle du Canada* (Toronto: Carswell, 1996) at 53, note 154. See also his submissions to the Senate Standing Committee on Legal and Constitutional Affairs, 42nd Parl, 2nd Sess (27 November 2013) at 1:37 [Senate Standing Committee].

21 Patrick J. Monahan and Byron Shaw, *Constitutional Law,* 4th ed (Toronto: Irwin, 2013) at 204.

22 *Ibid.*

23 Daly, *supra* note 16 at 22, citing James Ross Hurley, *La modification de la Constitution du Canada: Historique, processus, problemes et perspectives d'avenir* (Ottawa: Government of Canada, 1996) at 81.

24 As Daly suggests in his Senate submissions, *supra* note 16 at 21, one can read the Quebec Court of Appeal's decision in *Projet de loi federal relative au Senat (Re),* 2013 QCCA 1807 at paras 30, 33–34, as standing for a particularly radical version of this teleological approach.

25 Peter Oliver, "Canada, Quebec and Constitutional Amendment" (1999) 49 UTLJ 519 at 580.

26 Warren Newman, "The Constitutional Status of the Supreme Court of Canada" (2009), 74 SCLR (2nd) 429 at 435.

27 Attorney General of Canada, Supreme Court of Canada, Factums on Appeal, No 35586, *In the Matter of Section 53 of the Supreme Court Act, RSC 1985, c S-26,* at para 90 [Factums on Appeal], online: <https://www.scc-csc.ca/case-dossier/info/af-ma-eng.aspx?cas=35586>.

28 *Re: Authority of Parliament in relation to the Upper House,* [1980] 1 SCR 54.

29 Attorney General of Canada, Factums on Appeal, *supra* note 27 at 36.

30 Newman, *supra* note 26 at 436.

31 *Ibid* at 439.

32 Daly, *supra* note 16 at 25.

33 Senate Standing Committee, *supra* note 20 at 1:41.

34 *Ibid* at 1:49.

35 *Reference, supra* note 19 at 443.

36 House of Commons, Standing Committee on Justice and Human Rights, 41st Parl, 2nd Sess, No 006, Evidence (21 November 2013) at 0920 [Standing Committee on Justice and Human Rights], online: <https://www.ourcommons.ca/DocumentViewer/en/41-2/JUST/meeting-6/evidence>.

37 Hugo Cyr, "The Bungling of Justice Nadon's Appointment to the Supreme Court of Canada" (2014) 67 SCLR (2nd) 73 at 83. In particular, the scandal involving the expense claims of Harper-appointed senator Mike Duffy had started to heat up only a few months earlier.

38 Senate Standing Committee, *supra* note 20 at 1:35 (Bastarache).

39 *Ibid* at 1:46 (Mathen) and 1:48 (Mathen, Bastarache).

40 See *Reference re: Anti-inflation Act (Canada),* [1976] SCJ No 12, [1976] 2 SCR 373, 68 DLR (3d) 452 (SCC). Standing Committee on Justice and Human Rights, *supra* note 36 at 0850.

41 See Supreme Court of Canada, Case Information, Docket 3558, "In the Matter of Section 53 of the Supreme Court Act, R.S.C. 1985, c. S-26; et al.," online: <http://www.scc-csc.gc.ca/case-dossier/info/dock-regi-eng.aspx?cas=35586>. See also Bruce Cheadle, "Supreme Court Quarantines Marc Nadon Until Challenge Heard" *Toronto Star* (3 November 2013), online: <http://www.thestar.com/news/canada/2013/11/03/supreme_court_quarantines_marc_nadon_until_challenge_heard.html>.

CHAPTER 5: THE LEGAL SHOWDOWN

1 Supreme Court Act, RSC 1985, c S-26, s 53. There is a further section, s 54, which permits references from the Senate and House of Commons, but it is

largely defunct. Provinces may initiate references in the various courts operating in the provinces, from which there is an automatic right of appeal: s 36.

2 The former justices were Robert Décary, Alice Desjardins, and Gilles Létourneau.

3 Marshall Rothstein, telephone interview, 5 September 2018. Indeed, Rothstein can be seen in a photograph at Nadon's swearing-in ceremony at the Federal Court in 1993.

4 The suggestion that Justice Rothstein recused for this reason was floated by Paul Daly at the time: Paul Daly, "L'affaire Nadon: A Note on Justice Rosthein's Recusal" (10 December 2013) *Paul Daly: Administrative Law Matters* (blog), online: <http://www.administrativelawmatters.com/blog/2013/12/10/laffaire-nadon-a-note-on-justice-rothsteins-recusal/>.

5 Alison Crawford, "Supreme Court Justice Rothstein Won't Hear Nadon Reference" *CBC News* (10 December 2013), online: <http://www.cbc.ca/news/politics/supreme-court-justice-rothstein-won-t-hear-nadon-reference-1.2458371>.

6 The same is not true for references initiated by provincial governments. These must first be heard by provincial courts of appeal (or, rarely, superior courts), the results of which may be appealed. *Supreme Court Act,* RSC, 1985, c S-26, s 36.

7 Michael Plaxton and Carissima Mathen, "Purposive Interpretation, Quebec, and the *Supreme Court Act*" (2013) 22 Const Forum Const 15. Note, though, that we did not strongly press this interpretation.

8 *Reference re Supreme Court Act, ss 5 and 6,* 2014 SCC 21, [2014] 1 SCR 433 at para 21 [*Supreme Court Act Reference*] [emphasis in original]:

> 4. Her Majesty may appoint, by letters patent, under the Great Seal of Canada, one person, who is, or has been, a Judge of one of the Superior Courts in any of the Provinces forming part of the Dominion of Canada, or who is a Barrister or Advocate of at least ten years' standing at the Bar of any one of the said Provinces, to be Chief Justice of the said Court, and five persons *who are, or have been, respectively, Judges* of one of the said Superior Courts, *or who are Barristers or Advocates* of at least ten years' standing at the Bar of one of the said Provinces, to be Puisne Judges of the said Court, *two of whom at least shall be taken from among the Judges of the Superior Court or Court of Queen's Bench, or the Barristers or Advocates of the Province of Quebec.*
>
> 4. Sa Majesté pourra nommer, par lettres patentes sous le grand sceau du Canada, – comme juge en chef de cette cour, – une personne étant ou ayant été juge de l'une des cours supérieures dans quelqu'une des provinces formant la Puissance du Canada, ou un avocat ayant pratiqué pendant au moins dix ans au barreau de quelqu'une de ces provinces, et, – comme juges puînés de cette cour, – cinq personnes *étant ou ayant*

> *été respectivement juges* de l'une de ces cours supérieures, *ou étant avocats* de pas moins de dix ans de pratique au barreau de quelqu'une de ces provinces, *dont deux au moins seront pris parmi les juges de la Cour Supérieure ou de la Cour du Banc de la Reine, ou parmi les procureurs ou avocats de la province de Québec.*

9 Attorney General of Canada, Supreme Court of Canada, Factums on Appeal, No 35586, *In the Matter of Section 53 of the Supreme Court Act, RSC 1985, c S-26,* at para 20 [Factums on Appeal], online: <https://www.scc-csc.ca/case-dossier/info/af-ma-eng.aspx?cas=35586>.

10 *Ibid* at paras 21–25 [in-text citations removed; emphasis added].

11 *Ibid* at paras 53–54.

12 See the discussion of the strategy in Chapter 4.

13 Attorney General of Canada, Factums on Appeal, *supra* note 9 at para 77; Federal Courts Act, RSC 1985, c F-7, as am., ss 5.3, 5.4; Judges Act, RSC 1985, c J-1, as am., s 3.

14 *The Attorney-General of Ontario and others v The Attorney-General of Canada and others and The Attorney-General of Quebec (Canada)* [1947] UKPC 1.

15 Attorney General of Canada, Factums on Appeal, *supra* note 9 at para 84. Here, Canada cites *An Act to amend the Federal Court Act, the Crown Liability Act, the Supreme Court Act and other Acts in consequence thereof,* SC 1990, c 8, ss 33–49; *Miscellaneous Statute Law Amendment Act,* 1993, SC 1993, c 34, ss 115–17; *Criminal Law Amendment Act,* 1994, SC 1994, c 44, ss 98–102; *Criminal Law Improvement Act,* 1996, SC 1997, c 18, ss 98–102; *Courts Administration Service Act,* SC 2002, c 8, s 175; *Interpretation Act,* RSC 1985, c I-21, s 11, s 42.

16 See the discussion of the "empty vessel" theory in Chapter 4.

17 Attorney General of Canada, Factums on Appeal, *supra* note 9 at paras 75–76 [emphasis added].

18 In the Matter of Section 53 of the Supreme Court Act, RSC 1985, c S-26, et al (Webcast, 15 January 2015), online: <https://www.scc-csc.ca/case-dossier/info/webcastview-webdiffusionvue-eng.aspx?cas=35586&id=2014/2014-01-15--35586&date=2014-01-15&fp=n&audio=n 1:06:05>.

19 In this respect, its strategy was similar to the one employed in the *Senate Reform Reference,* [2014] 1 SCR 704, argued only a few months earlier.

20 Attorney General of Quebec, Factums on Appeal, *supra* note 9 at para 118. "Quebec culture is not confined, in legal matters, to the pure civil law. On the contrary, it extends to everything that emanates from the Quebec legislature and even infuses those laws that the legislature borrows from other legal systems. Thus, for example, the Consumer Protection Act is as much 'civil law' as the Civil Code; and the responsibility of municipalities and corporations, although established by common law, must be assessed in 'civilian' terms."

21 The term "incorporationist" is borrowed from US constitutional law. Incorporation was the doctrine whereby the obligations in the first ten amendments in the Bill of Rights – which on their face apply only to the US federal government – were deemed to have been incorporated into the due process clause of the Fourteenth Amendment and, thus, made binding upon the individual states. See, e.g., *Gitlow v New York* 268 US 652 (1925) (First Amendment).

22 Attorney General of Quebec, Factums on Appeal, *supra* note 9 at para 37.

23 In August 2017, Monahan was appointed to the Ontario Superior Court of Justice: Province of Ontario, News Release, "New Judges Appointed to the Ontario Court of Justice" (28 August 2014), online: <https://news.ontario.ca/mag/en/2014/08/new-judges-appointed-to-the-ontario-court-of-justice-5.html>.

24 See the discussion in Chapter 4.

25 Attorney General of Ontario, Factums on Appeal, *supra* note 9 at para 4. At the hearing, Ontario also stated that such membership could be obtained in separate periods rather than in a continuous ten-year period.

26 *Ibid* at para 48. Normally, such an amendment would fall under the general formula, which requires the assent of both houses of Parliament plus the legislatures of seven provinces with at least 50 percent of the population of the provinces. One would expect that a change to s 101 that affected the court's composition would be subject to the unanimity formula, but Ontario did not specify the appropriate route.

27 *Ibid* at para 33.

28 In the Matter of Section 53 of the Supreme Court Act, RSC 1985, c S-26, et al (Webcast 15 January 2015), online: https://www.scc-csc.ca/case-dossier/info/webcastview-webdiffusionvue-eng.aspx?cas=35586&id=2014/2014-01-15--35586&date=2014-01-15&fp=n&audio=n 4:17:00; 4:34:30.

29 *Ibid* at 4:23:00.

30 *Ibid* at 4:29:00.

31 Though note that the court occasionally has exercised a discretion not to answer questions: see *Reference re Same-Sex Marriage,* [2004] 3 SCR 698, 2004 SCC 79 at para 63; Carissima Mathen, *Courts without Cases: The Law and Politics of Advisory Opinions* (London: Hart, 2019) at ch 4.

32 *Supra* note 28 at 4:15:00.

33 *Ibid* at 4:31:00.

34 *Ibid* at 4:54:00.

35 *Ibid* at 4:46:00.

36 "Rocco Galati Challenges Bank of Canada to Offer Interest-Free Loans" *CBC News* (8 May 2015), online: <https://www.cbc.ca/news/business/rocco-galati-challenges-bank-of-canada-to-offer-interest-free-loans-1.3065650>.

37 Sean Fine, "The Lawyer Who Challenged the Harper Government and Won" *Globe and Mail* (22 August 2014), online: <https://www.theglobeandmail.

com/report-on-business/careers/careers-leadership/rocco-galati-is-always-fighting-for-long-shots/article20176185/>.

38 *Ibid.*

39 *Ibid.*

40 See *Felipa v Canada (Citizenship and Immigration)*, 2011 FCA 272 (CanLII).

41 Michael McKiernan, "Judging the Judges" *Canadian Lawyer Magazine* (6 February 2012), online: <http://www.canadianlawyermag.com/author/michael-mckiernan/judging-the-judges-1484/>.

42 *Ibid.*

43 Jason Markusoff, Charlie Gillis, and Michael Friscolanti, "The Robin Camp Case: Who Judges Judges?" *Maclean's* (14 September 2016), online: <http://www.macleans.ca/news/robin-camp-case-who-judges-the-judges/>.

44 Application for judicial review submitted by Alex Chapman, Federal Court, No T-1789-12, online: <https://www.cjc-ccm.gc.ca/cmslib/general/Douglas_Docs/Chapman%20JR%20Application%202012-09-26.pdf>; Christie Blatchford, "Inquiry Decisions in Judge Douglas Case Should Be Overturned" *Canada.com* (20 August 2012), online: <http://o.canada.com/news/inquiry-decisions-in-judge-douglas-case-should-be-overturned-2>.

45 Shannon Kari, "Galati Questions Appointment of Law Prof to Appeal Court" *Law Times* (12 January 2015), online: <http://www.lawtimesnews.com/author/shannon-kari/galati-questions-appointment-of-law-prof-to-appeal-court-11664/>.

46 *Ibid.*

47 *Galati v Harper,* 2014 FC 1088.

48 *Galati v Harper,* 2016 FCA 39 (CanLII) at paras 35–36. See also Canadian Press, "Judge Slams 'Gonzo Logic' of Two Lawyers Who Want $70,000 for Fighting Supreme Court Appointment" *National Post* (9 February 2016), online: <http://nationalpost.com/news/politics/judge-slams-gonzo-logic-of-two-lawyers-who-want-70000-for-fighting-supreme-court-appointment>.

49 Rocco Galati, Factums on Appeal, *supra* note 9 at para 6.

50 *Ibid* at paras 37–38.

51 *Ibid* at paras 40–47.

52 *Ibid* at para 6 [emphasis added].

53 *Ibid* at para 56 [emphasis added].

54 *Supra* note 28 at 5:16:00.

55 The principal point of distinction between inferior and superior courts is that the latter are not created by the legislative branch. They exist by virtue of their own force that predates Confederation and that is protected from interference by the doctrine of judicial independence.

56 But see cases in which it was argued that judicial remuneration schemes and processes compromised judicial independence: *Ref re Remuneration of Judges of*

Prov Court of PEI; Ref re Independence and Impartiality of Judges of Prov Court of PEI; R v Campbell; R v Ekmecic; R v Wickman; Manitoba Prov Judges Assn v Manitoba (Min of Justice), [1998] 2 SCR 443.

57 See the discussion in Chapter 3.

58 Canadian Association of Provincial Court Judges, Factums on Appeal, *supra* note 9 at para 15.

59 *Ibid.*

60 *Supra* note 28 at 1:40:00.

61 *Ibid* at 1:45:00.

62 Interview with *CTV Power Play*, 14 March 2014.

63 *Reference, supra* note 8 at para 71.

64 *Ibid* at para 152:

> My colleagues have chosen not to address the scope of the currency requirement under section 6, i.e. whether one day's renewed membership at the Quebec bar is sufficient to qualify as an advocate or whether something more is needed – six months, two years, five years, or perhaps even a continuous 10-year period immediately preceding the appointment.
>
> In my view, currency means exactly that. A former Quebec superior court judge or advocate of 10 years standing at the Quebec bar could rejoin that bar for a day and thereby regain his or her eligibility for appointment to this Court. In my view, this exposes the hollowness of the currency requirement. Surely nothing is accomplished by what is essentially an administrative act. Any interpretation of section 6 that requires a former advocate of at least 10 years standing at the Quebec bar, or a former judge of the Quebec Court of Appeal or Superior Court, to rejoin the Quebec bar for a day in order to be eligible for appointment to this Court makes no practical sense. Respectfully, I find it difficult to believe that the people of Quebec would somehow have more confidence in this candidate on Friday than they had on Thursday.

65 *Ibid* at para 152.

CHAPTER 6: THE OPINION AND ITS CRITICS

1 The majority was a rare joint opinion signed by each one of the six judges who agreed with it. Plainly, they had hoped to issue a *per curiam* or "by the court" opinion, but the dissent made that impossible. The majority, therefore, has no single identifiable author; it has, rather, six of them. In a recent paper, Peter MacCormick used linguistic analysis to conclude that Chief Justice McLachlin was the "most likely author of the initial draft": see "Nom de Plume: Who Writes the Supreme Court's 'By the Court' Judgments?" (2016) 39 Dal LJ 77 at 117.

2 *Reference re Supreme Court Act, ss 5 and 6,* 2014 SCC 21 at paras 28–34 [*Reference*].

3 *Ibid* at paras 39–45.

4 *Ibid* at para 49.

5 *Ibid.*

6 Peter H. Russell, *The Supreme Court of Canada as a Bilingual and Bicultural Institution,* Documents of the Royal Commission on Bilingualism and Biculturalism, vol 1 (Ottawa: Queen's Printer, 1969) at 8 [original emphasis].

7 *Ibid* at para 54 citing Canada, *House of Commons Debates* (27 March 1875) at 940.

8 *Reference, supra* note 2 at para 56.

9 *Ibid* at para 57.

10 *Ibid* at para 58.

11 *Ibid* at para 60.

12 *Ibid* at para 63.

13 *Ibid* at paras 63–66.

14 *Ibid* at para 67.

15 *Ibid* at para 139.

16 *Ibid* at para 74.

17 *Ibid* at para 82.

18 *Ibid* at para 83, citing *Reference re Securities Act,* 2011 SCC 66 at para 55; *Reference re Secession of Quebec,* [1998] 2 SCR 217 at para 53.

19 *Reference, supra* note 2 at para 85.

20 *Ibid* at para 86, citing *R v Henry,* 2005 SCC 76 at para 53.

21 *Reference, supra* note 2 at para 89, citing *Hunter v Southam,* [1984] 2 SCR 145 at 155.

22 *Reference, supra* note 2 at para 90.

23 *Ibid* at para 92.

24 *Ibid* at para 93.

25 *Ibid* at para 98.

26 *Ibid* at para 100.

27 *Ibid* at para 99.

28 *Ibid* at paras 102–3.

29 Grant Huscroft, "The Supreme Court's Faulty Logic on Nadon" *National Post* (25 March 2014), online: <http://news.nationalpost.com/full-comment/grant-huscroft-the-supreme-courts-faulty-logic-on-nadon>.

30 *Ibid.*

31 Andrew Coyne, "Flaky Supreme Court Ruling Meets Dubious Appointment" *National Post* (24 March 2014), online: <http://news.nationalpost.com/full-comment/andrew-coyne-on-marc-nadon-flaky-supreme-court-ruling-meets-dubious-appointment>.

32 *Ibid.*

33 *Ibid.*

34 Leonid Sirota, "What You Wish For" (22 March 2014) *Double Aspect Blog,* online: <https://doubleaspect.blog/2014/03/22/what-you-wish-for/>.

35 Tonda MacCharles, "Former Supreme Court Judge Critical of Both Harper and Court's Ruling on Marc Nadon" *Toronto Star* (27 May 2014), online: <https://www.thestar.com/news/canada/2014/05/27/former_supreme_court_judge_critical_of_both_harper_and_courts_ruling_on_marc_nadon.html>.

36 Louise Charron, telephone interview with authors, 17 May 2018. *Brown v Allen,* 344 US 443 (1953): "We are not final because we are infallible, but we are infallible only because we are final" (per Justice Jackson, concurring).

37 Sean Fine, "Supreme Court's Rejection of Nadon Is a Legal Marker and a Political Blow" *Globe and Mail* (21 March 2014), online: <http://www.theglobeandmail.com/news/politics/supreme-courts-rejection-of-nadon-is-a-legal-marker-and-a-political-blow/article17625541/>.

38 John Geddes, "Q & A: Supreme Court of Canada Rejects Harper Appointment" *Maclean's* (21 March 2014), online: <http://www.macleans.ca/politics/ottawa/q-a-supreme-court-of-canadas-rejects-a-harper-appointment/>. See also Carissima Mathen, "Nadon Ruling Hits Like an Earthquake" *Ottawa Citizen* (21 March 2014) A8.

39 John Geddes, "The 'Free the Beer' Ruling and the Supreme Court's Record of Putting the Brakes on Change" *Maclean's* (19 April 2018), online: <http://www.macleans.ca/politics/ottawa/the-supreme-courts-record-of-putting-the-brakes-on-change/>.

40 Laura Stone, "Justice Marc Nadon Speaks 'At Least This Has Certainly Ended the Uncertainty'" *Global News* (25 March 2014), online: <https://globalnews.ca/news/1229811/nadon/>.

41 See Margaret Jane Radin "Risk-of-Error Rules and Non-ideal Justification" (1986) 28 Nomos 33. On "bounded rationality," see Daniel Kahneman, *Thinking Fast and Slow* (Toronto: Anchor Canada, 2012) at ch 13; Richard Thaler and Cass Sunstein, *Nudge: Improving Decisions about Health, Wealth, and Happiness* (New York: Penguin, 2009).

42 See, e.g., *Palmore v Sidoti,* 466 US 429 (1984), as discussed in Frederick Schauer, *Playing by the Rules: A Philosophical Examination of Rule-Based Decision-Making in Law and in Life* (Oxford: Clarendon, 1991) at 151.

43 See Kahneman, *supra* note 41 at ch 13; Thaler and Sunstein, *supra* note 41.

44 Kahneman, *supra* note 41 at 224.

45 In the American context, see Michael J. Saks and Barbara A. Spellman, *The Psychological Foundations of Evidence Law* (New York: NYU Press, 2016).

46 See Pierre Schlag, "Rules and Standards" (1985) 33 UCLA L Rev 379; Schauer, *supra* note 42 at 137–38.

47 Schauer, *supra* note 42 at 159. See also Kathleen M. Sullivan, "Foreword: The Justices of Rules and Standards" (1992) 106 Harv L Rev 22 at 64–66; Antonin Scalia, "The Rule of Law as a Law of Rules" (1989) 56 U Chicago L Rev 1175 at 1179–82.

48 Schauer, *supra* note 42 at 159.

49 For a particularly emphatic argument that the discretion of administrative actors should be subject, where possible, to highly specific, rule-based constraints, see Kenneth Culp Davis, *Discretionary Justice: A Preliminary Inquiry* (Baton Rouge: Louisiana State University Press, 1969). Consider also the critiques of discretionary power by administrative actors in F.A. Hayek, *The Constitution of Liberty* (Chicago: University of Chicago Press) at 207–12; F.W. Maitland, *A Historical Sketch of Liberty and Equality* (Indianapolis: Liberty Fund, 1875) at 110.

50 To some extent, this idea finds expression in the "void for vagueness" case authorities in Canada: see *R v Nova Scotia Pharmaceuticals,* [1992] 2 SCR 606; Marc Ribeiro, *Limiting Arbitrary Power: The Vagueness Doctrine in Canadian Constitutional Law* (Vancouver: UBC Press, 2004). See also Lon Fuller, *The Morality of Law,* revised ed (New Haven: Yale University Press, 1969).

51 Likewise, most of us would find it unconscionable and dangerous for a law to give social workers a roving power to strip parents of custody of their children whenever doing so would be in the child's "best interests" – without limiting in any way what the social worker can consider in that calculation. See, e.g., *Baars v Children's Aid Society of Hamilton,* 2018 ONSC 1487 (CanLII).

52 This, moreover, leaves aside the compelling interest an individual or institution may have in binding oneself: see, on this point, Jon Elster, *Ulysses and the Sirens: Studies in Rationality and Irrationality* (Cambridge: Cambridge University Press, 1979).

53 Schauer, *supra* note 42 at 159. See also Sullivan, *supra* note 47 at 64–66; Antonin Scalia, "The Rule of Law as a Law of Rules" (1989) 56 U Chicago L Rev 1175 at 1179–82.

54 Schauer, *supra* note 42.

55 The majority in the reference explicitly rejected any suggestion that Federal Court judges are less skilled than other judges: *Reference, supra* note 2 at para 60. Generally, commentators agree with this conclusion. A rare exception was an intervention at a debate between Carissima Mathen and Andrew Coyne during a Q & A session at the Canadian Constitution Foundation Conference in January 2015. An audience member offered a spirited argument that, by nature of their limited jurisdiction, federal courts are, in fact, not the equivalent of superior courts. The comment elicited gasps from those present.

56 See the highly unusual speech made by the chief justice of the Federal Court: Cristin Schmitz, "Chief Justice Noel's Remarks Spark Debate over How Far to Go" *Lawyers Weekly* (26 December 2014) at 3.

57 See Guido Calabresi, *The Cost of Accidents* (New Haven: Yale University Press, 1970).

58 The classic examples of this can be found in the Enron and Torture Memos scandals: see David Luban, *Legal Ethics and Human Dignity* (Cambridge: Cambridge University Press, 2007) at ch 3; Jeremy Waldron, "Torture and Positive Law: Jurisprudence for the White House" (2005) 105 Columbia L Rev 1681.

59 See Jon Elster, *Ulysses and the Sirens: Studies in Rationality and Irrationality* (Cambridge: Cambridge University Press, 1979).

60 It is worth observing that, by and large, bills of rights are framed as broad standards rather than as bright-line rules.

CHAPTER 7: THE AFTERMATH

1 Sean Fine, "The Nadon Hearings: 10 Key Issues in the Supreme Court Showdown" *Globe and Mail* (13 January 2014), online: <https://www.theglobeandmail.com/news/politics/the-nadon-hearings-10-key-issues-in-the-supreme-court-showdown/article16293479/>.

2 Canadian Press, "Harper Comments 'Inappropriate' Says Lawyer Who Mounted Nadon Challenge" *CBC News* (5 May 2014), online: <http://www.cbc.ca/news/politics/harper-comments-inappropriate-says-lawyer-who-mounted-nadon-challenge-1.2631997>.

3 Emmett Macfarlane, "The Supreme Court Act Reference" *CBA National Magazine* (February 2014), online: <http://www.nationalmagazine.ca/Articles/February-2014-WEB/The-Supreme-Court-Act-reference.aspx>. See also Macfarlane's remarks after the reference was decided: Emmett Macfarlane, "The Supreme Court's Remarkable Rejection of Marc Nadon" *Maclean's* (21 March 2014), online: <http://www.macleans.ca/politics/the-supreme-courts-remarkable-rejection-of-marc-nadon/>.

4 Dennis Baker and Rainer Knopff, "A Few Questions for Beverley McLachlin" *National Post* (7 May 2014), online: <https://nationalpost.com/opinion/baker-knopff-stephen-harper-vs-the-supreme-court>.

5 *Bedford v Canada*, 2013 SCC 72.

6 John Ivison, "Tories Incensed with Supreme Court As Some Allege Chief Justice Lobbied against Marc Nadon Appointment" *National Post* (1 May 2014), online: <http://nationalpost.com/news/politics/tories-incensed-with-supreme-court-as-some-allege-chief-justice-lobbied-against-marc-nadon-appointment>.

7 *Ibid.*

8 *Ibid.*

9 John Ibbitson, *Stephen Harper* (New York: Signal, 2015) at 385.

10 Ivison, *supra* note 6.

11 John Ivison, telephone interview, 22 May 2018.

12 Aaron Wherry, "The Prime Minister's Office vs the Chief Justice" *Maclean's* (2 May 2014), online: <https://www.macleans.ca/politics/marc-nadon-prime-ministers-office-vs-the-chief-justice/>.

13 *Ibid.*

14 *Ibid.*

15 Howard Anglin, telephone interview with authors, 11 May 2018.

16 Ivison, interview.

17 Mark Kennedy, "PMO Says Harper Avoided Inappropriate Call from Chief Justice on Nadon" *Ottawa Citizen* (20 May 2014), online: <http://ottawacitizen.com/entertainment/pmo-says-harper-avoided-inappropriate-call-from-chief-justice-on-nadon> <emphasis added>.

18 Anglin, interview. Aaron Wherry, "Bob Dechert: 'Nobody Is Attacking the Chief Justice's Credibility Here'" *Maclean's* (6 May 2014), online: <https://www.macleans.ca/politics/bob-dechert-nobody-is-attacking-the-credibility-of-the-chief-justice/>.

19 Sean Fine, "Harper Alleges Supreme Court Chief Justice Broke Key Rule with Phone Call" *Globe and Mail* (1 May 2014), online: <https://www.theglobeandmail.com/news/politics/harper-alleges-supreme-court-chief-justice-broke-key-rule-with-phone-call/article18382971/>.

20 Karina Roman, "Stephen Harper Weighs in on Spat with Chief Justice Beverley McLachlin" *CBC News* (2 May 2014), online: <http://www.cbc.ca/news/politics/stephen-harper-weighs-in-on-spat-with-chief-justice-beverley-mclachlin-1.2629853>.

21 Lorne Sossin, "Court Dismissed" *The Walrus* (18 January 2015), online: <https://thewalrus.ca/court-dismissed/>.

22 Kathleen Harris and Rosemary Barton, "'Shocked': Retiring Chief Justice Was Blindsided by Stephen Harper's Public Attack" *CBC News* (14 December 2017), online: <http://www.cbc.ca/news/politics/mclachlin-supreme-court-harper-battle-1.4433283>. See also her discussion of the whole affair in Beverley McLachlin, *Truth Be Told: My Journey Through Life and the Law* (Toronto: Simon and Schuster, 2019).

23 Supreme Court of Canada, News Release (2 May 2014), online: <https://scc-csc.lexum.com/scc-csc/news/en/item/4602/index.do>.

24 *Ibid.*

25 Sean Fine, "Mackay Repeats Allegations against Top Court Judge" *Globe and Mail* (5 May 2014), online: <https://www.theglobeandmail.com/news/politics/mackay-repeats-allegations-against-top-court-judge-defies-calls-to-withdraw/article18476754/>.

26 Aaron Wherry, "The Justice Minister Suggests the Chief Justice Started It" *Maclean's* (7 May 2014), online: <http://www.macleans.ca/politics/justice-minister-to-chief-justice-you-started-it/> [Wherry, "Justice Minister Suggests"].

27 Canada, *House of Commons Debates,* 41st Parl, 2nd Sess, No 082 (7 May 2014) at 5505; Wherry, "Justice Minister Suggests," *supra* note 26.

28 Wherry, "Justice Minister Suggests," *supra* note 26.

29 Ibbitson, *supra* note 9 at 386. A possible exception is the dispute between William Osgoode, chief justice of Lower Canada, and the governor, Robert Prescott. That contretemps occurred in 1794. See "Harper v McLachlin Is a Supreme Spat" *CBC Radio* (18 May 2014), online: <https://www.cbc.ca/radio/thesundayedition/harper-v-mclachlin-michael-s-essay-justice-for-residential-school-survivors-mail-ira-basen-s-listumentary-an-ode-to-the-oboe-vancouver-the-most-asian-city-outside-of-asia-frank-faulk-goes-to-butchering-school-1.2905066/harper-v-mclachlin-is-a-supreme-spat-1.2905071>.

30 Lorne Sossin, "Court Dismissed" *The Walrus* (18 January 2015), online: <https://thewalrus.ca/court-dismissed/>.

31 Tonda MacCharles, "Canada's Legal Community Steps Up Its Demand That Stephen Harper Withdraw Criticism of Chief Justice" *Toronto Star* (13 May 2014), online: <https://www.thestar.com/news/canada/2014/05/13/canadas_legal_community_steps_up_its_demand_that_stephen_harper_withdraw_criticism_of_chief_justice.html>.

32 Glenn Kauth, "Bar Alarmed at Extraordinary Situation between Harper and McLachlin" *Canadian Lawyer Magazine* (5 May 2014), online: <http://www.canadianlawyermag.com/legalfeeds/author/glenn-kauth/bar-alarmed-at-extraordinary-situation-between-harper-mclachlin-5718/>.

33 Tonda MacCharles, "Joe Clark, Paul Martin Criticize PM's Attack on Chief Justice" *Toronto Star* (20 May 2014), online: <https://www.thestar.com/news/canada/2014/05/20/joe_clark_paul_martin_criticize_pms_attack_on_chief_justice.html>.

34 Letter from Gerald Heckman to Wilder Tayler (n.d.), online: <http://voices-voix.ca/sites/voices-voix.ca/files/icj-submission.pdf>.

35 Sean Fine, "Harper, MacKay Should Apologize to Chief Justice, Commission Says" *Globe and Mail* (25 July 2014), online: <https://www.theglobeandmail.com/news/politics/harper-mackay-should-apologize-to-chief-justice-mclachlin-commission-says/article19765357/>; Tonda MacCharles, "Chief Justice Cleared in Spat with Stephen Harper Government" *Toronto Star* (25 July 2014), online: <https://www.thestar.com/news/canada/2014/07/25/chief_justice_cleared_in_spat_with_stephen_harper_government.html>.

36 Colin Perkel, "International Law Group Raps Harper over Supreme Court Feud" *Maclean's* (25 July 2014), online: <http://www.macleans.ca/politics/ottawa/international-law-group-raps-harper-over-supreme-court-feud/>.

37 Letter from Peter MacKay, Minister of Justice, to Gerald Hickman (23 July 2014), online: <http://voices-voix.ca/sites/voices-voix.ca/files/mackay_response_letter.pdf>

38 Canadian Press, "Beverley McLachlin Says She's Moved on from Spat with Harper, Mackay" *CBC News* (14 August 2014), online: <http://www.cbc.ca/news/politics/beverley-mclachlin-says-she-s-moved-on-from-spat-with-harper-mackay-1.2736594>. Some of the remarks in her memoirs put this claim into context: see Beverley McLachlin, *Truth Be Told: My Journey Through Life and the Law* (Toronto: Simon and Schuster, 2019).

39 Ibbitson, *supra* note 9 at 386.

40 *Ibid.*

41 Lawrence David, "I-CONnect Symposium on the Legacy of Chief Justice Beverley McLachlin – Part V: The Face of an Institution: Beverley McLachlin's Reinvention of the Role of the Chief Justice of Canada" (7 December 2017) *Int'l J Const L Blog*, online: <http://www.iconnectblog.com/2017/12/david-on-Chief-Justice-McLachlin>.

42 Comments made at a symposium held at University of Ottawa, 11 April 2018.

43 See Sean Fine, "The Secret Short List That Provoked the Rift between Chief Justice and PMO" *Globe and Mail* (23 May 2014), online: <https://www.theglobeandmail.com/news/politics/the-secret-short-list-that-caused-a-rift-between-chief-justice-and-pmo/article18823392/> [Fine, "Secret Short List"].

44 Order/Address of House of Commons, Q-437 (1 April 2014) at (ss), online: <http://www.macleans.ca/wp-content/uploads/2014/05/Q-437.pdf>.

45 See Chapter 2.

46 There was a leak of the short list in 2006, when Justice Rothstein was appointed. See Richard Blackwell, "Supreme Court Short List Tests Conservative Mettle" *Globe and Mail* (22 February 2006), online: <https://www.theglobeandmail.com/news/national/supreme-court-short-list-tests-conservative-mettle/article1095505/>.

47 John Gomery, interview by Evan Solomon (10 May 2014), *The House, CBC Radio*, online: <http://www.cbc.ca/player/News/Politics/Audio/ID/2455409481/>.

48 Aaron Wherry, "You Think It's Easy to Make Supreme Court Appointments" *Maclean's* (26 May 2014), online: <http://www.macleans.ca/politics/you-think-its-easy-to-make-supreme-court-appointments/>; Geoffrey Stevens, "Building a Supreme Court with the 'Right' View" *The Record.com* (26 May 2014), online: <https://www.therecord.com/opinion-story/4539465-building-a-supreme-court-with-the-right-view/>; Sean Fine, "Supreme Court's Rejection of Nadon Is a Legal Marker and a Political Blow" *Globe and Mail* (21 March 2014), online: <http://www.aqaad.com/documents-publiques/supreme_courts_rejection_of_nadon_is_a_legal_marker.pdf>; Geoff Stevens, "Trying to Make the Supremes Sing Right" (26 May 2014) *Rabble.ca blogs*, online: <http://rabble.ca/blogs/bloggers/geoff-stevens/2014/05/trying-to-make-supremes-sing-right>.

49 Fine, "Secret Short List," *supra* note 43.

50 Indeed, Sean Fine reported in October 2014 that Justice Gascon had "declined to give interviews since his appointment in June": Sean Fine, "Unvetted Quebec Judge Clement Gascon Takes Supreme Court Seat" *Globe and Mail* (5 October 2014), online: <https://www.theglobeandmail.com/news/national/unvetted-quebec-judge-clement-gascon-takes-supreme-court-seat/article20938996/> [Fine, "Unvetted Quebec Judge"].

51 Tonda MacCharles, "Quebec Court of Appeal Judge Nominated to Supreme Court" *Toronto Star* (3 June 2014), online: <https://www.administrativelawmatters.com/media/quebec-court-of-appeal-judge-nominated-to-supreme-court-of-canada/>.

52 *Ibid.*

53 *Ibid.* A similar statement was made several months later: Fine, "Unvetted Quebec Judge."

54 Tonda MacCharles, "Quebec Lawyer Suzanne Côté Named to Supreme Court of Canada" *Toronto Star* (27 November 2014), online: <https://www.thestar.com/news/canada/2014/11/27/quebec_lawyer_suzanne_ct_named_to_supreme_court_of_canada.html>; Drew Hasselback, "New Supreme Court of Canada Appointee Suzanne Côté Has National Profile, Known for Taking on Big Cases" *Financial Post* (27 November 2014), online: <http://business.financialpost.com/legal-post/new-supreme-court-of-canada-appointee-suzanne-cote-has-national-profile-known-for-taking-on-big-cases>.

55 "Editorial: Harper Abandons Openness with Latest Nomination to Supreme Court" *Toronto Star* (28 July 2015), online: <https://www.thestar.com/opinion/editorials/2015/07/28/harper-abandons-openness-with-latest-nomination-to-supreme-court-editorial.html>.

56 Under ss 96–98 of the *Constitution Act, 1867* the prime minister appoints the judges of the provincial superior and appellate courts. Under s 100–1, the prime minister appoints the judges of the federal courts, including the Supreme Court of Canada.

57 Coauthor Carissima Mathen was one of them. The full list was not released, but a numbers of individuals known to the authors were consulted. Some confirmed their discussions with the Prime Minister's Office on social media.

58 Office of the Commissioner for Federal Judicial Affairs Canada, "Qualifications and Assessment Criteria," online: <https://www.fja-cmf.gc.ca/scc-csc/2019/qualifications-eng.html>.

59 Justin Trudeau, "Why Canada Has a New Way to Choose Supreme Court Judges" *Globe and Mail* (2 August 2016), online: <https://www.theglobeandmail.com/opinion/why-canada-has-a-new-way-to-choose-supreme-court-judges/article31220275/>. The op-ed was also published in a French-language newspaper.

60 Office of the Commissioner for Federal Judicial Affairs Canada, "Supreme Court of Canada Appointment Process – 2016," online: <https://www.fja.gc.ca/scc-csc/2016-MalcolmRowe/index-eng.html>.

61 House of Commons, Standing Committee on Justice and Human Rights, 42 Parl, 1st Sess, No 023, Evidence (11 August 2013), online: <http://www.ourcommons.ca/Content/Committee/421/JUST/Evidence/EV8398115/JUSTEV23-E.PDF>.

62 In the first iteration of the process (with Malcolm Rowe), this hearing took place at the University of Ottawa. In the second, involving Sheilah Martin, the venue was moved to the John A. Macdonald Building, within the parliamentary precinct.

63 *Supra* note 60.

64 Office of the Commissioner for Federal Judicial Affairs Canada, SCC Appointments, "Supreme Court of Canada Appointment Process – 2017": Sheilah Martin, online: <https://www.fja.gc.ca/scc-csc/2017-SheilahMartin/index-eng.html> and Malcolm Rowe <http://www.fja.gc.ca/scc-csc/2016-MalcolmRowe/nominee-candidat-eng.html>.

65 In 2004, former Supreme Court justice Claire L'Heureux-Dubé told the parliamentary committee that she had not known that she was being considered (though she harboured suspicions) until Prime Minister Mulroney called to offer her the job:

> *Mr. Chuck Cadman:* Thank you, Mr. Chair. This is a personal question, but it's not very often I get to question a judge. In your own personal case, would you mind letting us know at what point in the process you became aware that you were being considered as a candidate? When you were appointed, how were you informed of that, and who did it?
>
> *Hon. Claire L'Heureux-Dubé:* I'll tell you very frankly. Everybody knows. Rumours were circulating at the court. I was at the court of appeal, and the judges used to lunch together. Somebody said, "Tonight is the night someone will be called." I didn't know anything about that. My name had been circulated, with others. So I said, "Oh, I don't want to go so I'm going to hide in my office" – which I did.
>
> I stayed in my office until about 11 o'clock. I was so happy I didn't get the call – and then I got the call from Mr. Mulroney. That was it. That was all I knew.

House of Commons, Standing Committee on Justice, Human Rights, Public Safety and Emergency Preparedness, 37th Parl, 3rd sess, No 8, Evidence (30 March 2004) at 1620, online: <https://www.ourcommons.ca/DocumentViewer/en/37-3/

JUST/meeting-7/evidence>. See also Constance Backhouse, *Claire L'Heureux-Dubé: A Life* (Vancouver: UBC Press, 2017).

66 Office of the Commissioner for Federal Judicial Affairs Canada, SCC Appointments, "The Independent Advisory Board for Supreme Court of Canada Judicial Appointments," online: <http://www.fja.gc.ca/scc-csc/2016-MalcolmRowe/establishment-creation-eng.html>.

67 Beatrice Britneff, "SCC Will Get an Indigenous Judge … Eventually: Campbell" (4 December 2017) *iPolitics Blog,* online: <https://ipolitics.ca/2017/12/04/scc-will-get-indigenous-judge-eventually-campbell/>.

68 Leslie MacKinnon, "Bob Rae Criticizes Process for Picking Supreme Court Justices" (26 October 2017) *iPolitics Blog,* online: <https://ipolitics.ca/2017/10/26/bob-rae-criticizes-process-for-picking-supreme-court-justices/>.

69 At the time of writing, Nicholas Kasirer had just been appointed to fill the vacancy left by Justice Gascon.

CHAPTER 8: JUDICIAL APPOINTMENTS LAW

1 Laura Stone, "Another Marc Nadon? Conservatives Appoint Federal Judge to Quebec Court" *Global News* (13 June 2014), online: <https://globalnews.ca/news/1393231/another-marc-nadon-conservatives-appoint-federal-judge-to-quebec-court/>.

2 *Constitution Act, 1867* 30 and 31 Victoria, c. 3 (UK).

3 Robert Décary, "Cachez ces juges que je ne saurais voir!" *Droit-Inc* (14 July 2014), online: <http://www.droit-inc.com/article13139-Cachez-ces-juges-que-je-ne-saurais-voir>. See also Hugo Cyr and Maxime Sainte-Hilaire, "Une menace pour la culture juridique québécoise" *Le Devoir* (25 June 2014), online: <http://www.ledevoir.com/opinion/idees/411814/nomination-du-juge-mainville-une-menace-pour-la-culture-juridique-quebecoise>; Maxime St-Hilaire, "Le festival harpérien de l'insconstitutionnalié se poursuit: La nomination du juge Mainville à la Cour d'appel du Québec" (24 June 2014) *Double Aspect* (blog), online: <https://doubleaspect.blog/2014/06/24/le-festival-harperien-de-linsconstitutionnalite-se-poursuit-la-nomination-du-juge-mainville-a-la-cour-dappel-du-quebec/>.

4 Leonid Sirota, "The Mainville Hearing: Beyond Interpretation" (8 December 2014) *Double Aspect* (blog), online: <https://doubleaspect.blog/2014/12/08/the-mainville-hearing-beyond-interpretation/>.

5 *Ibid.*

6 *Quebec (Attorney General) v Canada (Attorney General)*, 2014 QCCA 2365.

7 *Ibid* at paras 49–57.

8 *Ibid* at para 36.

9 See Sean Fine, "Latest PM Court Move Suggests Supreme Court Appointment in Making" *Globe and Mail* (13 June 2014), online: <https://www.theglobeandmail.com/news/national/pm-moves-judge-from-federal-court-to-quebec-court/article19171876/>.

10 Sean Fine, "The Secret Short List That Provoked the Rift between Chief Justice and PMO" *Globe and Mail* (23 May 2014), online: https://www.theglobeandmail.com/news/politics/the-secret-short-list-that-caused-a-rift-between-chief-justice-and-pmo/article18823392/.

11 *Ibid.*

12 Tonda MacCharles, "Quebec Lawyer Suzanne Côté Named to Supreme Court of Canada" *Toronto Star* (27 November 2014), online: <https://www.thestar.com/news/canada/2014/11/27/quebec_lawyer_suzanne_ct_named_to_supreme_court_of_canada.html>.

13 See, e.g., Andrew Coyne, "Flaky Supreme Court Ruling Meets Dubious Appointment" *National Post* (24 March 2014), online: <http://news.nationalpost.com/full-comment/andrew-coyne-on-marc-nadon-flaky-supreme-court-ruling-meets-dubious-appointment>.

14 Paul Daly, "Judicial Musical Chairs" (15 June 2014) *Paul Daly: Administrative Law Matters* (blog), online: <http://www.administrativelawmatters.com/blog/2014/06/15/judicial-musical-chairs/>.

15 Geoffrey Marshall and Graeme Moodie, *Some Problems of the Constitution* (London: Hutchinson and Co, 1959). See also Andrew Heard, *Canadian Constitutional Conventions: The Marriage of Law and Politics,* 2nd ed (Toronto: Oxford University Press, 2014) at ch 1.

16 A.V. Dicey, *An Introduction to the Study of the Law of the Constitution,* 10th ed (London: Macmillan Press, 1959) at 417.

17 *Ibid* at 30–32: "With conventions or understandings he has no direct concern. They vary from generation to generation, almost from year to year. Whether a Ministry defeated at the polling booths ought to retire on the day when the result of the election is known, or may more properly retain office until after a defeat in Parliament, is or may be a question of practical importance ... The subject, however, is not one of law but of politics, and need trouble no lawyer or the class of any professor of law. If he is concerned with it at all, he is only so far as he may be called upon to show what is the connection (if any there be) between the conventions of the constitution and the law of the constitution. This, the true constitutional law, is his only real concern. His proper function is to show what are the legal rules (i.e. rules recognised by the courts) which are to be found in the several parts of the constitution."

18 This point has also been made with regard to the United Kingdom and the United States: see, e.g., Herbert W. Horwill, *The Usages of the American Constitution*

(New York: Oxford University Press, 1925); Jon Elster, "Forces and Mechanisms in the Constitution-Making Process" (1995) 45 Duke LJ 364 at 365; Rodney Brazier, *Constitutional Practice: The Foundations of British Government,* 3d ed (Oxford: Oxford University Press, 1999) at 3.

19 The Honourable Eugene A. Forsey, "The Courts and the Conventions of the Constitution" (1984) 33 UNBLJ 11 at 12.

20 Andrew Heard, *Canadian Constitutional Conventions: The Marriage of Law and Politics,* 2nd ed (Toronto: Oxford University Press, 2014) at 24.

21 Ivor Jennings, *The Law and the Constitution,* 5th ed (London: University of London Press, 1959) at 68–74. See also E.C.S. Wade, Introduction to A.V. Dicey, *An Introduction to the Study of the Law of the Constitution,* 10th ed (London: Macmillan Press, 1959), at cxxxvi–cxlvi.

22 See Adam Tomkins, *Public Law,* Clarendon Law Series (Oxford: Oxford University Press, 2003), at 9. See also David A. Strauss, "Common Law Constitutional Interpretation" (1996) 63 U Chicago L Rev 877 at 924 (observing that there is little practical difference between the United Kingdom's unwritten constitution and the United States' written one).

23 But note that there have clearly been Cabinet disputes over the years concerning the appropriateness of the regional representation convention and what it entails: see, e.g., "Judicial Appointment – Supreme Court of Canada," 30 October 1962, Library and Archives Canada, RG 2, Privy Council Office, Series A-5-a, Vol 6193, online: <http://www.bac-lac.gc.ca/eng/CollectionSearch/Pages/record.aspx?app=CabCon&IdNumber=21700> (concerning whether British Columbia is entitled to a seat and whether there should be any regional convention at all).

24 Ian MacLeod, "Supreme Court Facing Another Vacancy with Rothstein Retirement" *Ottawa Citizen* (24 April 2015), online: <http://ottawacitizen.com/news/politics/supreme-court-facing-another-vacancy-with-rothstein-retirement>; Shannon Kari, "Tricky to Predict Who Will Replace Justice Rothstein" *Canadian Lawyer Magazine* (28 April 2015), online: <http://www.canadianlawyermag.com/legalfeeds/author/shannon-kari/tricky-to-predict-who-will-replace-justice-rothstein-6309/>.

25 MacLeod, *supra* note 24.

26 Michael Plaxton, "Rothstein's Replacement: Some Early Thoughts to Guide the Speculation" *Policy Options* (29 April 2015), online: <http://policyoptions.irpp.org/2015/04/29/rothsteins-replacement-some-early-thoughts-to-guide-the-speculation/>.

27 *Ibid.*

28 Justin Trudeau, "Why Canada Has a New Way to Choose Supreme Court Judges" *Globe and Mail* (2 August 2016), online: <https://www.theglobeandmail.com/opinion/why-canada-has-a-new-way-to-choose-supreme-court-judges/article31220275/>.

29 CBC News, "Keep Atlantic Representation on Top Court, Says Canadian Bar Association" *CBC News* (10 August 2016), online: <http://www.cbc.ca/news/politics/atlantic-representation-supreme-court-cba-1.3715801>.

30 Anjuli Patil, "Atlantic Canadian Voice Should Remain on Supreme Court, Stephen McNeil Says" *CBC News* (3 August 2016), online: <http://www.cbc.ca/news/canada/nova-scotia/michel-samson-atlantic-canada-supreme-court-1.3704997>.

31 Justin Trudeau, "Mandate Letter (Members) – Independent Advisory Board for Supreme Court of Canada Judicial Appointments," *Justin Trudeau, Prime Minister of Canada,* at 4, online: <https://pm.gc.ca/eng/news/2016/08/04/mandate-letter-members-independent-advisory-board-supreme-court-canada-judicial> [emphasis added].

32 House of Commons, Standing Committee on Justice and Human Rights, 42 Parl, 1st Sess, No 023 (11 August 2016), online: <http://www.ourcommons.ca/Content/Committee/421/JUST/Evidence/EV8398115/JUSTEV23-E.PDF>.

33 Patil, *supra* note 30; "Keep Atlantic Representation on Top Court, Says Canadian Bar Association" *CBC News* (10 August 2016), online: <http://www.cbc.ca/news/politics/atlantic-representation-supreme-court-cba-1.3715801>.

34 John Paul Tasker, "Atlantic Canada Being Treated Like a 'Backwater' with Supreme Court Snub: Lisa Raitt" *CBC News* (6 August 2016), online: <http://www.cbc.ca/news/politics/supreme-court-snub-atlantic-canada-raitt-1.3709018>.

35 Peter Cowan, "Ottawa Stripped Atlantic Canada of Inclusion on Supreme Court with Barely a Peep" *CBC News* (10 August 2016), online: <http://www.cbc.ca/news/canada/newfoundland-labrador/supreme-court-appointments-justin-trudeau-policy-atlantic-canada-1.3713759>.

36 Letter from Janet M. Fuhrer to Justin Trudeau and Jody Wilson-Raybould (10 August 2016), online: <http://www.cba.org/CMSPages/GetFile.aspx?guid=d09d6b68-0029-46ad-ba75-aafed4f093e4>.

37 "Remarks of the Right Honourable Beverley McLachlin, P.C. Chief Justice of Canada," Supreme Court of Canada (Speech to Council of the Canadian Bar Association Canadian Legal Conference, Ottawa, 11 August 2016), online: <https://www.scc-csc.ca/judges-juges/spe-dis/bm-2016-08-11-eng.aspx>. The quoted remarks, however, are not included.

38 Canadian Press, "Atlantic Canada Lawyers Challenge Trudeau on Changes to Supreme Court Appointment Process" *CBC News* (19 September 2016), online: <http://www.cbc.ca/news/politics/atlantic-lawyers-supreme-court-1.3769108>; Joanna Smith, "Atlantic Canadian Judges Will Be Considered for High Court" *CTV News* (11 August 2016), online: <https://www.ctvnews.ca/politics/atlantic-canadian-judges-will-be-considered-for-high-court-wilson-raybould-1.3024337>.

39 Atlantic Province's Trial Lawyers Association, Press Release, "Supreme Court of Canada Judicial Appointment – Notice of Application Filed at the Nova Scotia

Supreme Court" (19 September 2016) [APTLA Press Release]; Canadian Press, "Atlantic Canada Lawyers Challenge Trudeau on Changes to Supreme Court Appointment Process" *CBC News* (19 September 2016), online: <http://www.cbc.ca/news/politics/atlantic-lawyers-supreme-court-1.3769108>.

40 APTLA Press Release, *supra* note 38.

41 *Re Resolution to Amend the Constitution,* [1981] 1 SCR 753.

42 Canada, *House of Commons Debates,* 42nd Parl, 1st Sess, No 79 (22 September 2016) at 4951 (Mr. Nicholson).

43 *Ibid.*

44 *Ibid.*

45 *Ibid.*

46 *Ibid.*

47 Katie Simpson, "MPs Unanimously Support Regional Representation for Supreme Court" *CBC News* (27 September 2016), online: <http://www.cbc.ca/news/politics/mps-vote-in-favour-of-regional-representation-scc-custom-1.3781520>.

48 Sean Fine, "Trudeau Waffles on Approach to Appointing Supreme Court Judge" *Globe and Mail* (27 September 2016), online: <https://www.theglobeandmail.com/news/national/trudeau-waffles-on-approach-to-appointing-supreme-court-judge/article32094612/> [Fine, "Trudeau Waffles"].

49 Section 5 of the *Supreme Court Act* states: "Any person may be appointed a judge who is or has been a judge of a superior court of a province or a barrister or advocate of at least ten years standing at the bar of a province." The Provincial Court of Saskatchewan is not a superior court. Furthermore, Turpel-Lafond does not appear to have been a member of any provincial bar for ten years. From her call in Nova Scotia, she was a member of its bar from 1991 until her 1998 appointment in Saskatchewan. (She was also a member of the Saskatchewan bar for three to four years, but this overlapped with the period during which she was a member of the Nova Scotia bar.) At first glance, then, Turpel-Lafond satisfies neither of the eligibility criteria for the Supreme Court.

50 Fine, "Trudeau Waffles," *supra* note 48.

51 Justin Trudeau, News Release, "Prime Minister of Canada Announces Appointment of Mr. Justice Malcolm Rowe to Supreme Court of Canada" (28 October 2016), online: <https://pm.gc.ca/eng/news/2016/10/28/prime-minister-canada-announces-appointment-mr-justice-malcolm-rowe-supreme-court>.

52 Justin Trudeau, News Release, "Prime Minister Opens the Process to Select the Next Justice of the Supreme Court of Canada" (14 July 2017), online: <https://pm.gc.ca/eng/news/2017/07/14/prime-minister-opens-process-select-next-justice-supreme-court-canada>.

53 Canadian Bar Association, News Release, "CBA President's Statement on Selection Process for SCC Vacancy" (14 July 2017), online: <http://www.cba.org/News-Media/News/2017/July/CBA-President%E2%80%99s-statement-on-selection-process-to?_ga=2.158236082.901441289.1519789749-645469156.1519789749>.

54 Beatrice Britneff, "A Supreme Court Justice from the North?" (14 July 2017) *iPolitics Blog*, online: <https://ipolitics.ca/2017/07/14/a-supreme-court-justice-from-the-north/>.

55 It is worth noting, however, that Justice Russell Brown, though widely viewed as an "Alberta judge," grew up, attended university, articled, and practised law in British Columbia – illustrating the difficulties in identifying appointments with discrete geographical regions. We are grateful to an anonymous reviewer for pointing this out.

56 Canada, *House of Commons Debates,* 3rd Parl, 2nd Sess, vol 1 (30 March 1875) at 974 (Mr. Bunster).

57 Tasneem Karbani, "Tradition Trumps: A New Guard for Canada's Supreme Court" *Law Now* (5 January 2018), online: <https://www.lawnow.org/viewpoint-42-3-tradition-triumphs-new-guard-canadas-supreme-court/>.

58 Laura Lynch, "BC Now Shut Out of Canada's Highest Court: Does It Matter?" *CBC News* (29 December 2017), online: <http://www.cbc.ca/news/canada/british-columbia/b-c-now-shut-out-of-canada-s-highest-court-does-it-matter-1.4461559>. See also the remarks of Arthur Grant, "A New Appointment to the Supreme Court of Canada: Congratulations (and Some Unintended Consequences)" (29 November 2017) *Constitutionally Canadian* (blog), online: <https://constitutionalcanadian.com/2017/11/29/a-new-appointment-to-the-supreme-court-of-canada-congratulations-and-some-unintended-consequences/#more-2841>.

59 Lynch, *supra* note 58.

60 Sean Fine, "Trudeau's Decision on Supreme Court Appointment Tangled in Race, Gender Politics" *Globe and Mail* (16 November 2017), online: <https://www.theglobeandmail.com/news/national/trudeaus-decision-on-supreme-court-appointment-tangled-in-race-gender-politics/article36999295/>; Robert Fife and Sean Fine, "Trudeau to Name New Supreme Court Judge, Maintaining Gender Split" *Globe and Mail* (28 November 2017), online: <https://www.theglobeandmail.com/news/politics/trudeau-set-to-name-new-supreme-court-judge-to-replace-beverley-mclachlin/article37121259/>; Tonda MacCharles, "Trudeau to Name New Supreme Court Judge" *Toronto Star* (28 November 2017), online: <https://www.thestar.com/news/canada/2017/11/28/trudeau-to-name-new-supreme-court-judge.html>; Cristin Schmitz, "Rae Skewers Liberals' SCC Appointment Process" *Lawyers Daily* (26 October 2017), online: <https://www.thelawyersdaily.ca/

articles/5005/rae-skewers-liberals-scc-appointment-process>; Cristin Schmitz, "PM Picks Feminist Constitutional Scholar from Alberta for SCC" *Lawyers Daily* (29 November 2017), online: <https://www.thelawyersdaily.ca/articles/5308/pm-picks-feminist-constitutional-scholar-from-alberta-for-scc>.

61 Karbani, *supra* note 57.

62 Ian MacLeod and Jason Fekete, "Pressure to Name the First Indigenous Supreme Court Judge Could See Trudeau Shaking Up the Rules" *National Post* (16 September 2016), online: <https://nationalpost.com/news/politics/pressure-to-name-first-indigenous-supreme-court-judge-could-see-trudeau-shaking-up-rules>.

63 "Stephen Harper Asks Governor General to Dissolve Parliament, Kicking Off Long Election Campaign" *National Post* (2 August 2015), online: <http://news.nationalpost.com/news/canada/canadian-politics/stephen-harper-asks-governor-general-to-dissolve-parliament-and-kick-of-long-federal-election-campaign>.

64 See Privy Council Office, *Guidelines on the Conduct of Ministers, Secretaries of State, Exempt Staff and Public Servants during an Election* (Ottawa: Privy Council Office, 2015), online: <http://publications.gc.ca/collections/collection_2017/bcp-pco/CP22-125-2015-eng.pdf>.

65 See Michael Plaxton, "The Caretaker Convention and Supreme Court Appointments" (2016) 72 SCLR (2nd) 449.

66 Jason Markusoff, "How Conservative Is New Supreme Court Judge, Russell Brown?" *Maclean's* (28 July 2015), online: <https://www.macleans.ca/news/canada/how-conservative-is-new-supreme-court-judge-russell-brown/>.

67 A similar issue arose in the appointment of Justice Nicholas Kasirer, which crystallized during the 2019 federal election campaign.

CHAPTER 9: A COURT FROZEN IN AMBER

1 See, e.g., *Reference re Remuneration of Judges of the Provincial Court of PEI,* [1997] 3 SCR 3 [*Provincial Judges Reference*].

2 *Ibid.*

3 See Kate Glover, "Structure, Substance and Spirit: Lessons in Constitutional Architecture from the Senate Reform Reference" (2014) 67 SCLR (2nd) 221 at 221–22.

4 *Reference re Alberta Statutes,* [1938] SCR 100 at 132–33.

5 *Ibid.*

6 *Ibid* at 133.

7 *Switzman v Elbling,* [1957] SCR 285 at 327–28.

8 *Ontario (Attorney General) v OPSEU,* [1987] 2 SCR 2 at para 151.

9 *Roncarelli v Duplessis,* [1959] SCR 121 at 142.

10 *Reference re Manitoba Language Rights,* [1985] 1 SCR 721 at 750–51.

11 *Provincial Judges Reference, supra* note 1 at para 108.

12 *Reference re Secession of Quebec,* [1998] 2 SCR 217 at para 49.

13 *Ibid* at para 50.

14 *R v Demers,* [2004] 2 SCR 489 at para 83.

15 See Robin Elliott, "References, Structural Argumentation and the Organizing Principles of Canada's Constitution" (2001) 80 Can Bar Rev 67.

16 See also *Lalonde v Ontario (Commission de restructuration des services de santé)* (2001), 56 OR (3d) 577 at para 180 (CA).

17 See Guy Régimbald and Dwight Newman, *The Law of the Canadian Constitution,* 2nd ed (Toronto: LexisNexis, 2017) at 121–24.

18 See Jean Leclair, "Canada's Unfathomable Unwritten Constitutional Principles" (2001) 27 Queen's LJ 389 at 420.

19 *Babcock v Canada (Attorney General)*, [2002] 3 SCR 2 at para 55.

20 *British Columbia v Imperial Tobacco Canada Ltd,* [2005] 2 SCR 473 at para 66.

21 See, e.g., *Bacon v Saskatchewan Crop Insurance Corp*, [1999] 11 WWR 51 at para 36 (Sask CA); *Hogan v Newfoundland (Attorney General)* (2000), 183 DLR (4th) 225 at para 59 (Nfld CA); *Singh v Canada,* [2000] 3 FC 185 at para 12 (FCA); *Baie d'Urfé (Ville) c Quebec (Procureur general)*, [2001] RJQ 2520 at paras 91–93 (QCA).

22 It is important to note that, as an advisory opinion, the reference did not formally strike down the declaratory legislation. Technically, since references are not binding *per se,* the court did not issue a judgment at all. It merely provided an opinion to the governor-in-council that ss 5.1 and 6.2 were *ultra vires* the Parliament of Canada. (Indeed, if one looks to the Act today, one finds both provisions still in place. It may be that the reference has made governments hesitant to propose *any* further amendments to the Act. For clarity's sake, however, it would be preferable for these clauses to be removed.) In practice, of course, references issuing from Canadian courts are difficult to distinguish from cases. In any event, the broader point holds: the court used an unwritten constitutional principle – the underlying norm of federalism – to explain why duly enacted legislation was inconsistent with the Constitution. This was, in itself, a radical departure from prior practice.

23 For a historical discussion of the era of mega-constitutional politics see Peter Russell, *Constitutional Odyssey: Can Canadians Become a Sovereign People?*, 3rd ed (Toronto: University of Toronto Press, 2004).

24 See *Re: Resolution to Amend the Constitution,* [1981] 1 SCR 753; A.V. Dicey, *An Introduction to the Study of the Law of the Constitution,* 10th ed (London: Macmillan Press, 1959).

25 For analogous criticism in the context of Senate reform, see Emmett Macfarlane, "Unsteady Architecture: Ambiguity, the Senate Reference, and the Future of Constitutional Amendment in Canada" (2015) 60 McGill LJ 883.

26 *Criminal Code,* RSC 1985, c C-46, s 691(1).

27 Supreme Court of Canada, Statistics Report 2017, "03 Appeals Heard," online: <https://www.scc-csc.ca/case-dossier/stat/cat3-eng.aspx#cat3c>.

28 *Judges Act,* RSC 1985, c J-1.

29 *Supreme Court Act,* RSC 1985, c 2-26, s 9(2) [*Supreme Court Act*].

30 S.A. Scott, "Pussycat, Pussycat or Patriation and the New Constitutional Amendment Processes" (1982) 20 UWOL Rev 247 at 272.

31 *Supreme Court Act, supra* note 29, s 53. For further discussion, see Carissima Mathen, *Courts without Cases: The Law and Politics of Advisory Opinions* (Oxford: Hart, 2019).

32 Section 54 of the *Supreme Court Act* does provide that "[t]he Court, or any two of the judges, shall examine and report on any private bill or petition for a private bill presented to the Senate or House of Commons and referred to the Court under any rules or orders made by the Senate or House of Commons." It is quite different from the general reference power. First, it restricts the advisory function to private bills or petitions of same. Second, s 54 refers to "rules or orders" made by either chamber, suggesting that each retains the authority to determine the procedure by which a request would be made. Third, it permits a report issuing from as few as two members of the court, while GIC references are heard and released just like cases. The above limitations have led to s 54 becoming, more or less, a dead letter. The last s 54 reference was in 1882. Mathen, *supra* note 31, at ch 4.

33 See, for example, Bill S-34, *An Act to amend the Department of Justice Act and the Supreme Court Act to remove certain doubts with respect to the constitutional role of the Attorney General of Canada and to clarify the constitutional relationship between the Attorney General of Canada and Parliament,* 1st Sess, 38 Parl, 2005.

34 Graham Fraser, "In Defence of a Bilingual Supreme Court" *Maclean's* (2 August 2016), online: <http://www.macleans.ca/politics/ottawa/in-defence-of-a-bilingual-supreme-court/>.

35 Kirk Makin, "One Supreme Court Nominee Confident at Hearing, the Other Struggles" *Globe and Mail* (19 October 2011), online: <https://www.theglobeandmail.com/news/politics/one-supreme-court-nominee-confident-at-hearing-the-other-struggles/article4182537/>.

36 Canadian Bar Association, Resolution 10-03-A, "Institutional Bilingualism at Supreme Court of Canada," carried 14–15 August 2010, online: <https://www.cba.org/getattachment/Our-Work/Resolutions/Resolutions/2010/Bilinguisme-institutionnel-a-la-Cour-supreme-du-Ca/10-03-A.pdf>.

37 Tonda MacCharles, "Bilingual Supreme Court 'essential', Quebec Bar Association President Says at Richard Wagner's Swearing-in" Toronto Star (3

December 2012), online: <https://www.thestar.com/news/canada/2012/12/03/bilingual_supreme_court_essential_quebec_bar_association_president_says_at_richard_wagners_swearingin.html>; Drew Hasselback, "Is Requiring Bilingualism for Judges Double-Talk?" *Financial Post* (31 August 2011), online: <http://business.financialpost.com/legal-post/drew-hasselback-is-requiring-bilingualism-for-judges-double-talk>.

38 Sebastien Grammond and Mark Power, "Should Supreme Court Judges Be Required to Be Bilingual?" in Nadia Verrelli, ed, *Democratic Dilemma: Reforming Canada's Supreme Court* (Montreal and Kingston: McGill-Queen's University Press, 2013) 49.

39 *R v Daoust,* [2004] 1 SCR 217 at para 28.

40 Office of the Commissioner for Federal Judicial Affairs Canada, "Qualifications and Assessment Criteria," online: <http://www.fja-cmf.gc.ca/scc-csc/qualifications-eng.html>.

41 Justin Trudeau, "Mandate Letter (Members) – Independent Advisory Board for Supreme Court of Canada Judicial Appointments," *Justin Trudeau, Prime Minister of Canada,* at 4, online: <https://pm.gc.ca/eng/news/2016/08/04/mandate-letter-members-independent-advisory-board-supreme-court-canada-judicial>.

42 Bill C-203, *An Act to amend the Supreme Court Act (understanding the official languages),* 1st Sess, 42 Parl, 2015, online: <http://www.parl.ca/Content/Bills/421/Private/C-203/C-203_1/C-203_1.PDF>. In 2010, a fellow NDP MP had introduced a similar bill: "Bilingualism for Top Court Judges Essential: MP" *CBC News* (6 April 2010), online: <http://www.cbc.ca/news/canada/new-brunswick/bilingualism-for-top-court-judges-essential-mp-1.866178>.

43 Canada, *House of Commons Debates*, 1st Sess, 42 Parl, No 148 (6 March 2017) at 1925. It is worth noting that these constitutional arguments were strikingly absent when the bill was again debated the following October.

44 Sebastien Grammond, "Can Parliament Enact a Requirement That Supreme Court Judges Be Bilingual?" (13 May 2016) *Paul Daly: Administrative Law Matters* (blog), online: <http://www.administrativelawmatters.com/blog/2016/05/13/guest-post-sebastien-grammond-can-parliament-enact-a-requirement-that-supreme-court-judges-be-bilingual/>.

45 *Ibid.*

46 Leonid Sirota, "The Comprehension of 'Composition'" (16 May 2016) *Double Aspect* (blog), online: <https://doubleaspect.blog/2016/05/16/my-comprehension-of-composition/>.

47 *Ibid.*

48 Kate Glover, "A Third View on Legislating Two Language at the SCC" (18 May 2016) *Double Aspect* (blog), online: <https://doubleaspect.blog/author/kateeglover/>.

49 *Reference re Supreme Court Act, ss 5 and 6,* 2013 SCC 21 at para 101.

50 *Ibid* at para 93.

51 Glover, *supra* note 48 [emphasis added].

52 *Ibid.*

53 For a critique of this claim, see Fraser, *supra* note 34.

54 Recently, former Ontario Court of Appeal justice Harry LaForme, the first and thus far only Indigenous judge to sit on a provincial court of appeal, called out the bilingualism requirement as unfair to Indigenous persons. LaForme noted that the requirement "trumped what I think is an even more precious notion for the Supreme Court, of having an aboriginal person there." Sean Fine, "Harry LaForme, a Groundbreaking Indigenous Judge, Looks Back in Anger at the Milestone Canada Missed" *Globe and Mail* (21 November 2018), online: <https://www.theglobeandmail.com/canada/article-harry-laforme-a-pioneering-indigenous-judge-looks-back-in-anger-at/>. See also David Butt, "French Proficiency Shouldn't Be Mandatory for Canada's Supreme Court Judges" *Globe and Mail* (10 December 2018), online: <https://www.theglobeandmail.com/opinion/article-french-proficiency-shouldnt-be-mandatory-for-canadas-supreme-court/>.

55 Beatrice Britneff, "Indigenous Groups Disappointed in PM's Supreme Court Pick" (30 November 2017) *iPolitics Blog,* online: <https://ipolitics.ca/2017/11/30/indigenous-groups-disappointed-pms-supreme-court-pick/>; Kristy Kirkup, "Top Court's Bilingual Rule a Barrier to Indigenous Judges: Sinclair, Bellegarde" *Globe and Mail* (22 September 2016), online: <https://www.theglobeandmail.com/news/national/supreme-courts-bilingual-requirement-unfair-sinclair-bellegarde/article32011596/>. See also Christina Gray, "A Place for Indigenous Peoples on Canada's Top Bench" *Policy Options* (21 February 2018), online: <http://policyoptions.irpp.org/magazines/february-2018/a-place-for-indigenous-peoples-on-canadas-top-bench/>. In 2017, when it was unclear who would replace the soon-to-retire Chief Justice McLachlin, it was thought significant that Professor John Borrows, who was believed to be a front-runner, had recently taken steps to learn French: Cristin Schmitz, "Insistence on French for SCC Judges Could Block Historic Appointment of First Indigenous Judge" *Lawyers Daily* (1 August 2017), online: <https://www.thelawyersdaily.ca/articles/4316>.

56 See *R v Gladue,* [1999] 1 SCR 688; *R v Ipeelee,* 2012 SCC 13.

57 See, e.g., Sean Fine, "Hope for Indigenous Supreme Court Justice Swells As Appointment Recommendations Loom" *Globe and Mail* (22 October 2017), online: <https://www.theglobeandmail.com/news/national/hope-for-indigenous-supreme-court-justice-swells-as-appointment-recommendations-loom/article36686760/> [Fine, "Hope"]; Tonda MacCharles, "More Indigenous Judges Needed in Lower Courts to Develop Skills for Supreme Court: Beverley McLachlin" *Toronto Star* (10 August 2016), online: <https://www.thestar.com/news/canada/2016/08/10/

more-indigenous-judges-needed-in-lower-courts-to-develop-skills-for-supreme-court-beverley-mclachlin.html>.

58 Andrew Griffith, "Diversity among Federal and Provincial Judges" *Policy Options* (4 May 2016), online: <http://policyoptions.irpp.org/2016/05/04/diversity-among-federal-provincial-judges/>. It is worth pointing out that Statistics Canada suggested in 2011 that only 4.3 percent of the total population had an Indigenous identity and that 2.6 percent of the population had a First Nations identity: Statistics Canada, "Aboriginal Peoples in Canada: First Nations, Métis and Inuit," online: <http://www12.statcan.gc.ca/nhs-enm/2011/as-sa/99-011-x/99-011-x2011001-eng.cfm>. Without making too much of this point, we wish only to use it to observe that issues of diversity and representation must be approached as the complicated questions they are.

59 Media reports speculated that the prime minister was considering a Dalhousie University law professor, Naomi Metallic, as a "private bar" appointee, but she did not yet have ten years' membership in the bar: Ian MacLeod, "Pressure to Name First Indigenous Supreme Court Judge to See Trudeau Shaking Up Rules" *National Post* (16 September 2016), online: <https://nationalpost.com/news/politics/pressure-to-name-first-indigenous-supreme-court-judge-could-see-trudeau-shaking-up-rules>.

60 Sean Fine, "Chief Justice Beverley McLachlin to Retire after Decades of Pushing Boundaries" *Globe and Mail* (12 June 2017), online: <https://www.theglobeandmail.com/news/politics/chief-justice-beverley-mclachlin-to-retire-after-decades-of-pushing-boundaries/article35286239/>.

61 Fine, "Hope," *supra* note 57.

62 Lorne Sossin, interview, *CTV Your Morning*, 8 November 2017.

63 In March 2019, anonymous sources informed the Canadian Press that there had been a dispute between the minister of justice and the prime minister concerning who should be appointed to the vacant seat. According to the reports, the minister of justice, Jody Wilson-Raybould, had preferred Manitoba Chief Justice Glenn Joyal. Brian Platt, "Liberal MPs on Justice Committee Reject Motion to Study Leak Surrounding Supreme Court Judge Nomination" *National Post* (11 April 2019), online: <https://nationalpost.com/news/politics/liberal-mps-on-justice-committee-reject-motion-to-study-leak-surrounding-supreme-court-judge-nomination>; Jolson Lim, "Liberals Block Committee Probe into SCC Nominee Leaks" (11 April 2019) *iPolitics Blog*, online: <https://ipolitics.ca/2019/04/11/liberals-block-committee-probe-into-scc-nominee-leaks/>.

64 Tonda MacCharles, "Absence of Indigenous Candidate a 'Missed Opportunity,' Lawyers Say" *Toronto Star* (29 November 2017), online: <https://www.thestar.com/news/canada/2017/11/29/absence-of-indigenous-candidate-a

-great-missed-opportunity-law-expert-says.html> [MacCharles, "Absence of Indigenous Candidate"]; John Geddes, "Indigenous Lawyers Upset over Trudeau's Supreme Court Pick" *Maclean's* (29 November 2017), online: <http://www.macleans.ca/politics/ottawa/first-nations-lawyers-upset-over-trudeaus-supreme-court-pick/>.

65 MacCharles, "Absence of Indigenous Candidate," *supra* note 64. An earlier report by Robert Fife and Sean Fine had indicated that Mary Ellen Turpel-Lafond was on the short list: Robert Fife and Sean Fine, "Trudeau to Name New Supreme Court Judge, Maintaining Gender Split" *Globe and Mail* (28 November 2017), online: <https://www.theglobeandmail.com/news/politics/trudeau-set-to-name-new-supreme-court-judge-to-replace-beverley-mclachlin/article37121259/>. To our knowledge, however, the subsequent report by Tonda MacCharles has not been disputed.

66 MacCharles, "Absence of Indigenous Candidate," *supra* note 64.

67 See Rosemary Cairns Way, "Deliberate Disregard: Judicial Appointments under the Harper Government" (2014) 67 SCLR (2nd) 43.

68 US Supreme Court Justice Ruth Bader Ginsburg made headlines in 2012 when she expressed her desire for nine female judges. "Ginsburg Wants to See All-Female Supreme Court" *CBS DC* (27 November 2012), online: <https://washington.cbslocal.com/2012/11/27/ginsburg-wants-to-see-all-female-supreme-court/>.

69 See, e.g., Bertha Wilson, "Will Women Judges Really Make a Difference?" (Paper delivered at the Fourth Annual Barbara Betcherman Memorial Lecture, Osgoode Hall Law School, 8 February 1990); Peter McCormick and Twyla Job, "Do Women Judges Make a Difference? An Analysis by Appeal Court Data" (1993) 8 CJLS 135; James Stribopoulos and Moin Yahya, "Does a Judge's Party of Appointment or Gender Matter to Case Outcomes? An Empirical Study of the Court of Appeal for Ontario" (2007) 45 Osgoode Hall LJ 315; Isabel Grant and Lynn Smith, "Gender Representation in the Canadian Judiciary" in Ontario Law Reform Commission, *Appointing Judges: Philosophy, Politics and Practice* (Toronto: Ontario Law Reform Commission, 1991) 57. For the most part, the literature and study on this has not yet caught up with the increasing complexity of gender identity, but this question, too, must be considered in any analysis.

70 See Samreen Beg and Lorne Sossin, "Diversity, Transparency and Inclusion in Canada's Judiciary" in Graham Gee and Erika Rackley, eds, *Debating Judicial Appointments in an Age of Diversity* (London: Routledge, 2017) 118 at 139 (observing: "the fact that the *Supreme Court Act* requires three judges from Quebec but no indigenous judges is not sustainable").

71 "Cabinet Conclusions – 2170," Library and Archives Canada, RG 2, Privy Council Office, Series A-5-a, Vol 6193, online: <http://www.bac-lac.gc.ca/eng/CollectionSearch/Pages/record.aspx?app=CabCon&IdNumber=21700>.

72 A Cabinet document from 1957 appears to suggest that there was some doubt as to whether any one of the Prairie provinces had a claim to the "Prairie seat" in a given year: "Cabinet Conclusions – 16657," *ibid*, online: <http://www.bac-lac.gc.ca/eng/CollectionSearch/Pages/record.aspx?app=cabcon&IdNumber=16657>.

73 *Reference re Senate Reform*, 2014 SCC 32 at para 70.

74 House of Commons, Standing Committee on Justice and Human Rights, 42 Parl, 1st Sess, No 023, Evidence (11 August 2016) at 14:38.

75 *Provincial Judges Reference*, *supra* note 1.

76 In early 2019, news reports stated that during the first three years of the Trudeau Liberal government, the minister of justice, Jody Wilson-Raybould, had sought to limit the role of the Prime Minister's Office (and, by extension, the prime minister himself) in judicial appointments. The reports do not focus on the Supreme Court specifically, however: Daniel LeBlanc and Robert Fife, "Wilson-Raybould Sought to Limit PMO Involvement in Judicial Appointments" *Globe and Mail* (22 February 2019), online: <https://www.theglobeandmail.com/politics/article-wilson-raybould-sought-to-limit-pmo-involvement-in-judicial/>.

CONCLUSION

1 Laura Stone, "Nadon Appointment Rejected on Technicality, Justice Cromwell Says" *Globe and Mail* (14 September 2016), online: <https://www.theglobeandmail.com/news/politics/nadon-appointment-rejected-on-technicality-justice-cromwell-says/article31891826/>.

2 Sean Fine, "The Lawyer Who Challenged the Harper Government and Won" *Globe and Mail* (22 August 2014), online: <https://www.theglobeandmail.com/report-on-business/careers/careers-leadership/rocco-galati-is-always-fighting-for-long-shots/article20176185/>.

3 See, e.g., John Geedes, "Q & A: Supreme Court of Canada Rejects a Harper Appointment" *Maclean's* (21 March 2014), online: <http://www.macleans.ca/politics/ottawa/q-a-supreme-court-of-canadas-rejects-a-harper-appointment/>.

4 Marc Nadon, telephone interview with authors, 4 June 2018.

Selected Bibliography

JURISPRUDENCE

Alberta v Hutterian Brethren of Wilson Colony, 2009 SCC 37.

The Attorney-General of Ontario and others v The Attorney-General of Canada and others and The Attorney-General of Quebec (Canada) [1947] UKPC 1.

Baars v Children's Aid Society of Hamilton, 2018 ONSC 1487 (CanLII).

Babcock v Canada (Attorney General), [2002] 3 SCR 2.

Bacon v Saskatchewan Crop Insurance Corp., [1999] 11 WWR 51 (Sask CA).

Baie d'Urfé (Ville) c Québec (Procureur général), [2001] RJQ 2520 (QCA).

Bedford v Canada, 2013 SCC 72.

Bennett v Canada (AG), 2013 FCA 161 (CanLII).

British Columbia v Imperial Tobacco Canada Ltd, [2005] 2 SCR 473.

Brown v Allen, 344 US 443 (1953).

Brown v Board of Education, 347 US 483 (1954).

Canada (Attorney General) v Jodhon, 2012 FCA 161.

Canada (Prime Minister) v Khadr, 2009 FCA 246.

Canada (Prime Minister) v Khadr, 2010 SCC 3.

Carter v Canada, 2015 SCC 5.

Cojocaru v British Columbia Women's Hospital and Health Centre, 2013 SCC 30.

Crevier v AG (Québec) et al, [1981] 2 SCR 220.

Doucet-Boudreau v Nova Scotia (Minister of Education), [2003] 3 SCR 3, 2003 SCC 62.

EGALE Canada v Canada (AG), 2003 BCCA 251, 13 BCLR (4th) 1 (CA).

Es-Sayyid v Canada (Public Safety and Emergency Preparedness), 2012 FCA 59 (CanLII).

Felipa v Canada (Citizenship and Immigration), 2011 FCA 272 (CanLII).

Fuller's Case, 12 Co Rep 63, 65, 77 Eng Rep 1342, 1343 (1607).

Galati v Harper, 2016 FCA 39.

Gitlow v New York 268 US 652 (1925).

Halpern v Toronto (City) (2003), 65 OR (3d) 151 (CA).

Harper v Canada, 2004 SCC 33.

Hendricks c Québec (PG), [2004] RJQ 851 (CA).

Hogan v Newfoundland (Attorney General) (2000), 183 DLR (4th) 225 (Nfld CA).

Lalonde v Ontario (Commission de restructuration des services de santé) (2001), 56 OR (3d) 577 (CA).

Marbury v Madison, 5 US 137 (1803).

Martin v Canada (Attorney General), 2013 FCA 15 (CanLII).

May v CBC/Radio Canada, 2011 FCA 130 (CanLII).

McCulloch v Maryland, 17 US 316 (1819).

Morgentaler [1988] 1 SCR 30.

Mugesera v Canada (Minister of Citizenship and Immigration), [2005] 2 SCR 91, 2005 SCC 39.

Ontario (Attorney General) v OPSEU, [1987] 2 SCR 2.

Palmore v Sidoti, 466 US 429 (1984).

Quebec (Attorney General) v Canada (Attorney General), 2014 QCCA 2365.

Quebec (Attorney General) v Canada (Attorney General), 2015 SCC 22.

R v Buzizi, 2013 SCC 27.

R v Conway, 2004 SCC 20.

R v Daoust, [2004] 1 SCR 217.

R v Demers, [2004] [2004] 2 SCR 489.

R v Gladue, [1999] 1 SCR 688.

R v Gomboc, 2010 SCC 55.

R v Ipeelee, 2012 SCC 13.

R v Mills, [1999] 3 SCR 668.

R v O'Connor, [1995] 4 SCR 411.

R v Singh, 2007 SCC 48.

Re Authority of Parliament in relation to the Upper House, [1980] 1 SCR 54.

Re Projet de loi federal relative au Senat, 2013 QCCA 1807.

Re Resolution to Amend the Constitution, [1981] 1 SCR 753.

Ref re Remuneration of Judges of Prov Court of PEI; Ref re Independence and Impartiality of Judges of Prov Court of PEI; R v Campbell; R v Ekmecic; R v Wickman; Manitoba Prov Judges Assn v Manitoba (Min of Justice), [1998] 2 SCR 443.

Reference re Alberta Statutes, [1938] SCR 100.

Reference re Anti-inflation Act (Canada), [1976] SCJ No 12, [1976] 2 SCR 373, 68 DLR (3d) 452.

Reference re Manitoba Language Rights, [1985] 1 SCR 721.

Reference re Remuneration of Judges of the Provincial Court of PEI, [1997] 3 SCR 3.

Reference re Remuneration of Judges of the Provincial Court (PEI), [1998] 2 SCR 44.

Reference re Same-Sex Marriage, [2004] 3 SCR 698.

Reference re Secession of Quebec, [1998] 2 SCR 217.
Reference re Senate Reform, 2014 SCC 32, [2014] 1 SCR 704.
Reference re Supreme Court Act, ss 5 and 6, 2014 SCC 21.
Régie des rentes du Québec v Canada Bread Company Ltd, [2013] SCJ No 46, [2013] 3 SCR 125, 2013 SCC 46.
Roncarelli v Duplessis, [1959] SCR 121.
Schmidt v Attorney General of Canada, 2016 FC 269.
Singh v Canada, [2000] 3 FC 185 (FCA).
Switzman v Elbling, [1957] SCR 285.
Vancouver v Ward, 2010 SCC 27.

NEWSPAPERS AND MAGAZINES

Canadian Lawyer Magazine
Globe and Mail
Maclean's
National Post
Ottawa Citizen
Toronto Star
The Walrus

OTHER SOURCES

Abella, Rosalie Silberman. *Equality in Employment: A Royal Commission Report,* Royal Commission on Equality in Employment (Ottawa: Minister of Supply and Service Canada, 1984).

Adams, Eric. "The Constitutionality of Prorogation" (2009) 18 Const Forum Const 17.

Alarie, Benjamin, and Andrew Green. "Policy Preference Change and Appointments to the Supreme Court of Canada" (2009) 47 Osgoode Hall LJ 1.

Angus, William H. "Judicial Selection in Canada: The Historical Perspective" (1966) 3 Can Legal Stud 220.

Beg, Samreen, and Lorne Sossin. "Diversity, Transparency and Inclusion in Canada's Judiciary" in Graham Gee and Erika Rackley, eds, *Debating Judicial Appointments in an Age of Diversity* (London: Routledge, 2017) 118.

Bonga, Melissa. "The Coalition Crisis and Competing Visions of Canadian Democracy" (2010) 33 Can Parliamentary Rev 8.

Boult, Reynald. "Ad Hoc Judges of the Supreme Court of Canada" (1979) 26 Chitty's LJ 289.

Brazier, Rodney. *Constitutional Practice: The Foundations of British Government,* 3rd ed (Oxford: Oxford University Press, 1999).

Brodie, Ian. "Interest Group Litigation and the Embedded State" (2001) 34 Can J Political Science 357.

Brunet, Mélanie. *Out of the Shadows: The Civil Law Tradition in the Department of Justice Canada, 1868–2000* (Ottawa: Department of Justice, 2000).

Bushnell, Ian. *The Captive Court: A Study of the Supreme Court of Canada* (Montreal and Kingston: McGill-Queen's University Press, 1992).

–. *The Federal Court of Canada: A History, 1975–1992* (Toronto: Osgoode Society for Canadian Legal History, 1997).

Cairns Way, Rosemary. "Deliberate Disregard: Judicial Appointments under the Harper Government" (2014) 67 SCLR (2nd) 43.

Calabresi, Guido. *The Cost of Accidents* (New Haven: Yale University Press, 1970).

Cotler, Irwin. "The Supreme Court Appointment Process: Chronology, Context and Reform" (2007) 58 UNBLJ 133.

Crane, Brian A., Robert Mainville, and Martin W. Mason. *First Nations Governance Law,* 2nd ed (Toronto: LexisNexis, 2008).

Culp Davis, Kenneth. *Discretionary Justice: A Preliminary Inquiry* (Baton Rouge: Louisiana State University Press, 1969).

Cyr, Hugo. "The Bungling of Justice Nadon's Appointment to the Supreme Court of Canada" (2014) 67 SCLR (2nd) 73.

–. "De la formation du gouvernement" (2013) 43 RGD 381.

Devlin, Richard, and Adam Dodek. "The Achilles Heel of the Canadian Judiciary: The Ethics of Judicial Appointments in Canada" (2017) 20 Leg Ethics 43.

Dicey, A.V. *An Introduction to the Study of the Law of the Constitution,* 10th ed (London: Macmillan Press, 1959).

Diefenbaker, John G. *One Canada: The Tumultuous Years, 1962–1967* (Toronto: Macmillan, 1977).

Dodek, Adam. "Omnibus Bills: Constitutional Constraints and Legislative Liberations" (2017) 48 Ottawa L Rev 1.

–. "Reforming the Supreme Court Appointment Process, 2004–2014: A 10-Year Democratic Audit" (2014) 67 SCLR (2nd) 111.

Elliott, Robin. "References, Structural Argumentation and the Organizing Principles of Canada's Constitution" (2001) 80 Can Bar Rev 67.

Elster, Jon. "Forces and Mechanisms in the Constitution-Making Process" (1995) 45 Duke LJ 364.

–. *Ulysses and the Sirens: Studies in Rationality and Irrationality* (Cambridge: Cambridge University Press, 1979).

Epstein, Lee, and Jeffrey A. Segal. *Advice and Consent: The Politics of Judicial Appointments* (Oxford: Oxford University Press, 2006).

Fletcher, Joseph, and Paul Howe. "Public Opinion and Canada's Courts" in Paul Howe and Peter H. Russell, eds, *Judicial Power and Canadian Democracy* (Montreal and Kingston: McGill-Queen's University Press, 2001) 255.

Forsey, Eugene A. "The Courts and the Conventions of the Constitution" (1984) 33 UNBLJ 11.

Friedland, Martin. *A Place Apart: Judicial Independence and Accountability in Canada* (Ottawa: Canadian Judicial Council, 1995).

–. "Appointment, Discipline and the Removal of Judges in Canada" in H.P. Lee, ed, *Judiciaries in Comparative Perspective* (Cambridge: Cambridge University Press, 2011) 46.

Fuller, Lon. *The Morality of Law,* revised ed (New Haven: Yale University Press, 1969).

Glover, Kate. "Structure, Substance and Spirit: Lessons in Constitutional Architecture from the Senate Reform Reference" (2014) 67 SCLR (2nd) 221.

Grammond, Sebastien, and Mark Power. "Should Supreme Court Judges Be Required to Be Bilingual?" in Nadia Verrelli, ed, *Democratic Dilemma: Reforming Canada's Supreme Court* (Montreal and Kingston: McGill-Queen's University Press, 2013) 49.

Grant, Isabel, and Lynn Smith. "Gender Representation in the Canadian Judiciary" in *Appointing Judges: Philosophy, Politics and Practice* (Toronto: Ontario Law Reform Commission, 1990) 57.

Hayek, F.A. *The Constitution of Liberty* (Chicago: University of Chicago Press, 1960).

Heard, Andrew. *Canadian Constitutional Conventions: The Marriage of Law and Politics,* 2nd ed (Toronto: Oxford University Press, 2014).

–. "The Governor General's Decision to Prorogue Parliament: A Chronology and Assessment" (2009) 18 Const Forum Const 1.

Hicks, Bruce M. "British and Canadian Experience with the Royal Prerogative" (2010) 33 Can Parliamentary Rev 18.

Hogg, Peter. "Appointment of Justice Marshall Rothstein to the Supreme Court of Canada" (2006) 44 Osgoode Hall LJ 527.

–. *Constitutional Law of Canada,* 5th ed Supp (Toronto: Thomson Carswell, 2007).

Horwill, Herbert W. *The Usages of the American Constitution* (New York: Oxford University Press, 1925).

Hurley, James Ross. *La modification de la Constitution du Canada: Historique, processus, problemes et perspectives d'avenir* (Ottawa: Government of Canada, 1996).

Hutchinson, Allan C. "Looking for the Good Judge: Merit and Ideology" in Nadia Verrelli, ed, *The Democratic Dilemma: Reforming Canada's Supreme Court* (Montreal and Kingston: McGill-Queen's University Press, 2013) 99.

Ibbitson, John. *Stephen Harper* (New York: Signal, 2015).

Jennings, Ivor. *The Law and the Constitution,* 5th ed (London: University of London Press, 1959).

Kahneman, Daniel. *Thinking Fast and Slow* (Toronto: Doubleday, 2011).

Kelly, James B., and Kate Puddister. "Criminal Justice Policy during the Harper Era: Private Member's Bills, Penal Populism, and the Criminal Code of Canada" (2017) 32 CJLS 391.

Kheiriddin, Tasha. "Law and Order in the Harper Years" in Jennifer Ditchburn and Graham Fox, eds, *The Harper Factor: Assessing a Prime Minister's Policy Legacy* (Montreal and Kingston: McGill-Queen's University Press, 2016) 196.

Leclair, Jean. "Canada's Unfathomable Unwritten Constitutional Principles" (2001) 27 Queen's LJ 389.

Luban, David. *Legal Ethics and Human Dignity* (Cambridge: Cambridge University Press, 2007).

MacCormick, Peter. "Nom de Plume: Who Writes the Supreme Court's 'By the Court' Judgments?" (2016) 39 Dal LJ 77.

Macfarlane, Emmett. "Conservative with the Constitution? Moderation, Strategy, and Institutional Distrust" in J.P. Lewis and Joanna Everitt, eds, *The Blueprint: Conservative Parties and Their Impact on Canadian Politics* (Toronto: University of Toronto Press, 2017) 221.

–. "Unsteady Architecture: Ambiguity, the Senate Reference, and the Future of Constitutional Amendment in Canada" (2015) 60 McGill LJ 883.

Mackinnon, Frank. "The Establishment of the Supreme Court of Canada" in W.R. Lederman, ed, *The Courts and the Canadian Constitution* (Toronto: McClelland and Stewart, 1964) 106.

Maitland, F.W. *A Historical Sketch of Liberty and Equality* (Indianapolis: Liberty Fund, 1875).

Mallory, J.R. *The Structure of Canadian Government* (Toronto: Macmillan, 1971).

Marshall, Geoffrey, and Graeme Moodie. *Some Problems of the Constitution* (London: Hutchinson and Co, 1959).

Massicotte, Louis. "Omnibus Bills in Theory and Practice" (2013) Can Parliamentary Rev 13.

Mathen, Carissima. "Choices and Controversy: Judicial Appointments in Canada" (2007) 58 UNBLJ 52.

–. *Courts without Cases: The Law and Politics of Advisory Opinions* (London: Hart 2019).

–. "Developments in Constitutional Law: The 2004–2005 Term – A Court in Transition" (2005) 50 SCLR (2nd) 89.

McCormick, Peter, and Twyla Job. "Do Women Judges Make a Difference? An Analysis by Appeal Court Data" (1993) 8 CJLS 135.

McLellan, Anne. "Foreword" (2000) 38 Alta L Rev 603.

McWhinney, Edward. "The Constitutional and Political Aspects of the Office of the Governor General" (2009) 32 Can Parliamentary Rev 2.

Miller, Bradley W. "Proroguing Parliament: A Matter of Convention" (2009) 20 Public L Rev 100.

Monahan, Patrick J., and Byron Shaw. *Constitutional Law,* 4th ed (Toronto: Irwin, 2013).

Morton, F.L. "Judicial Appointments in Post-Charter Canada: A System in Transition" in Kate Malleson and Peter H. Russell, eds, *Appointing Judges in an Age of Judicial Power: Critical Perspectives from around the World* (Toronto: University of Toronto Press, 2006) 56.

–. "The Meaning of *Morgentaler:* A Political Analysis" in Ian Gentles, ed, *A Time to Choose Life: Women, Abortion and Human Rights* (Toronto: Stoddart, 1990).

Morton, F.L., and Rainer Knopff. *The Charter Revolution and the Court Party* (Toronto: University of Toronto Press, 2000).

Munro, Kenneth. "The Turmoil Surrounding the Prorogation of Canada's 40th Parliament and the Crown" (2009) 18 Const Forum Const 13.

Newman, Warren. "The Constitutional Status of the Supreme Court of Canada" (2009), 74 SCLR (2nd) 429.

Nicholson, Patrick. *Vision and Indecision* (Don Mills, ON: Longmans, 1968).

Oliver, Peter. "Canada, Quebec and Constitutional Amendment" (1999) 49 UTLJ 519.

Ostberg, C.L., and Matthew J. Wetstein. *Attitudinal Decision Making in the Supreme Court of Canada* (Vancouver: UBC Press, 2007).

Pelletier, Benoit. *La modification constitutiionelle du Canada* (Toronto: Carswell, 1996).

Plaxton, Michael. "The Caretaker Convention and Supreme Court Appointments" (2016) 72 SCLR (2nd) 449.

–. "The Neutrality Thesis and the Rothstein Hearing" (2008) 58 UNBLJ 92.

Plaxton, Michael, and Carissima Mathen. "Purposive Interpretation, Quebec, and the *Supreme Court Act*" (2013) 22 Const Forum Const 15.

Radin, Margaret Jane. "Risk-of-Error Rules and Non-ideal Justification" (1986) 28 Nomos 33.

Régimbald, Guy, and Dwight Newman. *The Law of the Canadian Constitution,* 2nd ed (Toronto: LexisNexis, 2017).

Ribeiro, Marc. *Limiting Arbitrary Power: The Vagueness Doctrine in Canadian Constitutional Law* (Vancouver: UBC Press, 2004).

Riddell, Troy, Lori Hausegger, and Matthew Hennigar. "Federal Judicial Appointments: A Look at Patronage in Federal Appointments since 1988" (2008) 58 UTLJ 39.

Roberts, Edward. "Ensuring Constitutional Wisdom during Unconventional Times" (2009) 32 Can Parliamentary Rev 13.

Roussy, Alain. "Cut-and-Paste Justice: A Case Comment on *Cojocaru v British Columbia Women's Hospital and Health Centre*" (2015) 52 Alta L Rev 761.

Russell, Peter. *Constitutional Odyssey: Can Canadians Become a Sovereign People?*, 3rd ed (Toronto: University of Toronto Press, 2004).

–. *The Supreme Court of Canada as a Bilingual and Bicultural Institution* (Ottawa: Queen's Printer, 1969).

Russell, Peter H., and Jacob Ziegel. "Federal Judicial Appointments: An Appraisal of the First Mulroney Government's Appointments and the New Judicial Advisory Committees" (1991) 41 UTLJ 4.

Saks, Michael J., and Barbara A. Spellman. *The Psychological Foundations of Evidence Law* (New York: New York University Press, 2016).

Sauvageau, Florian, David Schneiderman, and David Taras. *The Last Word: Media Coverage of the Supreme Court of Canada* (Vancouver: UBC Press, 2006).

Savoie, Donald J. *What Is Government Good At? A Canadian Answer* (Montreal and Kingston: McGill-Queen's University Press, 2015).

Scalia, Antonin. "The Rule of Law as a Law of Rules" (1989) 56 U Chicago L Rev 1175.

Schauer, Frederick. *Playing by the Rules: A Philosophical Examination of Rule-Based Decision-Making in Law and in Life* (Oxford: Clarendon, 1991).

Schlag, Pierre. "Rules and Standards" (1985) 33 UCLA L Rev 379.

Schneiderman, David. *Red, White, and Kind of Blue? The Conservatives and the Americanization of Canadian Constitutional Culture* (Toronto: University of Toronto Press, 2015).

Scott, S.A. "Pussycat, Pussycat or Patriation and the New Constitutional Amendment Processes" (1982) 20 UWOL Rev 247.

Skogstad, Grace. "Western Canada and the 'Illegitimacy' of the Liberal-NDP Coalition" in Peter H. Russell, Lorne Sossin, and Adrienne Clarkson, eds, *Parliamentary Democracy in Crisis* (Toronto: University of Toronto Press, 2014) 163.

Snell, James G., and Frederick Vaughan. *The Supreme Court of Canada: History of the Institution* (Toronto: Osgoode Society for Canadian Legal History, 1985).

Songer, Donald. *Transformation of the Supreme Court of Canada* (Toronto: University of Toronto Press, 2008).

Strauss, David A. "Common Law Constitutional Interpretation" (1996) 63 U Chicago L Rev 877.

Stribopoulos, James, and Moin Yahya. "Does a Judge's Party of Appointment or Gender Matter to Case Outcomes? An Empirical Study of the Court of Appeal for Ontario" (2007) 45 Osgoode Hall LJ 315.

Sullivan, Kathleen M. "Foreword: The Justices of Rules and Standards" (1992) 106 Harvard L Rev 22.

Tetley, William, and Marc Nadon. *Marine Cargo Claims* (Toronto: Butterworths, 1978).

Thaler, Richard, and Cass Sunstein. *Nudge* (New York: Penguin, 2009).

Tomkins, Adam. *Public Law,* Clarendon Law Series (Oxford: Oxford University Press, 2003).

Trudeau, Pierre Elliott. "The Constitution and the People of Canada: An Approach to the Objectives of Confederation, the Rights of People and the Institutions of Government (1968)," reproduced in Anne F. Bayefsky, ed, *Canada's Constitutional Act 1982 and Amendments: A Documentary History* (Toronto: McGraw-Hill Ryerson, 1989) 78.

Valpy, Michael. "The 'Crisis': A Narrative" in Peter H. Russell, Lorne Sossin, and Adrienne Clarkson, eds, *Parliamentary Democracy in Crisis* (Toronto: University of Toronto Press, 2014) 3.

Waite, P.B. *Arduous Destiny: Canada, 1874–1896* (Toronto: McClelland and Stewart, 1971).

Waldron, Jeremy. "Torture and Positive Law: Jurisprudence for the White House" (2005) 105 Columbia L Rev 1681.

–. "Vagueness and the Guidance of Action" in Andrei Marmor and Scott Soames, eds, *Philosophical Foundations of Language in the Law* (Oxford: Oxford University Press, 2011) 58.

Walters, Mark D. "The Law behind the Conventions of the Constitution: Re-assessing the Prorogation Debate" (2012) 5 JPPL 127.

Willis, John. "Methods of Appointing Judges: An Introduction" (1967) 4 Can Legal Stud 217.

Wilson, Bertha. "Will Women Judges Really Make a Difference?" (Paper delivered at the Fourth Annual Barbara Betcherman Memorial Lecture, Osgoode Hall Law School, 8 February 1990).

Wittes, Benjamin. *Confirmation Wars: Preserving Independent Courts in Angry Times* (Lanham, MD: Rowman and Littlefield, 2006).

Ziegel, Jacob. "Merit Selection and Democratization of Appointments to the Supreme Court of Canada" in Paul Howe and Peter H. Russell, eds, *Judicial Power and Canadian Democracy* (Montreal and Kingston: McGill-Queen's University Press, 2001) 131.

–. "Merit Selection and Democratization of Appointments to the Supreme Court of Canada" (June 1999) 5:2 Choices 3.

Index of Cases

Index

The Rain Belongs Here

THE RAIN BELONGS

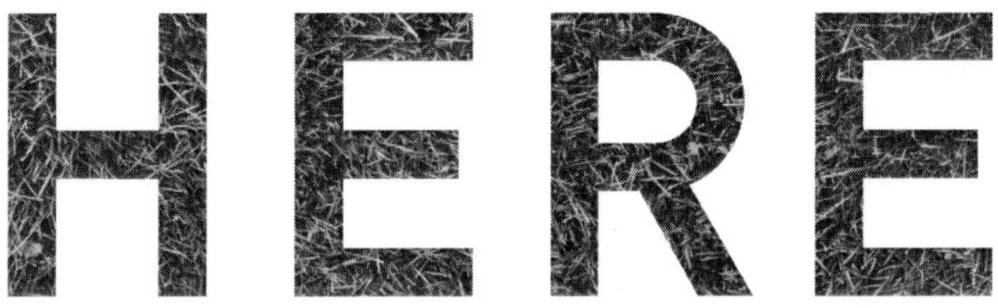

The Rain Belongs Here

First edition

ISBN 978-1-9992540-0-1

To my beloved partner, Sky, who taught me
that there is no separation between art and life.

CHAPTER 1

13 MARCH 2064. Since she started living in her station wagon, in this neglected corner of the City, Ana rarely sleeps through the night. It's not the sirens that bother her or the icy wind blowing through her car's rusted body. Not the drone of street lamps or lumpy seats. It's the shock of Finn's absence that she can't shake. She pictures his lifeless body rotting in a ditch or folded into someone's deep freeze. On bad days, she fears that nothing happened to him at all. He simply walked away.

A row of barren birch trees extends along the side of the parking lot, their limbs heavy with ice. Branches groan and snap off, sketching messages on a fresh blanket of snow.

She's not alone. A Volvo is parked across from her, its parts long gone, the passenger door permanently open. And a trailer

shelters a woman and her twelve-year old boy, Spit. Every morning Spit's mother walks across the lot in her mustard colored cafeteria uniform, her hair pinned into a net. The boy stays behind. When he's not harassing Ana with questions or showing her his collection of things – dull pennies, a ball he's woven from bits of yarn – she catches him studying her through the trees.

"Let's hang out," he begs her. "We could watch a movie on your screen. A comedy maybe. You won't notice I'm there." But she would. Even twenty feet away, his presence is overwhelming.

If Finn were here, he'd be kinder. He'd gather firewood for the woman and show the boy how to make paper airplanes and forage for food under the snow. But then if her brother hadn't disappeared, she wouldn't be in this parking lot in the first place.

It's been ninety days since Finn and four of his friends went missing, eighty since she quit university to look for him, sixty since she ran out of money, forty since she returned to her apartment to find strangers cooking in her kitchen, her belongings piled high in the hallway.

Her home now is a brandless station wagon that she helped her father and brother assemble from salvaged parts that almost fit together. This is how she learned the geography of the City, hunting in corners for brake pads and wheel bearings. It saved her and Finn from boredom. What they couldn't find, they bartered for. Sometimes a part would appear in front of their door, a gift from an anonymous friend. The car became the pride of their neighborhood in the early days. Something to watch unfold. Now it's practically the only thing of value she has left of them.

She shakes off her blankets. A whole heap of them. She was born onto the smallest one, an orange and green crocheted bedspread a neighbor made from a bag full of polyester sweaters he'd found at the dump. The kind that get washed wrong and are too bent out of shape to be worn and too artificial to become fertilizer. Its orange flowers, tightly woven into a beautiful mess of green, have always seemed alive to her, as if they're constantly reknitting themselves into new varieties.

She takes her map out of the glove compartment and marks a warehouse she searched yesterday. The map is failing after ninety days of opening and closing, dead pixels in its deep folds.

It'll take a year to search every building in the City. Longer to interview everyone. Who's next on her list? A cousin of one of the other four who disappeared. He didn't say anything at the meeting with the police, but he didn't ask the usual questions either. The idea of visiting him fills her with dread. Another dead end to mark off her list. But someone knows where Finn is. Maybe it's him.

She rifles through her clothes basket for something to wear. Everything is dirty except for a pair of worn underwear and a pink jacket of her mother's that she wouldn't be caught dead in. Last night she slept in jeans she's been wearing all month and an old shirt of her father's that smells of sawdust. She can hear Finn's voice in her head. *"Really Ana? You fell this quickly after I left you? A lunatic recluse in a parking lot? When's the last time you had a conversation with anyone that didn't have to do with me? I didn't ask you to look for me. I don't want to be found."* The voice

is compelling, but then she imagines Finn and the others locked away in someone's garden shed with nothing but a paint can to piss in. He's waiting for her, wondering what's taking her so damn long.

She piles her clothes into the basket on the back of her bike, secures them with bungee cords and rides to the community pool, wheels crunching through half frozen puddles.

In the distance, the wall that surrounds her City defines the edges of possibility. Thirty miles around, built from the bricks of crumbled factories, always a dead bird or two hanging by a wing from the wires.

She passes the warehouses where materials from collapsing buildings have been consolidated and categorized over the years – steel, wood, copper and bricks – but they're mostly empty now, their contents reinvented over and over until their final use was found. Finn could be in one of them.

She crosses through the quiet market, row upon row of empty tables. In an hour, people will be haggling over coarse bread and shriveled beets.

She rides along Kennedy Avenue through a mile-long trail of office towers that have been converted into modest residences, the laundry of their tenants hanging from rooftop racks, each tower a world of its own with matchbox-sized apartments, classrooms, greenhouses and performance spaces. All of them crowded with children like her that know nothing of the time before, that have only ever known the City.

It was thirty years ago, in her old building, in the aftermath,

that a handful of neighbors got the idea that something beyond mere survival might be possible in the City. There's a faded mural in the front entrance of multi-colored people holding hands, slogans written in bold colors across the top: "a community without greed and corruption", "power comes from contributing to the community, not controlling it", "no one prospers unless everyone does".

The parks and empty lots she passes through are mostly gardens now because everything has to have a purpose in the City. Even the old baseball field behind her old building has been tilled and made ready for corn. All that's left of the old playground is a lone swing set. But there's still beauty. She catches her breath briefly by the old greenhouse her father built in the parking lot, red tomatoes on green vines pressing against its glass walls.

She reaches the pool as the clouds finally lift, revealing the City in all its splendor. The pool, over a century old, smells of mildew. A few carefully placed buckets collect water from leaking skylights.

There's a small radio on a shelf over the row of sinks in the women's change room. She turns it on. By the end of morning news, three of the sinks are filled with her clothes, water and soap made of lavender and lard. There's never anyone at the pool at this hour except for the janitor and he never bothers her, although sometimes she catches him pausing with his mop by the deep end.

She changes into her suit and dives in, letting the water warm her chilled bones.

She showers, washing out the remaining filth of a week of street living – nail dirt from foraging under the snow for roots, mud that sprays up on her clothes from the rust hole under the driver's seat and sweat from endless walking. Then she starts in on the clothes. It takes her over an hour to complete her routine – sudsing, scrubbing, rinsing and wringing them out, drying them under hand dryers. When she's done, she looks for food in the garbage bins in the pool snack shop.

She'd never eaten from a trash bin until last month. She grew food in their greenhouse until she got evicted. When Finn was still around, they shopped at the market with his modest teaching wages and her student stipend. Even after she moved into her car, she had things to bargain with. But she's been carrying on like this too long.

She avoids the sandwiches, the bread usually soggy or moldy. Half-eaten apples might have a maggot or two in them, but they can be picked off. She looks for food that is nutritious but unpopular, something a parent would pack for an ungrateful child. But there were no ungrateful children at the pool today.

CHAPTER 2

15 MARCH 2064. Saturday night. 10:00 p.m. If Finn weren't missing, she'd be out with her friends. She had a lot of them before she became a hermit. They'd hang out at someone's house listening to music and debating the state of their world, as if they might have something original to say. If they happened to find privacy, like a linen closet or balcony, a rare thing in a City where whole families share a room, they'd take turns pairing off and making out. Eventually, the entire group would migrate to a café, order a single plate of fries between them. Stay as long as the owner would put up with them. On nights like that she felt happy, like a speck of dust suspended in a sunbeam. But since Finn disappeared, she avoids anything that might make her forget him.

Her car battery died an hour ago. Everything went dark. Heat hemorrhaged out of the car's cracks. Her fingers became so numb she couldn't get the glove compartment open to find her mittens. She jabbed a screwdriver at the latch until it finally gave. How long does it take for frostbite to set in? Spit will find her body tomorrow, blue hands frozen to the steering wheel as if she had somewhere to go. Go. She has to leave. Get moving. Things can't freeze when they're in motion.

She tries the doors, but they're iced shut. All of them. She swears and bounces her head off the steering wheel in frustration. Likes the feeling of it and does it again, harder than intended. For a fleeting second, she considers that the impossible might actually happen. She could die in this car tonight.

She gets a rush of adrenaline, scrambles over her loose belongings in the back seat into the trunk and searches for a safety latch. Did they bother with one? But it's there, right where it should be. She pops it and kicks at the hatch until the ice finally gives. Doesn't care if it ever closes again. She can't go on much longer like this anyway.

She walks to the nearest street that will have something open. Every noise she hears behind her – the shudder of a ladder, a bottle rolling across the pavement – she thinks could be Finn. He'll grab her from behind around the waist. She'll wrestle him to the ground and demand to know where he's been. He'll say casually, *"It was a government thing. Couldn't tell you anything about it – for your own safety of course – but we're back. I'm taking you home."*

When she reaches King's Avenue, she finds what she's looking

for, the Tall Poppy restaurant. It's busy and expensive, not a place where her friends would go. She can be anonymous there.

She stops at the restaurant's window to examine her reflection. Gaunt, unkempt. She pulls off a mitten and runs her fingers through her long black hair. Puts colored beeswax on her lips. Almost looks like her old self. She squeezes through an exiting crowd of men and approaches the hostess, a short and peppy girl. Her dress looks like something from the time before. Black, tight and shiny. Slightly frayed at the sleeves.

"For how many?" the hostess asks.

"Two," Ana answers.

"The tables are fully booked, but you can sit at the bar."

She seats Ana next to the kitchen door. Waiters fly past within an inch of her with trays of food. She puts her jacket on the back of her chair and goes to the toilet. Once she's alone, she looks for a plug for her battery. Finds one inside the vanity. In an hour, she'll have enough charge to stave off hypothermia for the night if she keeps the heat low.

They might kick her out before then if her plan doesn't work. She'll go back to the bar. They'll offer her a menu. Ask if she wants anything to drink while she waits for her friend. She'll say she'll order when he gets there. They'll tell her the specials and she'll ask detailed questions like "Are there mushrooms in it? I don't like mushrooms," as if she plans to order. After an hour of uncomfortable looks, she'll apologize and say he must have got the time or place wrong. She'll take her battery and go. She almost always gets away with this scheme.

When she returns, a man is seated two bar stools away. He's vaguely familiar. He nods in greeting as if he recognizes her as well. But from where? He's attractive in a sort of unassuming way despite scars slashing across one arm. There are needles on the wool jacket slung across the back of his stool. He must have been walking in the forest. She should do the same once she's warm. If she gets up the nerve, she'll ask him to join her and she can pretend for a night that's she's normal, maybe even crash at his place. He doesn't know her. They could talk about something ordinary, like a movie they've both seen. A night off from this insanity. Screw Finn.

She reconsiders when she notices the L2 tattoo on his left hand, the mark of a convicted criminal. L2 could mean anything – theft, fraud, corruption. Anything short of major violence. If there'd been violence, it would have been an L3 offense. They don't usually bother tattooing the L3s; they just banish them. They don't tattoo the L1s either. Squatting in a parking lot is probably an L1 offence, but they won't bother her about it. There's still a certain amount of sympathy towards destitution in the City.

Where *did* she meet him? The Neighborhood Justice Center where she volunteered last year as a mediator? Was he a client? No, it was at the library auditorium at one of those meetings Finn dragged her to. The group called themselves the "Movement". A generic name for an unremarkable group. Finn got involved with them a couple of years ago after their dad died. She never understood why. They were supposed to be activists, but

they mostly just listened to themselves talk, at least until Finn joined them. Finn was better than them. This guy had showed up at a few meetings. Aaron. That was his name. He'd helped her stack chairs once.

As she recalls, Aaron hadn't been that committed to the Movement either. He stopped showing up long before Finn disappeared. Was it his criminal conviction that brought him there? An attempt at redemption?

She pulls out her screen and makes notes from her meeting with the cousin she interviewed earlier in the day. *Mark was friendly enough at first. Said he had lunch with his cousin Carly the day before they disappeared and didn't sense anything suspicious. They had plans for indoor tennis that weekend. They grew up together. Were more like siblings than cousins. Did say Carly had spent a lot of time with Finn in the past, but there'd been a falling out. Some kind of argument. Didn't know what the issue was. He suddenly turned on me. What did I know? Was I holding stuff back from the police? Made excuses and got out of there in a hurry. Dead end number ninety.*

"Pretentious place, isn't it?" Aaron asks.

She can hardly hear him over the music. Loud busy jazz. A piano that needs to be tuned. She closes her screen and looks up at him to make sure he's talking to her. His eyes scan the place and then meet hers.

"It's warm in here," she says, relieved that her vocal cords still work. "That's all I care about." It's not a bad place actually. If you can overlook the inflated prices and pretense of

the staff, it's actually kind of homey. Massive oak doors have been turned into long communal tables. Candles in blue medicine jars light up every surface. The place is dangerously comfortable.

"True," he says, eyeing her stiff fingers and pushing his warm mug of tea towards her. What does he want her to do with it, warm her hands or drink it?

A waitress brings out two bowls of leek and potato soup and puts one directly in front of her.

"I didn't order this," she says. That's all she needs, getting stuck with a bill she can't pay. But maybe a night in a warm cell wouldn't be so bad.

"*He* did," the waitress answers confused.

"I'm waiting for someone," she says to Aaron, her eyes glued to the soup.

"So, you'll keep me company until he comes?" he says.

She considers the implications of his offer. The guy's a criminal. But he can't be that bad if he helped her stack chairs once. She can always slip out the back exit.

He waits until her bowl is empty before he speaks again. "Three months," he says, nodding toward her screen. "You sure he wants to be found?"

He must have been reading over her shoulder. She should be more careful.

"You think he disappeared on purpose?" she asks, trying to sound more amused than pissed off. No one had ever suggested that Finn left intentionally. The assumption is that some-

thing sinister happened to them. When she was still talking to her friends, they had all sorts of theories. Finn and the others found some off-the-grid warehouse to meet in and got carbon monoxide poisoning. They took a canoe out and got swallowed by the dam. They locked themselves into one of those walk-in industrial fridges. But if Aaron's right about Finn leaving on purpose, then he can also come back when he's ready. He could be alive.

"Pretty sure he did," he answers, buttering some bread casually and handing it to her.

This isn't a chance meeting.

"What do you want?" she asks.

"I think maybe you'd like to talk to some of my friends about this," he says, with his mouth full, as if he's discussing an art exhibit she might want to see.

"Friends?"

"People interested in what your brother was doing. We could help each other."

For a fleeting second, she thinks this is it. She's finally found someone who actually knows where Finn is. Finn might have sent him. But he could also be the reason Finn is gone. Something feels wrong.

The waitress brings out more food – two plates of homemade noodles with real meat sauce, not the faux stuff. Aaron lifts Ana's screen to make room for their feast and her instincts tell her to grab her screen from his hand and run. But curiosity keeps her rooted to her stool.

"I wouldn't be much help to you," she says. "I'm no closer to figuring this out than I was when I started."

"We know," he says.

"How?"

"We've been watching you," he says.

She looks down at his L2 tattoo. He notices and drops his hand casually to his lap out of view. She twirls some noodles, but they don't make it to her mouth. She's too distracted by the thought that this man has been stalking her. He's been watching her pick food out of garbage bins and urinate behind the trees next to her car. He's probably seen her naked, cleaning her armpits with chunks of snow.

"Who are your friends?" she asks, running through the handful of subversive groups he might belong to in her head.

"The Council," he says, as if he's just said a bad word.

"You're government?" she asks, clearly disappointed. That's why he was at those Movement meetings. He was there to spy; to assess the threat of the Movement. But that's not how the government would spin it. They'd say they were trying to understand what's important to the people so that they can serve us better. In any event, the last person she wants to talk to is someone from the state. For all she knows, they're the reason Finn and the others disappeared.

"I'm not interested," she says, climbing down from her stool. She'll find some other restaurant to loiter in.

"Don't leave yet," he says, putting his hand loosely over her wrist. "I have something you'll want to see first."

She obeys for the sole reason that if she doesn't talk to him now, he'll probably show up at her car tomorrow with a warrant and haul her into an interrogation room.

The music becomes louder. Those who are actually listening are cheering and whistling. They yell out songs they want to hear. The smell of the food, the lights, the noise all make her head swirl. She can barely breathe. She eyes the exit longingly.

He pulls out his own screen from his leather shoulder bag, stretches it out, brings up a photo, and hands it to her. A body. A body on a gurney. A gurney in the morgue. A bullet wound through his jaw. Benjamin Anderson. One of the missing four. He flips to a second image. Annie Redmond. Twenty-seven. School teacher. Bullet wound through her ribcage. The wounds are all over the place and sloppy, the bodies decomposed and practically unrecognizable. She shuts it off before she sees the one photo she can't bring herself to look at. The one she sees every night when she's trying to sleep. So that's it then. They're all dead. Finn is dead. Murdered in a City where crime is non-existent. She should be crying, shouldn't she? Scream maybe. Fall off her stool? But only if all of this is real and it obviously isn't.

"When?" she asks.

"At least two months ago."

"Who killed them?"

"We have a suspect," Aaron says.

"Who?"

"Someone who isn't in the photos," he answers, turning the screen back on and angling it toward her.

She flips through each photo trying to discern his meaning. Same haphazard bullet wounds, same gurney, same morgue, different faces. But one photo is missing. Finn. Finn is not there. He's not among the dead. Finn's their suspect. She looks through the photos again, absorbing the horror of them, trying to decide how to respond. She can see that Aaron is struggling to read her reaction, gauging whether she knows anything about this.

"You think Finn murdered his friends?"

"My bosses do," he says.

"They have evidence?"

"Enough."

"And you expect me to help you so that you can arrest him for murder?"

"Yes," he says, glancing between her and the last image on the screen, a dead blond girl. Carly. The cousin. She was seventeen. Chess champion. She'd taken every class Finn had taught. He would never hurt her.

"You're crazy," she answers.

He takes another bite, not the least bit disturbed. "I get it. It's an impossible offer. But you're not going to find him without us," he says.

"How can you be so sure?"

He returns his screen to his bag, takes a pen out and writes something on the palm of her hand – an address and time.

"Come and we'll tell you," he says, putting some coins on the table and leaving her with two plates of spaghetti that she has no appetite for now.

CHAPTER 3

16 MARCH 2064. Ana spends the morning in an abandoned store in a strip mall, two blocks down from her parking lot and across the street. Flooding has made the building unusable to anyone but Ana. Soon they'll put a new roof over it and paint it up. And then the citizens of the City will fight over every inch of it. She hasn't been here since sleet hit the City, turning the concrete floor into a bumpy skating rink.

Photos of Finn and the other four are pinned to a wall along with useless bits of information – where they lived, what they studied, their connection to Finn. She knows what each one was doing the last day they were seen. No one was packing bags or hoarding provisions. Whatever happened came as a surprise. Her display spreads vine-like, mostly a map of

what she doesn't know. A monument to her failure as a sister.

She can almost sense Finn in the room. Maybe that's why she chose the place.

They escaped here together sometimes as kids, before it underwent its various transformations – daycare, art center, medical clinic. The first time was the day after her sixth birthday. The City's walls had just been expanded to include this neighborhood. Like most areas surrounding the City, it had been abandoned when everyone fled to military camps. The Council's policy back then was that if the City didn't have enough resources or land, they should simply push the walls outward. And by doing so, the City swallowed up this little strip mall and her parking lot.

Her father, Aavai, had been hired to catalogue the contents of some of the newly acquired buildings and he was taking his family with him. They would be the first to explore the place and salvage things their people could use. She'd anticipated this day all week.

The sun had finally reappeared that morning after a cloudy winter. For months, it had been so overcast that the greenhouses had barely produced. And spring came late. People were tempted to abandon the City in search of food, but once they left, they wouldn't be allowed to return.

Their father took their bikes out of the storage shed.

"It's cold Papi," Ana complained. "Can't we take the car?"

"But there's so much to see out in the world today," he said. "Come look." He showed her a mayfly on a leaf caught in a

puddle in front of their apartment building. And out of the waterlogged grass he lifted a perfect sphere of ice to her like a lens to his world.

They spent hours oiling and adjusting the bikes. His was the old racing bike with peeling purple paint and rusted gears that Ana now uses. Finn's was a woman's bike with a painted wicker basket and shiny fender. Ana's was too small, pink and green with plastic streamers in the wheels that clicked when she pedaled.

Their mother's was shiny and silver. Not a scratch on it. He always gave her the best of everything.

The idea of exploring a new place was almost too much for Ana to handle. The outside world was something to be feared and they'd just allowed a piece of it inside. But what if there was something there that would change everything? An explanation maybe.

They rode proudly through the City streets, energized by the buzz of people finally emerging from their apartments into the sun. Neighbors worked together to clean out greenhouses. Children pushed wheelbarrows of dirt. Families exchanged seeds. Emergency money was spent on sweets to celebrate.

When they got to the strip mall, they rested their bikes against an old drive-through bank. Although the parking lot was broken up and mounds of debris dulled the shininess of the place, the promise of the neat line of buildings was overwhelming, each store a portal to an unknown world. Which one would they explore first? The biggest one – what they used

to call a department store, with its isles of flowing silk, cotton and cashmere? They would try on sequined dresses and shoes that made her a foot taller and clip bobbly things to their ears. The kitchen store, with its slicers and blenders? No. That would remind her how hungry she was. Maybe the toy store, the office supply depot, the sports store? She imagined a new ping pong table in the rec room of her apartment building, one with paddles that still had rubber on them. They ruled out the grocery store at the far end. Although some process must have long ago removed all traces of flesh, pulp and fiber that were left behind on that day the humans evacuated, there was still a lingering stench.

Finn chose the electronics store. The blue and yellow sign had faded and the letters that had once coursed with electricity were hanging off threads of wire, but he desperately wanted what was inside – wires, circuits and motors. They crowded around their father as he worked on the chain with his bolt cutters. Aavai had become too thin that winter. He wore a large woolen belt to keep his pants from falling down. His faded blue sweatshirt was wide and stretched out at the bottom and threadbare at the collar. His long curly black locks splayed across his face in damp clumps.

He broke through the links, but the door had shifted over the years and it took the four of them to wrestle it open. The rusted bolts broke, unhinging the door. They carefully set it inside, leaving the contents open and vulnerable. Later, they'd cover the wound in plastic.

They walked down the aisles, marveling at the objects, Ana trusting Finn's mostly fabricated explanations of their use.

"This one makes people unable to speak," he said, showing her a pair of noise-cancelling headphones.

"And this smartwatch?" she asked him. "Does it make you intelligent?"

"Only if you know the codes," he sighed.

"Do you know the codes?" she asked optimistically.

"I'll figure them out," he said.

She reached out and took Finn's hand. He looked down at her fingers laced through his. For a moment she was afraid he'd shake her off, but he didn't. He swung their arms up and down into the air while they skipped through the aisles.

Ana explored on her own, finding a pile of magazines in the back office. Their father never let them pilfer anything when they went on these expeditions, except for old magazines. She had stacks of Time, The New Yorker and Vogue. She would skim the articles, but what she devoured was the advertisements. She found it fascinating that people had to be convinced they needed something. She would cut out the pictures of perfume and alcohol, glue them onto cardboard and arrange them on her shelf.

When she came back, Finn was writing down model numbers on an inventory list while their father took pictures. The following day, a team would come and take everything away to one of the warehouses. The packages would be opened, the objects broken down into components that would eventually find their way into the City's more evolved technology.

left through the broken door in search of her mother. She walked the length of the strip mall, following her footprints in the muddy snow. She tracked her to a dumpster, crawled on top of it and up a fire escape to the roof of a steak restaurant where she found her mother sitting on her coat. The wall in this new section of the City wasn't quite finished, the bricks only a few feet high, a temporary force field blurring the world beyond. But she saw them. They were there on the other side of the wall where there weren't supposed to be people now, walking in a field amongst half-finished houses, cement trucks with flat tires and miles of pipe that would never find its way into the ground now. A man and a boy and a wagon full of dried corn. The outside man saw them too. He covered the boy's eyes and turned him in the opposite direction.

And then her father was there beside them and from up on that roof he seemed to tower over the whole universe. Finn was there too, a wire peeking out of his back pocket. He'd swiped something. Her father lifted her onto his shoulders. If he was bothered by the people on the other side, he never said anything. They all just stared into the distance, glimpsing a rare scene that would soon be obscured by bricks. What they saw was more dangerous than pilfering from the store.

"You shouldn't have left your father," her mother snapped at her. "You're always getting lost. Someday we'll lose you for good."

But that never happened. One by one they all left her.

SHE STARES AT her work on the wall trying to force it all to make sense, especially now that she knows Finn's friends are dead. All those bits of info she thought were irrelevant resurface in light of Aaron's accusations. The cousin said Finn had had a falling out with Carly. When was the last time Finn made anyone angry, anyone but Ana? She forces herself to imagine Finn with a gun in his hand, shooting his friends point blank. It's ludicrous. Finn can't bring himself to kill the rats in their apartment. He makes her do it.

The facts don't point to Finn being a murderer, but they do tell her something. Someone killed those people and Finn witnessed it. He has good reason to hide.

CHAPTER 4

16 MARCH 2064. “Do you know what I’m going to do to you today?” her interrogator asks. She’s secured to a table in a room she’s never been in. It’s an ordinary looking living room, other than the shaded windows. A bookshelf in the corner is stacked with old board games – Scrabble, Operation. A one-way mirror separates the room from what would normally be a kitchen. The whitish carpet is musty and gag worthy.

“Ask questions I can’t answer,” she replies.

“You’ll answer them,” he says, nodding toward a tray of knives, plastic bags and a bucket. Next to the tray is a container with needles and rolls of bandages.

He goes over to a chest by the dining room table, lifts the lid and sticks in a data key.

His face is pretty. That's the only way she can describe it. Delicate, sensitive. Long lashes. Not the kind of guy that cuts people for a living. And his voice. It's sickeningly cheerful.

How did she get here? She tries to remember the last thing that happened before she woke up in this chair. She was in the electronics store. The night before, she'd been at the Tall Poppy. Aaron gave her an address. He wanted her to meet some friends of his in the government. Is this his friend? Where is Aaron? Why is she forgetting?

"You don't mind a little music, do you?" he asks.

"I guess," she says.

He puts on something classical she's never heard. A waltz maybe.

"You hungry?" he asks, "I could fix you a sandwich before we begin."

"No," she finally answers after a hard swallow.

"Suit yourself. Let's talk for a bit then," he says, sitting on a chair next to her, cleaning his nails with a square piece of metal. She stops herself from imagining what else he might do with it.

"What do you want to know?" she asks with as little emotion as possible.

"How do we catch criminals in the City?" he asks, putting down the metal. He picks up a roll of bandages and cuts a large square and then another and another.

She hesitates, trying to understand what he wants from her. Her voice comes out thin and distant, as if someone else is speaking through her. "Is this a test of some sort?"

"Humor me. I want to make sure you understand why we're here."

"We don't need to catch criminals because it's virtually impossible to commit a crime."

"It's not impossible; you just can't get away with it. But walk me through it."

She repeats the usual spiel. They're being monitored all the time. Not just a few cameras occasionally catching someone in the act. The cameras are in every tree, every device, every corner of every building. Wherever you stand, you are being observed from a thousand angles. But all these images are meaningless on their own. They produce a mass of data that can't be accessed without good reason. It's those privacy laws that make it all legitimate, that ensure that nobody can argue they live in a totalitarian state.

The cameras are integrated with internal sensors that constantly record your vitals. If there is a sudden change – a spike in adrenaline, like if you fall down the stairs – only then will one of the ladies in the monitoring room be alerted to access the footage. It's called legal data access or LDA for short. Someone will be there in minutes to help you. It means your grandmother with Alzheimer's can live alone in her apartment. A dad can leave his kids in the park while he gets ice cream down the block. No need to worry that they'll be kidnapped like in the old days.

When it comes to crime, say some guy tries to rip off your screen, your adrenaline will trip your sensor, someone will view the scene and the police will come. The simplicity of the system

lies in what happens later. You don't need a prolonged investigation and trial to convict. No need for unreliable witnesses. The evidence is all there. It's just a matter of interpreting it. You either like it or hate it. Both views have merit. You can always leave and try your luck on the outside.

Ana looks down at her left forearm, her own sensor pulsating under her skin. But no one will come, will they? Not here. He's found a way around things.

"An excellent system, isn't it? Takes care of itself. Violence is futile."

"Yes, it is," she says emphatically.

"Except ..." he starts.

"Except what?" she asks a little too quickly.

"If a series of unlikely events converge. A broken camera. A faulty sensor. A power outage in the monitoring room. It's rare, but it happens – what do we do then?"

It never occurred to her that that was a possibility. She looks away from the tray towards the front door.

"That's when they call me. I don't get hired very often – too embarrassing for the government to rely on someone like me when we're supposed to be so enlightened now – but when they need me, they don't hesitate. Because if they fail to respond to anomalies, people lose faith in the system. Are you listening to me?" he asks, offended that she's staring at the door instead of him.

"Yes," she answers, turning her gaze to the bandages, wondering where they will end up, what kind of damage the man will inflict. Will she scream or take it in silence?

"You're interested in this?" he asks, holding up a scalpel.

She doesn't answer him.

"I suppose you're curious what these are for."

She looks for something she can defend herself with if she gets the chance, but there's nothing within reach and her hands are bound.

"Each of these instruments is designed to hurt you," he says, putting the scalpel back in its spot. "I'm going to try one at a time until I find the 'one' and then I am going to use it repeatedly until you tell me where Finn is."

"You seem to enjoy this," she says, surprising herself.

He shrugs. "Oh, I don't know if I enjoy it. I don't have much personality, you know. It's not possible to have personality and hurt people – unless of course you are a psychopath or liar, neither of which I am. Are you a good liar, Ana?"

"No," she mouths, but no sound comes out.

"Well then, this won't take long," he says, kind of disappointed.

He circles her, maybe looking for signs that she's sufficiently terrified to begin his work.

"I like the smell of fear – it's faintly skunk-like," he says, putting his greasy nose close to her neck.

She doesn't flinch. She won't give him the satisfaction.

"Shall we begin then?" he asks, getting serious. "I like to start with one of these," he says, looking through a stack of plastic bags for the perfect one, inspecting them for holes. "Less clean-up after and suffocation often achieves surprising results." Then

he stops and smiles as if he's had a brilliant thought. "No. You are special Ana. An extraordinary tool is needed. He retrieves the shard of metal from his back pocket and runs the *dull* side under her chin. "Where is your brother Ana?" he asks.

"I don't know. He didn't tell me." Her words come out in whispers.

He rolls the shard end to end between his thumb and each finger, considering where to start, like an artist contemplating a bare canvas. "Oh yes," he says, running the sharp point vertically down the left side of her back and then horizontally to the right while she shudders, the blade bumping over scars and vertebrae. She can feel blood drip down and pool at the waistband of her underwear.

"An L for liar." He puts the shard down, a dissatisfied look on his face.

"Maybe we'll try suffocation after all," he says, picking up a plastic bag.

SHE WAKES UP, her head twisted in blankets, a loose spring from the passenger seat cutting into the underside of her arm. It was only a nightmare. She takes deep breaths and then tries to shake off the dream, but it keeps returning like a pesky fly. She doesn't go back to sleep that night or read or look at her map. She imagines plastic bags, hundreds of them, billowing and shuddering, rising above the wall, catching in its wires.

CHAPTER 5

17 MARCH 2064. It's a quaint building Aaron has sent her to, an old convenience store with a faded blue Pepsi symbol on its orange stucco façade. Two bikes are locked to a rack in front, their pedals spinning backwards in the wind. Piles of plastic milk crates are stacked around the side under the eaves, snow blowing through their slats.

She opens the door with difficulty and removes the hood of her parka. The walls have been gutted. Only studs, lath and crumbling plaster remain. Even the copper piping has been removed. A round table with four chairs stands in the middle with a bowl of walnuts and some paper files on it. One of them is open.

"You made it," Aaron says, as if he'd invited her to a party

and not an interrogation. He's by the window talking to Councillor Palmer, one of the nine members of the City's Council, an old colleague of her mother's. She should be surprised that the Council is interested in a criminal case but, then again, it's the first of its kind.

Wet to the bone, they wipe themselves down with a wadded-up t-shirt. Palmer's dressed in a tight suit that she likely had made when she was twenty pounds thinner. She has grease stains on her arm and a blood smear on her blouse.

There are noises from another room, swearing. A man emerges with a bike.

"You've managed to fix the wretched thing Noah?" Palmer asks, taking her bike from him. "I made the mistake of biking here," she says directly to Ana. "It's good for the heart they say. Had a little accident though on the front sidewalk because of this guy," she says, nodding accusingly to something small moving behind Aaron.

He bends down and picks it up affectionately and hands it to Ana. A black and grey husky, hardly more than a pup. It's more surprising than anything else in that room. Dogs are a rare sight in the City. They have no utility. They take up resources and space. If it's Aaron's, there must be something frivolous or even subversive about him.

Remembering her dream, she looks around for weapons and torture instruments, but there are none. Just the dog. He's their weapon. He completely disarms her.

"Have a seat Ana," Palmer says. Ana last saw her when she

spoke at her father's funeral. She took Ana aside afterwards and told her that people like her father made the City worth living in. But Ana isn't sure he had the same respect for her. Not at that point anyway.

And she's seen Noah before as well, although she's never spoken to him. He plays guitar with a popular band. He's performed at a few house parties she's been to. And once, she walked in on him getting it on with a girl in a broom closet. A woman with a glistening black afro and a mask of pretty freckles.

He doesn't look like government. He's more tattooed than not and not exactly muscular. There's no shadow of emotion on his face except disdain as he takes a chair. If anyone is about to torture her, it's him. Clearly, he's decided Finn is guilty, making her an outlaw by association. But at least he doesn't handcuff her or pull out a tray of scalpels and bandages.

Aaron and Noah seem like an odd couple, but then they aren't likely friends. They're government employees hired to play roles. She looks closely at Noah's tattoos, considering whether they are real or part of some cover.

"What is this place?" she asks, touching the stripped walls with her free hand. Nothing happens when she glances her hand over the light panel. "There's no electricity. Are there even …"

"Cameras?" Noah responds. "No. The place is slated for demolition. Has been for years," he says matter-of-factly. Now she's worried. Although she despises the cameras, without them these people can hurt her, and no one will know. She notices now the device in Aaron's back pocket – a stun gun maybe,

and is that a knife protruding from Noah's boot? There are zip ties hanging from Noah's belt. Maybe these three killed Finn, possibly even in a place like this, dissolved him in acid, carried his body out in pieces and fed him to the birds. The whole story about Finn murdering those people was a ruse designed to get her into this unmonitored room so that they can dispose of her as well.

She looks around for evidence of containers of chemicals, plastic tarps, sponges or hacksaws. There's nothing but a chewed-up broom and a bent fork covered in paint. Then she notices the light of the sensor in her arm. It glows warmly, its steady blue pulse calming her. At least *it's* on.

She finally takes a chair but pushes it two feet away from the table. The puppy jumps out of her arms and into Aaron's lap and does that head tilt thing that dogs do.

"How committed are you to finding your brother?" Noah asks, turning to her. When she doesn't answer right away, he looks over at Aaron and sighs, as if bored by this thing they're doing, dragged into it against his will. Where would he rather be, she wonders.

"If you've been watching me, you know the answer," she says.

Palmer takes a photo from one of the paper files and puts it in front of Ana. Noah seems surprised. He reaches to stop her but then hesitates. Perhaps they were going to wait until later to spring it on her, after they'd interrogated her. But Palmer is on the Council. She can play this how she wants.

The photo is of Finn. He's with a group of people Ana

doesn't recognize by a fire pit, behind them a river she's never seen. They're in shorts. It was from last summer when Finn let his hair grow long.

"Where was this taken?" she asks.

"Not in the City," Palmer answers.

She's lying. No one leaves the City and returns. The gate is a one-way exit. Finn was here through the fall, long after the photo was taken. But then if it's true, it explains why she hasn't found any trace of him. Her face turns red; not from embarrassment, but anger. Finn left the City and excluded her. She wasn't good enough to go with him. She doesn't speak until she can compose herself.

She picks up one of the files on the table and leafs through it – photos and notes in Finn's handwriting. A map of places outside the City.

Aaron takes it from her and closes it.

"Will you help us?" he asks.

"Do what?"

"Interpret his files," he says.

"Are you going out there to look for him?" she asks.

"Aaron will," Noah answers.

"Can I go with him?"

"Sure," Noah answers emphatically.

"It's a possibility," Aaron corrects him.

"Why would you want my help?"

They give each other a look like the answer is obvious.

"Because no one else is as motivated to find him as you are,"

Aaron says. "And you're obviously resourceful."

"And you think maybe his allies out there are more likely to cooperate with his sister than you?" Ana adds, beginning to see this for what it is. The people in the photo are likely protecting him. They're not going to answer a detective's questions. Maybe Aaron has already been out there and failed. But Ana is a different story. They might trust a sister. But something still doesn't add up. Why look for him at all? The punishment for murder is banishment. He's already banished himself.

"You don't really think he killed them, do you?" she says, hoping they're not reading her thoughts.

"Your parents were lovely people, Ana," Palmer says. "But ever since your father died, your brother's behavior has occasionally been erratic. We don't know what he's capable of and I don't think you do either."

"You'll be compensated," Aaron says, putting an envelope of silver in front of her as an enticement.

"You think I'm interested in money?" she asks, pushing it back toward him.

"No, of course not," Noah answers sarcastically, as if he has her figured out. She could have abandoned her search for Finn at any point and taken some kind of job. Money is the least of her concerns. But they're willing to give her Finn's files and a means to leave the City to find him. Refusing their offer means giving up on him. And what if they find him without her? Will he even make it back?

"Okay then. What now?" Ana says in defeat.

Palmer puts a screen in front of her and pulls up a document.

"What's this?"

"A contract."

"What am I agreeing to?"

"That you're not going to discuss this with anyone outside this room. If you do, it will be considered treason," Palmer says.

"You have to understand that few people have left the City in thirty years. Few that have returned anyway. If it were to get out that you had been outside the City …" Aaron starts.

Few he said. So there have been others who have left the walls and returned.

"I get it. What else?"

"That you might sustain physical and other injuries should you agree to provide your services," Noah adds, almost mockingly.

"What injuries?" she asks.

"You're leaving the City," Noah says, as if that clearly answers her question.

"You're also agreeing that there is no permanent contract," Palmer continues. "You're not an employee of the Council."

As if she would ever want to be.

"Nor are you entitled to the usual benefits."

"Just envelopes of silver?" she answers Palmer sarcastically.

"Yes," Palmer says, pushing it back across the table. "One a week."

But Ana doesn't take it. She leaves it there for everyone to stare at uncomfortably. She fingerprints their document. She'll do what they want – she'll go out there with them, help them track him – but as soon as she finds him, she'll make sure neither of them returns.

CHAPTER 6

18 MARCH 2064. Spit has a fire going. He's caught something, a squirrel perhaps. It's hard to tell, hairless and skewered on a stick.

"You hungry?" Spit asks, walking over from the trailer, hand extended. Even though the boy is short and thin boned, he somehow manages to fill the space around him. It's his nervous energy. She takes the charbroiled mass from his greasy fingers.

"Squirrel?" she asks, putting on a mask of politeness.

"Bird," he says ripping a bite off the leg in his other hand.

He's not looking at her. He's guilty about something. Probably snuck her screen and dropped it in a puddle.

"I'm not very hungry," she says, but she eats it gristle and all. "Where'd you get it?" she asks as an afterthought, afraid maybe that she's eating a rotting carcass from the road.

"Stupid bird hit the window of the trailer," he says, flicking the bone and picking up some twigs and pine needles to add to his collection under a makeshift awning.

She made the mistake of telling him about Finn last month. Now he wants a daily report on her search – her walks for hours on end exploring underpasses, caves by the river, the places of her and Finn's childhood. But she won't be looking for him in the City now. She'll be working with the government – Finn's new enemy – trying to impress them so they'll let her leave the City with them. But she can't tell Spit about this. She's a pitiful liar so she'll just have to avoid him.

"You okay?" he asks.

"Tired. Think I'll hit the hay early."

"You've got that look my mother gets when she has nothing left to trade."

"I'm fine," she says.

"Does it have something to do with that man?" he persists.

"What man?" she asks.

"The one who was in your car this morning."

"Spit, who was in my car?" she asks.

"He had a tattoo on his hand," he says, excited maybe that he has information for her.

"Aaron?" she asks.

"Didn't say his name. Said he was a friend of yours."

"Not a friend," she says. "What was he doing?"

His eyes light up, the freckles on his face joining in a single brown blob and then tells her what he knows. Aaron wasn't in

the car long. He was looking for something. Of course he was. They've been watching her. Why wouldn't they search her car, maybe plant an audio feed so they can hear her mumbling to herself in her sleep?

"Did you speak to him, Spit?" she asks.

"Maybe a little," he admits.

"What did he say?"

"He said to tell you to get ready. They're coming for you after the weekend."

She goes back to the car, takes an inventory of her belongings, searches every crevice for wires she doesn't recognize, looks beneath the hood, under the rusted bottom with a flashlight, Spit standing behind her. She finds nothing, not until she starts the car. For the first time in two years, the battery is full. She pulls it out and examines it. It's new. She traces the leads from the battery up to where they plug into the solar skin on the roof. Her old stripped wires, with electric tape all over them, have been replaced and the holes in the solar skin patched.

Aaron didn't do this to be nice. He wants to keep her alive until she can help them. She's no good to them frozen. Now he won't have to follow her into snooty restaurants. He can sit behind his camera back at headquarters in his cushy government-issued armchair eating popcorn.

"Stay away from that man, Spit."

Spit pokes at the ground with the stick he cooked the bird with and nods in understanding, even though he's just a kid and

can't know anything. She gathers the feathers and carcass of the bird, throws it in the bushes and covers the bloody mess with clean snow.

CHAPTER 7

19 MARCH 2064. He shovels the slush off the sidewalk in front of his confectionary with youthful enthusiasm, a slight drizzle pooling on the folds of his jacket, his face filled with joy. He's wearing his White Socks' baseball cap, a gift from a partner from another life.

Hooper's the closest thing to family she has now, an uncle of sorts. But she hasn't visited the old man since she dumped some of her family's junk in his basement when she got evicted. She hasn't returned any of his messages or thanked him for breaking into her car to leave baskets of food.

She's not here to ask for forgiveness though, but to search through Finn's boxes. To find an explanation, a map to the outside world maybe. Everyone leaves a crumb behind. Finn's has to be in Hooper's basement.

It occurred to her after the battery thing that leaving the City with Aaron might not be the best idea. How will she get away from him once Finn's found? Hit him over the head with a rock? Outrun him? What if Finn can't walk? Which leaves her with one option, find out how Finn left the City and leave on her own. By the time they realize she's gone, she'll be on the other side where their rules don't apply.

Hooper flips the sign on the door to "closed" and she leaves her car to go to him, shielding her head from the rain with her pack. There's no anger or disappointment on his face when he sees her, only happiness. He pulls her off her feet and she's surprised how good it feels to be in his arms. She drinks in his smell – a mixture of butter and rosemary. She presses her face against his stubble.

"You've made my day," he says, letting her go and leading her inside.

She enters the familiar store and, at once, feels at home amongst the Formica tables and shelves of objects that people have traded for candy over the years – kitchen appliances, children's toys, tools. Nothing stays on the shelves long though; he finds a home for even the strangest of things – a loom, a hand massager.

Hooper's confections are a cross between sculptures and chemistry experiments – an attempt to create something that can't be connected to the world that existed before – apple cilantro candy necklaces with raspberry veins that glow in the dark, ice pops in the shape of City monuments that stay frozen in the sun.

"Will you stay long?" he asks, after she explains that she's there to look for something in her boxes.

"Long enough for you to put me to work after."

"You don't owe me anything, Ana," he says.

But she does, especially Hooper.

He takes her to the basement, puts on a solitary lightbulb in the dank room and leaves her in the middle of her family's discarded possessions, things that might have meant something when they were alive, but now are a burden.

She starts with the biggest box, packed away years before she was forced to leave the apartment. She opens the lid and takes out two large plastic bags of toys, one with a sticker that says Finn on it, the other with NADA written in black marker.

Before she was Ana she was known as Nada. Finn was one of those rare children who couldn't speak before he was four and, then when he did, it was in complete sentences. But before then he could at least say what he thought was his sister's name. He said it with such conviction that soon everyone called her Nada.

The two of them had ten European-made plastic play sets. Every year back then, on Social Contract day, the day of the big parade, the Council would give out prizes – toys for the kids, a vacation at a bed and breakfast for the parents, or a side of beef. It was something for the people to look forward to. There were no raffle tickets to purchase. Instead, a member of the Council would stand on the stage and announce a name in each category, randomly picked by a computer.

In 2046, Finn won the ten sets. They were sealed in a gigantic box that was found in a toy store warehouse. No one even knew what was in it until it was opened. It could have been a box full of dried up markers. Not knowing what was in the box was part of the thrill.

The sets were all over their crammed apartment – a police station in the bathroom, a modernist house filled with plastic furniture in her bedroom, a coliseum in the living room in front of their book shelf.

For years Finn was known as *that* kid who won *that* prize.

When Ana was seven, she contracted a virus. She spent days cooped up in their apartment. It was summer and Finn had to stay home with her while their father worked. At one point, Aavai disappeared altogether for days. He did that a lot in his early years of being a single parent. But Finn knew how to take care of Nada. He brought her cool cloths when she got hot. Made her an icy bath when the cloths didn't bring the fever down and let her have his fire truck. He was getting too old for his toys by then. But she was in no mood to play. When she had cooled down, he tucked her in and read her a book about magic. After thirty-six hours, they ran out of food, but Finn knew where to find his father's stash of coins. He left Ana and went to the market himself, returning with candy from Hooper's and some vegetables from the market. Then he made soup from one of their mother's recipes.

On day five of her illness, their father returned to find Ana covered in scabs. He took one look at her and started weeping,

big droplets that he didn't bother to wipe away. Maybe it was guilt or just sadness that the three of them were alone now. That night – and only that night – he let her sleep with him. He didn't even move her when she was sound asleep.

The next morning, Finn decided they'd go for a walk. They packed up the coliseum in their wagon and walked to one of their favourite spots, the footbridge to a place called the Annex. The Annex isn't a place for kids. It's a small enclave where people are not monitored. You go there if you have no other place to go or if you need a taste of freedom. Anything can happen there.

Right in the middle of the bridge, six feet above the river, they set up their Roman universe, with its horses, gladiators and chariots.

Two boys came up to them. They were taking turns kicking a can from one end to the other. When they saw Ana and Finn they stopped and kicked it right into the middle of the coliseum.

"Your sister is gross," they said to Finn.

"She has a virus," Finn said.

"Is she always going to be that ugly?" the other one said.

Finn turned a little red, clenched his fist around a plastic soldier, but Finn couldn't hurt anyone. He was too reasonable, too understanding.

The boys wouldn't let it go.

"In the old days, they'd lock someone as ugly as her away in a tower."

"Or drown her at birth," the other one said.

Ana got up, smoothed down her pink skirt and preceded to

pin one of the boys down on the wooden slats of the bridge, his head dangling over the side. "Say you're sorry," she said, "or I'll pick off my scabs and put them in your mouth."

He laughed at her and so she did it. She picked a scab off her arm and smeared it across his lips.

Then the boy *did* say he was sorry.

Finn was like his father though. Always drawing out the good in people. He invited the boys to play with them. And when they left, he gave them a chariot. The boys gave Ana their tin can.

Most of the coliseum pieces are gone now, but the horse that went with the chariot is still there. She packs the toys back up – not bothering to sort them into the two bags – and turns to the other boxes.

Broken screens, clothes that she intended to take to a community exchange, Finn's fishing tackle, some ungraded papers from the class he was teaching. That's what she finds. There wasn't a note three months ago when she went through his things. And there's no note now, pictures of people on the outside or sketches of hidden tunnels under the wall.

Hooper is cleaning out cupboards when she returns to his kitchen. Jars are scattered on the small round table where she would sit every Sunday, often on her father's knee or under the table drawing while Hooper and her father talked endlessly about greenhouses.

There are signs of Finn everywhere – the beat-up wooden door that Hooper and Finn pulled across the City on a bike

trailer, the black marble tile that broke when they were playing catch with a glass water bottle, the wicker chair by the basement stairs where Finn would sit and read graphic novels when he was supposed to be at school. They both did that on occasion – leave school and sit in the corner, a book in one hand, exploding sponge toffee in the other.

Before it all happened, Hooper was a bored VP of a large chemical company, their father an unemployed architect working in a watch shop. Neither felt they had much to offer the old world, but in the City, they found their purpose.

"You can help me with something after all," he says, walking out the back door to his greenhouse, a tall narrow structure wedged in the back alley. He wheels around some scaffolding and locks it in place. Climbing to the top, Ana follows behind. The ventilation system is jammed. Together they free some branches and the flaps spring to life again.

"Your father and I never would have become friends if we hadn't been forced to build these wretched greenhouses together," he says.

They were rather different. Her father liked comics, trance music and misfits. He grew up in a devout Sikh family. Hooper liked sports and country music. But everyone was so different from her father, including her mother, that she hadn't noticed.

"I didn't know you were forced to work with him. I assumed he'd found you in a park and dragged you home," she says, as they climb back down the scaffolding. He walks over to a worktable in the greenhouse with tomato seedlings on it and inspects them.

"No. The Council had this bright idea that an architect – who had never actually worked as an architect – and a chemical engineer could build greenhouses. He would design them. I would handle fertilization and pest control."

He replants the seedlings into bigger pots, hands them to Ana, and she stacks them on the long shelves.

"Your father didn't have a clue what he was doing, but he had this marvelous way of surrounding himself with people who did. You remember that first greenhouse? The one at your old building?" She does. It fed her until she got evicted.

Hooper's face is flushed despite the air billowing through the vents now. Is it the memories or is he sick? She should be looking after him, not leaving the City. Soon he'll be grieving for her as well as Finn. It's not fair to him.

"But we still didn't really know each other, your father and I, after we built that first one," he goes on. "We had worked mostly separately until the last month, and when we were together I found him a little – well – irritatingly enthusiastic. But then we started helping others build the greenhouses. It wasn't part of our assignment, but your dad just got so excited that he wanted to get in there with his hammer and nails – although giving him a hammer was never a very good idea – and I couldn't say no to him. He was infectious. I got hooked. It was so rewarding to spend a Saturday with a family, finding materials, setting them up, watching in anticipation as they planted seeds. It was the happiest time of my life."

"And his," she says. She often walks up to the City's highest

hill and looks out over the sea of roofs dotted with greenhouses that her father designed. He's more present on those rooftops than he ever was with her.

Her father always spoke proudly of his time working with Hooper. Hooper was a legend in the City. He'd been in the original building where it all started thirty years ago, where the idea of the City was borne.

Apparently, after the world fell apart, he sat alone in his apartment watching the news until there was no more news. When his food ran out, he connected with a few families in his building purely out of necessity. People who had hardly spoken a word to him in all the years he'd lived there. They made supply runs together, but kept their makeshift weapons close, locked their doors as soon as they were done, didn't say a lot on their trips.

But after the shock passed, they stopped being scared of each other. People emerged from barricaded doors. They shared meals, played music, plowed parks to make communal gardens. They said there was this feeling of brotherhood they'd never experienced before. They were the ones who had made it; managed to escape humanity's fate. When they decided to create a new kind of community, Hooper was on the City's first Council. It wasn't until the wall was built, six years into their experiment, that he decided he had had enough of politics.

But he wasn't bored. In those early years there was a fervor amongst the City's artists and scientists. They refined solar energy, advanced agricultural practices, designed new

communications technology, held poetry evenings and set up art installations. It was a renaissance of sorts. The feeling of being free from the constraints of their old lives and jobs was exhilarating. Her parents and Hooper were at the center of it.

As a lawyer, her mother was soon elected to the Council. And while she sat on committees and drafted laws, her father collected lost souls. He'd get some idea, like starting a community daycare, a multi-faith study group on the meaning of life, or a tool exchange. He would carry it all over the neighborhood, interrupt men playing cards in front of teashops, religious leaders in their churches, synagogues and mosques, parents in parks with strollers. They would follow him home, where the thread of his idea would be woven into something not even he had envisioned. Finn and Ana would come home from school to a living room full of people they'd never met. Most had never met each other. Aavai would be in that red plaid shirt he always wore, his black hair uncombed, someone's toddler on his knee playing with one of Finn's toys.

There would always be a modest meal, some kind of stew that would be thinned out or added to as new guests arrived. What they filled up on though, after the ideas were shared, were stories, mostly from the time before. It was never clear how accurate their tales were. Their memories seemed to be tainted by subsequent events, as if all history had to be rewritten after that day everything collapsed. The adults would laugh and cry. Ana never understood what was so funny about humanity reaching its lowest point. But a memory of something horrific, like dead

bodies lying along the highway or a row of buildings being swept away would make them convulse and double over with laughter until their emotions were spent and then they'd stare at nothing in particular. To her and Finn, who had never experienced that time, it was fascinating.

Although some of the characters that he brought home were questionable, her father always found something interesting about them. With him, the promise of what they might have been was revived.

"He's a grumpy old man, dad. And he smells," Ana said about their neighbor.

"But Ana. He used to fix airplane engines. Can you imagine that? He has so much to teach us." And he *would* end up helping her take apart her first engine. Her father was right. He was always right. And as long as you were in his world, his love would suffuse you. But when you were out of it, he occasionally forgot you existed.

"DOES WHAT YOU'RE looking for in those boxes have anything to do with Finn?" Hooper asks, rousing her out her memories.

"Yes."

"But you're not going to tell me what?"

"No. Not yet."

He looks concerned. She thinks of the photos of dead bodies on gurneys, and the picture they showed him of Finn outside the City, but she wouldn't burden him with all that even if she hadn't signed their confidentiality agreement.

"And you didn't find it?"

"No."

"How long are you going to keep doing this?" he asks.

"As long as it takes."

"It's been months."

"I know."

"I don't think he wants to be found, Ana."

"It's a possibility," she answers soberly.

"His leaving has nothing to do with you Ana. You know that, don't you?"

"I'd like to believe that."

"He wasn't well, Ana."

"He was fine."

"You know he wasn't, Ana."

CHAPTER 8

20 MARCH 2064. The auditorium is dark, but the stage is set for a play – some kind of sea voyage. Few in the City have ever seen a large body of water or travelled on a boat. Professor Ekhart, the leader of the infamous Movement, stands in front of cardboard blue waves, tripping over the rays of a yellow fabric sun.

Ana never understood Finn's attraction to the Movement, but she let him drag her along anyway. Occasionally, she'd even get drawn into the hype, mostly to please him. Professor Ekhart had this way of transfixing people. He'd make them imagine what the City might be capable of without the walls and cameras. He'd talk about rebuilding their broken-down infrastructure with resources outside the walls, reconnecting them with potential survivors, eventually re-establishing a global society. It was a

nice story, but by Monday the spell would wear off. The stack of flyers Ana had agreed to distribute would be in the recycling bin.

Their own father was all about the doing. Talk was a waste of his time. If he saw a young mother struggling to drag a stroller up the stairs with three kids pulling at her, he'd immediately go to the building manager. He'd harass her with gentle urgings until she agreed to set up a stroller park in the entrance. He didn't care if anyone found out what he'd done. He didn't distinguish between big causes and little ones. You see a need you take care of it, he'd say.

As far as she can tell, Ekhart hasn't actually accomplished a thing since the collapse except get elected to the Council. But she should give him credit for that at least. He's the only quasi-revolutionary that has managed to infiltrate the City's leadership.

Maybe she's just jealous of him. Finn started confiding in her less and less after Ekhart became his new father figure. And when they talked alone in their apartment, it was always Ekhart this and that. But then how could she blame Finn? He needed someone to keep that side of him alive.

People turn to stare at her when her seat creaks. When they recognize her, they fixate on her longer than they should. She makes them uncomfortable.

"Good to see you," one of the regulars says. He seems to want to say more, but he stops himself. What can he say? Have you heard anything? It would be a stupid question. If there was news, everyone would have heard it by now.

There's none of the usual anticipation in the room, a far cry from the last meeting she attended before Finn left. There'd been five hundred that night. The Movement was starting to attract some high-level administrators and intellectuals. Their numbers had tripled since Finn and the other four had become involved. There was the usual enthusiastic clapping when Ekhart took the stage that night, but it was Finn's humble and more practical speech that seemed to resonate with them. There was talk of Finn getting elected to the Council. He was becoming more popular than Ekhart. The fact that their mother had been on the Council didn't hurt. And if Ekhart *and* Finn could get elected, the Movement would finally have influence.

She's not here to rally for the Movement though, but to interrogate Ekhart. She suspects he knows what Finn was doing outside the walls. Maybe he even sent him out there to prove that it's safe now or at least that the outside world has something they need. Isn't that the Movement's agenda, to reconnect the City with the world? As a Council member, Ekhart might have been able to help Finn leave. Actually, the whole situation doesn't seem that farfetched, except the murder part.

He has a thing about playing music before meetings, usually starting with a short piece of jazz, maybe Charlie Bird, John Coltrane or Miles Davis – never any of the women – no Ella, Sarah or Etta.

He limps slightly when he plugs in his data key, leaving a depression line in the carpet. Dark circles pull at his eyes.

He's from Denmark. Immigrated when he was seventeen. By

the time it all happened, he was a stockbroker teaching business at the University on the side, married to a Congolese super model.

He puts on Miles Davis' "Kind of Blue", which is entirely appropriate to the mood. And when he looks up into the crowd, assessing the crowd, he finally notices her. He momentarily looks concerned, but then covers his surprise with a smile and a nod.

When the clock approaches 8:00 p.m., the lights dim, and he invites a few "revolutionaries-in-training" to take up chairs beside him.

"Crisis and victory," he starts, "the two opposing forces at the heart of the progress of civilization that propel it forward. One inevitably follows the other. Fellow citizens, we're in a crisis. We've lost good people and, worse, we don't know what happened to them, what danger is lurking in our City ready to strike again. Where does that leave our mighty cause?" – he pauses for dramatic effect – "Not in as bad a state as one might think. Why, you ask me? Because underlying everything there's our will and our will is stronger than the very foundations of this City. And our will tells us we are done with the cameras, done living in a prison City. We want …" – he pauses again – "we need openness, land, everything God has to offer us to grow the seeds of change and we need it before it's too late, before the light is snuffed out of this place by those who are not fueled by hope, or knowledge or vision, but who subsist on the weak and tepid energy of fear. And you. All of you will be the victors in this conquest. You will be the Martin Luther Kings of the twenty-first century. Show others the way. But how you ask me? How

when some of those we have put our faith in have vanished? Well, I'll tell you how we are going to do it. And we *will* do it and we'll do it *now* …"

When he's finished, he turns to the four nervous women and men seated beside him wearing ill-fitting suits, rubbing their hands on their knees to quell their nerves. He gives them ten minutes each to talk about their projects. They stumble through presentations on non-invasive security protocols, empowerment programs for youth, etc. All good initiatives, but wasted in this room.

When the speeches are over, she waits in her seat while the audience greets Ekhart one by one, feigning optimism. He glances over at her from time to time.

"You look thin," he comments when she eventually follows him backstage.

"And you look battered," she responds. He does. There's a new scar over his left ear.

"I'm hungry. Join me?" he asks. She follows him out the loading dock. It's just rained and there's a greenish haze over everything, almost like a faded photograph. He takes her to a Mexican place she's never been to.

"Did they force you to work for them?" he asks, as he enters their order onto a screen, without asking her what she wants. So, he knows about Aaron's offer.

"I wasn't having much luck finding Finn on my own."

"No, I expect you weren't."

"You knew he was leaving the City, didn't you?" she asks.

"I've read the reports."

"I mean before he disappeared," she says.

"What are you getting at?"

"That you told him and the others how to leave? That it was your idea."

He looks at her almost amused, like a parent would regard a child having a tantrum.

"You're not the first to come to that conclusion. I've spent most of the last three months defending myself to the Council. They go through my garbage. They watch me in bed with my wife at night."

"Are they right?"

"No. The sad fact is that Finn and the others were increasingly excluding me. Maybe they thought it was time to replace me – thought I wasn't moving things along fast enough. They were wrong though, weren't they? The fact that the four of them died outside the walls hasn't helped our cause at all. If anything, people will want bigger walls now."

"Why have you been refusing to meet with me?" She tried to get a hold of him a few times after Finn vanished, but he never returned her messages.

"I'd been briefed about Finn's excursions to the outside. How could I meet with you and keep that from you? And what were you going to do with that information? There was no way for you to follow him. Besides …"

"What?"

"I can't answer your real question. You want to know why

he didn't tell you – why you were excluded. That's the hardest part of all of this, isn't it? He didn't ask you to leave with him." Sighing, he looks down at his hands. "But Ana. He didn't want me either."

Ana looks over at the waitress. She's watching a show on her screen. There are dishes on some of the tables that haven't been cleared.

"I want to help you Ana. Who do you think suggested they recruit you?" he says.

"It was you who put me into Aaron and Noah's hands?"

"Not them specifically. That was bad judgment on the Council's part."

She racks her brain trying to figure out how to get through to the man. He's not going to confess to sending Finn out there, not over a plate of enchiladas. He won't even hint at anything under the eyes of the ladies in the monitoring room. They obviously have a warrant to watch both of them. She can imagine the excitement in there right now. Their two prime leads together in one place having it out. But it can't be helped. She'll be in no worse position talking to him. So, what can she do? Plant seeds. It's up to Ekhart to do something with them if he can.

"I expect they'll be going out there any day now to look for him. Maybe they already have. Once Aaron and Noah find Finn, they'll get the truth out of him. The Council will know this was your idea," she says.

"It wasn't, Ana," he says, somewhat exasperated now. He's

come to the end of his rehearsed explanations. Now he's just annoyed.

"It'd be a shame if that happened. The Council would put an end to the Movement. If only …"

His eyes brighten just a little. She hopes he gets it. She's extending an invitation to him. Tell Ana how to leave. Where to go. She could get to him first. Make sure neither of them makes it back to the City. There would never be any evidence against Ekhart, nothing conclusive anyway.

"If only Finn would come back now and clear things up. It would make things so much easier," she says, covering.

They eat in silence, the waitress laughing periodically at her TV show by the cash. He makes an X with his knife and fork to signal that he's done and suddenly frowns at something behind her. She turns around to see what he's looking at. Across the street, a man puts air in his bike tire at a community pump. She can't see his face, but Noah's tattoos are unmistakable. They're following her.

Wow, she's that stupid. It never occurred to her before now that the reason they didn't take her straight into custody after their little meeting at the convenience store was because they wanted her to scramble. See who she talked to. As she took care of loose ends, they'd find out if they'd missed anything. They've probably gone through her boxes at Hooper's as well.

"I start at the Hive tomorrow," she says. He nods. He understands. He's got a day to get her out of the City if he can.

CHAPTER 9

21 MARCH 2064. The government headquarters, known as the Hive, was designed to be an example to the citizens of what might be possible in the new world. Like Hooper's crazy candy, the idea was to build something that didn't look, feel or even smell like any other building in their decaying City. It started in 2049 with the demolition of the airport. Every piece of the place, down to the last drywall screw, was dismantled, transformed and then reassembled to suit the imagination of its ambitious architect.

She had been here for the unveiling with her father. Heard the government's speeches praising their achievement. They toured the Council chamber that day, Ana hopping along the rows of benches while Finn grilled the architect with questions about load-bearing walls.

But it was the quiet spaces that Ana wanted to explore. The walls made of plant life, the inner gardens and courtyards. The building was so alive that it wasn't always clear whether you were outside or inside.

She hesitates as she approaches the entrance. Entering the Hive means an end to her freedom and the beginning of compromise. But Ekhart didn't come through for her and she failed to find Finn's exit on her own. There's no other choice.

The gate to the compound is a curtain of beads controlled by magnets, solid to the touch until released. There are no guards but that doesn't come as a surprise. The Council believes that humans should be in charge of activities that require rational thought or creativity; everything else should be left to technology.

She walks into the scanner and waits in a shower of splintering blue lights for it to identify her and part the gates.

There are rows of evergreen trees on the other side, some big enough to be from the time before, their scent crisp and fresh. Groups of government workers walk on stone paths between the rows, some in uniform, many with screens.

The Hive is in the distance, a round mound of interlaced tree branches, somewhat reminiscent of a giant plant burr, glowing from within. Surrounding the Hive are circles of gardens.

She walks down marble stairs and through the entrance into the underbelly of the sphere. The building extends three stories high and three below ground. Natural light flows into the lower levels through tunnels.

She wants to despise all of this, considering that most citizens live in squalor, but she can't hate something so beautiful and intelligent.

"Hmph. She actually showed up," Noah says to the air, as if she weren't there. How long has he been standing in the entrance waiting for her? He fingers her blouse, dotted with delicate red embroidered flowers. She's suddenly conscious of how shabby she must look in her mother's leftover clothes, with seams that have been re-stitched a dozen times. Maybe she wore it because she remembered her own mother dressing this way when she went to Council meetings.

What appears to be a single escalator winds around the perimeter in a spiral, stopping at each level. They get off at the top floor and walk down a long corridor with spongy floors.

"The floor mats harvest energy from our body heat and movement to power the screens and hard drives," Noah comments proudly, as if he built the place himself. He takes her wrist and feels her rapid pulse. "Fear produces a lot of energy," he says, smirking.

He's wrong. She's not afraid. Her pulse is racing because she's angry – at Finn for leaving without her, at herself for not noticing his transformation, at Ekhart for encouraging him, at Noah for his condescending gaze, at her parents for choosing to settle in this upside-down village.

A team in the hallway argues over a new camera camouflaged as tree bark that is malfunctioning. The other workers seem so clean cut. What do they think of Noah with

his tattoos and abrasive personality?

They walk through a courtyard, men and women sitting on wooden benches nestled into the building's concave walls. At the end is a small kitchen. Freshly cut oranges, a large bowl of lentil salad with petals on it and lavender tea are set out on a counter.

"You'll be hungry, I suppose," he says sarcastically, spooning out two bowls.

She wonders if chaperoning her is an inconvenience to him. Would he rather be looking for her brother beyond the walls, taking in the vast fields, looking for people who match the descriptions of their childhood horror stories, tales of savages and cannibals? She never believed the stories. Why would anyone need to be a cannibal with all the animals and fruit trees out there that humans are no longer competing over?

They end up in a large open room. A half dozen people work around a giant table that is also a screen, each taking up the space they need for their assignment. Some work two-dimensionally and others, three.

He seats her near a row of windows overlooking the ravine – a perfect spot for sledding – and they awkwardly size each other up. Noah has a homely sort of face that nevertheless draws you in. His gaze makes her skin crawl.

"Wait here," he says, getting up. "There's something I'd like to ask you about." A worker next to her transforms her table and chair into various scenes – a picnic table, a school desk, looking perhaps for the perfect setting. Ana touches the table and walls. They're covered in a tightly woven transparent fabric.

Noah returns with a file and inputs something into his screen. A tube descends over their area, the sounds of the other workers instantly erased, but light permeates through the opaque material. He pushes her bowl of lentils toward her, making room for his file.

"Here's the problem. This arrangement of ours, I'm not particularly comfortable with it," he says, rocking his chair on its back legs.

"This 'arrangement' wasn't my idea. I'm not thrilled with it either."

"Maybe you can explain something to me," he says.

"I doubt anything I say will satisfy you."

"You helped your brother with his social projects, attended Movement meetings with him, went to the same parties. You lived with him and shared meals. You shit in the same toilet."

"What's your point?"

"You had no idea he'd been leaving the City for two years?"

"No, but then neither did the government with all its cameras and monitors. Can you explain that?"

"You know what I was doing while Aaron was watching you – you didn't know that, did you, that *he* was the one watching you for countless hours. He's seen more of you than your mother ever did – I was studying your brother. Would you like to know what I found?"

He opens the file and pulls out a paper.

"Two awards for teaching excellence. He was very popular with his students."

He was. Finn was charismatic, a real people person, at least in public. But he could also spend an entire weekend alone in his dark room staring at the ceiling.

"And this one is interesting. He was behind getting the sewage treatment plant moved to a less densely populated area of the City. He was only twenty-one."

He puts a picture of the new sewage plant on top of the teacher's certificate. The stack of Finn's achievements is tall. She wonders how long this is going to take.

"And he liked children, didn't he? Volunteered at the free school he helped set up. Didn't teach though. He built paper airplanes and swords with the kids." He adds a paper airplane to the pile. He did like kids. Maybe that's why he was such an attentive older brother when they were young. It was a good thing she wasn't born first.

"Stellar citizen, wasn't he?"

He was. Much better than her.

"Of course, there was more to him, wasn't there, things that you aren't entirely clueless about?" He moves the bulk of the documents to the left side of the file. Two documents remain. He puts the first in front of her. A prescription for antidepressants.

"He was depressed after your father died?" he asks.

"We both were. That doesn't make him a criminal." She doesn't add that Finn's depression didn't start with their father's death. Either he knows or he doesn't. It's not up to her to enlighten him.

"Were *you* on anti-depressants?" he asks her.

"No," she answers. Maybe she should have been but at the time she didn't feel like she deserved to be happy.

"Are you aware that he abruptly stopped taking them a couple of months later?"

"No. We didn't talk about everything."

"Well that much is obvious." He takes a bite of his sprouted lentils and chews unnecessarily loud. "You weren't close then?"

"Do you have siblings?"

"No."

"Then I doubt I can explain our relationship to you."

What else can she say? They *were* close in the sense that they occupied the same apartment, sat at the same table for meals, hung the laundry together on Sundays. He helped her with her essays. She followed him to his meetings and occasionally entertained his friends at the house. But did they confide in one another? No. Not really. Not at that point.

"What's your explanation for this?" he says.

It's a photo of Finn with a swollen left eye. Finn never got into fights. He wasn't violent. Yeah, he became unhinged in private sometimes, but only Ana and Hooper ever saw that side of him.

"It must have happened outside the City."

"No, it happened here," he says emphatically.

"How can you be so sure?"

"Because I did it myself after he went on a paranoid rampage in Palmer's office a month before he left."

The screen lifts back up and Aaron stands in front of them with a distressed look on his face. "We agreed I would meet her," he says. Noah shrugs, gets up with his file under one arm, nods to them both and disappears between two trees.

Aaron shrugs apologetically. "Did he show you your new office at least?" he asks.

"Not yet." *I get an office?* she wants to ask.

He leads her through the monitoring room, dark except for the glow of an enormous screen with thousands of tiny boxes, each one eyeing a place or person, searching out threats. Some flip images at lightning speed; others show a still image, suspended for closer examination. A 3D image, projected in the middle of a round table, with three women in identical blue uniforms sitting around it, displays scenes that the computer has identified as important – a smashed window in an abandoned store, a potential fire in a warehouse, a woman injured by a falling branch. The women analyze whether the scene requires a police officer, an ambulance or social worker. They operate efficiently, as if they are of one mind. Calls are made to the appropriate authorities and loud speakers are used to talk directly to the criminals, victims and injured.

He deposits her in an office with two neon blue vinyl chairs and an old teak desk filled with pen marks and coffee cup rings from a previous century. It's out of place in this modern building. She feels the desk's surface carefully to determine if it's real, but she can't tell.

"Was Noah polite?" he asks, taking her brother's files out of a box and stacking them on the desk.

"Did you expect that he would be?"

"No."

"You needn't worry. I'm unharmed."

"That's something."

"Unlike my brother," she adds.

He looks up from the files at her questioningly and then shakes off whatever thought he has.

"Where did you find the files?" she asks, taking one. "The Commune" is written on the outside. There are photos of a village of huts and trailers. A barn with sheep and pigs and a large warehouse. She recognizes the river from the photo they showed her. There are images of people that Finn met and diary notes of their conversations. He's done research on each place in the City's archives – satellite photos from the old days, land deeds, historical documents, phone directories.

"We found them in a filing cabinet in the store we met you at the other day. We thought maybe you'd recognize the place, reveal something to us by being there. But clearly it was as foreign to you as it was to us." So, the convenience store was Finn's place. Another thing he kept from her. Maybe that's where she should have looked for Finn's exit.

"This is my job now, reading my brother's files?"

"Today you work here. Tomorrow we start your training," he says.

"For what?"

"You don't want to make it too easy for those savages outside to kill you, do you?" he asks.

"Ha," she replies, but his dour expression indicates that he wasn't joking.

"You find the idea of being molested out there amusing?"

"No, I'm laughing at the thought of me becoming some kind of soldier."

She sits down and picks up another file defiantly, an Orphanage run by a lone woman named Isla. Finn would have liked that – children being rescued from the roads. People with a purpose beyond merely surviving.

"It's going to get ugly out there," he says, leaning forward. "You can change your mind anytime."

"I signed a contract," she reminds him.

"They'd let you out of it if you failed your training or did something crazy," he says.

"How much time did you waste watching me?" she asks as he gets up to leave.

"I'm embarrassed to say," he answers, hovering in the doorway, his back to her.

"That much? Did you enjoy it?" she asks.

"It wasn't the worst thing they've made me do," he answers, leaving her alone in the room with the scraps of Finn's secret life.

CHAPTER 10

22 MARCH 2064. "Ever fire a gun?" Aaron asks.

"No," Ana answers, annoyed that he's bothering to ask her. Why would she have, living in a City where violence isn't an effective weapon?

He takes her hand and turns it over in his, examines her thin wrist and delicate skin and sighs.

"You have no scars," he says.

"Scars are a job requirement?" she asks.

"No. I'm just wondering what kind of shape you'll be in when we return to the City. I'm thinking maybe this is a mistake," he says. She doesn't argue with him. Leaving the City isn't a mistake but putting a gun in her hand is.

They walk through corridor after corridor of weapons and

grenades, things she doesn't know the names of – black, metallic and cold. Items scarcely touched in thirty years.

"You know how they used to decide if someone was guilty of a crime in the Middle Ages?" she asks him.

"No," he answers.

"They would subject the accused to a dangerous ordeal, such as fire or drowning. If he survived, he was innocent. Trial by ordeal they called it."

"Doesn't seem very just."

"No, it wasn't. Someone eventually got the idea that evidence and a trial were necessary. Here in the City we rarely need a trial now because everything we do is recorded."

"What's your point?"

"Don't you think humanity has evolved to the point where we don't need to hurt people to impose justice? Can't words be our weapon outside the City?" She wonders if these old guns even work after all these years.

"And if a savage out there tries to rape you, what will you do, negotiate with him?"

"I doubt a gun will help once he's on top of me."

"You have a point there," he says.

"And don't you think this fear-mongering about the outside world is a little overblown? They all seem pretty innocent from what I've read in Finn's files. A commune, an Orphanage, some Amish farmers."

"You haven't got to the file on the Band then?"

She had, but Finn didn't seem too concerned about them.

Although the Band is clearly the least humane of the organized groups outside the City, they seem to be easily avoided by staying off the main roads and away from their town. And since the Band travels in a large convoy, they can be heard from a mile away. But then there was that one disturbing passage in a file of Finn's from his early days outside:

I guessed the Band had been through the area, maybe the day before. I saw dogs feasting on the charred remains of what might have been a deer barbequed on the side of the road – at least I hoped it was a deer. And there was a trail of horse shit. But it wasn't until I saw the first body I was sure this was the Band's work. It was a boy, no older than sixteen. One of their own. He was wearing a deer hide like the rest of them. There was a bullet hole through his left eye. A note was pinned to his shirt. "This is what happens when you steal from Blackwell". Blackwell is their leader. And I saw one of the Amish, a heavyset man with bangs straight across his forehead. I stopped to see if he was alive. He had no pulse, but I couldn't see a wound. A day later there was an old man slumped against a tree, the back of his head crushed. I wondered if they'd killed him for sport.

"OKAY, YOU WIN. I'll learn to use a gun," she says.

"I'm guessing your experience with hand to hand combat is also limited?" he asks.

"Somewhat," she says.

"And can you take orders?" he asks.

"Probably not. I've never been given any."

"Take this jacket," he says, handing her a windbreaker. "It's cold where we're going."

A sinewy man with a humped back and a liver spotted face greets Ana with a warm handshake. Behind him is a gun cabinet, an old wall calendar with autumn scenes and an assortment of photos of World War II fighter planes.

"What do you want to try with her?" the old man asks enthusiastically, as if they're picking out a Christmas toy.

"How about a 9mm semi-automatic?" Aaron says.

"Oh," he says, somewhat disappointed. "Well alright then." He shuffles over to a round display case and finds one for a small hand. Aaron inspects it, looking for imperfections and then nods to the clerk, who proceeds to search for matching bullets.

They walk outside to a shooting range in a field and wait while the man sets up targets. Leaves from the fall before – crisp and browned – blow across the grass, swelling and lifting. The first few targets are swept away before he's managed to staple them to the boards.

While they wait, Aaron makes her hold the gun loosely in her hand until she's comfortable with its weight. He explains the mechanics of it, his voice barely audible above the wind, loads it and hands it back to her. She takes off the safety, waits for the old man to get out of the way, and makes her first shot.

"Are you a gun expert?" she asks, shaking out the sting from the recoil.

"That would be Noah," he says, squaring off her body and adjusting her hand position.

"And what's your expertise?" she asks, firing again and again until the cartridge is empty.

"I'm better with knives."

She wonders if she'll have a specialty once they're done with her. She was good at darts once. Can you kill with darts? Speaking of killing, will she be able to do it if she has to?

He removes the gun from her hand and brings up their targets.

"Passable," he declares, "for a first try." He's being generous. Half the bullets didn't even hit the sheet.

"So now I can kill someone?" she asks.

"No, now you can shoot a gun," Aaron responds. "I would avoid the killing part."

"Hand-to-hand combat now?" she suggests mockingly.

"Next week," he says in a serious tone that fills her with dread.

He removes the cartridge from her gun.

"This is yours now," he says, putting the gun back in its case. "You'll take it with you when we leave. If we leave."

She nods in understanding while the old man sets up targets for another group that has just arrived.

"It's for protection against them," he says, nodding to the void beyond the wall. "Don't think about using it against me out there," he says, only half joking.

CHAPTER 11

23 MARCH 2064. "Did you get to the part about his girlfriend?" Aaron asks, reading one of Finn's files over Ana's shoulder. Her desk is a mess of documents and stained mugs of cold tea. Everything is a blur, her eyes red and swollen from reading and lack of sleep. Last night she didn't bother to return to her room; she passed out on a bench in the atrium under a yucca tree.

It's as if Finn is a masterpiece that's been painted over and discovered at a garage sale. Her job is to chip away at the façade without damaging the underlying image, until the original work is revealed. But which is the real image now?

"He had a girlfriend?"

"Apparently."

"Couldn't he have gotten laid in the City?" Ana asks him.

"I suspect he didn't leave the City for that purpose," Aaron says. "Not at first anyway."

Of course, he didn't. He left because he'd lost his way, something she was partly to blame for.

"Maybe not, but she might be the reason he didn't come back."

Aaron takes the file from her and finds the notes he's referring to. They're dated 11 September 2063.

"You look as if you can't see straight. Would you like me to read it to you?" he asks, his tone somewhat devious. It's the first time she's seen Aaron since he gave her the gun.

"Please," she says.

He sits down on the corner of her desk and gives the paper a little shake in preparation. He's enjoying this. When he reads, she tries to imagine Finn's voice, but Aaron's relaxed and raspy tone is nothing like Finn's clear and forceful speech.

On my last trip to the Commune I spent some time with Gerald in the barn. We were putting fresh hay in the stalls. Gerald's gun was on an overturned milk crate a few feet away. It made me uncomfortable. In all the months I'd been travelling out there, I'd never held a weapon, not anything designed to be one anyway. Once I tried to show an interest in it, as if it were an art object or historical artifact, and not a means to end a life. But Gerald didn't let me touch it. He probably had more than one reason to avoid educating me on the finer points of killing.

I understand that the Commune needs its weapons. They don't have walls or cameras like the City. But guns – who thought of the

idea of creating something that would, at the very least, tear apart muscle and flesh and, in skilled hands, rupture a critical artery or decimate a vital organ. Such an inelegant way of winning an argument.

"I could get you some stun guns from the City," I offered him. "They don't cause any damage."

"The idea is *to inflict damage," he answered. "If we don't kill the intruder, what are we going to do with him? Send him on his way with a bag lunch? Adopt him?" I knew he was only trying to provoke me. The members of the Commune aren't killers unless they have to be, but I argued with him anyway.*

"So, being humane is inconvenient?" I said.

"Sometimes," he said.

He turned to examine some sheep droppings, weighing a clump in his big leather gloves. I had no idea why. Maybe he was just waiting for something clever to come to him. Maybe the sheep were ill. Gerald's hard to read with all that hair and Elvis sideburns. I have to find his eyes to figure out how he actually feels, which is difficult because he rarely looks at you straight on.

He apparently passed through the City once before the wall went up. Stayed a week or so. Even hooked up with a school teacher. He's probably spent the last twenty-eight years wondering if he should have stayed. He seems to mine our lengthy conversations for proof the City is a failed experiment, ignoring my tales of scientific advancement, community engagement and relative peace. He finds things to be critical of and is patronizing about them.

I don't understand why. The Commune is nothing special. Their

routines are predictable and dull, the only joy a bit of storytelling and singing. It feels claustrophobic even though it's surrounded by miles of mostly open fields. And there is a melancholy about the place. Something happened that no one wants to speak of.

They have no technology either, except for an old airplane Gerald keeps in a hangar a few miles from the settlement. If he has fuel for it, it would be stale by now.

And yet I keep coming back here. I can't stay away.

"How many laws do you have?" he asked me that day.

"Why?" I asked. It was cold in the barn. It had snowed for the first time the day before and, although it had melted, my fingertips were numb, and I could see my breath. I didn't know where they'd put my jacket. Since property is communal, they take everything I have when I arrive. As long I am with them, I have no more entitlement to my stuff than anyone else.

"We don't have any rules. We're anarchists," Gerald said.

"Bullshit. There's no such thing as anarchy. There are rules in every society, even if they aren't written down," I said.

"But the act of making laws explicit is the problem. People use those written laws as a means of exerting power over others."

"You're telling me that your unwritten rules don't result in power struggles? What happens to the guy who refuses to join in on the building of a new outhouse? He gets less to eat. There may not be a bed or blanket waiting for him that night."

"Maybe, but my head would spin with all those laws. I'd probably end up being banished for something I didn't know was a crime, like sleeping with someone's wife."

I doubt Gerald has slept with anyone in a long time.

"We don't have laws on moral behavior," I said. "We leave that to religion and conscience."

Gerald had fingerless mittens on. He could see that I was freezing, but he did nothing to help me. I had youth on my side. He probably thought the lack of mittens evened things out a little.

"Do you have to shovel shit in the City?" Gerald asked, with sheep droppings still in his hand.

"Sometimes. We have our twenty percent rule," I said.

"Twenty percent of what?"

"Eighty percent of our working hours are spent on our chosen work. The other twenty percent is our volunteer hours. Time devoted to the less desirable jobs like sewer work, garbage collection, demolition. It's a sort of tax."

"We don't have taxes or volunteer hours. People just know what they have to do here," Gerald said.

When we finished with the hay, we walked over to the henhouse to collect eggs, but Gerald just watched, resting on a rake, while I wrestled with the chickens. The henhouse was dark. There were no windows, but the sun was glinting through bullet holes in the side. When I asked about the holes once, he brushed me off.

"You get to pick what crap volunteer job you do?" Gerald said twisting his foot in a circle, playing with the light.

"The computer uses an algorithm. It matches what you want to do with what is needed, accounting of course for what you might be good at."

"And if you refuse?"

"You lose your entitlement to social benefits. But most of the time we don't mind the work. Some of my best friends are people I met sorting at the dump."

"All work here is grunt work. Maybe that explains why we're so happy," Gerald said. I couldn't tell if the old man was being sarcastic. Maybe he thought they were content. Isn't perception all that matters? Was I content? Maybe I finally was again.

Miriam walked in at some point. "I thought you might be cold," she said, handing me a parka, glaring at Gerald accusingly. "You'll have no one to talk to, old man, if you don't take better care of your guests" she said. I was just glad that Gerald hadn't shot me yet.

She took the bucket of eggs I had half-filled and headed back to the kitchen. It was torture sitting there with Gerald, waiting until I could make an excuse to visit her cabin. What was it that time, a frozen pipe? But I had to wait a long time – play a couple of chess games with Gerald and his friend, help the men bring in their catch when the boats came back, eat a bland meal of fish and turnips, tell a few stories from the City in front of a bonfire. Only then could I manage to go to her under cover of night. I watched her as inconspicuously as I could throughout the day, noting every gesture. The way her ears poked out of the bandana she tied her hair back with, her red, almost chapped cheeks, her quiet laugh, as if surprised that something could still amuse her.

"What is this thing we're doing?" I asked her one morning.

"I guess it's something for us both to look forward to until we no longer do," she said.

I wonder if some day she won't be happy to see me.

"So next time I come here I might find another man in your cabin with a pile of kindling in his arms."

"I doubt it," she said. "I haul my own wood."

"THERE'S MORE," Aaron says, giving it back to her. She flips to the next page. A drawing of Finn scaling fish with some of the men. The others look burdened, unsettled. What would it have been like for them to have Finn there reminding them how meager their existence was? Does their acceptance of the idea of communal property extend to sharing lovers? Would they have been jealous that Miriam chose to sleep with him? Finn seemed oblivious to any danger he might be in. But whoever drew the picture seemed to understand.

CHAPTER 12

24 MARCH 2064. The room is quiet except for two inharmonious beeps from an EKG machine. The nurse lays out the IV fluid, needle and IV catheter on a tray next to Ana's bed as if setting the table for lunch. He searches through cabinets looking for a tourniquet, wheezing and quietly swearing under his breath. He returns with one, lays it across the IV bag and cracks his knuckles. He's stout, his fingers so fat that his gloves are translucent around them.

"You don't have to go ahead with this," Aaron says to her. He's leaning against the wall, one eye fixed on the nurse.

"It's a minor procedure," she says. "No pain, they promised." They're replacing the monitor in her arm with a special one for government workers.

"It's not the procedure I'm worried about. It's what happens afterward."

The nurse ties the rubber strap around her arm and waits, breathing uncomfortably close to her ear.

"You don't remember me from before, do you?" Aaron asks.

"You were at a Movement meeting last year. We cleaned up together," she answers. She wants to add something disparaging about him spying on those poor fools.

"Before that, as children," he says.

She doesn't know what he's talking about. The nurse can't find a good vein. He palpates her arm, asks her to squeeze her hand and then inserts the needle roughly and unsuccessfully again.

"Elder Street. Back in '50. The testing room."

She knows Elder Street well, the place where they performed their tests on children. But she doesn't remember him.

"You sat in the front. I was in back."

"I didn't notice who was there," she says, finally letting out her breath when the nurse declares he's finally done it. The tubing is adjusted, and a Velcro strap secured over the catheter. The nurse attaches a nerve blocking probe to her other arm, two inches above her old monitor. She winces as he secures it, but then everything below her shoulder becomes numb.

"Well, I remember you," Aaron says. "That orange sundress you wore was the only color in the room. You gripped your pencil like a horse waiting to burst out of the gate. Once you started, you bit your lower lip and stayed that way the whole time. You

looked back every once in a while, not at me, but over me, at the clock."

"Were you the one with those balloon pants that were all the rage back then and a shaved head?"

"Guilty," he says.

"I hated going there."

"Why, you were exactly what they were looking for. Highest IQ in the room."

"It wasn't our intelligence they were interested in. They didn't even look at the results of those tests."

The testing started in '44. By that point, the Council was pretty proud of its achievements. They'd created a sort of utopia out of the ashes. The atheists thought their enlightened City reflected their own brilliance and fair-mindedness. The religious saw it as the beginnings of God's Kingdom on Earth. What they agreed on was that this experiment depended on a new race of children. They weren't entirely clear, at first, what qualities these children would need. IQ was obviously not decisive. Resilience was important, but not enough because an intelligent person could survive and still be a psychopath. They were looking for people, like the early settlers of the City, who had a high sense of justice. They had to have the intelligence to form strong opinions without being dissidents. They needed to be able to collaborate in a way that was neither overly competitive nor acquiescent. Those who abandoned their ideas too quickly weren't invited back. The select group of children who were invited to the sessions were carefully observed so that these essential

characteristics could be identified. Once the Council was clear what the new race should look like, they developed their ideas into a curriculum that was taught in the schools. The hope was that this group they had put together would also act as the leaven for the rest of them.

"How do you know all this?"

Hooper told her. As a former Council member, he knew about it. He'd let it slip. But she can't let Aaron know that. They'll be following him around next. Probably already are.

"I went back to grab my sweater once. Saw the examiner stuffing the IQ tests in the garbage without even looking at them. Then I started observing them. The receptionist had a weak bladder. When she was in the restroom, I glanced over the desk at some notes she'd taken on our 'personalities'. I did some digging and found out that she had a PhD in behavioral psychology. Everyone there, including the janitor, was acting. They were all part of the study."

That part is also true.

She's surprised that they share this memory, that at one point they were just two kids in a room with puzzles to solve.

"How long did you last?" she asks him.

"A year."

"Longer than most then." She was there every Wednesday for three years.

"You should know that what is about to happen to you is far worse than anything they put us through back then," he says, looking down at the pulsating light in her arm. The nurse tugs it

out with pliers, its nerves dangling like tentacles. He performs a nerve conduction test to determine if there's been any damage. Satisfied, he glues the wound.

"You recruited me. Why are you always trying to talk me out of this?" she asks.

"You were just a woman in some footage then."

"And now?"

"And now you talk."

"Don't do that," she says.

"What?"

"Pretend like I'm important to you. Are you forgetting that your job is to arrest my brother for murder?" she asks. "There's little chance you and I are ever going to become friends."

"I suppose not. Let me put it another way then. You're an important asset that I need to protect."

The nurse leaves them to find gauze.

"Nothing in your contract requires you to leave the City. I could go without you, keep you informed of my progress. You'll have your chance to defend Finn if we manage to bring him back. I'll make sure he does come back." That's what she's afraid of.

"Maybe you should tell me what this bad thing is that they're going to do?" Whatever it is, she's not too worried. They obviously did it to Aaron and Noah and they don't look too traumatized.

"The Council is worried we've become soft over the last thirty years. If we're ever attacked from the outside again – or even from within – they don't want us to hesitate."

"The training is brutal. That's hardly surprising."

"More than brutal. The problem is that they tell you it's virtual training, but they have ways of making us believe that what we see is real. We have memories of things that didn't happen, injuries that can never heal because there's nothing to repair. And they can do all this in a fraction of a second."

"You're exaggerating."

"I'm not."

"You just don't want me out there with you."

"You'll hate me when this is over," he answers, avoiding her question.

I already do, she wants to answer. Not him in particular – he's not so horrible as far as they go, which is likely why they chose him for this – but the whole machinery of government. They've always had it in for her family since her mother was out of the picture. They were never direct about it because both Finn and her father were popular, but popular makes you powerful and people don't like to share power.

She tries to will her fingers to move, but they won't.

"Why do I need a new monitor anyway?" she asks him.

"This one syncs with the training program and has built-in injections for pain and such," he adds, ominously. She wonders what the "such" means. The nurse inserts something into her IV, cleans up his mess, takes his cart and closes her curtain. If Aaron says anything more, she has no memory of it. All she recalls after that point is a feeling of total bliss. For the first time in years, she doesn't care about anything.

Then there's a doctor, speaking to her in soft tones, explaining every step and telling her to move into position. She can hear voices, even understand them, but it's as if she's observing. The nerve-blocking probe is moved to her lower back. More drugs are injected into her IV. When she slips back into consciousness, she's on her back again. Aaron is gone and so is the nurse. The room is dark except for the colorful lights of the machines surrounding her now.

The nurse returns, tells her they're giving her adrenaline and she's jolted out of her euphoric state. Her arm is sore, and it feels as if a piece of her back is missing now, like there's a big round hole right through her middle, but she can walk.

Two orderlies lead her, one on each side, to a virtual reality chamber, squirt contact gel all over her head and body and affix sensors. They put contacts in her eyes as well. She's shown various images – someone standing at the edge of a cliff looking down, children lined up outside a classroom, a knife flying through the air an inch away from a smiling toddler's head, a frozen body in the snow, puppies nestling together, birthday parties, a woman breastfeeding, her father washed up on the river bank with a gash in his forehead. Eventually a voice announces that calibration of her monitor is complete. The screen goes blank. She goes to the door to leave, but it's locked. She knocks, but no one comes to open it. She looks back into the room and sees herself still seated in the chair.

There's a flicker. She's in a scene now, in the alley behind Hooper's, but the greenhouse is gone. She looks at her hands,

rotates them, checks for the mole behind her left leg, the bruise on her foot from kicking Finn's boxes in frustration. They are all there in the virtual world. She jumps up and down. The motion is awkward at first – real but surreal. Certain things are missing; like the ache she's always had in her left hip from a skateboarding accident. They wouldn't know about that. And the gravity isn't quite right. She feels slightly less resistance when she moves. She goes into the store and touches things– a piece of marshmallow on the tester tray in the candy shop and a tea towel. They're a little sharper than normal. Too much sensation. She can smell burnt sugar and strawberries but not the lemon she puts to her nose. But humans are adaptable – we fill in the blanks quickly – and soon this place is as familiar as the real one.

There's a guttural noise coming from the kitchen. A man is strangling Hooper. She tries to pull him off. It's almost comical and she's painfully aware that they're watching her, taking notes, discussing her prowess. She's played video games before, even virtual ones. What the hell. She should just have fun with it.

He loosens his grip on Hooper and turns to confront her. After sizing her up, he laughs – of course, they would write intimidation into the program – seizes her easily by the arm and slams her against the wall, pushing her face into the white subway tiles over the recycling bin. Snaking his dirty hand up her shirt he grabs at her breast. Licks her neck while Hooper looks on distressed. She winces in pain when he pinches her nipple hard. Of course, they're worried about sexual violence on the outside. They're trying to prepare her for it.

He undoes his jeans with his free hand and pulls them down and then proceeds to pull at hers. Distracted, he doesn't see Hooper swing a two-by-four at his head. The man falls away from her. She picks up the wood just as the man's friend comes to his rescue and swings it wildly in the air, but he backs her into a corner. Hooper is weaponless.

A voice tells her to retrieve her gun. She didn't know she had one. Her 9mm is in a holster by her side. She fires it at the man, barely grazing him, but he stumbles, and she can exit into the alley. One of her attackers pulls out a small dagger and manages to jab her in the back by the kitchen door. It pierces through muscle and bounces off her rib cage with an exaggerated thud and scrape. Her back becomes slick with blood. The voice tells her to run. She reluctantly leaves Hooper behind – she'll draw them away – and finds her way into the market and loses them.

It's not the market she knows, but an Arab bazaar. She pushes through a crowd on a narrow stone path, stalls of colorful spices, wicker baskets, scarves and jewelry closing in on either side. At the end is a carpet stand. She weaves between blood red rugs suspended from a ceiling and slips out into openness again. Some programmer must have been bored and snuck that in.

She runs along the familiar street of office buildings that have been converted into apartments, each stride like three in the real world. A woman she passes is struggling to remove her groceries from the handle bars of her bike while a toddler teeters on the edge of her bike seat. She can't help them. They're testing her focus. The men are gaining on her now.

She steals a bike and rides along the North side of the wall to a grove of trees where she can hide. But the wall isn't there when she arrives. She's outside the City, surrounded by miles of mowed grass. The men catch up to her, one of them yanking her backwards, his fist full of her hair. The gun is still in her hand. She shoots her attacker in the foot, turns and pulls the trigger again. The men disappear. The screen goes blank. She can feel the chair under her. Something cold runs from her monitor through her spine.

That wasn't so bad, she tells herself.

But they're not done. A box in the corner records her heart rate. Each time it drops below 120, she's propelled into a new scene. An encounter with wolves. A lightning storm. Weeks go by. She eventually finds a boulder overlooking a thin stream of water and collapses onto her back. Finn is asleep beside her. It's the last thing she remembers.

CHAPTER 13

25 MARCH 2064. “Ana,” someone calls to her, rousing her, his hand on her thigh.

Stop touching me, she wants to shout. If he doesn’t stop right now, she’ll lunge at him. Put her thumb in his eye socket. Her mouth doesn’t want to move though. She kicks at him and he backs away. She hears noises like an animal. They’re coming from her.

She parts her eyes a little. They resist stubbornly, as if there’s nothing outside her head worth seeing. The light is painfully bright. Where is it coming from? Someone’s screen. One of the voices takes pity on her and turns it off. It takes a moment to adjust and then she sees the two of them clearly, Aaron and the nurse from earlier.

"How long has she been like this?" Aaron asks.

"All night," the nurse says.

"What have you given her?"

"Nothing. They said to run it by you first."

"Dammit. Can't you see that's she's suffering?"

"We couldn't reach you."

What is this all about? She wills her lids to open fully and takes in her room. A simple box. A bed and a dresser. Concrete floors. Her shoes by the foot of the bed. She remembers now. She's in her room in the Hive. Her clothes are drenched in sweat. How did she get here? They brought her back here, didn't they? Someone changed her into scrubs. They put her in that bed by the window. She was exhausted and fell asleep immediately, but then the visions started. She was sure she was back in the chair again. That all of this was part of their "training". She panicked. The door was locked. She pressed the red button they told her was for emergencies and waited in the corner shaking. No one came.

"I want to go back to my car. Get me out of here." Did she say that out loud? Did they hear her?

"Someone needs to be with you, Ana. Hold on a second, will you. Let me make some calls," Aaron says.

He helps her up and seats her on the window ledge. Spotlights below the window light up some branches, swaths of green bending in and out of darkness.

There's whispering in the hallway. Although they're quiet, she can tell Aaron is angry.

He comes back and sits beside her, his face full of worry.

"It won't be long, Ana. I'm going to help you."

"I can go back to my car?"

"Noah took your car. Don't you remember? It's being fixed up."

"I can't be here, Aaron."

"I know."

"I failed the test, didn't I?"

"It wasn't a test, Ana. You were just supposed to get through it. You should have seen me after my first session."

"I don't think there's any oxygen in here, Aaron. I can't breathe."

"It's just a panic attack. Imagine that you're doing jumping jacks. It helps."

"They've okayed it," the nurse says, coming to check her pulse. "She's your responsibility now. You know what it'll mean if you mess this up."

"We'll be fine."

"What's happening?"

"You're coming to stay with us. Is that okay, Ana? I can get you out of here, but you'll have to stay with Noah and me."

"Okay," she says, because she just wants to leave and breathe again.

They take the escalator to the top floor of the Hive. It's mostly dark in the corridor, just some exit lights illuminating their way. From the top floor they take a set of stairs. Her legs resist movement. They shake with every step. He puts her inside

a passenger drone and keys in an address. She's in there alone for some time while he talks to the nurse. She's afraid the door is going to close, and the drone will leave without him. Finally, he gets in beside her. It takes them to a housing block on the east end. One of those neighborhoods where the buildings all look the same. They have to paint them different colours, so you know which one is home. They land right on the street. There isn't a car or drone in sight other than his. The people here are too poor to own a vehicle. She's relieved to find out that Aaron lives on the first floor. She can't make it up another flight of stairs. The door is purple. He can barely open it with his key. When he does, the broken bottom scrapes loudly against the floor.

"They're sleeping," he says. "We'll have to keep it down." Who is *they* she wonders? Is the extra person Aaron's girlfriend or Noah's? He lights the room dimly with a table lamp and helps her onto the couch. He leaves her there awkwardly while he rummages through cupboards. He comes back with a pink duvet and sheets. "This will have to do for tonight. We'll make better arrangements tomorrow."

"It's okay, Aaron." She's starting to feel like herself.

"Take this," he says, handing her a pill. "It'll stop the panic."

She's not sure if the pill is for her benefit or his – probably doesn't want her screaming and waking up the others – but she's grateful anyway.

In the morning, there's a little person sitting on the edge of her couch in a long white nightie, her black hair tangled and sticking out at odd angles.

"That's my blanket," she says to Ana.

"Leave her be, Martha. She's our guest," Noah says, emphasizing the word guest as if it's an inconvenience.

"Who does she belong to?" Ana asks, looking under her blanket, hoping she has clothes on.

"Children aren't property," Noah says.

"Don't use your mad voice, daddy," the girl says.

Daddy? Ana has a hard time believing that Noah could have offspring.

The girl twists her dark arms in and around his pale ones. He extricates his arms from hers and the two of them do a two-minute long secret handshake that includes beat boxing and dance moves. She squeals with delight and Ana sees Noah smile for the first time. The two of them have the same chin now that she looks closer and the same Slavic eyes. She's just a darker version of him.

"What time is it?" Ana asks.

"Ten. You've slept half the morning away."

"Where is Aaron?"

"Don't worry, he'll meet us there."

"Where?"

"The Hive. But first I was told to get you into the shower. You smell like a locker room."

When she returns, transformed, from the bathroom, Noah is eating porridge with Martha on his lap. He tries to eat but can't get the spoon to his mouth with all her bouncing. He attempts a spoonful, but it lands on the floor. Resigned, he feeds

her instead. He's remarkably gentle. She leans over the bowl as he shovels it in. Wiry curls bob in and out of the mixture. A few are glued to her face.

The little girl is dressed now, her outfit perfectly matched, a green and pink kilt and pink t-shirt. A pink and gold earring in one earlobe. The other is slightly infected and red.

"Go and get your school bag and socks," he says, when she's had enough. He lifts her onto the floor and pushes her a little in the correct direction.

"You know her grandfather quite well, I think," he says casually when Martha is out of earshot.

"Do I?" she asks.

"Ekhart," he says, gauging her reaction.

Of course. The one and only time she met Noah was when she walked in on him at a party making out with that beautiful freckled girl with the afro. She never made the connection. The girl was Ekhart's daughter. But didn't Ekhart confide in her that his daughter was in a group home? That she suffered from mental distress as he put it? Maybe that's why Ekhart and Noah have both made disparaging remarks about one another. They had a falling out over Martha's mother.

"Okay, we can go," he says, when Martha is getting her shoes on. "We need to drop her off at daycare first. Are you okay to walk, Ana, or do I need to call for a ride?"

"I can walk," she says, although the idea of walking several kilometers with Noah isn't particularly compelling.

CHAPTER 14

26 MARCH 2064. Noah takes her to the training room, mirrors all around, the floor slightly bouncy beneath her feet.

"It stops," he says to her. "The flashbacks. In a few days."

"How comforting."

Her ordeal in the virtual chamber is already fading. She can at least distinguish fact from fiction now.

"I have no interest in comforting you. The reality outside the City will be far worse."

"Are you always so cynical?"

"I'd rather be that than unprepared."

"Can we hit each other now?"

"You'd like that, wouldn't you?" he asks.

"Yes," she says, without qualifying her answer. After living

in a virtual world, and the humiliating episode last night, she's anxious for the experience to be real at least. She suspects he understands.

"We'll start with some simple moves," he says, but there's nothing uncomplicated about what he teaches her. Getting out of a wrist hold. Levelling a blow to the knee. Breaking a nose in the most painful manner. Choke holds. Head butting. Elbow strikes to the temple. It all looks possible when he shows her on a dummy – the details of where to strike and how hard make sense – but even after everything they've done to her, she can't override her instinct to preserve life.

"Slow down," he says, when she's imitating a combination he just showed her, trying to be as aggressive as possible to impress him. "What's with the lightning speed?"

"What am I doing wrong now?"

"Do it in slow motion like I said. You have to train slowly. Don't worry, when you're angry everything will speed up. Right now, you're just trying to build muscle memory."

Noah doesn't ever praise or encourage her. The only clue that she's improving is when he lets her move on to something new.

This isn't entirely foreign to her. Finn and Ana used to watch Aikido videos on their screens. Dressed in black, and carrying broomstick handles, they'd go to the rooftops of the City's highest buildings and pretend to be ninjas. But it was all about making a crisp thwack with their wooden sticks, not about maiming or subduing.

In the afternoon, Noah hands her a case with contacts in it.

"These work with your new monitor and the implants in your ears," he says. She feels her ears. She must have been sedated for that part. She wonders if there are any other artificial parts in her now.

"Your training will be based on the psychological profile gathered during your virtual training. The program will give you instructions through your earpiece."

He doesn't give her any clues as to her performance in the virtual training chair. It's a small mercy. She'd rather not know.

"This will work out there?" she asks.

She hangs on to his every word. He's cantankerous and clearly distrusting of her, but his training might make the difference between life and death out there. She doesn't have to like him.

"No. Once you're outside the walls, you'll be offline. You won't be connected to the network anymore. But it might help you figure out what you're capable of."

He lifts a padded suit off a hook and hands it to her. The material on the side closest to her skin is a mesh of microscopic beads. It's soft until Noah moves his hand towards her and then the beads move together to form a hard shield. The same technology as the gate to the Hive. The outside is padded, likely to prevent Noah from being injured when he pummels her.

"Go ahead," he says once he has his own suit on. They move in a slow circle watching each other. The voice in her head tells her to grab his shoulders and try to knee him in the groin, but she can't respond fast enough. He hits her in the stomach. She's thrown to the ground, but there's no pain, only pressure.

"If you don't listen to the tech, you can't learn," he says. She's exhausted. So is he. She fantasizes about floating in the pool or maybe walking in the forest outside the Hive. And she's tired of looking at Noah's face. She's memorized every mole and pimple scar.

The voice tells her to stand and aim for his throat with the side of her wrist. She attempts this, but he blocks her again and grabs her by the waist, twisting her down. An image shows her how to bring her elbow down hard on his kidneys. She executes the move, but it's sloppy. The voice is too fast, Noah too quick. He pulls her onto the ground, immobilizing her with one arm across her chest.

Aaron appears in the doorway in a padded suit. She hasn't seen him since last night. From the glance Noah gives him, he's not supposed to be there.

The two of them demonstrate a full-on fight and she realizes then how far she is from being able to do this. They move from one side of the room to the other, pinning each other and continually extricating themselves from impossible holds. When they pull off their masks, she can see that, despite the padding, there's minor damage. Large red splotches mark their faces, but they're both exhilarated. They like this.

Aaron continues her training while Noah watches from the sidelines, smirking. It's a good idea. They need to learn how the other moves since they'll be partners. But Aaron doesn't hit Ana. He only defends himself. Noah calls a time-out.

"Aaron," he says emphatically. "Beat the shit out of her so she can learn something."

She agrees and so she grips him by the shoulders and knees him in the groin, hard enough to get him motivated. He grabs her by the wrist, twists her arm behind her, pushes her to the ground, his knee in her back. He's even faster than Noah. The voice tells her to reach around with her free hand and pull at his neck. She closes off his airway enough to get him to let go. He pushes her to the ground on her back, his elbow across her throat. He could just stay there – wait for Noah to call it – but he releases her. He gets up, shaking his head and leaves in frustration without saying a word to either of them.

That night and every night of her training, Aaron and she take the same drone back to his place. She shares the living room with Martha, Ana on a twin bed, Martha on a mat on the floor. The two of them play Go Fish. They build a Lego fire station. Ana puts her to bed at night and covers her with a soft pink and blue quilt that Martha's mother sent her. There are knitted items all over Martha's corner of the room – dolls, book covers, doilies, wall hangings with inspirational words woven into them like "peace" and "love". Weaving these words into art is her mother's only way of ensuring they come true now.

On day three, Martha sits glued to the living room window. Aaron is next to his stereo trying to find music he thinks Ana might like. He's failing miserably. Their tastes are not at all similar. He's stuck in the 1980s. She won't go lower than 2040. Noah is doing dishes in the tiny galley kitchen. It's so small that only

one person can be there at a time. The fridge makes a hum that you can hear over the music.

"Is she coming with us?" Martha asks.

"Where?" Noah asks.

"She wants to go sledding," Aaron says, coolly.

"You won't be going sledding," Noah says. His voice firm, but not unkind. Outside, a group of kids fly down a rather steep hill. A dining room chair is fastened to one of the sleds. It looks horribly dangerous and somewhat stupid, exactly the kind of thing she would have loved as a kid.

"Can I take her out there?" Ana offers.

"She's grounded," Noah says.

"What for?" She suddenly has sympathy for the little girl. She's also a bit jealous that Martha has adults in her life who care whether or not she's naughty. She and Finn did horrible and dangerous things; no one noticed.

"She poured water down her friend's underwear at daycare so that he'd be teased for peeing his pants."

"Did he get in trouble before they figured out you were behind it?" she asks Martha.

The girl doesn't answer. She just covers her eyes with her hands.

"And last week she poured juice into my guitar because she was upset I was going to a gig." Her fingers open slightly as she peers at Noah with large hazel eyes. "Oh. You didn't think we found out about that one, did you? Don't you know that adults know everything, and we read minds?"

"We're out of towels again," he says to Aaron.

"So, do a load of laundry," Aaron barks back.

"And the week before that, she encouraged one of the girls to stick a hair pin in an electrical outlet," he says, continuing his tale of Martha's escapades. "She's been kicked out of three day-cares this year. If she doesn't start behaving herself, one of us is going to have to quit working and stay home with her."

"Would you consider a brief suspension of her sentence?"

Aaron and Noah stop what they're doing and look at her with a horrified expression. She's violated the parenting code, but she can't take it back now.

"Let them go," Aaron says. "Double or nothing?" he asks Martha sternly.

"I swear. If I do anything naughty, you can hit me with a stick."

"Where does she get these things?" Noah asks Aaron. "No stick. You'll be grounded for four days."

"I accept," Martha says with a bow and curtsy. She smiles at Ana conspiratorially.

The girl's probation ends up lasting over an hour. Noah and Aaron join them. By the time the four of them return, they are pink-faced and exhausted. She's left alone with Martha while Aaron and Noah walk to the grocery store for hot chocolate ingredients. Martha will be allowed a cup if she gets ready for bed. Ana helps her and then reads her a story while they wait. Halfway through, Martha is snoring lightly. Ana has forgotten to make her brush her teeth. She would be a horrible parent.

She closes Martha's door quietly and explores the bedroom that Aaron and Noah share. There's a library of history books, organized chronologically from the beginning of time to the collapse, some textbooks on economic theory and a few Norwegian novels. The walls are empty except for a Father's Day card from Martha with a stick figure drawing of Aaron and Noah with swords in one hand, flowers in the other. Aaron is wearing a veil. They're getting married.

There are almost no clothes in their closet. Just a few worn shirts, unmatched socks and a small white t-shirt that could only have belonged to a woman. She finds a shoebox in Aaron's drawer with odd bits: a few polished rocks, some bullet casings, poetry and letters from a former girlfriend that she barely resists reading – the writing is offensively neat –, and a picture of a tall man, maybe his father. She feels slightly ashamed that she's invading their privacy but not enough to stop. Besides, wasn't Aaron watching her for months without her knowledge? Fair is fair. She searches the medicine cabinet as well, pushing the ceiling tiles up to look for hidden objects. But if they have more secrets, they're not hidden in this apartment.

CHAPTER 15

28 MARCH 2064. Week two begins with training videos that tell her how to do two things at once – talk to someone in a way that encourages them to cooperate while scanning the scene for dangers, potential weapons, exit routes, etc. She learns the ten most obvious places to hide weapons in a room. They tell her to be prepared for the worst, but to focus on persuasion, how to weigh whether to run or fight and, when she has to run, where to go.

"This part of the training actually make sense to me," she says to Aaron in the orange grove during a mid-morning break. "I think I might be good at running away."

"It does seem like the preferred option," he says, holding her performance report from yesterday in the crook of his arm.

Her "team" is continually assessing her, although she's never met them. Everyone but her gets to see the reports. She is simply the object of their experiment. She tries to make out some words, but he moves too quickly. All she catches is a blur of yellow highlight, which indicates the things she's struggling with. Today, the report is mostly yellow.

When they're done with the videos, Aaron takes her back to the procedure room. Just seeing the empty VR chairs makes her heart race.

"Don't worry, you'll never have to go back in there," he says. "Today we just sit." Electrodes that strengthen certain weak muscles are attached to their legs and arms. They're given various injections of vitamins, minerals and amino acids, followed by vaccinations. It's the first time that Aaron is also a patient. Her equal. It's promising. It means they're preparing them to leave together.

In the evening, the computer reviews her hand-to-hand combat performance from yesterday and gives her advice. It shows her alternative moves using her image.

When they're ready to leave, Aaron looks worried.

"I'm failing, aren't I?" she asks.

"Not exactly."

"You couldn't possibly have expected that I would become Wonder Woman in two weeks."

"Of course not."

"What do they want then?"

"There is only one purpose to the training," he says. "To

instill a desire in you to defend yourself, a survival instinct that few in the City have now."

"And have you done that?"

"No. Not yet. But before your training is over, I suspect Noah will manage it, no thanks to me."

"And if he doesn't?"

"Then you don't leave with me."

"Shouldn't that make you happy? You don't want me to pass."

"True, I don't. But he does, and I owe him."

"You're a very complicated person."

"Are you tired?"

"No," she says, although she could fall asleep right there on the training mat.

"Will you go somewhere with me?" he offers.

THE DRONE DROPS them off in a part of town where wealthy people used to live. She's never explored the area. Nothing about it has ever interested her. They stop in front of a large mansion on the highest hill in the City. It's dark, the two flower beds in front untended. Boards cover the windows. A basketball hoop hangs above the garage, its net in perfect condition.

"What is this place?" she asks.

"Noah's house," he says, so convincingly she almost believes it. But no individual in the City could have a place like this to himself. If he did own it, why live in a one-bedroom dump?

"There's a loose board in back. Come," he says.

"This is going to get us into trouble, isn't it?"

"Not if you keep your heart rate down. Can you do that, Ana?" He's taunting her. It's a side of him she's never seen before. In the few days she's known him, he's always toed the line. If it weren't for his L2 tattoo, she might accuse him of being boring.

"I can," she says, actually feeling confident. The one thing they've effectively taught her is how to slow her heart rate. Even if she never leaves the City, it's a skill that will come in handy.

The house is even bigger than it looks from the outside. Built on a ravine, it cascades down the hill. The entrance is on the top floor and all of the bedrooms on the lower levels, each with their own terrace. They enter through the kitchen. The marble counters are stained and chipped from years of cooking and the walls are filled with crayon marks, but it's clear that it was once a home of luxury. The library he takes her through is the most beautiful room she's ever seen. Two stories high. Scattered afghan rugs on the floor. Antiques that have somehow avoided destruction. Sculptures on plinths. More books than she can count.

There's a blurry photo on a bookshelf of a man at the City's gate. He's wearing a black trench coat, his hair long and slightly graying, an officer beside him. An enormous backpack leans against the City's wall with a rolled-up tent and sleeping bag attached to it. A pan dangles off to one side, a guitar off the other. There's a look of anticipation on his face, maybe even relief.

"Who is he?"

"Noah's father."

"Was he banished?"

"He was an asshole."

"A rich asshole, it seems."

"He owned real estate in the City when the collapse happened. Made a killing off the apocalypse."

"Must have been nice growing up in a palace."

"He didn't get a chance, actually. My mother was his nanny. And when his own mother passed, and my mother saw how neglected he was, she packed him up and moved him in with us to live in squalor."

"How did his father get banished?"

"My fault."

"Are you going to tell me about it?"

"You might think less of me."

"I don't think much of you as it is," she says, attempting a laugh. It doesn't go over well.

"It was senior year. My mother had a cooking gig at the farm. That's where she is now. There wasn't room for us there, so we decided to move back here for a while. Noah and his father were sort of getting along. Things were pretty good. Then Noah started dating Julia, Martha's mother. I don't think she liked him as much as he liked her – they were always fighting – but she hung out here nevertheless.

Noah's dad could be very charismatic. Sometimes we'd come home and find her talking to him. He'd be making her something elaborate in the kitchen or showing off his art collection. We didn't like it but what could we say? He'd argue he was just being a polite host.

Then, one day, I walked in on them. Her shirt was off. He was taking pictures of her naked. She was only sixteen. I attacked him. Noah walked in and got in on it as well. When it was over, Noah's dad got charged with sexual assault and banished and I got the L2 tattoo. Maybe they would have banished me too if it weren't for the circumstances. I was protecting a minor. Noah wasn't eighteen yet so he was only provisionally charged. If he stays clean, his record will be expunged."

"They tattooed you for hitting a pedophile?"

"I didn't just hit him, I almost killed him. Excessive force they called it. He gave back though," he says, nodding to the scars on his arm. "It's not my proudest moment. I don't consider myself to be violent. I didn't even know I had it in me."

"Who owns this place now?"

"Legally, Noah owns it and everything his father had, which is a good chunk of the City. But his assets are frozen. We're probationary citizens."

"What does that mean exactly?"

"Can't hold property. Reduced rations. No opportunity to go to University. Crappy daycares for Martha. Limited career advancement. They gave us a couple of choices. Work for the Council or at the pig processing plant. The Council paid better."

"I'm sorry, Aaron."

"Don't be. I did this to us. Problem is, now I have to get us out of it, even if I don't like it. They've promised to change our status if we're successful."

"If you find Finn, you get your life back?"

"Essentially. They want Finn *and* they want to seal up the exit he left through. I don't care about myself, but I want to see Noah's status restored. Martha deserves decent schools."

"And Noah thinks you can't do it without me."

"He does."

"Then I better pass."

CHAPTER 16

2 APRIL 2064. When Noah begins Ana's training on the last day, there are no padded suits. Instead, he gives her a holographic tire iron. Noah holds a virtual bat.

"Five minutes," he says. "That's how long you have to last."

"This is a test?"

"More like your last chance."

He hits her with his bat before she's even figured out her weapon. She looks at her throbbing arm. No physical damage. But the bat delivers virtual pain through her internal monitor. She retaliates, her tire iron making contact with his wrist, knocking his bat to the ground. The image sizzles out and is gone. He's weaponless.

She's enjoying this, even the pain. She's gotten better over the

last few days. Not his equal of course, but it's not so embarrassing now. But five minutes is a long time when you're fighting.

She can see him anticipating every move she makes. But she doesn't need to fight, she reminds herself, just to survive another 270 seconds.

Easier said than done. Noah fills in the gap between them, forcing her to make a move. She swipes at his legs, but he dodges the tire iron, goes for her leg to take her down. But she's faster than him. Speed, not strength, is her super power. She rolls to the side and springs back up on her feet.

Four minutes to go.

Aaron is watching from the corner of the room. What will he do if she fails? Probably take her back to her parking lot, her car full of food and supplies. "It's better this way," he'll say. "We'll find him on our own. We'll be okay."

She swings around in a circle and brings the iron down on Noah's shoulder. He grabs the tip with both hands and pulls it out of her hands, flinging it to the corner of the room. He steps toward her, his hands grabbing her by the shoulders, but she breaks the hold, knees him the groin, takes his head and butts him. Stunned, Noah steps back. She takes the opportunity for a sidekick. The move looked more fluid in the training video they showed her yesterday. She's done more damage to her foot than him.

Three minutes left.

He gets a hold of her wrist, twisting it into her forearm. She recalls a bully in her class giving her a snake bite once. This is

worse. She reaches with her free hand and rips a chunk of hair out of his head. He lets go of her wrist. Rolling sideways, she manages to retrieve the tire iron. She gets it in her hands, but he has the other end. She lets it go and Noah stumbles backwards. He's down, but he has her weapon. She kicks it out of his hand. He grabs her leg, pulls her down. This is not an elegant fight.

Two minutes.

He could kill her in two minutes, at the very least get her to tap out. If he pins her, it's over. Not much you can do after that. She kicks him with her free foot. It makes contact with his nose. He lets go. His face changes. She's got to him. He's no longer a demanding teacher. The fight's real. Noah can't see through the blood on his face. His eyes are black against the red stream, his pupils like saucers. This would be a good time to run. She sprints away, but he catches up to her in the corner a few feet from Aaron. She hears noises – grunting – is it coming from her? She levels a blow with an open fist to his Adam's apple while he swings at her.

One more minute.

He hits her on the side of her head, forcing her down. The pain is crushing. He has her backed against the wall, crouching. She grabs at his legs to pull him down, but he doesn't budge. With his hand around her neck he drags her to her feet. *Breathe. Defend yourself,* she screams in her head. She can feel consciousness fading. He's killing her. Maybe he never intended for her to succeed. It was all a lie. He wanted to get her into this room to kill her. What'll he say to the Council? It was an

accident? She was ill-prepared. They should never have agreed to train her.

Zero.

CHAPTER 17

(AARON)

2 APRIL 2064. "Why did we do it?" he asks Noah in the monitoring room. Noah is watching footage of Ana taking a steam in the women's change room. All they can see through the tempered glass is an amorphous pink blob. What is Noah doing? He may be many things, but he's no pervert.

"Do what, Aaron?" Noah asks, looking at Aaron with disdain when he turns the monitor off.

"Agree to train her. She's not prepared."

"Neither are you."

"I'm serious."

"So am I. You know nothing about the outside world. None of us do. She passed our test, at least. That's something."

"It was a controlled environment, the weapons holographic. What's she going to do when it gets real?" he points out.

"I've taken care of that," Noah says.

"I don't want to know what that means."

Noah turns the camera back on. Ana is no longer in the frame. She's piled her clothes into a sink. The tap is on. The sink overflows, an indigo swirl eddying around the floor drain. Noah adjusts the camera jerkily and finds her lying on a wooden bench, eyes closed. He focuses in on a large black bruise on her thigh. That's why he's watching her. He wants to make sure he didn't do too much damage.

"It should be you and me out there," Aaron says, looking away from the image. "She barely passed your test."

"You thought I was testing her?" he asks with one of his annoying smirks. "That was about you. Had to make sure torturing her didn't throw you off your game."

"Did I pass?"

"No, but it's too late to replace you."

Two days. That's how long Aaron has to convince everyone this is insane, but no one is budging – not Noah nor the Council. Especially not Ana.

"You know she has to go, Aaron. Finn's friends out there are not going to trust anyone sent by the Council." He's right of course, but Aaron keeps seeing the images of Benjamin Anderson, Annie Redmond and the others with sloppy bullet wounds all over them. Where will Ana's bullet wound be? In her head? Her heart?

“She despises us,” Aaron says.

“So, make her trust you.”

“I’ve tried. But why would she? We’re after her brother.”

“Because you’re all she has out there,” he says.

“The minute we leave she’s going to hit me over the head and dump me in a ditch so she can look for him herself,” he says, gathering some dirty plates and cups stacked on a table under the screen. Noah has been in the monitoring room a long time.

“You’re a slob,” Aaron says.

“Maybe I should hire some servants.”

“You should.”

“Then again, I don’t need to if I have you.”

“You’re an asshole.”

“I know,” Noah says. “But at least I did something for you.”

“And what was that?”

“Get the Council to recruit Ana.”

“How is that a good thing, Noah?”

“You want to touch her, don’t you?”

“Shove off.”

“Maybe you will someday.”

“Not likely. You’ve made her my enemy.”

“You did that on your own, but at least you’re near her now.”

“She hates you more than me, you know.”

“But I don’t care. That’s the difference. That’s how I know you want her.”

“You have no clue what I want.”

CHAPTER 18

3 APRIL 2064. When she returns to her room, there's an envelope on the table next to her bed. Inside is a blurred photo of Finn resting against a brick wall, knees up, face raised to the sun. His expression is soft, his eyes hopeful. It's summer. He's in their father's jeans and a V-neck white shirt. There's a blur of people on the street holding up signs. The caption under the picture reads "Social Contract day parade. 7 September 2063, 11:00 a.m." Finn was still in the City then. By noon he was with Ana on a float the kids from the free school had built. Hundreds of brightly colored papier-mâché birds suspended by wire from spinning posts. A banner in front read "we are many, we are one". On the back of the photo someone has written "Why was Finn at the Arc?"

The Arc is in the Annex, a suburb of the City still within the walls but on the other side of the river, away from the densely populated inner core. Its streets are lined with a jumble of windowless industrial buildings and boarded up character homes, all abandoned and ransacked in the last century. Plans to raze the neighborhood and build a casino had been half executed when the collapse happened, leaving the area dotted with empty lots. The surveillance is lax in the Annex, making it a haven for those with something to hide; the City's first attempt to give people a bit of freedom within the walls. Those who prefer safety, stay on this side of the river.

The Arc is one of the only inhabitable buildings left in the Annex. A former plastics factory that was converted into artists' studios in the last century, it's become a sort of flophouse.

It's late afternoon when Ana gets there. Surprisingly, no one stopped her when she left the Hive gate unaccompanied. They treated her like any employee leaving for the day. The river in front of the Arc is littered with junk that became immobilized when the City was surprised by an early winter – a rusted wheelbarrow, piles of dead branches, broken pottery. A group of men clean the embankment, while a posse of young boys eyes them lazily.

She pushes through a set of double doors into the Arena-like warehouse. There's a long line of stalls on two floors that have been converted into living quarters, most with closed curtains. The tenants have no more room than a horse in a stable. The second floor is ringed with a balcony. A few older men lean over the railing smoking, looking for something to catch their interest.

In an open classroom, in the center of the first floor, an elderly woman, probably from the City, teaches children an evening pottery class. Most Annex children attend school across the river, where they're also given meals, clothes and a screen to use while they're on the other side.

At a communal washing area, men and women clean their laundry. Some families cook in their stalls on camp stoves or in a community kitchen, but there's also a restaurant, a diner of sorts. The place smells of rancid oil.

What was this place to you Finn? A buffer between your real life and the outside world? Just a place to hide? Why couldn't you tell me?

She has no idea where to start. Secrets are respected here. If she asks about him directly, and he has friends here, they'll clam up.

She sits in the restaurant eating fries, watching. Some parents wash their children, naked in front of each other, with a spray hose.

However dire their living circumstances, there's a semblance of community life at least. Older children sit at a large table doing their homework together and talking. Some adults play cards. A man strums a guitar in the corner singing with the newly bathed children while a story is acted out with puppets. And a woman stops by each apartment to collect clothes for a clothing exchange, giving Ana a chance to see behind the curtains. The woman is slow, gathering gossip along with t-shirts and pants with holes in the knees.

When the woman is done, Ana leaves the restaurant and walks along the corridor as if she belongs there. She goes to the stalls that the woman didn't visit. Maybe Finn is hiding in one of them still. He's been here this whole time, but no one has seen him because there are no cameras in the building. She peaks behind the curtains. Some are empty, only a wash basin and bare mattress remaining. There's an old man sleeping on the floor of one and a half naked woman in another. She gets a glimpse of her when a man exits. He's doing up his zipper as he leaves. Another man waits outside for his turn. She carefully parts the curtain of the last room, half expecting to find Finn, but it's empty.

"He said you'd probably follow him here at some point," a man says, closing the curtain behind him.

His hands are calloused and blackened from work. He's missing a front tooth. He must be Chang, the owner of the place. From the stories she heard, she thought he'd be a lot older.

"Who?"

"Finn. You're his sister, aren't you?"

Finn obviously thought she was smarter than she is.

"Yes. You know why I'm here then?"

"You're looking for him, but he's gone."

"Did he leave anything behind?" she asks. Although her heart is beating faster now, she acts as if she's not the least bit surprised he caught her trespassing.

"Over here," he says, taking her through a door to an open space. Two men are wrestling each other while others watch.

She recognizes one of the men from her old apartment building.

"Fight league," he explains.

Behind the fighting ring there's a maintenance room and, behind that, a small closet.

"This is his room," he says.

There's a mattress on the floor. All those nights Finn said he was crashing at a friend's place or working through the night were likely spent here. The clip lamp her father frequently worked under is attached to a small bookshelf made of bricks and old boards. On the bottom shelf is her father's strong box. She puts her finger on the biometric sensor and opens it. She looks up at Chang. He takes the hint and leaves the room to give her privacy, but he doesn't stop talking.

"Your brother's an odd guy. Kept to himself. Didn't eat with anyone. Showered at 2:00 a.m. Moaned in his sleep." How does he know that, she wonders?

"Pretty though. The girls liked to look at him."

She lifts the first tray out and finds all of their parent's important documents, driver's licenses from before, pictures of Finn and her when they were young, envelopes of lost teeth and first haircuts. But there are things she doesn't recognize – a pile of head shots of children, at least a hundred of them, bound by a rubber band. Under the second tray she finds their inheritance. Bags of seeds. Not just plants from the time before, but experimental seeds that her father was gifted over the years by the grateful scientists he built greenhouses for. The collection is worth a fortune. She's glad Finn kept it here.

Otherwise, she would have traded most of it for food and shelter by now.

"You were friends with Finn?" she says through the closed door.

"Everyone's a friend here," he says, coming back in and leaning against the white wall inspecting her in a way that makes her uncomfortable.

"He really missing?" Chang asks, with a wink that suggests that their secret is safe with him.

"Yes," she answers.

"How did he do it?" Chang asks.

"If I knew, I wouldn't be looking for him," Ana says.

He invites Ana back to his quarters. She only agrees because she has more questions. His is the same size as every other unit even though he owns the place. It's stuffed with things – old screens, kitchen appliances and boxes of work boots.

"Some people pay their rent in goods," he says, seeing her eye his stuff.

A table is littered with unfinished drawings, mostly of buildings much like his.

"There are rules to visiting us," he says.

"What rules?" she says, feeling somewhat uneasy.

"We don't like to be bothered. We don't like people talking about what they've seen here."

"I don't plan to."

"The Finn that was here may not be the brother you're looking for."

"What does that mean?"

“People do things here they wouldn’t do on your side of the river.”

“Such as?”

“They’ve talked about cleaning up this place over the years, but they never have and likely never will,” he says, reaching into his mini fridge for a drink.

“And why is that?” she asks, watching his Adam’s apple move up and down with each swallow.

“The City needs this place,” he says, handing her the half empty bottle, which she freely downs. They’ve pumped her and Aaron so full of antivirals and vaccinations there is little chance of catching anything from him. “It’s a pressure valve for you people. You can’t leave the City, so you need a place of escape within because without a means to be immoral there is no point to free will. For most of you, the idea that there is a place where it’s possible to be bad is enough to keep you good. Others have to dip their toes into our waters, maybe swim in them for a while. They need to damage themselves just a little to remember why badness is undesirable. It orients them. They come home with bruises from a casual fight and then remember that they want humanity to be better.

He pauses, leafing through his music for something to play for her. “And then there are the virtuous ones who need to live amongst the bad, to care for them. Wherever there is darkness they appear brighter. In the world of the good, they’re practically invisible.”

“And which one are you?” she asks.

"I don't know," he answers with a slightly sarcastic laugh, but she can tell that he's happy she's interested in him. "I've always been here. I'm not bad or a voyeur. I'm a prop like the architecture."

"So, what did my brother do here then? Was his vice fighting, sleeping around, trading in black market goods?"

"Nothing. Nothing in a strange way if you know what I mean. He would sit for hours on the floor of his stall on a towel. I think he was meditating."

He leans over and brushes her hair to the side, letting his blackened fingers slowly fall down her cheek and neck. She understands now what he meant when he said everyone is a friend here. He wants something from her for helping. Even though she's slightly repulsed by him, she almost wants him to touch her – to feel something before she leaves the City, in case she gets so disoriented on the outside that she doubts the City was real. But Chang isn't what she needs.

He puts his hand on her thigh. She moves it gently back to his own knee and squeezes it affectionately, giving him the clear message that she's not offended, but not interested. At the same time, she scours the room for an object that could be used as a weapon. She settles on a wrench on his worktable a few feet away. He's stronger than her, but he won't be expecting it. She imagines him on the ground, his face sticking to the vinyl tiles, another tooth knocked out.

"Can I offer you something for your help?" she asks, looking away from the wrench.

"What could you offer me that I don't already have?" he asks, waving his arms at all his possessions as if he's the richest man in the City.

"This," she says, reaching into her pocket and pulling out the coins the Council gave her. She hasn't had an opportunity to spend any of them. "Finn must owe you as much in back rent."

Clearly disappointed, he nods and takes the envelope.

IT'S PITCH-BLACK outside when she leaves the building. The boys from earlier are carrying another load of garbage from the river to a junk pile behind the building, their way lighted by the light from one of their screens. They stop when she passes and whisper to each other. They finish and head back inside. The building is bolted down for the night, the streets empty now.

She walks along the river instead of the street. She used to come here with Finn sometimes when they were younger. Always in the daytime. They didn't want to explore the Annex but look at the City from this side.

It's cold or maybe it's fear that makes her tremble. She walks quickly. It's only five blocks to the bridge, where there are streetlights at least, and then a half mile through the park to her old parking lot and twenty minutes from there to Aaron's.

She hears a crack behind her; just branches blowing in the wind she tells herself or a squirrel. She turns around, but nothing is there. She scolds herself for being such a coward and walks quicker to the bridge. A block before she gets there, something

snaps behind her in the grass and when she turns it's too late for either of them.

"SHE'S OVER HERE," Noah says to Aaron.

"You asshole," he responds, "what were you thinking?" Aaron reaches the pile of leaves where she's lying still, her arms and legs reaching in opposite directions.

"It had to be done, Aaron. It had to get real at some point. It's what you wanted."

"You could have let me know. I would have watched from the side, intervened when it went too far."

"You said you didn't want to know. In any case, you should be more worried about him," Noah says pointing to a man lying on his face, the open strong box next to his head, blood oozing from a gash on his forehead, photos of children rolling across the ground like curled leaves. "He was doing this as a favor to me."

"She could be bleeding internally," Aaron says, brushing her hair off her face, inspecting Ana's body for puncture wounds. He lifts her over his shoulder and takes her across the bridge to a waiting ambulance, uninterested in the fate of the man who attacked her. For a person with so much presence, she weighs very little.

"There's nothing wrong with her. I programmed her monitor to sedate her once it was over. She's a bit bruised is all. I watched the whole thing. She was impressive. Lots of raw instinct to make up for her lack of skill."

"Your little test could have killed her," Aaron says.

“Look at the bright side,” Noah says. “At least we know that she can protect you out there.”

CHAPTER 19

5 APRIL 2064. Ana and Aaron plow through muck in heavy boots along the river in front of the Hive. It's the first time Ana's been outside since the incident in the Annex.

He helps her over fallen logs, his hand warm and steady, everything she isn't right now. But he doesn't need to know that every time a branch cracks or an animal burrows under leaves she imagines someone is behind her.

"Where are we going?" Ana asks, sounding a little too paranoid. *Is this more training? Another test?*

"The government farm." Aaron answers.

Ana hasn't been there since she was eight – a year-end class trip to visit the bees. She'd worn a green and yellow kilt. An idiot in her class provoked the bees. They swarmed her, flew between

her pleats, sending her screaming through the fields, skirt flying. She'd been mortified, not about the sting on her temple, or the three between her thighs, but an image of her soaring skirt and shabby underwear that circulated for weeks afterwards.

"What are we going to do there?" she asks.

"If there's a chance I won't make it back to the City, I'd like to spend my last day in the old farmhouse. You'll like it I think."

Tomorrow they leave the City. The Council has given them precisely fifteen days to find Finn. Fifteen days to search hundreds of miles. She spent ninety looking for him in this tiny place. Two weeks is nothing.

"My brother travelled outside the City regularly for more than two years. With all your training, you're bound to survive a couple of weeks."

His fingers lightly brush over the bruises on her arm from her attack, making the hair on her arm rise.

"You think so? I'm not so sure," he says.

She pulls away from him and turns toward the forest.

"I know this area," she says. "Follow me."

She takes him deeper into the woods to an overturned cedar that's managed to stay alive, a cave-like opening in its roots. They climb in and sit on some rocks that someone has dragged in.

"Finn and I ran away once and camped here."

"Why?"

"We were rebelling. My father had grounded us for playing ninjas."

"What's wrong with ninjas?

"We did it on the rooftop of buildings. Used a rickety extension ladder to cross from one building to another."

"You've always been attracted to danger then?"

"It was more like I needed to feel something that no one else was experiencing. It didn't have to be danger necessarily."

"Oh. And what exactly did you experience on those rooftops?"

"Sometimes an object would accidentally fall from one of our backpacks as we were crossing. There was this deep sense of satisfaction when it hit the pavement: a shattered mug on the sidewalk, a prized book face down in mud, its binding broken. I once sat in the middle of the ladder watching a cat pick at Finn's pulverized lunch."

"I think we might have missed something in your psychological profile."

"I'm glad there are aspects of my character that are still a mystery to the Council."

"Tell me more about this ninja business," he says.

Finn volunteered on weekends as an apprentice to a construction crew and had access to all kinds of tools – ladders, bolt cutters, harnesses. He and Ana carried these heavy items in their packs, an extension ladder between them and walked miles across town through crowds of curious faces.

On one occasion, they found a building that had been condemned before humanity's collapse; too rundown to repair and too complicated to demolish. The windows of the first three

stories had been boarded up, the only way in a padlocked revolving door on the ground floor.

Dressed in black, they took the stairs to the top of the office building next door. The building had been the headquarters of an insurance company in the time before but had been converted into a dorm for the elderly. It was a dump. Something always needed fixing. And so no one looked twice at the ladder being hauled from floor to floor, even though they were just kids.

"We're going to find something over there," Finn said, looking over the railing of the dorm, "something no one has seen in thirty years." They did find something unexpected.

He was fifteen then, Ana eleven. He'd tried shaving the night before and had nicked his jaw in a few places. She had a hard time taking him seriously.

He slid the ladder, suspended by two ropes, down to the rooftop of the condemned building – about sixteen feet across and four down. They secured their harnesses, cinched the straps of their packs, checked their zippers, took a drink of water and then they were ready.

He went first, as usual, so that he could hold the ladder for her on the other side. By the time it was her turn though, and she was halfway across, a pigeon was in front of her, making gurgling noises. She tried to shoo it away, but it wouldn't budge. She bounced the ladder a little. The bird lifted off temporarily and then settled back down, wings folded tight. She remembers the look of terror on Finn's face as she bounced the ladder again. The pigeon didn't move, but one of the ropes loosened and the

ladder twisted sideways. She was upside down now, a hundred feet above a concrete alley. Finn screamed. He was overreacting. They had harnesses. Even if the ladder collapsed she would swing down against the side of the building. If she didn't pass out from the impact, she would climb the rope back up.

But she didn't fall, and the pigeon was gone. Finn held his breath as she climbed downwards, rung to rung, feet dangling down, as if she were scaling monkey bars. When she finally crawled back over the top of the upside-down ladder and onto the rooftop Finn started swearing at her – a litany of words she wasn't even sure were proper swear words.

"How the hell are we going to get back?" he asked.

"Scaredy-cat," she said removing her harness, but her heart was beating in her throat now. He scowled at her and took out his bolt cutters.

Once they'd managed to break the lock on the access door, they took the stairs, flashlights in hand, down to an ordinary looking office floor. Caution tape across the elevator. Glass doors on either end of the floor. In the main room, particleboard workstations swelled from the damp. Clean white rectangles marked the walls where paintings once hung. She twirled around in the open space – there were few buildings in the City that weren't crowded with people – and glided into a pile of dirt someone had swept into a corner. There was a perfectly good nail file in it and some dice.

They found packages of panty liners in the women's restroom, a teakettle in the kitchen and a ream of paper near a photocopier.

Finn seemed a little disappointed. What was he expecting, a safe full of gold? She was happy enough with the paper; better than screens. Since their father wasn't there to judge them for taking what he would consider to be communal property, she filled their packs with their loot.

The final office she came to was locked, a blue curtain pulled across the glass wall. In front was a table with petrified donuts and a note announcing someone's birthday. Ana peered through a slit in the fabric, hoping to find something to add to her collection of oddities she kept under her bed, things she didn't want her father or even Finn to see. She saw a desk. On the carpet beside it was a bone all on its own – not a remnant of someone's lunch in Styrofoam like they'd seen before in old buildings. It was too big to belong to a chicken.

She smashed through the glass wall divider with their bolt cutters and crawled through the hole, avoiding the shards. What she saw made her freeze. A pile of bones, human bones, were stacked in a pyramid, about three bodies worth judging by the head count. Finn arrived, looked over the scene and, without asking her, took the teakettle, panty liners and reams of paper out of their backpacks and filled them instead with the bones – some white, others yellowish, some smooth, others pocked. He carried the two packs out of the building, one on each of his shoulders, reattached his harness and crossed the twisted ladder without second thought. He left their equipment behind – the ladder, bolt cutters, ropes.

There was something detached, almost robotic about his movements. He wouldn't have heard her if she'd yelled at him.

They walked into the forest and calmly dug a hole in mossy soil.

"Whatever crime this was, belongs to the people from before," she said, but he wasn't listening.

She handed him the bones, one at a time, and he placed them carefully in the soil. When the bones were covered, he murmured a prayer – a made up one but a good one nevertheless.

"I'M AMAZED YOU survived childhood," Aaron says.

"I made it to twenty, but thirty is looking less likely. But I doubt you were any less adventurous."

"Our old place was in the Annex," he says, as if this answers the question.

"The Arc?"

"No, a two-story walk up behind it. My mother wasn't a civil servant or a revolutionary like yours. I never met my father. And my friends didn't recite poetry or engage in social discourse."

"What did they do then?"

"For fun we hung out in an old school bus. Sometimes we gathered scrap metal in the garbage dump, the one the ski hill is built on now."

"You never met your father?"

"I didn't have a chance to. Come, let me show you," he says, leaving the mouth of the cave and leading her up a dirt path

to the farm. When they reach the cornfields, a yellow blanket stretches before them, waiting for the first planting.

There's a monument in the middle of the field; it would easily be missed if a small circle hadn't been mowed around it. A simple plaque to commemorate the spot where, in 2040, two thousand citizens rioted against the building of the wall. It was the first major incident of violence since the City was founded six years earlier. Some were killed. The leaders were banished. The rest were pardoned.

"He was here that day?" she asks. The riots aren't something people like to talk about. The City prides itself on being enlightened, non-violent. Matters are resolved through negotiation and, occasionally, a City-wide vote. In this case, there had been a vote and the majority of the citizens agreed to the wall. They didn't want anyone else coming in. Their new ideas needed time and space to incubate without being influenced by the dregs of civilization. And if people didn't like being cut off, they could always leave permanently.

But there were those who weren't happy with the decision.

"He moved to the City shortly before the riot."

"From where?"

"Florida and, before that, Ireland."

"He became a revolutionary that quickly?"

"No. He shouldn't have been here that day. Some new friends dragged him along."

He tells her the story his mother, Ariel, had told him. Elias Henderson had arrived in the City a week before the uprising,

his hands covered in cuts from the barbed wire fence. He was a tall man with sunken cheekbones from starvation and thick red brows that almost met in the middle. A sunburned face from spending most of the last six years in the wild gazing up at the sun.

Some men found him sleeping in their garden plot. They gave him clothes and got him a job at the plant. They took him to their favourite café to eat after his first day. He was wearing a new shirt he'd bartered for in the market. Ariel was a waitress there. She was kind to him – gave him an extra big portion – and so he came back every day. In the evenings, he walked her home. He liked her laugh and her innocence. Having always been in the City, it seemed as though the worst of the calamities had passed her by. Ariel hadn't taken a life or been violated. Never had to decide whether to give her last bit of food to a starving family.

He hadn't been all that interested in the idea of the riot. It didn't seem like such a bad idea to build a wall, but he went in support of his new friends and to impress Ariel. He never imagined it would turn bloody, that years later the son he would never meet would walk over his bones in this field.

"How was he killed?" Ana asks.

"Shot dragging away one of his friends who'd been trampled."

"And your mother was pregnant with you?"

"Barely. She didn't even know it at the time."

"I'm sorry," she says.

"It's not far to the farmhouse from here."

They turn in the direction of a dot on the horizon. A yellow brick structure surrounded by a fence with peeling white paint slowly comes into view. The old weathered oak door is open, and Aaron walks into the large dining room like it's his home. A tin ceiling has been perfectly restored and wide pine planks extend through every room. In the kitchen, rows of colorful preserves line wooden shelves along two walls – orange and red jams, pickles and asparagus standing on end.

"A good place to spend your last day," she says.

His mother left them some stew on the stove and fresh bread under a towel. They take their meal to a table on the back porch. The farm hands are done their lunch. Some are outside working on seeders, getting ready for the first planting.

"How did your mother end up in the City?" she asks. It's a question that every conversation between strangers eventually leads to.

"Before humanity's collapse, my mother worked for a large hotel chain not far from the City. On the day it happened, she was setting pastries out for the participants of a renewable energy conference. She had a tray of muffins in her arms when the news started coming in. The hotel quickly turned to chaos – the hallways became littered with luggage and overturned food trays. People huddled in front of a TV in the reception area, too afraid to return to their rooms alone, speculating about how bad it was going to get. A security guard was killed in the stairwell by a panicked guest and no one bothered to move him. Some guests

lost their minds and became worried about odd things – *will the Knicks game be cancelled, how much of my portfolio is in cash, should I still tip the cleaning lady?*

My mother admitted there was something exhilarating about it as well, like watching a car crash. It was as if humanity's longstanding appointment with fate had finally arrived and they were excited to be at the center of it.

Once the guests recovered from the initial shock, most tried to flee in cars, on foot, even on bicycles, but a dozen or so holed up in the hotel. Some were engineers experimenting with geothermal power generation. If they hadn't stayed, the City wouldn't have a reliable power source."

"My father knew those guys. Your mother was with them?"

"She kept them alive. Barely. She fed them condiments, oats and pancake mix. That's all they had after the first week. The hotel guests eventually found a truck and drove to a neighboring farm and bartered for potatoes and onions. Hunting and foraging became their main preoccupation. That and hoarding what they could find in abandoned houses.

For years, my mother made meals for an ever-widening group of people who made the hotel their home, pooling together their squirrels, deer, garden snakes and roots. In those early days, before they had power, they cooked in the parking lot behind the hotel, meat strung on lines between the balconies.

When the hotel burned down in a fire, they all moved on. A friend offered her the job at the café in the Annex and a bed in

her bachelor apartment in the walk-up. A year later, after I was born, she took the job as Noah's nanny."

A mangy cat leaps onto the porch and into his lap, purring before Aaron has even touched it.

"I've been thinking about what you said that day before your monitor was replaced," he says, stroking the cat affectionately, "that since my intention is to arrest your brother, there's little chance we are ever going to be friends."

"Yes."

"I accept that. I don't expect friendship from you. But you have me worried that once we get out there, you'll hit me on the head with a rock and go look for him yourself."

"The thought has crossed my mind," she says facetiously.

"I can't imagine we'll do a very good job finding your brother under those conditions. We're going to need to rely on each other. Especially since the Council has only given us fifteen days to find him. We can't cover much ground in that time if I always have to watch my back."

"Let me ask you a question," she says. "If we find Finn and he refuses to come with you, will you hurt him?"

"Not if I don't have to."

"But it could happen."

"It might."

"How do you expect me to forget that?"

"You'll just have to. Aren't I in the same position?"

"I don't know if I can."

"I thought about our little problem all night," he says. "I

know, by the way, what you've been up to, what you were looking for in the basement of your friend's store and when you met with Ekhart. So, I thought to myself, what if I just gave it to you? That might solve things."

"Give me what?"

"This," he says, handing her a slip of paper. On it is the address of the old brick factory in the Annex. Is it Finn's unsanctioned exit out of the City? He's taking a huge risk giving this to her under the eyes of the cameras.

"You have a choice now," he says. "There's no need to assault me if you want to find him on your own. You'll just disappear tonight. Noah will go with me instead. Maybe we'll cross paths out there; likely not."

He takes the paper back from her and burns it in a woodstove.

"But if you choose to do this with me, then you have to be all in. No crazy stuff. No deception. It's your decision. But if we do this right, we might actually find him.

"How did you get this?"

"We've had it all along. Another bit of Noah's inheritance. His father owned the building."

"Why haven't you told the Council? Isn't this what they want?"

"It's worth nothing unless we find Finn."

CHAPTER 20

6 APRIL 2064. Day 1 of 15. She's supposed to pick Aaron up at the market at 2:00. She arrives twenty minutes early, parks her large beast behind the spice vendor and watches him through bushels of oregano. He's wearing a black sweater and leather jacket she's never seen. His hair is the right degree of messy, as if he was lucky enough to wake up that way. She catches people sizing him up as he bargains with vendors.

He does an inordinate amount of shopping, loading up on jerky, nuts, dried fruit and spices. Does he think the outside world is a complete wasteland now? Is he too much of a snob for squirrel meat?

He eventually emerges from the crowd and stuffs his bags into the corners of her trunk. The influx of smells – dried sage in particular – permeate her car, knocking back the

lingering odors of spilled ice cream, rust and dead mouse.

"So, we're actually doing this?" he asks, as he settles into the passenger seat, wrestling with a bag of roasted chestnuts that is too hot to hold.

"Apparently."

When she got her car back from the mechanic yesterday, there was a pack in the trunk from Aaron. Everything she'd need to leave on her own – tent, water filters, thermal blankets, binoculars, a pocket survival guide. There was even a new screen that had been loaded with playlists. An envelope was tucked into the pocket, in it a note and some silver for trading. It said, "Stay off the roads. Don't be afraid to use your gun." She put the pack on, felt the weight of it, imagined crossing through hollow towns alone, sleeping in an abandoned school library. It wasn't a bad fantasy.

Then she pictured going out there with Aaron, pitching their tents, hunting and skinning squirrels together, getting into fights with feral men, having someone to bandage her up. She imagined the conversations they might have on the road about the things they'll see. She put the pack down, crawled into a ball and slept soundly for the first time in weeks.

As soon as she starts driving, Aaron opens and closes the glove compartment, knocking her gun against the apples she threw in there, her pathetic attempt at packing for the trip. He examines all the pockets and corners of her car, pausing briefly when he finds a school photo of Finn.

"What're you looking for?" she asks, turning in the direction of the Hive.

"Just taking inventory."

He pulls out a copy of "To Kill a Mockingbird" from a bin under the passenger seat, flips through it and puts it back. When she turns, he grips the dashboard hard.

"You're afraid to drive with me?" she laughs.

"That obvious?"

"I've been driving since I was ten. I'm pretty good at it. Besides, someone needs to be ready to shoot if need be. It would be best if that person wasn't also steering the car."

It was Noah's idea to take the car. It wasn't really much of a decision. The City's network doesn't operate outside the walls. None of the City's vehicles would work. He also thought her heap of junk would blend in better outside the City. But he insisted on outfitting it with massive airless tires and a new suspension system designed to weather the worst roads and fields. She has no idea where he found the parts. The proportions are all off now. It drives like an elongated Jeep. As a backup, he insisted they take a motorbike with them, which, to her great disappointment, is taking up most of the trunk.

Aaron directs her to an unexceptional cinderblock structure, the City's "emigration" center. A guard is waiting for them. He looks at the strange vehicle curiously but waves them through the gate anyway. There are no people inside, but an automated voice speaks to them: "You are being banished for anti-social behavior. No further contact with the City or its citizens will be possible; nor may you return to the City for any reason. Final

messages can be left in the box on the table. Any notes delivered to the gate after you leave will, under no circumstances, be delivered. Once you complete your messages, please proceed to station two where you will be given immunization and nutritional injections, as well as a survival kit. We wish you good fortune on the outside."

"I never knew they gave such a generous send-off," she says to Aaron, as they pass station two without taking anything. "Let's hope they're not serious about *not* letting us back in."

But he isn't laughing. In fact, he looks spooked.

They proceed to another, heavier, gate that opens automatically as the car approaches.

"You ready?" she asks him, hesitating.

"Get on with it already, will you?" he says, in an irritated voice she's never heard before.

She inches forward until the iron gate closes behind them and they find themselves on a bridge neither of them has ever seen. Packed with matted leaves, it has a mattress quality to it. They bump across it to the opposite side of the river. When they're on solid ground again, she turns the car around and looks back at the wall, the side she's never seen. There's some graffiti here and there, but otherwise it's almost new looking, not banged up like it is in the City from kids and the occasional drone accident. The world outside has mostly ignored it, as if it is of no interest to them.

Someone has cleared the road. Instead of removing the rusted-out vehicles, they've pushed them to either side. Other junk

has been piled on top over the years – chunks of broken concrete, umbrellas, vinyl suitcases, fallen branches, animal carcasses, furniture. What remains is a narrow path through a tunnel of wreckage, barely wide enough for a single car.

It's what's missing that she notices most though. No loud voices, sirens or lights. No cooking or garbage odors – just the clean smells of earth and ozone.

Aaron nods to her screen. "We're offline," he reports. No one knows where they are now or how fast their hearts are beating. All of their lives, they were connected to thirty thousand other souls, their images and data swirling in a giant digital swamp with everyone else's. Now they are truly alone. Alone, but together.

"I don't feel any different," she says, casually looking at the highway, her eye catching a pristine-looking gray plastic suitcase at the bottom of the pile. She wonders what's inside. Her father would have had a field day rummaging through this stuff. She barely resists the urge to get out of the car and start sorting through it.

They drive back and forth through the suburbs surrounding the City, looking for the ideal base. A place to stash supplies and meet up if they get separated. Many of the buildings they find have been burned down over the years with no one to put fires out. Others are not tall enough. They need something with a bit of a vantage point.

Just when they start talking about moving on to the next town, they find a compromise, an inconspicuous low-rise office building nestled between what was once a Greek restaurant and

a hardware store. From here, they'll be able to see a fair distance and it has an intact tin roof. It isn't exactly what they're looking for, but it's worth exploring. They park the car in the alley and take a weapon each with them.

The only footprints they see are those of animals and so they relax a little. The metal door in back is unlocked and Ana goes in ahead of him.

"Is anybody here?" she calls up the stairwell, but there's no response. They're alone, but there are signs of previous occupation – a plastic container of peach pits and a rain barrel fitted with a pipe to the outside.

"We should go as high as we can," he suggests.

They aren't the first to come to that conclusion. The loft on the top floor has clearly been used by other travelers.

A Japanese screen divides the main room from a sleeping area equipped with foam mattresses and pillows. Piles of perfectly folded clean sheets and blankets sit on top. They've left behind a jerry can and a generator connected to a lamp, a teakettle and a small heater. A stack of self-help books lies next to the bed, beside it a neat bowl of shell casings.

A garment rack covers one wall of the main room, stuffed with evening gowns. Six sewing stations line the wall opposite the windows. It must have been a garment factory.

Light streams in through a wall of glass tiles, all unbroken except for a tiny four-by-four-inch square that lets in wind. A puddle of water and leaves has accumulated on the floor under the hole. Ana takes some duct tape and a scarf out of

her pack and patches it, the fabric billowing in and out like a lung.

In an office, she finds a yellowed copy of the New York Times from 7 July 2034 lying on a coffee table. The world seemed so ordinary that day – an election in India, an increase in housing starts. She returns it to the table next to a green mug with dead fruit flies in it.

"Check this out," Aaron says.

There are faded messages pinned to a bulletin board from former residents. "13 June 2040. Dan is dead. Don't bother going west. I'll meet you at our place. Jane." "1 August 2058. Farmer at 44.7681° N, 85.6222° W offering peaches and oats in exchange for labor. Ben." "Farmer at 44.7681° N, 85.6222° W is a sexual predator. Go for the blueberries at 44.8632° N, 85.8760° W instead". "Adam, where the hell are you? I waited for over a week. Cara." Hundreds of messages, but none from Finn or his four dead friends.

A door from the office leads to a metal balcony, big enough for a small chair and coffee table. She steps onto it and fingers a mug with "world's best mom" inscribed on it.

She could ignore the collapse when she was in the City. It almost seemed like a fairytale the elders shared to entertain them or make them behave. But reading these notes, looking out at all the buildings, mostly destroyed and not a soul in sight, it can't be denied that it happened.

"You think there's a God?" she asks Aaron, who is behind her now, one hand on her arm just in case the balcony collapses.

Below, a cat claws at something trapped under the deflated tires of a van.

"You're asking me? Isn't that your area of expertise?"

Ana's father was famously religious. Although born Sikh, he seemed to slip in and out of faiths, not seeing a need to create walls between them. He championed them all.

"Not really. My dad did the "believing" on our behalf. Our "expertise" was challenging him. I never understood why a benevolent God would do this to humanity?"

"I think the standard response is that God didn't do it, we did."

"But if he's all-powerful, why not stop us from destroying this place?"

"Because God gave us free will. You can't very well let people make their own decisions and then intervene every time they make a bad one."

"That's actually a reasonable answer. Do you believe it?"

"I'll let you know when we get back. Now can we get off this rickety thing?" he asks, bending down to inspect the bolts holding the balcony in place. "Because if we don't, you may have an opportunity to ask God herself sooner than later."

CHAPTER 21

7 APRIL 2064. Day 2 of 15. They drive west to the Commune where Finn first met Miriam. It's the obvious place to start. He might even be there. Sometimes, the simplest answer is the right one. Finn just packed up and moved to the Commune. Decided to pursue what he really wanted. It wasn't because he resented Ana or their life together. He just wanted Miriam. She'll find him by the lake, tarring a fishing boat with his friend Gerald.

Sunlight flickers through slits in the tunnel of wreckage. They follow a map from the time before when it was a pristine six-lane highway. Every so often, the road opens up, a gas station, grain elevator or cell tower whizzing by.

She can imagine the anticipation Finn would have felt driving this route, looking forward to seeing his new friends,

especially Miriam. He would do his various jobs in the City all week – teach his classes, oversee his projects, vacuum their living room – all the while anticipating that moment when he would be on this road again.

How will he react when she finds him? Will he be angry? Will he hang his head in shame?

When they were kids, he was always looking for a place he could call his own. He'd find a hideout – maybe an unused mechanical room under an overpass – and claim it. He'd fill it with his possessions, leaving no room for anyone else.

Of course, if he's here, there'll be the small matter of what to do with Aaron. All morning she's been going through the options in her head. Kill him – no, she obviously couldn't do that. Knock him out – assuming that's even a possibility, what then? He'll know Finn lives at the Commune. They'll have to flee. She'll have ruined it for Finn.

AN HOUR IN, Ana sees a ribbon of blue rippling through the debris.

"Something wrong?" he asks.

"People," she says, pointing to a blue SUV bumping through the fields to their left.

"Head down," he says, pulling his gun out of the glove compartment calmly, as if he had been anticipating this moment since they left. He leans over her and unwinds her window.

The SUV veers towards the road through an opening and drives alongside them. She crouches down, eyes barely peeking

over the steering wheel. Is this it? One day in and the wrong decision might be the end of them.

"It's a woman and her boy," Aaron says as if it's no big deal, but the boy has a shotgun locked on Aaron, his eyes full of resolve.

As the tunnel narrows, Ana accelerates ahead of them. The woman nods slightly as Ana passes as if to say *we're not a threat, leave us alone.* In the split second that Aaron and the boy must decide whether to pull the trigger, an understanding is reached. They figure out who each other are. Violence is averted.

Ana takes the next exit and pulls over on the off-ramp. She cuts the motor, gets out and paces, her knees and hands shaking. Aaron joins her, clearly wanting to do something, but unsure what.

"They were just people," he says, putting his hand over hers to steady her. Her weakness embarrasses her. In her mind, she's almost fearless, but her body betrays her. Why is he so calm?

His eye catches something in the distance. He lets her hand go and walks down the winding off-ramp on a mission. When he returns, he's smiling. "Come see this," he says, dragging her along.

Someone, decades ago, thought to plant tulip bulbs by the side of the highway. Thousands of yellow flowers are in full bloom.

"Looks like the sun has melted onto the earth," he says.

"It's beautiful," she answers. "But we should go. We need to get there and back before dark."

They reach their destination just before noon, a grove of pear trees, the unofficial gate to the Commune. Their sharp branches twist like the arthritic fingers of an old woman. Something out of a horror movie.

Before they can decide how to proceed, two horses come into view, riders mounted on their backs, a man and a woman. The woman is oddly colorful. Her hair short and spiky, the tips died green. Her black leggings brightly sequined. The man is in baggy white hemp pants and a hemp shirt, almost monk-like. They're no older than Ana and Aaron.

As Ana pulls over, Aaron reaches into the glove compartment.

"No guns," she says. "Finn said they're not violent."

But it isn't guns he's after.

He gets out and walks as non-threateningly as he can toward the horses, Ana following behind.

"May I?" he asks, motioning to the apples in his hand. Their owners nod and he makes his offering to the horses.

"You lost?" the woman asks.

"We're here to speak to Gerald. He's a friend of my brother's," Ana says.

"Who's your brother," she asks.

"Finn."

She watches for signs that they recognize his name. The woman's expression is blank, but the man raises an eyebrow. He looks to the woman for a response.

"Gerald isn't available," she says.

"He's not here or he won't see me?"

"Take your pick," she says.

Why the hostility? Aren't these people her brother's friends?

"I'm not leaving until Gerald sees me," Ana says, moving in front of Aaron.

"If you have a message from your brother, I can deliver it."

"From" Finn, not "for" Finn, she said. So he's not here after all. She tries not to let her disappointment show.

"The message is that something bad has happened to him. He'd want Gerald to know."

"Hmph," she says. "And Miriam?"

"Missing," she says, although she's not sure that's true. Maybe she's exactly where she wants to be.

"Your trinkets," she says. "Can you do without them? We don't allow weapons of any kind on the property."

Aaron lifts his shirt to show her he is unarmed. Ana does the same.

"And that?" she asks, nodding to his boot.

He removes his ivory-handled knife and puts it in the glove compartment. Ana notices that he doesn't remove the smaller knife he keeps in his front pocket.

"Follow me," she says, turning her horse around.

They walk behind the horses to a village nestled in a forest. Early twenty-first century suburban homes mixed in with shacks made of mud and bricks. A large green barn a few hundred yards in the distance. Through the leafless trees a river can be seen, rows of canoes arranged at an angle along its shoreline. The riv-

er is still partly frozen, a thin relentless stream cutting through its middle.

A group sits in front of an open fire roasting a rabbit, the fire crackling loudly. It's the scene in Finn's photos, except that he's absent. She's comforted at least that he was once here, that she is finally amongst people who knew him outside the City, but something is wrong. She can see it in their secret glances and nervous gestures. Their escorts unmount and approach an elderly man and woman sitting on canvas chairs. The woman is pouring water over a whetstone while the man sharpens a knife. Hushed words are exchanged. He puts his knife downs and looks up at Ana with an aloof expression. He motions for her to come closer.

"You're his sister?" he grumbles. Ana shows him a photo of her with Finn and their father as proof. The man makes a sound at the back of his throat as he hands it back. His sideburns extend down to the edge of his chin. He wears a black parka and steel-toed boots. He has to be Gerald. Is that Finn's hat he's wearing?

"Sit and shake off the cold," the woman says. She wraps her coat, an assemblage of various furs, tightly around her, the browns and greys almost indistinguishable from her dreadlocks. She ladles water into an aluminum cup and offers it to Aaron.

He looks into the cup, hesitates, and then gulps it down. The woman refills it and hands it to Ana. She's never tasted spring water, only the recycled liquid from the City's waste treatment plant. It tastes sweeter, but slightly metallic.

Heads begin to poke out behind buildings, trees and outhouses and a crowd slowly converges on them. All of the women

have bird tattoos on their neck – blue jays, vultures, finches. Their clothes are bold, an odd assortment of mismatched items – multi-colored leg warmers, flowing patterned shirts cut into shreds in the back like feathers.

"What happened to him?" Gerald asks.

"He didn't return to the City."

"That all. Why would he? He has everything he wants now. He has her."

"Maybe, but some of his friends ended up dead out here. Finn's DNA is all over them. He was with them when it happened. He could be hurt or worse," Aaron says.

"We don't know about any of that. They aren't here, anyway." He gives his sharpened knife to the old woman to inspect. She puts her thumb to the blade and nods in approval. He smiles reassuringly at her. She keeps it in her hand instead of placing it with the others.

"Why did my brother come here?" Ana asks. "Was it just because of her?"

"To see what we had to offer," the old woman answers. "Because he didn't belong in your City anymore. He was running from something, looking for something, hiding something. Maybe just because of the girl. Who knows?"

"Whatever his reason, he didn't share it with us," Gerald adds. "He came. Had a lot of big ideas. Ate our food. Showed us how useless you City people are at farm work and then left." His face is redder than when they arrived. He keeps looking into the distance, as if expecting someone else.

"You don't mind if we look around?" Aaron asks. "Talk to a few people?"

"No point in that," Gerald says, giving Aaron a dirty look. "No one here can help you."

"Can't or won't?" Aaron says.

"You don't know Miriam," the woman says. "That girl kept to herself. Whatever her plans were, she didn't share them."

Ana takes a step towards the woman and puts her hand over the top of the blade.

"I get that you're mad at my brother for taking Miriam away. Maybe someday you can punish him for it, but not today. Today we're going to interview every person here because somebody will remember something. Even if it's a small detail, like what they took with them or what they were wearing," she says, lifting her hand off the knife. "Do you understand? We're staying here until we're done."

A look of disgust crosses Gerald's face. He grabs Ana by her jacket collar and slams her head onto the table next to him. With his other hand, he holds her head down, immobilizing her. Ana squirms unsuccessfully against the weight of his monstrous hand.

"We don't owe those two anything," he says.

The crowd of men on horses circles closer. Some look away, embarrassed. She can see Aaron reaching into his pocket for his knife. Ana catches his gaze and shakes her head imperceptibly as if to say *don't do it. Not yet.*

"Gerald. Stop messing with the girl," the woman says,

lifting his hand off Ana's hair and petting him like he's a skittish dog.

"Lay off, Nancy," he says, shrugging her off. "That asshole brought us nothing but trouble and now these two are here to bring us more."

"Come walk with me," Nancy says to Ana, ignoring Gerald and pulling Ana a safe distance from him. Aaron and Gerald both take a step closer. "We'll be alright on our own," she says to both of them.

The two women walk through the forest to a clearing. Ana sizes Nancy up. She's older, but not feeble. At least she's left the knife behind.

"That boy ain't gonna hurt Gerald, will he?" she asks Ana.

"I don't think so," Ana says, but nevertheless she listens for signs of conflict behind them.

"I think it's me that should be worried about Aaron," Ana says, rubbing her bruised face.

"He don't mean no harm," she says. "Gerald would'na hurt you."

Ana doesn't want to debate the point, but there's a small circle on her scalp where her hair is missing, and her ears are ringing. "I have to find my brother," she says.

"I know, dear," she answers.

"Is he really not here?"

"Haven't seen them for months. Haven't heard word of them either," she says anticipating her next question.

"Something's wrong here, isn't it?"

Nancy inhales deeply and then lets her breath out with a saddened expression.

"The Band was also here looking for your brother. He pissed them off somehow. Their leader, Blackwell, took his revenge out on Miriam's younger sister. Did it himself. Didn't even bother to make his cronies do it."

"I'm sorry," Ana says. "Is she okay?"

"No, she's not," Nancy says, nodding to a mound of freshly overturned earth ahead of them. A grave. "She was my nephew's partner. *She* was loyal to us."

Ana's heart sinks. They blame Finn for her death.

"What did Finn do to the Band?"

"They didn't take the time to say."

They reach a cemetery, a few dozen graves spilling down a hillside. Ana rubs at her bruised face.

"You gotta understand something about Gerald. He's not a bad man, but he's also not one of us. I suppose he stays because he balances us out. And he needs us to keep him from falling. I'm making him sound like a bad person. It's not that, he's just more hardened than us, more willing to compromise when he has to. Your brother and him were buddies. It's not like they were the same or anything. Finn could never hurt a fly. But Finn was an outsider like Gerald. They could talk about things the rest of us don't know anything about. And the two of them played chess."

She reaches down, takes a handful of pine needles and puts them to her nose.

"Every time your brother came, Gerald ignored him at first. He'd walk around with some tools and pretend to be busy doing something useful. But eventually he'd find your brother in front of the fire pit and then he'd ignore him just a little bit longer. But Finn understood the routine: it had to be on Gerald's terms. Then finally Gerald would sit next to Finn and say 'I suppose you'll be wanting to play some chess.' 'I can think of worse things to do,' your brother would say. Gerald would send one of the kids to fetch the board while he built up the fire. He'd whine about how the wood wasn't split right. But once the game was in front of them, it was just the two of them and that board until it got dark. Gerald was happy. So, no, it's not just that Finn broke our peace with the Band. It's also that he left Gerald behind."

"In that case, Gerald and I should get along well."

"Why is that?"

"Because Finn did the same thing to me."

Nancy laughs and nudges Ana in the arm like they're old friends.

"Look, there aren't any answers here. Go back to your City now with that boy of yours and tell your people to stay where they are. We've had enough of outsiders here. If you do that for me, I'll question my people myself. I'll send someone to the gate with a message if I learn anything."

"It's a kind offer, but I need to do this myself."

"There are two of you and forty of us," she says, threateningly.

"No, there are thirty thousand of us. If we don't return to the City, they'll send more. Maybe ten next time. They'll

bring guns. The City won't rest until this is dealt with."

"How long have you been out here, girl?"

"Less than a day."

"It won't be long before the Band gets word that Finn's sister is here. What do you think will happen to you, then?" she asks.

Ana doesn't have an answer.

"I'll tell you. You'll get strung up under a tree before you make it back. You'll be dead before that army of yours marches out here. You want to take that risk?"

"I do."

CHAPTER 22

7 APRIL 2064. By the time they're back on the highway, the sun is low on the horizon, blinding light reflecting off the asphalt. Aaron can't look Ana in the eye. He picks a clump of hair out of the hood of her jacket and swears.

Why is he so upset? So, Gerald pushed her face against a picnic table. She'd experienced worse in kindergarten – done worse for that matter.

"Tic tac toe," he says, pointing to her face.

"What?"

"The bruises on your face." She looks in the rearview mirror. He's right. Her bruise resembles a tic tac toe game.

"That was relatively unsuccessful, wasn't it?" she says of their visit to the Commune.

"A 3 out of 10," he answers, with a lopsided smile. "It was only our first stop, though."

They did interview everyone. One by one they brought the members of the Commune into the circle by the fire and asked them the same questions. No one from the Commune was permitted to witness the interview for fear that a sideways glance from Gerald might silence them. Ana asked the questions. Aaron watched their faces for signs that they were lying. If need be, he asked follow-up questions. It took hours. They found out what Finn liked to eat, how long he visited before he started sleeping in her cabin, what Finn told them about the City, what his mood was, how often he changed his socks. Everything but where they were going.

The only useful information – that the Band killed Miriam's sister and the old woman's warning about the Band – Ana keeps to herself. If Aaron found out, he would drag her back to the City.

IT ALMOST LOOKS like a mirage when she sees it, the four-by-four they passed earlier stopped perpendicular to the highway, its left signal light flashing, doors open. Pages of a coloring book circling the pavement, half obscuring the body of a woman. The mother. A dead man lies next to her.

"What do we do?" Ana asks next to the man. She wraps her jacket tighter around herself, maybe more as protection against the violent scene than the cold. Half his face is a bloody mess, his hand still on his gun. Aaron pries the

man's fingers off the weapon and puts it in his back pocket.

"He's gone," he says, casually.

"We should be careful," Ana says, looking into the field across the road. "Whoever did this could be watching us."

The woman is pale, but the pool of blood on the concrete is small.

"We can't leave her," he says. "She's still alive."

"What about her kid? He's gone."

"We'll deal with her first."

Ana takes her emergency kit out of her spare tire compartment and hands it to Aaron. He rifles through it, pulling out a pre-filled morphine injection.

"Where did you get this?" he asks.

"My dad took his emergency kit seriously."

He puts the kit down and unzips the woman's jacket. The blood has dried, gluing her wound to the fabric. He pours water over her chest to loosen it. They remove her shirt and ease down her jeans, exposing the entry point. Jagged scars – old ones – are visible across her lower abdomen. Her face is covered in pock marks. He rolls her over, revealing the exit wound. Ana squeezes iodine over her abdomen and back while Aaron looks into the distance for signs of movement. When she's done, he squeezes a tube of glue into the holes on both sides of her.

"Hold her up," he says.

He wraps the woman tightly in a bandage while Ana holds the woman by her shoulders. Then he deftly removes the needle from its packaging and administers half of it.

"That ought to hold her for now. We'll deal with her properly later," he says.

They move the woman to the back seat of Ana's car and search the SUV. It reeks of dirty clothes. There's a half-finished pancake next to a child's seat and a plastic container of markers, most with the lids off. The rifle the boy pointed at them earlier is on the ground next to the open car door. She puts the tip to her nose to smell it. It's recently been fired.

"I'm going to look for her children."

"It's getting dark," she says. That's one of the rules they've come up with, never travel on the highway at night. They'd need to put their headlights on, which would make them an easy target.

"I won't be long."

But it's half an hour before he comes back, alone.

"I found three sets of prints, one was an adult's. The dead guy must have been with someone who took the kids. I lost their trail in the field," he says. He's clearly distraught.

"We can help *her* at least," Ana says, although she's not sure how. "But it means we aren't going to make it back to the safe house tonight."

"We'll find some other place then," he says.

They drive under the thin light of a waning moon until they see a brick rancher with a steel roof, nestled in a valley.

They leave the woman in the car, draw their guns and walk the perimeter of the bungalow. No lights. No signs of life. Everything left untouched for years. Aaron picks the lock.

Animals have found their way in and burrowed holes in the drywall. The place reeks of stale urine, but at least they're out of sight.

The beds in the two bedrooms are stacked with decorative pillows and stuffed animals. The comforter dissolves when she pulls it back, no more solid than cotton candy now, but there's a pristine vinyl covered mattress underneath. She wipes it down and covers it with a clean thermal blanket from her backpack. They haul the woman from the car to the bed. Blood has soaked through her bandages.

"You got a sewing needle in that kit of yours?" he asks.

"You can't stitch her here."

"What choice do we have? The glue's not holding."

"Have you done this before?" she asks.

"There are a lot of things we never did in the City that we'll have to do out here," he answers.

His hand isn't steady, but he takes his time and his stitches come out neat and pretty even. Ana dresses her wound, shrouds her in another blanket and they leave her to rest.

Ana stashes the car a few hundred yards away in a densely-treed backyard of another house, while Aaron secures the front and back entrances to the house with his motion sensors. When she returns, they sit together and watch the woman's chest rise and fall.

"We should sleep. There's another bed in the other room," he says, as if it's nothing for them to sleep together.

Without speaking, they remake the bed with more thermal blankets and get under the covers awkwardly. The bed's small

and there's no way to avoid touching. It's that or fall off the side. He doesn't seem to mind. She considers moving to the car or sleeping on the mildewed carpet. While she's trying to make up her mind, she drifts off.

At the first hint of light she gets up. Aaron's shirt has ridden up in the night and she can't help but notice that the scar on his arm extends around to his back, ending at a small burn mark.

She checks on the woman and finds that her pulse has strengthened some. Aaron joins her, buttoning a new shirt in the doorframe. She stares at him despite her best efforts.

"You're not going to ask?" he says.

"About what?"

"The scars."

"None of my business," she responds, but there is something unsatisfactory about her answer, maybe for him as well. But she doesn't want to know. If she's going to pull this whole thing off, she needs to keep some distance from him.

The woman rouses, mumbling something about her son's guitar.

"What do we do now?" Ana asks.

"We've done all we can. We have to leave her." His mouth is saying one thing, his face another.

"You want to stay with her, don't you? Make sure she makes it through the worst of it. Find her kids," Ana says, as she lays out another needle and some bandages for later. Hopefully the next time the woman wakes, she'll be conscious enough to nurse herself.

"No," he answers. "We only have thirteen days left. We look for your brother. All the other problems out here are not our concern."

CHAPTER 23

8 APRIL 2064. Day 3 of 15. He puts on '80s pop music. Duran Duran, "A View to a Kill". That's what she hears as they drive north to the Orphanage – a tiny whizzing noise from the car's virtually silent electric motor, rubber squelching over wet concrete, and pop music.

There are two types in the City, people who mine old hard drives for cultural material from the time before and those who refuse to have anything to do with the past. Everything they create is new – people like Hooper with his odd candy experiments and Noah with his dissonant music. But you can't ignore history. Shouldn't. And so most people happily consume the old music and movies. That was one thing they did right before. They knew how to entertain.

"What can you tell me about the woman who runs the Orphanage?" she asks, turning the radio down.

Aaron has a dossier on all of Finn's contacts at the various settlements. He's matched old satellite photos and newspaper articles with Finn's descriptions. He interviewed some of the old-timers in the City to find out what they know about the places he and Ana are going. He even found someone who had actually worked at the warehouses where the Orphanage now stands.

"According to Finn's notes, she was just a kid when it all happened," he says. "Barely fourteen." He changes the song and turns it up slightly.

"Isla Bjorn is her name. She's forty-four now. Her father, Erik Bjorn, was the CEO of a building supply distributor. That's where the Orphanage is – at his company's old distribution warehouses."

"So, she just happened to be at her father's office that day? Did he forget to take her with him on his escape helicopter?"

"Probably had a heart attack when he realized everything he owned didn't have any value now."

"What made her decide to save children?"

"Who knows? Finn implied that she was a little unusual. Never makes eye contact. Awkward socially. Exceedingly organized in a sort of military fashion."

Ana thinks about fourteen-year-old Isla managing on her own, especially that first winter. She envisions this young teenager pushing carts of goods from Costco back to the warehouses,

picking up stray children along the way. At night, maybe they powered up a generator and watched movies on their screens, ate food packaged in plastic and metal as long as they could.

The road gets better thirty miles north of the City. No random trees pushing through cement or the green mossy film that covers everything on the other highways.

They spot a sign for a campground and veer off the highway. They leave the car in the sun to recharge. Aaron fills a cup with lake water and cleans the woman's blood off the back seat of the car. Ana almost wants to leave it. The car is like her own personal history book. Its dents, holes and odors all tell stories.

They eat their lunch on a dock, thirty feet into the water. Islands of ice sway on slow-moving waves, catching sun in their ascent, no shoreline visible in the distance. When they're done, they lay on their backs, close their eyes and listen to the straining and creaking of ice breaking apart.

"What are you thinking about?" Ana asks him eventually.

"The woman from the road."

"She'll be okay," Ana says, eyes closed. She was conscious when they left her. They did all they could and left her with supplies. Gave her half their antibiotics.

"I should have kept searching for her kids. I keep imagining what their kidnapper might do to them."

"You want to go back?" she asks, somewhat resigned. The one thing she hadn't anticipated when they left the City was that they might become entangled in problems far worse than her missing brother.

"No," he says emphatically, rising onto one elbow, his face slightly reddened from the sun. "We go to the Orphanage. One problem at a time."

ISLA LIVES IN a mid-century modern rectangular box – two walls made of glass and wood and the others of brick. It overlooks rows of dormitories, each one nearly identical to the next. In front of every dorm is a picnic bench. Everything is neat and tidy except for a few stray socks, broken water pistols and a forgotten kitchen rag. Far in the distance are the distribution warehouses. Dozens of them. All massive. A city unto itself.

Juan, one of Isla's guards, escorts them into her living room. Although he appeared amiable when he met them at the gate, he has an assortment of weapons and gardening tools tucked into his safari outfit that make her nervous.

Isla is cutting out paper dolls, carefully sorting the mannequins and their tabbed paper clothing into two separate boxes. Her red hair is twisted into a ring at the back of her head that threatens to come loose as she works. She's dressed simply in a blue linen dress.

"The little girls will love these," she says to an aged and severely bow-legged woman pinning children's drawings to the walls. "What a find."

The old woman wears an excessive amount of bobbly jewelry and a green velour tracksuit.

Juan clears his throat to announce their arrival and they both look up.

"She looks just like her brother, doesn't she, Margo?" Isla says to the older woman, not addressing them directly.

"Spittin' image of Finn," Margo says.

Juan invites them to sit on an L-shaped couch in a sitting area that smells of crayons.

"They'll want some coffee, Juan," Margo says. Her earrings are so heavy they look as if they're going to tear through her lobes at any moment.

Ana's never had coffee.

"That's right," Isla says, as if reading her thoughts. "No coffee in the City. Everything but coffee, your brother said. He had so many questions about our greenhouses. About everything actually."

Margo nods with pursed lips.

"Where is he then – your brother? Will he be joining you?" Isla asks excitedly, but without so much as a glance at Ana.

He's not at the Orphanage then, not unless Isla is playing games with her. Ana's eyes well up unexpectedly. Is it noticeable? Of course it is. Margo is looking at her with a pitiful expression.

"He's missing," Aaron says on her behalf.

The enthusiasm fades from Isla's face. "That's not good at all," she says, putting the last of the paper dolls in the Rubbermaid box and clipping the lid on.

"How long?"

"More than three months."

Juan brings out a thermos of coffee, a tray of biscuits and a handkerchief for Ana.

"We should have sent an escort with him, Margo, shouldn't we have? Now you have me worried."

"You two are here looking for him then?" Margo says, putting two spoonful's of honey in Isla's cup for her.

Ana nods.

The lamp in the corner flickers on and off. Isla catches Ana staring at it. The power here is sporadic. Only a few solar panels on the dorm roofs, is what Finn said in his notes.

"Can you tell me what he was doing here?" Ana asks.

"Hmm," Isla says, sitting back and crossing her legs ceremoniously. "So that's the situation then. You two have no clue why he was here? But you're not entirely in the dark, are you? He told you about this place or you wouldn't have found me. So why did he keep secrets from you?"

"He was protecting her?" Margo suggests.

"Possibly," Isla says. "Puts me in a bit of a quandary though, doesn't it? Who am I to second-guess Finn? We were friends, Ana, your brother and I. Friends don't reveal each other's confidences. If he wants to tell you his secrets, he'll have to do it himself."

Juan bends over and puts a biscuit on each of their plates, smiling sympathetically at Ana.

"You're right. He didn't want me to know what he was doing outside the City," Ana agrees. "But now he's probably strung up in someone's basement. That changes things, doesn't it?"

"There's only one group that's likely to string him up," Isla says, unconvinced.

"The Band?" Aaron asks.

"Yes. And I hesitate to say this, but if the Band took him and didn't have a reason to kill him instantly, they would have attempted to trade him to us, and no offer has been made. So that leaves us with only two possibilities."

"Which are?" Ana asks.

"He's not in this world anymore or he doesn't want to be found – even by you."

"Or he got himself caught in an animal trap," Margo suggests.

"Then he'd also be dead," Isla says, somewhat irritated at her friend.

"Dead people don't need to keep secrets," Aaron suggests.

"Maybe not," Isla answers. "Let me sleep on it. You'll stay in our guest cabin tonight. That'll give the children a chance to meet you."

ISLA TAKES THEM all in a golf cart fitted with a solar panel on top of a pole and power generating pedals. Juan sits beside he in the passenger seat, Ana and Aaron crowded in the back. On the way, Isla stops to greet children walking on the road. She knows them all by name. They're in brown pants and shirts and have dirty hands. After they high-five her and accept some honey candy, they head back to the greenhouse and fields.

"We all work here, even the children," Isla explains. "It's part of their school curriculum. I myself keep the banana grove free of weeds. Juan raises his eyebrows at this but doesn't contradict her.

"Where do the children come from?" Aaron asks.

"Most are strays, some are our own and a few are rescues."

"Rescues?"

"Children liberated from unpleasant circumstances," she explains with a tone of defensiveness.

Behind the greenhouse is a windowless bunker surrounded by a barbed wire fence and guards. A few kids play basketball in the courtyard.

"Some of our children require a period of adjustment. Much like a puppy needs to be kenneled in the beginning. Otherwise they throw the others off, you know. But they eventually get the hang of things," Isla says, as they round the bunker.

The children are pets to Isla. She cages them if necessary, makes them beg for treats. Showers affection on them when they're good. In exchange for her devoted care, they do all her labor for her.

Isla drops them off at a small cabin.

"I guess we're prisoners," Ana says to Aaron, when she spots a couple of guards out the window.

"There are three more on that side," Aaron says, nodding toward the back of the cabin. "At least there's a fire going."

"What will we do?" she asks.

"Scrabble," he answers, pointing to some board games in the corner. "Maybe a walk by the river with our armed escorts. Consider it a vacation from your vacation," but she isn't listening to him. She's looking at the bookshelf.

"He used to make a lot of these," she says, picking up a paper airplane from the shelf. She unfolds it, hoping to find

a hidden message from Finn, but there's nothing. She goes to throw it into the wood stove, but he stops her and puts it back on the shelf.

"It was a good day, Ana. Isla knows something."

"Maybe," she says, picking up a second airplane, opening it and then putting it back on the shelf unfolded.

Finn used to attach a paper airplane to his gifts, a card of sorts.

She should have gotten one on the day he disappeared. It was her birthday. The first blizzard of the year. There were snowplows everywhere; one almost drove over the milk courier. The snow was blowing so hard that as soon as it was moved off the road, the wind sent it right back.

When Ana finally made it home, she expected to find Finn in the apartment. He would usually cook spaghetti for her and then hand her some ridiculous gift, a vintage Barbie Dream House or something. It was easier to be humorous than to actually figure out what she wanted. It was dark in the apartment when she arrived. But that was the night the Movement was meeting. Finn was presenting something big, he said. Ana figured he was pacing back and forth in his office at the university, reciting his speech. He'd forgotten all about her. She called his office, but he didn't pick up. Then it occurred to her that maybe he was at Hooper's getting candy for her. She called there, but Hooper said he hadn't seen him in weeks. At seven that evening, he still wasn't home. She gave up and went over to the auditorium. The meeting had started.

She sat at the end of a row so she wouldn't have to climb over people to guilt him out when he finally got there. But he didn't come. She thought maybe he was backstage. This was a big event. There were even reporters. Finally, Ekhart introduced him and called for him to come to the stage, but his call went unanswered.

That's when it hit her. Something had actually happened to him. He'd been hit by a snowplow. After the commotion settled down, she went home and sat on the couch waiting for someone to bring her the bad news. No one came. He wasn't there in the morning, the next day or the following week. It eventually came out that his friends were missing as well. That's when she decided to look for him herself.

"We'll find him, Ana. Maybe at the Amish settlement or some other place," Aaron says.

"And he'll have a perfectly good explanation for all of this?"she adds.

"Probably more than one."

IN THE MORNING, snot-nosed giggling children press their faces against the windows of the cabin, staring at Ana and Aaron like they're on display in a zoo.

"Go away," Ana says under her breath, pulling the covers over her head.

"They're cute," Aaron says. "Don't you like children?"

"Not particularly."

"But you like Martha."

"She's different. She's just like me."

"I'm bringing them candy," he says, stealing her bag of treats from Hooper's out of her pack and going outside. Within minutes, they're crawling all over him. Juan is with them. When they come back inside, Aaron has a child on his shoulders, and one attached to each leg.

Juan and Aaron are chatting amiably.

"Juan was Isla's first rescue," Aaron announces. "Found him alone in a skateboard park."

"Or I found her. Hard to say who rescued whom," he says. Someone calls him on his radio. He walks to the porch to answer in private.

"Isla has something she wants you to see," he says, when he returns.

"I hope it involves food," Aaron whispers to her as he untangles the children knotted to him.

"Probably taking us to their prison," she answers.

AS THEY NEAR their destination, they hear the deafening noise of turbines, a familiar sound to anyone from the City. A steel superstructure comes into view, a geothermal power station, just like the one down the street from their old apartment. Finn had helped design it. A rather simple model.

"Your brother was helping us," Juan says. "She's beautiful, isn't she?"

This is Finn's secret. He built them a power station. It was something noble after all.

Juan takes them next to the old distribution warehouses to show them Isla's side of the bargain. The first is full of glass sheets, millions of them in various sizes and colors stacked in racks and large bins of recycled broken beakers ready to be melted down. A boy of about eleven sits on a chair on guard duty reading a graphic novel and eating sunflower seeds.

"He wanted glass?"

"Not just glass," he answers. "Drywall, lumber, tools, tiles, cement, hardware, even steel. Enough for the new apartment building he planned to build in your City."

"You don't need these things here?" Aaron asks.

"Look around," Juan says. "There's an endless supply of perfectly good buildings for the taking. And even if we wanted new ones, who would build them? The kids?"

For the City, this is a gold mine. The City ran out of building supplies twenty-eight years ago. And there's only so much recycling you can do. What does this mean? Finn wasn't fleeing the City; he was looking for a way to rebuild it.

"Funny thing though," Juan says. "Four months ago, he was supposed to get a progress payment. We loaded up a truck with everything he asked for. When we were set to give it to him, he changed his mind. Said he didn't want the stuff after all. Not yet anyway. He just wanted two of the children."

Children. A boy and a girl. Finn forfeited half his payment for a couple of kids and then didn't return to claim the building supplies. Whose kids? Juan doesn't know. Just a couple of strays. They aren't even connected to each other.

"We were somewhat relieved to be rid of them," he says, "the girl anyway. She was trouble."

"Was anyone else here with him, other people from the City?"

"No, not from the City. He had a team of workers, but they were locals, most of them from out east."

"And the power station? Is it finished?"

"Far as we can tell, it's done. He said he'd put it online once we'd finished the electric fence. We've done that now and Finn hasn't showed up to turn it on. No one here knows how to make that thing work."

"DO YOU UNDERSTAND any of this?" Aaron asks her when they're wandering through the lumber warehouse alone, Juan sneaking a smoke outside. Juan has taken them through six warehouses so far. He's insisting they see everything. He wants Ana and Aaron to go back to the City and convince them to send another engineer. They're treating them like royalty. Isla has filled her car with gifts, including a pound of her precious coffee, which she is to take directly to the Council. Ana doesn't have the heart to tell her that the Council will never help her. In eleven days, the gate will be sealed behind them. No one will come out again if they can help it.

"Sort of. I can imagine that Finn hyperventilated when he saw all of this. He's been wanting to build something since he got his first Lego kit. But abandoning his plan for two kids? No, I don't, but then there are obviously things he kept from me."

"You're frustrated."

"Worried. When you told me that he'd left the City, I thought, okay, he's got some plan. But now we know what that plan was and he's not doing it. He never came back to claim his prize. That means he's dead. What other explanation is there?"

"That your brother didn't like what Isla was doing here. This is a pretty twisted orphanage if you haven't noticed. These children are prisoners. They might not realize it, but the 'orphanage' is a work camp. I figure your brother didn't like the situation, either. He rescued a couple of them. Two that he was attached to. Now he's waiting somewhere for the right opportunity to come back and liberate them all."

CHAPTER 24

(FINN)

SPRING 2064. "Where are we going?" Simeon asks Finn, as they leave the gates of the Orphanage. It's freezing, but Finn is warm in his thin coat, too warm. His heart is racing. He's anxious to put as much white space between them and the Orphanage as possible. Clara looks to him for an answer. They're not afraid of him, he thinks – he's different from the other adults at the Orphanage. He knows little details about their interests – who their favorite superhero is, what they draw, the books they read when they're allowed.

But they are afraid. The children are taken to offsite places to work sometimes, but never on foot and not in the direction of the City. He couldn't tell them his plans, though, not until they got out of that place.

"Home," Finn says, stopping to pick up the long green scarf that has fallen off Clara's shoulders. What does that word mean to them? He wraps it over her head and around and around her neck. He stuffs the ends into her coat. She's maybe eleven. One of the feisty ones. Is sent to detention a lot. He takes the opportunity to reposition their belongings on their little wooden sleigh – a box of the boy's things, a cardboard tube of the girl's artwork and her pink plastic suitcase.

"The Commune?" the boy asks. "I don't know that place now."

"No. My home. The City."

"Why? Are we being punished?"

The boy would think that, wouldn't he? Finn's overheard the horror stories they tell the children about the City. It's a prison. It's full of greedy monsters. They weave all sorts of tales to convince them that living at the Orphanage is a great privilege. That they live in the best place left on earth.

"I'm rescuing you," Finn says sarcastically because he knows they won't see it that way, or at least the boy won't.

"I'd like to go back to my father," the girl finally says, her weak voice barely audible over the crunching of deep snow under their feet. She's only been at the Orphanage a year. She can still remember being happier before.

"We have a cabin. You could both stay there with us. It's beautiful. There's a great big window overlooking a lake."

"I know. I've been there," Finn says.

Her eyes widen and fill with tears. "You have?" she asks.

"We'll go to your father when we're done in the City," he says. The girl turns away disappointed, her tears freezing to her cheeks.

Finn didn't want to take her from the Orphanage. As bad as it is there, it's still better than returning her to her father. He's high every time Finn visits and he's become paranoid. One minute, Finn and he are old friends, the next he's grilling him for the tenth time about his motives, looking through Finn's stuff. And come to think of it, when did he ever see food there? But Finn has no choice. He agreed to return Clara in exchange for Dmitri's help.

Finn doesn't discuss his plans further with the children. He tells them stories of his childhood as they push through the snow. Tales of his and Ana's adventures by the river, exploring under bridges, collecting things. "You'd like Ana," he tells Clara. "She's strong-willed like you and – don't ever tell her I said this – she's smarter than I am. But she likes to make the adults around her mad. She pushes things a little too far.

"Did she used to get detention a lot?"

"No," he laughs. "There's no detention for children in the City."

Clara and Finn discuss things a child shouldn't know anything about – physics, using the sky to navigate – while the boy stares blankly ahead. She's learned a lot from her father. Simeon's been given only a rudimentary education at the Orphanage school and can barely read. Finn will change that. Big flakes of snow pile up on their coats and scarves, weighing them down.

Clara gets tired. Finn gives the box and the tube to Simeon, lifts the bony girl onto the sleigh, her long hair flowing behind her over the snow like red flames. He places their food on her lap and pulls the sled with one arm, her pink suitcase with the other.

At dusk, they spot an old barn. It smells of hay, leather and horses, although it must be his imagination because it's empty. Some boards have been pulled loose on one side. The boy and Finn find some metal sheeting to keep out the wind, but it's still cold, colder now that they've stopped moving. They leave the girl near a pile of brown dust that must once have been hay and look for something to burn. They find nothing but a few horse blankets. The three of them huddle together under the blankets, taking turns being in the middle.

In the morning, Clara is gone. Slipped out under cover of darkness and the shrill of the wind. "I know my way home," she wrote on one of her drawings. He finds it pinned to a hook over the saddle rack. She left the pink suitcase behind.

CHAPTER 25

11 APRIL 2064. Day 6 of 15. Ana crouches on the floor of a closet in what was once the manager's apartment at Blossom Gates, an upscale building in the center of the town of Woodfield with marble floors and a ten-foot-wide chandelier in its entrance. Under a gold embossed "valet parking" sign is a chicken coop and a cistern of water. There are some cows down the hall in number 105 – she saw them being taken out to pasture when they brought her here.

Her cell is four-by-three-feet. If she lies diagonally, she can sleep with her knees bent, head pressed into a built-in shelving unit from Oasis Closets. Instead of clothes, its drawers are filled with onions and garlic. They've given her two mason jars, one to pee in and one with drinking water.

This is all her doing. The plan was to stick to the peaceful communities for now. They might have got lucky and found Finn without any complications. The Amish were supposed to be next. No risk there. The more perilous places would be reserved for later when they ran out of options. But she wanted to go back to the beginning, to the place that first drew Finn out here.

That place was Blossom Gates. A haven, apparently, for those who had been banished from the City. He didn't keep a file on them, but she found a cursory reference to Blossom Gates in Finn's file on the Commune. It was buried in a story about a bonfire – a yearly event at the Commune to clean up garbage – old doors, broken crates, tree stumps. A lot of singing, storytelling, pear cider and deer sausages.

Finn compared the bonfire to one he'd experienced his first night outside the City. He'd sought shelter at Blossom Gates. There was a fire going in the parking lot when he arrived. Except that it wasn't a warm and friendly event. They were burning an old woman who had died. It was winter; no one wanted to dig her a grave. That should have been Ana's first clue that they should avoid the place.

It's been a long time since she last heard Aaron in the living room. They work on him periodically, taking turns. She can only make out the odd word when they question him. Then they do things to him – she doesn't know what. He either emits short grunts or longer moans.

How much can Aaron endure?

When she isn't panicking on his behalf, she worries about

herself. They'll come for her at some point. She psyches herself up. It will be just like the virtual training, painful, but eventually it'll be over. Everything ends. And she'll get breaks. Aaron's screaming is intermittent. Perhaps it's not even that bad. Some finger and wrist bending, minor burns, a few punches to the stomach. Things that will heal.

But last night when she tried to sleep – maybe she was dreaming – she heard dripping and imagined they'd slit his throat and were bleeding him to death.

Their arrival isn't the only news at Blossom Gates. Meg, a prized jersey, is expecting her first calf. They talk about it in the hallway in front of her room enthusiastically. It's not just the extra milk and cheese they're thrilled about – now that Meg will be lactating – it's that their family is expanding. It makes her think the whole torture thing is an act – you can't love cows and then kill people – but maybe you can.

Aaron tried to talk her out of it at first. "You sure it's a good idea to go there? We don't know anything about them."

She told him not to worry. She had a plan. Aaron would make sure his L2 tattoo was visible and tell the man they'd recently left the City. The people at Blossom Gates would assume they'd been banished, just like them, and welcome them into their fold. Then they'd get to the part about her brother already being out here somewhere and that he had friends at Blossom Gates. They'd find out what they needed to know, and they'd be gone in a couple of days. In return for their cooperation, she'd offer them information on their loved ones in the City. Aaron

has a database on his screen with information on every citizen. There are rules against randomly accessing the files, but these are exigent circumstances.

Her plan got derailed quickly. Some guards found them hovering around the front entrance and zip-tied them to a swing set in the playground. A man they called Martin came out to question them. He made some valid points she hadn't considered.

"Say you are from the City, are we supposed to owe you something because at one point we walked the same ground, had the same math tutor maybe, or shared the same bus route? Or do you suppose we'll be friends because we now have the same enemy?"

"Yes," she said. "Why not?"

"Are you that stupid? You think we have a special place in our hearts for violent criminals from the City? We have kids and animals here."

"We're not violent. And we only want to talk to Finn's friends here, so we know where to find him. Then we'll be gone." She laid out as much of the truth about Finn's disappearance as she knew, but he wasn't interested. They took them inside the building, strung Aaron up and took her to the closet.

THE DAY BEFORE yesterday, after they returned from the Orphanage, she was sitting on the safe house balcony planning this whole thing. She'd dragged a chair out there, anxiously waiting for Aaron to get ready. It was dry and windy. Bits of plastic blew down the road, catching on branches. Leaves were pulled loose

from the roofs of buildings. In the distance, she could see a ball of orange sunlight over the City.

She watched Aaron through the sliding glass window. He was making an inventory of his weapons, devising his strategy. Her idea to go to Blossom Gates made him nervous, but he didn't say no. His things were arranged in a circle: knives at three o'clock, a rifle at six, hand guns at nine and a pile of odd things she'd never seen before at twelve o'clock, amongst them a box of dead flies.

Aaron's eyes darted back and forth between the map and his weapons and he was mumbling to himself as he made notes. It was kind of endearing – Aaron kneeling on the parquet floor, the muscles in his thighs threatening to burst through his jeans, his t-shirt riding up in the back, revealing a thin line of flesh. He was just a man. That's when she first noticed the spray of tiny freckles on the back of his elbows. If she'd met him at a party, she would have been too intimidated to start a conversation with him. It would have been someone less attractive, more desperate, that she would have hung out with – probably discussing chess moves or twentieth-century science fiction films. But she would have eyed him, observing how he interacted with women, the way he made them feel, the pick-up lines he used. She could imagine him standing tall against the wall, shoulders relaxed, confidently flirting. If one of her friends had left with him, she'd have been jealous.

At some point in his preparations the dead flies came to life. They hovered above the map. One buzzed around on the sliding

glass window until it found a way out. The fly stopped on the arm of her chair, studying her. She dumped out her glass of water and covered it, the fly making a staccato hum against the side of the cup. Metal. Robotic. Tiny lights behind its eyes. The fly was a camera. She stuck her tongue out at it. He laughed from the other room.

He joined her when he finished packing. The wind picked up and it began to thunder. They watched lightening wreak havoc with the force field over the City, sending a spray of sparks into the sky.

Things were good that afternoon. She had to go and ruin it.

THE HANDLE TO the closet door turns, waking her. A woman comes into her closet, barely able to stand in the tight space and runs her blood-stained hands through her hair. She has multiple scars on her face, including a vertical line from her brow to the middle of her cheekbone. The woman laughs nervously when Ana's eyes move to her red hands.

"It's Meg's blood, not your friend's," she says, "although Meg looks a bit better than him at this point." He's alive then. That's something. It must be her turn now.

The woman takes what's left of the water in the mason jar and pours it over her hands into the pee jar.

"The midwife wants to see you." Midwife. That can't be bad.

The light coming through the sliding glass door in the living room is blinding after days in the dark. But she can see enough to know that the room is empty, the ropes that bound Aaron

still suspended from two beams in the ceiling, a sheet of plastic underneath. A sodden mop against the wall.

They take her to the penthouse where a group is assembled in the dining room. They're eating the dried fruit and nuts from Aaron's pack. The robotic flies are scattered across a coffee table, some smashed. Martin is massaging the shoulders of an older woman – presumably the midwife – while a boy sits at their feet with Aaron's screen. He's having fun stretching it in and out but is unable to turn it on. He brings it to Ana and asks her to make it work. She reluctantly brings it to life and hands it back to him. He flees down the hallway before anyone can take it from him.

Martin looks like a movie star from a surfer movie, tough but too pretty to be real, boyish blond curls around his face obscuring the fine lines of middle age. He's surprisingly unscarred.

The penthouse is filled with newish looking furniture, oil lamps and knick-knacks, but no electronic devices or appliances. They've put a woodstove in front of the sliding glass door and vented it out the balcony. Deer meat hangs down in strips in the kitchen and laundry baskets full of potatoes litter the floor. She can hear children in a bedroom jumping on beds.

Ana sees his shoe first, extending out from behind the couch. Aaron is propped against a wall, his face and arms a mess – nose out of joint, one eye swollen shut, bruises on his arms. The rest of the damage is hidden under his clothes. But he has all his limbs and he's semi-conscious. She goes to him and lifts his chin, checking that his pupils are still dilating. An expression of relief fills his face when he sees her. Maybe he thought they'd been

torturing her as well all this time. He takes her hand and pulls her down beside him.

"You can leave now," the midwife says to Martin.

"Not a good idea," he says.

"Shoo," she says. "I can handle myself. Go tell the others about Meg."

Martin puts Aaron's gun in the midwife's hand and reluctantly leaves the apartment, taking the children with him.

She walks over to Ana, lifts the back of her shirt and runs her finger up her back until she finds the birthmark on her right shoulder. The gesture is oddly unsettling and Ana jerks away from her.

"Do you know who I am?" she asks, laughing slightly.

Ana can't place her, but she's vaguely familiar – was she a vendor at the market or one of her father's projects?

"I do," Aaron answers. "Miranda Pape. You were banished from the City seven years ago."

"And what do they give as the reason in that device of yours?" she asks.

"Your children and husband died in a fire that was caused by your negligence."

"Negligence is a bit of a benign word. I started the fire on purpose, didn't I?"

"That's what they say."

"Are you curious why?" she asks him.

"Sure," he says, looking like he's about to pass out. The woman just saved them after all. He has to pretend to be interested.

"Because I hadn't felt anything in that place for a long time and I needed to. That's the best I can explain it. I didn't intend for them to die of course – only myself. They were supposed to be on their way to school. But here I am and they're in the ground behind the wall."

There's nothing they can say to that. Judge her and they might get sent back downstairs. It will be Ana's turn now. They could try being sympathetic, but it would sound insincere. Setting a building on fire when there's a severe housing shortage in the City is bad enough, let alone killing your own family.

"It was a shock when Finn showed up here. Didn't take him to be a troublemaker. Turns out he wasn't banished of course. He'd simply found a way to sneak out. He always was clever."

"You knew him?"

"I knew you both. I was your babysitter. You don't remember?" she asks, slightly disappointed. "Ah, but you were just three. Kids don't remember much at that age. Such a hyperactive child you were, climbing like a monkey up doorframes, jumping on furniture. I don't think your feet touched the ground that year I was with you – when you weren't flying off chairs, you always wanted to be held. But I liked you. Other children got bored and wanted to be entertained. Not you."

Aaron needs medical attention. The cloth they've given him for his nose is soaked. His eye doesn't look good. It's time to find a way out of here.

"Your brother and I stayed friends, you know. He'd come to my place sometimes to play with my girls."

"That's why he came to you when he first left?" Ana asks.

"Not just that. Something about your father's death that he was working through. He wanted absolution, I think. Probably thought that if I was able to live with myself after doing something horrible, maybe he could forgive himself for not saving him. That's where he stayed," she says, pointing to the room down the hall where the children had been jumping. "Didn't leave that room for the better part of a month."

"A month?" Ana asks. When was he away from her that long? That time is all a blur. There'd been the funeral. Then Finn said he was house-sitting for a friend. But had it been that long? Truthfully, she'd been avoiding him. She blamed herself for what happened.

Martin is back. He's hovering in the hallway.

"For the first week, your brother didn't even speak," Miranda says, when Martin's out of earshot again. Maybe Martin doesn't know any of this.

"Did he get what he needed here?" Ana asks.

"I think he did. We kind of thought he'd become a permanent feature. He was talking about piping water up from the river, maybe hooking us up with some solar panels. And then he just decided to go one day. I told him it was a good idea. He should return to the City and do someone some good there. It would make up for the wrong he thought he did. He said he planned on doing exactly that."

"If you knew who I was, why did you let them hurt my *friend*?" she asks, for lack of a better word.

"I didn't know you were here, but I don't blame Martin. The City banished us. Which is fine. We're not unhappy here. But you can't have it both ways. If we can't go back there, you shouldn't rightly be allowed here."

A LARGE CROWD assembles in the living room on the couches, the floor, even the kitchen island, legs dangling down. One by one, they look up names of family and friends left behind in the City in Aaron's database. Some smile through tears when they hear that a sibling or friend has done something extraordinary. Mostly it just makes them sad though. Martin goes silent when he hears that his wife is remarried to his old boss.

"They have kids now?" he asks. "Huh. Thought she didn't want kids."

"HOW BAD IS IT?" Ana asks, after Martin leaves them back at her car. She looks at his swollen face, Aaron seated on the hood. The air is thick with the scent of a smokehouse.

"I don't think it's broken," he says.

"I take it you didn't get a chance to look in the mirror then?" she asks, prodding it gently. "It's completely bent out of shape." Before he can open his mouth to respond, she crunches his nose back into place. His scream sends a wild turkey fleeing. "Didn't think I actually knew how to do that," she says.

"I'm not sure you did," he says.

She packs it with gauze to stop the bleeding and then turns her attention to the cut by his eye.

"I'm going to have to stitch that," she says.

"You? No. Just glue it."

When she's done, there's a large pile of bloody gauze, an empty bottle of disinfectant and a vial of skin glue between them.

"I'm not very good at apologizing," she says.

"So don't."

"I get these ideas and I'm so convinced I'm right."

"You were. We needed to go there."

"I keep imagining you hanging from those ropes, lifeless, me asking Martin to at least help me carry your dead body to the car."

"None of that happened."

"But look at your face."

"Why did Finn feel responsible for your father's death?" he asks. "Didn't he drown?"

"Let me see the rest of you," she says, pulling his shirt up. He pulls it back down.

"Are you going to answer me?" he asks.

My father wouldn't have died if we'd been better children. We both felt guilty after it happened." She inspects a bruise at the back of his neck she hadn't noticed before. It's more of a hematoma. "We might need to lance that one," she says.

"What could you possibly have done to prevent it?" he asks, pushing her hand away.

She's never actually talked about it with anyone. And she doesn't want to now, in the middle of this field. But she knows he won't let it go.

"You know that little cove off the river where you can swim?"

"The one that's always crowded?"

"Yes. That one," she says, digging a hole to bury their medical mess.

"My father came to me one night at 3:00 a.m. and woke me up, towels in one hand and our swimming suits in the other. It was the anniversary of my mother's death. I suspect that he'd been drinking a little. He said "Ana, it's a full moon. We have to go swimming. Maybe we'll get lucky and no one will be there." It was unusual for my father to want to do something with me. He wasn't a bad person. It's just that he seemed to think that everyone but his children needed him. I should have immediately said yes. Instead, I protested. Put the pillow over my head and told him to go away. He pleaded with me. He talked about how beautiful it would be. The moon reflecting on the still water. 'We could lie on our backs and float and imagine that we were anywhere in the world,' he said."

"Where was Finn?"

"In those years, Finn didn't always sleep at home. He often couch-surfed."

"So, it would have just been you and him that night?"

"If I'd said yes, but I couldn't bring myself to go with him."

"He went alone and had the accident?"

"He did. And now I frequently torture myself replaying that night over and over, except that in my fantasy I go with him to the water. He tells me stories of his childhood. About elephants in India and food so spicy you can't breathe. I ask him what I

should do with my life and he gives me that warm smile he reserved for the really needy. In my fantasy, he still slips and falls but I see it. I drag him out of the water before he drowns. An ambulance comes in time. Sometimes I imagine the years since. I go through everything that has happened except that dad is also there because I saved him."

"If it was you he asked to go with him, why did Finn feel so guilty?"

"He thinks he should have stayed home that night. We always commemorated the day together. But he ditched us without explanation."

"You and your brother have big egos."

"What's that supposed to mean?"

"That you think you're so powerful that you can control fate. Your father slipped and fell and died because the rock he was standing on had moss and dew on it. He died because he made a bad decision to combine alcohol and swimming. It wasn't because you didn't feel like waking up in the middle of the night. No one does. It wasn't because Finn stayed at a friend's house."

CHAPTER 26

12 APRIL 2064. Day 7 of 15. According to Ana's limited knowledge of the canine species, dogs wag their tails and are generally content when humans approach them, happy to lick a hand or submit to scratching and petting. Domesticated dogs anyway. But what about feral dogs? There aren't a lot of either kind in the City. Too much competition over food and space.

It was this morning that the dogs found them. They'd set up camp early the night before. Ana was worried that Aaron might expire in the front seat of her car if she drove any further. He was in pain. Couldn't get comfortable enough to sleep. Couldn't manage to get any food into his swollen mouth. She stopped, left him in the car and set up his tent. She was too tired to bother with hers and so they slept together. It was Aaron who woke her.

There was breathing and snorting outside. They speculated as to whether it might be a bear. But when she peaked out the flap, she saw three dogs licking the pan she used the night before. For reasons she still can't understand, this discovery somehow animated Aaron. He wasn't afraid of them. He went right up to the dogs, knelt down and put his hand out for them to sniff and spoke to them in a soft voice. They gave him something she hadn't managed to offer him.

Now they're jumping and slobbering all over him, making him wince in pain.

Two of them are kind of cute; mangy but endearing in a pathetic way. The third is just plain ugly – bulging eyes in a tiny head, wisps of grey wiry hair, yellow teeth. He's her favorite.

The dogs follow Ana and Aaron down to a stream and splash around at the edges of the cold water as Aaron cleans their pan and fills their water bottles. Ana throws sticks for them to fetch. The two relatively handsome dogs don't get along that well and she has to break up a skirmish over clams. When the conflict subsides, they compete over licking her.

"You're not so hard-hearted after all," he says.

"Oh, I am. I can't stand them. I'm just trying to get my exercise," she says. "How did you get to be so good with dogs?"

"There was a dog in the Annex. A black lab. Skippy. He used to live in the bus we all hung out in. We took turns keeping him fed. Didn't tell any of the adults, even when we all got itchy."

WHEN ANA AND AARON leave, the ugly one jumps into the back seat and the others look anxious to join him.

"Should I shoo them away?" Aaron asks.

"They probably have fleas."

"Most likely," he says.

"Might be good protection though."

"So, we can keep them?" he asks, as if there's a decision to be made.

"We'll need to name them," she says.

"Yours is Yippy. Mine are Jasper and Sassafras," he says emphatically. He probably named them the minute he met them.

CHAPTER 27

13 APRIL 2064. Day 8 of 15. Aaron's mother worked at a resort every summer before the collapse. When she told stories from the time before, they were always about that place – smoking a joint on the dock with her boss, sprinkling salt on her ankles to get rid of leeches, a manhunt for a kid who went missing for three days and was eventually found asleep in a log. Her stories had become a part of his DNA. The one thing he asked for when the trip was being planned was to spend a night there. It was an hour from the Amish settlement and so she had no reason to say no. He said that if the place was remote enough, they might even be able to have a fire.

But they can't find it. Maybe time swallowed it up. They pull up to an old auction house and examine a detailed map of the

county in a glass display case. The dogs take turns peeing against a phone booth.

"Where would you live if the City didn't exist?" he asks her. They play these games when they're bored on the road.

"I wouldn't live in one of those fully furnished 'never lived in' show homes Finn refers to in his files," she says, returning to the fantasy. "It would be a loft. Something like our safe house, with floor-to-ceiling windows, movable walls. High up so I can watch everything that's happening. Instead of furniture, I'd put a million pillows on the floor and there'd be stacks of books along the walls. I'd find a really good stereo and blast music – new music – not that '80s garbage you listen to."

"Would there be people with you in your loft?"

"A few friends. Intelligent people. We'd hang out on my balcony at night by candlelight and talk about Hegel and Rousseau. During the days we'd be on our own, building useful things and making art. On Sundays, we'd cook elaborate meals with everything we'd collected over the week – quail eggs, squirrel sausages and such."

"Waffles?"

"Yes, definitely waffles with those tiny strawberries that grow wild."

Yippy perks his head up at that. He eyes her with a confused, but loyal expression, one ear caked with dust from his explorations of the auction house. Her car will never be the same.

"Have you read much philosophy?"

"No, but in my fantasy I'm extremely well-read."

Aaron's imaginary home outside the City is a one-room cabin overlooking a river. Typical male fantasy.

"I'd fish," he says. "And on Sundays, I'd come to your brunches in town with a string of smoked cod and I'd join your philosophy reading club."

"Sounds good," she says. It actually does sound kind of nice. Not far off from some of the gatherings her father used to hold in their apartment.

AN HOUR LATER, Aaron spots what was once a backroad to the river under a crop of wild wheat. The old camp sign lies horizontal. They follow the road, plant life beating at the underbelly of the station wagon. When they can't go any further by car, they continue on foot, Aaron limping, but determined, until the wheat thins out and is replaced by cattails and thistles and the spongy earth becomes rocky sand. They find the camp office and, beyond it, a path to swimming pools filled with sludge.

"That's where she worked," he says, pointing to a round wooden hut with a neon "snack shop" sign.

She can imagine what it would have been like in its heyday. All those kids having a blast away from their parents.

"I'd like to swim," he says.

"Do you have a concussion?" she asks. There's nothing resembling water in the pools. He also isn't in any shape to be splashing around. He ignores her and continues on the path intently until they reach a circle of rocks enclosing a pool of water

on the edge of the river. He strips down to his underwear while she pulls her jacket tighter. It's cloudy and barely above freezing.

"You're on your own," she says. If he's delirious, maybe the cold water will knock some sense into him. At the very least, it will kill some of the pain.

He eases into the pool. When he doesn't scream, she tests the water with her hand. It's warm, with a slight sulfur odor. A hot spring. She strips and joins him. If it weren't for Aaron's mangled face, she could imagine they were on vacation, the kind her parents talked about from the old days – her mother's Christmas getaways to Florida, her father's family trips to India.

Ana and Aaron spend the afternoon like children, seeing how long they can hold their breath under water, Ana practicing handstands on the pebbled beach and jumping off boulders with the dogs.

When they get bored of the water, they explore the fishing shack, a cross-country ski hut, some of the cabins, the park restaurant. She imagines eating in front of the large dining hall fireplace. She looks at a plastic-covered menu lying on the hostess' podium and fantasizes about ordering a Shirley Temple or Harvey Wallbanger, whatever they are. He'll order a seafood appetizer – ceviche. For an entrée, they'll have a T-bone steak and baked potato.

She gathers clams along the shoreline, while he inspects a rack of canoes.

"You want to go fishing, don't you?" she asks.

"It's on my bucket list," he says.

"I saw rods and tackle in the camp store."

"We could use some real food," he says, guiltily.

THEY ASSEMBLE the necessary gear, choose a bright red canoe, carry it over their heads to the edge of the river and drop it in clumsily, icy water splashing into her shoes. The dogs refuse to join them in the boat. Instead, they run around on the sand and bark at the departing canoe. They row downstream to a small island. Aaron immediately gets to work on the rod, struggling to spool the reel and string it – it's much harder than it looks – while Ana unearths worms from under a bolder. When he finally manages it – not entirely the right way, she thinks – he stands at the edge of some rocks, swinging the rod over his shoulder, while she collects more clams.

The fish he catches are tiny, the kind you should release, but she screeches in delight each time he plops one into the bucket. After an hour, she takes over and hardly does any better. The fish have become smarter since humans left.

"Did you ever fish with Finn?" Aaron asks, when they're side-by-side on a washed-up oil barrel.

"Yes. In the bathtub with magnets, over the bridge with a stick and string. Always pretend."

"Have you forgiven him for leaving you?"

"Not yet."

"But you miss him?"

"I don't know. I'm not doing this because I miss him. It's just the way it is. Finn helps other people. I save him."

She puts the rod down and a toad hops over it. There are hundreds of them in the swampy grass all around them.

"In some ways it's actually easier with him gone."

"How so?"

"Finn was complicated. He was charismatic. Confident. Inspired. He'd get an idea in his head – like the time he wanted to move the water treatment plant – and he'd talk to people about it in a way that got them hyped up. It was just a damn plant where they treated human waste, but he'd make them think that their entire life story culminated in that single goal – getting it moved downwind. He was selling them hope. Every resource they had, their intelligence, money, time, connections, would get mobilized and it'd be like a giant hurricane pushing this stupid little idea along. The momentum he created became much bigger than the thing itself and the result much more than he could have imagined. Yeah, the sewage plant got moved but, more than that, people changed, they connected, community happened. Everything felt new again. You could see it at the Orphanage with Isla and her people. He got that from our father, of course. But he was even better at it.

But then there was the other side of him. That light would come and go and when he went dark he could suck the energy out of everything and everyone around him. Drain it completely. When that happened, he would make sure he was alone so that no one else would feel it. Only Hooper and I would get sucked into his vortex. I hated it. I resented that his depression held me hostage like that. That any energy

Hooper might have had for me needed to go to Finn.

You all think Finn didn't tell me about his trips because he was protecting me from the violence out here. That wasn't it. And he wasn't worried that I would get implicated in his little crime and get arrested in the City. And it wasn't because I wasn't good enough or would have been a liability. It was because he didn't want me telling him he shouldn't go, that he was too unbalanced for this. He didn't want *me* protecting *him*. But it's my job. Finn falls apart, and then I make him whole again so that he can make the world a better place."

"It doesn't have to be that way. You could save the world all on your own. Cut out the middle man."

"I'm not that smart, Aaron. I'm not even likable."

"You're forgetting I've read your file. I've seen your test results, performance evaluations and report cards. They say you have your mother's mind."

"Maybe. I wouldn't know."

"And as for being likable, he likes you," Aaron says, nodding to the shoreline where Yippy waits for her, chasing flies.

CHAPTER 28

2034. Emily Bentham graduated from law school four years before the calamities. She immediately started working for a firm her father handpicked for her on Bay Street. She would have preferred to do something to make the world a better place, like work for the UN or a charitable organization. She had a friend who, when he wasn't lawyering, negotiated with warlords in Africa to free child soldiers. But there weren't a lot of jobs like that, none her family would have "facilitated" anyway. And so, like most of her fellow graduates, she ended up using her legal skills, in the metropolis of Toronto, to keep the corporate world from dissolving too quickly. They assigned her to a partner in mergers and acquisitions, which was a lucrative area considering the economic crisis – corporations needed to restructure or go bankrupt.

She was competent and had a good rapport with clients. People went to her when a difficult personality was standing in the way of a deal. It helped that her family held a significant number of shares in one of the country's oldest steel companies. Her connections had been relied on more than once to bring in new clients. It made her feel dirty.

When she talked about those times, she said she was generally unhappy. It was like wearing shoes all day that were a size too small. It could be done but was uncomfortable. She would rebel in hidden ways – not shaving her legs, attending Green Party information nights, staying in rough motels when she travelled on business. Many of her peers were content enough, learning from the best, saving for a down payment on a condo near the water, eating out at trendy restaurants. They were addicted to the thrill of being a new lawyer – the high-stake deals, aggressive negotiating positions – not that they were part of all that. They mostly sat behind their laptops researching and writing briefs.

To escape the Bay Street world, she would take long walks down Queen Street West, talk to strangers – some, but not all, homeless – buy beads, yarn, fountain pens or other non-essential items at eclectic shops.

It was in her fourth year of practice that she walked into the clock and watch store where Aavai worked. Her mother had sent her there to get some antique watches appraised for insurance purposes. She resented wasting her lunch break running errands for her mother, who didn't need to work

and never understood what having a regular job entailed. Emily felt these errands were her mother's way of putting her in her place.

There was only one clerk in the store, a man about her age, Sikh, with a light blue turban. Something about all those dinner parties at her home in Rosedale with affluent white people made her gravitate to anyone with a little color. She wondered how her parents could live in such a multicultural city and keep their world so small.

He didn't notice her at first. He was reading a graphic novel tucked into a textbook.

"Can I help you," he finally said when he eventually noticed her. She was surprised that he had an American accent.

According to Ana's father's version of the story, he was so shell-shocked when he set eyes on her that he could barely string two words together. Her mother didn't remember it that way. She said everything he said was interesting, that he put on a good show of intellectual prowess.

He was studying architecture at Ryerson, working at a relative's shop part-time. In the fall, he was starting a co-op at a firm in Mississauga. His parents lived in Texas.

She explained what she needed and handed him the insurance forms, but he was having a hard time concentrating on her words. He did manage to take the watches from her and get down her phone number, six of the seven digits anyway.

"I'm not particularly good at this," he said. "You probably know more about your watches than I do."

"I know nothing about watches except that people *used* to wear them," Emily said.

After they were done, she felt glued to the counter she was leaning over, unable to return to the office. Although there was an uncomfortable silence as they both figured out what came next, neither of them moved.

"Do you want to get something to eat later?" she asked.

She had a dinner to go to that night with clients. Her whole team was invited. She would be missed, but she hated those things. She knew how it would go. Small talk about whatever was in the news, followed by a discussion of the best golf courses in Ontario. They'd banter about wine and the latest microbrew, a cruise they went on last summer, horror stories of nightmare home renovations. They weren't bad people, they just had little interest in refugees or clean water in Africa. It wasn't their fault; it was hers. She didn't belong there. And what was she doing about the problem in Syria anyway? She was such a hypocrite.

She returned to the office, had a couple of meetings with clients, and then took Aavai out for Persian food in the evening. They discussed the failings of their education, a documentary they'd both watched at the Toronto Film Festival on aberrant weather patterns. He told her about his interest in studying religion. He'd studied them all – Islam, the Bahá'í Faith, Judaism, Buddhism, Christianity. He had a Bahá'í friend who made solar stoves in India. If he didn't get a job after his co-op, he was going there.

"I'm not sure I believe in God," she said, "but I respect your convictions."

"I probably don't believe in the God you don't believe in either. What do you believe in?" he asked, amused.

"Doing meaningful things with whatever the universe has given you. I'm going back to school to get my master's degree in Human Rights law," she added, although the idea hadn't even occurred to her until that moment. Her phone kept vibrating; she ignored it. When they were finished eating, he took her back to his one-room flat and made her coffee. It was a noisy building, full of the aromas of international cuisine. Homey. She considered asking him if she could move in and split the rent. She was still living with her parents at the time. Not because she wanted to; she was too busy to think about moving.

The next day she woke up back in her Rosedale house feeling dazed. The night before seemed like it almost didn't happen. What was she supposed to do now, go to the office and quit her job or suck it up and live with her lot? The idea of going back to school seemed like a childish fantasy now.

It didn't help that he didn't call her in the days that followed. After a few weeks of waiting in vain for some kind of communication, she realized that that night could not be reconciled with the rest of her life. She went to work, put him out of her mind and forgot that she was slightly miserable. His boss faxed the appraisal to the insurance company, so Emily had no reason to go back there. At Christmas, she went to Florida with some

colleagues at work. Five months later she moved into a condo on the waterfront.

The morning of 8 July 2034, she got a call from Aavai. He had spent a significant part of the intervening months trying to figure out what the missing seventh digit of her phone number might be. Was it the last number or the first that he'd missed? A number in the middle maybe? There were endless possibilities. Normally, he would have googled her, but he didn't know her last name and there were over a hundred lawyers named Emily in Toronto. He was surprised when he got to the sixty-seventh on his list and she answered. Of course, he didn't tell her any of this until years later.

"I'm not a stalker," he said matter-of-factly, without a hint of the emotion that was now overwhelming him. "I just thought we had more to talk about."

"I need a walk. Can I come over now?" she asked.

"I could make time for you?" he said.

It was a perfect day, with a balmy breeze fanning over the city from Lake Ontario. She told her assistant she was taking her screen to a café to work and left.

She walked down Spadina, past her old law school. By the time she got to Queen Street, pedestrians were leaving offices and stores in a hurry. Any vehicle unfortunate enough to be on a road, rather than airborne, was stuck in traffic, people honking incessantly. Had there been a terrorist attack? She looked to the sky for signs of smoke, but it was as blue as a robin's egg. People eventually left their cars and moved in droves in opposing directions.

When she got to the watch store, Aavai was putting his graphic novels and the cash from the till into his bag. He was on speakerphone with his mother in San Francisco.

"Just get out of the city, Aavai, to your aunt's house in Windsor. We'll meet you there."

"What's going on?" Emily asked him.

"Do you have some place to go?"

"No," she answered, even though she could have walked the five miles to her new, unfurnished condo and wait out whatever was going on.

"You'll come with me then?" he asked, hopefully. He paused only long enough to determine if she was willing. She was, not because the world as she knew it was ending – she couldn't have known at the time – but because she wanted to. She figured that out as soon as she saw him packing his bag. She would make solar stoves with him and his Bahá'í friend in India.

They went through a backdoor to the alley where he parked his e-bike. It was garbage day and reeked of food waste from a nearby Vietnamese restaurant. There was barely room for the both of them and his stuff. She threw her computer bag over her shoulder and leaned into him. And when he looked back at her to make sure she was ready, he smiled, and she knew then she'd made the right decision. That's how she told it anyway.

Did she really know that? Ana always wondered, or did she need to remember it that way. In any event, Aavai drove off with her pinned to his back.

He found his way around the stalled cars to the expressway. The highway was like a stadium parking lot. Nothing moved. Even the dirt roads were jammed, but on his bike, he could weave around anything.

Instead of going to Windsor, as his mother suggested, they rode north, stopping every three hours to wait for his solar battery to charge and to call his mother. Emily tried her parents once, but their cleaning lady Rita answered and said she hadn't been able to get a hold of them all day. They were in New York.

That night, they slept under the stars in a field of flax that was dotted with the blankets and tents of other families fleeing south to the military camps, the rooftops of their cars piled high with things that, on that day at least, seemed so important. They joined someone's fire and sang songs, as if they were all at summer camp. All night, Aavai doted on her. He bargained for some blankets and let her sleep closest to the fire where the black flies weren't too bad.

By the end of the second night, they were at a family cottage in the Bruce Peninsula, alone.

"Why didn't you take me to Windsor?" she asked him.

"You wouldn't fit in there."

"Because I'm not Sikh."

"No, because you're sane."

But there was another reason. Last summer, he'd been here and befriended a survivalist down the road. He'd given Aavai a tour of his cellar. Tin cans, wheat berries and powdered milk. He even had freeze-dried camping food, generators and first aid

kits. If he was there, he could maybe give Aavai some advice on making it through until things settled down, lend him a hunting rifle and water purifier maybe.

The guy never showed up and, eventually, Emily and Aavai decided it wouldn't be so bad to raid his supplies. When the easy food was gone, they ate mostly coarse flat bread made from hand ground wheat berries and drank wheat grass juice. Occasionally, she managed to kill something edible – rabbits and fish. They slept arm in arm until noon some days, swam in Cyprus Lake, foraged, fought over extraneous facts they could no longer google, like how many kilometers the earth's diameter is.

The two of them became synchronized, an engine of sorts with distinct, yet well-aligned, parts. Gone were her suits, leg waxes and conference calls with Beijing.

At first, they thought maybe they'd made a mistake. They should go to one of the camps. There must be a reason why everyone thought they were safer down south, but they just didn't want to. Aavai built his first greenhouse their second summer up north. He put it right on the lake, a floating greenhouse, so he wouldn't have to haul buckets of water up the escarpment. It was a good summer.

Then, in September, worms got into their wheat supply. A heavy storm sunk the greenhouse just before the first snowfall. Emily miscarried.

They met a couple from the south on a supply run, invited them back to their cottage. The couple were friendly, also of Indian descent, but Hindu. They were thrilled to taste bread again,

even though it was unleavened and rough. They told them about a functioning city halfway across the continent. They said it was "experimental".

"Utopian?" Aavai asked. He had read a lot of science fiction.

"Doubt it," the guy said. "They have food, though, and work."

"Is it run by a psychopath?" Emily asked. She had watched a few too many post-apocalyptic TV series.

"Doesn't seem like it," he said. "It's run by committee."

"So why aren't you going there?" Aavai asked.

"We've had enough of cities," their new friends said.

Over the next four months they fixed up his bike and gathered what they needed for the long journey. When they weren't working, they hung out with their friends. Eventually, they said goodbye and started the long journey southwest. Along the way, they traded wheat for a better solar battery and dried jerky.

They arrived in March 2036, two years after the City became a thing, four years before the wall cut them off from the rest of the world, six months before Finn was born.

CHAPTER 29

14 APRIL 2064. Day 9 of 15. "Out," she orders, somewhere between the resort and the Amish farm.

"You want to ditch me by the side of the road? So soon?"

"I'm teaching you to drive," she says.

His face lights up, as if the thought had never occurred to him.

"Why?" he asks.

"You might need to drive my body back to the City," she says. He laughs at this, but then shakes the idea away as if maybe there's truth to it.

He's been watching her drive, asking questions here and there, but when he actually gets in front of the wheel, he doesn't seem to know where to start.

She talks him through each step patiently as her father did with her. Shows him how to start it, put it in drive, accelerate and brake. When he accelerates in reverse and then jerks forward, causing their few remaining possessions and the dogs to fly off the back seat, she doesn't complain.

She lets him control the wheel all the way to the Amish farm, one arm eventually relaxing casually by his side; the other poised on the wheel like a pro.

He looks dissatisfied when they reach the farm.

"You don't want to stop, do you?" she asks.

"I could drive for hundreds of miles. But don't get any ideas. I still want to go home," he says.

"Homesick already?"

"You don't, do you?"

"What?"

"Want to go back. You won't leave him once you find him," he says casually, looking up to gauge her reaction. "That's what this driving lesson is all about. I'm going to have to drive myself home."

This a test. If she confirms his suspicion, he'll be better prepared when the big confrontation comes – the moment when he wants to take Finn back and she stops him. If she lies, he'll see through it. He won't trust anything she says.

Is Aaron wrong? Will she stay out here with Finn when she finds him? That was her plan when she left, but now? Even if Finn welcomes her into his new world, will she want to stay with him? The person she thought he was, the brother who walked

her to her first day of school, who snuck silver from their grocery fund to buy her new shoes, who explained puberty to her because there were no women in her life, was overtaken a long time ago by someone who was merely playing along as Finn out of habit or as an act of kindness to her.

"I need to find him. What happens after that is uncertain," she says. It's a neutral enough answer.

THE AMISH SETTLEMENT is deserted, the cluster of white buildings as still as the dirt road they just exited, the only noise a string of clothes pins clattering against a metal pole. Aaron parks by a burnt-out schoolhouse. A pile of charred desks and books, wet from the recent rain, lies under a heap of half-burnt studs, an acrid smell hanging in the air.

They search the stables and barns. No horse-drawn buggies. The pumps have been disconnected. Nothing of value left. The few rusted tools that remain have been put away on hooks and shelves. The closets and chests in the houses have been emptied of their heavy black clothing and bonnets.

She thinks maybe Finn was just making up stories. He went crazy and started imaging people where there were none. Then she spies the greenhouse. They stroll through it, plucking cucumbers, tomatoes and greens, putting them straight into their mouths, warm liquid dripping down their forearms.

"They didn't plan on leaving," she says, running her free hand along a row of tiny sprouts waiting to be transferred to the freshly plowed kitchen garden outside the community hall. The

seedlings are no more than two weeks old and the vegetables are just beginning to dry out from lack of attention.

"No, they didn't, but they had enough time to bury their dead," he says, pointing at two new graves in a small cemetery next to the community hall.

They leave the dogs rolling in the grass and walk over to a house on a hill, away from the other white homes. It too is deserted. In an upstairs bedroom, the owners have left behind a rocking horse and bookshelf with a single dog-eared copy of *Pride and Prejudice* on it that had once been a library book.

Noises outside the house interrupt them. They move to either side of the bedroom window. She can see four men, coils of hair – maybe human – hanging off their belts, jeans encrusted with something viscous, vacuous faces. Not Amish. They're young, aggressive and curious. They peer into Ana's car, kick the tires. One of them pulls out what looks to be a pick axe and is about to smash the back window in but changes his mind.

A feeling of dread overcomes her. She didn't tell Aaron about the old woman's warning that the Band will come for Ana once they know she's out here. She thought she was still safe.

The strangers follow their footprints to the front porch of the house. Aaron and Ana tiptoe back into the hallway, down the back stairs and out the kitchen door.

There's a forest not far from the house. They disappear under its cover and run. When they're out of breath, they lean against a tree. But the men know they are there. They hear them inching closer, brushing against branches. The dogs bark

in the distance, furious. What have they done to them?

They load their guns and disengage the safety. There's something very natural about this act, a mere adjustment to their routine, like veering around debris on the highway. They could try to lose them, but since confrontation seems inevitable, they may as well stand their ground.

"Don't use your gun if you don't have to," he whispers. "There could be others. The noise will draw them to us."

When minutes go by, Ana thinks maybe they've lost them. Her heart rate starts to slow. She nods back in the direction they've come from, as if to suggest they should return to the car and get the hell out of there.

Before he can respond, there's a rustling and two of the boys emerge from behind some trees. No doubt, the one reliable bit of education they've had is tracking and hunting. And they know how to keep quiet.

They're so young, maybe sixteen, sinewy and thin boned, acne on their faces, oily bangs covering their eyes. One dark and olive-skinned; the other pale and red haired. Ana and the latter dance around each other for a while, while Aaron chases the other into the forest. The boy jabs at her with his knife playfully. She deftly sidesteps him, the gun slack in her right hand. "Make this easy on me" he says mockingly, "your gun's not even loaded". Of course the boy thinks that. Bullets must be scarce out here now. The next time he strikes at her, she grabs his arm and brings it down hard on her knee, his knife dropping onto a bed of needles.

A look of shame crosses his face. He barrels into her, the two of them landing in a soft bed of moss. He immobilizes her with the full weight of his body while groping for his knife two feet away. When his head is turned, she buffalos him on the side of his head with the cylinder of her gun, stunning him just enough for her to get onto her hands and knees.

"Shit," he says, one hand nursing his head while the other still seeks his knife. "I wasn't gonna hurt you that bad."

She pulls herself to her feet and strikes him again – harder – just as he rises with the knife. He stumbles against a tree.

She tells herself this is a play – she auditioned and got the role of kickass girl. This forest is her stage, the gun in her hand a prop. When the curtain goes down, she'll bow and walk away. She and this guy will have drinks backstage, laugh about how his pants were practically falling off when he fell on her. She thinks about this as she rams his head into the trunk of the tree, his ear bloody and raw now, one eye twitching. He falls over onto his back, a bloody monograph of the tree imprinted on his face.

Aaron has his guy against a narrow tree, hands zip tied behind the trunk. He hesitates, a conflicted look on his face. Maybe he wants her to leave – doesn't like the idea of her seeing what he's going to do to the boy. He eyes Ana's assailant lying on a bed of needles, possibly dead, and appears to make up his mind. He shrugs, unhappy with what he must do but resigned. He gets out his pocketknife, puts his boot on one of the boy's outstretched legs and makes a small cut to the corner of the guy's eye as he squirms against his restraints. He moves the knife to his neck.

"Who are you?" Aaron asks.

"Nobody," he answers loudly, spitting at Aaron's face.

"You're with the Band?" Aaron asks.

The guy tries to head butt Aaron, but Aaron is prepared for this and tilts to the side. He presses his boot down hard on the boy's kneecap.

"What are you looking for?" Aaron persists.

"I ain't telling you shit," he says.

"Bloody hell," Aaron says, barely audibly. "This is going to be a long night," but Ana isn't listening, her ears focused instead on the tiny whiz of her car's motor retreating into the distance. Someone has claimed her car.

CHAPTER 30

15 APRIL 2064. Day 10 of 15. "If we were any good at this, we would have offed those Band boys," Ana says, the dogs trailing behind her.

"Well, we aren't. Do you want to be good at killing people?" Aaron replies.

"No," she says, but she's not so sure. What if they follow them?

"Good, then can we turn to the subject of food. We haven't eaten in twenty-four hours.

"We have food at the safe house."

"But no car to get there."

"*Please* don't talk about my car," she says, irritated. Aaron is mute after that.

There's a glint ahead in the road and she thinks maybe they got lucky – that the fools who stole her car abandoned it when it ran out of juice. She runs ahead, Aaron trailing behind her, but it's just a hubcap.

She wonders what the men from the Band are doing in her car. Visions of pimply faces rubbing against the upholstery and strands of human hair caught in the rust hole under the back seat haunt her.

"How far is the safe house, do you think?" he asks.

"I don't know. Another day maybe."

"I'll eat an entire bag of hemp jerky when we get there," he says.

"You hate that stuff."

"I don't care."

There's a pristine blanket of dust over the town of Birch Lake, not a footprint disturbing it. It's a tiny town, one mile of road down the center. They find a park at the end of main street, almost out of town. Ana walks up the stuck teeter totter like it's a balancing beam and settles down on the plastic seat, suspended a good two feet above Aaron. The dogs play with a swing, barking at it when it gets animated by a gust of wind and then squealing when it nails them on its way down.

Ana eyes a sign for a steakhouse in the distance. "Noodles," she says. "That's what I'm craving. You remember that meal you bought me when we first met? You had me all worked up. I only ate a few bites even though I hadn't eaten hot food in days."

“I could make us noodles,” he says. “Once we get back to the safe house, and after I’ve cleaned this blood off me, I could put something like that together.”

“We’ll both fall asleep before any of that happens.”

“True,” he says.

They’ve been lucky with the weather. No clouds. The constellations lighting up the road just enough for them to put one foot in front of the other in a sort of stupor. Somewhere in the middle of the night, they put Ana’s pack on Sassafras’s back, and he’s been carrying it for her ever since.

“Why do you think the Amish boys started a fight with the Band?” Ana asks him.

“Because they were young and stupid. I’m feeling a little like them right now.”

Their hostage, after considerable effort, told them that the Amish had caused trouble for the Band last month. They’d tampered with the brakes on one of the Band’s supply trucks and it took a dive down a ravine. The Amish bishop and his wife were killed as an example to the others, justifiably the boy pointed out. The rest of the community left after that, maybe a week ago. He thought maybe they’d gone west to join another settlement. He and his friends had come to raid the greenhouse. They’d never heard of Finn.

FURTHER DOWN the road they find a blueberry farm but it’s too early for berries and the bushes have long since been overtaken by chickweed and other wild plants.

"We can boil the chickweed," she says optimistically. "It helps with healing."

"I'm not settling for chickweed. We'll try to snare something," Aaron says.

They follow some prints to the river and find dandelions. They stuff several heads in their mouths. Ana puts roots in her bag to roast later to make tea with.

"We're officially no longer starving," she says.

"Speak for yourself. If I don't find food soon, I might end up eating you, although there's not much meat on you."

Sassafras reappears after a long hiatus. He's an adept hunter. He brought them a mouse at the hot springs, which they rejected. Now he's got a squirrel in his teeth. Still warm.

"We can eat that," Aaron says.

"I guess ..." she answers.

Ana guts it and skins it while Aaron struggles to find dry wood for a fire. When they finally manage to cook it, the five of them only get a couple of bites each. It's not bad. Kind of porklike. After their meal, Aaron takes their water bottles and filters and looks for a stream, while Ana puts out the fire. Sassafras follows him while Jasper and Yippy work on the squirrel bones.

Aaron is gone too long. Eventually she hears Sassafras yelp in the distance. The dogs run in his direction. Ana follows them to a line of trees a few hundred yards from the highway. A fox emerges out of a path between the trees. Half his hair is gone and he's walking in an uncoordinated manner. There's blood on his mouth. He bares his teeth, but without much force. Eventually

he sits down, drool accumulating in a pool on the grass. She takes a step towards him and he makes a choking crying noise.

"Shoot him," Aaron says, coming out of the path behind the fox, carrying Sassafras. "You'll be doing him a favor".

It takes a single shot to take the fox down. In the state he was in, even the sound of the gun firing would have been enough to do him in. It surprises her how easily she manages the task. No pause for reflection on the moral dimensions of the act.

"You think it had rabies?" she asks. She notices that Aaron's hand is shaking a little as he eases Sassafras to the ground.

"He wouldn't be out in the middle of the day acting like that if he didn't."

"Did he get Sassafras?"

"Yes," he says, pulling back the dog's fur to reveal a two-inch gash.

"We'll have to put him down," she says.

"I know," he says, clearly devastated. "Will you do it?"

"I'll take care of it," she says. "Any bites on you?"

"If I say yes, will you euthanize me as well?"

"Definitely."

"No then, but I tripped running away from him," he says. She lifts his pant leg and inspects his ankle. It's already swelling.

"It's not broken. If it was broken, you'd be screaming."

But it's still a problem. It's a day's walk to the safe house and they'll be a lot slower now.

She makes him soak the ankle in the icy river. Then she wraps it in a tensor band, pads it with a wadded-up shirt and

cuts a brace out of the padding in her backpack. She forces him to lie down and elevate it on a log. The dogs curl around him. She wants to lie down on the heap of warm bodies. She's never been this drained in her life, but there's more to be done.

"I'm going to find firewood," she says, cinching the ties on the brace.

He nods in agreement, takes her hand affectionately and then lets it go.

"I screwed up, didn't I?" he says.

"You didn't do anything wrong," she answers, but she can't hide the fact that she's worried. She touches his forehead with the back of her hand. He's warm.

Car, Ana thinks. *We need a car. But the cars out here are all rust buckets with dead batteries and flat tires. You can figure this out, Ana. You've faced worse.*

Garages. There might be cars in garages that aren't rusted. The batteries will be dead. So, you take the car out of the garage into the sun and the battery recharges. But how would you move it to a power source if it's dead? You need power to put it in neutral.

What will happen if you don't figure this out? Another few days of walking slowly without food. Aaron's fever will get worse.

The houses nearby are mostly farm houses, hundreds of acres between them. For hours, she runs in and out of one and then on to the next, her plan becoming increasingly farfetched. She eventually comes to a settlement of identical townhouses that looks promising. The entire complex is covered in a solar roof. Inside, they each have a solar battery on the wall, but

the cars are all gone. In one of them, she finds an electric bike under a tarp. She thinks it's a mirage maybe. Starvation is making her delirious. It's made to look vintage. Black and chrome. Thin wheels. Lights like bug eyes. Nothing visibly damaged. She finds the charger exactly where it should be, a few feet from the bike, unplugged. Rats have chewed through it. She'll have to splice it.

She carefully opens the garage door into the house and finds a mess of birds' nests. A single black sneaker in the hallway to the living room. To the right of the stove, there's a magnetic rack with knives stuck to it. She uses a paring knife and her teeth to cut out the mangled parts of the cord, peels the casing off a few inches of good wire, twists the strands together and tapes it all up, thankful for the duct tape in her pack. It's a little flimsy – a definite fire hazard – but the battery on the bike flickers on when she plugs it into the wall battery, which, miraculously, must still be connected to the panels. She watches the bike charge – one percent … two percent … five percent. While it's charging, she fills the tires with a bicycle pump, cleans and oils the bike's parts. It takes an hour to get to twenty-five percent and then it plateaus.

Aaron is sleeping when she returns with the bike, Jasper, Sassafras and Yippy folded around him. She checks Aaron's head. Still warm. She rubs Sassafras's snout. He lifts his head, blinks a few times and then settles back onto Aaron's chest, his eyes still open. The bite mark on his neck is hardening over; he protects it with his paw.

"Come," she says. "Let them sleep." He jerks his head in understanding and pulls himself up unsteadily on his legs. The two of them walk over to a field. She wraps her jacket around the butt of her gun to muffle the noise. She strokes the top of Sassafras's head with her left hand until his eyes roll back in pleasure, the gun steady in her right. He wriggles on his back in the grass, one last moment of pleasure, and then lies perfectly still, not wanting to make it hard on her.

CHAPTER 31

16 APRIL 2064. Day 11 of 15. Lying on the back seat of a truck, hands and feet zip tied, she replays the last hour. Sassafras was lying in that hole uncovered, his black eyes glasslike, hind legs pointing stiffly into the air. It was almost dawn, a sliver of pink reflecting off the river. Already twenty degrees. They'd gone from winter to summer, no spring in between. She was pushing clumps of grass and dirt over him that were full of earth worms. She was smoothing over the dirt, as if she had just planted a garden, when something sharp pressed into the back of her ear.

It was refreshingly cold.

If they wanted to kill me, I'd already be dead, she told herself. *I can get out of this.* She reacted mechanically and efficiently. Pushed the gun aside, elbowed his chest, turned around, kneed

his groin. It might have been enough had he been alone. His partner had her zip tied to the child seat hook in the back of their truck before she could subdue his friend. They appear now, through her blindfold, as amorphous blobs.

"He said to be gentle," the passenger says to the driver. "Not a single bruise."

"Have you seen my face? Nailed you pretty good too, didn't she? I saw you jumping around holding your privates while I was taking a beating."

"I'm just saying. He isn't gonna be happy."

The gag in her mouth tastes like it was pulled out of a compost bin. Her lip is folded under it. With every bump, her incisors draw blood. And when she takes a deep breath, pain ripples through her insides.

She memorizes the car's movements. Two right turns, three left, a steep hill. Another valley, a left turn, a bridge maybe. Her ears pop. They must be high up. But it's pointless. She loses track eventually.

They finally stop and both men get out. Rain hammers the roof, muting the argument in front of the car. The back door opens, and she's pulled out and laid on the ground like a corpse on a mudslide. When the blindfold is removed, she sees the point of a long beard hanging over her, funneling rain onto her forehead.

"What did they do to you, Solnyshko?" a man says to her, inspecting her. Only one man has ever called her that.

"Dmitri?" she asks.

The Russian prince they called him. Banished from the City years ago. Or did he leave voluntarily?

He's wearing nothing but grey underwear and a thin silk robe. He's thinner than she remembers. But beneath his mane of wiry silver hair, a familiar inquisitive countenance greets her. He lifts her like a baby and carries her onto a couch inside his cabin.

Dmitri had been a good citizen once. He was given a medal of honor for designing a mineral recycling program. But the City had had a hard time containing an unpredictable mind like his. He dabbled in fusion, invented rockets that blew a hole through the force field, hacked into surveillance cameras, created a virtual private network outside the Council's control. Brilliant, but lacking sufficient loyalty to the City's social contract, he eventually became a liability.

In the early days of the City, he'd given Hooper and her father some advice on their greenhouses and the three had stayed friends. Ana had been to his lab a few times and he'd been kind to her, keeping her occupied with increasingly difficult math problems. He came to her seventh birthday party, brought kebabs and performed magic tricks for her friends. His departure from the City came as a real blow to her father. It made him start to wonder if there was still a place for him in the City. Dmitri brings her a cool towel and wipes blood from her face. Where is the blood coming from? Her ear? Everything is numb. He rinses it in his kitchen sink, wrings it out and tenderly wipes mud off her arms and back.

She's cold. So cold.

"Help is coming," he promises her, throwing the soiled towel in a plastic bucket and covering her in a wool blanket. It's then that she notices the needle marks on his arm. The yellowed skin.

He sits across from her, lights his pipe and takes a long draw, blinking as the smoke hits his eye.

"Why the commando team?" she asks, holding her head to relieve the throbbing.

"We keep our location hidden," he says. "We didn't think you'd resist. Who taught you to fight like that?"

"A friend." He doesn't need to know that she sold her soul to the Council to get out here.

"What do you want with me, Dmitri?" She can't move an inch without crushing pain. She just wants to be back with Aaron and the dogs. How will she find him now?

"We've been waiting for your brother to come back," he says. "Miranda told us you were out here looking for him. Have you found him?"

"No. Not even a trace."

"Shit," he says, dropping his head between his legs. He launches into a tirade of Russian profanity. "How much do you know?" he asks, once his outburst is over.

"Very little. Do me a favor and tell me everything, Dmitri. No one else will."

He takes increasingly deeper draws on his pipe. His eyes dart between her and his front door.

"Okay, you'll get your answers," he says, putting his hand affectionately on her knee. He's frowning though. It can't be good.

He sighs, gets up and pulls out a piece of paper from under some books on his cluttered dining room table and shows it to her. It's a child's faded drawing of a rocket shop. There are other drawings strewn across the walls of his cottage. Intricate sketches of tulips behind his samovar and Snow White in her glass coffin next to a floor lamp.

"My daughter's," he says.

"Where is she?" she asks.

"The Band took her and sold her to Isla."

It's been going on since the beginning, he tells her. The Band kidnaps children from the road. Not just orphans. Often, they're forcibly taken from their parents. It's not unusual for a parent to get beaten – even to death – in the process. The Band brings them to Isla and, in exchange, she supplies the Band with a share of her crops. Isla believes she's helping the children, that they're better off with her than their parents. The collapse was caused by the adults. In order to break the cycle, the children need to be cleansed of their influence. At the Orphanage, the stain of arrogance and aggression is slowly removed.

"There was a woman on the road," Ana says. "They shot her and took her kids."

"Most likely a traveler. People around here know better."

"And your daughter? How was she taken?"

"Foolishness. I gave into her just the once. Took her to an art supply store a few hundred miles west of here that one of my men told her about. Imbecile. She was so happy leafing through all those pads of paper and pencils. We filled dozens of boxes. She

was never going to be bored again. I was so impressed with myself for taking her there. When I returned to the store after taking a load to my truck she was gone. That was a year ago."

"Finn left the Orphanage with two children. She was one of them?" Ana asks.

"Yes."

"And the other?"

"Finn had a girlfriend, Miriam."

"That much I know."

"The other child was her son."

"Finn's?"

"Not his. She'd been married before. The father was killed when the boy was taken from them."

Ana tries to reposition herself, but the effort tears her apart. Dmitri looks sick. He keeps looking at the door. Is it her? Is something wrong with her?

"Did you have something to do with the power plant he was helping Isla build?"

"A little. I helped him source supplies out here."

"And he agreed to get your daughter back in exchange?"

"It wasn't a business deal. Just two friends helping each other out."

"And his plan to build an apartment building in the City, was it just a ruse?"

"Your brother was ambitious. He wanted to do both. He had to, actually. That was Ekhart's price. He would keep Finn's escapades a secret. And somehow Finn would get the City some

steel and concrete. The Movement would end up looking good. I didn't pay much attention to that part."

So Ekhart *was* part of the plan. How could he lie to her face like that?

Dmitri looks down at her affectionately. Taking her chin in his hand, he searches her eyes. "You should rest now, Ana. We can talk more later."

"Was it Ekhart who told Finn how to leave the City? Has he been sending people out here all along?" she asks, unwilling to end the conversation until she hears everything.

"Ekhart didn't know anything about it. He found out later. It was some cop who told him. His father was a big developer from the old days. The tunnel was a family secret."

Noah? This should surprise her, but it doesn't. He'd had a fight with Finn. He wanted to be rid of him. But does the Council know? Was it guilt that made Noah recruit and train her? Or does Noah want to be rid of her as well? Does Aaron know?

Dmitri finishes with his pipe, gets up and washes his hands.

"What are you going to do about your daughter, Dmitri?"

"You know, your father and I used to play video games together in my lab," he says, avoiding the question.

"Was he any good?"

"What do you think? He was just looking for an excuse to have a conversation."

"Sounds like him."

"Your father had this way of asking questions that relate to your life's purpose and then, as you answered them, out of

the recesses of your mind some idea would spring, something borne of your higher nature, but that you'd never conceived of. It would be your idea, an expression of your own will and conscience, but he would have drawn it out of you. It felt like a lecture, except that you would end up lecturing yourself. You know what I mean?"

"I do."

"I miss thinking that way."

"What are you planning, Dmitri?"

"Nothing. I can't leave here, Ana. I'm not well", he says, rubbing his arm. "And I'm not loved out there. There's a reason we're hidden. I've asked all my allies for help. Even Miranda. They've all said no."

"I haven't."

"This isn't something you can do. The Band likely has them. If you go near there, you'll be no better off than your brother."

The door that Dmitri was staring at finally opens and relief floods over his face. Instead of a weapon, the man carries a medical kit. He gets down on his knees next to her and looks her over. He knows what he's doing. He binds her ribs with Dmitri's assistance, sterilizes and glues the cut by her ear and puts a tablet of bitter herbs into her mouth. Dmitri pays him in what appears to be drugs and he leaves without a word.

Dmitri settles her into a bed to rest. She doesn't remember falling asleep, but when she wakes, it's nighttime. She's lying on the back seat of the truck again and Dmitri is saying goodbye. How long was she out?

He rolls up a blanket under her head, puts a handful of pain tablets in her hand and folds her fingers over them. "I'm so sorry for what they did to you," he says. She touches her closed fist to his face. "Don't worry," he says. The Band won't harm the children. They will eventually end up back with Isla. They will be fine."

But not Finn. Finn won't be fine.

SOMEONE HAS HACKED at the lock on the safe house door. There are gouges all over it. They've spray painted "asshole" across the door. What right did Ana and Aaron have to claim this refuge as their own?

Dmitri's men hold her up as she puts her thumb on the scanner and opens it. They push her and her bike inside. Something rips through her and she collapses onto the bottom step. They look at her helplessly, unsure whether they are obliged to do anything more. She orders them to leave. It takes two more of Dmitri's pills before she can drag herself up to the loft.

Her window patch is on the floor in a pool of water. She steps around it and turns on the light attached to the generator. She sees the neat pile of food packages in the kitchen and thinks of Aaron. Is he still asleep in that ditch with the dogs? Is he limping, half-starved, down the I-90? As soon as she can stand properly, she'll go after him.

From this high up, she can see the wall, the forcefield suspended above it like an orange sunset. For the first time, she longs to be back there. She can almost feel the buzz of activity – an anomaly in this wasteland. A well-tended garden in the wild.

She eases off her jeans, lies on a mattress and stares at the ceiling. The objects around the room seem to lift around her as her body sinks into the floorboards.

A LOUD BANG wakes her. Metal against metal. She bolts upright. Hauls her body to the window. It's just a deer crossing the street below. Knocked a sign post maybe. An entire herd of them disappear between two buildings.

She should pack and leave. She starts making a list. Something to bind his ankle better, food packages, a change of clothes. She can do this. Her insides feel like they've been turned inside out but at least she's upright. She drinks a liter of water as she takes apart her gun and reassembles it.

There's another clang, this time echoing through the empty space of the building. She must have forgotten to lock up. Idiot. Is it another traveler? Or the Band coming for her? She puts the magazine back in her gun and braces herself for a fight she's in no shape to win.

The footsteps move into the upstairs hallway. She removes the safety as the handle on the loft door turns.

"Leave," she says.

His scar appears before anything else, a raised line winding up his arm. The sleeve of his shirt. Then his face, filled with relief.

"I thought we agreed you weren't going to shoot me," Aaron says, throwing his pack down and limping over to her.

"How did you get here so quickly?"

"Quickly? I've been walking for nearly two days."

She glances at her screen. She's been out for almost a day. She won't be taking any more of Dmitri's pills.

Stopping in front of her, he traces the line of a bruise over her left eye.

"Tell me the other guy looks worse," he says.

Eyeing the bandages, he lifts the edge of her t-shirt and frowns. He unwinds the strips in wide swirls. Walking in a slow circle, he takes in the damage.

"It's not too bad," she says.

"What are you on?" he asks, examining her pupils. He starts to say something more but stops himself.

She puts his hand to her breast. His thumb moves cautiously over the top of it. Maybe it's the drugs, but the fact that this is likely a mistake is easily exiled to the recesses of her mind. She needs him to touch her. He steps closer, his hand now tracing the unmarked curve of her hip.

"You frightened the hell out of me," he says, leaning his head against her forehead and taking her face in his hands.

She pulls at the top button of his shirt as his mouth brushes her ear.

"Ana, what are you doing?"

"Stop talking."

"Order me not to touch you," he pleads. "I'm too weak to control myself."

She takes in the smell of campfire on his neck, the rasp of his stubble. Wasn't the idea of them always there? Something they couldn't acknowledge until they ended up totally messed up in

this loft? Why is joy always for other people, another time? Why can't now be that time for her?

She puts her mouth on his. It feels even better than Dmitri's pills.

He props her gently against the wall and kisses her back as if he always knew what he'd do to her when he got the chance. But when he pulls her tighter to him, she folds over in pain.

He looks at her, confused. A pigeon lands on the windowsill and pecks at a stray piece of duct tape dangling from the hole. He walks over to the window and knocks it harder than necessary until it flees. When he returns, he examines her with fresh eyes. Sighing, he carries her to a mattress.

She begins to laugh hysterically at the ridiculousness of their situation, but her convulsions cause more pain.

"I'm not that broken," she says.

"I'd trade anything in the world for that to be true."

"You don't look so great yourself."

"Have you seen your stomach? Blood is pooling under your skin." He runs his fingers lightly over her damaged skin. "I'm taking you home."

"I have so much to tell you Aaron. I know where he is, or at least who has Finn." She spills out everything. The Band's ongoing trade arrangement with the Orphanage. Miriam's son. His arrangement with Dmitri. The fact that Finn was expected back at Dmitri's over a month ago.

"Are you listening. What are you doing with that thing?" she asks, his head buried in her screen now.

"Hoping to fix you," he says. "Here it is. Blunt force trauma." He's reading their first aid manual.

"Did you know that it was Noah who told Finn how to leave the City?"

"No," he says. "But I'm not surprised."

"Why?"

"His wife had a crush on Finn. I don't think your brother did anything to encourage it – she wasn't his only groupie – but Noah wasn't happy about it. Now stop talking, you're distracting me," he says. "Listen to this, *Internal bleeding is one of the most serious consequences of trauma. Usually, the bleeding results from obvious injuries that require rapid medical attention. If the bleeding continues or is severe, surgery is required to correct it.* You understand now why I have to take you back?"

"Let me see that," she says, grabbing it from him. "*Internal bleeding may also occur after a less severe trauma. Some internal bleeding due to trauma stops on its own.* That's what I have. Minor trauma. Minor bleeding."

He raises an eyebrow at her as he checks her pulse and then applies a blood pressure cuff.

"The numbers aren't good. You're in shock," he says.

"What do you know? In any event, if you're right, moving me will kill me."

"What do you suggest then?"

"An IV. Pump me up. If I get better by tomorrow, we go to the Band. If I get worse, you take me home."

In answer, he disinfects his hands, gets an emergency kit and puts the screen on auto execute. A holograph projection appears above her arm. All he has to do is replace the virtual tourniquet with a real one and follow the motions of the projection precisely. If he doesn't, his screen will beep. It looks easier than it is. Once he gets it on, he palpates her arm looking for a viable vein to work with. The screen finds one before he does.

"Is that really a vein or another bruise?" he asks, looking at the faint mark on her hand.

"Just do it."

He inserts the needle through her skin and then carefully reduces the angle of insertion as he advances it into her vein. He puts pressure on her skin, pulls the needle back a little, pushes the catheter further in. She looks away as he secures it and removes the needle. He prepares the bag, hanging it on a garment rack. When the line hits the floor, he swears.

"Have you done it?"

"I think so."

"Why is it beeping then?"

"It wants me to do a couple more things and you're not going to like it."

"What then?"

"I have to sedate you."

"Please don't. You don't *have* to listen to that thing."

"I do. Your body will heal better if you stop arguing with it."

"And the second thing?"

She isn't conscious long enough to find out.

CHAPTER 32

DAY 15 OF 15. Ana wakes up sometime in the night in a new bed. The floor is littered with wrappers and syringes. Her IV bag is half full. A couple of empties are on the floor. He's even managed a catheter.

Aaron, still in his clothes, is asleep on a mattress in the corner. Her screen has fallen off the bed, projecting a map on the sewing machine wall at a skewed angle. A route to the Band.

She pulls the catheter out, then her IV, revealing a mess of caked blood and a nasty bubble. Aaron makes a small noise in his sleep but doesn't stir. She covers him in her blanket and carefully lifts the screen off the floor and checks it. More than two days have passed. How long did he stay awake watching her?

It's 5:00 a.m., 20 April 2064. The Council's deadline ends

in three hours. They've failed. But she hasn't. Their timeline no longer matters to her. She has to do this right, though. Make it so the Council doesn't blame Aaron for what she's about to do.

She scurries around the loft and up and down the stairs in her socks, moving as fast as her bruises will allow. When she's finally ready to leave, she finds some paper in the kitchen and writes him a note. Tacks it to the bulletin board with the others.

Aaron,

You remember when you said you were worried I was going to hit you over the head and run off? That time has come. I have to go, Aaron. In three hours, we won't be able to return to the City. If I wake you now, there are two possibilities. One, you'll force me to return and I'll never forgive you for it. Two, you'll decide to come with me. I can't let you do that. You'll never see Martha or your mother again. You'll be stuck in a world that you clearly despise. I was always going to leave you. It was just a matter of time.

Don't follow me, Aaron. I know you'll think about it, but I have the weapons and the bike. On that ankle, it will take you a century to catch up to me. By that time, this will all be over. Do something for me. Tell the Council what's going on out here. We need to help the children. And there is so much out here for us. It's time to reconnect with the outside world. When we do, I'll be able to come home. Make that happen from the inside.

CHAPTER 33

20 APRIL 2064. That first day on her own, the highway is still. Only her bike is in motion, like an ant crawling across a photo.

She follows the route that Aaron prepared. It takes her parallel to highway I-90 but farther south. An old road along a river. Mostly washed out. His route ends where the road intersects the highway north. There will be traffic there. She'll hire someone to get information. She doesn't even know if the Band has him. No sense going to the Band guns blazing only to find out that Finn is on the other side of the country.

She'll need a new identity. Can't play the distraught sister anymore. A bounty hunter maybe. Who do they hate the least out here? People who feed them. She'll be a farmer.

Aaron's absence is intolerable. She didn't used to mind being alone, but his sociability has tainted her. Her thoughts drift back to their early days together on the outside, Aaron in the passenger seat beside her, his face buried in a map, his hand lightly tapping a beat. Stopping her from littering out the window. Entertaining her with horror stories from his youth.

But she was always going to go farther than him.

Doubt starts to creep in after a few miles. Who is she to think she can do this on her own? And what about the map on the wall? If he was planning their route, he wasn't going to drag her home. He was on her side. There's still time. She could go back. She'll probably find him in the safe house still, frantically trying to improvise a weapon. Will he yell at her? "Okay, we'll go back to the City," she'll say. He'll nod sheepishly and they'll drive to the gate. When it opens, they'll ride along Central Avenue to the market. People will be jogging and grabbing fruit on their way to work, as if it's an ordinary day. After a long boring briefing at the Hive, she'll head to the employment office. They'll assign her farm work for now. She'll sleep above the candy shop on Hooper's couch because her car is gone. She and Aaron will stay friends. She'll be okay. The City is a good place. It's her place.

But she'll never be at peace. Not for the rest of her life.

She puts on headphones and listens to heavy metal. Metallica. It's horrible. No melody. But it matches the screaming in her head.

She catches herself talking out loud. Just a word here or there. Then the odd phrase. Then an entire monologue.

Maybe she's losing her mind. Her brother did.

That first night, she pulls up to a barn off the highway, walks down to a stream and splashes cold water on her face. When several eyes gaze at her in the dark – skunks or racoons – she flees back to the barn. Her weakness is laughable. How is she going to face the Band if she's afraid of a little wildlife?

Inside, she rewraps her ribs – her wounds yellow and green now, much better than purple and red – and makes an uncomfortable bed next to the door in case she needs to bolt. She flips through old movies looking for something to distract her. Finding nothing, her eye lands on her notes folder. She should document her trip. If she doesn't make it, and someone discovers her body a decade from now, her diary might be important to someone. She's surprised to find a file from yesterday in the folder. A voice recording. She presses play and Aaron's voice blasts into her headphones. He must have made it when she was out cold. She listens to it four times. She no longer feels alone.

I'm wondering, Ana, what's going through that head of yours in your sleep? You look so alive but I'm afraid you're dissolving from the inside out. I don't know if I made the right call. Your spleen could be ruptured. This could be worse than I imagined and I'm just sitting here next to you waiting for you to die. I've reached the end of my abilities. If I ever get my status restored, remind me not to study medicine.

But if I take you back, you might wish you were dead anyway. You'll want to kill me. An hour ago, I almost did it. I started to pack our things, but then I checked you again and your pulse was slightly stronger and I thought of the damage I would do running

down the stairs with you over my shoulder. There's no way I can win this.

But I want to take you home. I want you to live with me in my apartment. There's room. We'll go to my mother's for brunch on Sunday. We'll start that philosopher's club. We'll both go back to University and study together in the library.

I'm rambling. No time to edit this. It's 3:00 a.m. I've spent the last hour watching a rat go back and forth along the floor in a grid pattern trying to find crumbs.

I'd like to clear up a few things while I'm here. Things I should have said before. A confession of sorts. It's narcissistic isn't it? Taking up airtime talking about myself, thinking it might somehow make you laugh if you ever hear this. But of course, you won't. Like the last ten messages I've dictated to you on the rare moments I've been alone with your screen, I'll be erasing it.

First fact. I'm not really a stalker. While it's technically true – I watched one hundred and seventy-four hours of you, including moments when you were unclothed and I didn't look away – you should know that I protested at first. It was never my idea to take the assignment. Noah would have been better at it. He finds things I don't even know to look for. I haven't actually been trained for that kind of surveillance. Which relates to fact number two. Before you, the most important gig I had was directing traffic when the lights went down. They used to make me clean out the fridge in the officer's lounge. No, really. I think I might have made it sound like I was a bigger deal at the Hive than I was. You should see my last performance review. Mediocre. I was

recruited for this assignment as aggressively as you were. They wanted us together.

Fact number three. I have deep respect for your family. I want to help you because I like you, but it's more than that. I want to believe in the idea of a family like yours. You came from socialist royalty. I was just a poor bastard.

Am I boring you? It doesn't matter. I have the mike. I have all the power. You could press pause or even delete this if you want, but it won't matter because I'm not doing this for you. This whole exercise is entirely for my benefit.

Fact number four. I think I might also have exaggerated my badass past. I was actually a freakishly obedient child. I'm that kid who sat on his mom's lap until he was nine. Despite my humble beginnings, I did my homework. Didn't burn down crap in the alley or get into street fights. My hobby was fencing. And don't let Noah's tattoos fool you either. Before the age of twelve, his main obsession was collecting things, in particular old boy scout badges that he hadn't earned. We were nerds. Worse than that, we were self-righteous nerds.

I think I told you that some of my friends and I used to hang out in an old school bus with our dog. We were all stuck in the Annex for different reasons. My mother because she chose to practice cello with me over working more hours. Some of my friends for reasons far worse than poverty. Neglect is the one crime that the monitors can't catch. The monitors don't notice if you haven't bathed your kids in a week or if you spend your baby stipend on VR instead of socks for your kids.

There were a couple of kids in that bus whose parents moved to the Annex because they didn't want anyone noticing they were shitty parents. Alice Miller was one of them. Quiet until you pushed her to the edge and then she'd attack. It was anxiety she said. Nothing personal. She was my first girlfriend. Left a few scars on me. Her little brother Phoenix had a knack for comedy. Turned every sad episode of those years into a stand-up routine. Their parents' issue was drugs. In the Annex, the skinnier the kid, the more the parents were using. Phoenix and Alice were rake thin. But all of us in that bus parented each other, especially Noah. We made sure everyone got fed occasionally.

Me being the idiot that I was, I thought the solution was to steal their parents' drugs. Thought if I did, they'd detox and stay clean long enough to notice they had kids. Make some changes.

I built up a major stash in my vent. But, of course, it backfired. They still wanted their fix, so they spent even more food money on drugs. So here I was with a stockpile of meth and those kids were getting skinnier. And people were after me, offering rewards for information on the Annex thief. I racked my brain trying to come up with a new plan. Then this rich guy comes to our neighborhood and asks Noah where he can get a fix, thinking every twelve-year old in the Annex should know. He brings the guy to our place and sells him my entire stash. We had a ton of coinage to burn through after that. Spent it on food of course. And I also bought three dozen pairs of socks because the bus reeked. It became a rule. You couldn't have stinky feet in the bus.

So, we get this little business going. All the kids with addict

parents start stealing from them. I handle sales. Take a small cut. The miracle is that we were never caught by the authorities. Actually, it might have been better if we had because, when the shit hit the fan, I got a beating from my mother worse than anything they would have done. Not a physical one, of course. I was grounded for twelve months. She forced me to spend every free moment on the farm hauling bags of wheat. We moved out of the Annex, back into the land of the cameras. So, there you have it. My badass past is hardly attractive.

Fact five. I loathe the outside world. I hate what it's doing to me. What it turned me into so quickly. The things I did to that kid at the Amish farm. It disgusts me.

Fact six or is it seven, I'm losing count? I have a lot to confess …

It stops there. He must have got up to change her IV bag. Maybe there was more but he erased it. She'll never know.

ON HER SECOND day alone, the highway comes alive again. Wind pulls at the debris on the side of the road. A clothes hanger rolls down the highway almost as fast as her car. She passes vultures pecking away at the carcass of a deer, a dog carrying a rodent in its mouth. And she sees her first human. A girl walking along the highway pulling a wagon, making no effort to conceal herself. Ana cuts the motor and watches her disappear between two houses.

She gets out and examines the girl's footprints. Two sets. Both small. One foot turned inward slightly. She bends to touch the tiny toe indentations.

Following her path, Ana comes out into the middle of what was once a grand backyard. She reaches down and checks her holster, even though she can feel the weight of her gun on her hip.

The girl is kneeling in the shadows under an oak tree on a quilt, fumbling with a black case. She opens its latches and pulls out the pieces – a pink violin, bow and box of rosin – organizing them around her. She stands up and puts the violin to her neck, her thin hair falling over the fingerboard. Gripping the bow awkwardly, she draws it across the untuned strings. She plays reverently, eyes closed, turning in circles.

Ana waits, afraid to startle her. When the girl finally stops to rosin the bow, Ana calls out to her. "Excuse me," she says, thinking of nothing better.

The girl turns her head slowly, eyes wide, and then bolts with the violin tucked under her arm. Ana runs after her but then stops abruptly. There, on the quilt, amongst the girl's abandoned possessions, is a small familiar book. A book of poetry – Rumi. Finn's. She opens it to the middle and feels the pages, the familiar raised type. She can still recite a few of the poems from memory. She recognizes a drawing she made on page 43 of a princess. She turns to the first page and sees her father's pigeon scrawl. "May your life be filled with words organized in meaningful and soul stirring patterns. Dad 2042."

Finn is here. The girl must have run to him. Hope makes her ribs hurt.

She gathers up the girl's discarded belongings and follows

her trail through a neighborhood of half constructed houses and a boggy field. The mud prints stop in front of a locked fuel station.

"What do you want with her?" a voice says from behind her.

Not Finn. A boy. He has the sharp-boned face of a teenager, but his body is tiny and emaciated.

"I'm no threat to you," Ana says to him.

"That 9mm says otherwise," he says. "Do me a favor. Take me. Leave her behind. They won't want her. She's mostly deaf."

"You think I want to sell you?"

"Don't you?"

"I'm looking for the owner of this book," she says, showing it to him.

"Can't help you with that. Found it earlier today but it wasn't attached to a person," he says spitting to the side.

"You sure about that? You're not with anyone else?"

"We fly solo. Haven't seen another person in weeks."

"Show me where you found it."

"What are you offering?" the boy asks.

"I'm offering not to sell you. That'll have to be enough."

"We leave her here. Deal?"

"Fine."

"And you put that away in your pack," he says, nodding to the gun.

Ana sizes him up. He doesn't seem like much of a threat but then neither did Noah and he almost choked her to death. These kids are out here alone, unscathed. Who knows what resources

they have at their disposal? He could be leading her to a whole tribe of them.

"Not a chance," she says.

"THAT'S WHERE I found it," the boy says, pointing to a blue house on the highest point of a ridge overlooking a golf course, a latticework of criss-crossing wires connecting it to the neighbors' solar panels. There are no signs of people from below, but she can smell garbage.

They climb over a chain-link fence and up the hill to the house. The yard reeks of organic waste. A pile of peelings overflows next to a trampoline.

She can hear music playing inside.

"Finn?" she says, opening the door to the kitchen. The wind sucks it shut behind them and the boy jumps.

There's a plastic wrapper on the table with a sticker on it – girl's dress size 10X. On the counter, she finds rows of empty jars and a cracked bucket, a small pan of dried up oatmeal. A few crumpled drawings behind the bedroom door like the ones at Dmitri's place. In the basement, Finn's set up a workshop. A bunch of radios are in various states of assembly. The music is coming from a speaker on a shelf over the worktop. The same song loops over and over.

"Maybe he's out hunting for the day," the boy says.

"No one has been here in a long time."

"He have kids with him?"

"Yeah."

"Too bad for them," he says.

She sits down on the edge of the mattress in the master bedroom and lets herself weep for the first time in months, while the boy stands in the doorway helpless. She doesn't wail or shake. Bloated drops just roll down her face, soaking her shirt.

"We should go. The Band could still be in the area," he says, putting his hand affectionately on her shoulder.

Pulling herself off the bed, she trips over clothes – a bra and underwear, Miriam's maybe – and a torn t-shirt, the right arm soaked in blood. Finn's. She puts them in her pack, along with a decent-looking battery and the plastic wrap, as if, cumulatively, these objects will lead her to him.

"When did you last eat?" she asks the boy as they're leaving.

"Had potatoes this morning."

"Will you eat with me?" Ana asks.

"Who was he?"

Was not *is*, he said.

"My brother," she says, not bothering to lie.

WHEN THEY RETURN, a truce ensues. Her new friends, Jason and Amber, sit on one end of the quilt, Ana on the other, her entire food supply spread out between them.

"Why are you traveling alone?" Amber asks.

"There was someone else, but I had to leave him."

"That's sad," she says. "Everyone needs someone. You could come with us."

"No, she can't," Jason says.

When Ana tells her new friends that she's from the City, they get excited, although they try to play it down. They ask a lot of questions – what kind of shelter did she have, is it dangerous, what are their leaders like? Ana tells them about the good and the bad. The cameras and the house parties.

"Is it beautiful?" Amber asks.

When Ana describes the Hive, and the forest around it, they become forlorn, like they hadn't imagined such a place could exist and now that they know about it, their world has paled in comparison.

Amber and Jason have a screen that they pilfered from an old library. They show it off to Ana. It's 2D technology from long before the collapse with a frayed solar wrap. A great big crack down the middle. But to the kids, it's the greatest treasure imaginable. It's loaded up with old movies and "how to" videos that they've watched over and over. They've memorized the 10 episodes of Ray Mears Bushcraft they have. Ray – they talk about him like he's a friend – taught them how to make fires and forage.

"Where are your people?" Ana asks.

"We don't remember," Amber says casually.

The two of them were taken by the Band in a truck as young children.

"The Band kept stopping and rounding up more kids. If the parents resisted, they killed them," Amber says. "There were a bunch of us."

They got away when the truck slipped on ice and skidded into a ditch. Jason hurt his foot in the accident and it healed

crooked. After being together for a month, they decided not to separate. They became nomads, changing their camp every week or so. Until recently, they were in the north where the Band doesn't go.

"Sometimes we think we'll end up in a town and someone will recognize us. They'll say, *we know your parents. We'll take you to them*. But it's never happened."

Amber gets excited when she talks. The freckles on her face dance around. Surprisingly, she doesn't have a mark on her. Lying on the grass, dressed in a colorful purple shirt and yellow shorts, she twirls her feet. They should be more scared. How have these two managed to survive?

"You can't go too far north though. Or too far south. There are busted nuclear plants everywhere out there. Your babies will be born without arms," Amber says.

"We're getting married," the boy says as if in explanation, "when she becomes a woman," he adds.

They've obviously got some kind of video on human sexuality on their screen. They have it all planned. In another year or so they can start 'coupling', have babies and start their own community. They aren't the least bit embarrassed to talk about this with her. No one has taught them social convention.

"But for now, we'll keep on the move," she says.

"We don't like staying in fancy places," he says, looking at the big house. "It makes us soft, but this place is too good to pass up," Jason says.

"That's where we found the violin," Amber says.

"She's been wanting one for ages. She'll learn how to play it too," he adds. "She can learn anything."

"What I really want," she says, "is to see one of those houses that turn on like in the movies."

When Ana looks at her confused, Jason explains. "She means a house with electricity. With light switches that work and TVs and vacuum cleaners."

"I think I can do something about that," Ana says.

FASCINATED, THEY watch her work, fetching tools and things they don't know the names of. This is going to become her trade on the outside. Showing people how easy it is to produce power. It's a good distraction. When she finally gets Finn's battery hooked up to the electrical panel and switches the breakers on, action and noise erupt all around them. The pump in the well vibrates. Lights turn on. An alarm system is triggered. The kitchen tap runs, first with brown and then clear water.

"I think we'll stay here after all," Jason says, hardly able to contain his excitement. "For now, anyway."

"No," the girl says. "The Band will easily find us. When Ana leaves, we leave."

THE HOUSE IS still full of useful things. Musty sheets. Even boxes of laundry soap. The girl wants to try washing clothes in a machine and Ana shows her how.

A little after midnight, the three of them cozy up in front of an electric fireplace on clean blankets that smell of lemons,

still warm from the dryer. Amber falls asleep just as the battery finally dies.

"Is your brother as smart as you?" the boy asks.

"Smarter."

"Then maybe the Band didn't kill him."

"I don't think they did," she says. "I would feel it."

"What are you going to do?" he asks, blowing the bangs out of his face.

"Try to trade for him."

"You're pretty," he says. "Whatever you offer them won't be as valuable as you. A bird in hand. That's what you are," he says, propping himself up on one elbow.

"I'm not stupid," she says, although she suddenly feels decades younger than him. "I'll hire someone to do it for me. An adult," she adds, in case he gets any heroic notions in his head.

"They don't trade with many people. Mostly just the Orphanage. We have a friend down here. Gus. He trades with Blackwell sometimes. He might help you."

"Is he dangerous?"

"Not usually."

THERE'S A BRIEF moment of longing in Amber's face when Ana turns to leave. They cling to each other tightly. Jason and Amber seem to have everything they want except a community. But by the time Ana is two feet away, they're laughing again, spraying each other with a hose, reluctant to leave.

CHAPTER 34

22 APRIL 2064. Gus's place is where the kids said it would be. A trailer park near a lake. He's joined some of the mobile homes together in a line, five long, two wide, a tin palace.

He's skinning a rabbit on his deck, his head bent over a pail. He looks up at Ana and casually moves his gun within reach, as if the act is no more important than putting on the kettle.

"Amber and Jason sent me. Gave me this to give to you," she says, handing him two rolled up sheets of paper wrapped in brown string.

"Oh yeah?" he says, taking the papers, unrolling them and smiling. He points to a lawn chair for her to sit on. "Those two back in these parts then?"

"About an hour south-east of here. I can help you with that," Ana says, nodding to a string of freshly gutted rabbits.

"Please yourself," he says.

She unties one and starts skinning it with Aaron's ivory-handled knife. He'll miss it. It was his father's. But she had to leave him with nothing or her plan wouldn't have worked. She's skinned rabbits before. She slits it around the feet and up through the legs on the backside, then draws the fur over the rabbit's neck like pulling a shirt inside out.

"Haven't seen you before," Gus says, taking the bloody mess from her, his eyes sizing her up like a meaty buck that's wandered into his woods. He puts the skinned rabbit in a soup pot and the hide in a bucket of cold water, adding a cup of salt and some battery acid.

"I'm new to the area," Ana says.

"It's gonna rain. Best come on in," Gus says. They get the pots of fur and skinned rabbits into one of the trailers just as it starts to pour.

Although the trailers look haphazard on the outside, inside they're clean and organized. He walks her through trailers for sleeping, exercise, reading, bathing, growing things and, finally, the kitchen. They're all well stocked, as if he's emptied out an entire shopping mall. There's a whole unit full of clothes with price tags on them.

"You live alone?" she asks, noticing a picture of a woman and teenaged girl next to the fridge. It looks as if it might have come with the frame.

“Not really,” he answers. He puts the meat on the counter and takes up a big butcher knife with Japanese writing on it. There’s a table saw and a tile cutter in the corner. Some new kitchen cabinets are half assembled. Three black and white cats sit on the ledge of a large window looking out over the lake.

“There’s wild boar, a dozen or so cats ... but you mean humans. People do visit me, but no one stays very long.”

He throws Ana an onion.

“Knives are over there, or you could just use the one in your boot,” he says, raising his eyes a little as if to say, “don’t think of trying anything”. She chooses one from a butcher block, Gus following her every move.

He has a large growth on the side of his face. It looks painful and oozes when he moves his jaw. He’s well fed though. The large tire around his middle looks out of place attached to a set of matchstick legs and a narrow face.

“Amber and Jason made me this,” he says, showing off a binder filled with maps of the places they’ve been. They’re marked with little notes – fallen bridge, possible safe house, raspberries, bears. He opens the rings and inserts the pages she’s just given him and then clicks it shut. “We help each other out sometimes. Can’t convince them to settle here even though it’d be safer for them.”

“They think they’re invincible,” she says. “Maybe they are.”

He adds some leeks to the rabbit pot, pulls some herbs straight into it off a string hanging over the stove. The rest of the parts he puts in plastic bags that he organizes into his

large freezer. He works quickly, as if time is running out.

"Why'd they send you to me?" Gus asks.

"I'm from out east. Got a farm going with some friends. A man stayed with us last month and said he'd help us set up an irrigation system. He just needed some supplies. Came out here trading. Took all our silver and didn't come back. Rumor has it he got into a little trouble and that the Band might have him. The kids thought maybe you could find out for me." She's surprised how easily the lies come to her.

"Got a picture?"

She shows him her screen. He wipes his bloody hands on a towel before he takes it from her. Turning it over and over he examines every detail.

"How did you get so many rabbits?" Ana asks.

"Can't get rid of the damn bastards. Garden's full of them. At least they're edible."

He stretches out the screen and then contracts it. Rolls and unrolls it. He inadvertently brings up a few photos, almost dropping the thing when the image of Finn extends into the room. He turns it off and puts it gingerly on the counter away from the meat.

"It's from the City," she says by way of explanation. "My friend used to live there. Got banished two years ago. You ever been there? I mean before the wall?"

"A couple of times to trade. Wasn't my thing. You?"

"No. My friend said he could get me inside. I didn't believe him though. So, have you seen him?" she asks.

"Nope."

"You know anybody you can ask about him?"

"If they have him, then what?"

"We trade."

"What are you offering?"

"I'd rather not say," she says. "They'll want it though. I'm sure of that."

He takes the whiskey bottle off the table and tips it back and forth.

"What are you doing?" Ana asks.

"Trying to figure out how much I've had to drink today."

"Why?'

"Because I'm not sure that you're real."

"I'm real," she says, touching his arm. Somewhat alarmed, he steps back and slides his fingers through his hair, as if to make himself more presentable.

He invites her to sit on his long deck overlooking the lake. It might have been a peaceful scene – lily pads and water so clear it's as if the logs and plants beneath are under a microscope – but the view is interrupted by an overturned wind turbine.

"You swim in there?" she asks him.

"I've fallen in a few times," he says, smiling, but the movement hurts his face. "I wonder if they have cancer in the City?" he says, pointing to his face.

"Probably not."

He pours two drinks. When she doesn't take one, he downs both himself.

She surveys the fence he's built, the neat rows of his garden, the rain barrel shower.

"You've got a nice setup here," she says.

He leans back in his chair and tilts his head ambiguously.

"As far as places go, this one's pretty good."

A duck emerges out of the water and shakes itself off.

"I'd love to eat one of those," he says.

"So why don't you?"

"There are only two of them. Doesn't seem right."

"I suppose not," she answers. Gus shifts in his chair uncomfortably, briefly glancing up at her. He's obviously not used to making conversation.

"So, will you help me?" she asks.

"I don't even know you. Why would I do you a favor?" he asks, matter-of-factly.

"Back where I come from, people help each other out."

"Yeah? What are you going to do for me?"

She shrugs, suddenly uncomfortable. "Name your price."

He gets up and throws some bread to the ducks. When he's done, he takes a long-handled pool net and skims some sludge floating on the surface by the dock. He's thinking. He hasn't said no. There's hope. But what if she can't give him what he wants?

"I'll take your screen," he says.

Her screen has everything on it that connects her to the City. A year's worth of entertainment. A lifetime of books. The message from Aaron.

"Make the deal and you can have it," she says.

AFTER EATING rabbit on turnip mush, they retire to Gus's "library". Three of the walls are covered in record jackets leaning on little white plastic rails. He's suspended colorful streamers from the ceiling. They sit down on giant cushions made from rabbit fur.

"Do you listen to all these records or are they just decoration?" she asks, riffling through a few albums.

"A bit of both. I didn't have much interest in music when I was your age. Had a few playlists on my phone, whatever was on the radio, mostly downloaded by girlfriends, but I didn't need music."

"And now?"

"After it all happened, I wandered into this ghetto area of town where all the pawn shops were and there was this one colorful little shop. The records were on the walls just like this, museum like. Something made me want to touch them, pull out the sleeves, read the liner notes. Smell them even. The whole world had gone to shit and yet here was proof that humanity could create something wonderful. I spent the entire day on the floor of that place surrounded by them. Then I brought them all here. Now I listen to music every night. They're my friends," he says, putting on Bob Dylan's "Blood on the Tracks".

"You live close to the Band. You're not worried?"

"They're no threat to me," he says, bending over awkwardly to attach a couple of speakers. The room fills with more sound than either of them can absorb.

"Why? You have something on them?" she asks. Gus is on his fourth drink now, each one bigger than the last, and he's starting to slur a little.

"Not sure it's such an interesting story," he says, turning the music down.

"I'd like to hear it," Ana says, taking a record out of its sleeve. Joni Mitchell. He snatches it from her. These are his babies.

"I had this teacher once when I was seventeen," he starts, once it's safely back on the shelf. "He was maybe twenty-five, fresh out of college. It was the first class I took in high school that I actually did well in. Civics and Careers." He pauses, gauging Ana's reaction. "You weren't expecting a story from the old days, were you?"

"I have no expectations," she says.

"He gave me an A-. I never got anything above a C before that. Maybe my mother dropped me on the head. Anyway, this Mr. Blackwell took a special interest in my education. We did pretend job interviews. He made me a resume and told me how to dress right. He could spin all those defects my mother nagged me about into a job asset."

The record skips. He takes it off, examines it, swears and chucks it into his vinyl graveyard, a painted wooden box.

"Before I even finished high school, he fixed me up with a job at FedEx. I figured I owed him, so I took him to my parents' restaurant after my first day of work. They hit it off well. He became a family friend. My parents liked him better than I did. We kept him fed when the school board redrew the boundaries

and he was out of a job. 'Now that's a decent man,' my mother would say every time he left."

Ana has never heard the album he puts on now – Janis Joplin – music that didn't end up in the City's collective database. Makes her wonder what else the City is missing.

"So, after it all went down, my parents decided we should go to one of the military camps. But I didn't show up at the bus we were supposed to take. Instead, I came here."

"Your family had a trailer here?"

"No. I had a crush. There was this popular Christian girl who was sort of nice to me at work. Her family had a summer place here. She always talked about going to the lake on weekends. I never did anything like that. My parents ran a restaurant. Never took vacations. I hoped one day she'd invite me and we'd go windsurfing. I was pretty good-looking back then. So, when it happened, and people were leaving town, I had this idea she would come here and I would take care of her."

"But she wasn't here," Ana said.

"No. Never saw anyone. And then one day I'm wandering around these trailers and this guy jumped me from behind. He wanted my food and weapons. I thought he was going to kill me, so I turned around to face him. He looked like all them Band guys. Animal vest. Dirty. Blood under his nails. But then I saw that it was my old teacher, Mr. Blackwell. He got all embarrassed and dropped my bag down in front of me and we stared at each other for a spell and then he left without a word. He's the leader of the Band now. Crazy, isn't? It

had only been a year since it all happened."

"People bend in whatever direction the wind is blowing," she says.

"Maybe you're right. I guess they have to."

The song they're listening to becomes melancholy and Gus settles deeper into his chair and stares at the spinning disk. Maybe this is why people have a fetish for old records. They're hypnotizing.

"No one from the Band has laid a finger on me in the twenty-nine years since," he says, turning to her, "on account of Blackwell being my protector. But *you* should be afraid of him."

"So I've heard."

"Hope this guy's worth your investment," he says, with a smile full of pity. He reaches for a black marker and draws a line on his bottle two inches below its current level. "You see this line," he says. "When I get close to it, you best go into the guest room beyond the kitchen and lock yourself in."

"Why?"

"The calamities might have turned Mr. Blackwell into someone else, but it's this stuff that makes me crazy. Actually, I don't even know if that's true because I can't remember anything that happens. I just see evidence of it in the morning: broken plates, bruises, holes in the drywall. I even found a mutilated cougar floating in the lake once. "But I need it you know. The pain's too much otherwise."

She considers this carefully. If she had any sense, she'd get out of there, find a place to camp far away from him. Some of his

looks haven't been innocent. But this guy is friends with Blackwell. He can find out if they have Finn. Besides, she can defend herself against a drunk. The real issue is that she might do actual damage to him. He won't be of help to her if he's incapacitated.

They set out his alarm system – strings of cowbells – and lock up for the night. When the bottle gets close to the line, she does as he says. Leaving him in his armchair, surrounded by his vinyl companions, she goes to her guest room. She jams a chair under the door handle, puts her loaded gun next to her pillow and lies down pretending to sleep.

At 2:00 a.m., he comes staggering into the kitchen, knocking over a chair. She can hear him opening the fridge and making something to eat. He mumbles to a non-existent person, one of the cats maybe.

After he eats, he hums, eventually breaking into song. "Beautiful farmer lady from the east," he sings over and over. He drums his empty cup to his tune and then heartily laughs. He lumbers down the hall toward her room. "I'm going to respect you," he says. "Yes, Gus is Mr. Nice Guy and nice guys don't get laid, do they?" Then he sinks to the floor, back against her door and weeps. The last thing she hears is Gus snoring.

CHAPTER 35

23 APRIL 2016. "What's that noise, Ana? You're not touching my records, are you?" Gus asks over the radio.

"I would *never*," she says, turning the volume down on his stereo. "What's your status?"

"Blackwell's heavy into something. Can't see me, they say. Put me on the list for next week, but no guarantees. I'm heading home soon. Just waiting on a buddy of mine. He knows someone who knows someone who might know if they have this engineer of yours."

"Good work Gus," she says, although he can probably hear the disappointment in her voice – even over his useless radios. "But Gus, this engineer's no good to me dead you know. Tell your friend to keep him safe until you meet with Blackwell."

"Will do. I'll check in again in an hour."

"Copy that."

"And Ana. I know you're not a farmer."

"What gives you that idea?"

"Farmers have leathery skin from the sun and spots on their hands."

"I'm twenty-two, Gus. Plenty of time for that."

"Whoever this guy is to you, Ana, he doesn't deserve you."

"He's just an asset, Gus."

"Far left. Second shelf down. Ten from the right. You'll like it," he says before he goes dark. "Don't get any fingerprints on it."

José Feliciano. A blind guitarist from the last century. Doesn't look promising. She puts on "Ain't no sunshine" and pulls out one of Gus' cookbooks and reads it by the pond. French food. He's bookmarked all of the pages with rabbit recipes. The music makes her cry. Nothing in the City ever made her cry like that. Maybe it won't be so bad living on the outside after all.

CHAPTER 36

22 APRIL 2064. He's bound tightly in a blue and white blanket in a concrete room that smells of disinfectant. It's not a hospital. A glass wall separates his room from a large warehouse space, empty except for a skateboard ramp. Jasper and Yippy bark at him from behind the glass.

He's not sure what they're doing to him, but it's messing with his head. He sees flashes – Sassafras sitting at the front of his bed scratching at a hole in his head. Ana cleaning her gun. The boy from the Band he almost beat to death with his face pressed against the window. Sometimes the visions speak to him, but he can only make out a few words, as if their universe and his are only partially aligned. Occasionally, he smells things that can't be there – lilac bushes and the coffee Isla served them.

Earlier, he was on a dock with Ana, Finn's dead friends bobbing up and down in the water.

They took him yesterday. Or maybe it was two days ago. He's not sure how long he's been under. Two guards in hazmat suits escorted him straight from the gate.

Noah is next to him in a hazmat suit. He's dozed off, one hand clenching and unclenching the armrest of his chair in his sleep. He stays too long to be an aberration.

"Wake up, you bastard," he says. Noah stirs casually as if trying to downplay the fact that he drifted off.

"I actually had a father for a while. You're the bastard," Noah says.

"What's with all of this?" he asks, nodding toward the tubes and machines.

"She said you'd protest."

"Who?"

"Ana."

"She's back?"

"She's not coming back, Aaron."

"So how the hell is she communicating with you?"

"A message from your screen. It must have gone through when you got back inside."

Shit, she is smarter than I am, he thinks.

"What lies did she tell you?"

"That you have rabies."

"One of our dogs had rabies. Not me. We put it down."

"You had dogs together? How quaint."

"Shut up and get me out of here."

"Couldn't if I tried. Not until they're done running tests."

"I *don't* have rabies."

"It's protocol. You didn't think they were going to let you loose in the City after you returned? You remember that flu epidemic last year. They're blaming it on Finn now. Consider it a well-deserved vacation. It's not fun for me either. I haven't had help with Martha for weeks. She got in trouble again. Cut up some books in the library. Said she was making art. How long can a five-year-old sustain this level of delinquency?"

"When can I leave?"

"In a few days, if you're on your best behavior."

"It will all be over by then."

"I think that was her intention. Just in case."

A nurse interrupts them. He takes his vitals, records some numbers on his chart, tilting his head at Noah somewhat optimistically. Of course, his stats are good. He was never sick.

"Cameras?" Aaron asks, when the nurse is gone.

"None. The Council wants no record of you ever being here. You never left the City. Remember?"

"Why did you do it?"

"Do what?"

"Help Finn leave the City?"

"You're delusional."

Aaron raises his eyebrows at him.

"What?" he asks, looking sideways at the blood pressure machine. "It just sort of slipped out."

"What caused it to *slip out?*"

"He was friendly with my wife."

"He was never interested in her. It was one-sided. Your wife came on to everyone, even me. You can't blame Finn for that."

"But he was very sympathetic to her."

"He was helping her. They had similar struggles."

"Really? Finn's not perfect?"

"No, he's not. No one is. Especially you. You're the reason we're all in this position."

"He would have abandoned the City eventually anyway. I just sped things up."

"Why would he do that?"

He pulls his screen out of his back pocket and presses it to the glass divider. A photo of Miranda Pape and two dark-haired girls.

"Ana briefed me on your visit with Miranda Pape. I've done some digging."

He could care less about Miranda.

"Not all of Miranda's family were burned in the fire. Just her son and husband," he says.

"And?"

"Miranda took her two daughters with her. There was some kind of hearing. The girls wanted to stay in the City, but the court went along with Miranda's wishes. Finn's Miriam may be Miranda's daughter, his childhood friend. Which means he left the City to find her. Probably never got over her leaving."

"He met Miriam at the Commune, not Blossom Gates. Can't be her."

"Maybe her daughters ran away from her. Their mother is a psychopath, after all. I figure Finn went to Blossom Gates to find Miriam and stayed just long enough to figure out that she had moved to the Commune with her sister. And then he got embroiled in this mess with the Orphanage."

"She's out there alone, Noah. Isn't there anything you can do?"

"If you're asking if I can go after her, maybe I should share with you the rest of the news."

"What have you done, Noah?"

"Not me. Her. It's not entirely bad. Look at your hand."

There's a bandage over his left hand. He assumed it was from whatever sedative they gave him. He rips it off and finds his tattoo gone.

"Congratulations. Your status is restored."

"How?"

"Ana sent a message to the Council. Told them about *Finn's* way out. Said *you* figured it out yourself and performed admirably out there."

"But I didn't bring him back."

"That wasn't your fault. In any case, once they seal the exit, Finn can't come back and no one else will be leaving illegally. That's good enough for the Council. Truthfully, I think it's because Palmer has a soft spot for you."

"Lucky me."

"Tell me. Why *did* you come back? Why not follow her?"

"Are you an idiot? Of course I'm going after her. I came back for wheels and weapons. I had no choice. She left me with nothing."

"Oh," he says, staring at his hands.

"What aren't you telling me?"

"It's just that I'm in negotiations with the Council myself. I might need to part with a few of my properties, but it looks like we'll be getting the old house back soon. Even the money. If there's no more trouble they say."

"Define trouble."

"You banishing yourself, for example."

So that's it then. If he goes, Noah doesn't get his inheritance. They stay in that dump the rest of their lives. Martha doesn't get to go to a good school. There's no way out for him now.

"Don't look so glum, Aaron. It was always going to play out this way. They never expected her to come back. They didn't want her to."

CHAPTER 37

30 APRIL 2064. Gus left over a week ago. Probably went on a bender and is sleeping it off in a ditch. She has to believe that he got her message to Blackwell, that Finn is safe until they can come to an arrangement.

She spends her days looking for distractions to calm herself down. She forces herself to sip sage tea in front of the pond and feed the ducks. It would be peaceful if she weren't so agitated.

When she isn't obsessively trying the radio, she frequently listens to Aaron's message. She should stop herself, but soon her screen will belong to Gus anyway.

Every morning, she hikes the length of his trapline, string and knife in hand. Can't have dead animals rotting in traps. It'll scare the rest away. This morning, she found one still alive.

It was completely white except for a few drops of blood on its clamped foot. She let it go. The idea of ever eating rabbit again repulses her.

She's working out in his exercise room when she hears the cowbells clink outside. She goes to the window and sees a robin settle on a powerline.

She tries the radio again. Static.

She unpacks and repacks her bag. Rolls the tent tighter. Takes a shower. Tries the radio again. Avoids Aaron's message. Riffles through Gus' clothing collection. Tries on a sleazy black dress. Goes to the sundeck. Climbs the ladder to the roof. Takes a nap on the upper deck. Gets a bad sunburn. Listens to Aaron's message. If Gus doesn't come back by tomorrow, she'll leave.

At dusk, she hears the cowbells again, but this time they're immediately muffled. An animal wouldn't do that. It has to be Gus. Relieved, she rolls over the sundeck to the edge. She's about to call out to him but stops herself in time. It's two women. One looks somewhat like her but a decade older. Long black hair that's a little wavy. Green eyes. Broader shoulders. The other one is older. Short-haired, wiry and grey. They're equipped, both carrying large semi-automatics. They dress like the boys from the Band. Grimy. Jackets made of pelts. She hears them searching through the trailers. She can't make out their conversation until they come out at the deck below her. They're less than four feet from her now and the older one leans against the ladder to her hiding spot.

"She's gone," the younger one says, throwing a stone at one of the ducks.

"Nah. Her pack's here. Leave the poor duck alone."

"So she went to the lake maybe. We wait."

They're here for her.

"Without her shoes? Would you do that? You're here aren't you, Ana?" she yells into the darkness.

They stop and listen for her reaction but Ana stays absolutely still. She shifts onto her side soundlessly, reaching for her weapon. Maybe they mean her no harm. They're here because Blackwell got her message. *But what do your instincts tell you, Ana? They know your name. Gus never came back. They have big guns. They're not saying anything friendly. Finn pissed Blackwell off.* She squirms back a foot and steadies her gun.

"You search the trailers on the left. I'll search right," the older woman says. "We'll start at the ends and meet in the middle. And if you see any antibiotics, take them. This guy has everything."

"And if we find her?" the younger one asks.

"Do what you have to. She needs to be able to speak but it doesn't matter what she looks like."

It'll be a couple of minutes before they end up back in middle where Ana is. Now's her chance to run. There are only two places to go from here: back into the trailer or into the pond. She chooses the pond.

The ladder is loose and rattles a little as she climbs down. She curses herself for not being more careful. Shoeless, she creeps

across the deck and soundlessly sinks into the water, barely disturbing it. Swimming as close to the bottom as she can, she makes it to the fallen wind turbine. Swimming is the one thing she's done a lot of since Finn left, especially on laundry days, but she'd be faster if it weren't for the stupid dress getting tangled between her legs.

A bullet flies to her right and then one to her left.

"Blackwell wants to talk. That's what you want, isn't it?" the older one yells across the pond.

"We're your escorts," the younger one says. "Your protection."

"Where's Gus?" Ana yells.

"Don't worry about him. You want your friend from the City, don't you?"

Gus is dead, Ana thinks. She's next. The older one was clear. They can do whatever they want to her as long as she can speak.

She dips back below the water and swims to the other end of the pond, pulls herself onto a branch and then runs over thistles, gravel and broken glass, until her feet are battered and bloody. The one lesson she passed with flying colors in her training was knowing when to run. When she finally stops in the middle of a field, sheltered by weeds, she forces herself to examine the damage in the fading light. Her feet are a mess of blisters and slivers. She pulls out a shard of glass embedded in her heel. Shoes would have been a good idea. At least she has her gun.

She lies flat and listens for movement, alert to every creaking weather vane and rush of wind over the weeds. She's made it pretty far, but the trail she made through the field couldn't

have been clearer had she drawn them a map. She needs to get to water again. Water covers tracks. She struggles to remember the map Aaron projected on the wall. Gus' pond is near a large lake, the same lake she was following west to get to the Band. But where? The sun is setting to her right, so she must be facing south. The lake is south. She crawls out of her hiding spot and runs south, crouched down.

After a kilometer, she finds the road she'd been travelling on. It's completely dark now, which also means it'll be harder to track her. She walks past the Harrington Yacht Club, only one wall of it now standing, to a stack of kayaks. A few are in decent shape, but she can't take a boat. They'll see it. Swimming is her only option, but which direction? Back to the safe house to rethink this naïve plan of hers or into the heart of the Band's territory?

Before she can make up her mind, she hears the faint whizz of two motorcycles coming closer. She has no choice but to stand her ground now. It's only the two of them after all. Crouching amongst the kayaks, she waits. The older one passes her first. Ana shoots at her tire and misses. She brakes, skids on the sandy road and turns abruptly. But she doesn't fire at Ana. It's too dark and they need her alive. The woman takes cover behind a garden shed just as the other one arrives. Ana can hear them whispering.

They have bikes. Ana will have better odds if she disables them. The motor of the older woman's bike gleams in the moonlight. An easy target.

She hears one of them swear when her bullet makes contact.

Ana creeps around what's left of the yacht club. The two women walk in opposite directions. Ana is ready for them. She finds a tin can and throws it at a metal pole. The younger woman turns in the direction of the noise. The distraction is just enough for Ana to get close to her. She shoots her in the thigh, nicking it and then kicks the gun out of her hand. Ana can barely hear the older woman coming up behind her over the swearing of the younger one.

"The more damage you do to us, the more we do to you," the older one says.

"That's not necessarily how it works," Ana says, slowly turning so that she can see both of them at the same time.

"Stop being foolish," she says.

"She's going to bleed out," Ana says, nodding to the younger one.

"She can take care of herself."

The older one and Ana have their weapons pointed at each other. The woman inches toward Ana, forcing her to back up a little if she wants to keep them both in view. The fallen gun is a couple of feet away.

"Where is Finn?" Ana asks.

"Blackwell will tell you. You just need to come with us now."

"I'm not going anywhere. He can come to me. Then he'll get what I'm offering."

"Blackwell doesn't leave his throne for anyone."

"Someone makes his deals for him. Send me that person."

"You're nuts."

"The way that leg's bleeding, she won't last long," Ana says, crouching down to pick up the other gun. Now she has one on each of them. "Better send someone quickly and leave me your radio."

"He'll like you," she says, laughing. She slides her radio to Ana, gets on the good bike and takes off without even glancing back at her partner.

CHAPTER 38

30 April 2064

Dear Ana,

I've been shedding my possessions. What do I need them for? I've read all those history books on my shelf in our apartment. They don't tell us how to live now anyway. And I don't need a second screen. My stereo hisses and I'm never going to get around to fixing it. I had a little more difficulty parting with the undershirt you left under our couch.

You may wonder why I'm discarding my stuff. I haven't taken a vow of poverty or anything. It's just a thought I had when I was walking back to our safe house – before you left me. I was exhausted and needed to hide somewhere and nap for a few minutes. I saw a

metal building near an old airport. It seemed as good as any place to sleep. It turned out to be a hangar with three airplanes in it. I was thinking maybe I would find a bunch of dead bodies inside. I wondered if their flesh would be gone or if the lack of oxygen would have preserved them somehow. I pushed one of those movable staircases to the biggest one. The doors were a little complicated, but no locks. The inside was strange, not like the airplanes I'd seen in old movies. More like a spaceship. It was a hollow round tube, silver and white with tracks and hooks in the floor to secure cargo. It was as long as a park, divided into numbered sections. Although it was mostly empty, there were a few pallets secured to the front end stacked with boxes. I opened a bunch of them. Even read people's invoices and printed birthday greetings. I held their mail order objects – curling irons, books, puffer jackets. I felt sick to my stomach. All those dead people, their only legacy a blender they never got to use. A book they never read. So that's why I'm giving away all my stuff. If I die, I don't want anyone finding my things and thinking they define me – an old t-shirt, some photos in a box, a pair of shoes I never wore because they were too small in the first place.

I've been out of quarantine for six days. They let me out early, no thanks to you. When they released me, all I could think of was candy. It was all the stories you told me. I went to that weird shop and met your friend Hooper. I bought two pounds of sponge toffee. I said I worked with you and asked for a tour of the place. He obliged me. Showed me everything from the basement to his apartment above the store. I asked him a lot of questions to keep him talking – how does he thicken his candy, what temperature does he cook the

caramel at, where does he get his ideas? It was getting near dinnertime and so he heated up some food one of his customers had brought him yesterday – couscous with meat. We sat in his greenhouse for two hours – he said I would like the air in there and I did – mostly talking about his days on the Council. You didn't tell me he had been on the first Council. I just thought he was some crazy guy who built greenhouses with your father. Finally, he asked me why I was really there? Was I trying to buy his place? Did the Council send me to interrogate him? He said it in a kind way, as if he expected it. I admitted it was because of you. I told him you had totally destroyed me and that I just wanted to be someplace where you had been. He said I should tell you *how I feel. When I didn't respond, he said "she's left the City, hasn't she?" Then his eyes filled with tears. Maybe mine did too.*

We didn't speak of it further. He walked back into his kitchen, got a rickety old chair and climbed onto a counter. He moved around some old mixing bowls and muffin tins and produced an old VR headset.

"Take this home and fix it," he said. "It might bring you some comfort. But bring it back, please."

The old thing was dead and I didn't think I'd be able to find a plug for it. I asked one of the junk dealers at the market and he said he didn't have a cord but he offered to buy it from me 'as is'. I asked the evidence guys at the Hive. They'd never seen anything like it. They offered to take it apart and try to extract the data. I said I'd think about it. I finally broke down and told Noah t hat I'd found this thing and did he have any ideas. I didn't tell

him who I got it from or what I hoped was on it.

He'd just gotten the keys to his old place back and he said maybe we could find something there. We spent a morning in his basement looking through boxes of old electronics. Finally, we found a game console in a plastic bag with some controllers attached. The cord fit into the old headset. We plugged everything in and a little green light went on.

I asked Noah to leave me alone, but he shook his head. He said whatever was on there, he wanted to see it. He'd earned it. I said fine. Just let me watch it alone first.

I put the headset on and was transported back into the candy shop, a scene of you and Finn cooking with Hooper. You couldn't have been more than five. The little version of you ran around the kitchen. Just like Miranda said, you were never on the floor. You jumped from chair to chair, counter to counter, like an animal, your little black bob springing up and down.

"Come help me invent some new candy recipes," Hooper said to you. He wasn't the least bit concerned about you being totally hyper.

He put a mountain of ingredients in front of you to experiment with. Your little head could hardly be seen above the pile.

You stringed together candy necklaces made out of black licorice gumballs. Your neck and face became covered in sticky black smears. Finn didn't do any cooking. He was preoccupied with the idea of inventing a vending machine that could make candy to order. He was making intricate drawings, using a cookie sheet as a ruler. Hooper didn't discourage him; he just asked questions like 'will there be a cooling device to ensure the butter doesn't melt?' Finn answered

emphatically that there would of course, as if he'd already thought of this. You were wearing the green jumper that appears in several images from those days – did you only have the one outfit?

Your mother walked into the kitchen. It couldn't have been long before she died. She turned and smiled at the camera. Who was behind the camera, I wonder? Your father? She looked exhausted and leaned into the table to support herself. There were dark circles under her eyes and she had a scarf around her head, but she still looked beautiful.

"Have you done your homework?" she asked Finn. He shrugged and went back to his drawings. She smiled at him, but his face was down, and he didn't see it. He likely never knew that she smiled at him with so much love that day. You started talking to your mother a mile a minute. She looked at you so intently, hanging on to every word. You put your wet sticky black licorice gumball necklace around her neck and then the scene cut out.

It was at that precise moment that I accepted my fate. I'm staying in the City and it's okay. In fact, in a way, there's more of you here then out there. I have my files on you. This little video. And now I have your friend.

I went back to Hooper's to return the headset and told him I'd had enough of working for the Council. My status had been restored and I could do whatever I wanted. Would he take me on as an apprentice? He asked me if I liked candy and I said it was growing on me. He said fine, he would give me a try.

Now I'm in his apartment sleeping on his couch with almost no possessions because I've sold them all.

But I'm enjoying my monastic life. I prefer this tiny quiet place to Noah's big empty mansion. And there's nothing like the smell of burnt sugar and meringue. In the morning, there's a line-up of customers down the block, all smiling. No matter how busy we are, Hooper takes the time to visit with each of them. I have new friends now. No wonder the old man gave up politics for this life.

I've been subsisting on caramels. Tell me. How many cavities did you get as a child? My teeth are already starting to hurt. I've also put on five pounds, but I think you'll still recognize me when you see me again. If you see me again. But how could that happen?

Noah pesters me with polite messages regarding Martha. Will I still be getting her from school on Wednesdays now that I've moved to Hooper's? Will I be picking up the laundry I left in the dryer? Would I mind if he invited a few of our friends to move into the mansion with him?

He's testing me. He's seen me shedding my possessions. He's afraid I'm going to leave. Let him wonder. He did this to us.

Martha asks about you. I didn't know you two had become such great buddies. Did you knit that Barbie doll skirt for her? Okay, so it had a few dropped stitches, but I was moderately impressed.

Palmer came to the shop today. She all but accused me of being in the throes of a mental breakdown. Return to work, she urged me. We should all just know what we're good at and accept it. My calling isn't candy, she said. I note, though, that she left with a pound of my meringue.

I loathe the Hive now. Yesterday, I visited my mother at the farm. I walked the long way along the river to avoid catching

a glimpse of it. I've paid my dues for my crime. I'm never going back there.

I'm concerned about Hooper. On Saturday, he charged a woman double for a pound of mint patties. She paid it without a word. I found burnt jelly in the compost. He came into the shop today in that sweater vest he likes and pajama bottoms. How did I become his family? You should be figuring out what to do with him. I'm taking him to the doctor tomorrow. He was reluctant, but I said statistically people who get regular check-ups in the City live longer. He bought it. We've actually become very chummy, the two of us. I think I might finally understand what he and his friends were all about when they started this City.

I dreamt last night of you in the safe house in one of those evening gowns from the clothing rack, the emerald green one. You were so beautiful, but then you hacked away the arms and frills, anything that could get in your way. Maybe I am having a breakdown. Perhaps everyone should have a breakdown at some point.

CHAPTER 39

30 APRIL 2064. Blood drips down the woman's jeans to her ankles. She looks at her thigh, stunned, trying to comprehend the impossible.

"If I'd hit an artery, you'd be dead," Ana says, inspecting the wound. "And good news. The bullet went straight through." If this were the City, she'd be more compassionate. She'd apologize. But then no one shot at her in the City.

Ana zip ties the woman to the kayak rack. She cuts off a strip from the bottom of her dress and ties it around the wound. Without supplies, there's not a lot more she can do.

She checks the woman's gun. Empty. She wasted her only two bullets on Ana trying to chase her out of the water.

"Can you walk?" Ana asks, patting her down for other weapons. She finds a couple of knives, a hair tie and a little bracelet that would only fit a child's hand.

"Does it look like I can walk?" she asks sarcastically.

"I'll come back for you," she says. "Don't think about trying to get loose."

"I'm pretty sure I wouldn't get far."

"Your name?" Ana asks.

"Sarah."

"How long before your friend gets to Blackwell do you think?"

"A day or so."

Enough time then. It'll be slow getting back to Gus' place in the dark. She'll need to change and pack up her stuff, get her bike from its hiding place and come back for Sarah. She can't take too long or Sarah might not make it.

"He'll come with an army," Sarah says, as Ana turns to leave.

"It doesn't matter," Ana says.

"You and your brother aren't both getting away."

"I know," she says. "I never expected to." It isn't Sarah's warning that makes Ana shudder. It's the fact that she knows Finn is her brother. Even Gus didn't know that.

IT'S ALMOST MORNING by the time they finally get to the safe house. It was an awkward ride. Sarah rode behind, her arms around Ana's waist, her wrists zip-tied to a lip of chrome on the seat. It's a good thing they were because, sometime in the night,

Sarah fell asleep and the two of them almost fell over. Getting Sarah up the stairs to the loft is another long ordeal.

When they finally make it to the top, Ana drags a mattress to the window and helps Sarah onto it. She secures her to the radiator pipe. It takes every bit of will power she has not to plop down on the mattress herself.

"I'm going to dress your wound properly, okay? You aren't going to kick me, are you, because I can't hold my gun and tape you at the same time?"

"Sure whatever," Sarah says, spreading her legs into a wide V so that her injured leg is closer to Ana.

Ana cuts through her pants, wipes up the mess of blood, squirts iodine into the hole and glues it. Then she moves Sarah onto her side and does the same with the exit wound. As far as she can tell, it went straight through muscle. No chipped bones. She covers the entire leg with gauze and bandages, then gives her a shot of antibiotics. Surprisingly, Sarah flinches more at the site of the needle than anything else.

Ana inspects the loft using her screen as a light. Everything of Aaron's is gone. His pack, his clothes, his books. He hasn't even left her a note on the bulletin board. How angry was he when he finally admitted defeat and went back to the gate? Is there a chance he didn't go?

She makes Sarah a plate of dried fruit and nuts, undoing one hand so she can eat it. She doesn't get a thank you.

"I need to take a piss."

She brings her a bucket.

"I don't care how many weapons you have," Sarah says, as Ana unzips what's left of her pants and helps her squat over the bucket on one leg. "He's got more. And there'll be a hundred men outside here by morning."

"I'm counting on it," Ana says.

"You're either really stupid or a lot smarter than your brother."

"I'm both," Ana says, pouring the contents of the bucket down the kitchen sink, hoping it will end up outside the building.

She leaves the loft, goes to the second floor where she hid all of their weapons, sets up Aaron's motion sensors outside the building, makes sure the lock is properly secured. She assesses their food and water supplies. They have enough for a week, at most, if they end up trapped here.

When everything is ready, she considers what to do with Sarah. She can't let her guard down for even a second. She sets up a motion sensor just beyond Sarah's reach, a grid of red lights lighting up the room.

"If you move out of range of the lights, an alarm will go off. If I don't disarm it within thirty seconds, that thing will blow."

"You're bluffing."

"I'd demonstrate, but then I'd be down a weapon. Take your chances if you'd like," she says, as she readies a dose of morphine. She's pretty sure Sarah passes out before the needle even goes in.

Ana drags her own mattress a few feet away, lies down, her hand on the radio, trying to forget that the last time she slept here, Aaron was beside her.

Sometime in the night, a voice breaks through static.

"Am I speaking to the infamous Ana Singh?"

"Yes," she says, sitting up, her voice breaking up a little. No sense lying about her identity now.

"You're a bit of a nuisance, aren't you?"

"I can be." She'd give anything for a glass of water.

"You didn't like the envoy I sent you?"

"I liked them just fine, Mr. Blackwell – it is you, isn't it? – but if you want to get on with this, send me someone with the authority to negotiate, not a couple of thugs with no brains."

"You have my attention. What is it you want exactly?"

"You have my brother. I have something you could use. I'd like to make a trade and then we can be done with each other."

"And if I don't want to make a deal with you?"

"Suit yourself. You should know though that I'm relentless. You think I'm annoying now. Just wait. You won't see it coming. Maybe one day everyone gets sick and you find out your water supply has been tampered with. Let's just say I left the City prepared."

"I doubt you have the stomach for something like that. You're from the City."

"You go ahead and think that. I hope it gives you comfort."

"You've damaged one of my assets."

"Is that a question?"

"That was excessive, don't you think?"

"I negotiate at the level of my opponent. If my opponent acts like a Neanderthal then so do I. It gets bloody. No one gains much in a negotiation like that, though. Is that what you are,

Mr. Blackwell, a Neanderthal? Because, if so, we can both imagine how this is going to turn out."

"You're smart, Ana. I could use you here. Maybe I should trade you for your brother."

"You probably should."

"So now what?"

"You give me proof that you have Finn and then we discuss terms. There are infinite possibilities." She'd like to ask about Gus but that would just give Blackwell more power over the situation.

"Intriguing, but we're a little busy here right now, Little Miss Singhshine. *Adult* business. It might be a while before someone can get back to you."

"Take all the time you need. I'll just be sitting here twiddling my thumbs, thinking of ways to terrorize you. Oh, and Mr. Blackwell, what do you want me to do with Sarah? I don't have any medical training."

The radio cuts out mid-sentence.

Little Miss Singshine? Really? It's like he's taken a page out of a negotiation manual. I guess he's not aware she's been volunteering as a mediator for years at the neighborhood justice center. She's glad now that they forced her to take all those weekend conflict resolution courses. At the time, she thought it was one step up from sorting garbage at the dump.

Here's what they teach about old-style negotiation. Rule one: use disrespectful and diminutive language to make your opponent feel less powerful. Men, in negotiating with women,

often use words like girl, miss, honey, sweetie or even little lady to imply that the woman is less mature and weaker. A variation on this theme is to use language that pisses your opponent off. Her instructor told them a story from his early days as a clerk at a law firm. The partner he was assigned to repeatedly mispronounced the name of a witness she was examining. The witness got increasingly flustered until he finally blew and, in the process, gave the lawyer all the ammunition she needed to attack his credibility. Bring it on, Blackwell.

And she definitely beat him on rule number two: try to get what you want without negotiating at all. In Blackwell's world, this translated into sending two lackies to take her and whatever she was offering and that didn't exactly work out for him.

Blackwell did moderately better on rule three: stall. He's counting on her becoming more desperate the longer she waits. More importantly, stalling gives Blackwell time to prepare. Controlling the time frame also puts him in charge of the process. She didn't do so bad herself in responding. Her best option was to pretend like it didn't matter how long he took. And then there's Sarah. If he cares what happens to her, he'll contact her again soon. She could have done more to hurry him up, like threatening to kill Sarah, but that would violate rule number four: never make threats you're not prepared to follow through on.

She also won on rule five: don't get stuck in a win-lose situation. She made it clear that they could both come out ahead. Anyone who has negotiated with a toddler knows that it's rarely

a good idea to end up in a situation where there can be only one winner. The toddler will win.

There's only one thing that's disturbing her about their interaction. He hasn't shown any interest in what she's offering. That means one of two things. He doesn't want to make a deal with her at all. He's stalling so that he can carry out his original plan uninterrupted. The second possibility is that he has his own idea of what he wants from her and he'll let her know when he's ready.

Which brings her to rules six and seven: never underestimate your opponent and always get as much information as possible before you start.

Anyway, the real problem is rule eight: always be willing to walk away from a negotiation. She can't and he knows it. Maybe he's already clued in that she gave up living in the City for this. But that doesn't mean she's lost. Blackwell has his price. She just needs to figure out what it is.

In the meantime, she has her own strategy. Be completely unpredictable. Do things that make absolutely no sense. It confuses your opponent, which makes them happy to make any kind of deal that's at all sensible.

SHORTLY AFTER breakfast, another voice comes on the line, deeper than Blackwell's.

"Ana?"

"Gus?" she asks, halfway through tacking up fabric over the windows. "You're alright?"

"I'm okay. Talked to Blackwell, finally. I think we can make this happen, Ana."

"No thanks to you. Where have you been?"

"Delayed."

"I think I know what that means."

"What are you offering them, Ana? Blackwell is ready to talk terms."

"In addition to agreeing not to pester the Band, I have seeds."

"They're not farmers, Ana."

"These aren't ordinary seeds. They're my inheritance. The Band settled on infertile land. These seeds will grow anywhere."

"Mr. Blackwell wouldn't be interested in your seeds even if they grew magical beanstalks."

"I would think they'd want to be less dependent on Isla."

"It's not who they are."

"I have weapons. And bullets."

"They have more weapons than they know what to do with. Bullets are good, but not enough to trade for your brother. How many?"

"How about you tell me how many it would take and then I'll tell you if I have enough?"

"Let me be honest with you Ana. This entire discussion is pointless. There is something they want. They're actually as desperate for it as you are for your brother, but it's not seeds or weapons."

"What then?"

"He'd like the use of your skills. In fact, yesterday was an audition of sorts and you passed."

"Audition for what?"

"A very delicate negotiation."

"With who?"

"Your brother, actually."

Ana drops the fabric she's been holding. An entire bolt of black velvet unrolls all the way to the sewing machines. It takes every ounce of control she has not to scream. If they want her to negotiate with Finn, he must be okay.

"They want something from him?"

"It'll soon become clear."

"Let me talk to him."

"That's not exactly possible at the moment. It's like this, Ana. Sarah can take you to him. And once you're there, it'll all make sense. Does that sound reasonable?"

"Not at all. How do I know Sarah isn't going to drive me into a field full of her people? Maybe Finn won't be there when we arrive."

"You have a point. They're prepared to do whatever you'd like to guarantee your safety. As I said, this is important to them."

"Bring him to me then."

"Also not possible. I have an idea. What you need is leverage. Sarah isn't enough. I get that. How would you feel about taking me along for the ride? Anybody tries anything on you, you'll have both of us. And believe me, we're very valuable to him. It's a generous offer. It involves trust."

Something about what he's saying doesn't compute. Whose side is he on?

"You're very good, aren't you, Gus?"

"At what?"

"You're not just some old friend of Blackwell's. You work with him, don't you? You told him where I'd be."

"We do business. It can hardly come as a surprise."

"You knew all along it was my brother I was after?"

"Everyone out here knows about Finn, Ana."

"Did Finn trade with you, Gus? Those long-range radios you have. They look an awful lot like the ones I found where he was staying."

"Yes, Ana, and yes I told Blackwell where he was. Whatever you are imagining is probably true. But none of these questions are going to get you closer to your brother."

Is she that stupid that she didn't see this coming?

"I'll consider your offer and get back to you in an hour."

"Hold up. One more thing. You should know something about your brother. He's injured. Can't say how bad it is. Maybe it's a scratch but they say he needs antibiotics. I'm just saying. You may not want to wait too long to go to him."

He could be telling the truth. There *was* a lot of blood on Finn's t-shirt.

"And Ana."

"What now, Gus?"

"I'm just wondering whether these motion sensors of yours are armed as well. I'm about a foot away from one of them."

He's downstairs. She peeks behind the velvet to confirm. He's in front of the restaurant across the street.

"Yes, they're armed."

SHE GETS TIRED of watching him pace back and forth and lets him in. Mostly because she has questions, not because she pities him. He doesn't seem the least bit perturbed that she took so long. He has a perpetually optimistic expression on his face.

"I like this place," he says, when he gets to the third floor.

"You've been here?"

"Everyone has."

"That stuff edible?" he asks, nodding to a packet of teriyaki hemp steak on the counter. He goes through her food box like he owns it.

"Are you going to fill me in on what's actually going on?" she asks.

"It's a mess really. And neither side is budging. You're familiar with Dmitri?"

Hearing his name makes her ribs hurt. "I know him."

"Well, that's where your brother is and he's not letting us in. That Dmitri is a freak, you know. Has the place armed to the hilt. We go in, we die. Problem is, they can't leave. Eventually they'll starve. They've got kids in there, you know."

"What does he want with Finn?"

"Nothing of consequence to your brother. I'm surprised he hasn't caved. I'm not entirely sure your brother isn't a bit off. It's about this power plant business."

Of course, the Band wouldn't like the power plant. The more power Isla has, the less they have.

"They don't want her to have it?"

"No, they want it for themselves."

"So why not take it?"

"They have. Your brother still has the software though. Blackwell wants him to hand it over so they can get the thing fired up. What's the big deal?"

"So the Band gets electricity but the kids don't?"

"That'll be up to him."

He looks out the window, anxiously. Maybe he's brought others. Or he's worried an army from the City is coming.

"Do you steal kids for him, Gus?"

"There are no kids now."

"But did you?"

"I regret some of the things I did in the past, Ana, but I never hurt any of those children. I helped them. They were better off with Isla. Some parents even asked me to take their kids. Heck, I would have sent my own kids to her if I had any."

"Did you hurt their parents, Gus?"

"No. I drew the line at that."

"And Amber and Jason, why haven't you traded them? They don't have parents."

"I almost did. But I just couldn't. There was something about them."

"Like the ducks in your pond."

"Yes."

"And you've been protecting them ever since. You're the reason they're untouched?"

"Mostly, but they're also clever."

She checks on Sarah. She's still asleep from her morning dose of morphine.

"You said to me before that some people move in whatever direction the wind is blowing," Gus says. "That was me before, but not now."

She's not convinced. "You told Blackwell where my brother was."

"I just thought he wanted to talk to him. I didn't know Blackwell meant your brother harm."

"*Does* he mean my brother harm? If Finn gives Blackwell what he wants, will he leave him alone?

"I'm not going to lie, Ana. He won't. Your brother is a wild card. A leader can't afford to have someone smarter than him lurking in the background, threatening his order. Blackwell will deal with him eventually if he stays around here. You'll need to get him away."

"What will he do to *me* when this is over?"

"Nothing. I've made sure of that," he says, his head turned away from her.

She wonders what this small concession has cost him.

"My brother isn't going to listen to me, Gus."

"Well, if he doesn't, he starves, unless he dies of an infection first. Or maybe Blackwell gets tired of waiting, sacrifices a few good men, and goes in. I can't see a scenario where your

brother wins. But you can get him out of this."

A DOZEN OF BLACKWELL'S men surround Dmitri's compound. A few are lying on the grass with their heads propped against a log. Others walk the perimeter casually. One of the men meets them by the back porch and hands Ana a radio.

"Convince them to let us in," Gus says.

She hesitates. Finn is on the other end of the radio. She's not even sure she can get her voice to work. Her heart feels like it's jammed into her voice box. She's been at this for four months and yet she feels entirely unprepared.

"Go on, Ana," Gus says.

She nods and takes it.

"Finn," she says.

"Ana," Dmitri answers.

"Let me talk to him, Dmitri," she says.

"I can't let you do that."

"Why?"

"Because Finn will never agree to you coming in here."

"But you will?"

"Yes. This has to end."

It's all coming clear. Dmitri is on the Band's side now.

"Take my screen out of my bag," she orders Sarah. "Take it inside and take a photo of every person in there."

Sarah looks to Gus for approval. He nods.

"Dmitri," Ana says. I'm sending a woman in there. I want

proof Finn is inside before I'm coming in. Open the door for her."

Sarah stands by the back door waiting. The others also look at the door with anticipation as if they've spent a very long time being bored and they're excited the impasse might finally be over. But it's a few minutes before the door opens and a long time before she comes out again.

"Show me," Ana says.

"Don't know how to use your screen," Sarah answers. "He took the pictures," she says, presumably implying Dmitri. Gus takes it from her and scrolls through the images hastily in front of Ana, her own hands full. Two children. Miriam. Dmitri. The two men who roughed her up. Another man she doesn't recognize. And then she sees him. Finn asleep on a mattress, his pale skin covered in sweat, a bandaged arm. This is her brother now, eroded like the soil at the edge of the riverbank she and Finn used to jump from. Her heart contracts and releases, almost as if it's chewing itself up.

"Now, we go in?" Sarah asks.

Ana doesn't answer, she nudges her gun in the direction of the door and Gus and Sarah go in ahead of her.

Ana hands Miriam her pack. "Food," she says, her first words to the woman who took her brother from her. Miriam nods gratefully and starts unpacking it, the two children staring into it expectantly. How long have they been without food?

"Is that her?" the boy, who must be Simeon, asks. He fondles the food, but his eyes are on Ana.

The girl, Clara, elbows him in the chest to keep quiet.

"Let Dmitri feed the children," Ana says to Miriam. "I need you to make sure these two don't leave this house. Can you do that?" she asks Miriam.

"I can," she answers.

Ana hands her one of her loaded guns. For a moment Miriam's hand rests on hers, almost motherly and she smiles. She's thin and weak herself, but there is something superior about her, as if none of this tragedy fazes here.

"Do you know how to use it?" Ana asks.

"Of course," Miriam answers.

"Good, because these two are our leverage. Don't let them out of your sight for a second. And I don't want anyone near Finn and I until I say."

"I understand," she says. "But Ana..."

"What?"

"He's not going to be happy that you're here."

ANA LEAVES THE others and finds Finn, finally, in the front room on the same couch she slept on a week ago. They probably missed each other by a day. She closes the French doors behind her and sits next to him.

"Finn," she says, waking him carefully. He has a thick beard now, a couple of hairs prematurely greying. He looks more like her father than the Finn she remembers. There's a purple shadow under his eyes and two deep creases in his forehead. His dry mouth moves a little when she shakes him, but he hardly

stirs. She could use that IV kit that Aaron wasted on her.

"It's Ana," she says, her face an inch from his. His eyes open a slit.

"No," he says, when he recognizes her, recoiling as if she's just threatened him with a knife. "Oh God, no," he says, moaning. "I ordered them not to involve you."

"And you thought they'd listen?"

His eyes fully open and he strokes her face. She puts her forehead to his and they stay like that until she can feel him convulse a little, stifling emotion. He tries to sit up but he's too weak to do it alone. Worse than she thought. She helps him get comfortable, puts two antibiotics in his palm and hands him her water bottle. He seems more anxious for the water than the pills.

"Ana, leave. It's a trap. Dmitri is worse than Blackwell. Walk out of here and tell them I don't have what they want."

"And then what, Finn? If he believes me, he has no reason to keep you alive."

"We're doomed anyway. And now you are too."

"No need to be fatalistic."

His face falls as he takes her hand.

"I knew they'd use you like this if you came out here."

"I'm going to fix you up and then you'll tell me everything. Can you give Blackwell what he wants? Can you make that contraption work?"

"Yes, but I don't want to."

"Why not end this?"

"Isla is twisted, but she's all those kids have. If I hand that

plant over to him, where does it stop? He'll be one step closer to taking over everything out here."

He downs the rest of the water in one go. She only has three bottles left. She curses herself for not bringing more. She thought food was their problem. She should have asked more questions.

She inspects his elbow. It's a sticky mess of puss. The tip of the bone is missing and it smells off. She traces the red streaks reaching out of the wound.

"When did this happen?"

"A month ago," he answers. "It was healing okay but then it got infected again. Pretty, isn't it?" he asks, as she douses antiseptic all over it. Neither of them discusses what's on their mind. That if the antibiotics don't take, he's going to lose it.

"Do you have morphine?" he asks, hopefully.

"Enough," she says. "But it's not going to come to that."

He nods, smiling weakly. "You look good," he says.

"Relative to you, I guess I do," she says.

"Hooper?"

"He's fine. Tortured by your absence, but he always forgives you."

"I went to Isla about a year ago," he starts, wincing as she applies gauze. "I was there to get *him*," he says, his eyes peering at Simeon, whose face is pressed to the glass door. "I didn't tell Isla why I was there of course." Finn's voice is raspy. Each word a struggle. "I studied her. It didn't take long to figure out how I could become indispensable. I fixed a few things the others

were clueless about. I did just enough to make her happy to see me every time I came. But what she needed most was power. Not just electricity. They had their little arrangement with the Band. Food in exchange for "helping" stray children and providing protection. But there aren't a lot of children now. And Isla hardly needs protection against the Amish and the banished. Blackwell was her only real threat. She was essentially feeding him to prevent him from turning on her. I thought what she needed was a wall."

"Ironic. You offered her the very thing you fled from."

She takes his vitals. He has a temperature but his pulse is strong.

"What did Blackwell think of what you were doing?"

"We started with a simple fence. There's a rabbit epidemic, so he didn't question it until he saw that it was ten feet high. But when he confronted her, she said the deer were also a problem. She was just being a good farmer, something he knew nothing about.

We built the plant slowly and in secret. She didn't even tell her own people in case there were spies. When it was finally done, Blackwell clued in and went ballistic. She stupidly informed him that he would have to start paying proper currency for her produce. And that's how we ended up in this position."

"What happened to your arm?"

"Clara. We'd been arguing about whether to return her to her father. She kept running away from us. She got my gun somehow. She's just a kid. She was determined."

"What about your friends from the City? The Council thinks you murdered them."

"Of course, they would. I'm tired, Ana. I'll tell you everything, but not now."

"We need to decide what the plan is, Finn. You're not going to be able to stay here much longer."

"If I give Blackwell the software, he'll have no reason to keep us alive."

"He can't hurt you if you're not here. This is what we'll do. You'll drive out of here with the kids. When you're long gone, *I'll* hand it over to him."

"And what happens to you?"

"Nothing. I've been assured that I'll be fine. Besides. It's a simple equation, Finn. You, Miriam and her boy, or me? You can't save all of us. Don't look so glum. I have a better chance than the rest of you."

"I can't," Finn says emphatically. "I won't."

She adjusts his blanket. For a moment, she's back in her old apartment with him. They're alone. He's having another one of his episodes. She's covering him with their mother's quilt, urging him to take his pills. He always got through the bad days eventually. Sometimes he was even better afterwards. Time is all he needs. But they don't have time.

"No, you're right Finn. You can't do this."

IT ISN'T THE goodbye she wanted. It's much more unsettling. She doesn't learn what happened to the others or why Finn kept

her in the dark all these years. She's not at all sure of his mental state. Finn never says that he loves her or forgives her. But she doesn't need an apology or confession. She just needs to know that he's safe.

Within minutes of leaving that couch, an unlikely pact is struck between Dmitri, Ana and Gus. Dmitri and his men force her brother, Miriam and Simeon into a car and Blackwell doesn't stop them from leaving. What choice does he have? Ana has Finn's screen and she's proven to Gus that she can open it. And if she can open it, she can delete the software and he'll get nothing. Maybe that's all they ever needed from her, her ability to access that thing.

Moments later, Blackwell's people are in a Jeep driving in the opposite direction, excited about their victory and their stupid power plant. Dmitri's compound is eerily quiet. In that moment, Ana feels something resembling relief.

As she packs her things, Dmitri watches her from the kitchen table, where he's been chain smoking since Finn left.

"Do you know where your brother is going?" he asks her.

"No. Don't you?" she asks. Dimitri shakes his head and a sudden panic overcomes her. She'd assumed now that Blackwell's people were gone, Dmitri would tell her how to find Finn. Her plan was to go stay with him for a while. They'd have that conversation they hadn't had time for. Once she knew he was okay and there was peace between them again, she'd find her own place to settle. She never considered the possibility that no one knew where he was going.

She leans against the couch for support. Finn's bandages are still there next to a green rag they'd been cooling him down with. She can hear Clara in the kitchen bringing in water.

A million thoughts race through her mind. Could Dmitri be lying? Did Finn say anything she'd missed? When it all happened – when Dmitri's men forced the three of them into that car – she wasn't even near him. She watched from a distance. Ana's only concern was that no one followed them.

"Why didn't he tell you, Dmitri?"

"He wanted to, but I shut him down. Blackwell would eventually get it out of me. You know that I'm weak."

"So what? Blackwell has what he wants. Why would Finn be at risk?"

"Your brother is smarter than him, which means Blackwell will always be wondering if Finn is planning something against him. Can't have a loose cannon around threatening your kingdom."

That's exactly what Gus said.

"You look pale, Ana, sit down." He helps her onto the couch and offers her one of his homemade tablets, but she waves it away.

Now what? She never sees Finn again? Another item to add to her list of lost things – her parents, her education, her apartment, Aaron, most of her possessions, her City, her car.

"It's better this way, Ana. You can't be with him. He's a threat to you as well. We all are. Go back to the City. Forget about all the garbage out here."

She doesn't correct him. He doesn't need to know she can't go back.

"Tell you what. I have to take care of a few things. Clara will sit with you until one of my guys can take you to the gates. In a month, this will all just be a distant memory."

She nods, mostly because she wants him to leave her alone to figure all of this out.

He squeezes her shoulder and starts to get up.

"Dmitri," she says, pulling him back down by his arm. "One more thing. Finn didn't come out here alone. Four of his friends were also here. They were found dead in front of the gates. Did Finn tell you what happened?"

Maybe she can live without seeing her brother again, but she needs to know that he's not a murderer.

"I don't know anything about that, Ana," he says, pulling away.

CLARA SITS MUTELY on the edge of the couch for so long that Ana begins to wonder if there is something wrong with her.

"I saw them," Clara finally says. "We were here before. Your brother brought me home. We were so cold. Your brother especially. He'd pulled Simeon and me on a sled here. I put the kettle on and called out for dad, but he didn't answer. I figured he was out back. I'd go see him as soon as I got the others warm."

Clara looks down at the cup in her own hand and turns it clockwise and then counter clockwise in a very precise manner before she speaks again.

"I was so happy that I was finally home that I started talking to them like a crazy person, telling them about my horses and the mushrooms out back. I was bragging to them about my dad. Your brother was nice. He just listened and helped me clean some cups. The kitchen was a real mess."

Ana looks around. Other than Finn's bandages, there are no signs of the disarray that was apparent last time she was here. Clara has straightened everything, as if a little cleaning could solve everything.

"There was blood in front of his workshop. I was worried something had happened to him, so I ran in calling for him. He wasn't inside though. There was a puddle of blood on the workshop floor, splatters on all the walls and his equipment. I followed the blood to the trailer we sometimes hook up to the horses. The four of them were there, under a pile of hay. I didn't have a clue who they were or that they were from the City. But your brother must have heard me scream and soon he was beside me. Simeon too. Your brother was swearing and then crying. He pulled the hay off and started working on them, not believing they were dead. Finally, he just stopped. He said we had to go. We took the trailer and a couple of horses and brought the four of them to the gates. I thought we'd go back afterwards, but Finn said no. He said I wasn't safe there now. My dad wasn't who he used to be."

"And you went along with his decision?" It suddenly occurs to Ana that maybe this girl still needs protecting – she isn't safe with Dmitri and he's likely to neglect her – but she doesn't have

any more fight in her.

"Yeah I went along with it," she says defensively. "I'm not scared of my dad; it wasn't that. I just didn't want him to know that I knew what he'd done to those people. I didn't want the shame of it between us."

"He still doesn't know, does he?"

"No. But when we came back last week, I overheard Finn and my dad yelling about it. All I know is that those people were looking for Finn. He'd let them down. They were upset that he'd traded that power plant for me and Simeon. They'd been promised a truckload of glass. My dad told Finn they were fools. One of them waved around a gun. It was their fault, he claimed. It was all a big accident."

Is that all murder is out here, an accident?

"Thank you for telling me," Ana says, as coldly as she can manage.

"You won't tell him I know?"

"I won't."

CHAPTER 40

10 DECEMBER 2064. Gus and Ana play guitar all afternoon. She's got D minor, E minor and C major pretty much down – well maybe not C. Her fingers are numb and have nice little dents in them that she shows off to Gus. She cools them in a glass of iced cold root beer while Gus talks about suspended sevenths and beats his guitar like a drum. She's never had rhythm. Still doesn't. This is the first instrument she's learned, but she feels oddly confident about it. She has this illusion that maybe her and Gus can form a band and tour the state – go from bonfire to bonfire and play for venison and hides.

There's a Christmas tree in the corner. A real one with a few actual ornaments, colorful bulbs and a few candles. Underneath the tree, there are presents for her, Amber, Jason, Gus and his cats.

Gus doesn't start drinking until 6:00 p.m. now. He's been pushing his start time up by 5 minutes every day. By summer, he plans on drinking only on Sundays. He's very OCD about it all, recording the exact time on a chart he keeps pinned next to his bathroom mirror. He's excited about what he can do with all those extra hours of sobriety. Finding a girlfriend is high on his bucket list.

"Can't get a girlfriend unless I'm at least sober until dinner time," he told her, as if it's a fixed rule.

It's the medicine she brought him that's turned him around. It was a long shot. A cream she found in her kit for radiation burns, which were not uncommon in the City in the early years. It's not exactly a miracle cure, but his lesion is slowly closing.

When they get bored of the music, he models his wardrobe for her. She waits in his living room while he puts outfits together in his clothing trailer. Then he struts out, does runway moves, juts his hip forward when he stops in front of the Christmas tree and asks for a score out of 10.

A big ropey scar is forming over the edges of the lesion. Sporting a black tux and baby blue cummerbund he points to it and says, "tell me honestly, is it a turnoff?"

"Have you seen the women out here?" she responds. The women who might date him have pock parks, warts, wrinkles, gouges and dents, not to mention missing patches of hair due to untreated hormone imbalances.

His fantasy woman wears a red dress that crisscrosses at her breasts and black Jimmy Choo pumps. She's a composite of a

librarian he fanaticized about when he was twelve and his aunt Carlotta – she had an extensive shoe collection.

"You need some friends," Gus says to her.

"Why? I have you."

"You need girlfriends."

"I have girlfriends."

"No, you don't."

"Jennifer, Janine, Mercedes."

"You're making up names."

She's not. Ana befriended some of the girls at the Orphanage. They're only a couple of years younger than her. She took them to find lamps for their dorm now that they have power. Ana's never been one to hang out with girls. But yesterday, she actually enjoyed spending an afternoon with the orphans, putting on makeup and curling their hair. They read her a poorly written romance novel that got her fanaticizing about going on a road trip and finding some reclusive lumberjack to shack up with.

The Orphanage is where she mostly lives now. They've offered her Isla's house, but she prefers the old cook's quarters above the cafeteria. It's the only place with a view.

She didn't plan on moving there. When she left Dmitri's, she rode to the campground she'd visited with Aaron. She arrived at the south entrance welcome gate. The camp rules, etched into a wooden board, were as clear as they would have been before the calamities. A statute of a smiling gopher waved to her.

In the camp store, the plastic box filled with brochures was exactly where Ana and Aaron had left it. The fishing rod they

used was back on the shelf, some dried weeds stuck to it. She walked down the boardwalk to the warm pool on the edge of the lake. It was still, as if nothing had disturbed it since the two of them were last there, Ana doing cartwheels off a large flat boulder, Aaron with his battered face talking excitedly about fishing.

She dove in, hoping to be revived. Instead, the water pulled her down. She stayed deep below, suspended, flirting with oblivion. A large tree leaned over the pond, it's leaves dripping with sunlight. It extended one of its branches to her. She pulled herself out and lied on the mossy bank. The sky was cloudless that day, the humidity stifling. There was no relief from the heat, either in the water or outside of it.

She swatted mosquitos until she became so tired that she drifted off. When she woke up, her legs and arms look all measled. Red ants, black flies and mosquitoes had been feasting on her all afternoon.

She took out one of the canoes and a fishing rod and rowed to their island. The water level was higher than before, but the fish were generous. Maybe it was because she was alone and quiet but three heavy ones were laying limp on a tarp by the end of the day.

That's when she decided to stay there for the summer. Maybe she secretly believed that Aaron would come looking for her there.

It was her home until the leaves fell and it was too cold at night in her cabin even with a fire going. By the time she left, she'd learned to smoke fish. She could identify all of the deer

families that came through. There was even a black bear that she came to know from a safe distance.

But she was done being alone.

She went back to the safe house. The door was unlocked now but her supplies were still untouched on the second floor under a tarp where she left them. Everything was the same in the loft, except for a new note pinned to the bulletin board. "11 September 2064. Isla is dead."

She thought maybe Isla died of natural causes. Or one of the kids in detention offed her. It could have been a mutiny. It was only a matter of time. Many of the kids were adults now. She put it out of her mind. Planned a trip north. There are other communities up there. Saner people. Farmers and religious groups. She would find people she could tolerate.

But she needed winter gear – something she never thought to bring with her – and the only person she knew with decent stuff was Gus. It was that or start sewing and piece together a rabbit coat.

What he told her was exactly what Finn had warned her of. Once Blackwell had his power plant, there was nothing stopping him from taking control of the Orphanage altogether. Why trade for food, when he could have direct access to it? But when he hung Isla for all the kids to see, in front of the cafeteria, it didn't scare them into submission. There *was* a mutiny. The orphans refused to work. It got violent on both sides. When she came to Gus for a jacket and mittens, things were still not resolved.

Finn had caused all of this and Ana felt responsible. She changed her plans. Helped broker a temporary deal. Blackwell would stop acting like he owned the Orphanage. It wouldn't be a complete withdrawal – he'd leave a dozen of his men behind for show. The kids would start tending the fields again without making trouble. He'd get the best of their crops. The kids would have access to unlimited electricity. Blackwell didn't like it; neither did the kids. But they all accepted it because they thought it was temporary. The Orphans expected they'd eventually get rid of him and Blackwell believed he'd eventually absorb the Orphanage into his kingdom. For now, they'd compromise.

Then Ana started helping out at the Orphanage. Just small things at first. She had to stay in case Blackwell got ambitious again. But, within weeks, she was hooked. She convinced the remaining adults to let some of the children go home. And there would be no more kidnappings. Some families even settled at the Orphanage with their lost children. They got the idea to build new houses. Ana found the children of the woman they rescued from the road, but their mother never came for them. Maybe, despite everything they did for her, she never made it.

Ana did her best to solve everyone's problems but her own.

Then she thought about Aaron again. He should be her lumberjack guy.

CHAPTER 41

7 JULY 2065. "Why are you doing this?" Juan asks her for the fourth time that week. "You don't care about them anymore, do you?"

"Of course I do, Juan. The City is my home. But that doesn't mean I love you any less," she says, kissing his cheek, making him turn red. He's been lost without Isla. For reasons she can't understand, he's been leaning on her more and more.

Finn's first shipment had been loaded into a large truck months ago. He'd done it himself. It just hadn't been delivered. She'd inspected it carefully. The whole thing was filled with glass, the one resource there is no substitute for in the City.

She drives the truck herself to the City's gate, a dozen children running behind it for the first kilometer. They've been

doing that a lot, venturing farther and farther out of the gates unaccompanied. It's a bit foolish – there are still wild animals and strangers to contend with, but it isn't her job to constrain them.

The shipment stays in front of the gate untouched for weeks. The letter to Aaron clipped under the windshield wiper bleeds and becomes mush. She replaces it with another and another.

On 1 August 2065, Ana is returning to the Orphanage from a trip north. The children swarm her. She picks up a little girl and throws her on her shoulders and tickles her hard.

"Did you hear?" she asks, pulling Ana's hair into a ponytail.

"What is it? Did you find a new family of toads?"

"It's gone," she says. "They finally took your stuff."

No one had seen it happen, but the City had indeed swallowed her offering and spit the truck back out empty. And they swallowed the next five shipments and a dozen or so letters to Aaron as well.

CHAPTER 42
(AARON)

4 SEPTEMBER 2065. "Crank it up a bit," Hooper says.

"It's on max," Aaron says.

"Well, tune it in better then," he says somewhat irritated, his elbows on his knees, hands under his chin, toes tapping nervously.

"That's as good as we're going to get it." An announcer is sharing his opinions on what Ana's shipments are doing for the City.

"They won't do it," he says.

"Who won't do what?"

"The people. They won't vote for a Council that's in favor of knocking down the walls."

"No one is talking about destroying the walls. That would be stupid."

"Even leaving. They won't allow it."

"Want to wager?"

"Twenty coins says it'll be the same damn nine. You get to know a little about psychology when you're my age. People want to imagine another place, but deep down they're scared. Trust me, may as well turn those coins over to me now."

"My tummy hurts," Martha interjects. "I'm hungry." We've been ignoring her all day, glued to the news. Did she get lunch? No, probably just snuck some candy. You can always tell when she's been into the toffee. She rolls around on the carpet with Yippy and Jasper until her hair is full of static. Then she stares at you with wide creepy eyes. Grilled cheese. That'll be quick. But no, we're out of ketchup again.

"Bottom shelf in the basement," Hooper says, reading Aaron's mind again. The guy can't remember his middle name now but knows exactly what others are thinking.

"I'm leaving," Hooper says. "If there isn't a change, I'm heading outside the City with the protesters. I'll find Ana."

"And if she's long gone?"

"You know she's not. She's sending you letters. And anyways, who the hell cares what happens to me? So, I die out there. I won't remember who I am in six months anyway."

"But Martha and I will."

In the past, there was little interest in Council elections. Partly because the City did away with party politics a long time ago. And the elections are boring. Every five years virtually the same Council gets elected.

But this year is different because of Ana's shipments. Now the people know there's something valuable out there and they can't unlearn that fact. It's all anyone talks about. When the first load was delivered, the Council ignored it. They thought it was a Trojan horse. They inspected every inch of the truck, expecting to find a bomb or anthrax. But the bomb wasn't physical, so they came up empty. The explosion she delivered was hope.

There have been protests. A large group has decided to leave the City if the election result isn't in their favor. Someone started setting up speaker booths all over the City to debate the issues. Aaron spoke at one last week. He told stories about his two weeks outside. He was just trying to provide a little entertainment until someone else volunteered, but before long he was preaching about change. How much would be too much or too little? He described Isla's warehouses and what new buildings could mean to the City. He didn't even know these were his opinions until he spoke. It was like Finn and Ekhart were speaking through him. People seemed to respond to what he had to say. In truth, he had developed a bit of a cult following because of Ana. She and her shipments had become a legend and everyone knew that her letters were written to him.

MARTHA HAS KETCHUP on her shirt. She sits on Hooper's lap, rubbing it all over his apron. He doesn't notice. His knees are bouncing up and down in excitement. She's enjoying the motion.

"The results are coming up on the screen now," the announcer says. "They'll be read in order of highest to lowest votes. And

here they are: Jessica Palmer, Joshua Smith, Karen McLeod, Brian Herstfield, Dave Glover … the remaining names can't be heard over the screaming. Screaming in the room from Hooper's own mouth. Cheering from outside in the market, where thousands are glued to a large projection. The first five are all left of center and most under forty. No one needs to hear the rest of the names.

"Daddy," Martha says when things calm down. "Why did that man say your name?"

"Well I'll be damned," Hooper says, handing Aaron twenty coins. "You're on the Council. You're number nine."

CHAPTER 43

4 OCTOBER 2065. When Ana isn't at the Orphanage, she visits the farmhouse she found last month. A mere four miles north. Corn was growing straight through the front porch. But inside it looked similar to the farmhouse at the Hive that Aaron took her to. The wood floors buckle in only a few places. The owners kept a wood stove on the back porch and a big white enamel cook stove in the kitchen. She's thinking maybe she won't bother with solar panels.

In the basement, she found boxes of mason jars and canning equipment. She plans to make jam in the fall. The farm has an orchard. Although most of the trees have died, she found a few buds on some peach trees that give her hope of fruit. In a few years, she'll clear the fields and plant her inheritance.

The old owners converted their guest room into a music room. Three electric guitars and some African drums crowd one corner. The opposite wall is covered in big sheets of paper where they let their children draw. It's mostly covered in airplanes and Japanese anime.

Ana leafed through the documents they left behind in their basement office. A week before the calamities, the mother was charged with impaired driving. Something to do with prescription pain killers. Ana wonders if she ever told her husband. A court appearance was scheduled for the following Wednesday. One of the children had severe asthma. There was a receipt for inhalers and rental of an oxygen tent in a medical file. The dad was on disability – a work-related injury. Someone had a birthday coming up. There was a gift in a Walmart bag – a spiralizer – and a blank birthday card.

When she stays overnight, she sleeps on a bunkbed in the boys' room. They were twins she thinks, judging by the similar-sized clothes they left behind. Their floor is covered in plastic glow-in-the-dark stars that were once stuck to the ceiling.

She's been slowly bringing supplies here – farm implements, chicken wire and shovels. The son of one of the big farming families up north has offered to help her rebuild the porch and get the pump for the well working. She's not sure how she feels about having a man her age around for several weeks.

That's the thing about living out here, though. You accept help wherever it comes from. There's no room for pride if you want to make a decent life. And it gets lonely without people.

That's been the best part of all of this. Every week she meets someone with a different story that they want to share.

Today, there is a celebration at the Orphanage. The Amish have set up a long table in the glass house, an orange cloth covering the length of it. It's dotted with indigo napkins the art class made and lopsided white plates. They're making piles of sausages and potato salad.

Ana joins the women in Isla's house. They cut vegetables and make iced tea. They gossip about some Amish girls who are former orphans. They clearly don't belong either at the Orphanage or with their families now. They bicker with their mothers, wear their Orphanage clothes and speak together in a lingo only they understand. Their mothers don't know what to do with them.

Ana is by Isla's stereo changing the music when Gus walks in, barely suppressing a smile.

"Your friends are here," he says.

"Who?" Ana asks. Probably the farmer from up north and his son.

Before he can answer, Hooper comes through the screen door, a basket of candy in tow. Ana's knees go weak. It must be an apparition. She's developed a brain tumor maybe. He puts it down on the coffee table, makes his way through a crowd of teenagers fighting over the basket and squeezes her so hard she's pulled off her feet. Why is he here? Did he get tired of waiting for Finn to return?

But Gus said "friends." Plural.

She tries to see through a cluster of women looking out the window. Martha is hopping in and out of view in the garden.

Hooper sees the disappointment on her face. "He's in the parking lot," he says. "Waiting for you."

Aaron is next to a car. Not a station wagon. Smaller and more modern. She practically falls into him, her head fitting against his shoulder as if that spot had always been reserved for her.

"Ana," is all he manages to get out.

"How?"

"Your doing, of course," he says. "It's only for a couple of days, though." He pushes her away to inspect her. For once, she isn't covered in scratches, bites and cuts. She's even fixed herself up for the party, one of Gus' blue cocktail dresses that spins wide when she twirls. He seems relieved but confused by her transformation. "Can we talk to you alone?"

She takes Hooper and Aaron to her apartment above the cafeteria. Hooper looks around as if, for a moment, he's forgotten where he is. When Aaron hands him his leather bag, he seems to get oriented again.

"Your shipments have changed things, Ana," Aaron says.

"How?" She looks at his hand and notices that the tattoo is gone. He looks healthier and even more comfortable in his skin, but something weighs on him.

"The Council wants to start opening things up. They'll take it slowly. Begin by trading with you. Build some trust. Maybe send a handful of families out here to settle. Good people with technical knowledge they could share."

"We can't trust the Council."

"Ana, Aaron *is* the Council now," Hooper says.

"How is that possible?"

"Your letters and shipments. You couldn't have run a more effective election campaign had you tried," Hooper says.

"And will this be reciprocal? Will people here be able to move to the City?" she asks.

"Not in the beginning. Not even our settlers. No in and out movement, just out. But after a while, they'll allow people in, even non-citizens. Even you, Ana."

"Aren't I a criminal?"

"If you agree to help us, you'll receive a full pardon in time. You'll be allowed to come and go."

"These people are my responsibility now. I represent their interests, not the City's."

"Of course, your loyalties have shifted, which is exactly why you should advocate for them. You know what the City has that they could use. You'll make sure they're treated fairly. The City has a lot to offer – access to our technology, help with farming, health care," Aaron says. "With our technology, there would be less need for labor. The kids could spend more time learning."

"The orphans do just fine as it is."

"We could help you make sure Blackwell never touches them again," he says, the first convincing argument he's made.

"And they're willing to let you come back, Ana," Hooper interjects, a little hurt and surprised maybe that she isn't jumping at the offer. Aaron understands her better.

She watches her new friends through the window. They're holding hands around the table reciting their dinner song. Isla had songs and recitations for everything, even brushing teeth.

"Go tell them we'll be a while," Hooper says to Aaron.

Aaron looks at Ana, confused. He clearly doesn't want to leave her. She doesn't want him to go either, but neither of them will disrespect Hooper.

"We'll be down in a minute," she says, opening the door for him, a clear signal to Hooper to keep this private meeting short.

"Tell me about Finn," Hooper says, behind her, once the door is closed.

"I saw him, but only briefly."

"Aaron read me your letters. What I want to know is if he'll ever come back."

"Not as long as Blackwell is alive."

"And you? Are you okay?"

"Physically, but I don't know what I'm doing here. We're always on the brink of an all-out war. One nasty glance from either side and violence will erupt. Finn had good intentions. I don't understand how his actions turned everything upside down."

"Your brother has a good soul. His mind is sharp. He can make almost anything happen. But he's not wise. When he decided to give power to Isla, both literally and figuratively, he was taking sides. As soon as you do that, you create enemies."

"He was trying to help the children. How could he not side with them?"

"Sure, but what did he think Blackwell would say, lucky them? How nice? By choosing the children, he forced the Band to react. My generation did this all the time. We would decide who we thought had the moral high ground. We'd pick our winners – Israel versus Palestine, Iraq versus Iran. We'd give them armies and weapons. It only made things worse. But what do I know, Ana?" he asks, fingering her seedlings, clearly impressed with her work. "Maybe I'm wrong. We tried to do things differently in the City and perhaps we failed too. But I know this. Nature gets it right. The sun shines on all living things equally, both weeds and flowers. It doesn't discriminate. Rain doesn't only fall in rivers. It belongs to everything. It flows to the dirtiest places. To the lowest point. It's humble.

"What am I supposed to do with that tidbit of wisdom, Hooper? This is real life. Blackwell turns the power off anytime he feels like it. The kids start fires in the Band's village." She eyes Aaron outside struggling to get Martha into a chair. Martha is clearly curious about the Amish women. She puts her napkin on her head, imitating their bonnets.

"Don't pick sides. Help everyone, even the Band. If there's an issue you can solve, do it. It will confuse them all at first. But then they'll see the wisdom in it. They'll even copy you."

His eyes glaze over. He looks scared even. With fierce determination, he rearranges her seedlings on the window sill as if trying to solve a puzzle. "I'm forgetting again, aren't I?" he asks.

"What's wrong, Hooper?"

"A little memory loss. Probably a concussion from falling off

the greenhouse ladder too many times. It comes and goes. It's getting better."

That doesn't sound good. She'll have to ask Aaron about it later.

"Is that why you wanted to talk to me alone, to tell me to take the moral high ground out here?"

"No. It's about the past. Something I should have told you a long time ago. Your generation has romantic notions about that time. It's our fault. We indulge you with our fantastical stories. But you can't imagine what it was really like to have no rule of law. You weren't even sure if you should stop at an intersection."

"I can imagine," she says. It's exactly how she feels out here even now. The rules are unclear.

"I met Isla. She was hardly more than a girl," Hooper says, staring out the window at the new houses in the distance.

"How?"

"There was a meeting. Me, Blackwell, your mother, Isla. I know you think they're evil, but they did something right. They created order where there was none. Their systems were imperfect, but chaos was worse," he says. "Your mother and I thought we should come to some agreement with them. This was long before the wall. People were coming and going between settlements, trying to figure out where they fit in."

How could Ana not have known this? What other secrets did their mother keep from them?

"Isla was almost impossible to talk to. Sarcastic. Angry. But with the mind of a general. She had a master plan for everything.

Farming, educating the kids, protecting themselves. Some of her ideas were naïve, but she'd thought everything through. It was only two years after the calamities and her people were doing okay. And Blackwell was managing to keep thousands alive as well." He speaks very quickly, as if this brief window of clarity might close at any moment.

"And what, you formed a pact?"

Hooper turns his eyes back to her. He smiles at what he sees, probably as relieved as Aaron was to find out that she still has all her limbs.

"You could call it that. Blackwell agreed to protect Isla and the children. If he found stray kids, he would bring them to her. He didn't even want anything in return back then."

"And what concessions did the City make?"

"That we wouldn't nuke them provided they left us alone. We had the strongest position in terms of technology. And we agreed to wait a while before building the wall. They wanted us to give people time to make sure they were where they needed to be. And once people had chosen, we could all erect our walls, real or psychological."

"And then people just had to accept the world they'd picked? No opposition?"

"Can I have some water?" Hooper asks. "The road was dustier than I thought."

She finds her old filter from the City and pours him a glass.

"Opposition wasn't forbidden in the City," he says. "It was actually cultivated. Every community needs its outliers. In a

classroom, you need that one kid who questions the system. Who refuses to line up or sit obediently at a desk. Because he tells you what you're doing wrong and what you can do better. That's how societies evolve. A system that doesn't evolve dies. That's what the testing room was all about."

Hooper's description hits home and Ana is dumbfounded.

"My parents knew about this?" she asks.

"As a Council member, your mother did. Not your father. We were on a good path. We had our social contract. No corruption. Protect the weak. Support the industrious. Collaboration over competition. There was no need to tell people that we were looking for dissidents. You might recall that I quit the Council."

"Because you hated the wall."

"No, it was because I decided that my role would be different. I took it upon myself to cultivate the outliers. Good ones. Helpful ones."

"Who?"

"Your father, Ekhart and then Finn."

"You were grooming them all those years to challenge the Council?"

"I did very little. I just found them. And your father was perfect. He made everyone want to be better without inciting riots." Hooper's tone is wistful, but then his expression saddens. "But I made a mistake with Finn. He became more than the City's outlier. He destabilized things out here as well and didn't know what he was doing. Don't look at me like that, Ana. I'm not mad at him. It was my fault. I failed him."

They all did, Ana thinks. Everyone expected too much from him.

"I'm here to say sorry, Ana. Finn wasn't the one we needed. It was always you. I couldn't see it. You're his antidote both inside and out here. You probably don't want to come back, Ana, but if you ever did, it would be different. Both worlds would be open to you. You could help all of us."

She looks away from his hopeful expression. She suddenly finds it hard to swallow. She's not sure she can give him what he wants.

SHE SITS BETWEEN Hooper and Martha during dinner. Halfway through, Martha finds her way onto Ana's lap. But it's Hooper who takes care of Martha, wiping her face with his napkin, forcing another spoonful of green beans into her mouth. They have become a family in her absence.

Aaron helps Gus with the bonfire, searching through the woodpile for dry wood. Despite her best efforts to avert her gaze, she can't help but stare at him when his back is turned. He's tanned from working at the Hive farm. More self-assured from being on the Council.

Gus takes out his guitar and some others join in and play trance-like music. A setar appears and poetry is recited. The kids dance and laugh at themselves, while the adults sit, almost stoned, staring at the flames. Some of the kids have disappeared. They're behind the glass warehouse having their own celebration.

They've ended up across the fire from one another. Ana

glances up at Aaron – quickly and inconspicuously. When they happen to do it at the same time, he smiles at her, almost shyly. She doesn't let him look away. It's time that they talk away from the others. Whatever life he has now without her, she wants to hear about it. She'd like to tell him about hers. He nods in understanding, as if reading her mind, sighs nervously and stands up. He walks toward her, helps her off her tree stump and they leave her circle of friends in the direction she often hikes now, radio and gun in tow. Aaron holds his weapon awkwardly, as if it's a foreign object to him now.

They don't go far. They can still hear music and the occasional laughter. She takes him to one of the new houses that's under construction. The foundation has been laid, the walls framed. Sheets of plastic sway in a slow breeze. They sit down on canvas drop sheets in what will one day be the living room, legs outstretched, their backs against the wall facing the hole where the window will be, the light quickly fading. He laces his fingers tentatively through hers, his heart beating visibly in his throat. The feel of his skin on hers makes her ache.

Clearly, they're not the same two people that met in a café over a year ago and she is glad of that. But it makes them strangers. And yet it feels as if it has always been just the two of them in this room. But what does he want? He's here to ask for help, not her. Perhaps he's nervous because he wants to tell her he's moved on.

"Should we be doing this?" he says, rubbing his thumb lightly over her knuckles.

"Hanging out at a construction site?" she asks, her voice slightly higher than she intended. "Would you like a hard hat?"

"No. The things I've been fantasizing about since I saw you this afternoon," he says.

"Oh."

"Is there someone else?" he asks, letting go of her hand. "Tell me about him." He sounds sincere.

"No one. You?"

"There was a whole string of them after you left. Had to beat them off with a stick when they heard I'd been outside the City. I haven't slept in a year."

"So no one then?" she laughs.

"No. I don't have time for it anyway. Not with Martha and Hooper and the Council."

"Oh," she says, slightly relieved, although she feels guilty for it. She doesn't want him to be alone.

"Will you move into one of these houses?" he asks, getting up and running his hand along the stretched plastic. But his eyes are on her. He's waiting for her reaction. He's asking if she wants to accept their offer.

"I don't want a new house."

"But you like your farmhouse?"

"Yes. I wish you could see it."

"So, you're not coming back?"

"I'm considering it. A place in the City. My farm out here. Doesn't sound bad."

"You could have your old apartment."

"My old apartment?"

"Noah owns the building. He's told the tenants they'll have to leave when – if – you come back."

"You could move in with me," she says, surprising herself. All that he's admitted to is that he's been thinking about her all day, not that he wants a relationship with her if she returns, let alone move in with her.

"Is that what you want?" he asks. "You want there to be an us?"

"I'd prefer it to the alternative," she says, seating herself in the window frame. "Do I sound insane?"

"I've just told a woman I haven't seen in a year that I've been fantasizing about her all afternoon. I don't think I'm in a position to judge."

He joins her on the window frame, the two of them staring into the expanse of yellow growth, the sun, low to the ground, lighting up the corn stocks.

"We should get on with this, don't you think?" he says, inching closer to her. "I'm afraid I'll lose my nerve if I don't get my hands on you soon."

"We could be well into it by now if you'd stop chatting like a …."

He sets his mouth on hers. There is nothing tentative about his actions now or her reaction. They both know what they want. She had forgotten how good this feels, his warm hands moving up her thighs, the feel of the skin of his back, muscle tight against bone.

He moves his hands under her dress and peels it away as if *it* was the impediment all this time. He lets her unbutton his shirt even though she's painfully slow at it.

His nakedness stuns her a little. It's not as if she hasn't seen him without clothes. They've skinny dipped and lain together half clothed in the tent – they were never shy about their bodies – but not with the intention of possessing each other.

They lie together on the canvas drop sheet and it all falls away, the pain of the past year, the people they've lost, their separation. They touch each other so thoroughly, move together so tenderly, as if to make up for all the pleasure they'll be denied until they see each other again. It was this night everything had been leading up to and every subsequent one would be measured by its distance from this room.

CHAPTER 44
(AARON)

3 MARCH 2066. The new deep freezer, delivered an hour ago, is jammed in the doorway to the cellar storage room. Hooper promised to clear out the room yesterday to make room for it. The much smaller old one, now broken, is on the street waiting to be recycled. A delivery of frozen blueberries is coming in an hour. Of the thirty-seven boxes of junk in the room, Aaron has managed to get Hooper to part with one. As soon as they make progress, Hooper leaves under the pretense of some other imperative task – a recipe he has to write down. He's recording all his recipes and stories from the early days of the City in case he forgets them, but that's not how it works. It's his short-term memory that's going. He'll ask Aaron the same question over and over. Did he turn off the stove? How many dozen meringue

are left? But every memory from before six months ago is as clear as the day it happened.

"A lot of this is junk from Ana's parents that she didn't want," Aaron says, nodding toward a wall of broken screens, failed chemistry experiments, old architectural models, stained and ripped bedding. "She told us to chuck it all."

"I can't," he says. "It all meant something at one time or another."

"Once it's gone, no one will remember it ever existed." That was a mistake. He shouldn't have mentioned anything to do with memory.

"That's what I'm afraid of. So many people disappeared thirty years ago that nobody remembers now. Does that mean their lives never mattered?"

"Do you trust me, old man?"

"Not particularly."

"Well, I guess that's not imperative. In any event, since you're no help with this junk, I'm making an executive decision to bin half of it. I promise I'll leave the good stuff. You know that whatever we get rid of will be recycled into something useful. You don't want to deprive the City of possible resources, do you?"

He nods – not out of agreement but to signal that he's too weak to argue.

With renewed hope, Aaron goes through a box of stained linens. "I can't imagine Ana would want these," he says, pulling one out to show Hooper the state of the moth-eaten cloth. A

small notebook falls out. Inside is a bundle of pictures bound in an elastic band.

Aaron recognizes the familiar shots of Ana and Finn, photos of their parents at meetings, community gatherings, the Hive. He's seen them all, or images like them, in the files on Ana. And he remembers the childhood version of her from their time together at the testing room and VR clip.

"Where is this?" he asks Hooper, showing him a polaroid of a cabin.

"I've never seen it," he says, looking at it curiously. "Unless… it could be… would they have had a photo of the place?"

"What place?"

"The cottage they lived in. They didn't come straight here after the collapse. They fled north to the Bruce Peninsula in Canada. Aavai said it was the best year of his life. He talked about going back there one day, but he never would have. He was too attached to people and there weren't many of them up there. Probably even fewer now." Aaron doesn't ask anything more about it. He slips the photo into his back pocket when Hooper is distracted.

Over the next few days, he searches old satellite images of the Bruce Peninsula and finds the cottage. It's a small place, sandwiched in between other small cottages, on a cliff high above the water. It's days away but he decides it's worth the risk. Of course, there is the little matter of the Council letting him go. Technically, he shouldn't be allowed to come back. And he's indispensable to the Council now. He

tells them he's leaving whether or not they agree.

He hasn't spent much money since he moved in with Hooper. Once the Council grants him permission to leave, he takes a year's worth of wages and buys a decent motorbike with plenty of room for supplies, a better tent than the one he and Ana slept in on the road and all the camping gear he can find in the City.

He packs enough dried goods for a week. He'll fish along the way. He goes light on the weapons – a gun, a grenade, a knife. He'll go alone. He won't write to Ana about it. They'll visit the place at a later point if it pans out.

It's still a bit cool, but that's better – no sun beating down on his head. Music – he'll need music without her there to keep him company. Hooper gifted him a curiously good playlist last week. Stuff from the early days of the Paris jazz scene.

He starts out on a Tuesday. The gate has been renovated since he last left. The reception area, previously a tiny room, is now a two-story building. Four counters on the main floor. Right now, they're only processing people wanting to leave, but on 1 August they will be open to immigration. A new health center will take up the entire second floor, code word for quarantine. People will be interviewed. The vetting process will be onerous, but the Council is still expecting hundreds of people to try to get in.

He goes to the second floor, presents his vaccination exemption to the sole nurse on duty – he's already been inoculated against every virus known to man – and waits for his physical. There's a group waiting with him. They're heading to the west coast. Now that the citizens know that there are people out there

and it's not the hell they've been taught to believe, people have been trickling out.

He enters his assigned cubicle, removes his clothes, changes into a hospital gown, puts on the shoes provided and gets on a treadmill. The nurse checks his vitals, takes blood, gives him nutrition shots and sends him back to the waiting room.

When he's finally cleared to leave, it's almost dusk. There are workers on the other side of the river cleaning up the bank of debris, installing cameras in the trees and cables to allow for communication outside the walls. They're not permitted to stray more than fifty feet.

He heads east of the City on a road that he and Ana never took. It's in bad repair, some of the off ramps collapsed. The radiation levels are higher here from a decommissioned nuclear plant. He wonders what the animals out here think of this strange human in white protective gear on a silver bike.

There are no sporadic enclaves of population up here. No one has raided the old stores. He's seen only a couple of birds since he got to the hot zone. No lights flicker in the dark. It's just him, his bike and a single headlight making their way slowly down the road.

He eventually reaches the border to Canada around midnight of the second day. Barricades block the neat line of booths where, thirty-two years ago, cars attempted to flee in either direction only to be turned around. Solar lights, still operational, flood the pavement with light. He has the feeling he's being watched, but he knows there's no one left here. He squeezes

between two rusted black and white patrol cars, rides through the express lane and over the bridge. On the other side, the door to the duty-free shop is open, the windows smashed in, the road littered with crushed liquor bottles.

He sleeps in a provincial park, making a fire by the water on the white sand. He listens to Radiohead and eats jerky. He sets up his security perimeter, checks the pollution levels of the water, boils some and then lies down on his air mattress in his tent reading until well after midnight.

When he finally reaches the Bruce Peninsula, he gets lost in overgrown trees, impassable fields and roads that don't match with the map he's drawn. There's no one to ask directions from. He finds a lighthouse ten miles from the cottage that's on his map and traces his way backward. There might not be people around, but there are bears and wolves. He begins to regret his decision.

There's no security around the cottage. The lights are on though. They could be from before, like at the border. But the wood stacked by the side looks green. And there are cups and plates on a picnic table.

The cabin is small, but tidy. The roof and some of the windows have been patched with plywood and plastic.

He sees her first, a bird tattoo on her neck. When she turns her face to him, there is no doubt in his mind that she's Miriam. She carries a toddler on one hip, a plate of freshly cut cucumbers in the other. A boy emerges from over the edge of a cliff with a pail of shells, his arm pulling from the weight of it. There were

no pictures of him in the files. He must be Simeon. They don't have weapons on them. He waits for the woman to put down the platter.

"Hello," he says, moving within view with his hands above his head, his pistol in his hand pointed behind him.

The boy drops the bucket and moves in front of the woman and toddler protectively.

"You lost?" the boy asks, trying to sound casual. The woman glances towards the house and then back again.

"No," Aaron says. "Not now. I'm exactly where I need to be."

"What do you want?" the woman asks, but her voice is drowned out by the sound of the porch door slamming shut. A shirtless man emerges with a shotgun. His right arm is scarred and twists back at the elbow.

"You're from the City?" the man asks, nodding towards Aaron's bike. He doesn't seem angry, just curious.

"Yes," Aaron says.

"What are you looking for then?"

"Not what, who," he answers.

"Who then?"

"Finn. You are Finn, aren't you?" But there's no doubt. He recognizes Finn from the files he studied for months.

"What do you want with me?" he asks walking within a few feet of him, somewhat more anxious now. He looks back at the boy and the woman to reassure them. He takes the toddler from the woman with his good arm and plants it on his hip. The baby buries his head in his armpit.

"Want? Nothing," he says. So this is it, Aaron thinks. The culmination of months, now years, of searching, the expenditure of too many City resources. Losing Ana. This is where it ends. He has found Finn.

"I'm here on behalf of Ana. You should know that she's fine."

"Oh," Finn responds, dropping his head.

When he was a boy once, Aaron saw a middle-aged man in a coffee shop after his wife's funeral. All of his friends were around him eating, mostly pretending the man wasn't there because they didn't know how to console him. His children, a couple of them pretty young, were hiding under the tables. The man didn't even notice them though. He just sat there looking at the picture of his wife on the funeral program. He had a look of intense guilt, like he hadn't done right by her.

That's the look on Finn's face now. He leans onto the edge of the table, supported by his bad arm. He lets the toddler drop from him and run to his brother.

When he recovers enough, he disappears into his cabin. Miriam offers Aaron some water. Some neighbors arrive. An older couple. They have a truck full of chicken wire with them. They drive it out to the site of what appears to be a new chicken coop. They nod to Aaron through the truck window when they pass by, curious and a little concerned, but they don't ask. Finn eventually comes out with a bag. He secures it to Aaron's bike. Then he takes his son, puts him on his knee and feeds him supper.

"You're leaving with this man?" Miriam asks.

"Yes."

"Will you come back?" she asks.

"Of course I will," he says, looking over at Aaron for reassurance. "But I won't be alone. I'm bringing Ana back with me."

ACKNOWLEDGMENTS

I owe my partner, Sky, and children a debt of gratitude for tolerating my absence while I hid in my room writing this novel with noise cancelling headphones on. Thank you Ella, Lewis, Martha and Edward for graciously accepting underwhelming meals, wearing your dirty clothes yet another day and agreeing to do your homework on your own.

In particular, thank you Ella for being my first, and most enthusiastic, reader; Sky for teaching me that there is no separation between art and life; Martha for advising me on cover design; Edward for his million stories that fed my imagination; and Lewis for being an example to us all. Thank you to my parents, Barb and Don Rogers, for being the first to make it all the way through the first draft.

Thank you to Catherine Chapman for letting me talk your ear off when life got complicated and being an endless fountain of wisdom.

I am sincerely grateful to Josanne Blokker, my editor and colleague, who is an expert at noticing all of the little details while not losing sight of the big picture. I hope this is the first of many collaborations. And thank you to May Phan for designing the cover and Angela Caravan for designing the interior.

And, finally, I would like to acknowledge Jami Attenberg for mentoring me at the beginning of this project through the Humber College Creative Writing Program. Without your guidance, I'd likely still be stuck on page 1.

Manufactured by Amazon.ca
Acheson, AB

12168318R00217

Printed and bound in Canada by Friesens
Set in Garamond by Artegraphica Design Co. Ltd.
Copy editor: Lesley Erickson
Proofreader: Judith Earnshaw
Indexer: Judy Dunlop
Cover designer: Will Brown